# LOVE AND
## MR. LEWISHAM
### &
## MARRIAGE

# LOVE AND MR. LEWISHAM

and

# MARRIAGE

by

## H. G. WELLS

ODHAMS PRESS LIMITED
LONDON, W.C.2

Printed in Great Britain

# LOVE AND
# MR. LEWISHAM

" Great Spirits and Great Businesse doe keepe out this weak Passion . . . yet Love can finde Entrance not only into an open Heart but also into a Heart well fortified, if Watch be not well kept."—FRANCIS BACON.

# CONTENTS

# CONTENTS

# CHAPTER ONE

## INTRODUCES MR. LEWISHAM

THE opening chapter does not concern itself with Love—indeed that antagonist does not certainly appear until the third—and Mr. Lewisham is seen at his studies. It was ten years ago ; and in those days he was assistant master in the Whortley Proprietary School, Whortley, Sussex, and his wages were forty pounds a year, out of which he had to afford fifteen shillings a week during term time to lodge with Mrs. Munday, at the little shop in the West Street. He was called " Mr." to distinguish him from the bigger boys, whose duty it was to learn, and it was a matter of stringent regulation that he should be addressed as " Sir."

He wore ready-made clothes, his black jacket of rigid line was dusted about the front and sleeves with scholastic chalk, and his face was downy and his moustache incipient. He was a passable-looking youngster of eighteen, fair-haired, indifferently barbered and with a quite unnecessary pair of glasses on his fairly prominent nose—he wore these to make himself look older, that discipline might be maintained. At the particular moment when this story begins he was in his bedroom. An attic it was, with lead-framed dormer windows, a slanting ceiling and a bulging wall, covered, as a number of torn places witnessed, with innumerable strata of florid old-fashioned paper.

To judge by the room, Mr. Lewisham thought little of Love but much on Greatness. Over the head of the bed, for example, where good folks hang texts, these truths asserted themselves, written in a clear, bold, youthfully flourishing hand : " Knowledge is Power," and " What man has done man can do "—man in the second instance referring to Mr. Lewisham. Never for a moment were these things to be forgotten. Mr. Lewisham could see them afresh every morning as his head came through his shirt. And over the yellow-painted box upon which—for lack of shelves—Mr. Lewisham's library was arranged, was a " *Schema*." (Why he should not have headed it " Scheme," the editor of the *Church Times*, who calls his miscellaneous notes " Varia," is better able to say than I.) In this scheme, 1892 was indicated as the year in which Mr. Lewisham proposed to take his B.A. degree at the London University with " hons. in all subjects," and 1895 as the date of his " gold medal." Subsequently there were to be " pamphlets in the Liberal interest," and such-like things duly dated. " Who would control others must first control himself," remarked the wall over the wash-hand stand, and behind the door against the Sunday trousers was a portrait of Carlyle.

These were no mere threats against the universe ; operations had begun. Jostling *Shakespeare*, Emerson's *Essays*, and the penny *Life of Confucius*, there were battered and defaced school books, a number of the excellent manuals of the Universal Correspondence Association, exercise books, ink (red and black) in penny bottles, and an india-rubber stamp with Mr. Lewisham's name. A trophy of bluish green South Kensington certificates for geometrical drawing, astronomy, physiology, physiography, and inorganic chemistry, adorned his farther wall. And against the Carlyle portrait was a manuscript list of French irregular verbs.

Attached by a drawing-pin to the roof over the wash-hand stand, which—the room being an attic—sloped almost dangerously, dangled a Time-Table. Mr. Lewisham was to rise at five, and that this was no vain boasting, a cheap American alarum clock by the books on the box witnessed. The lumps of mellow chocolate on the papered ledge by the bed-head, endorsed that evidence. " French until eight," said the time-table curtly. Breakfast was to be eaten in twenty minutes ; then twenty-five minutes of " literature "—to be precise, learning extracts (preferably pompous) from the plays of William Shakespeare—and then to school and duty. The time-table further prescribed Latin Composition for the recess and the dinner hour (" literature," however, during the meal), and varied its injunctions for the rest of the twenty-four hours according to the day of the week. Not a moment for Satan and that " mischief still " of his. Only three-score and ten has the confidence, as well as the time, to be idle.

But just think of the admirable quality of such a scheme ! Up and busy at five, with all the world about one horizontal, warm, dreamy-brained or stupidly dullish ; if roused, roused only to grunt and sigh and roll over again into oblivion. By eight three hours' clear start, three hours' knowledge ahead of every one. It takes, I have been told by an eminent scholar, about a thousand hours of sincere work to learn a language completely—after three or four languages much less—which gives you, even at the outset, one each a year before breakfast. The gift of tongues—picked up like mushrooms ! Then that " literature "—an astonishing conception ! In the afternoon mathematics and the sciences. Could anything be simpler or more magnificent ? In six years Mr. Lewisham will have his five or six languages, a sound, all-round education, a habit of tremendous industry, and be still but four-and-twenty. He will already have honour in his university and ampler means. One realises that those pamphlets in the Liberal interest will be no obscure platitudes. Where Mr. Lewisham will be at thirty stirs the imagination. There will be modifications of the Schema, of course, as experience widens. But the spirit of it—the spirit of it is a devouring flame !

He was sitting facing the diamond-framed window, writing,

writing fast, on a second yellow box that was turned on end and empty, and the lid was open, and his knees were conveniently stuck into the cavity. The bed was strewn with books and copygraphed sheets of instructions from his remote correspondence tutors. Pursuant to the dangling time-table he was, you would have noticed, translating Latin into English.

Imperceptibly the speed of his writing diminished. " *Urit me Glyceræ nitor* " lay ahead and troubled him. " Urit me," he murmured, and his eyes travelled from his book out of the window to the vicar's roof opposite and its ivied chimneys. His brows were knit at first and then relaxed. " *Urit me !* " He had put his pen into his mouth and glanced about for his dictionary. *Urare ?*

Suddenly his expression changed. Movement dictionaryward ceased. He was listening to a light tapping sound—it was a footfall—outside.

He stood up abruptly, and stretching his neck peered through his unnecessary glasses and the diamond panes down into the street. Looking acutely downward he could see a hat daintily trimmed with pinkish white blossom, the shoulder of a jacket, and just the tips of nose and chin. Certainly the stranger who sat under the gallery last Sunday next the Frobishers. Then, too, he had seen her only obliquely. . . .

He watched her until she passed beyond the window frame. He strained to see impossibly round the corner. . . .

Then he started, frowned, took his pen from his mouth. " This wandering attention ! " he said. " The slightest thing ! Where was I ? Tcha ! " He made a noise with his teeth to express his irritation, sat down, and replaced his knees in the upturned box. " Urit me," he said, biting the end of his pen and looking for his dictionary.

It was a Wednesday half-holiday late in March, a spring day glorious in amber light, dazzling white clouds and the intensest blue, casting a powder of wonderful green hither and thither among the trees and rousing all the birds to tumultuous rejoicings ; a rousing day, a clamatory insistent day, a veritable herald of summer. The stir of that anticipation was in the air, the warm earth was parting above the swelling seeds, and all the pine-woods were full of the minute crepitation of opening bud scales. And not only was the stir of Mother Nature's awakening in the earth and the air and the trees, but also in Mr. Lewisham's youthful blood, bidding him rouse himself to live—live in a sense quite other than that the Schema indicated.

He saw the dictionary peeping from under a paper, looked up " Urit me," appreciated the shining " nitor " of Glycera's shoulders, and so fell idle again to rouse himself abruptly.

" I *can't* fix my attention," said Mr. Lewisham. He took off the needless glasses, wiped them, and blinked his eyes.

This confounded Horace and his stimulating epithets ! A walk ?

" I won't be beat," he said—incorrectly—replaced his glasses, brought his elbows down on either side of his box with resonant violence, and clutched the hair over his ears with both hands. . . .

In five minutes' time he found himself watching the swallows curving through the blue over the vicarage garden.

" Did ever man have such a bother with himself as me ? " he asked vaguely but vehemently. " It's self-indulgence does it—sitting down's the beginning of laziness."

So he stood up to his work, and came into permanent view of the village street. " If she has gone round the corner by the post office, she will come in sight over the palings above the allotments," suggested the unexplored and undisciplined region of Mr. Lewisham's mind. . . .

She did not come into sight. Apparently she had not gone round by the post office after all. It made one wonder where she had gone. Did she go up through the town to the avenue on these occasions ? . . . Then abruptly a cloud drove across the sunlight, the glowing street went cold and Mr. Lewisham's imagination submitted to control. So " *Mater sæva cupidinum*," " The untameable mother of desires "—Horace (Book II. of the Odes) was the author appointed by the university for Mr. Lewisham's matriculation—was, after all, translated to its prophetic end.

Precisely as the church clock struck five Mr. Lewisham, with a punctuality that was indeed almost too prompt for a really earnest student, shut his Horace, took up his Shakespeare, and descended the narrow curved uncarpeted staircase that led from his garret to the living-room in which he had his tea with his landlady, Mrs. Munday. That good lady was alone, and after a few civilities Mr. Lewisham opened his Shakespeare and read from a mark onward—that mark, by the bye, was in the middle of a scene—while he consumed mechanically a number of slices of bread and whort jam.

Mrs. Munday watched him over her spectacles and thought how bad so much reading must be for the eyes, until the tinkling of her shop-bell called her away to a customer. At twenty-five minutes to six he put the book back in the window-sill, dashed a few crumbs from his jacket, assumed a mortar-board cap that was lying on the tea-caddy, and went forth to his evening " preparation duty."

The West Street was empty and shining golden with the sunset. Its beauty seized upon him, and he forgot to repeat the passage from *Henry VIII.* that should have occupied him down the street. Instead he was presently thinking of that insubordinate glance from his window and of little chins and nose-tips. His eyes became remote in their expression. . . .

The school door was opened by an obsequious little boy with " lines " to be examined.

Mr. Lewisham felt a curious change of atmosphere on his entry. The door slammed behind him. The hall with its insistent scholastic suggestions, its yellow marbled paper, its long rows of hat-pegs, its disreputable array of umbrellas, a broken mortar-board and a tattered and scattered *Principia*, seemed dim and dull in contrast with the luminous stir of the early March evening outside. An unusual sense of the greyness of a teacher's life, of the greyness indeed of the life of all studious souls, came and went in his mind. He took the " lines," written painfully over three pages of exercise book, and obliterated them with a huge G. E. L., scrawled monstrously across each page. He heard the familiar mingled noises of the playground drifting in to him through the open schoolroom door.

# CHAPTER TWO

## " AS THE WIND BLOWS "

A FLAW in that pentagram of a time-table, that pentagram by which the demons of distraction were to be excluded from Mr. Lewisham's career to Greatness, was the absence of a clause forbidding study out of doors. It was the day after the trivial window peeping of the last chapter that this gap in the time-table became apparent, a day if possible more gracious and alluring than its predecessor, and at half-past twelve, instead of returning from the school directly to his lodging, Mr. Lewisham escaped through the omission and made his way—Horace in pocket—to the park gates and so to the avenue of ancient trees that encircles the broad Whortley domain. He dismissed a suspicion of his motive with perfect success. In the avenue—for the path is but little frequented—one might expect to read undisturbed. The open air, the erect attitude, are surely better than sitting in a stuffy, enervating bedroom. The open air is distinctly healthy, hardy, simple. . . .

The day was breezy, and there was a perpetual rustling, a going and coming in the budding trees.

The net work ofthe beaches was full of golden sunlight, and all the lower branches were shot with horizontal dashes of new-born green.

> " *Tu, nisi ventis*
> *Debes ludibrium, cave* "

was the appropriate matter of Mr. Lewisham's thoughts, and he was mechanically trying to keep the book open in three places at once, at the text, the notes and the literal translation, while he turned up the vocabulary for *ludibrium*, when his attention, wandering dangerously near the top of the page, fell over the edge and escaped with incredible swiftness down the avenue. . . .

A girl wearing a straw hat adorned with white blossom, was advancing towards him. Her occupation, too, was literary. Indeed, she was so busy writing that evidently she did not perceive him :

Unreasonable emotions descended upon Mr. Lewisham— emotions that are unaccountable on the mere hypothesis of a casual meeting. Something was whispered ; it sounded suspiciously like " It's her ! " He advanced with his fingers in his book, ready to retreat to its pages if she looked up, and watched her over it. *Ludibrium* passed out of his universe. She was clearly unaware of his nearness, he thought, intent upon her writing, whatever that might be. He wondered what it might be. Her face, foreshortened by her downward

16

regard, seemed infantile. Her fluttering skirt was short, and showed her shoes and ankles. He noted her graceful, easy steps. A figure of health and lightness it was, sunlit, and advancing towards him, something, as he afterwards recalled, with a certain astonishment, quite outside the Schema.

Nearer she came and nearer, her eyes still downcast. He was full of vague, stupid promptings towards an uncalled-for intercourse. It was curious she did not see him. He began to expect almost painfully the moment when she would look up, though what there was to expect—— ! He thought of what she would see when she discovered him, and wondered where the tassel of his cap might be hanging—it sometimes occluded one eye. It was of course quite impossible to put up a hand and investigate. He was near trembling with excitement. His paces, acts which are usually automatic, became uncertain and difficult. One might have thought he had never passed a human being before. Still nearer, ten yards now, nine, eight. Would she go past without looking up ? . . .

Then their eyes met.

She had hazel eyes, but Mr. Lewisham being quite an amateur about eyes, could find no words for them. She looked demurely into his face. She seemed to find nothing there. She glanced away from him among the trees, and passed, and nothing remained in front of him but an empty avenue, a sunlit, green-shot void.

The incident was over.

From far away the soughing of the breeze swept towards him, and in a moment all the twigs about him were quivering and rustling and the boughs creaking with a gust of wind. It seemed to urge him away from her. The faded dead leaves that had once been green and young sprang up, raced one another, leapt, danced and pirouetted, and then something large struck him on the neck, stayed for a startling moment, and drove past him up the avenue.

Something vividly white ! A sheet of paper—the sheet upon which she had been writing !

For what seemed a long time he did not grasp the situation. He glanced over his shoulder and understood suddenly. His awkwardness vanished. Horace in hand, he gave chase, and in ten paces had secured the fugitive document. He turned towards her, flushed with triumph, the quarry in his hand. He had as he picked it up seen what was written, but the situation dominated him for the instant. He made a stride towards her, and only then understood what he had seen. Lines of a measured length and capitals ! Could it really be—— ? He stopped. He looked again, eyebrows rising. He held it before him, staring now quite frankly. It had been written with a stylographic pen. Thus it ran :

"*Come !  Sharp's the word.*"

And then again,

" *Come !   Sharp's the word.*"
And then,
" *Come !   Sharp's the word.*"
" *Come !   Sharp's the word.*"
And so on all down the page, in a boyish hand uncommonly
like Frobisher ii.'s.

Surely !   " I say ! " said Mr. Lewisham, struggling with
the new aspect and forgetting all his manners in his surprise. . . .   He remembered giving the imposition quite well :
Frobisher ii. had repeated the exhortation just a little too
loudly—had brought the thing upon himself.   To find her
doing this jarred oddly upon certain vague preconceptions
he had formed of her.   Somehow it seemed as if she had
betrayed him.   That of course was only for the instant.

She had come up with him now.   " May I have my sheet
of paper, please ? " she said with a catching of her breath.
She was a couple of inches less in height than he.   Do you
observe her open-half lips, said Mother Nature in a noiseless
aside to Mr. Lewisham—a thing he afterwards recalled.   In
her eyes was a touch of apprehension.

" I say," he said, with protest still uppermost.   " You
oughtn't to do this."

" Do what ? "

" This.   Impositions.   For my boys."

She raised her eyebrows, then knitted them momentarily,
and looked at him.   " Are *you* Mr. Lewisham ? " she asked
with an affectation of entire ignorance and discovery.

She knew him perfectly well, which was one reason why
she was writing the imposition, but pretending not to know
gave her something to say.

Mr. Lewisham nodded.

" Of all people !   Then "—frankly—" you have just found
me out."

" I am afraid I have," said Lewisham.   " I am afraid I
*have* found you out."

They looked at one another for the next move.   She decided
to plead in extenuation.

" Teddy Frobisher is my cousin.   I know it's very wrong,
but he seemed to have such a lot to do and to be in *such*
trouble.   And I had nothing to do.   In fact, it was *I* who
offered. . . ."

She stopped and looked at him.   She seemed to consider
her remark complete.

That meeting of the eyes had an oddly disconcerting
quality.   He tried to keep to the business of the imposition.
" You ought not to have done that," he said, encountering
her steadfastly.

She looked down and then into his face again.   " No," she
said, " I suppose I ought not to.   I'm very sorry."

Her looking down and up again produced another unreasonable effect. It seemed to Lewisham that they were discussing something quite other than the topic of their conversation ; a persuasion patently absurd and only to be accounted for by the general disorder of his faculties. He made a serious attempt to keep his footing of reproof.

" I should have detected the writing, you know."

" Of course you would. It was very wrong of me to persuade him. But I did—I assure you. He seemed in such trouble. And I thought——"

She made another break, and there was a faint deepening of colour in her cheeks. Suddenly, stupidly, his own adolescent cheeks began to glow. It became necessary to banish that sense of a duplicate topic forthwith.

" I can assure you," he said, now very earnestly, " I never give a punishment, never, unless it is merited. I make that a rule. I—er—*always* make that a rule. I am very careful indeed."

" I am really sorry," she interrupted with frank contrition. " It *was* silly of me."

Lewisham felt unaccountably sorry she should have to apologise, and he spoke at once with the idea of checking the reddening of his face. " I don't think *that*," he said with a sort of belated alacrity. " Really, it was kind of you, you know—very kind of you indeed. And I know that—I can quite understand that—er—your kindness . . ."

" Ran away with me. And now poor little Teddy will get into worse trouble for letting me . . ."

" Oh no," said Mr. Lewisham, perceiving an opportunity and trying not to smile his appreciation of what he was saying. " I had no business to read it as I picked it up— absolutely no business. Consequently . . ."

" You won't take any notice of it ? Really ! "

" Certainly not," said Mr. Lewisham.

Her face lit with a smile, and Mr. Lewisham's relaxed in sympathy. " It is nothing—it's the proper thing for me to do, you know."

" But so many people wouldn't do it. Schoolmasters are not usually so—chivalrous."

He was chivalrous ! The phrase acted like a spur. He obeyed a foolish impulse.

" If you like——" he said.

" What ? "

" He needn't do this. The Impot., I mean. I'll let him off."

" Really ? "

" I can."

" It's awfully kind of you."

" I don't mind," he said. " It's nothing much. If you really think . . ."

He was full of self-applause for this scandalous sacrifice of justice.

" It's awfully kind of you," she said.

" It's nothing, really," he explained, " nothing."

" Most people wouldn't——"

" I know."

Pause.

" It's all right," he said.   " Really."

He would have given worlds for something more to say, something witty and original, but nothing came.

The pause lengthened.   She glanced over her shoulder down the vacant avenue.   This interview—this momentous series of things unsaid was coming to an end !   She looked at him hesitatingly and smiled again.   She held out her hand. No doubt that was the proper thing to do.   He took it, searching a void, tumultuous mind in vain.

" It's awfully kind of you," she said again as she did so.

" It don't matter a bit," said Mr. Lewisham, and sought vainly for some other saying, some doorway remark into new topics.   Her hand was cool and soft and firm, the most delightful thing to grasp, and this observation ousted all other things.   He held it for a moment, but nothing would come.

They discovered themselves hand in hand.   They both laughed and felt " silly."   They shook hands in the manner of quite intimate friends, and snatched their hands away awkwardly.   She turned, glanced timidly at him over her shoulder, and hesitated.   " Good-bye," she said, and was suddenly walking from him.

He bowed to her receding back, made a seventeenth-century sweep with his college cap, and then some hitherto unexplored regions of his mind flashed into revolt.

Hardly had she gone six paces when he was at her side again.

" I say," he said with a fearful sense of his temerity and raising his mortar-board awkwardly as though he was passing a funeral.   " But that sheet of paper. . . ."

" Yes," she said, surprised—quite naturally.

" May I have it ? "

" Why ? "

He felt a breathless pleasure, like that of sliding down a slope of snow.   " I would like to have it."

She smiled and raised her eyebrows, but his excitement was now too great for smiling.   " Look here ! " she said, and displayed the sheet crumpled into a ball.   She laughed—with a touch of effort.

" I don't mind that," said Mr. Lewisham laughing too. He captured the paper by an insistent gesture and smoothed it out with fingers that trembled.

" You don't mind ? " he said.

" Mind what ? "

" If I keep it ? "

" Why should I ? "

Pause. Their eyes met again. There was an odd constraint about both of them, a palpitating interval of silence.

" I really *must* be going," she said suddenly, breaking the spell by an effort. She turned about and left him with the crumpled piece of paper in the fist that held the book, the other hand once more lifting the mortar-board in a dignified salute.

He watched her receding figure. His heart was beating with remarkable rapidity. How light, how living she seemed ! Little round flakes of sunlight raced down her as she went. She walked fast, then slowly, looking sideways once or twice but not back, until she reached the park gates. Then she looked towards him, a remote, friendly little figure, made a gesture of farewell, and disappeared.

His face was flushed and his eyes bright. Curiously enough, he was out of breath. He stared for a long time at the vacant end of the avenue. Then he turned his eyes to his trophy gripped against the closed and forgotten Horace in his hand.

## CHAPTER THREE

### THE WONDERFUL DISCOVERY

ON Sunday it was Lewisham's duty to accompany the boarders twice to church. The boys sat in the gallery above the choir, facing the organ loft and at right angles to the general congregation. It was a prominent position, and made him feel painfully conspicuous, except in moods of exceptional vanity when he used to imagine that all these people were thinking how his forehead and his certificates accorded. He thought a lot in those days of his certificates and forehead, but little of his honest, healthy face beneath it. (To tell the truth there was nothing very wonderful about his forehead.) He rarely looked down the church, as he fancied to do so would be to meet the collective eye of the congregation regarding him. So that in the morning he was not able to see that the Frobishers' pew was empty until the litany.

But in the evening, on the way to church, the Frobishers and their guest crossed the market-square as his string of boys marched along the west side. And the guest was arrayed in a gay new dress, as if it were already Easter, and her face set in its dark hair came with a strange effect of mingled freshness and familiarity. She looked at him calmly ! He felt very awkward and was for cutting his new acquaintance. Then hesitated, and raised his hat with a jerk as if to Mrs. Frobisher. Neither lady acknowledged his salute, which may possibly have been a little unexpected. Then young Siddons dropped his hymn-book, stooped to pick it up, and Lewisham almost fell over him. . . . He entered church in a mood of black despair.

But consolation of a sort came soon enough. As *she* took her seat she distinctly glanced up at the gallery, and afterwards as he knelt to pray, he peeped between his fingers and saw her looking up again. She was certainly not laughing at him.

In those days much of Lewisham's mind was still an unknown land to him. He believed among other things that he was always the same consistent intelligent human being, whereas under certain stimuli he became no longer reasonable and disciplined but a purely imaginative and emotional person. Music, for instance, carried him away, and particularly the effect of many voices in unison whirled him off from almost any state of mind to a fine massive emotionality. And the evening service at Whortley church—at the evening service surplices were worn—the chanting and singing, the vague brilliance of the numerous candle flames, the multitudinous unanimity of the congregation down there, kneeling,

rising, thunderously responding, invariably inebriated him.
Inspired him, if you will, and turned the prose of his life into
poetry. And Chance, coming to the aid of Dame Nature,
dropped just the apt suggestion into his now highly responsive
ear.

The second hymn was a simple and popular one, dealing
with the theme of Faith, Hope and Charity, and having each
verse ending with the word " Love." Conceive it, long
drawn out and disarticulate—

> Faith will van . . . ish in . . . to sight,
> Hope be emp . . . tied in deli . . . ight,
> Love in Heaven will shine more bri . . . ight
> There . . . fore gi . . . ve us . . . Love.

At the third repetition of the refrain, Lewisham looked down
across the chancel and met her eyes for a brief instant. . . .

He stopped singing abruptly. Then the consciousness of
the serried ranks of faces below there, came with almost
overwhelming force upon him, and he dared not look at her
again. He felt the blood rushing to his face.

Love ! The greatest of these. The greatest of all things.
Better than fame. Better than knowledge. So came the
great discovery like a flood across his mind, pouring over it
with the cadence of the hymn and sending a tide of pink in
sympathy across his forehead. The rest of the service was
phantasmagorial background to that great reality—a phantasmagorial background a little inclined to stare. He, Mr.
Lewisham, was in Love.

" A . . . men." He was so preoccupied that he found
the whole congregation subsiding into their seats, and himself
still standing, rapt. He sat down spasmodically, with an
impact that seemed to him to re-echo through the church.

As they came out of the porch into the thickening night
he seemed to see her everywhere. He fancied she had gone
on in front, and he hurried up the boys in the hope of overtaking her. They pushed through the throng of dim people
going homeward. Should he raise his hat to her again ? . . .
But it was Susie Hopbrow in a light-coloured dress—a raven
in dove's plumage. He felt a curious mixture of relief and
disappointment. He would see her no more that night.

He hurried from the school to his lodging. He wanted
very urgently to be alone. He went upstairs to his little
room and sat before the upturned box on which his Butler's
*Analogy* was spread open. He did not go to the formality
of lighting the candle. He leant back and gazed blissfully
at the solitary planet that hung over the vicarage garden.

He took out of his pocket a crumpled sheet of paper,
smoothed and carefully refolded, covered with a writing not
unlike that of Frobisher ii., and after some maidenly hesita-

tion pressed this treasure to his lips. The Schema and the
time-table hung in the darkness like the mere ghosts of
themselves.

Mrs. Munday called him thrice to his supper.

He went out immediately after it was eaten and wandered
under the stars until he came over the hill behind the town
again, and clambered up the back to the stile in sight of the
Frobishers' house. He selected the only lit window as hers.
Behind the blind, Mrs. Frobisher (thirty-eight) was busy with
her curl-papers—she used papers because they were better
for the hair—and discussing certain neighbours in a fragmentary way with Mr. Frobisher, who was in bed. Presently
she moved the candle to examine a faint discolouration of
her complexion that rendered her uneasy.

Outside, Mr. Lewisham (eighteen) stood watching the orange
oblong for the best part of half an hour, until it vanished
and left the house black and blank. Then he sighed deeply
and returned home in a very glorious mood indeed.

He awoke the next morning feeling extremely serious, but
not clearly remembering the overnight occurrences. His eye
fell on his clock. The time was six and he had not heard
the alarum ; as a matter of fact the alarum had not been
wound up. He jumped out of bed at once and alighted upon
his best trousers amorphously dropped on the floor instead
of methodically cast over a chair. As he soaped his head he
tried, according to his rules of revision, to remember the
overnight reading. He could not for the life of him. The
truth came to him as he was getting into his shirt. His head,
struggling in its recesses, became motionless, the handless
cuffs ceased to dangle for a minute. . . .

Then his head came through slowly with a surprised expression upon his face. He remembered. He remembered
the thing as a bald discovery, and without a touch of emotion.
With all the achromatic clearness, the unromantic colour-
lessness of the early morning. . . .

Yes. He had it now quite distinctly. There had been no
overnight reading. He was in Love.

The proposition jarred with some vague thing in his mind.
He stood staring for a space, and then began looking about
absent-mindedly for his collar-stud. He paused in front of
his Schema, regarding it.

# CHAPTER FOUR

"WORK must be done anyhow," said Mr. Lewisham. But never had the extraordinary advantages of open-air study presented themselves so vividly. Before breakfast he took half an hour of open-air reading along the allotments land near the Frobishers' house ; after breakfast and before school he went through the avenue with a book, and returned from school to his lodgings circuitously through the avenue, and so back to the avenue for thirty minutes or so before afternoon school. When during these periods of open-air study Mr. Lewisham was not looking over the top of his book, then commonly he was glancing over his shoulder. And at last whom should he see but——!

He saw her out of the corner of his eye, and he turned away at once, pretending not to have seen her. His whole being was suddenly irradiated with emotion. The hands holding his book gripped it very tightly. He did not glance back again, but walked slowly and steadfastly, reading an ode that he could not have translated to save his life, and listening acutely for her approach. And after an interminable time, as it seemed, came a faint footfall and the swish of skirts behind him.

He felt as though his head was directed forward by a clutch of iron.

"Mr. Lewisham," she said close to him, and he turned with a quality of movement that was almost convulsive. He raised his cap clumsily.

He took her extended hand by an afterthought, and held it until she withdrew it. "I am so glad to have met you," she said.

"So am I," said Lewisham simply.

They stood facing one another for an expressive moment, and then by a movement she indicated her intention to walk along the avenue with him. "I wanted so much," she said looking down at her feet, "to thank you for letting Teddy off, you know. That is why I wanted to see you." Lewisham took his first step beside her. "And it's odd, isn't it," she said looking up into his face, "that I should meet you here in just the same place. I believe. . . . Yes. The very same place we met before."

Mr. Lewisham was tongue-tied.

"Do you often come here ? " she said.

"Well," he considered—and his voice was most unreasonably hoarse when he spoke—"No. No. . . . That is—— At least not often. Now and then. In fact I like it rather for reading and that sort of thing. It's so quiet."

" I suppose you read a great deal ? "

" When one teaches one has to."

" But you. . . ."

" I'm rather fond of reading, certainly.   Are you ? "

" I *love* it."

Mr. Lewisham was glad she loved reading.  He would have been disappointed had she answered differently.  But she spoke with real fervour.  She *loved* reading !  It was pleasant.  She would understand him a little perhaps.  " Of course," she went on, " I'm not clever like some people are. And I have to read books as I get hold of them."

" So do I," said Mr. Lewisham, " for the matter of that. . . Have you read . . . Carlyle ? "

The conversation was now fairly under way.  They were walking side by side beneath the swaying boughs.  Mr. Lewisham's sensations were ecstatic, marred only by a dread of some casual boy coming upon them.  She had not read *much* Carlyle.  She had always wanted to, even from quite a little girl—she had heard so much about him.  She knew he was a Really Great Writer, a *very* Great Writer indeed.  All she *had* read of him she liked.  She could say that.  As much as she liked anything.  And she had seen his house in Chelsea.

Lewisham, whose knowledge of London had been obtained by excursion trips on six or seven isolated days, was much impressed by this.  It seemed to put her at once on a footing of intimacy with this imposing Personality.  It had never occurred to him at all vividly that these Great Writers had real abiding places.  She gave him a few descriptive touches that made the house suddenly real and distinctive to him. She lived quite near, she said, at least within walking distance, in Clapham.  He instantly forgot the vague design of lending her his *Sartor Resartus* in his curiosity to learn more about her home.  " Clapham—that's almost in London, isn't it ? " he said.

" Quite," she said, but she volunteered no further information about her domestic circumstances.  " I like London," she generalised, " and especially in winter."  And she proceeded to praise London, its public libraries, its shops, the multitudes of people, the facilities for " doing what you like," the concerts one could go to, the theatres.  (It seemed she moved in fairly good society.)  " There's always something to see even if you only go out for a walk," she said, " and down here there's nothing to read but idle novels.  And those not new."

Mr. Lewisham had regretfully to admit the lack of such culture and mental activity in Whortley.  It made him feel terribly her inferior.  He had only his bookishness and his certificates to set against it all—and she had seen Carlyle's house !  " Down here," she said, " there's nothing to talk about but scandal."  It was too true.

At the corner by the stile, beyond which the willows were splendid against the blue with silvery aments and golden pollen, they turned by mutual impulse and retraced their steps. " I've simply had no one to talk to down here," she said. " Not what *I* call talking."

" I hope," said Lewisham, making a resolute plunge, " perhaps while you are staying at Whortley . . ."

He paused perceptibly, and she, following his eyes, saw a voluminous black figure approaching. " We may," said Mr. Lewisham, resuming his remark, " chance to meet again, perhaps."

He had been about to challenge her to a deliberate meeting. A certain delightful tangle of paths that followed the bank of the river had been in his mind. But the apparition of Mr. George Bonover, headmaster of the Whortley Proprietary School, chilled him amazingly. Dame Nature no doubt had arranged the meeting of our young couple, but about Bonover she seems to have been culpably careless. She now receded illimitably, and Mr. Lewisham, with the most unpleasant feelings, found himself face to face with a typical representative of a social organisation which objects very strongly *inter alia* to promiscuous conversation on the part of the young unmarried junior master.

" —chance to meet again, perhaps," said Mr. Lewisham, with a sudden lack of spirit.

" I hope so too," she said.

Pause. Mr. Bonover's features, and particularly a bushy pair of black eyebrows, were now very near, those eyebrows already raised, apparently to express a refined astonishment.

" Is this Mr. Bonover coming ? " she asked.

" Yes."

Prolonged pause.

Would he stop and accost them ? At any rate this frightful silence must end. Mr. Lewisham sought in his mind for some remark wherewith to cover his employer's approach. He was surprised to find his mind a desert. He made a colossal effort. If they could only talk, if they could only seem at their ease ! But this blank incapacity was eloquent of guilt. Ah !

" It's a lovely day, though," said Mr. Lewisham. " Isn't it ? "

She agreed with him. " Isn't it ? " she said.

And then Mr. Bonover passed, forehead tight reefed so to speak, and lips impressively compressed. Mr. Lewisham raised his mortar-board, and to his astonishment, Mr. Bonover responded with a markedly formal salute—mock clerical hat sweeping circuitously—and the regard of a searching, disapproving eye, and so passed. Lewisham was overcome with astonishment at this improvement on the nod of their

ordinary commerce.    And so this terrible incident terminated
for the time.

He felt a momentary gust of indignation.    After all, why
should Bonover or any one interfere with his talking to a
girl if he chose ?    And for all he knew they might have been
properly introduced.    By young Frobisher, say.    Nevertheless, Lewisham's spring-tide mood relapsed into winter.    He
was, he felt, singularly stupid for the rest of their conversation, and the delightful feeling of enterprise that had hitherto
inspired and astonished him when talking to her had shrivelled
beyond    contempt.    He    was    glad—positively    glad—when
things came to an end.

At the park gates she held out her hand.    "I'm afraid
I have interrupted your reading," she said.

"Not a bit," said Mr. Lewisham warming slightly.    "I
don't know when I've enjoyed a conversation . . ."

"It was—a breach of etiquette, I am afraid, my speaking
to you, but I did so want to thank you. . . ."

"Don't mention it," said Mr. Lewisham, secretly impressed
by the etiquette.

"Good-bye."    He stood hesitating by the lodge, and then
turned back up the avenue in order not to be seen to follow
her too closely up the West Street.

And then, still walking away from her, he remembered that
he had not lent her a book as he had planned, nor made
any arrangement ever to meet her again.    She might leave
Whortley anywhen for the amenities of Clapham.    He stopped
and stood irresolute.    Should he run after her ?    Then he
recalled Bonover's enigmatical expression of face.    He decided that to pursue her would be altogether too conspicuous.
Yet. . . . So · he stood in inglorious hesitation, while the
seconds passed.

He reached his lodging at last to find Mrs. Munday half-way
through dinner.

"You get them books of yours," said Mrs. Munday, who
took a motherly interest in him, " and you read and you read,
and you take no account of time.    And now you'll have to eat
your dinner half cold and no time for it to settle proper before
you goes off to school.    It's ruination to a stummik—such
ways."

"Oh, never mind my stomach, Mrs. Munday," said Lewisham, roused from a tangled and apparently gloomy meditation ; " that's *my* affair."    Quite crossly he spoke for him.

"I'd rather have a good sensible actin' stummik than a
full head," said Mrs. Munday, " any day."

"I'm different, you see," snapped Mr. Lewisham, and relapsed into silence and gloom.

("Hoity toity ! " said Mrs. Munday under her breath.)

# CHAPTER FIVE

## HESITATIONS

M R. BONOVER, having fully matured a Hint suitable for the occasion, dropped it in the afternoon while Lewisham was superintending cricket practice. He made a few remarks about the prospects of the first eleven by way of introduction, and Lewisham agreed with him that Frobisher i. looked like shaping very well this season.

A pause followed and the headmaster hummed. " By the bye," he said, as if making conversation and still watching the play ; " I, ah—understood that you, ah—were a *stranger* to Whortley."

" Yes," said Lewisham, " that's so."

" You have made friends in the neighbourhood ? "

Lewisham was troubled with a cough and his ears—those confounded ears — brightened. " Yes," he said, recovering. " Oh yes. Yes. I have."

" Local people, I presume."

" Well, no. Not exactly." The brightness spread from Lewisham's ears over his face.

" I saw you," said Bonover, " talking to a young lady in the avenue. Her face was somehow quite familiar to me. Who *was* she ? "

Should he say she was a friend of the Frobishers ? In that case Bonover, in his insidious amiable way, might talk to the Frobisher parents and make things disagreeable for her. " She was," said Lewisham, flushing deeply with the stress on his honesty and dropping his voice to a mumble, " a . . . a . . . an old friend of my mother's. In fact, I met her once at Salisbury."

" Where ? "

" Salisbury."

" And her name ? "

" Smith," said Lewisham, a little hastily and repenting the lie even as it left his lips.

" Well *hit*, Harris ! " shouted Bonover, and began to clap his hands. " Well *hit*, sir."

" Harris shapes very well," said Mr. Lewisham.

" Very," said Mr. Bonover. " And—what was it ? Ah ! I was just remarking the odd resemblances there are in the world. There is a Miss Henderson—or Henson—stopping with the Frobishers—in the very same town, in fact, the very picture of your Miss . . ."

" Smith," said Lewisham, meeting his eye and recovering the full crimson note of his first blush.

" It's odd," said Bonover, regarding him pensively.

B

" Very odd," mumbled Lewisham, cursing his own stupidity and looking away.

" *Very*—very odd," said Bonover.

" In fact," said Bonover, turning towards the schoolhouse, " I hardly expected it of you, Mr. Lewisham."

" Expected what, sir ? "

But Mr. Bonover feigned to be already out of earshot.

" Damn ! " said Mr. Lewisham. " Oh !—*damn !* "—a most objectionable expression and rare with him in those days. He had half a mind to follow the headmaster and ask him if he doubted his word. It was only too evident what the answer would be.

He stood for a minute undecided, then turned on his heel and marched homeward with savage steps. His muscles quivered as he walked, and his face twitched. The tumult of his mind settled at last into angry indignation.

" Confound him ! " said Mr. Lewisham, arguing the matter out with the bedroom furniture. " Why the *devil* can't he mind his own business ? "

" Mind your own business, sir ! " shouted Mr. Lewisham at the wash-hand stand. " Confound you, sir, mind your own business ! "

The wash-hand stand did.

" You overrate your power, sir," said Mr. Lewisham a little mollified. " Understand me ! I am my own master out of school."

Nevertheless, for four days and some hours after Mr. Bonover's Hint, Mr. Lewisham so far observed its implications as to abandon open-air study and struggle with diminished success to observe the spirit as well as the letter of his time-table prescriptions. For the most part he fretted at accumulating tasks, did them with slipshod energy or looking out of window. The Career constituent insisted that to meet and talk to this girl again meant reproof, worry, interference with his work for his matriculation, the destruction of all " Discipline," and he saw the entire justice of the insistence. It was nonsense this being in love ; there wasn't such a thing as love outside trashy novelettes. And forthwith his mind went off at a tangent to her eyes under the shadow of her hat brim, and had to be lugged back by main force. On Thursday when he was returning from school he saw her far away down the street, and hurried in to avoid her, looking ostentatiously in the opposite direction. But that was the turning-point. Shame overtook him. On Friday his belief in love was warm and living again, and his heart full of remorse for laggard days.

On Saturday morning his preoccupation with her was so vivid that it distracted him even while he was teaching that most teachable subject, algebra ; and by the end of the school hours the issue was decided and the Career in headlong rout. That afternoon he would go whatever happened, and see her and speak to her again. The thought of Bonover arose only to be dismissed. And besides——

Bonover took a siesta early in the afternoon.

Yes, he would go out and find her and speak to her. Nothing should stop him.

Once that decision was taken his imagination became riotous with things he might say, attitudes he might strike, and a multitude of vague fine dreams about her. He would say this, he would say that, his mind would do nothing but circle round this wonderful pose of lover. What a cur he had been to hide from her so long ! What could he have been thinking about ? How *could* he explain it to her, when the meeting really came ? Suppose he was very frank——

He considered the limits of frankness. Would she believe he had not seen her on Thursday ?—if he assured her that it was so ?

And, most horrible, in the midst of all this came Bonover with a request that he would take " duty " in the cricket field instead of Dunkerley that afternoon. Dunkerley was the senior assistant master, Lewisham's sole colleague. The last vestige of disapprobation had vanished from Bonover's manner ; asking a favour was his autocratic way of proffering the olive branch. But it came to Lewisham as a cruel imposition. For a fateful moment he trembled on the brink of acquiescence. In a flash came a vision of the long duty of the afternoon—she possibly packing for Clapham all the while. He turned white. Mr. Bonover watched his face.

" *No*," said Lewisham bluntly, saying all he was sure of, and forthwith racking his unpractised mind for an excuse. " I'm sorry I can't oblige you, but . . . my arrangements . . . I've made arrangements, in fact, for the afternoon."

Mr. Bonover's eyebrows went up at this obvious lie, and the glow of his suavity faded. " You see," he said, " Mrs. Bonover expects a friend this afternoon, and we rather want Mr. Dunkerley to make four at croquet. . . ."

" I'm sorry," said Mr. Lewisham, still resolute, and making a mental note that Bonover would be playing croquet.

" You don't play croquet by any chance ? " asked Bonover.

" No," said Lewisham, " I haven't an idea."

" If Mr. Dunkerley had asked you ? . . ." persisted Bonover, knowing Lewisham's respect for etiquette.

" Oh ! it wasn't on that account," said Lewisham, and Bonover with eyebrows still raised and a general air of outraged astonishment left him standing there, white and stiff, and wondering at his extraordinary temerity.

# CHAPTER SIX

## THE SCANDALOUS RAMBLE

As soon as school was dismissed Lewisham made a gaol-delivery of his outstanding impositions, and hurried back to his lodgings, to spend the time until his dinner was ready—Well ? . . . It seems hardly fair, perhaps, to Lewisham to tell this ; it is doubtful, indeed, whether a male novelist's duty to his sex should not restrain him, but, as the wall in the shadow by the diamond-framed window insisted, "*Magna est veritas et prævalebit.*" Mr. Lewisham brushed his hair with elaboration, and ruffled it picturesquely, tried the effect of all his ties and selected a white one, dusted his boots with an old pocket-handkerchief, changed his trousers because the week-day pair was minutely frayed at the heels, and inked the elbows of his coat where the stitches were a little white. And, to be still more intimate, he studied his callow appearance in the glass from various points of view, and decided that his nose might have been a little smaller with advantage. . . .

Directly after dinner he went out, and by the shortest path to the allotment lane, telling himself he did not care if he met Bonover forthwith in the street. He did not know precisely what he intended to do, but he was quite clear that he meant to see the girl he had met in the avenue. He knew he should see her. A sense of obstacles merely braced him and was pleasurable. He went up the stone steps out of the lane to the stile that overlooked the Frobishers', the stile from which he had watched the Frobisher bedroom. There he seated himself with his arms folded, in full view of the house.

That was at ten minutes to two. At twenty minutes to three he was still sitting there, but his hands were deep in his jacket pockets, and he was scowling and kicking his foot against the step with an impatient monotony. His needless glasses had been thrust into his waistcoat pocket—where they remained throughout the afternoon—and his cap was tilted a little back from his forehead and exposed a wisp of hair. One or two people had gone down the lane, and he had pretended not to see them, and a couple of hedge-sparrows chasing each other along the side of the sunlit, wind-rippled field had been his chief entertainment. It is unaccountable, no doubt, but he felt angry with her as the time crept on. His expression lowered.

He heard some one going by in the lane behind him. He would not look round—it annoyed him to think of people seeing him in this position. His once eminent discretion, though overthrown, still made muffled protests at the afternoon's enterprise. The feet down the lane stopped close at hand.

"Stare away," said Lewisham between his teeth. And then began mysterious noises, a violent rustle of hedge twigs, a something like a very light foot-tapping.

Curiosity boarded Lewisham and carried him after the briefest struggle. He looked round, and there she was, her back to him, reaching after the spiky blossoming blackthorn that crested the opposite hedge. Remarkable accident! She had not seen him!

In a moment Lewisham's legs were flying over the stile. He went down the steps in the bank with such impetus that it carried him up into the prickly bushes beside her. "Allow me," he said, too excited to see she was not astonished.

"Mr. Lewisham!" she said in feigned surprise, and stood away to give him room at the blackthorn.

"Which spike will you have?" he cried overjoyed. "The whitest? The highest? Any!"

"That piece," she chose haphazard, "with the black spike sticking out from it."

A mass of snowy blossom it was against the April sky, and Lewisham, struggling for it—it was by no means the most accessible—saw with fantastic satisfaction a lengthy scratch flash white on his hand, and turn to red.

"Higher up the lane," he said, descending triumphant and breathless, "there is blackthorn. . . . This cannot compare for a moment. . . ."

She laughed and looked at him as he stood there flushed, his eyes triumphant, with an unpremeditated approval. In church, in the gallery, with his face foreshortened, he had been effective in a way, but this was different. "Show me," she said, though she knew this was the only place for blackthorn for a mile in either direction.

"I knew I should see you," he said by way of answer. "I felt sure I should see you to-day."

"It was our last chance almost," she answered with as frank a quality of avowal. "I'm going home to London on Monday."

"I knew," he cried in triumph. "To Clapham?" he asked.

"Yes. I have got a situation. You did not know that I was a shorthand clerk and typist, did you? I am. I have just left the school, the Grogram School. And now there is an old gentleman who wants an amanuensis."

"So you know shorthand?" said he. "That accounts for the stylographic pen. Those lines were written. . . . I have them still."

She smiled and raised her eyebrows. "Here," said Mr. Lewisham tapping his breast-pocket.

"This lane," he said—their talk was curiously inconsecutive—"some way along this lane, over the hill and down, there is a gate, and that goes—I mean, it opens into the path that runs along the river bank. Have you been?"

" No," she said.

" It's the best walk about Whortley.  It brings you out upon Immering Common.  You *must*—before you go."

" *Now ?* " she said with her eyes dancing.

" Why not ? "

" I told Mrs. Frobisher I should be back by four," she said.

" It's a walk not to be lost."

" Very well," said she.

" The trees are all budding," said Mr. Lewisham, " the rushes are shooting, and all along the edge of the river there are millions of little white flowers floating on the water.  *I* don't know the names of them, but they're fine. . . . May I carry that branch of blossom ? "

As he took it their hands touched momentarily . . . and there came another of those significant gaps.

" Look at those clouds," said Lewisham abruptly remembering the remark he had been about to make and waving the white froth of blackthorn.  "And look at the blue between them."

" It's perfectly splendid.  Of all the fine weather the best has been kept for now.  My last day.  My very last day."

And off these two young people went together in a highly electrical state—to the infinite astonishment of Mrs. Frobisher, who was looking out of the attic window—stepping out manfully and finding the whole world lit and splendid for their entertainment.  The things they discovered and told each other that afternoon down by the river !—that spring was wonderful, young leaves beautiful, bud scales astonishing things, and clouds dazzling and stately !—with an air of supreme originality !  And their naïve astonishment to find one another in agreement upon these novel delights !  It seemed to them quite outside the play of accident that they should have met each other.

They went by the path that runs among the trees along the river bank, and she must needs repent and wish to take the lower one, the towing path, before they had gone three hundred yards.  So Lewisham had to find a place fit for her descent, where a friendly tree proffered its protruding roots as a convenient balustrade, and down she clambered with her hand in his.

Then a water-vole washing his whiskers gave occasion for a sudden touching of hands and the intimate confidence of whispers and silence together.  After which Lewisham essayed to gather her a marsh mallow at the peril, as it was judged, of his life, and gained it together with a bootful of water.  And at the gate by the black and shiny lock, where the path breaks away from the river, she overcame him by an unexpected feat, climbing gleefully to the top rail with the support of his hand, and leaping down, a figure of light and gace, to the ground.

They struck boldly across the meadows, which were gay with lady's-smock, and he walked, by special request, between her and three matronly cows—feeling as Perseus might have done when he fended off the sea-monster. And so by the mill, and up a steep path to Immering Common. Across the meadows Lewisham had broached the subject of her occupation. "And are you really going away from here to be an amanuensis ? " he said, and started her upon the theme of herself, a theme she treated with a specialist's enthusiasm. They dealt with it by the comparative method, and neither noticed the light was out of the sky until the soft feet of the advancing shower had stolen right upon them.

"Look ! " said he. "Yonder ! A shed," and they ran together. She ran laughing, and yet swiftly and lightly. He pulled her through the hedge by both hands, and released her skirt from an amorous bramble, and so they came into a little black shed in which sheltered a rusty harrow of gigantic proportions. He noted how she still kept her breath after that run.

She sat down on the harrow and hesitated. " I *must* take off my hat," she said, " that rain will spot it," and so he had a chance of admiring the sincerity of her curls—not that he had ever doubted them. She stooped over her hat, pocket-handkerchief in hand, daintily wiping off the silvery drops. He stood up at the opening of the shed and looked at the country outside through the veil of the soft vehemence of the April shower.

"There's room for two on this harrow," she said.

He made inarticulate sounds of refusal, and then came and sat down beside her, close beside her, so that he was almost touching her. He felt a fantastic desire to take her in his arms and kiss her, and overcame the madness by an effort. " I don't even know your name," he said, taking refuge from his whirling thoughts in conversation.

" Henderson," she said.

" *Miss* Henderson ? "

She smiled in his face—hesitated. " Yes—*Miss* Henderson."

Her eyes, her atmosphere were wonderful. He had never felt quite the same sensation before, a strange excitement, almost like a faint echo of tears. He was for demanding her Christian name. For calling her " dear " and seeing what she would say. He plunged headlong into a rambling description of Bonover and how he had told a lie about her and called her Miss Smith, and so escaped this unaccountable emotional crisis. . . .

The whispering of the rain about them sank and died, and the sunlight struck vividly across the distant woods beyond Immering. Just then they had fallen again into a silence that was full of daring thoughts for Mr. Lewisham. He moved his arm suddenly and placed it so that it was behind her on the frame of the harrow.

"Let us go on now," she said abruptly. "The rain has stopped."

"That little path goes straight to Immering," said Mr. Lewisham.

"But, four o'clock?"

He drew out his watch and his eyebrows went up. It was already nearly a quarter past four.

"Is it past four?" she asked, and abruptly they were face to face with parting. That Lewisham had to take "duty" at half-past five seemed a thing utterly trivial. "Surely," he said, only slowly realising what this parting meant. "But must you? I—I want to talk to you."

"Haven't you been talking to me?"

"It isn't that. Besides—no."

She stood looking at him. "I promised to be home by four," she said. "Mrs Frobisher has tea. . . ."

"We may never have a chance to see one another again."

"Well?"

Lewisham suddenly turned very white.

"Don't leave me," he said, breaking a tense silence and with a sudden stress in his voice. "Don't leave me. Stop with me yet—for a little while. . . . You . . . You can lose your way."

"You seem to think," she said, forcing a laugh, "that I live without eating and drinking."

"I have wanted to talk to you so much. The first time I saw you. . . . At first I dared not . . . I did not know you would let me talk. . . . And now, just as I am—happy, you are going."

He stopped abruptly. Her eyes were downcast. "No," she said, tracing a curve with the point of her shoe. "No. I am not going."

Lewisham restrained an impulse to shout. "You will come to Immering?" he cried, and as they went along the narrow path through the wet grass, he began to tell her with simple frankness how he cared for her company. "I would not change this," he said, casting about for an offer to reject, "for—anything in the world. . . . I shall not be back for duty. I don't care. I don't care what happens so long as we have this afternoon."

"Nor I," she said.

"Thank you for coming," he said in an outburst of gratitude. "Oh, thank you for coming," and held out his hand. She took it and pressed it, and so they went on hand in hand until the village street was reached. Their high resolve to play truant at all costs had begotten a wonderful sense of fellowship. "I can't call you Miss Henderson," he said. "You know I can't. You know . . . I must have your Christian name."

" Ethel," she told him.

" Ethel," he said and looked at her, gathering courage as he did so. " Ethel," he repeated. " It is a pretty name. But no name is quite pretty enough for you, Ethel . . . *dear*. . . ."

The small shop in Immering lay back behind a garden full of wallflowers, and was kept by a very fat and very cheerful little woman, who insisted on regarding them as brother and sister, and calling them both " dearie." These points conceded she gave them an admirable tea of astonishing cheapness. Lewisham did not like the second condition very much, because it seemed to touch on his latest enterprise. But the tea and the bread and butter and the whort jam were like no food on earth. There were wallflowers, heavy scented, in a jug upon the table, and Ethel admired them, and when they set out again the little old lady insisted on her taking a bunch with her.

It was after they left Immering that this ramble, properly speaking, became scandalous. The sun was already a golden ball above the blue hills in the west—it turned our two young people into figures of flame—and yet, instead of going homeward, they took the Wentworth road that plunges into the Forshaw woods. Behind them the moon, almost full, hung in the blue sky above the tree-tops, ghostly and indistinct, and slowly gathered to itself such light as the setting sun left for it in the sky.

Going out of Immering they began to talk of the future. And for the very young lover there is no future but the immediate future.

" You must write to me," he said, and she told him she wrote such *silly* letters. " But I shall have reams to write to you," he told her.

" How are you to write to me ? " she asked, and they discussed a new obstacle between them. It would never do to write home—never. She was sure of that with an absolute assurance. " My mother——" she said and stopped.

That prohibition cut him, for at that time he had the makings of a voluminous letter-writer. Yet it was only what one might expect. The whole world was unpropitious—obdurate indeed. . . . A splendid isolation *à deux*.

Perhaps she might find some place where letters might be sent to her ? Yet that seemed to her deceitful.

So these two young people wandered on, full of their discovery of love, and yet so full too of the shyness of adolescence that the word " Love " never passed their lips that day. Yet as they talked on, and the kindly dusk gathered about them, their speech and their hearts came very close together. But their speech would seem so threadbare, written down in cold blood, that I must not put it here. To them it was not threadbare.

When at last they came down the long road into Whortley,

the silent trees were black as ink and the moonlight made her
face pallid and wonderful, and her eyes shone like stars. She
still carried the blackthorn from which most of the blossoms
had fallen. The fragrant wallflowers were fragrant still.
And far away, softened by the distance, the Whortley band,
performing publicly outside the vicarage for the first time that
year, was playing with unctuous slowness a sentimental air.
I don't know if the reader remembers it, that favourite melody
of the early 'eighties :

> " Sweet dreamland faces, passing to and fro (pum, pum)
>   Bring back to Mem'ry days of long ago-o-o-oh "

was the essence of it, very slow and tender and with an accompaniment of pum, pum. Pathetically cheerful that pum, pum,
hopelessly cheerful indeed against the dirge of the air, a dirge
accentuated by sporadic vocalisation. But to young people
things come differently.

" I *love* music," she said.

" So do I," said he.

They came on down the steepness of West Street. They
walked athwart the metallic and leathery tumult of sound
into the light cast by the little circle of yellow lamps. Several
people saw them and wondered what the boys and girls were
coming to nowadays, and one eye-witness even subsequently
described their carriage as " brazen." Mr. Lewisham was
wearing his mortar-board cap of office—there was no mistaking
him. They passed the Proprietary School and saw a yellow
picture framed and glazed, of Mr. Bonover taking duty for his
aberrant assistant master. And outside the Frobisher house
at last they parted perforce.

" Good-bye," he said for the third time. " Good-bye,
Ethel."

She hesitated. Then suddenly she darted towards him.
He felt her hands upon his shoulders, her lips soft and warm
upon his cheek, and before he could take hold of her she had
eluded him, and had flitted into the shadow of the house.
" Good-bye," came her sweet, clear voice out of the shadow,
and while he yet hesitated an answer, the door opened. He
saw her, black in the doorway, heard some indistinct words,
and then the door closed and he was alone in the moonlight,
his cheek still glowing from her lips. . . .

So ended Mr. Lewisham's first day with Love.

# CHAPTER SEVEN

## THE RECKONING

AND after the day of Love came the days of Reckoning.
Mr. Lewisham was astonished—overwhelmed almost—
by that Reckoning, as it slowly and steadily unfolded
itself. The wonderful emotions of Saturday carried him
through Sunday, and he made it up with the neglected Schema
by assuring it that She was his Inspiration, and that he would
work for Her a thousand times better than he could possibly
work for himself. That was certainly not true, and indeed
he found himself wondering whither the interest had vanished
out of his theological examination of Butler's *Analogy*. The
Frobishers were not at church for either service. He speculated rather anxiously why ?

Monday dawned coldly and clearly—a Herbert Spencer of
a day—and he went to school sedulously assuring himself
there was nothing to apprehend. Day boys were whispering
in the morning apparently about him, and Frobisher ii. was
in great request. Lewisham overheard a fragment. " My
mother *was* in a wax," said Frobisher ii.

At twelve came an interview with Bonover, and voices
presently rising in angry altercation and audible to Senior-
assistant Dunkerley through the closed study door. Then
Lewisham walked across the schoolroom, staring straight
before him, his cheeks very bright.

Thereby Dunkerley's mind was prepared for the news that
came the next morning over the exercise books. " When ? "
said Dunkerley.

" End of next term," said Lewisham.

" About this girl that's been staying at the Frobishers ? "

" Yes."

" She's a pretty bit of goods. But it will mess up your
matric next June," said Dunkerley.

" That's what I'm sorry for."

" It's scarcely to be expected he'll give you leave to attend
the exam. . . ."

" He won't," said Lewisham shortly, and opened his first
exercise book. He found it difficult to talk.

" He's a greaser," said Dunkerley. " But there !—what
can you expect from Durham ? " For Bonover had only a
Durham degree and Dunkerley, having none, inclined to be
particular. Therewith Dunkerley lapsed into a sympathetic
and busy rustling over his own pile of exercises. It was not
until the heap had been reduced to a book or so that he spoke
again—an elaborate point.

" Male and female created He them," said Dunkerley,

39

ticking his way down the page. "Which (tick, tick) was damned hard (tick, tick) on assistant masters."

He closed the book with a snap and flung it on the floor behind him. "You're lucky," he said. "I *did* think I should be first to get out of this scandalising hole. You're lucky. It's always acting down here. Running on parents and guardians round every corner. That's what I object to in life in the country : it's so confoundedly artificial. *I* shall take jolly good care *I* get out of it just as soon as ever I can. You bet."

" And work those patents ? "

" Rather, my boy. Yes. Work those patents. The Patent Square Top Bottle ! Lord ! Once let me get to London. . . ."

" I think *I* shall have a shot at London," said Lewisham.

And then the experienced Dunkerley, being one of the kindest young men alive, forgot certain private ambitions of his own—he cherished dreams of amazing patents—and bethought him of agents. He proceeded to give a list of these necessary helpers of the assistant master at the gangway— Orellana, Gabbitas, The Lancaster Gate Agency, and the rest of them. He knew them all—intimately. He had been a " nix " eight years. " Of course that Kensington thing may come off," said Dunkerley, " but it's best not to wait. I tell you frankly—the chances are against you."

The " Kensington thing " was an application for admission to the Normal School of Science at South Kensington, which Lewisham had made in a sanguine moment. There being an inadequate supply of qualified science teachers in England, the Science and Art Department is wont to offer free instruction at its great central school, and a guinea a week, to select young pedagogues who will bind themselves to teach science after their training is over. Dunkerley had been in the habit of applying for several years, always in vain, and Lewisham had seen no harm in following his example. But then Dunkerley had no green-grey certificates.

So Lewisham spent all that " duty " left him of the next day composing a letter to copy out and send the several scholastic agencies. In this he gave a brief but appreciative sketch of his life, and enlarged upon his discipline and educational methods. At the end was a long and decorative schedule of his certificates and distinctions, beginning with a good-conduct prize at the age of eight. A considerable amount of time was required to recopy this document, but his modesty upheld him. After a careful consideration of the time-table, he set aside the midday hour for " Correspondence."

He found that his work in mathematics and classics was already some time in arrears, and a " test " he had sent to his correspondence tutor during those troublous days after the meeting with Bonover in the Avenue, came back blottesquely

indorsed : " Below Pass Standard." This last experience
was so unprecedented and annoyed him so much that for a
space he contemplated retorting with a sarcastic letter to the
tutor. And then came the Easter recess, and he had to go
home and tell his mother, with a careful suppression of details,
that he was leaving Whortley. " Where you have been getting
on so well ! " cried his mother.

But that dear old lady had one consolation. She observed
he had given up his glasses—he had forgotten to bring them
with him—and her secret fear of grave optical troubles that
were being " kept " from her, was alleviated.

Sometimes he had moods of intense regret for the folly of
that walk. One such came after the holidays, when the
necessity of revising the dates of the Schema brought before
his mind, for the first time quite clearly, the practical issue of
this first struggle with those mysterious and powerful influences the springtime sets a-stirring. His dream of success and
fame had been very real and dear to him, and the realisation of the inevitable postponement of his long anticipated
matriculation, the doorway to all the other great things,
took him abruptly like an actual physical sensation in his chest.

He sprang up, pen in hand, in the midst of his corrections,
and began pacing up and down the room. " What a fool I
have been ! " he cried. " What a fool I have been ! "

He flung the pen on the floor and made a rush at an ill-
drawn attempt upon a girl's face that adorned the end of his
room, the visible witness of his slavery. He tore this down
and sent the fragments of it scattering. . . .

" Fool ! "

It was a relief—a definite abandonment. He stared for a
moment at the destruction he had made, and then went
back to the revision of the time-table, with a mutter about
" silly spooning."

That was one mood. The rarer one. He watched the
posts with far more eagerness for the address to which he
might write to her than for any reply to those reiterated letters
of application, the writing of which now ousted Horace and the
higher mathematics (Lewisham's term for conics) from his
attention. Indeed he spent more time meditating the letter
to her than even the schedule of his virtues had required.

Yet the letters of application were wonderful compositions ;
each had a new pen to itself and was for the first page at least
in a handwriting far above even his usual high standard.
And day after day passed and that particular letter he hoped
for still did not come.

His moods were complicated by the fact that, in spite of his
studied reticence on the subject, the reason of his departure
did in an amazingly short time get " all over Whortley." It
was understood that he had been discovered to be " fast,"
and Ethel's behaviour was animadverted upon with com-

placent indignation—if the phrase may be allowed—by the ladies of the place. Pretty looks were too often a snare. One boy—his ear was warmed therefor—once called aloud " Ethel," as Lewisham went by. The curate, a curate of the pale-faced, large-knuckled, nervous sort, now passed him without acknowledgment of his existence. Mrs. Bonover took occasion to tell him that he was a " mere boy," and once Mrs. Frobisher sniffed quite threateningly at him when she passed him in the street. She did it so suddenly she made him jump.

This general disapproval inclined him at times to depression, but in certain moods he found it exhilarating, and several times he professed himself to Dunkerley not a little of a blade. In others, he told himself he bore it for *her* sake. Anyhow he had to bear it.

He began to find out too, how little the world feels the need of a young man of nineteen—he called himself nineteen, though he had several months of eighteen still to run—even though he adds prizes for good conduct, general improvement, and arithmetic, and advanced certificates signed by a distinguished engineer and headed with the Royal Arms, guaranteeing his knowledge of geometrical drawing, nautical astronomy, animal physiology, physiography, inorganic chemistry and building construction, to his youth and strength and energy. At first he had imagined headmasters clutching at the chance of him, and presently he found himself clutching eagerly at them. He began to put a certain urgency into his applications for vacant posts, an urgency that helped him not at all. The applications grew longer and longer until they ran to four sheets of note-paper—a pennyworth in fact. " I can assure you," he would write, ' that you will find me a loyal and devoted assistant." Much in that strain. Dunkerley pointed out that Bonover's testimonial ignored the question of moral character and discipline in a marked manner, and Bonover refused to alter it. He was willing to do what he could to help Lewisham, in spite of the way he had been treated, but unfortunately his conscience . . .

Once or twice Lewisham misquoted the testimonial— to no purpose. And May was half-way through, and South Kensington was silent. The future was grey.

And in the depths of his doubt and disappointment came her letter. It was typewritten on thin paper. " Dear," she wrote simply, and it seemed to him the most sweet and wonderful of all possible modes of address, though as a matter of fact it was because she had forgotten his Christian name and afterwards forgotten the blank she had left for it.

" Dear, I could not write before because I have no room at home now where I can write a letter, and Mrs. Frobisher told my mother falsehoods about you. My mother has surprised me dreadfully—I did not think it of her. She told me nothing

But of that I must tell you in another letter. I am too angry to write about it now. Even now you cannot write back, for *you must not send letters here.* It would *never* do. But I think of you, dear "—the " dear " had been erased and rewritten—" and I must write and tell you so, and of that nice walk we had, if I never write again. I am very busy now. My work is rather difficult and I am afraid I am a little stupid. It is hard to be interested in anything just because that is how you have to live, is it not ? I dare say you sometimes feel the same of school. But I suppose everybody is doing things they don't like. I don't know when I shall come to Whortley again, if ever, but very likely you will be coming to London. Mrs. Frobisher said the most horrid things. It would be nice if you could come to London, because then perhaps you might see me. There is a big boys' school at Chelsea, and when I go by it every morning I wish you were there. Then you would come out in your cap and gown as I went by. Suppose some day I was to see you there suddenly ! "

So it ran, with singularly little information in it, and ended quite abruptly, " Good-bye, dear. Good-bye, dear," scribbled in pencil. And then, " Think of me sometimes."

Reading it, and especially that opening " dear," made Lewisham feel the strangest sensation in his throat and chest, almost as though he was going to cry. So he laughed instead and read it again, and went to and fro in his little room with his eyes bright and that precious writing held in his hand. That " dear " was just as if she had spoken—a voice suddenly heard. He thought of her farewell, clear and sweet, out of the shadow of the moonlit house.

But why that " If I never write again," and that abrupt ending ? Of course he would think of her.

It was her only letter. In a little time its creases were worn through.

Early in June came a loneliness that suddenly changed into almost intolerable longing to see her. He had vague dreams of going to London, to Clapham, to find her. But you do not find people in Clapham as you do in Whortley. He spent an afternoon writing and rewriting a lengthy letter, against the day when her address should come. If it was to come. He prowled about the village disconsolately, and at last set off about seven and retraced by moonlight almost every step of that one memorable walk of theirs.

In the blackness of the shed he worked himself up to the pitch of talking as if she were present. And he said some fine brave things.

He found the little old lady of the wallflowers with a candle in her window, and drank a bottle of ginger beer with a sacramental air. The little old lady asked him, a trifle archly, after his sister, and he promised to bring her again some day.

" I'll certainly bring her," he said. Talking to the little old lady somehow blunted his sense of desolation. And then home through the white indistinctness in a state of melancholy that became at last so fine as to be almost pleasurable.

The day after that mood a new " text " attracted and perplexed Mrs. Munday, an inscription at once mysterious and familiar, and this inscription was :

$$\mathfrak{Mizpah}.$$

It was in Old English lettering and evidently very carefully executed.

Where had she seen it before ?

It dominated all the rest of the room at first, it flaunted like a flag of triumph over " discipline " and the time-table and the Schema. Once indeed it was taken down, but the day after it reappeared. Later a list of scholastic vacancies partially obscured it, and some pencil memoranda were written on the margin.

And when at last the time came for him to pack up and leave Whortley, he took it down and used it with several other suitable papers—the Schema and the time-table were its next-door neighbours—to line the bottom of the yellow box in which he packed his books : chiefly books for that matriculation that had now to be postponed.

# CHAPTER EIGHT

THERE is an interval of two years and a half and the story resumes with a much maturer Mr. Lewisham, indeed no longer a youth but a man, a legal man, at any rate, of one-and-twenty years. Its scene is no longer little Whortley embedded among its trees, ruddy banks, parks and common land, but the grey spaciousness of West London.

And it does not resume with Ethel at all. For that promised second letter never reached him, and though he spent many an afternoon during his first few months in London, wandering about Clapham, that arid waste of people, the meeting that he longed for never came. Until at last after the manner of youth, so gloriously recuperative in body, heart, and soul, he began to forget.

The quest of a " crib " had ended in the unexpected fruition of Dunkerley's blue paper. The green-blue certificates had, it seemed, a value beyond mural decoration, and when Lewisham was already despairing of any employment for the rest of his life, came a marvellous blue document from the Education Department promising inconceivable things. He was to go to London and be paid a guinea a week for listening to lectures—lectures beyond his most ambitious dreams ! Among the names that swam before his eyes was Huxley— Huxley and then Lockyer ! What a chance to get ! Is it any wonder that for three memorable years the Career prevailed with him ?

You figure him on his way to the Normal School of Science at the opening of his third year of study there. (They call the place the Royal College of Science in these latter days.) He carried in his right hand a shiny black bag, well stuffed with textbooks, notes, and apparatus for the forthcoming session ; and in his left was a book that the bag had no place for, a book with gilt edges, and its binding very carefully protected by a brown paper cover.

The lapse of time had asserted itself upon his upper lip in an inaggressive but indisputable moustache, in an added inch or so of stature, and in his less conscious carriage. For he no longer felt that universal attention he believed in at eighteen ; it was beginning to dawn on him indeed that quite a number of people were entirely indifferent to the fact of his existence. But if less conscious, his carriage was decidedly more confident—as of one with whom the world goes well.

His costume was, with one exception, a tempered black— mourning put to hard uses, and " cutting up rusty." The mourning was for his mother, who had died more than a year before the date when this story resumes, and had left him

45

property that capitalised at nearly a hundred pounds, a sum which Lewisham hoarded jealously in the Savings Bank, paying only for such essentials as university fees, and the books and instruments his brilliant career as a student demanded. For he was having a brilliant career after all, in spite of the Whortley check, licking up paper certificates indeed like a devouring flame.

(Surveying him, Madam, your eye would inevitably have fallen to his collar—curiously shiny, a surface like wet gum. Although it has practically nothing to do with this story, I must, I know, dispose of that before I go on, or you will be inattentive. London has its mysteries, but this strange gloss on his linen ! " Cheap laundresses always make your things blue," protests the lady. " It ought to have been blue-stained, generously frayed, and loose about the button, fretting his neck. But this gloss . . ." You would have looked nearer, and finally you would have touched—a charnel-house surface, dank and cool ! You see, Madam, the collar was a patent waterproof one. One of those you wash over-night with a tooth-brush, and hang on the back of your chair to dry, and there you have it next morning, rejuvenesced. It was the only collar he had in the world, it saved three pence a week at least, and that, to a South Kensington " science teacher in training," living on the guinea a week allowed by a parental but parsimonious government, is a sum to consider. It had come to Lewisham as a great discovery. He had seen it first in a shop window full of indiarubber goods, and it lay at the bottom of a glass bowl in which goldfish drifted discontentedly to and fro. And he told himself that he rather liked that gloss.)

But the wearing of a bright red tie would have been unexpected—a bright red tie after the fashion of a South-Western railway guard's ! The rest of him by no means dandiacal, even the vanity of glasses long since abandoned. You would have reflected. . . . Where had you seen a crowd—red ties abundant and in some way significant ? The truth has to be told. Mr. Lewisham had become a Socialist !

That red tie was indeed but one outward and visible sign of much inward and spiritual development. Lewisham, in spite of the demands of a studious career, had read his Butler's *Analogy* through by this time, and some other books ; he had argued, had had doubts, and called upon God for " Faith " in the silence of the night—" Faith " to be delivered immediately if Mr. Lewisham's patronage was valued, and which nevertheless was not so delivered. . . . And his conception of his destiny in this world was no longer an avenue of examinations to a remote Bar and political eminence " in the Liberal interest (D.V.)." He had begun to realise certain aspects of our social order that Whortley did not demonstrate, begun to feel something of the dull stress deepening to absolute wretched-

ness and pain, which is the colour of so much human life in
modern London.    One vivid contrast hung in his mind symbolical.    On the one hand were the coalies of the Westbourne
Park yards, on strike and gaunt and hungry, children begging
in the black slush, and starving loungers outside a soup
kitchen ;  and on the other, Westbourne Grove, two streets
further, a blazing array of crowded shops, a stirring traffic of
cabs and carriages, and such a spate of spending that a tired
student in leaky boots and graceless clothes hurrying home
was continually impeded in the whirl of skirts and parcels and
sweetly pretty womanliness.    No doubt the tired student's
own inglorious sensations pointed the moral.    But that was
only one of a perpetually recurring series of vivid approxi-
mations.

Lewisham had a strong persuasion, an instinct it may be,
that human beings should not be happy while others near
them were wretched, and this gay glitter of prosperity had
touched him with a sense of crime.    He still believed people
were responsible for their own lives ;  in those days he had
still to gauge the possibilities of moral stupidity in himself
and his fellow-men.    He happened upon *Progress and Poverty*
just then, and some casual numbers of the *Commonweal*, and
it was only too easy to accept the theory of cunning, plotting
capitalists and landowners, and faultless, righteous, martyr
workers.    He became a Socialist forthwith.    The necessity
to do something at once to manifest the new faith that was
in him was naturally urgent.    So he went out and (historical
moment) bought that red tie !

" Blood colour, please," said Lewisham meekly to the
young lady at the counter.

" *What* colour ? " said the young lady at the counter,
sharply.

" A bright scarlet, please," said Lewisham, blushing.
And he spent the best part of the evening and much of his
temper in finding out how to tie this into a neat bow.    It was
a plunge into novel handicraft—for previously he had been
accustomed to made-up ties.

So it was that Lewisham proclaimed the Social Revolution.
The first time that symbol went abroad a string of stalwart
policemen were walking in single file along the Brompton
Road.    In the opposite direction marched Lewisham.    He
began to hum.    He passed the policemen with a significant
eye and humming the " Marseillaise."  .  .  .

But that was months ago, and by this time the red tie was
a thing of use and wont.

He turned out of the Exhibition Road through a gateway
of wrought iron, and entered the hall of the Normal School.
The hall was crowded with students carrying books, bags, and
boxes of instruments, students standing and chattering,
students reading the framed and glazed notices of the Debating

Friendship in general, and things like that, down the Burlington Arcade during the lunch time—Burlington Arcade undisguisedly amused by her learned dinginess and his red tie—
and among other things that were said she reproached him for
not reading poetry.   When they parted in Piccadilly after the
examination, they agreed to write about poetry and themselves
during the holidays, and then she lent him, with a touch of
hesitation, Rossetti's poems.   He began to forget what had
at first been very evident to him, that she was two or three
years older than he.

Lewisham spent the vacation with an unsympathetic but
kindly uncle who was a plumber and builder.   His uncle
had a family of six, the eldest eleven, and Lewisham made himself agreeable and instructive.   Moreover he worked hard for
the culminating third year of his studies (in which he had
decided to do great things) and he learnt to ride the Ordinary
Bicycle.   He also thought about Miss Heydinger, and she, it
would seem, thought about him.

He argued on social questions with his uncle, who was a
prominent local Conservative.   His uncle's controversial
methods were coarse in the extreme.   Socialists, he said, were
thieves.   The object of Socialism was to take away what a
man earned and give it to " a lot of lazy scoundrels."   Also
rich people were necessary.   " If there weren't well-off people,
how d'ye think I'd get a livin' ?   Hey ?   And where'd *you* be
then ? "   Socialism, his uncle assured him, was " got up " by
agitators.   " They get money out of young Gabies like you,
and they spend it on champagne."   And thereafter he met
Mr. Lewisham's arguments with the word " Champagne "
uttered in an irritating voice, followed by a luscious panto-
mime of drinking.

Naturally Lewisham felt a little lonely, and perhaps he laid
stress upon it in his letters to Miss Heydinger.   It came to
light that she felt rather lonely too.   They discussed the
question of True as distinguished from Ordinary Friendship,
and from that they passed to Goethe and Elective Affinities.
He told her how he looked for her letters, and they became
more frequent.   Her letters were indisputably well written.
Had he been a journalist with a knowledge of " *per thou.*" he
would have known each for a day's work.   After the practical
plumber had been asking what he expected to make by this
here science of his, re-reading her letters was balsamic.   He
liked Rossetti—the exquisite sense of separation in " The
Blessed Damozel " touched him.   But on the whole he was a
little surprised at Miss Heydinger's taste in poetry.   Rossetti
was so sensuous . . . so florid.   He had scarcely expected
that sort of thing.

Altogether he had returned to the schools decidedly more
interested in her than when they had parted.   And the curious
vague memories of her appearance as something a little frayed

and careless, vanished at sight of her emerging from the darkness of the lift. Her hair was in order, as the light glanced through it it looked even pretty, and she wore a well-made dark-green and black dress, loose-gathered as was the fashion in those days, that somehow gave a needed touch of warmth to her face. Her hat too was a change from the careless lumpishness of last year, a hat that, to a feminine mind, would have indicated design. It suited her—these things are past a male novelist's explaining.

" I have this book of yours, Miss Heydinger," he said.

" I am glad you have written that paper on Socialism," she replied, taking the brown-covered volume.

They walked along the little passage towards the biological laboratory side by side, and she stopped at the hat pegs to remove her hat. For that was the shameless way of the place, a girl student had to take her hat off publicly, and publicly assume the holland apron that was to protect her in the laboratory. Not even a looking-glass !

" I shall come and hear your paper," she said.

" I hope you will like it," said Lewisham at the door of the laboratory.

" And in the vacation I have been collecting evidence about ghosts—you remember our arguments. Though I did not tell you in my letters."

" I'm sorry you're still obdurate," said Lewisham. " I thought that was over."

" And have you read *Looking Backwards* ? "

" I want to."

" I have it here with my other books, if you'd care for me to lend it to you. Wait till I reach my table. My hands are so full."

They entered the laboratory together, Lewisham holding the door open courtly-wise, Miss Heydinger taking a reassuring pat at her hair. Near the door was a group of four girls, which Miss Heydinger joined, holding the brown-covered book as inconspicuously as possible. Three of them had been through the previous two years with her, and they greeted her by her Christian name. They had previously exchanged glances at her appearance in Lewisham's company.

A morose elderly young demonstrator brightened momentarily at the sight of Lewisham. " Well, we've got one of the decent ones anyhow," said the morose elderly young demonstrator, who was apparently taking an inventory, and then brightening still more at a fresh entry. " Ah ! and here's Smithers."

# CHAPTER TEN

## IN THE GALLERY OF OLD IRON

As one goes into the South Kensington Art Museum from the Brompton Road, the Gallery of Old Iron is overhead to the right. But the way thither is exceedingly devious and not to be revealed to everybody, since the young people who pursue science and art thereabouts set a peculiar value on its seclusion. The gallery is long and narrow and dark, and set with iron gates, iron-bound chests, locks, bolts and bars, fantastic great keys, lamps, and the like, and over the balustrade one may lean and talk of one's finer feelings and regard Michael Angelo's horned Moses, or Trajan's Column (in plaster) rising gigantic out of the hall below and far above the level of the gallery. And here on a Wednesday afternoon were Lewisham and Miss Heydinger, the Wednesday afternoon immediately following that paper upon Socialism that you saw announced on the notice-board in the hall.

The paper had been an immense success, closely reasoned, delivered with a disciplined emotion, the redoubtable Smithers practically converted, the reply after the debate methodical and complete, and it may be there were symptoms of that febrile affection known to the vulgar as " swelled 'ed." Lewisham regarded Moses and spoke of his future, Miss Heydinger for the most part watched his face.

" And then ? " said Miss Heydinger.

" One must bring these views prominently before people. I believe still in pamphlets. I have thought . . .." Lewisham paused, it is to be hoped through modesty.

" Yes ? " said Miss Heydinger.

" Well—Luther, you know. There is room, I think, in Socialism, for a Luther."

" Yes," said Miss Heydinger, imagining it. " Yes—that would be a grand way."

So it seemed to many people in those days. But eminent reformers have been now for more than seven years going about the walls of the Social Jericho, blowing their own trumpets and shouting—wtih such small result beyond incidental displays of ill-temper within, that it is hard to recover the fine hopefulness of those departed days.

" Yes," said Miss Heydinger. " That would be a grand way."

Lewisham appreciated the quality of personal emotion in her voice. He turned his face towards her, and saw unstinted admiration in her eyes. " It would be a great thing to do," he said, and added, quite modestly, " if only one could do it."

" *You* could do it."

" You think I could ? " Lewisham blushed vividly—with
pleasure.

" I do. Certainly you could set out to do it. Even to fail
hopelessly would be Great. Sometimes . . ."

She hesitated. He looked expectation. " I think sometimes it is greater even to fail than to succeed."

" I don't see that," said the proposed Luther, and his eyes
went back to the Moses. She was about to speak and changed
her mind.

Contemplative pause.

" And then, when a great number of people have heard of
your views ? " she said presently.

" Then I suppose we must form a party and . . . bring
things about."

Another pause—full, no doubt, of elevated thoughts.

" I say," said Lewisham quite suddenly. " You do put—
well—courage into a chap. I shouldn't have done that
Socialism paper if it hadn't been for you." He turned round
and stood leaning with his back to the Moses, and smiling at
her. " You do help a fellow," he said.

That was one of the vivid moments of Miss Heydinger's
life. She changed colour a little. " Do I ? " she said, standing straight and awkward and looking into his face. " I'm
. . . glad."

" I haven't thanked you for your letters," said Lewisham.
" And I've been thinking . . ."

" Yes ? "

" We're first-rate friends, aren't we ? The best of friends."

She held out her hand and drew a breath. " Yes," she said
as they gripped. He hesitated whether to hold her hand.
He looked into her eyes, and at that moment she would have
given three-quarters of the years she had still to live, to have
had eyes and features that could have expressed her. Instead
she felt her face hard, the little muscles of her mouth twitching
insubordinate, and fancied that her self-consciousness made her
eyes dishonest.

" What I mean," said Lewisham, " is—that this will go on.
We're always going to be friends, side by side."

" Always. Just as I am able to help you—I will help you.
However I can help you, I will."

" We two," said Lewisham gripping her hand.

Her face lit. Her eyes were for a moment touched with the
beauty of simple emotion. " We two," she said, and her lips
trembled and her throat seemed to swell. She snatched her
hand back suddenly and turned her face away. Abruptly she
walked towards the end of the gallery, and he saw her fumbling
for her handkerchief in the folds of the green and black dress.

She was going to cry !

It set Lewisham marvelling—this totally inappropriate
emotion.

He followed her and stood by her. Why cry ? He hoped no one would come into the little gallery until her handkerchief was put away. Nevertheless he felt vaguely flattered. She controlled herself, dashed her tears away, and smiled bravely at him with reddened eyes. " I'm sorry," she said, gulping.

" I am so glad," she explained.

" But we will fight together. We two. I *can* help you. I know I can help you. And there is such Work to be done in the world ! "

" You are very good to help me," said Lewisham, quoting a phrase from what he had intended to say before he found out that he had a hold upon her emotions.

" No !

" Has it ever occurred to you," she said abruptly, " how little a woman can do alone in the world ? "

" Or a man," he answered after a momentary meditation.

So it was Lewisham enrolled his first ally in the cause of the red tie—of the red tie and of the Greatness that was presently to come. His first ally ; for hitherto—save for the indiscretion of his mural inscriptions—he had made a secret of his private ambitions. In that now half-forgotten love affair at Whortley even, he had, in spite of the considerable degree of intimacy attained, said absolutely nothing about his Career.

# CHAPTER ELEVEN

## MANIFESTATIONS

**M**ISS HEYDINGER declined to disbelieve in the spirits of the dead, and this led to controversy in the laboratory over Tea. For the girl students, being in a majority that year, had organised Tea between four o'clock and the advent of the extinguishing policeman at five. And the men students were occasionally invited to Tea. But not more than two of them at a time really participated, because there were only two spare cups after that confounded Simmons broke the third.

Smithers, the square-headed student with the hard grey eyes, argued against the spirits of the dead with positive animosity, while Bletherley, who displayed an orange tie and lank hair in unshorn abundance, was vaguely open-minded. " What is love ? " asked Bletherley, " surely that at any rate is immortal ! " His remark was considered irrelevant and ignored.

Lewisham, as became the most promising student of the year, weighed the evidence—comprehensively under headings. He dismissed the mediumistic séances as trickery.

" Rot and imposture," said Smithers loudly, and with an oblique glance to see if his challenge reached its mark. Its mark was a grizzled little old man with a very small face and very big grey eyes, who had been standing listlessly at one of the laboratory windows until the discussion caught him. He wore a brown velvet jacket and was reputed to be enormously rich. His name was Lagune. He was not a regular attendant, but one of those casual outsiders who are admitted to laboratories that are not completely full. He was known to be an ardent spiritualist—it was even said that he had challenged Huxley to a public discussion on materialism, and he came to the biological lectures and worked intermittently in order, he explained, to fight disbelief with its own weapons. He rose greedily to Smithers' controversial bait.

" I say *no !* " he said, calling down the narrow laboratory and following his voice. He spoke with the ghost of a lisp. " Pardon my interrupting, sir. The question interests me profoundly. I hope I don't intrude. Excuse me, sir. Make it personal. Am I a—fool, or an impostor ? "

" Well," parried Smithers with all a South Kensington student's want of polish, " that's a bit personal."

" Assume, sir, that I am an honest observer."

" Well ? "

" I have *seen* spirits, *heard* spirits, *felt* the touch of spirits." He opened his pale eyes very widely.

" Fool, then," said Smithers in an undertone which did not reach the ears of the spiritualist.

" You may have been deceived," paraphrased Lewisham.

" I can assure you . . . others can see, hear, feel. I have tested, sir. Tested ! I have some scientific training and I have employed tests. Scientific and exhaustive tests ! Every possible way. I ask you, sir—have you given the spirits a chance ? "

" It is only paying guineas to humbugs," said Smithers.

" There you are ! Prejudice ! Here is a man denies the facts and consequently *won't* see them, won't go near them."

" But you wouldn't have every man in the three kingdoms who disbelieved in spirits attend séances before he should be allowed to deny ? "

" Most assuredly yes. Most assuredly yes ! He knows nothing about till then."

The argument became heated. The little old gentleman was soon under way. He knew a person of the most extraordinary gifts, a medium . . .

" Paid ? " asked Smithers.

" Would you muzzle the ox that treadeth out the corn ? " said Lagune promptly.

Smithers' derision was manifest.

" Would you distrust a balance because you bought it ? Come and see." Lagune was now very excited and inclined to gesticulate and raise his voice. He invited the whole class incontinently to a series of special séances. " Not all at once —the spirits—new influences." But in sections. " I warn you we may get nothing. But the chances are . . . I would rejoice infinitely. . . ."

So it came about that Lewisham consented to witness a spirit-raising. Miss Heydinger it was arranged should be there, and the sceptic Smithers, Lagune, his typist and the medium would complete the party. Afterwards there was to be another party for the others. Lewisham was glad he had the moral support of Smithers. " It's an evening wasted," said Smithers, who had gallantly resolved to make the running for Lewisham in the contest for the Forbes medal. " But I'll prove my case. You see if I don't." They were given an address in Chelsea.

The house, when Lewisham found it at last, proved a large one with such an air of mellowed dignity that he was abashed. He hung his hat up for himself beside a green-trimmed hat of straw in the wide, rich-toned hall. Through an open door he had a glimpse of a palatial study, book-shelves bearing white busts, a huge writing-table lit by a green-shaded electric lamp and covered thickly with papers. The housemaid looked, he thought, with infinite disdain at the rusty mourning and flamboyant tie, and flounced about and led him upstairs.

She rapped, and there was a discussion within. " They're

at it already, I believe," she said to Lewisham confidentially. " Mr. Lagune's always at it."

There were sounds of chairs being moved, Smithers' extensive voice making a suggestion and laughing nervously. Lagune appeared opening the door. His grizzled face seemed smaller and his grey eyes larger than usual.

" We were just going to begin without you," he whispered. " Come along."

The room was furnished even more splendidly than the drawing-room of the Whortley Grammar School, hitherto the finest room (except certain of the State Apartments at Windsor) known to Lewisham. The furniture struck him in a general way as akin to that in the South Kensington Museum. His first impression was an appreciation of the vast social superiority of the chairs ; it seemed impertinent to think of sitting on anything quite so stately. He perceived Smithers standing with an air of bashful hostility against a bookcase. Then he was aware that Lagune was asking them all to sit down. Already seated at the table was the Medium, Chaffery, a benevolent-looking, faintly shabby gentleman with bushy iron-grey side-whiskers, a wide, thin-lipped mouth tucked in at the corners, and a chin like the toe of a boot. He regarded Lewisham critically and disconcertingly over gilt glasses. Miss Heydinger was quite at her ease and began talking at once. Lewisham's replies were less confident than they had been in the Gallery of Old Iron ; indeed there was almost a reversal of their positions. She led and he was abashed. He felt obscurely that she had taken an advantage of him. He became aware of another girlish figure in a dark dress on his right.

Every one moved towards the round table in the centre of the room, on which lay a tambourine and a little green box. Lagune developed unsuspected lengths of knobby wrist and finger directing his guests to their seats. Lewisham was to sit next to him, between him and the Medium ; beyond the Medium sat Smithers with Miss Heydinger on the other side of him, linked to Lagune by the typist. So sceptics compassed the Medium about. The company was already seated before Lewisham looked across Lagune and met the eyes of the girl next that gentleman. It was Ethel ! The close green dress, the absence of a hat, and a certain loss of colour made her seem less familiar, but did not prevent the instant recognition. And there was recognition in her eyes.

Immediately she looked away. At first his only emotion was surprise.  He would have spoken, but a little thing robbed him of speech. For a moment he was unable to remember her surname. Moreover, the strangeness of his surroundings made him undecided. He did not know what was the proper way to address her—and he still held to the superstition of etiquette. Besides—to speak to her would involve a general explanation to all these people. . . .

" Just leave a pin-point of gas, Mr. Smithers, please," said Lagune, and suddenly the one surviving jet of the gas chandelier was turned down and they were in darkness. The moment for recognition had passed.

The joining of hands was punctiliously verified, the circle was linked little finger to little finger. Lewisham's abstraction received a rebuke from Smithers. The Medium, speaking in an affable voice, premised that he could promise nothing, he had no " *directing* " power over manifestations. Thereafter ensued a silence. . . .

For a space Lewisham was inattentive to all that happened. He sat in the breathing darkness, staring at the dim elusive shape that had presented that remembered face. His mind was astonishment mingled with annoyance. He had settled that this girl was lost to him for ever. The spell of the old days of longing, of the afternoons that he had spent after his arrival in London, wandering through Clapham with a fading hope of meeting her, had not returned to him. But he was ashamed of his stupid silence, and irritated by the awkwardness of the situation. At one moment he was on the very verge of breaking the compact and saying " Miss Henderson " across the table. . . .

How was it he had forgotten that " Henderson " ? He was still young enough to be surprised at forgetfulness.

Smithers coughed, one might imagine with a warning intention.

Lewisham, recalling his detective responsibility with an effort, peered about him, but the room was very dark. The silence was broken ever and again by deep sighs and a restless stirring from the Medium. Out of this mental confusion Lewisham's personal vanity was first to emerge. What did she think of him ? Was she peering at him through the darkness even as he peered at her ? Should he pretend to see her for the first time when the lights were restored ? As the minutes lengthened it seemed as though the silence grew deeper and deeper. There was no fire in the room, and it looked for lack of that glow chilly. A curious scepticism arose in his mind as to whether he had actually seen Ethel or only mistaken some one else for her. He wanted the séance over in order that he might look at her again. The old days at Whortley came out of his memory with astonishing detail and yet astonishingly free from emotion. . . .

He became aware of a peculiar sensation down his back, that he tried to account for as a draught. . . .

Suddenly a beam of cold air came like a touch against his face, and made him shudder convulsively. Then he hoped that she had not marked his shudder. He thought of laughing a low laugh to show he was not afraid. Some one else shuddered too, and he perceived an extraordinarily vivid odour of violets. Lagune's finger communicated a nervous quivering

What was happening ?

The musical box somewhere on the table began playing a rather trivial, rather plaintive air that was strange to him. It seemed to deepen the silence about him, an accent on the expectant stillness, a thread of tinkling melody spanning an abyss.

Lewisham took himself in hand at this stage. What *was* happening ? He must attend. Was he really watching as he should do ? He had been wool-gathering. There were no such things as spirits, mediums were humbugs, and he was here to prove that sole remaining Gospel. But he must keep up with things—he was missing points. What was that scent of violets ? And who had set the musical box going. The Medium of course ; but how ? He tried to recall whether he had heard a rustling or detected any movement before the music began. He could not recollect. Come ! he must be more on the alert than this !

He became acutely desirous of a successful exposure. He figured the dramatic moment he had prepared with Smithers—Ethel a spectator. He peered suspiciously into the darkness.

Somebody shuddered again, some one opposite him this time. He felt Lagune's finger quiver still more palpably, and then suddenly the raps began, abruptly, all about him. *Rap !*—making him start violently. A swift percussive sound, tap, rap, dap, under the table, under the chair, in the air, round the cornices. The Medium groaned again and shuddered, and his nervous agitation passed sympathetically round the circle. The music seemed to fade to the vanishing point and grew louder again.

How was it done ?

He heard Lagune's voice next him speaking with a peculiar quality of breathless reverence. " The alphabet ? " he asked, " shall we—shall we use the alphabet ? "

A forcible rap under the table.

" No ! " interpreted the voice of the Medium.

The raps were continued everywhere.

Of course it was trickery. Lewisham endeavoured to think what the mechanism was. He tried to determine whether he really had the Medium's little finger touching his. He peered at the dark shape next him. There was a violent rapping with an almost metallic resonance far away behind them. Then the raps ceased, and over the healing silence the little jet of melody from the musical box played alone. And after a moment that ceased also. . . .

The stillness was profound. Mr. Lewisham was now highly strung. Doubts assailed him suddenly, and an overwhelming apprehension, a sense of vast occurrences gathered above him. The darkness was a physical oppression. . . .

He started. Something had stirred on the table. There was the sharp ping of metal being struck. A number of little crepitating sounds like paper being smoothed. The sound of wind without the movement of air. A sense of a presence hovering over the table.

The excitement of Lagune communicated itself in convulsive tremblings ; the Medium's hand quivered. In the darkness on the table something faintly luminous, a greenish-white patch, stirred and hopped slowly among the dim shapes. The object, whatever it was, hopped higher, rose slowly in the air, expanded. Lewisham's attention followed this slavishly. It was ghostly—unaccountable—marvellous. For the moment he forgot even Ethel. Higher and higher this pallid luminosity rose overhead, and then he saw that it was a ghostly hand and arm, rising, rising. Slowly, deliberately, it crossed the table, seemed to touch Lagune, who shivered. It moved slowly round and touched Lewisham. He gritted his teeth.

There was no mistaking the touch, firm and yet soft, of finger-tips. Almost simultaneously, Miss Heydinger cried out that something was smoothing her hair, and suddenly the musical box set off again with a reel. The faint oval of the tambourine rose, jangled, and Lewisham heard it pat Smithers in the face. It seemed to pass overhead. Immediately a table somewhere beyond the Medium began moving audibly on its castors.

It seemed impossible that the Medium, sitting so still beside him, could be doing all these things—grotesquely unmeaning though they might be. After all . . .

The ghostly hand was hovering almost directly in front of Mr. Lewisham's eyes. It hung with a slight quivering. Ever and again its fingers flapped down and rose stiffly again.

Noise ! A loud noise it seemed. Something moving ? What was it he had to do !

Lewisham suddenly missed the Medium's little finger. He tried to recover it. He could not find it. He caught, held and lost an arm. There was an exclamation. A faint report. A curse close to him bitten in half by the quick effort to suppress it. Tzit ! The little pin-point of light flew up with a hiss.

Lewisham, standing, saw a circle of blinking faces turned to the group of two this sizzling light revealed. Smithers was the chief figure of the group ; he stood triumphant, one hand on the gas tap, the other gripping the Medium's wrist, and in the Medium's hand—the incriminatory tambourine.

" How's this, Lewisham," cried Smithers, with the shadows on his face jumping as the gas flared.

" *Caught !* " said Lewisham loudly, rising in his place and avoiding Ethel's eyes.

" What's this ? " cried the Medium.

" Cheating," panted Smithers.

" Not so," cried the Medium. " When you turned up the

light . . . put my hand up . . . caught tambourine . . . to save head.''

"Mr. Smithers," cried Lagune. "Mr. Smithers, this is very wrong. This—shock——"

The tambourine fell noisily to the floor. The Medium's face changed, he groaned strangely and staggered back. Lagune cried out for a glass of water. Every one looked at the man, expecting him to fall, save Lewisham. The thought of Ethel had flashed back into his mind. He turned to see how she took this exposure in which he was such a prominent actor. He saw her leaning over the table as if to pick up something that lay across it. She was not looking at him, she was looking at the Medium. Her face was set and white. Then, as if she felt his glance, her eyes met his.

She started back, stood erect, facing him with a strange hardness in her eyes.

At the moment Lewisham did not grasp the situation. He wanted to show that he was acting upon equal terms with Smithers in the exposure, and for the moment her action simply directed his attention to the object towards which she had been leaning, a thing of shrivelled membrane, a pneumatic glove, lying on the table. This was evidently part of the mediumistic apparatus. He pounced and seized it.

"Look!" he said, holding it towards Smithers. "Here is more! What is this?"

He perceived that the girl started. He saw Chaffery, the Medium, look instantly over Smithers' shoulders, saw his swift glance of reproach at the girl. Abruptly the situation appeared to Lewisham; he perceived her complicity. And he stood, still in the attitude of triumph, with the evidence against her in his hand! But his triumph had vanished.

"Ah!" cried Smithers, leaning across the table to secure it. "*Good* old Lewisham! . . . Now we *have* it. This is better than the tambourine."

His eyes shone with triumph. "Do you see, Mr. Lagune?" said Smithers. "The Medium held this in his teeth and blew it out. There's no denying this. This wasn't falling on your head, Mr. Medium, was it? *This*—this was the luminous hand!"

# CHAPTER TWELVE

THAT night, as she went with him to Chelsea station, Miss Heydinger discovered an extraordinary moodiness in Lewisham. She had been vividly impressed by the scene in which they had just participated. For a time she had believed in the manifestations, and the swift exposure had violently revolutionised her ideas. The details of the crisis were a little confused in her mind. She ranked Lewisham with Smithers in the scientific triumph of the evening. On the whole she felt elated. She had no objection to being confuted by Lewisham. But she was angry with the Medium. " It is dreadful," she said. " Living a lie ! How can the world grow better, when sane, educated people use their sanity and enlightenment to darken others ? It is dreadful !

" He was a horrible man—such an oily, dishonest voice. And the girl—I was sorry for her. She must have been oh !— bitterly ashamed or why should she have burst out crying ? That *did* distress me. Fancy crying like that ! It was—yes— *abandon*. But what can one do ? "

She paused. Lewisham was walking along, looking straight before him, lost in some grim argument with himself.

" It makes me think of ' Sludge, the Medium,' " she said.

He made no answer.

She glanced at him suddenly. " Have you read ' Sludge, the Medium ' ? "

" Eigh ? " he said, coming back out of infinity. " What ? I beg your pardon. Sludge, the Medium ? I thought his name was—it *was*—Chaffery."

He looked at her, clearly very anxious upon this question of fact.

" But I mean Browning's ' Sludge.' You know—the poem."

" No—I'm afraid I don't," said Lewisham.

" I must lend it to you," she said. " It's splendid. It goes to the very bottom of this business."

" Does it ? "

" It never occurred to me before. But I see the point clearly now. If people, poor people, are offered money if phenomena happen, it's too much. They are *bound* to cheat. It's bribery—immorality ! "

She talked in panting little sentences, because Lewisham was walking in heedless big strides. " I wonder how much— such people—could earn honestly."

Lewisham slowly became aware of the question at his ear. He hurried back from infinity. " How much they could earn honestly ? I haven't the slightest idea."

He paused.  " The whole of this business puzzles me," he said.   " I want to think."

" It's frightfully complex, isn't it ? " she said—a little staggered.

But the rest of the way to the station was silence.  They parted with the hand-clasp they took a pride in—a little perfunctory so far as Lewisham was concerned on this occasion. She scrutinised his face as the train moved out of the station, and tried to account for his mood.  He was staring before him at unknown things—as if he had already forgotten her.

He wanted to think !  But two heads, she thought, were better than one in a matter of opinion.   It troubled her to be so ignorant of his mental states.   " How we are wrapped and swathed about—soul from soul ! " she thought, staring out of the window at the dim things flying by outside.

Suddenly a fit of depression came upon her.   She felt alone—absolutely alone—in a void world.

Presently she returned to external things.   She became aware of two people in the next compartment eyeing her critically.   Her hand went patting at her hair.

# CHAPTER THIRTEEN

## LEWISHAM INSISTS

ETHEL HENDERSON sat at her machine before the window of Mr. Lagune's study, and stared blankly at the greys and blues of the November twilight. Her face was white, her eyelids were red from recent weeping, and her hands lay motionless in her lap. The door had just slammed behind Lagune.

"Heigh-ho !" she said. "I wish I was dead. Oh ! I wish I was out of it all."

She became passive again. "I wonder what I have *done,*" she said, "that I should be punished like this."

She certainly looked anything but a Fate-haunted soul, being indeed visibly and immediately a very pretty girl. Her head was shapely and covered with curly dark hair, and the eyebrows above her hazel eyes were clear and dark. Her lips were finely shaped, her mouth was not too small to be expressive, her chin small, and her neck white and full and pretty. There is no need to lay stress upon her nose—it sufficed. She was of a mediocre height, sturdy rather than slender, and her dress was of a pleasant, golden-brown material with the easy sleeves and graceful line of those æsthetic days. And she sat at her typewriter and wished she was dead and wondered what she had *done.*

The room was lined with bookshelves and conspicuous therein was a long row of foolish pretentious volumes, the " works " of Lagune—the witless, meandering imitation of philosophy that occupied his life. Along the cornices were busts of Plato, Socrates and Newton. Behind Ethel was the great man's desk with its green-shaded electric light, and littered with proofs and copies of *Hesperus,* " A Paper for Doubters," which with her assistance he edited, published, compiled, wrote, and (without her help) paid for and read. A pen, flung down forcibly, quivered erect with its one surviving nib in the blotting pad. Mr. Lagune had flung it down.

The collapse of the previous night had distressed him dreadfully, and ever and again before his retreat he had been breaking into passionate monologue. The ruin of a life-work it was, no less. Surely she had known that Chaffery was a cheat. Had she not known ? Silence. " After so many kindnesses——"

She had interrupted him with a wailing " Oh, I know—I know."

But Lagune had been remorseless and insisted she had betrayed him, worse—made him ridiculous ! Look at the " work " he had undertaken at South Kensington—how could he go on with that now ? How could he find the heart ?

When his own typist sacrificed him to her stepfather's trickery?
" Trickery ! "

The gesticulating hands became active, the grey eyes
dilated with indignation, the piping voice eloquent.

" If he hadn't cheated you, some one else would," was
Ethel's inadequate muttered retort, unheard by the seeker
after phenomena.

It was perhaps not so bad as dismissal, but it certainly
lasted longer. And at home was Chaffery, grimly malignant
at her failure to secure that pneumatic glove. He had no
right to blame her, he really had not ; but a disturbed temper
is apt to falsify the scales of justice. The tambourine, he
insisted, he could have explained by saying he put up his hand
to catch it and protect his head directly Smithers moved. But
the pneumatic glove there was no explaining. He had made a
chance for her to secure it when he had pretended to faint. It
was rubbish to say any one could have been looking on the
table then—rubbish.

Beside that significant wreck of a pen stood a little carriage
clock in a case, and this suddenly lifted a slender voice and
announced *five*. She turned round on her stool and sat staring
at the clock. She smiled with the corners of her mouth
down. " Home," she said, " and begin again. It's like
battledore and shuttlecock. . . .

" I *was* silly. . . .

" I suppose I've brought it on myself. I ought to have
picked it up, I suppose. I had time. . . .

" Cheats . . . just cheats.

" I never thought I should see him again. . . .

" He was ashamed, of course. . . . He had his own friends."

For a space she sat still, staring blankly before her. She
sighed, rubbed a knuckle in a reddened eye, rose.

She went into the hall where her hat, transfixed by a couple
of hat-pins, hung above her jacket, assumed these garments,
and let herself out into the cold grey street.

She had hardly gone twenty yards from Lagune's door
before she became aware of a man overtaking her and walking
beside her. That kind of thing is a common enough experience to girls who go to and from work in London, and she had
had perforce to learn many things since her adventurous
Whortley days. She looked stiffly in front of her. The man
deliberately got in her way so that she had to stop. She lifted
eyes of indignant protest. It was Lewisham—and his face
was white.

He hesitated awkwardly and then in silence held out his
hand. She took it mechanically. He found his voice.
" Miss Henderson," he said.

" What do you want ? " she asked faintly.

" I don't know," he said. . . . " I want to talk to you."

" Yes ? "   Her heart was beating fast.

He found the thing unexpectedly difficult.

" May I—— ? Are you expecting—— ? Have you far to go ? I would like to talk to you. There is a lot . . ."

" I walk to Clapham," she said. " If you care . . . to come part of the way. . . ."

She moved awkwardly. Lewisham took his place at her side. They walked side by side for a moment, their manner constrained, having so much to say that they could not find a word to begin upon.

" Have you forgotten Whortley ? " he asked abruptly.

" No."

He glanced at her ; her face was downcast. " Why did you never write ? " he asked bitterly.

" I wrote."

" Again, I mean."

" I did—in July."

" I never had it."

" It came back."

" But Mrs. Munday. . . ."

" I had forgotten her name. I sent it to the Grammar School."

Lewisham suppressed an exclamation.

" I am very sorry," she said.

They went on again in silence. " Last night," said Lewisham at length. " I have no business to ask. But——"

She took a long breath. " Mr. Lewisham," she said, " that man you saw—the Medium—was my stepfather."

" Well ? "

" Isn't that enough ? "

Lewisham paused. " No," he said.

There was another constrained silence. " No," he said less dubiously. " I don't care a rap what your stepfather is. Were *you* cheating ? "

Her face turned white. Her mouth opened and closed. " Mr. Lewisham," she said deliberately, " you may not believe it, it may sound impossible, but on my honour . . . I did not know—I did not know for certain, that is—that my stepfather . . ."

" Ah ! " said Lewisham, leaping at conviction. " Then I was right. . . ."

For a moment she stared at him, and then, " I *did* know," she said, suddenly beginning to cry. " How can I tell you ? It is a lie. I *did* know. I *did* know all the time."

He stared at her in white astonishment. He fell behind her one step, and then in a stride came level again. Then, a silence, a silence that it seemed would never end. She had stopped crying, she was one huge suspense, not daring even to look at his face. And at last he spoke.

" No," he said slowly. " I don't mind even that. I don't care—even if it was that."

Abruptly they turned into the King's Road, with its roar of wheeled traffic and hurrying foot-passengers, and forthwith a crowd of boys with a broken-spirited Guy involved and separated them. In a busy highway of a night one must needs talk disconnectedly in shouted snatches or else hold one's peace. He glanced at her face and saw that it was set again. Presently she turned southward out of the tumult into a street of darkness and warm blinds, and they could go on talking again.

"I understand what you mean," said Lewisham. "I know I do. You knew but you did not want to know. It was like that."

But her mind had been active. "At the end of this road," she said, gulping a sob, "you must go back. It was kind of you to come, Mr. Lewisham. But you were ashamed—you are sure to be ashamed. My employer is a spiritualist, and my stepfather is a professional Medium, and my mother is a spiritualist. You were quite right not to speak to me last night. Quite. It was kind of you to come, but you must go back. Life is hard enough as it is. . . . You must go back at the end of the road. Go back at the end of the road. . . ."

Lewisham made no reply for a hundred yards. "I'm coming on to Clapham," he said.

They came to the end of the road in silence. Then at the kerb corner she turned and faced him. "Go back," she whispered.

"No," he said obstinately, and they stood face to face at the cardinal point of their lives.

"Listen to me," said Lewisham. "It is hard to say what I feel. I don't know myself. . . . But I'm not going to lose you like this. I'm not going to let you slip a second time. I was awake about it all last night. I don't care where you are, what your people are, nor very much whether you've kept quite clear of this medium humbug. I don't. You will in future. Anyhow. I've had a day and night to think it over. I had to come and try to find you. It's you. I've never forgotten you. Never. I'm not going to be sent back like this."

"It can be no good for either of us," she said as resolute as he.

"I shan't leave you."

"But what is the good ? . . ."

"I'm coming," said Lewisham, dogmatically.

And he came.

He asked her a question point blank and she would not answer him, and for some way they walked in grim silence. Presently she spoke with a twitching mouth. "I wish you would leave me," she said. "You are quite different from what I am. You felt that last night. You helped find us out. . . ."

" When first I came to London I used to wander about Clapham looking for you," said Lewisham, " week after week."

They had crossed the bridge and were in a narrow little street of shabby shops near Clapham Junction before they talked again. She kept her face averted and expressionless.

" I'm sorry," said Lewisham, with a sort of stiff civility, " if I seem to be forcing myself upon you. I don't want to pry into your affairs—if you don't wish me to. The sight of you has somehow brought back a lot of things. . . . I can't explain it. Perhaps—I had to come to find you—I kept on thinking of your face, of how you used to smile, how you jumped from the gate by the lock, and how we had tea . . . a lot of things."

He stopped again.

" A lot of things."

" If I may come ? " he said, and went unanswered. They crossed the wide streets by the Junction and went on towards the Common.

" I live down this road," she said stopping abruptly at a corner. " I would rather . . ."

" But I have said nothing."

She looked at him with her face white, unable to speak for a space. " It can do no good," she said. " I am mixed up with this. . . ."

She stopped.

He spoke deliberately. " I shall come," he said, " to-morrow night."

" No," she said.

" But I shall come."

" No," she whispered.

" I shall come." She could hide the gladness of her heart from herself no longer. She was frightened that he had come, but she was glad and she knew he knew that she was glad. She made no further protest. She held out her hand dumbly. And on the morrow she found him awaiting her even as he had said.

# CHAPTER FOURTEEN

FOR three days the Laboratory at South Kensington saw nothing of Lagune, and then he came back more invincibly voluble than ever. Every one had expected him to return apostate, but he thought back an invigorated faith, a propaganda unashamed. From some source he had derived strength and conviction afresh. Even the rhetorical Smithers availed nothing. There was a joined battle over the insufficient tea-cups, and the elderly young assistant demonstrator hovered on the verge of the discussion, rejoicing, it is supposed, over the entanglements of Smithers. For at the outset Smithers displayed an overweening confidence and civility, and at the end his ears were red and his finer manners lost to him.

Lewisham, it was remarked by Miss Heydinger, made but a poor figure in this discussion. Once or twice he seemed about to address Lagune, and thought better of it with the words upon his lips.

Lagune's treatment of the exposure was light and vigorous. "The man Chaffery," he said, " has made a clean breast of it. His point of view——"

" Facts are facts," said Smithers.

" A fact is a synthesis of impressions," said Lagune ; " but that you will learn when you are older. The thing is that we were at cross purposes. I told Chaffery you were beginners. He treated you as beginners—arranged a demonstration."

" It *was* a demonstration," said Smithers.

" Precisely. If it had not been for your interruptions. . . ."

" Ah ! "

" He forged elementary effects. . . ."

" You can't but admit that."

" I don't attempt to deny it. But, as he explained—the thing is necessary—justifiable. Psychic phenomena are subtle, a certain training of the observation is necessary. A medium is a more subtle instrument than a balance or a borax bead, and see how long it is before you can get assured results with a borax bead ! In the elementary class, in the introductory phase, conditions are too crude. . . ."

" For honesty."

" Wait a moment. *Is* it dishonest—rigging a demonstration ? "

" Of course it is."

" Your professors do it."

" I deny that *in toto*," said Smithers, and repeated with satisfaction, " *in toto*."

" That's all right," said Lagune, " because I have the facts. Your chemical lecturers—you may go downstairs now and ask, if you disbelieve me—always cheat over the indestructibility of matter experiment—always. And then another—a physiography thing. You know the experiment I mean ? To demonstrate the existence of the earth's rotation. They use—they use——"

" Foucault's pendulum," said Lewisham. " They use a rubber ball with a pin-hole hidden in the hand, and blow the pendulum round the way it ought to go."

" But that's different," said Smithers.

" Wait a moment," said Lagune, and produced a piece of folded printed paper from his pocket. " Here is a review from *Nature* of the work of no less a person than Professor Greenhill. And see—a convenient pin is introduced into the apparatus for the demonstration of virtual velocities ! Read it—if you doubt me. I suppose you doubt me."

Smithers abruptly abandoned his position of denial " *in toto.*" " This isn't my point, Mr. Lagune ; this isn't my point," he said. " These things that are done in the lecture theatre are not to prove facts, but to give ideas."

" So was my demonstration," said Lagune.

" We didn't understand it in that light."

" Nor does the ordinary person who goes to Science lectures understand it in that light. He is comforted by the thought that he is seeing things with his own eyes."

" Well, I don't care," said Smithers ; " two wrongs don't make a right. To rig demonstrations is wrong."

" There I agree with you. I have spoken plainly with this man Chaffery. He's not a full-blown professor, you know, a highly salaried ornament of the rock of truth like your demonstration-rigging professors here, and so I can speak plainly to him without offence. He takes quite the view they would take. But I am more rigorous. I insist that there shall be no more of this. . . ."

" Next time——" said Smithers with irony.

" There will be no next time. I have done with elementary exhibitions. You must take the word of the trained observer —just as you do in the matter of chemical analysis."

" Do you mean you are going on with that chap when he's been caught cheating under your very nose ? "

" Certainly. Why not ? "

Smithers set out to explain why not, and happened on confusion. " I still believe the man has powers," said Lagune.

" Of deception," said Smithers.

" Those I must eliminate," said Lagune. " You might as well refuse to study electricity because it escaped through your body. All new science is elusive. No investigator in his senses would refuse to investigate a compound because it did unexpected things. Either this dissolves in acid or I have nothing more to do with it—eh ? That's fine research ! "

Then it was the last vestiges of Smithers' manners vanished. "I don't care *what* you say," said Smithers. "It's all rot —it's all just rot. Argue if you like—but have you convinced anybody ? Put it to the vote ? "

"That's democracy with a vengeance," said Lagune. "A general election of the truth half-yearly, eh ? "

"That's simply wriggling out of it," said Smithers. "That hasn't anything to do with it at all."

Lagune, flushed but cheerful, was on his way downstairs when Lewisham overtook him. He was pale and out of breath, but as the staircase invariably rendered Lagune breathless he did not remark the younger man's disturbance. "Interesting talk," panted Lewisham. "Very interesting talk, sir."

"I'm glad you found it so—very," said Lagune.

There was a pause, and then Lewisham plunged desperately. "There is a young lady—she is your typist. . . ."

He stopped from sheer loss of breath.

"Yes ? " said Lagune.

"Is she a medium or anything of that sort ? "

"Well," Lagune reflected. "She is not a medium, certainly. But—why do you ask ? "

"Oh ! . . . I wondered."

"You noticed her eyes, perhaps. She is the stepdaughter of that man Chaffery—a queer character but indisputably mediumistic. It's odd the thing should have struck you. Curiously enough I myself have fancied she might be something of a psychic—judging from her face."

"A what ? "

"A psychic—undeveloped of course. I have thought once or twice. Only a little while ago I was speaking to that man Chaffery about her."

"Were you ? "

"Yes. He of course would like to see any latent powers developed. But it's a little difficult to begin, you know."

"You mean—she won't ? "

"Not at present. She is a good girl, but in this matter she is—timid. There is often a sort of disinclination—a queer sort of feeling—one might almost call it modesty."

"I see," said Lewisham.

"One can override it usually. I don't despair."

"No," said Lewisham shortly. They were at the foot of the staircase now. He hesitated. "You've given me a lot to think about," he said with an attempt at an offhand manner. "The way you talked upstairs "; and turned towards the book he had to sign.

"I'm glad you don't take up quite such an intolerant attitude as Mr. Smithers," said Lagune ; "very glad. I must lend you a book or two. If your *cramming* here leaves you any time, that is."

" Thanks," said Lewisham shortly, and walked away from him. The studiously characteristic signature quivered and sprawled in an unfamiliar manner.

" I'm *damned* if he overrides it," said Lewisham, under his breath.

# CHAPTER FIFTEEN

### LOVE IN THE STREETS

LEWISHAM was not quite clear what course he meant to take in the high enterprise of foiling Lagune, and indeed he was anything but clear about the entire situation. His logical processes, his emotions and his imagination seemed playing some sort of snatching game with his will. Enormous things hung imminent, but it worked out to this, that he walked home with Ethel night after night for—to be exact—seven and sixty nights. Every week night through November and December, save once when he had to go into the far East to buy himself an overcoat, he was waiting to walk with her home. A curious, inconclusive affair, that walk, to which he came nightly full of vague longings and which ended invariably under an odd shadow of disappointment. It began outside Lagune's most punctually at five, and ended—mysteriously—at the corner of a side road in Clapham, a road of little yellow houses with sunk basements and tawdry decorations of stone. Up that road she vanished night after night, into a grey mist and the shadow beyond a feeble yellow gas-lamp, and he would watch her vanish, and then sigh and turn back towards his lodgings.

They talked of this and that, their little superficial ideas about themselves and of their circumstances and tastes, and always there was something, something that was with them unspoken, unacknowledged, which made all these things unreal and insincere.

Yet out of their talk he began to form vague ideas of the home from which she came. There was, of course, no servant, and the mother was something meandering, furtive, tearful in the face of troubles. Sometimes of an afternoon or evening she grew garrulous. "Mother does talk so—sometimes." She rarely went out of doors. Chaffery always rose late, and would sometimes go away for days together. He was mean, he allowed only a weekly twenty-five shillings for housekeeping and sometimes things grew unsatisfactory at the week-end. There seemed to be little sympathy between mother and daughter ; the widow had been flighty in a dingy fashion, and her marriage with her chief lodger Chaffery had led to unforgettable sayings. It was to facilitate this marriage that Ethel had been sent to Whortley, so that was counted a mitigated evil. But these were far-off things, remote and unreal down the long, ill-lit vista of the suburban street which swallowed up Ethel nightly. The walk, her warmth and light and motion close to him, her clear little voice and the touch of her hand ; that was reality.

The shadow of Chaffery and his deceptions lay indeed

across all these things, sometimes faint, sometimes dark and present. Then Lewisham became insistent, his sentimental memories ceased, and he asked questions that verged on gulfs of doubt. Had she ever " helped " ? She had not, she declared. Then she added that twice at home she had " sat down " to complete the circle. She would never help again. That she promised—if it needed promising. There had already been dreadful trouble at home about the exposure at Lagune's. Her mother had sided with her stepfather and joined in blaming her. But was she to blame ?

" Of *course* you were not to blame," said Lewisham.

Lagune, he learnt, had been unhappy and restless for the three days after the séance—indulging in wearisome monologue with Ethel as sole auditor (at twenty-one shillings a week). Then he had decided to give Chaffery a second lecture on his disastrous dishonesty. But it was Chaffery gave the lecture. Smithers, had he only known it, had been overthrown by a better brain than Lagune's, albeit it spoke through Lagune's treble.

Ethel did not like talking of Chaffery and these other things. " If you knew how sweet it was to forget it all," she would say ; " to be just us two together for a little while." And, " What good *does* it do to keep on ? " when Lewisham was pressing. Lewisham wanted very much to keep on at times, but the good of it was a little hard to demonstrate. So his knowledge of the situation remained imperfect and the weeks drifted by.

Wonderfully varied were those seven-and-sixty nights, as he came to remember in after life. These were nights of damp and drizzle, and then thick fogs, beautiful, isolating, grey-white veils, turning every yard of pavement into a private room. Grand indeed were these fogs, things to rejoice at mightily, since then it was no longer a thing for public scorn that two young people hurried along arm in arm, and one could do a thousand impudent, significant things with varying pressure and the fondling of a little hand (a hand in a greatly mended glove of cheap kid). Then indeed one seemed to be nearer that elusive something that threaded it together. And the dangers of the street corners, the horses looming up suddenly out of the dark, the carters with lanterns at their horses' heads, the street lamps, blurred smoky orange at one's nearest, and vanishing at twenty yards into dim haze, seemed to accentuate the infinite need of protection on the part of a delicate young lady who had already traversed three winters of fogs, thornily alone. Moreover, one could come right down the quiet street where she lived, half-way to the steps of her house, with a delightful sense of enterprise.

The fogs passed all too soon into a hard frost, into nights of starlight and presently moonlight, when the lamps looked hard, flashing like rows of yellow gems, and their reflections and the glare of the shop windows were sharp and frosty and even the stars hard and bright, snapping noiselessly (if one may say so) instead of twinkling. A jacket trimmed with imitation Astrakhan replaced Ethel's lighter coat, and a round cap of Astrakhan her hat, and her eyes shone hard and bright, and her forehead was broad and white beneath it. It was exhilarating, but one got home too soon and so the way from Chelsea to Clapham was lengthened, first into a loop of side streets, and then when the first pulverulent snows told that Christmas was at hand, into a new loop down King's Road, and once even through the Brompton Road and Sloane Street, where the shops were full of decorations and entertaining things.

And under circumstances of infinite gravity, Mr. Lewisham secretly spent three-and-twenty shillings out of the vestiges of that hundred pounds, and bought Ethel a little gold ring set with pearls. With that there must needs be a cere- monial, and on the verge of the snowy, foggy Common she took off her glove and the ring was placed on her finger. Whereupon he was moved to kiss her—on the frost-pink knuckles next to an inky nail.

" It's silly of us," she said. " What can we do ?—ever ? "

" You wait," he said, and his tone was full of vague promises.

Afterwards he thought over those promises, and another evening went into the matter more fully, telling her of all the brilliant things that he held it was possible for a South Kensington student to do and be—of headmasterships, northern science schools, inspectorships, demonstratorships, yea, even professorships. And then, and then—— To all of which she lent a willing and incredulous ear, finding in that dreaming a quality of fear as well as delight.

The putting on of the pearl-set ring was mere ceremonial, of course ; she could not wear it either at Lagune's or at home, so instead she threaded it on a little white satin ribbon and wore it round her neck—" next her heart." He thought of it there warm " next her heart."

When he had bought the ring he had meant to save it for Christmas before he gave it to her. But the desire to see her pleasure had been too strong for him.

Christmas Eve, I know not by what deceit on her part, these young people spent together all day. Lagune was down with a touch of bronchitis and had given his typist a holiday. Perhaps she forgot to mention it at home. The Royal College was in vacation and Lewisham was free. He declined the plumber's invitation ; " work " kept him in London, he said, though it meant a pound or more of added expenditure. These absurd young people walked sixteen miles that Christmas Eve, and parted warm and glowing.

There had been a hard frost and a little snow, the sky was a colourless grey, icicles hung from the arms of the street lamps, and the pavements were patterned out with frond-like forms that were trodden into slides as the day grew older. The Thames they knew was a wonderful sight, but that they kept until last. They went first along the Brompton Road. . . .

And it is well that you should have the picture of them right ; Lewisham in the ready-made overcoat, blue cloth and velvet collar, dirty tan gloves, red tie, and bowler hat ; Ethel in a two-year-old jacket, and hat of curly Astrakhan ; both pink-cheeked from the keen air, shyly arm in arm occasionally, and very alert to miss no possible spectacle. The shops were varied and interesting along the Brompton Road, but nothing to compare with Piccadilly. There were windows in Piccadilly so full of costly little things it took fifteen minutes to get them done, card shops, drapers' shops full of foolish, entertaining attractions. Lewisham, in spite of his old animosities, forgot to be severe on the Shopping Class, Ethel was so vastly entertained by all these pretty follies.

Then up Regent Street by the place where the sham diamonds are, and the place where the girls display their long hair, and the place where the little chickens run about in the window, and so into Oxford Street, Holborn, through to Ludgate Hill, St. Paul's Churchyard, and on to Leadenhall and the markets where turkeys, geese, ducklings, and chickens—turkeys predominant, however—hang in rows by the thousand.

" I *must* buy you something," said Lewisham, resuming a topic.

" No, no," said Ethel with her eye down a vista of innumerable birds.

" But I *must*," said Lewisham. " You had better choose it, or I shall get something wrong." His mind ran on brooches and clasps.

" You mustn't waste your money, and besides, I have that ring."

But Lewisham insisted.

" Then—if you must—I am starving. Buy me something to eat."

An immense and memorable joke. Lewisham plunged recklessly—orientally—into an awe-inspiring place with mitred napkins. They lunched on cutlets—stripped the cutlets to the bone—and little crisp brown potatoes, and they drank between them a whole half bottle of—some white wine or other, selected by Lewisham in an offhand way from the list. Neither of them had ever taken wine at a meal before. One-and-ninepence it cost him, Sir, and the name of it was Capri ! It was really very passable Capri—a manufactured product, no doubt, but warming and aromatic. Ethel was aghast at his magnificence and drank a glass and a half.

Then, very warm and comfortable, they went down by the Tower, and the Tower Bridge with its crest of snow, huge pendant icicles, and the ice blocks choked in its side arches, was seasonable seeing. And as they had had enough of shops and crowds they set off resolutely along the desolate Embankment homeward.

But indeed the Thames was a wonderful sight that year ! Ice-fringed along either shore, and with drift-ice in the middle reflecting a luminous scarlet from the broad red setting sun, and moving steadily, incessantly seaward. A swarm of mewing gulls went to and fro, and with them mingled pigeons and crows. The buildings on the Surrey side were dim and grey and very mysterious, the moored, ice-blocked barges silent and deserted, and here and there a lit window shone warm. The sun sank right out of sight into a bank of blue, and the Surrey side dissolved in mist save for a few insoluble spots of yellow light, that presently became many. And after our lovers had come under Charing Cross Bridge the Houses of Parliament rose before them at the end of a great crescent of golden lamps, blue and faint, half-way between the earth and sky. And the clock on the Tower was like a November sun.

It was a day without a flaw, or at most but the slightest speck. And that only came at the very end.

" Good-bye, dear," she said. " I have been very happy to-day."

His face came very close to hers. " Good-bye," he said, pressing her hand and looking into her eyes.

She glanced round, she drew nearer to him. " *Dearest* one," she whispered very softly, and then, " Good-bye."

Suddenly he became unaccountably petulant, he dropped her hand. " It's always like this. We are happy. *I* am happy. And then—then you are taken away. . . ."

There was a silence of mute interrogations.

" Dear," she whispered, " we must wait."

A moment's pause. " *Wait !* " he said, and broke off. He hesitated. " Good-bye," he said as though he was snapping a thread that held them together.

# CHAPTER SIXTEEN

## MISS HEYDINGER'S PRIVATE THOUGHTS

THE way from Chelsea to Clapham and the way from South Kensington to Battersea, especially if the former is looped about a little to make it longer, come very near to each other. One night close upon Christmas two friends of Lewisham's passed him and Ethel. But Lewisham did not see them, because he was looking at Ethel's face.

"Did you see ? " said the other girl, a little maliciously.

"Mr. Lewisham—wasn't it ? " said Miss Heydinger in a perfectly indifferent tone.

Miss Heydinger sat in the room her younger sister called her "Sanctum." Her Sanctum was only too evidently an intellectualised bedroom, and a cheap wallpaper of silvery roses peeped coquettishly from between her draped furniture. Her particular glories were the writing-desk in the middle of the room and the microscope on the unsteady octagonal table under the window. There were bookshelves of workmanship patently feminine in their facile decoration and structural instability, and on them an array of glittering poets, Shelley, Rossetti, Keats, Browning, and odd volumes of Ruskin, South Place Sermons, Socialistic publications in torn paper covers, and above, science textbooks and notebooks in an oppressive abundance. The autotypes that hung about the room were eloquent of æsthetic ambitions and of a certain impermeability to implicit meanings. There was the "Mirror of Venus" by Burne-Jones, Rossetti's "Annunciation," Lippi's "Annunciation," and the "Love and Life" and "Love and Death" of Watts. And among other photographs was one of last year's Debating Society Committee, Lewisham smiling a little weakly near the centre, and Miss Heydinger out of focus in the right wing. And Miss Heydinger sat with her back to all these things in her black horsehair armchair, staring into the fire, her eyes hot and her chin on her hand.

"I might have guessed—before," she said. "Ever since that séance. It has been different. . . ."

She smiled bitterly. "Some shop girl. . . ."

She mused. "They are all alike, I suppose. They come back—a little damaged, as the woman says in *Lady Windermere's Fan*. Perhaps he will. I wonder. . . .

"Why should he be so deceitful ? Why should he act to me ? . . .

"Pretty, pretty, pretty—that is our business. What man hesitates in the choice ? He goes his own way, thinks his own thoughts, does his own work. . . .

" His dissection is getting behind—one can see he takes scarcely any notes. . . ."

For a long time she was silent. Her face became more intent. She began to bite her thumb, at first slowly, then faster. She broke out at last into words again.

" The things he might do, the great things he might do. He is able, he is dogged, he is strong. And then comes a pretty face ! Oh God ! *Why* was I made with heart and brain ? " She sprang to her feet, with her hands clenched and her face contorted. But she shed no tears.

Her attitude fell limp in a moment. One hand dropped by her side, the other rested on a fossil on the mantelshelf, and she stared down into the red fire.

" To think of all we might have done ! It maddens me !

" To work, and think, and learn. To hope and wait. To despise the petty arts of womanliness, to trust to the sanity of man . . .

" To awake like the foolish virgins," she said, " and find the hour of life is past ! "

Her face, her pose, softened into self-pity.

" Futility . . .

" It's no good. . . ." Her voice broke.

" I shall never be happy. . . ."

She saw the grandiose vision of the future she had cherished, suddenly rolled aside and vanishing, more and more splendid as it grew more and more remote—like a dream at the waking moment. The vision of her inevitable loneliness came to replace it, clear and acute. She saw herself alone and small in a huge desolation—infinitely pitiful, Lewisham callously receding. With " some shop girl." The tears came, came faster, until they were streaming down her face. She turned as if looking for something. She flung herself upon her knees before the little armchair, and began an incoherent sobbing prayer for the pity and comfort of God.

The next day one of the other girls in the biological course remarked to her friend that " Heydinger-dingery " had relapsed. Her friend glanced down the laboratory. " It's a bad relapse," she said. " Really . . . I couldn't . . . wear my hair like that."

She continued to regard Miss Heydinger with a critical eye. She was free to do this because Miss Heydinger was standing, lost in thought, staring at the December fog outside the laboratory windows. " She looks white," said the girl who had originally spoken. " I wonder if she works hard."

" It makes precious little difference if she does," said her friend. " I asked her yesterday what were the bones in the parietal segment, and she didn't know one. Not one."

The next day Miss Heydinger's place was vacant. She was ill—from overstudy—and her illness lasted to within three weeks of the terminal examination. Then she came back with a pallid face and a strenuous unavailing industry.

# CHAPTER SEVENTEEN

## IN THE RAPHAEL GALLERY

IT was nearly three o'clock, and in the Biological Laboratory the lamps were all alight. The class was busy with razors cutting sections of the root of a fern to examine it microscopically. A certain silent frog-like boy, a private student who plays no further part in this story, was working intently, looking more like a frog than usual—his expression modest with a touch of effort. Behind Miss Heydinger, jaded and untidy in her early manner again, was a vacant seat, an abandoned microscope and scattered pencils and notebooks.

On the door of the classroom was a list of those who had passed the Christmas examination. At the head of it was the name of the aforesaid frog-like boy ; next to him came Smithers and one of the girls bracketed together. Lewisham ingloriously headed the second class, and Miss Heydinger's name did not appear—there was, the list asserted, "one failure." So the student pays for the finer emotions.

And in the spacious solitude of the museum gallery devoted to the Raphael cartoons, sat Lewisham, plunged in gloomy meditation. A negligent hand pulled thoughtfully at the indisputable moustache, with particular attention to such portions as were long enough to gnaw.

He was trying to see the situation clearly. The shadow of that defeat lay across everything, blotted out the light of his pride, shaded his honour, threw everything into a new perspective. The rich prettiness of his love-making had fled to some remote quarter of his being. Against the frog-like youngster he felt a savage animosity. And Smithers had betrayed him. He was angry, bitterly angry with "swats" and "muggers" who spent their whole time grinding for these foolish chancy examinations. Nor had the practical examination been altogether fair, and one of the questions in the written portion was quite outside the lectures. Biver, Professor Biver, was an indiscriminating ass, he felt assured, and so too was Weeks, the demonstrator. But these obstacles could not blind his intelligence to the manifest cause of his overthrow, the waste of more than half his available evening, the best time for study in the twenty-four hours, day after day. And that was going on steadily, a perpetual leakage of time. To-night he would go to meet her again, and begin to accumulate to himself ignominy in the second part of the course, the botanical section, also. And so, reluctantly rejecting one cloudy excuse after another, he clearly focussed the antagonism between his relations to Ethel and his immediate ambitions.

Things had come so easily to him for the last two years

that he had taken his steady upward progress in life as assured. It had never occurred to him, when he went to intercept Ethel after that séance, that he went into any peril of that sort. Now he had had a sharp reminder. He began to shape a picture of the frog-like boy at home—he was a private student of the upper middle class—sitting in a convenient study with a writing-table, book-shelves and a shaded lamp—Lewisham worked at his chest of drawers with his great-coat on, and his feet in the lowest drawer wrapped in all his available linen—and in the midst of incredible conveniences the frog-like boy was working, working, working. Meanwhile Lewisham toiled through the foggy streets, Chelsea-ward, or, after he had left her, tramped homeward—full of foolish imaginings.

He began to think with bloodless lucidity of his entire relationship to Ethel. His softer emotions were in abeyance, but he told himself no lies. He cared for her, he loved to be with her and to talk to her and please her, but that was not all his desire. He thought of the bitter words of an orator at Hammersmith, who had complained that in our present civilisation even the elemental need of marriage was denied. Virtue had become a vice. "We marry in fear and trembling, sex for a home is the woman's traffic, and the man comes to his heart's desire when his heart's desire is dead." The thing which had seemed a mere flourish, came back now with a terrible air of truth. Lewisham saw that it was a case of divergent ways. On the one hand that shining staircase to fame and power that had been his dream from the very dawn of his adolescence, and on the other hand—Ethel.

And if he chose Ethel, even then would he have his choice ? What would come of it ?   A few walks more or less !   She was hopelessly poor, he was hopelessly poor, and this cheat of a Medium was her stepfather !   After all she was not well-educated, she did not understand his work and his aims. . . .

He suddenly perceived with absolute conviction that after the séance he should have gone home and forgotten her. Why had he felt that irresistible impulse to seek her out ?   Why had his imagination spun such a strange web of possibilities about her ?   He was involved now, foolishly involved. . . . All his future was a sacrifice to this transitory ghost of love-making in the streets.   He pulled spitefully at his moustache.

His picture began to shape itself into Ethel and her mysterious mother and the vague dexterous Chaffery holding him back, entangled in an impalpable net, from that bright and glorious ascent to performance and distinction.   Leaky boots and the splashings of cabs as his portion for all his life.   Already the Forbes Medal, the immediate step, was as good as lost. . . .

What on earth had he been thinking about ?   He fell foul of his upbringing.   Men of the upper or middle classes were put up to these things by their parents ; they were properly warned against involving themselves in this love nonsense before they were independent. It was much better. . . .

Everything was going. Not only his work—his scientific career, but the Debating Society, the political movement, all his work for Humanity. . . . Why not be resolute—even now ? . . . Why not put the thing clearly and plainly to her ? Or write ? If he wrote now he could get the advantage of the evening at the Library. He must ask her to forgo these walks home—at least until the next examination. *She* would understand. He had a qualm of doubt whether she would understand. . . . He grew angry at this possibility. But it was no good mincing matters. If once he began to consider her—— Why should he consider her in that way ? Simply because she was unreasonable !

Lewisham had a transitory gust of anger.

Yet that abandonment of the walks insisted on looking mean to him. And she would think it mean. Which was very much worse, somehow. *Why* mean ? Why should she think it mean ? He grew angry again.

The portly museum policeman who had been watching him furtively, wondering why a student should sit in front of the " Sacrifice of Lystra," and gnaw lips and nails and moustache, and scowl and glare at that masterpiece, saw him rise suddenly to his feet with an air of resolution, spin on his heel, and set off with a quick step out of the gallery. He looked neither to the right nor the left. He passed out of sight down the staircase.

" Gone to get some more moustache to eat, I suppose," said the policeman reflectively. . . .

" One 'ud think something had bit him."

After some pensive moments the policeman strolled along down the gallery and came to a stop opposite the cartoon.

" Figgers is a bit big for the houses," said the policeman, anxious to do impartial justice. " But that's Art. I lay '*e* couldn't do anything . . . not arf so good."

# CHAPTER EIGHTEEN

## THE FRIENDS OF PROGRESS MEET

THE night next but one after this meditation saw a new order in the world. A young lady dressed in an Astrakhan-edged jacket and with a face of diminished cheerfulness marched from Chelsea to Clapham alone, and Lewisham sat in the flickering electric light of the Education Library, staring blankly over a business-like pile of books at unseen things.

The arrangement had not been effected without friction, the explanation had proved difficult. Evidently she did not appreciate the full seriousness of Lewisham's mediocre position in the list. "But you have *passed* all right," she said. Neither could she grasp the importance of evening study. "Of course I don't know," she said judicially; "but I thought you were learning all day." She calculated the time consumed by their walk as half an hour, "just one half-hour," she forgot that he had to get to Chelsea and then to return to his lodgings. Her customary tenderness was veiled by an only too apparent resentment. First at him, and then when he protested, at Fate. "I suppose it *has* to be," she said. "Of course it doesn't matter, I suppose, if we *don't* see each other quite so often," with a quiver of pale lips.

He had returned from the parting with an uneasy mind, and that evening had gone in the composition of a letter that was to make things clearer. But his scientific studies rendered his prose style hard, and things he could whisper he could not write. His justification indeed did him no sort of justice. But her reception of it made her seem a very unreasonable person. He had some violent fluctuations. At times he was bitterly angry with her for her failure to see things as he did. He would wander about the museum conducting imaginary discussions with her and even making scathing remarks. At other times he had to summon all his powers of acrid discipline and all his memories of her resentful retorts, to keep himself from a headlong rush to Chelsea and unmanly capitulation.

And this new disposition of things endured for two weeks. It did not take Miss Heydinger all that time to discover that the disaster of the examination had wrought a change in Lewisham. She perceived those nightly walks were over. It was speedily evident to her that he was working with a kind of dogged fury; he came early, he went late. The wholesome freshness of his cheek paled. He was to be seen on each of the late nights amidst a pile of diagrams and text-books in one of the less draughty corners of the Educational

Library, accumulating piles of memoranda. And nightly in the Students' " club " he wrote a letter addressed to a stationer shop in Clapham, but that she did not see. For the most part these letters were brief, for Lewisham, South Kensington fashion, prided himself upon not being " literary," and some of the more despatch-like wounded a heart perhaps too hungry for tender words.

He did not meet Miss Heydinger's renewed advances with invariable kindness. Yet something of the old relations were presently restored. He would talk well to her for a time, and then snap like a dry twig. But the loaning of books was resumed, the subtle process of his æsthetic education that Miss Heydinger had devised. " Here is a book I promised you," she said one day, and he tried to remember the promise.

The book was a collection of *Browning's Poems*, and it contained " Sludge " ; it also happened that it contained " The Statue and the Bust "—that stimulating lecture on half-hearted constraints. " Sludge " did not interest Lewisham, it was not at all his idea of a medium, but he read and re-read " The Statue and the Bust." It had the profoundest effect upon him. He went to sleep—he used to read his literature in bed because it was warmer there, and over literature nowadays it did not matter as it did with science if one dozed a little—with these lines stimulating his emotions :

" So weeks grew months, years ; gleam by gleam
The glory dropped from their youth and love,
And both perceived they had dreamed a dream."

By way of fruit it may be to such seed, he dreamed a dream that night. It concerned Ethel, and at last they were a-marrying. He drew her to his arms. He bent to kiss her. And suddenly he saw her lips were shrivelled and her eyes were dull, saw the wrinkles seaming her face ! She was old ! She was intolerably old ! He woke in a kind of horror and lay awake and very dismal until dawn, thinking of their separation and of her solitary walk through the muddy streets, thinking of his position, the leeway he had lost and the chances there were against him in the battle of the world. He perceived the colourless truth ; the Career was improbable, and that Ethel should be added to it was almost hopeless. Clearly the question was between these two. Or should he vacillate and lose both ? And then his wretchedness gave place to that anger that comes of perpetually thwarted desires. . . .

It was on the day after this dream that he insulted Parkson so grossly. He insulted Parkson after a meeting of the " Friends of Progress " at Parkson's rooms.

No type of English student nowadays quite realises the noble ideal of plain living and high thinking. Our admirable examination system admits of extremely little thinking at any level, high or low. But the Kensington student's living is at any rate insufficient, and he makes occasional signs of recognition towards the cosmic process.

One such sign was the periodic gathering of these "Friends of Progress," an association begotten of Lewisham's paper on Socialism. It was understood that strenuous things were to be done to make the world better, but so far no decisive action had been taken.

They met in Parkson's sitting-room, because Parkson, being a Whitworth Scholar and in receipt of one hundred pounds a year, was the only one of the Friends opulent enough to have a sitting-room. The Friends were of various ages, mostly very young. Several smoked and others held pipes which they had discontinued smoking—but there was nothing to drink except coffee, because that was the utmost they could afford. Dunkerley, an assistant master in a suburban school, and Lewisham's former colleague at Whortley, attended these assemblies through the introduction of Lewisham. All the Friends wore red ties except Bletherly, who wore an orange one to show that he was aware of Art, and Dunkerley wore a black one with blue specks because assistant masters in small private schools have to keep up appearances. And their simple procedure was that each talked as much as the others would suffer.

Usually the self-proposed "Luther of Socialism"—ridiculous Lewisham !—had a thesis or so to maintain, but this night he was depressed and inattentive. He sat with his legs over the arm of his chair by way of indicating the state of his mind. He had a packet of Algerian cigarettes (twenty for fivepence) and appeared chiefly concerned to smoke them all before the evening was out. Bletherley was going to discourse of "Woman under Socialism," and he brought a big American edition of Shelley's works and a volume of Tennyson, including the "Princess," both bristling with paper tongues against his marked quotations. He was all for the abolition of "monopolies," and the crèche was to replace the family. He was unctuous when he was not pretty-pretty, and his views were evidently unpopular.

Parkson was a man from Lancashire, and a devout Quaker ; his third and completing factor was Ruskin, with whose work and phraseology he was saturated. He listened to Bletherley with a marked disapproval, and opened a vigorous defence of that ancient tradition of loyalty that Bletherley had called the monopolist institution of marriage. " The pure and simple old theory—love and faithfulness," said Parkson, " suffices for me. If we are to smear our political movements with this sort of stuff . . ."

" Does it work ? " interjected Lewisham, speaking for the first time.

" What work ? "

" The pure and simple old theory. I know the theory. I believe in the theory. Bletherley's Shelley-witted. But it's theory. You meet the inevitable girl. The theory says you may meet her anywhen. You meet too young. You fall in love. You marry—in spite of obstacles. Love laughs at locksmiths. You have children. That's the theory. All very well for a man whose father can leave him five hundred a year. But how does it work for a shopman ? . . . An assistant master like Dunkerley ? Or . . . Me ? "

" In these cases one must exercise restraint," said Parkson. " Have faith. A man that is worth having is worth waiting for."

" Worth growing old for ? " said Lewisham.

" Chap ought to fight," said Dunkerley. " Don't see your difficulty, Lewisham. Struggle for existence keen, no doubt, tremendous in fact—still. In it—may as well struggle. Two —join forces—pool the luck. If I saw a girl I fancied so that I wanted to, I'd marry her to-morrow. And my market value is seventy *non res.*"

Lewisham looked round at him eagerly, suddenly interested. " *Would* you ? " he said. Dunkerley's face was slightly flushed.

" Like a shot. Why not ? "

" But how are you to live ? "

" That comes after. If . . ."

" I can't agree with you, Mr. Dunkerley," said Parkson. " I don't know if you have read *Sesame and Lilies*, but there you have, set forth far more fairly than any words of mine could do, an ideal of a woman's place . . ."

" All rot—*Sesame and Lilies*," interrupted Dunkerley. " Read bits. Couldn't stand it. Never *can* stand Ruskin. Too many prepositions. Tremendous English, no doubt, but not my style. Sort of thing a wholesale grocer's daughter might read to get refined. *We* can't afford to get refined."

" But would you really marry a girl . . . ? " began Lewisham, with an unprecedented admiration for Dunkerley in his eyes.

" Why not ? "

" On—— ? " Lewisham hesitated.

" Forty pounds a year *res.* Whack ! Yes."

A silent youngster began to speak, cleared an accumulated huskiness from this throat and said, " Consider the girl."

" Why *marry* ? " asked Bletherley, unregarded.

" You must admit you are asking a great thing when you want a girl . . ." began Parkson.

" Not so. When a girl's chosen a man, and he chooses her, her place is with him. What is the good of hankering ? Mutual. Fight together."

" Good ! " said Lewisham suddenly emotional. " You talk like a man, Dunkerley. I'm hanged if you don't."

" The place of Woman," insisted Parkson, " is the Home. And if there is no home——! I hold that, if need be, a man should toil seven years—as Jacob did for Rachel—ruling his passions, to make the home fitting and sweet for her . . ."

" Get the hutch for the pet animal," said Dunkerley. " No. I mean to marry a *woman.* Female sex always *has* been in the struggle for existence—no great damage so far—always will be. Tremendous idea—that struggle for existence. Only sensible theory you've got hold of, Lewisham. Woman who isn't fighting square side by side with a man—woman who's just kept and fed and petted is . . ." He hesitated.

A lad with a spotted face and a bulldog pipe between his teeth supplied a Biblical word.

" That's shag," said Dunkerley. " I was going to say ' a harem of one.' "

The youngster was puzzled for a moment. " I smoke Perique," he said.

" It will make you just as sick," said Dunkerley.

" Refinement's so beastly vulgar," was the belated answer of the smoker of Perique.

That was the interesting part of the evening to Lewisham. Parkson suddenly rose, got down *Sesame and Lilies,* and insisted upon reading a lengthy mellifluous extract that went like a garden roller over the debate, and afterwards Bletherley became the centre of a wrangle that left him grossly insulted and in a minority of one. The institution of marriage, so far as the South Kensington student is concerned, is in no immediate danger.

Parkson turned out with the rest of them at half-past ten, for a walk. The night was warm for February and the waxing moon bright. Parkson fixed himself upon Lewisham and Dunkerley, to Lewisham's intense annoyance—for he had a few intimate things he could have said to the man of Ideas that night. Dunkerley lived north, so that the three went up Exhibition Road to High Street, Kensington. There they parted from Dunkerley, and Lewisham and Parkson turned southward again for Lewisham's new lodging in Chelsea.

Parkson was one of those exponents of virtue for whom the discussion of sexual matters has an irresistible attraction. The meeting had left him eloquent. He had argued with Dunkerley to the verge of indelicacy, and now he poured out a vast and increasingly confidential flow of talk upon Lewisham. Lewisham was distraught. He walked as fast as he could. His sole object was to get rid of Parkson. Parkson's sole object was to tell him interesting secrets about himself and a Certain Person with a mind of extraordinary Purity of whom Lewisham had heard before.

Ages passed.

Lewisham suddenly found himself being shown a photograph under a lamp. It represented an asymmetrical face singularly void of expression, the upper part of an " art " dress, and a fringe of curls. He perceived he was being given to understand that this was a Paragon of Purity, and that she was the particular property of Parkson. Parkson was regarding him proudly and apparently awaiting his verdict.

Lewisham struggled with the truth. " It's an interesting face," he said.

" It is a face essentially beautiful," said Parkson quietly but firmly. " Do you notice the eyes, Lewisham ? "

" Oh, yes," said Lewisham. " Yes. I see the eyes."

" They are . . . innocent. They are the eyes of a little child."

" Yes. They look that sort of eye. Very nice, old man. I congratulate you. Where does she live ? "

" You never saw a face like that in London," said Parkson.

" *Never*," said Lewisham decisively.

" I would not show that to every one," said Parkson. " You can scarcely judge all that pure-hearted, wonderful girl is to me." He returned the photograph solemnly to its envelope, regarding Lewisham with an air of one who has performed the ceremony of blood-brotherhood. Then taking Lewisham's arm affectionately—a thing Lewisham detested— he went on to a copious outpouring on Love—with illustrative anecdotes of the Paragon. It was just sufficiently cognate to the matter of Lewisham's thoughts to demand attention. Every now and then he had to answer, and he felt an idiotic desire—albeit he clearly perceived its idiocy—to reciprocate confidences. The necessity of fleeing Parkson became urgent —Lewisham's temper under these multitudinous stresses was going.

" Every man needs a Lode Star," said Parkson—and Lewisham swore under his breath.

Parkson's lodgings were now near at hand to the left, and it occurred to him this boredom would be soonest ended if he took Parkson home. Parkson consented mechanically, still discoursing.

" I have often seen you talking to Miss Heydinger," he said. " If you will pardon my saying it . . ."

" We are excellent friends," admitted Lewisham. " But here we are at your diggings."

Parkson stared at his " diggings." " There's Heaps I want to talk about. I'll come part of the way at any rate to Battersea. Your Miss Heydinger, I was saying . . ."

From that point onwards he made casual appeals to a supposed confidence between Lewisham and Miss Heydinger, each of which increased Lewisham's exasperation. " It will not be long before you also, Lewisham, will begin to know the infinite purification of a Pure Love. . . ." Then suddenly, with a vague idea of suppressing Parkson's unendurable chatter, as one motive at least, Lewisham rushed into the confidential.

"I know," he said. "You talk to me as though . . . I've marked out my destiny these three years." His confidential impulse died as he relieved it.

"You don't mean to say Miss Heydinger—— ? " asked Parkson.

"Oh, *damn* Miss Heydinger ! " said Lewisham, and suddenly, abruptly, uncivilly, he turned away from Parkson at the end of the street and began walking away southward, leaving Parkson in mid-sentence at the crossing.

Parkson stared in astonishment at his receding back and ran after him to ask for the grounds of this sudden offence. Lewisham walked on for a space with Parkson trotting by his side. Then suddenly he turned. His face was quite white and he spoke in a tired voice.

"Parkson," he said, "you are a fool ! . . . You have the face of a sheep, the manners of a buffalo, and the conversation of a bore. Pewrity indeed ! . . . The girl whose photograph you showed me has eyes that don't match. She looks as loathsome as one would naturally expect. . . . I'm not joking now. . . . Go away ! "

After that Lewisham went on his southward way alone. He did not go straight to his room in Chelsea, but spent some hours in a street in Battersea, pacing to and fro in front of a possible house. His passion changed from savagery to a tender longing. If only he could see her to-night ! He knew his own mind now. To-morrow he was resolved he would fling work to the dogs and meet her. The things Dunkerley had said had filled his mind with wonderful novel thoughts. If only he could see her now !

His wish was granted. At the corner of the street two figures passed him : one of these, a tall man in glasses and a quasi-clerical hat, with coat collar turned up under his grey side-whiskers, he recognised as Chaffery ; the other he knew only too well. The pair passed him without seeing him, but for an instant the lamplight fell upon her face and showed it white and tired.

Lewisham stopped dead at the corner, staring in blank astonishment after these two figures as they receded into the haze under the lights. He was dumbfounded. A clock struck slowly. It was midnight. Presently down the road came the slamming of their door.

Long after the echo died away he stood there. " She has been at a séance ; she has broken her promise. She has been at a séance, she has broken her promise," sang in perpetual reiteration through his brain.

And then came the interpretation. " She has done it because I have left her. I might have told it from her letters. She has done it because she thinks I am not in earnest, that my love-making was just boyishness . . .

" I knew she would never understand."

# CHAPTER NINETEEN

THE next morning Lewisham learnt from Lagune that his intuition was correct, that Ethel had at last succumbed to pressure and consented to attempt thought-reading. " We made a good beginning," said Lagune, rubbing his hands. " I am sure we shall do well with her. Certainly she has powers. I have always felt it in her face. She has powers."

" Was much . . . pressure necessary ? " asked Lewisham by an effort.

" We had—considerable difficulty. Considerable. But of course—as I pointed out to her—it was scarcely possible for her to continue as my typist unless she was disposed to take an interest in my investigations——"

" You did that ? "

" Had to. Fortunately Chaffery—it was his idea. I must admit——"

Lagune stopped astonished. Lewisham, after making an odd sort of movement with his hands, had turned round and was walking away down the laboratory. Lagune stared, confronted by a psychic phenomenon beyond his circle of ideas. " Odd ! " he said at last, and began to unpack his bag. Ever and again he stopped and stared at Lewisham, who was now sitting in his own place and drumming on the table with both hands.

Presently Miss Heydinger came out of the specimen room and addressed a remark to the young man. He appeared to answer with considerable brevity. He then stood up, hesitated for a moment between the three doors of the laboratory, and walked out by that opening on the back staircase. Lagune did not see him again until the afternoon.

That night Ethel had Lewisham's company again on her way home and their voices were earnest. She did not go straight home, but instead they went up under the gas lamps to the vague spaces of Clapham Common to talk there at length. And the talk that night was a momentous one. " Why have you broken your promise ? " he said.

Her excuses were vague and weak. " I thought you did not care so much as you did," she said. " And when you stopped these walks—nothing seemed to matter. Besides—it is not like séances with spirits. . . ."

At first Lewisham was passionate and forcible. His anger at Lagune and Chaffery blinded him to her turpitude. He talked her defences down. " It is cheating," he said. " Well —even if what *you* do is not cheating, it is delusion—unconscious cheating. Even if there is something in it, it is wrong.

True or not, it is wrong. Why don't they thought-read each other ? Why should they want you ? Your mind is your own. It is sacred. To probe it !—I won't have it ! I won't have it ! At least you are mine to that extent. I can't think of you like that—bandaged. And that little fool pressing his hand on the back of your neck and asking questions. I won't have it ! I would rather kill you than that."

" They don't do that ! "

" I don't care ! that is what it will come to. The bandage is the beginning. People must not get their living in that way anyhow. I've thought it out. Let them thought-read their daughters and hypnotise their aunts, and leave their typists alone."

" But what am I to do ? "

" That's not it. There are things one must not suffer anyhow, whatever happens ! Or else—one might be made to do anything. Honour ! Just because we are poor—— Let him dismiss you ! *Let* him dismiss you. You can get another place——"

" Not at a guinea a week."

" Then take less."

" But I have to pay sixteen shillings every week."

" That doesn't matter."

She caught at a sob. " But to leave London—I can't do it. I can't."

" But how ?—— Leave London ? " Lewisham's face changed.

" Oh ! life is *hard*," she said. " I can't. They—they wouldn't let me stop in London."

" What do you mean ? "

She explained if Lagune dismissed her she was to go into the country to an aunt, a sister of Chaffery's who needed a companion. Chaffery insisted upon that. " Companion they call it. I shall be just a servant—she has no servant. My mother cries when I talk to her. She tells me she doesn't want me to go away from her. But she's afraid of him. ' Why don't you do what he wants ? ' she says."

She sat staring in front of her at the gathering night. She spoke again in an even tone.

" I hate telling you these things. It is you . . . If you didn't mind. . . . But you make it all different. I could do it —if it wasn't for you. I was . . . I *was* helping . . . I had gone meaning to help if anything went wrong at Mr. Lagune's. Yes—that night. No . . . don't ! It was too hard before to tell you. But I really did not feel it . . . until I saw you there. Then all at once I felt shabby and mean."

" Well ? " said Lewisham.

" That's all. I may have done thought-reading, but I have never really cheated since—*never*. . . . If you knew how hard it is . . ."

LML—M                                                    D

" I wish you had told me that before."

" I couldn't. Before you came it was different. He used to make fun of the people—used to imitate Lagune and make me laugh. It seemed a sort of joke." She stopped abruptly. " Why did you ever come on with me ? I told you not to—you *know* I did."

She was near wailing. For a minute she was silent.

" I can't go to his sister's," she cried. " I may be a coward —but I can't."

Pause. And then Lewisham saw his solution straight and clear. Suddenly his secret desire had become his manifest duty.

" Look here," he said, not looking at her and pulling his moustache, " I won't have you doing any more of that damned cheating. You shan't soil yourself any more. And I won't have you leaving London."

" But what am I to do ? " Her voice went up.

" Well—there is one thing you can do. If you dare."

" What is it ? "

He made no answer for some seconds. Then he turned round and sat looking at her. Their eyes met. . . .

The grey of his mind began to colour. Her face was white and she was looking at him, in fear and perplexity. A new tenderness for her sprang up in him—a new feeling. Hitherto he had loved and desired her sweetness and animation—but now she was white and weary-eyed. He felt as though he had forgotten her and suddenly remembered. A great longing came into his mind.

" But what is the other thing I can do ? "

It was strangely hard to say. There came a peculiar sensation in his throat and facial muscles, a nervous stress between laughing and crying. All the world vanished before that great desire. And he was afraid she would not dare, that she would not take him seriously.

" What is it ? " she said again.

" Don't you see that we can marry ? " he said, with the flood of his resolution suddenly strong and steady. " Don't you see that is the only thing for us ? The dead lane we are in ! You must come out of your cheating, and I must come out of my . . . cramming. And we—we must marry."

He paused and then became eloquent. " The world is against us, against—us. To you it offers money to cheat— to be ignoble. For it *is* ignoble ! It offers you no honest way, only a miserable drudgery. And it keeps you from me. And me too it bribes with the promise of success—if I will desert you. . . . You don't know all. . . . We may have to wait for years—we may have to wait for ever, if we wait until life is safe. We may be separated. . . . We may lose one another altogether. . . . Let us fight against it. Why should we separate ? Unless True Love is like the other things—an empty cant. This is the only way. We two—who belong to one another."

She looked at him, her face perplexed with this new idea, her heart beating very fast. "We are so young," she said. "And how are we to live ? You get a guinea."

"I can get more—I can earn more. I have thought it out. I have been thinking of it these two days. I have been thinking what we could do. I have money."

"You have money ? "

"Nearly a hundred pounds."

"But we are so young—— And my mother . . ."

"We won't ask her. We will ask no one. This is *our* affair. Ethel ! this is *our* affair. It is not a question of ways and means—even before this—— I have thought . . . Dear one !—*don't* you love me ? "

She did not grasp his emotional quality. She looked at him with puzzled eyes—still practical—making the suggestion arithmetical.

"I could typewrite if I had a machine. I have heard——"

"It's not a question of ways and means. Now. Ethel—I have longed——"

He stopped. She looked at his face, at his eyes now eager and eloquent with the things that never shaped themselves into words.

"*Dare* you come with me ? " he whispered.

Suddenly the world opened out in reality to her as sometimes it had opened out to her in wistful dreams. And she quailed before it. She dropped her eyes from his. She became a fellow-conspirator. "But, how—— ? "

"I will think how. Trust me ! Surely we know each other now—— Think ! We two——"

"But I have never thought——"

"I could get apartments for us both. It would be so easy. And think of it—think—of what life would be ! "

"How can I ? "

"You will come ? "

She looked at him, startled. "You know," she said, " you must know I would like—I would love——"

"You will come."

"But, dear—— ! Dear, if you *make* me——"

"Yes ! " cried Lewisham triumphantly. "You will come." He glanced round and his voice dropped. "Oh ! my dearest ! my dearest ! . . ."

His voice sank to an inaudible whisper. But his face was eloquent. Two garrulous, home-going clerks passed opportunely to remind him that his emotions were in a public place.

# CHAPTER TWENTY

## THE CAREER IS SUSPENDED

ON the Wednesday afternoon following this—it was hard upon the botanical examination—Mr. Lewisham was observed by Smithers in the big Education Library reading in a volume of the *British Encyclopædia*. Beside him were the current *Whitaker's Almanack*, an open notebook, a book from the Contemporary Science Series, and the Science and Art Department's *Directory*. Smithers, who had a profound sense of Lewisham's superiority in the art of obtaining facts of value in examinations, wondered for some minutes what valuable tip for a student in botany might be hidden in *Whitaker*, and on reaching his lodgings spent some time over the landlady's copy. But really Lewisham was not studying botany, but the art of marriage according to the best authorities. (The book from the Contemporary Science Series was Professor Letourneau's *Evolution of Marriage*. It was interesting certainly, but of little immediate use.)

From *Whitaker* Lewisham learnt that it would be possible at a cost of £2 6s. 1d. or £2 7s. 1d. (one of the items was ambiguous) to get married within the week—that charge being exclusive of vails—at the district registry office. He did little addition sums in the notebook. The church fees he found were variable, but for more personal reasons he rejected a marriage at church. Marriage by certificate at a registrar's involved an inconvenient delay. It would have to be £2 7s. 1d. Vails—ten shillings, say.

Afterwards, without needless ostentation, he produced a cheque-book and a deposit-book, and proceeded to further arithmetic. He found that he was master of £61 4s. 7d. Not a hundred as he had said, but a fine big sum—men have started great businesses on less. It had been a hundred originally. Allowing five pounds for the marriage and moving, this would leave about £56. Plenty. No provision was made for flowers, carriages or the honeymoon. But there would be a typewriter to buy. Ethel was to do her share. . . .

"It will be a devilish close thing," said Lewisham with a quite unreasonable exultation. For, strangely enough, the affair was beginning to take on a flavour of adventure not at all unpleasant. He leant back in his chair with the notebook closed in his hand. . . .

But there was much to see to that afternoon. First of all he had to discover the district superintendent registrar, and then to find a lodging whither he should take Ethel—their lodging, where they were to live together.

At the thought of that new life together that was drawing so near, she came into his head, vivid and near and warm. . . .

96

He recovered himself from a day dream. He became aware of a library attendant down the room leaning forward over his desk, gnawing the tip of a paper knife after the fashion of South Kensington library attendants, and staring at him curiously. It occurred to Lewisham that thought reading was one of the most possible things in the world. He blushed, rose clumsily and took the volume of the *Encyclopædia* back to its shelf.

He found the selection of lodgings a difficult business. After his first essay he began to fancy himself a suspicious-looking character, and that perhaps hampered him. He had chosen the district southward of the Brompton Road. It had one disadvantage—he might blunder into a house with a fellow-student. . . . Not that it mattered vitally. But the fact is, it is rather unusual for married couples to live permanently in furnished lodgings in London. People who are too poor to take a house or a flat commonly find it best to take part of a house or unfurnished apartments. There are in London to every couple living in furnished apartments, a hundred in unfurnished rooms (" with the use of kitchen "). To the discreet landlady the absence of furniture predicates a dangerous want of capital. The first landlady Lewisham interviewed didn't like ladies, they required such a lot of attendance, the second was of the same mind, the third told Mr. Lewisham he was " youngish to be married," the fourth said she only " did " for single " gents." The fifth was a young person with an arch manner, who liked to know all about people she took in, and subjected Lewisham to a searching cross-examination. When she had spitted him in a downright lie or so, she expressed an opinion that her rooms " would scarcely do," and bowed him amiably out.

He cooled his ears and cheeks by walking up and down the street for a space, and then tried again. This landlady was a terrible and pitiful person, so grey and dusty she was, and her face deep lined with dust and trouble and labour. She wore a dirty cap that was all askew. She took Lewisham up into a threadbare room on the first floor. " There's the use of a piano," she said, and indicated an instrument with a front of torn green silk. Lewisham opened the keyboard and evoked a vibration of broken strings. He took one further survey of the dismal place. " Eighteen shillings," he said. " Thank you . . . I'll let you know." The woman smiled with the corners of her mouth down, and without a word moved wearily towards the door. Lewisham felt a transient wonder at her hopeless position, but he did not pursue the inquiry.

The next landlady sufficed. She was a clean-looking German woman, rather smartly dressed ; she had a fringe of flaxen curls and a voluble flow of words, for the most part recognisably English. With this she sketched out remarks. Fifteen shillings was her demand for a minute bedroom and a small sitting-room, separated by folding-doors on the ground floor, and her personal services. Coals were to be " sixpence a kettle," she said—a pretty substitute for scuttle. She had not understood Lewisham to say he was married. But she had no hesitation. " Aayteen shillin'," she said imperturbably. " Paid furs day ich wik. . . . See ? " Mr. Lewisham surveyed the rooms again. They looked clean, and the bonus tea vases, the rancid, gilt-framed oleographs, two toilet tidies used as ornaments, and the fact that the chest of drawers had been crowded out of the bedroom into the sitting-room, simply appealed to his sense of humour. " I'll take 'em from Saturday next," he said.

She was sure he would like them and proposed to give him his book forthwith. She mentioned casually that the previous lodger had been a captain and had stayed three years. (One never hears by chance of lodgers stopping for a shorter period.) Something happened (German) and now he kept his carriage— apparently an outcome of his stay. She returned with a small penny account-book, a bottle of ink and an execrable pen, wrote Lewisham's name on the cover of this, and a receipt for eighteen shillings on the first page. She was evidently a person of considerable business aptitude. Lewisham paid, and the transaction terminated. " Szhure to be gomfortable," followed him comfortingly to the street.

Then he went on to Chelsea and interviewed a fatherly gentleman at the Registrar's office. The fatherly gentleman was chubby-faced and spectacled, and his manner was sympathetic but business-like. He " called-back " each item of the interview. " And what can I do for you ? You wish to be married ! By licence ? "

" By licence."

" By licence ! "

And so forth. He opened a book and made neat entries of the particulars.

" The lady's age ? "

" Twenty-one."

" A very suitable age . . . for a lady."

He advised Lewisham to get a ring and said he would need two witnesses.

" *Well*——" hesitated Lewisham.

" There is always some one about," said the superintendent registrar. " And they are quite used to it."

Thursday and Friday Lewisham passed in exceedingly high spirits. No consciousness of the practical destruction of the Career seems to have troubled him at this time. Doubt had vanished from his universe for a space. He wanted to dance along the corridors. He felt curiously irresponsible and threw up an unpleasant sort of humour that pleased nobody. He wished Miss Heydinger many happy returns of the day, *apropos* of nothing, and he threw a bun across the refreshment room at Smithers and hit one of the Art School officials. Both were extremely silly things to do. In the first instance he was penitent immediately after the outrage, but in the second he added insult to injury by going across the room and asking in an offensively suspicious manner if any one had seen his bun. He crawled under a table and found it at last, rather dusty but quite eatable, under the chair of a lady art student. He sat down by Smithers to eat it, while he argued with the Art official. The Art official said the manners of the Science students were getting unbearable, and threatened to bring the matter before the refreshment-room Committee. Lewisham said it was a pity to make such a fuss about a trivial thing, and proposed that the Art official should throw his lunch—steak and kidney pudding—across the room at him, Lewisham, and so get immediate satisfaction. He then apologised to the official and pointed out in extenuation that it was a very long and difficult shot he had attempted. The official then drank a crumb, or breathed some beer, or something of that sort, and the discussion terminated. In the afternoon, however, Lewisham, to his undying honour, felt acutely ashamed of himself. Miss Heydinger would not speak to him.

On Saturday morning he absented himself from the schools, pleading by post a slight indisposition, and took all his earthly goods to the booking-office at Vauxhall Station. Chaffery's sister lived at Tongham, near Farnham, and Ethel, dismissed a week since by Lagune, had started that morning, under her mother's maudlin supervision, to begin her new slavery. She was to alight either at Farnham or Woking, as opportunity arose, and return to Vauxhall to meet him. So that Lewisham's vigil on the main platform was of indefinite duration.

At first he felt the exhilaration of a great adventure. Then, as he paced the long platform, came a philosophical mood, a sense of entire detachment from the world. He saw a bundle of uprooted plants beside the portmanteau of a fellow-passenger and it suggested a grotesque simile. His roots, his earthly possessions, were all downstairs in the booking-office. What a flimsy thing he was ! A box of books and a trunk of clothes, some certificates and scraps of paper, an entry here and an entry there, a body not over strong—and the vast multitude of people about him—against him—the huge world in which he found himself ! Did it matter anything to one human soul save her if he ceased to exist forthwith ? And miles away perhaps she also was feeling little and lonely. . . .

Would she have trouble with her luggage ? Suppose her aunt were to come to Farnham Junction to meet her ? Suppose some one stole her purse ? Suppose she came too late ! The marriage was to take place at two. . . . Suppose she never came at all ! After three trains in succession had disappointed him his vague feelings of dread gave place to a profound depression. . . .

But she came at last, and it was twenty-three minutes to two. He hurried her luggage downstairs, booked it with his own, and in another minute they were in a hansom—their first experience of that species of conveyance—on the way to the Registrar's office. They had said scarcely anything to one another, save hasty directions from Lewisham, but their eyes were full of excitement, and under the apron of the cab their hands were gripped together.

The little old gentleman was business-like but kindly. They made their vows to him, to a lean black-bearded clerk and a lady who took off an apron in the nether part of the building to attend. The little old gentleman made no long speeches. "You are young people," he said slowly, "and life together is a difficult thing. . . . Be kind to each other." He smiled, and held out a friendly hand.

Ethel's eyes glistened and she found she could not speak.

# CHAPTER TWENTY-ONE

## HOME

THEN a furtive payment of witnesses, and Lewisham was beside her. His face was radiant. A steady current of workers going home to their half-holiday rest poured along the street. On the steps before them lay a few grains of rice from some more public nuptials.

A critical little girl eyed our couple curiously and made some remark to her ragamuffin friend.

" Not them," said the ragamuffin friend. " They've only been askin' questions."

The ragamuffin friend was no judge of faces.

They walked back through the thronged streets to Vauxhall Station, saying little to one another, and there Lewisham, assuming as indifferent a manner as he could command, recovered their possession from the booking-office by means of two separate tickets and put them aboard a four-wheeler. His luggage went outside, but the little brown portmanteau containing Ethel's trousseau was small enough to go on the seat in front of them. You must figure a rather broken-down four-wheeler bearing the yellow-painted box and the experienced trunk and Mr. Lewisham and all his fortunes, a despondent fitful horse, and a threadbare venerable driver, blasphemous *sotto voce* and flagellant, and an ancient coat with capes. When our two young people found themselves in the cab again a certain stiffness of manner between them vanished and there was more squeezing of hands. " Ethel *Lewisham*," said Lewisham several times, and Ethel reciprocated with " Husbander " and "Hubby dear," and took off her glove to look again in an ostentatious manner at a ring. And she kissed the ring.

They were resolved that their newly-married state should not appear, and with considerable ceremony it was arranged that he should treat her with off-hand brusqueness when they arrived at their lodging. The Teutonic landlady appeared in the passage with an amiable smile and the hope that they had had a pleasant journey, and became voluble with promises of comfort. Lewisham having assisted the slatternly general servant to carry in his boxes, paid the cabman a florin in a resolute manner and followed the ladies into the sitting-room.

Ethel answered Madam Gadow's inquiries with admirable self-possession, followed her through the folding-doors and displayed an intelligent interest in a new spring mattress. Presently the folding-doors were closed again. Lewisham hovered about the front room pulling his moustache and pretending to admire the oleographs, surprised to find himself trembling. . . .

The slatternly general servant reappeared with the chops and tinned salmon he had asked Madam Gadow to prepare for them. He went and stared out of the window, heard the door close behind the girl, and turned at a sound as Ethel appeared shyly through the folding-doors.

She was suddenly domestic. Hitherto he had seen her without a hat and jacket only on one indistinct dramatic occasion. Now she wore a little blouse of soft, dark red material, with a white froth about the wrists and that pretty neck of hers. And her hair was a new wonderland of curls and soft strands. How delicate she looked and sweet as she stood hesitating there. These gracious moments in life! He took two steps and held out his arms. She glanced at the closed door of the room and came flitting towards him. . .

# CHAPTER TWENTY-TWO

FOR three indelible days Lewisham's existence was a fabric of fine emotions, life was too wonderful and beautiful for any doubts or forethought. To be with Ethel was perpetual delight—she astonished this sisterless youngster with a thousand feminine niceties and refinements. She shamed him for his strength and clumsiness. And the light in her eyes and the warmth in her heart that lit them !

Even to be away from her was a wonder and in its way delightful. He was no common Student, he was a man with a Secret Life. To part from her on Monday near South Kensington station and go up Exhibition Road among all the fellows who lived in sordid, lonely lodgings and were boys to his day-old experience ! To neglect one's work and sit back and dream of meeting again ! To slip off to the shady churchyard behind the Oratory when, or even a little before, the midday bell woke the great staircase to activity, and to meet a smiling face and hear a soft voice saying sweet foolish things ! And after four another meeting and the walk home—their own home.

No little form now went from him and flitted past a gas lamp down a foggy vista, taking his desire with her. Never more was that to be. Lewisham's long hours in the laboratory were spent largely in a dreamy meditation, in—to tell the truth—the invention of foolish terms of endearment : " Dear Wife," " Dear Little Wife Thing," " Sweetest Dearest Little Wife," " Dillywigs." A pretty employment ! And these are quite a fair specimen of his originality during those wonderful days. A moment of heart-searching in that particular matter led to the discovery of hitherto undreamt-of kindred with Swift. For Lewisham, like Swift and most other people, had hit upon the Little Language. Indeed it was a very foolish time.

Such section cutting as he did that third day of his married life—and he did very little—was a thing to marvel at. Bindon, the botany professor, under the fresh shock of his performance, protested to a colleague in the grill-room that never had a student been so foolishly overrated.

And Ethel too had a fine emotional time. She was mistress of a home—*their* home together. She shopped and was called " Ma'am " by respectful good-looking shopmen ; she designed meals and copied out papers of notes with a rich sense of helpfulness. And ever and again she would stop writing and sit dreaming. And for four bright week-days she went to and fro to accompany and meet Lewisham and listen greedily to the latest fruits of his imagination.

The landlady was very polite and conversed entertainingly about the very extraordinary and dissolute servants that had fallen to her lot. And Ethel disguised her newly wedded state by a series of ingenious prevarications. She wrote a letter that Saturday evening to her mother—Lewisham had helped her to write it—making a sort of proclamation of her heroic departure and promising a speedy visit. They posted the letter so that it might not be delivered until Monday.

She was quite sure with Lewisham that only the possible dishonour of mediumship could have brought their marriage about—she sank the mutual attraction beyond even her own vision. There was more than a touch of magnificence, you perceive, about this affair.

It was Lewisham had persuaded her to delay that reassuring visit until Monday night. "One whole day of honeymoon," he insisted, was to be theirs. In his prenuptial meditations he had not clearly focussed the fact that even after marriage some sort of relations with Mr. and Mrs. Chaffery would still go on. Even now he was exceedingly disinclined to face that obvious necessity. He foresaw, in spite of a resolute attempt to ignore it, that there would be explanatory scenes of some little difficulty. But the prevailing magnificence carried him over this trouble.

" Let us at least have this little time for ourselves," he said, and that seemed to settle their position.

Save for its brevity and these intimations of future trouble it was a very fine time indeed. Their midday dinner together, for example—it was a little cold when at last they came to it on Saturday—was immense fun. There was no marked subsidence of appetite ; they ate extremely well in spite of the meeting of their souls, and in spite of certain shiftings of chairs and hand claspings and similar delays. He really made the acquaintance of her hand then for the first time, plump white hands with short white fingers, and the engagement ring had come out of its tender hiding-place and acted as keeper to the wedding ring. Their eyes were perpetually flitting about the room and coming back to mutual smiles. All their movements were faintly tremulous.

She professed to be vastly interested and amused by the room and its furniture and her position, and he was delighted by her delight. She was particularly entertained by the chest of drawers in the living-room, and by Lewisham's witticisms at the toilet tidies and the oleographs.

And after the chops and most of the tinned salmon and the very new loaf were gone they fell to with fine effect upon a tapioca pudding. Their talk was fragmentary. "Did you hear her call me *Madame* ? *Mádáme*—so ! " And presently "I must go out and do some shopping. There are all the things for Sunday and Monday morning to get. I must make a list.

It will never do to let her know how little I know about things. . . . I wish I knew more."

At the time Lewisham regarded her confession of domestic ignorance as a fine basis for facetiousness. He developed a fresh line of thought, and condoled with her on the inglorious circumstances of their wedding. "No bridesmaids," he said ; "no little children scattering flowers, no carriages, no police-men to guard the wedding presents, nothing proper—nothing right. Not even a white favour. Only you and I."

"Only you and I. *Oh !* "

"This is nonsense," said Lewisham, after an interval.

"And think what we lose in the way of speeches," he re-sumed. "Cannot you imagine the best man rising—' Ladies and gentleman—the health of the bride.' That is what the best man has to do, isn't it ? "

By way of answer she extended her hand.

"And do you know," he said, after that had received due recognition, "we have never been introduced ! "

"Neither have we ! " said Ethel. "Neither have we ! We have never been introduced ! "

For some inscrutable reason it delighted them both enor-mously to think that they had never been introduced. . . .

In the later afternoon Lewisham, having unpacked his books to a certain extent and so forth, was visible to all men, visibly in the highest spirits, carrying home Ethel's shopping. There were parcels and cones in blue and parcels in rough grey paper and a bag of confectionery, and out of one of the side pockets of that East-end overcoat the tail of a haddock protruded from its paper. Under such magnificent sanctions and amid such ignoble circumstances did this honeymoon begin.

On Sunday evening they went for a long rambling walk through the quiet streets, coming out at last into Hyde Park. The early spring night was mild and clear and the kindly moonlight was about them. They went to the bridge and looked down the Serpentine, with the lights of Paddington yellow and remote. They stood there, dim little figures and very close together. They whispered and became silent.

Presently it seemed that something passed, and Lewisham began talking in his magnificent vein. He likened the Ser-pentine to Life, and found Meaning in the dark banks of Kensington Gardens and the remote bright lights. "The long struggle," he said, "and the lights at the end "—though he really did not know what he meant by the lights at the end. Neither did Ethel, though the emotion was indisputable. "We are Fighting the World," he said, finding great satis-faction in the thought. "All the world is against us—and we are fighting it all."

"We will not be beaten," said Ethel.

"How could we be beaten—together ? " said Lewisham "For you I would fight a dozen worlds."

It seemed a very sweet and noble thing to them under the sympathetic moonlight, almost indeed too easy for their courage, to be merely fighting the world."

"You 'aven't bin married ver' long," said Madam Gadow with an insinuating smile, when she readmitted Ethel on Monday morning after Lewisham had been swallowed up by the Schools.

"No, I haven't *very* long," admitted Ethel.

"You are ver' 'appy," said Madam Gadow, and sighed.

"I was ver' 'appy," said Madam Gadow.

# CHAPTER TWENTY-THREE

## MR. CHAFFERY AT HOME

THE golden mists of delight lifted a little on Monday, when Mr. and Mrs. G. E. Lewisham went to call on his mother-in-law and Mr. Chaffery. Mrs. Lewisham went in evident apprehension, but clouds of glory still hung about Lewisham's head, and his manner was heroic. He wore a cotton shirt and linen collar, and a very nice black satin tie that Mrs. Lewisham had bought on her own responsibility during the day. She naturally wanted him to look all right.

Mrs. Chaffery appeared in the half-light of the passage as the top of a grimy cap over Ethel's shoulder and two black sleeves about her neck. She emerged as a small, middle-aged woman, with a thin little nose between silver-rimmed spectacles, a weak mouth and perplexed eyes, a queer little dust-lined woman with the oddest resemblance to Ethel in her face. She was trembling visibly with nervous agitation.

She hesitated, peering, and then kissed Mr. Lewisham effusively. "And this is Mr. Lewisham!" she said as she did so.

She was the third thing feminine to kiss Lewisham since the promiscuous days of his babyhood. "I was so afraid—— There!" She laughed hysterically.

"You'll excuse my saying that it's comforting to see you—honest-like and young. Not but what Ethel . . . *He* has been something dreadful," said Mrs. Chaffery. "You didn't ought to have written about that mesmerising. And of all letters that which Jane wrote—there! But he's waiting and listening——"

"Are we to go downstairs, Mums?" asked Ethel.

"He's waiting for you there," said Mrs. Chaffery. She held a dismal little oil lamp, and they descended a tenebrous spiral structure into an underground breakfast-room lit by gas that shone through a partially frosted globe with cut-glass stars. That descent had a distinctly depressing effect upon Lewisham. He went first. He took a deep breath at the door. What on earth was Chaffery going to say? Not that he cared, of course.

Chaffery was standing with his back to the fire, trimming his finger-nails with a pocket-knife. His gilt glasses were tilted forward so as to make an inflamed knob at the top of his long nose, and he regarded Mr. and Mrs. Lewisham over them with—Lewisham doubted his eyes for a moment—but it was positively a smile, an essentially waggish smile.

"You've come back," he said quite cheerfully over Lewisham to Ethel. There was a hint of falsetto in his voice.

" She has called to see her mother," said Lewisham.   " You,
I believe, are Mr. Chaffery ? "

" I would like to know who the Deuce *you* are ? " said
Chaffery, suddenly tilting his head back so as to look through
his glasses instead of over them, and laughing genially.   " For
thorough-going Cheek I'm inclined to think you take the Cake.
Are you the Mr. Lewisham to whom this misguided girl refers
in her letter ? "

" I am."

" Maggie," said Mr. Chaffery to Mrs. Chaffery, " there is a
class of being upon whom delicacy is lost—to whom delicacy
is practically unknown.   Has your daughter got her marriage
lines ? "

" Mr. Chaffery ! " said Lewisham, and Mrs. Chaffery
exlaimed, " James !   How *can* you ? "

Chaffery shut his penknife with a click and slipped it into
his vest-pocket.   Then he looked up again, speaking in the
same equal voice.   " I presume we are civilised persons
prepared to manage our affairs in a civilised way.   My stepdaughter vanishes for two nights and returns with an alleged
husband.   I at least am not disposed to be careless about
her legal position."

" You ought to know her better——" began Lewisham.

" Why argue about it ? " said Chaffery gaily, pointing a
lean finger at Ethel's gesture, " when she has 'em in her
pocket ?   She may just as well show me now.   I thought so.
Don't be alarmed at my handling them.   Fresh copies can
always be got at the nominal price of two-and-seven.   Thank
you.   Lewisham, George Edgar.   One-and-twenty.   And
. . . You—one-and-twenty !   I never did know your age,
my dear, exactly, and now your mother won't say.   Student !
Thank you.   I am greatly obliged.   Indeed I am greatly
relieved.   And now, what have you got to say for yourselves
in this remarkable affair ? "

" You had a letter," said Lewisham.

" I had a letter of excuses—the personalities I overlook. . . .
Yes, sir—they were excuses.   You young people wanted to
marry—and you seized an occasion.   You did not even refer
to the fact that you wanted to marry in your letter.   Pure
modesty !   But now you have come here married.   It dis-
organises this household, it inflicts endless bother on people,
but never you mind that !   I'm not blaming *you*.   Nature's
to blame !   Neither of you know what you are in for yet.
You will.   You're married and that is the great essential
thing. . . . (Ethel, my dear, just put your husband's hat
and stick behind the door.)   And you, sir, are so good as to
disapprove of the way in which I earn my living ? "

" Well," said Lewisham.   " Yes—I'm bound to say I do."

" You are really *not* bound to say it.   The modesty of
inexperience would excuse you."

' Yes, but it isn't right—it isn't straight."

"Dogma," said Chaffery. "Dogma !"

"What do you mean by dogma ?" asked Lewisham.

"I mean, dogma. But we must argue this out in comfort.
It is our supper hour, and I'm not the man to fight against
accomplished facts. We have intermarried. There it is.
You must stop to supper—and you and I must thresh these
things out. We've involved ourselves with each other and
we've got to make the best of it. Your wife and mine will
spread the board, and we will go on talking. Why not sit in
that chair instead of leaning on the back ? This is a home—
*domus*—not a debating society—humble in spite of my manifest frauds. . . . That's better. And in the first place I
hope—I do so hope "—Chaffery was suddenly very impressive
—" that you're not a Dissenter."

"Eh !" said Lewisham, and then, "No! I am *not* a
Dissenter."

"That's better," said Mr. Chaffery. "I'm glad of that.
I was just a little afraid—— Something in your manner. I
can't stand Dissenters. I've a peculiar dislike to Dissenters.
To my mind it's the great drawback of this Clapham. You
see . . . I have invariably found them deceitful—invariably."

He grimaced and dropped his glasses with a click against
his waistcoat buttons. "I'm very glad of that," he said,
replacing them. "The Dissenter, the Non-conformist Conscience, the Puritan, you know, the Vegetarian and Total
Abstainer, and all that sort of thing, I cannot away with them.
I have cleared my mind of cant and formulæ. I've a nature
essentially Hellenic. Have you ever read Matthew Arnold ?"

"Beyond my scientific reading——"

"Ah ! you *should* read Matthew Arnold—a mind of singular
clarity. In him you would find a certain quality that is
sometimes a little wanting in your scientific men. They are
apt to be a little too phenomenal, you know, a little too
objective. Now I seek after noumena. Noumena, Mr.
Lewisham ! If you follow me—— ?"

He paused, and his eyes behind the glasses were mildly
interrogative. Ethel re-entered without her hat and jacket,
and with a noisy square black tray, a white cloth, some plates
and knives and glasses, and began to lay the table.

"*I* follow you," said Lewisham, reddening. He had not
the courage to admit ignorance of this remarkable word.
"You state your case."

"I seek after *noumena*," repeated Chaffery with great
satisfaction, and gesticulated with his hand, waving away
everything but that. "I cannot do with surfaces and appearances. I am one of those nympholepts, you know, nympholepts. . . . Must pursue the truth of things ! the elusive
fundamental. . . . I make a rule, I never tell myself lies—
never. There are few who can say that. To my mind—

truth begins at home. And for the most part—stops there.
Safest and seemliest! *you* know. With most men—with
your typical Dissenter *par excellence*—it's always gadding
abroad, calling on the neighbours. You see my point of
view ? "

He glanced at Lewisham, who was conscious of an unwonted
opacity of mind. He became wary, as wary as he could
manage to be on the spur of the moment.

" It's a little surprising, you know," he said very carefully,
" if I may say so—and considering what happened—to hear
*you* . . ."

" Speaking of truth ? Not when you understand my
position. Not when you see where I stand. That is what
I am getting at. That is what I am naturally anxious to
make clear to you now that we have intermarried, now that
you are my stepson-in-law. You're young, you know, you're
young, and you're hard and fast. Only years can give a mind
*tone*—mitigate the varnish of education. I gather from this
letter—and your face—that you are one of the party that
participated in that little affair at Lagune's."

He stuck out a finger at a point he had just seen. " By the
bye !—That accounts for Ethel," he said.

Ethel rapped down the mustard on the table. " It does,"
she said, but not very loudly.

" But you had met before ? " said Chaffery.

" At Whortley," said Lewisham.

" I see," said Chaffery.

" I was in—— I was one of those who arranged the
exposure," said Lewisham. " And now you have raised the
matter, I am bound to say——"

" I knew," interrupted Chaffery. " But what a shock that
was for Lagune ! " He looked down at his toes for a moment
with the corners of his mouth tucked in. " The hand dodge
wasn't bad, you know," he said with a queer sidelong smile.

Lewisham was very busy for a moment trying to get this
remark in focus. " I don't see it in the same light as you do,"
he explained at last.

" Can't get away from your moral bias, eh ? Well, well.
We'll go into all that. But apart from its moral merits—
simply as an artistic trick—it was not bad."

" I don't know much about tricks——"

" So few who undertake exposures do. You admit you
never heard or thought of that before—the bladder, I mean.
Yet it's as obvious as tintacks that a medium who's hampered
at his hands will do all he can with his teeth, and what *could*
be so self-evident as a bladder under one's lapel ? What
could be ? Yet I know psychic literature pretty well and it's
never been suggested even ! Never. It's a perpetual surprise
to me how many things are *not* thought of by investigators.
For one thing, they never count the odds against them, and

that puts them wrong at the start. Look at it! I am by
nature tricky. I spend all my leisure standing or sitting
about and thinking up or practising new little tricks, because
it amuses me immensely to do so. The whole thing amuses
me. Well—what is the result of these meditations? Take
one thing: I know eight-and-forty ways of making raps—of
which at least ten are original. Ten original ways of making
raps." His manner was very impressive. "And, some of
them simply tremendous raps. There!"

A confirmatory rap exploded—as it seemed between
Lewisham and Chaffery.

"*Eh?*" said Chaffery.

The mantelpiece opened a dropping fire, and the table went
off under Lewisham's nose like a cracker.

"You see?" said Chaffery, putting his hands under the
tail of his coat. The whole room seemed snapping its fingers
at Lewisham for a space.

"Very well, and now take the other side. Take the severest
test I ever tried. Two respectable professors of physics—not
Newtons, you understand, but good, worthy, self-important
professors of physics—a lady anxious to prove there's a life
beyond the grave, a journalist who wants stuff to write—a
person, that is, who gets his living by these researches just as
I do—undertook to test me. Test *me*! . . . Of course they
had their other work to do, professing physics, professing
religion, organising research, and so forth. At the outside
they don't think an hour a day about it, and most of them
had never cheated anybody in their existence, and couldn't,
for example, travel without a ticket for a three-mile journey
and not get caught, to save their lives. . . . Well—you see the
odds?"

He paused. Lewisham appeared involved in some interior
struggle.

"You know," explained Chaffery, "it was quite an accident
you got me—quite. The thing slipped out of my mouth.
Or your friend with the flat voice wouldn't have had a chance.
Not a chance."

Lewisham spoke like a man who is lifting a weight. "All
*this*, you know, is off the question. I'm not disputing your
ability. But the thing is . . . it isn't right."

"We're coming to that," said Chaffery.

"It's evident we look at things in a different light."

"That's it. That's just what we've got to discuss. Exactly!"

"Cheating is cheating. You can't get away from that.
That's simple enough."

"Wait till I've done with it," said Chaffery with a certain
zest. "Of course it's imperative you should understand my
position. It isn't as though I hadn't one. Ever since I read
your letter I've been thinking over that. Really!—a justi-

fication ! In a way you might almost say I had a mission. A sort of prophet. You really don't see the beginning of it yet."

" Oh, but hang it ! " protested Lewisham.

" Ah ! you're young, you're crude. My dear young man, you're only at the beginning of things. You really must concede a certain possibility of wider views to a man more than twice your age. But here's supper. For a little while at any rate we'll call a truce."

Ethel had come in again bearing an additional chair, and Mrs. Chaffery appeared behind her, crowning the preparations with a jug of small beer. The cloth, Lewisham observed, as he turned towards it, had several undarned holes and dis-coloured places, and in the centre stood a tarnished cruet which contained mustard, pepper, vinegar, and three ambiguous dried-up bottles. The bread was on an ample board with a pious rim, and an honest wedge of cheese loomed dispro-portionate on a little plate. Mr. and Mrs. Lewisham were seated facing one another, and Mrs. Chaffery sat in the broken chair because she understood its ways.

" This cheese is as nutritious and unattractive and in-digestible as Science," remarked Chaffery, cutting and passing wedges. " But crush it—so—under your fork, add a little of this good Dorset butter, a dab of mustard, pepper—the pepper is very necessary—and some malt vinegar, and crush together. You get a compound called Crab and by no means disagreeable. So the wise deal with the facts of life, neither bolting nor rejecting, but adapting."

" As though pepper and mustard were not facts," said Lewisham, scoring his solitary point that evening.

Chaffery admitted the collapse of his image in very compli-mentary terms, and Lewisham could not avoid a glance across the table at Ethel. He remembered immediately afterwards that Chaffery was a slippery scoundrel whose blame was better than his praise.

For a time the Crab engaged Chaffery, and the conversation languished. Mrs. Chaffery asked Ethel formal questions about their lodgings, and Ethel's answers were buoyant. " You must come and have tea one day," said Ethel, not waiting for Lewisham's endorsement, " and see it all."

Chaffery astonished Lewisham by suddenly displaying a complete acquaintance with his status as a South Kensington teacher in training. " I suppose you have some money beyond that guinea," said Chaffery, off-handedly.

" Enough to go on with," said Lewisham, reddening.

" And you look to them at South Kensington to do some-thing for you—a hundred a year or so, when your scholarship is up ? "

." Yes," said Lewisham, a little reluctantly. " Yes. A hundred a year or so. That's the sort of idea. And there's lots of places beyond South Kensington, of course, even if they don't put me up there."

"I see," said Chaffery ; "but it will be a pretty close shave for all that—one hundred a year. Well, well—there's many a deserving man has to do with less," and after a meditative pause he asked Lewisham to pass the beer.

"Hev you a mother living, Mr. Lewisham ? " said Mrs. Chaffery suddenly, and pursued him through the tale of his connections. When he came to the plumber, Mrs. Chaffery remarked with an unexpected air of consequence, that most families have their poor relations. Then the air of consequence vanished again into the past from which it had arisen.

Supper finished, Chaffery poured the residuum of the beer into his glass, produced a Broseley clay of the longest sort, and invited Lewisham to smoke. "Honest smoking," said Chaffery, tapping the bowl of his clay, and added : "In this country—cigars—sound cigars—and honesty rarely meet."

Lewisham fumbled in his pocket for his Algerian cigarettes, and Chaffery having regarded them unfavourably through his glasses, took up the thread of his promised apologia. The ladies retired to wash up the supper things.

"You see," said Chaffery, opening abruptly so soon as the clay was drawing, "about this cheating—I do not find life such a simple matter as you do."

"*I* don't find life simple," said Lewisham, "but I do think there's a Right and a Wrong in things. And I don't think you have said anything so far to show that spiritualistic cheating is Right."

"Let us thresh the matter out," said Chaffery, crossing his legs ; "let us thresh the matter out. Now "—he drew at his pipe—" I don't think you fully appreciate the importance of Illusion in life, the Essential Nature of Lies and Deception of the body politic. You are inclined to discredit one particular form of Imposture, because it is not generally admitted—carries a certain discredit, and—witness the heel edges of my trouser legs, witness yonder viands—small rewards."

"It's not that," said Lewisham.

"Now I am prepared to maintain," said Chaffery, proceeding with his proposition, "that Honesty is essentially an anarchistic and disintegrating force in society, that communities are held together and the progress of civilisation made possibly only by vigorous and sometimes even violent Lying ; that the Social Contract is nothing more nor less than a vast conspiracy of human beings to lie to and humbug themselves and one another for the general Good. Lies are the mortar that bind the savage individual man into the social masonry. There is the general thesis upon which I base my justification. My mediumship, I can assure you, is a particular instance of the general assertion. Were I not of a profoundly indolent, restless, adventurous nature, and horribly averse to writing, I would make a great book of this and live honoured by every profound duffer in the world."

" But how are you going to prove it ? "

" Prove it ! It simply needs pointing out. Even now there are men—Bernard Shaw, Ibsen, and such like—who have seen bits of it in a new-gospel-grubbing sort of fashion. What is man ? Lust and greed tempered by fear and an irrational vanity."

" I don't agree with that," said Mr. Lewisham.

" You will as you grow older," said Chaffery. " There's truths you have to grow into. But about this matter of Lies—let us look at the fabric of society, let us compare the savage. You will discover the only essential difference between savage and civilised is this : The former hasn't learnt to shirk the truth of things, and the latter has. Take the most obvious difference—the clothing of the civilised man, his invention of decency. What *is* clothing ? The concealment of essential facts. What is decorum ? Suppression ! I don't argue against decency and decorum, mind you, but there they are—essentials to civilisation and essentially ' *suppressio veri.*' And in the pockets of his clothes our citizen carries money. The pure savage has no money. To him a lump of metal is a lump of metal—possibly ornamental— no more. That's right. To any lucid-minded man it's the same or different only through the gross folly of his fellows. But to the common civilised man the universal exchangeability of this gold is a sacred and fundamental fact. Think of it ! Why should it be ? There isn't a why ! I live in perpetual amazement at the gullibility of my fellow-creatures. Of a morning sometimes, I can assure you, I lie in bed fancying that people may have found out this swindle in the night, expect to hear a tumult downstairs and see your mother-in- law come rushing into the room with a rejected shilling from the milkman. ' What's this ? ' says he. ' This Muck for milk ? ' But it never happens. Never. If it did, if people suddenly cleared their minds of this cant of money, what would happen ? The true nature of man would appear. I should whip out of bed, seize some weapon, and after the milkman forthwith. It's becoming to keep the peace, but it's necessary to have milk. The neighbours would come pouring out—also after milk. Milkman, suddenly enlightened, would start clattering up the street. After him ! Clutch—tear ! Got him ! Over goes the cart ! Fight if you like, but don't upset the can ! . . . Don't you see it all—perfectly reasonable every bit of it. I should return, bruised and bloody, with the milk- can under my arm. Yes—*I* should have the milk-can—I should keep my eye on that. . . . But why go on ? You of all men should know that life is a struggle for existence, a fight for food. Money is just the lie that mitigates our fury."

" No," said Lewisham ; " no ! I'm not prepared to admit that."

" What *is* money ? "

Mr. Lewisham dodged. " You state your case first," he said. " I really don't see what all this has to do with cheating at a séance."

" I weave my defence from this loom, though. Take some aggressively respectable sort of man—a bishop, for example."

" Well," said Lewisham, " I don't much hold with bishops."

" It doesn't matter. Take a professor of science, walking the earth. Remark his clothing, making him a decent citizen, concealing the fact that physically he is a flabby, pot-bellied degenerate. That is the first Lie of his being. No fringes round *his* trousers, my boy. Notice his hair, groomed and clipped, the tacit lie that its average length is half an inch, whereas in nature he would wave a few score yard-long hairs of ginger grey to the winds of heaven. Notice the smug suppressions of his face. In his mouth are Lies in the shape of false teeth. Then on the earth somewhere poor devils are toiling to get him meat and corn and wine. He is clothed in the lives of bent and thwarted weavers, his way is lit by phossy jaw, he eats from lead-glazed crockery—all his ways are paved with the lives of men. . . . Think of the chubby, comfortable creature ! And, as Swift has it—to think that such a thing should deal in pride ! . . . He pretends that his blessed little researches are in some way a fair return to these remote beings for their toil, their suffering ; pretends that he and his parasitic career are payment for their thwarted desires. Imagine him bullying his gardener over some transplanted geraniums, the thick mist of lies they stand in, so that the man does not immediately, with the edge of a spade, smite down his impertinence to the dust from which it rose. . . . And his case is the case of all comfortable lives. What a lie and sham all civility is, all good breeding, all culture and refinement, while one poor ragged wretch drags hungry on the earth ! "

" But this is Socialism ! " said Lewisham. " *I*—— "

" No Ism," said Chaffery, raising his rich voice. " Only the ghastly truth of things—the truth that the warp and the woof of the world of men is Lying. Socialism is no remedy, no *ism* is a remedy ; things are so."

" I don't agree—— " began Lewisham.

" Not with the hopelessness, because you are young, but with the description you do."

" Well—within limits."

" You agree that most respectable positions in the world are tainted with the fraud of our social conditions. If they were not tainted with fraud they would not be respectable. Even your own position—— Who gave you the right to marry and prosecute interesting scientific studies while other young men rot in mines ? "

" I admit——"

" You can't help admitting. And here is my position. Since all ways of life are tainted with fraud, since to live and speak the truth is beyond human strength and courage—as one finds it—is it not better for a man that he engage in some straightforward comparatively harmless cheating, than if he risk his mental integrity in some ambiguous position and fall at last into self-deception and self-righteousness ? That is the essential danger. That is the thing I always guard against. Heed that ! It is the master sin. Self-righteousness."

Mr. Lewisham pulled at his moustache.

" You begin to take me. And after all, these worthy people do not suffer so greatly. If I did not take their money some other impostor would. Their huge conceit of intelligence would breed perhaps some viler swindle than my facetious rappings. That's the line our doubting bishops take, and why shouldn't I ? For example, these people might give it to Public Charities, minister to the fattened secretary, the prodigal younger son. After all, at worst, I am a sort of latter-day Robin Hood ; I take from the rich according to their incomes. I don't give to the poor certainly, I don't get enough. But—there are other good works. Many a poor weakling have I comforted with Lies, great thumping, silly Lies, about the grave ! Compare me with one of those rascals who disseminate phossy jaw and lead poisons, compare me with a millionaire who runs a music hall with an eye to feminine talent, or an underwriter, or the common stockbroker. Or any sort of lawyer. . . .

" There are bishops," said Chaffery, " who believe in Darwin and doubt Moses. Now I hold myself better than they—analogous perhaps but better—for I do at least invent something of the tricks I play—I do do that."

" That's all very well," began Lewisham.

" I might forgive them their dishonesty," said Chaffery, " but the stupidity of it, the mental self-abnegation—Lord ! If a solicitor doesn't swindle in the proper shabby-magnificent way, they chuck him for unprofessional conduct." He paused. He became meditative, and smiled faintly.

" Now some of *my* dodges," he said with a sudden change of voice, turning towards Lewisham, his eyes smiling over his glasses and an emphatic hand patting the table-cloth ; " some of *my* dodges are *damned* ingenious, you know—*damned* ingenious—and well worth double the money they bring me—double."

He turned towards the fire again, pulling at his smouldering pipe and eyeing Lewisham over the corner of his glasses.

" One or two of my little things would make Maskelyne sit up," he said presently. " They would set that mechanical orchestra playing out of pure astonishment. I really must explain some of them to you—now we have intermarried."

It took Mr. Lewisham a minute or so to re-form the regiment of his mind, disordered by its headlong pursuit of Chaffery's flying arguments. " But on your principles you might do almost anything ! " he said.

" Precisely ! " said Chaffery.

" But——"

" It is rather a curious method," protested Chaffery, " to test one's principles of action by judging the resultant actions on some other principle, isn't it ? "

Lewisham took a moment to think. " I suppose that is so," he said, in the manner of a man convinced against his will.

He perceived his logic insufficient. He suddenly thrust the delicacies of argument aside. Certain sentences he had brought ready for use in his mind came up and he delivered them abruptly. " Anyhow," he said, " I don't agree with this cheating. In spite of what you say, I hold to what I said in my letter. Ethel's connection with all these things is at an end. I shan't go out of my way to expose you, of course, but if it comes in my way I shall speak my mind of all these spiritualistic phenomena. It's just as well that we should know about where we are."

" That is clearly understood, my dear stepson-in-law," said Chaffery. " Our present object is discussion."

" But Ethel——"

" Ethel is yours," said Chaffery. " Ethel is yours," he repeated after an interval, and added pensively—" to keep.

" But talking of Illusion," he resumed, dismissing the sordid with a sigh of relief, " I sometimes think with Bishop Berkeley, that all experience is probably something quite different from reality. That consciousness is *essentially* hallucination. I here, and you, and our talk—it is all Illusion. Bring your Science to bear—what am I ? A cloudy multitude of atoms, an infinite interplay of little cells. Is this hand that I hold out, me ? This head ? Is the surface of my skin any more than a rude average boundary ? You say it is my mind that is me ? But consider the war of motives. Suppose I have an impulse that I resist—it is *I* resist it—the impulse is outside me, eh ? But suppose that impulse carries me and I do the thing—that impulse is part of me, is it not ? Ah ! My brain reels at these mysteries ! Lord ! what flimsy fluctuating things we are—first this, then that, a thought, an impulse, a deed and a forgetting, and all the time madly cocksure we are ourselves. And as for you—you who have hardly learned to think for more than five or six short years, there you sit, assured, coherent, there you sit in all your inherited original sin—Hallucinatory Windlestraw !—judging and condemning. *You* know Right from Wrong ! My boy, so did Adam and Eve . . . *so soon as they'd had dealings with the father of lies !* "

At the end of the evening whisky and hot water were produced, and Chaffery, now in a mood of great urbanity, said he had rarely enjoyed any one's conversation so much as Lewisham's, and insisted upon every one having whisky. Mrs. Chaffery and Ethel added sugar and lemon. Lewisham felt an instantaneous mild surprise at the sight of Ethel drinking grog.

At the door Mrs. Chaffery kissed Lewisham an effusive good-bye and told Ethel she really believed it was all for the best.

On the way home Lewisham was thoughtful and pre-occupied. The problem of Chaffery assumed enormous proportions. At times indeed even that good man's own philosophical sketch of himself as a practical exponent of mental sincerity touched with humour and the artistic spirit, seemed plausible. Lagune was an undeniable ass, and conceivably psychic research was an incentive to trickery. Then he remembered the matter in his relation to Ethel. . . .

" Your stepfather is a little hard to follow," he said at last, sitting on the bed and taking off one boot. " He's dodgy—he's so confoundedly dodgy. One doesn't know where to take hold of him. He's got such a break he's clean bowled me again and again."

He thought for a space, and then removed his boot and sat with it on his knee. " Of course ! . . . all that he said was wrong—quite wrong. Right is right and cheating is cheating, whatever you say about it."

" That's what I feel about him," said Ethel at the looking-glass. " That's exactly how it seems to me."

# CHAPTER TWENTY-FOUR

## THE CAMPAIGN OPENS

ON Saturday Lewisham was first through the folding-doors. In a moment he reappeared with a document extended. Mrs. Lewisham stood arrested with her dress skirt in her hand, astonished at the astonishment on his face. " *I* say ! " said Lewisham ; " just look here ! "

She looked at the book that he held open before her, and perceived that its vertical ruling betokened a sordid import, that its list of items in an illegible mixture of English and German was lengthy. " 1 kettle of coals 6d." occurred regularly down that portentous array and buttoned it all together. It was Madam Gadow's first bill. Ethel took it out of his hand and examined it closer. It looked no smaller closer. The overcharges were scandalous. It was curious how the humour of calling a scuttle " kettle " had evaporated.

That document, I take it, was the end of Mr. Lewisham's informal honeymoon. Its advent was the snap of that bright Prince Rupert's drop ; and in a moment—Dust. For a glorious week he had lived in the persuasion that life was made of love and mystery, and now he was reminded with singular clearness that it was begotten of a struggle for existence and the Will to Live. " Confounded imposition ! " fumed Mr. Lewisham, and the breakfast table was novel and ominous, mutterings towards anger on the one hand and a certain consternation on the other. " I must give her a talking to this afternoon," said Lewisham at his watch, and after he had bundled his books into the shiny black bag, he gave the first of his kisses that was not a distinct and self-subsisting ceremony. It was usage and done in a hurry, and the door slammed as he went his way to the schools. Ethel was not coming that morning, because by special request and because she wanted to help him she was going to copy out some of his botanical notes which had fallen into arrears.

On his way to the schools Lewisham felt something suspiciously near a sinking of the heart. His preoccupation was essentially arithmetical. The thing that engaged his mind to the exclusion of all other matters is best expressed in the recognised business form.

From this it will be manifest to the most unbusiness-like that, disregarding the extraordinary expenditure on the marriage, and the by no means final " few little things " Ethel had bought, outgoings exceeded income by two pounds and more, and a brief excursion into arithmetic will demonstrate that in five-and-twenty weeks the balance of the account would be nothing.

| *Dr.* | | £ | s. | d. | *Cr.* | £ | s. | d. |
|---|---|---|---|---|---|---|---|---|
| Cash in hand | | | | | By bus fares to South Kensington (late) | 0 | 0 | 2 |
| Mr. L. . | . | 13 | 10 | 4½ | By 6 lunches at the Students' Club | 0 | 5 | 2¼ |
| Mrs. L. | . | 0 | 12 | 7 | By 2 packets of cigarettes (to smoke after dinner) | 0 | 0 | 6 |
| At Bank . | . | 45 | 0 | 0 | By marriage and elopement | 4 | 18 | 10 |
| To Scholarship | . | 1 | 1 | 0 | By necessary subsequent additions to bride's trousseau | 0 | 16 | 1 |
| | | | | | By housekeeping exs. . | 1 | 1 | 4½ |
| | | | | | By " A few little things " bought by housekeeper . | 0 | 15 | 3½ |
| | | | | | By Madam Gadow for coal, lodging and attendance (as per account rendered) . | 1 | 15 | 0 |
| | | | | | By missing . | 0 | 0 | 4 |
| | | | | | By balance . | 50 | 11 | 2 |
| | | £60 | 3 | 11½ | | £60 | 3 | 11½ |

But that guinea a week was not to go on for five-and-twenty weeks, but simply for fifteen, and then the net outgoings will be well over three guineas, reducing the " law " accorded our young couple to two-and-twenty weeks. These details are tiresome and disagreeable, no doubt, to the refined reader, but just imagine how much more disagreeable they were to Mr. Lewisham, trudging meditative to the schools. You will understand his slipping out of the laboratory and betaking himself to the Educational Reading-room ; and how it was that the observant Smithers, grinding his lecture notes against the now imminent second examination for the " Forbes," was presently perplexed to the centre of his being by the spectacle of Lewisham intent upon a pile of current periodicals, the *Educational Times*, the *Journal of Education*, the *Schoolmaster*, *Science and Art*, the *University Correspondent*, *Nature*, the *Athenæum*, the *Academy*, and the *Author*.

Smithers remarked the appearance of a notebook, the jotting down of memoranda. He edged into the bay nearest Lewisham's table and approached him suddenly from the flank. " What are *you* after ? " said Smithers in a noisy whisper and with a detective eye on the papers. He perceived Lewisham was scrutinising the advertisement columns, and his perplexity increased.

" Oh—nothing," said Lewisham blandly, with his hand falling casually over his memoranda ; " what's your particular little game ? "

" Nothing much," said Smithers, " just mooching round. You weren't at the meeting last Friday ? "

He turned a chair, knelt on it, and began whispering over the back about Debating Society politics. Lewisham was inattentive and brief. What had he to do with these puerilities ? At last Smithers went away foiled, and met Parkson by the entrance. Parkson, by the bye, had not spoken to Lewisham since their painful misunderstanding. He made a wide détour to his seat at the end table, and so, and by a singular rectitude of bearing and a dignified expression, showed himself aware of Lewisham's offensive presence.

Lewisham's investigations were twofold. He wanted to discover some way of adding materially to that weekly guinea by his own exertions, and he wanted to learn the conditions of the market for typewriting. For himself he had a vague idea, an idea subsequently abandoned, that it was possible to get teaching work in evening classes during the month of March. But except by reason of sudden death, no evening class in London changes its staff after September until July comes round again. Private tuition, moreover, offered many attractions to him, but no definite proposals. His ideas of his own possibilities were youthful, or he would not have spent time in noting the conditions of application for a vacant professorship in physics at the Melbourne University. He also made a note of the vacant editorship of a monthly magazine devoted to social questions. He would not have minded doing that sort of thing at all, though the proprietor might. There was also a vacant curatorship in the Museum of Eton College.

The typewriting business was less varied and more definite. Those were the days before the violent competition of the half-educated had brought things down to an impossible tenpence the thousand words, and the prevailing price was as high as one-and-six. Calculating that Ethel could do a thousand words in an hour and that she could work five or six hours in the day, it was evident that her contributions to the household expenses would be by no means despicable ; thirty shillings a week perhaps. Lewisham was naturally elated at this discovery. He could find no advertisements of authors or others seeking typewriting, but he saw that a great number of typists advertised themselves in the literary papers. It was evident Ethel also must advertise. " ' Scientific phraseology a speciality ' might be put," meditated Lewisham. He returned to his lodgings in a hopeful mood with quite a bundle of memoranda of possible employment. He spent five shillings upon stamps on the way.

After lunch, Lewisham—a little short of breath—asked to see Madam Gadow. She came up in the most affable frame of mind ; nothing could be further from the normal indignation of the British landlady. She was very voluble, gesticulatory and lucid, but unhappily bi-lingual, and at all the crucial points German. Mr. Lewisham's natural politeness restrained him from too close a pursuit across the boundary of the two imperial tongues. Quite half an hour's amicable discussion led at last to a reduction of sixpence, and all parties professed themselves satisfied with this result.

Madam Gadow was quite cool even at the end. Mr. Lewisham was flushed in the face, red-eared, and his hair slightly disordered ; but that sixpence was at any rate an admission of the justice of his claim. " She was evidently trying it on," he said almost apologetically to Ethel. " It was absolutely necessary to present a firm front to her. I doubt if we shall have any trouble again. . . .

" Of course what she says about kitchen coals is perfectly just."

Then the young couple went for a walk in Kensington Gardens, and—the spring afternoon was so warm and pleasant —sat on two attractive green chairs near the band-stand, for which Lewisham had subsequently to pay twopence. They had what Ethel called a " serious talk." She was really wonderfully sensible and discussed the situation exhaustively. She was particularly insistent upon the importance of economy in her domestic disbursements and deplored her general ignorance very earnestly. It was decided that Lewisham should get a good elementary text-book of domestic economy for her private study. At home Mrs. Chaffery guided her house by the oracular items of *Enquire Within upon Everything*, but Lewisham considered that work unscientific.

Ethel was also of opinion that much might be learnt from the sixpenny ladies' papers—the penny ones had hardly begun in those days. She had bought such publications during seasons of affluence, but chiefly, as she now deplored, with an eye to the trimming of hats and such-like vanities. The sooner the typewriter came the better. It occurred to Lewisham with unpleasant suddenness that he had not allowed for the purchase of a typewriter in his estimate of their resources. It brought their " law " down to twelve or thirteen weeks.

They spent the evening in writing and copying a number of letters, addressing envelopes and enclosing stamps. There were optimistic moments.

" Melbourne's a fine city," said Lewisham, " and we should have a glorious voyage out." He read the application for the Melbourne professorship out loud to her, just to see how it read, and she was greatly impressed by the list of his accomplishments and successes. " I did not know you knew *half* those things," she said, and became depressed at her relative illiteracy. It was natural, after such encouragement, to write to the scholastic agents in a tone of assured consequence.

The advertisement for typewriting in the *Athenæum* troubled his conscience a little. After he had copied out his draft with its " Scientific phraseology a speciality," fine and large, he saw the notes she had written out for him. Her handwriting was still round and boyish, even as it had appeared in the Whortley avenue, but her punctuation was confined to the erratic comma and the dash, and there was a disposition to spell the imperfectly legible along the line of least resistance. However, he dismissed that matter with a resolve to read over and correct anything in that way that she might have sent her to do. It would not be a bad idea, he thought parenthetically, if he himself read up some sound authority on the punctuation of sentences.

They sat at this business quite late, heedless of the examination in botany that came on the morrow. It was very bright and cosy in their little room with their fire burning, the gas lit and the curtains drawn, and the number of applications they had written made them hopeful. She was flushed and enthusiastic, now flitting about the room, now coming close to him and leaning over him to see what he had done. At Lewisham's request she got him the envelopes from the chest of drawers. "You *are* a help to a chap," said Lewisham, leaning back from the table. " I feel I could do anything for a girl like you—anything."

" *Really !* " she cried. " Really ! Am I really a help ? "

Lewisham's face and gesture were all assent. She gave a little cry of delight, stood for a moment, and then by way of practical demonstration of her unflinching helpfulness, hurried round the table towards him with arms extended. " You dear ! " she cried.

Lewisham, partially embraced, pushed his chair back with his disengaged arm, so that she might sit on his knee. . . .

Who could doubt that she was a help ?

# CHAPTER TWENTY-FIVE

## THE FIRST BATTLE

Lewisham's inquiries for evening teaching and private tuition were essentially provisional measures. His proposals for a more permanent establishment displayed a certain defect in his sense of proportion. That Melbourne professorship, for example, was beyond his merits, and there were aspects of things that would have affected the welcome of himself and his wife at Eton. At the outset he was inclined to regard the South Kensington scholar as the intellectual salt of the earth, to overrate the abundance of " decent things " yielding from one hundred and fifty to three hundred a year, and to disregard the competition of such inferior enterprises as the universities of Oxford, Cambridge, and the literate North. But the scholastic agents to whom he went on the following Saturday did much in a quiet way to disabuse his mind.

Mr. Blendershin's chief assistant in the grimy little office in Oxford Street cleared up the matter so vigorously that Lewisham was angered. " Head Master of an endowed school, perhaps ! " said Mr. Blendershin's chief assistant. " Lord !— why not a bishopric ? I say "—as Mr. Blendershin entered smoking an assertive cigar—" one-and-twenty, *no* degree, *no* games, two years' experience as junior—wants a headmastership of an endowed school ! " He spoke so loudly that it was inevitable the selectors of clients in the waiting-room should hear, and he pointed with his pen.

" Look here ! " said Lewisham hotly ; " if I knew the ways of the market I shouldn't come to you."

Mr. Blendershin stared at Lewisham for a moment. " What's he done in the way of certificates ? " asked Mr. Blendershin of the assistant.

The assistant read a list of 'ologies and 'ographies. " Fifty-resident," said Mr. Blendershin concisely—" that's your figure. Sixty, if you're lucky."

" *What ?* " said Mr. Lewisham.

" Not enough for you ? "

" Not nearly."

" You can get a Cambridge graduate for eighty resident—and grateful," said Mr. Blendershin.

" But I don't want a resident post," said Lewisham.

" Precious few non-resident shops," said Mr. Blendershin. " Precious few. They want you for dormitory supervision—and they're afraid of your taking pups outside."

" Not married by any chance ? " said the assistant suddenly, after an attentive study of Lewisham's face.

" Well—er." Lewisham met Mr. Blendershins eye. " Yes," he said.

The assistant was briefly unprintable. " Lord ! you'll have to keep that dark," said Mr. Blendershin. " But you have got a tough bit of hoeing before you. If I was you I'd go on and get my degree now you're so near it. You'll stand a better chance."

Pause.

" The fact is," said Lewisham slowly and looking at his boot toes, " I must be doing *something* while I am getting my degree."

The assistant whistled softly.

" Might get you a visiting job, perhaps," said Mr. Blendershin speculatively. " Just read me those items again, Binks." He listened attentively. " Objects to religious teaching !— Eh ? " He stopped the reading by a gesture. " That's nonsense. You can't have everything, you know. Scratch that out. You won't get a place in any middle-class school in England if you object to religious teaching. It's the mothers— bless 'em ! Say nothing about it. Don't believe—who does ? There's hundreds like you, you know—hundreds. Parsons— all sorts. Say nothing about it——"

" But if I'm asked ? "

" Church of England. Every man in this country who has not dissented belongs to the Church of England. It'll be hard enough to get you anything without that."

" But——" said Mr. Lewisham. " It's lying."

" Legal fiction," said Mr. Blendershin. " Every one under- stands. If you don't do that, my dear chap, we can't do any- thing for you. It's journalism, or London docks. Well, considering your experience—say docks."

Lewisham's face flushed irregularly. He did not answer. He scowled and tugged at the still by no means ample mous- tache.

" Compromise, you know," said Mr. Blendershin, watching him kindly. " Compromise."

For the first time in his life Lewisham faced the necessity of telling a lie in cold blood. He glissaded from the austere altitudes of his self-respect and his next words were already disingenuous.

" I won't promise to tell lies if I'm asked," he said aloud. " I can't do that."

" Scratch it out," said Blendershin to the clerk. " You needn't mention it. Then you don't say you can teach drawing."

" I can't," said Lewisham.

" You just give out the copies," said Blendershin, " and take care they don't see you draw, you know."

" But that's not teaching drawing——"

" It's what's understood by it in *this* country," said Blender-

shin. " Don't you go corrupting your mind with peda-
gogueries. They're the ruin of assistants. Put down drawing. Then there's shorthand——"

" Here, I say ! " said Lewisham.

" There's shorthand, French, book-keeping, commercial
geography, land measuring——"

" But I can't teach any of those things ! "

" Look here," said Blendershin, and paused. " Has your
wife or you a private income ? "

" No," said Lewisham.

" Well ? "

A pause of further moral descent, and a whack against an
obstacle. " But they will find me out," said Lewisham.

Blendershin smiled. " It's not so much ability as willing-
ness to teach, you know. And *they* won't find you out. The
sort of schoolmaster we deal with can't find anything out.
He can't teach any of these things himself—and consequently
he doesn't believe they *can* be taught. Talk to him of peda-
gogics and he talks of practical experience. But he puts 'em
on his prospectus, you know, and he wants 'em on his time-
table. Some of these subjects—— There's commercial geography, for instance. What *is* commercial geography ? "

" Barilla," said the assistant biting the end of his pen, and
added pensively, " *and* blethers."

" Fad," said Blendershin. " Just fad. Newspapers talk
rot about commercial education, Duke of Devonshire catches
on and talks ditto—pretends he thought of it himself—much
*he* cares—parents get hold of it—schoolmasters obliged to put
something down, consequently assistants must. And that's
the end of the matter ! "

" *All* right," said Lewisham catching his breath in a faint
sob of shame. " Stick 'em down. But mind—a non-resident
place."

" Well," said Blendershin, " your science may pull you
through. But I tell you it's hard. Some grant-earning
grammar school may want that. And that's about all, I
think. Make a note of the address. . . ."

The assistant made a noise, something between a whistle
and the word " Fee." Blendershin glanced at Lewisham and
nodded doubtfully.

" Fee for booking," said the assistant ; " half a crown.
Postage—in advance—half a crown."

But Lewisham remembered certain advice Dunkerley had
given him in the old Whortley days. He hesitated. " No,"
he said. " I don't pay that. If you get me anything there's
the commission—if you don't——"

" We lose," supplied the assistant.

" And you ought to," said Lewisham. " It's a fair game."

" Living in London ? " asked Blendershin.

" Yes," said the clerk.

" That's all right," said Mr. Blendershin.' " We won't say anything about the postage in that case. Of course it's the off season, and you mustn't expect anything at present very much. Sometimes there's a shift or so at Easter. . . . There's nothing more. . . . Afternoon. Any one else, Binks ? "

Messrs. Maskelyne, Smith and Thrums did a higher class of work than Blendershin, whose specialities were lower class private establishments and the cheaper sort of endowed schools. Indeed, so superior were Maskelyne, Smith and Thrums that they enraged Lewisham by refusing at first to put him on their books. He was interviewed briefly by a young man dressed and speaking with offensive precision, whose eye adhered rigidly to the waterproof collar throughout the interview.

" Hardly our line," he said, and pushed Lewisham a form to fill up. " Mostly upper class and good preparatory schools here, you know."

As Lewisham filled up the form with his multitudinous " 'ologies " and " 'ographies," a youth of ducal appearance entered and greeted the precise young man in a friendly way. Lewisham, bending down to write, perceived that this professional rival wore a very long frock-coat, patent-leather boots, and the most beautiful grey trousers. His conceptions of competition enlarged. The precise young man by a motion of his eyes directed the newcomer's attention to Lewisham's waterproof collar, and was answered by raised eyebrows and a faint tightening of the mouth. " That bounder at Castleford has answered me," said the newcomer in a fine rich voice. " Is he any bally good ? "

When the bounder at Castleford had been discussed Lewisham presented his paper, and the precise young man with his eye still fixed on the waterproof collar took the document in the manner of one who reaches across a gulf. " I doubt if we shall be able to do anything for you," he said reassuringly. " But an English mastership may chance to be vacant. Science doesn't count for much in *our* sort of schools, you know. Classics and good games—that's our sort of thing."

" I see," said Lewisham.

"Good games, good form, you know, and all that sort of thing."

" I see," said Lewisham.

" You don't happen to be a public-school boy ? " asked the precise young man.

" No," said Lewisham.

" Where were you educated ? "

Lewisham's face grew hot. " Does that matter ? " he asked with his eye on the exquisite grey trousering.

" In our sort of school—decidedly. It's a question of tone, you know."

" I see," said Lewisham, beginning to realise new limitations. His immediate impulse was to escape the eye of the nicely dressed assistant master. " You'll write, I suppose, if you have anything," he said, and the precise young man responded with alacrity to his doorward motion.

" Often get that kind of thing ? " asked the nicely dressed young man when Lewisham had departed.

" Rather. Not quite so bad as that, you know. That waterproof collar—did you notice it ? Ugh ! And—' I see.' And the scowl and the clumsiness of it. Of course *he* hasn't any decent clothes—he'd go to a new shop with one tin box ! But that sort of thing—and board-school teachers—they're getting everywhere ! Only the other day—Rowton was here."

" Not Rowton of Pinner ? "

" Yes, Rowton of Pinner. And he asked right out for a board-school master. He said, ' I want some one who can teach arithmetic.' "

He laughed. The nicely dressed young man meditated over the handle of his cane. " A bounder of that kind can't have a particularly nice time," he said, " anyhow. If he does get into a decent school, he must get tremendously cut by all the decent men."

" Too thick-skinned to mind that sort of thing, I fancy," said the scholastic agent. " He's a new type. This South Kensington place and the polytechnics are turning him out by the hundred. . . ."

Lewisham forgot his resentment at having to profess a religion he did not believe, in this new discovery of the scholastic importance of clothing. He went along with an eye to all the shop windows that afforded a view of his person. Indisputably his trousers *were* ungainly, flapping abominably over his boots and bagging terribly at the knees, and his boots were not only worn and ugly but extremely ill blacked. His wrists projected offensively from his coat sleeves, he perceived a huge asymmetry in the collar of his jacket, his red tie was askew and ill tied, and that waterproof collar ! It was shiny, slightly discoloured, suddenly clammy to the neck. What if he did happen to be well equipped for science teaching ? That was nothing. He speculated on the cost of a complete outfit. It would be difficult to get such grey trousers as those he had seen for less than sixteen shillings and he reckoned a frock-coat at forty shillings at least—possibly even more. He knew good clothes were very expensive. He hesitated at Poole's door and turned away. The thing was out of the question. He crossed Leicester Square and went down Bedford Street disliking every well-dressed person he met.

Messrs. Danks and Wimborne inhabited a bank-like establishment near Chancery Lane, and without any conversation presented him with forms to fill up. Religion ? asked the form. Lewisham paused and wrote " Church of England."

Thence he went to the College of Pedagogues in Holborn.

The College of Pedagogues presented itself as a long-bearded, corpulent, comfortable person with a thin gold watch chain and fat hands. He wore gilt glasses and had a kindly confidential manner that did much to heal Lewisham's wounded feelings. The 'ologies and 'ographies were taken down with polite surprise at their number. " You ought to take one of our diplomas," said the stout man. " You would find no difficulty. No competition. And there are prizes—several prizes—in money."

Lewisham was not aware that the waterproof collar had found a sympathetic observer.

" We give courses of lectures, and have an examination in the theory and practice of education. It is the only examination in the theory and practice of education for men engaged in middle and upper class teaching in this country. Except the Teacher's Diploma. And so few come—not two hundred a year. Mostly governesses. The men prefer to teach by rule of thumb, you know. English characteristic—rule of thumb. It doesn't do to say anything of course, but there's bound to be—something happen—something a little disagreeable—somewhen, if things go on as they do. American schools keep on getting better—German too. What used to do won't do now. I tell this to you, you know, but it doesn't do to tell every one. It doesn't do. It doesn't do to do anything. So much has to be considered. However . . . But you'd do well to get a diploma and make yourself efficient. Though that's looking ahead."

He spoke of looking ahead with an apologetic laugh as though it was an amiable weakness of his. He turned from such abstruse matters and furnished Lewisham with the particulars of the college diplomas, and proceeded to other possibilities. " There's private tuition," he said. " Would you mind a backward boy ? Then we are occasionally asked for visiting masters. Mostly by girls' schools. But that's for older men—married men, you know."

" I am married," said Lewisham.

" Eh ? " said the College of Pedagogues, startled.

" I am married," said Lewisham.

" Dear me," said the College of Pedagogues gravely, and regarding Mr. Lewisham over gold-rimmed glasses. " Dear me ! And I am more than twice your age, and I am not married at all. One-and-twenty ! Have you—have you been married long ? "

" A few weeks," said Lewisham.

" That's very remarkable," said the College of Pedagogues. " Very interesting. . . . Really ! Your wife must be a very courageous young person. . . . Excuse me ! You know—— You will really have a hard fight for a position. However— it certainly makes you eligible for girls' schools ; it does do that. To a certain extent, that is."

The evidently enhanced respect of the College of Pedagogues pleased Lewisham extremely. But his encounter
with the Medical, Scholastic and Clerical Agency that holds
by Waterloo Bridge was depressing again, and after that he
set out to walk home. Long before he reached home he was
tired, and his simple pride in being married and in active
grapple with an unsympathetic world had passed. His surrender on the religious question had left a rankling bitterness
behind it; the problem of the clothes was acutely painful.
He was still far from a firm grasp of the fact that his market
price was under rather than over one hundred pounds a year,
but that persuasion was gaining ground in his mind.

The day was a greyish one, with a dull cold wind, and a nail
in one of his boots took upon itself to be objectionable. Certain
wild shots and disastrous lapses in his recent botanical
examination, that he had managed to keep out of his mind
hitherto, forced their way on his attention. For the first
time since his marriage he harboured premonitions of
failure.

When he got in he wanted to sit down at once in the little
creaky chair by the fire, but Ethel came flitting from the
newly bought typewriter with arms extended and prevented
him. "Oh!—it *has* been dull," she said.

He missed the compliment. "*I* haven't had such a giddy
time that you should grumble," he said, in a tone that was
novel to her. He disengaged himself from her arms and sat
down. He noticed the expression of her face.

"I'm rather tired," he said by way of apology. "And
there's a confounded nail I must hammer down in my boot.
It's tiring work hunting up these agents, but of course it's
better to go and see them. How have you been getting
on?"

"All right," she said regarding him. And then, "You *are*
tired. We'll have some tea. And—let me take off your
boot for you, dear. Yes—I will."

She rang the bell, bustled out of the room, called for tea
at the staircase, came back, pulled out Madam Gadow's
ungainly hassock and began unlacing his boot. Lewisham's
mood changed. "You *are* a trump, Ethel," he said; "I'm
hanged if you're not." As the laces flicked he bent forward
and kissed her ear. The unlacing was suspended and there
were reciprocal endearments. . . .

Presently he was sitting in his slippers, with a cup of tea
in his hand, and Ethel, kneeling on the hearthrug with the
firelight on her face, was telling him of an answer that had
come that afternoon to her advertisement in the *Athenæum*.

"That's good," said Lewisham.

"It's a novelist," she said with a light of pride in her
eyes, and handed him the letter. "Lucas Holderness, the
author of *The Furnace of Sin* and other stories."

" That's first rate," said Lewisham with just a touch of envy, and bent forward to read by the firelight.

The letter was from an address in Judd Street, Euston Road, written on good paper and in a fair round hand such as one might imagine a novelist using. " Dear Madam," said the letter ; " I propose to send you, by registered letter, the MS. of a three-volume novel. It is about 90,000 words—but you must count the exact number."

" How I shall count I don't know," said Ethel.

" I'll show you a way," said Lewisham. " There's no difficulty in that. You count the words on three or four pages, strike an average, and multiply."

" But of course, before doing so I must have a satisfactory guarantee that my confidence in putting my work in your hands will not be misplaced and that your execution is of the necessary high quality."

" Oh ! " said Lewisham ; " that's a bother."

" Accordingly I must ask you for references."

" That's a downright nuisance," said Lewisham. " I suppose that ass Lagune. . . . But what's this ? ' Or, failing references, for a deposit . . .' That's reasonable, I suppose."

It was such a moderate deposit too—merely a guinea. Even had the doubt been stronger, the aspect of helpful hopeful little Ethel eager for work might well have thrust it aside. " Sending him a cheque will show him we have a banking account behind us," said Lewisham—his banking was still sufficiently recent for pride. " We will send him a cheque. That'll settle *him* all right."

That evening after the guinea cheque had been despatched, things were further brightened by the arrival of a letter of atrociously jellygraphed advices from Messrs. Danks and Wimborne. They all referred to resident vacancies for which Lewisham was manifestly unsuitable, nevertheless their arrival brought an encouraging assurance of things going on, of shifting and unstable places in the defences of the beleaguered world. Afterwards, with occasional endearments for Ethel, he set himself to a revision of his last year's notebooks, for now the botany was finished, the advanced zoological course—the last lap, as it were, for the Forbes medal—was beginning. She got her best hat from the next room to make certain changes in the arrangement of its trimming. She sat in the little chair, while Lewisham, with documents spread before him, sat at the table.

Presently she looked up from an experimental arrangement of her cornflowers, and discovered Lewisham no longer reading, but staring blankly at the middle of the tablecloth with an extraordinary misery in his eyes. She forgot the cornflowers and stared at him.

" Penny," she said after an interval.

Lewisham started and looked up. " *Eh ?* "

" Why were you looking so miserable ? " she asked.

" *Was* I looking miserable ? "

" Yes.   And *cross* ! "

" I was thinking just then that I would like to boil a bishop or so in oil."

" My dear ! "

" They know perfectly well the case against what they teach, they know it's neither madness nor wickedness nor any great harm to others, not to believe, they know perfectly well that a man may be as honest as the day, and right—right and decent in every way—and not believe in what they teach. And they know that it only wants the edge off a man's honour, for him to profess anything in the way of belief.   Just anything.   And they won't say so.   I suppose they want the edge off every man's honour.   If a man is well off they will truckle to him no end, though he laughs at all their teaching. They'll take gold plate from company promoters and rent from insanitary houses.   But if a man is poor and doesn't profess to believe in what some of them scarcely believe themselves, they wouldn't lift a finger to help him against the ignorance of their followers.   Your stepfather was right enough there.   They know what's going on.   They know that it means lying and humbug for any number of people, and they don't care.   Why should they ?   *They've* got it down all right.   They're spoilt and why shouldn't we be ? "

Lewisham having selected the bishops as scapegoats for his turpitude, was inclined to ascribe even the nail in his boot to their agency.

Mrs. Lewisham looked puzzled.   She realised his drift.

" You're not," she said, and dropped her voice, " an *infidel* ? "

Lewisham nodded gloomily.   " Aren't you ? " he said.

" Oh no," said Mrs. Lewisham.

" But you don't go to church, you don't——"

" No, I don't," said Mrs. Lewisham ; and then with more assurance, " But I'm not an infidel."

" Christian ? "

" I suppose so."

" But a Christian—— What do you believe ? "

" Oh !  to tell the truth, and do right, and not hurt or injure people and all that."

" That's not a Christian.   A Christian is one who believes."

" It's what *I* mean by a Christian," said Mrs. Lewisham.

" Oh !  at that rate any one's a Christian," said Lewisham. 'We all think it's right to do right and wrong to do wrong."

" But we don't all do it," said Mrs. Lewisham, taking up the cornflowers again.

" No," said Lewisham, a little taken aback by the feminine method of discussion.   " We don't all do it—certainly." He stared at her for a moment—her head was a little on one side and her eyes on the cornflowers—and his mind was full of a strange discovery. He seemed on the verge of speaking, and turned to his notebook again.

Very soon the centre of the tablecloth resumed its sway.

The following day Mr. Lucas Holderness received his cheque for a guinea. Unhappily it was crossed. He meditated for some time and then took pen and ink and improved Lewisham's careless "one" to "five" and touched up his unticked figure one to correspond.

You perceive him, a lank, cadaverous, good-looking man with long black hair and a semi-clerical costume of quite painful rustiness. He made the emendations with grave carefulness. He took the cheque round to his grocer. His grocer looked at it suspiciously.

"You pay it in," said Mr. Lucas Holderness, "if you've any doubts about it. Pay it in. *I* don't know the man or what he is. He may be a swindler for all I can tell. *I* can't answer for him. Pay it in and see. Leave the change till then. I can wait. I'll call round in a few days' time."

"All right, wasn't it ? " said Mr. Lucas Holderness in a casual tone two days later.

"Quite, sir," said the grocer with enhanced respect, and handed him his four pounds thirteen and sixpence change.

Mr. Lucas Holderness, who had been eyeing the grocer's stock with a curious intensity, immediately became animated and bought a tin of salmon. He went out of the shop with the rest of the money in his hand, for the pockets of his clothes were old and untrustworthy. At the baker's he bought a new roll.

He bit a huge piece of the roll directly he was out of the shop, and went on his way gnawing. It was so large a piece that his gnawing mouth was contorted into the ugliest shapes. He swallowed by an effort, stretching his neck each time. His eyes expressed an animal satisfaction. He turned the corner of Judd Street biting again at the roll, and the reader of this story, like the Lewishams, hear of him no more.

# CHAPTER TWENTY-SIX

AFTER all, the rosy love-making and marrying and Epithalamy are no more than the dawns of things, and to follow comes all the spacious interval of white laborious light. Try as we may to stay those delightful moments, they fade and pass remorselessly ; there is no returning, no recovering, only—for the foolish—the vilest peep-shows and imitations in dens and darkened rooms. We go on—we grow. At least we age. Our young couple, emerging presently from an atmosphere of dusk and morning stars, found the sky gathering greyly overhead and saw one another for the first time clearly in the light of every day.

It might perhaps witness better to Lewisham's refinement if one could tell only of a moderated and dignified cooling, of pathetic little concealments of disappointment and a decent maintenance of the sentimental atmosphere. And so at last daylight. But our young couple were too crude for that. The first intimations of their lack of identity have already been described, but it would be tedious and pitiful to tell of all the little intensifications, shade by shade, of the conflict of their individualities. They fell out, dear lady ! they came to conflict of words. The stress of perpetual worry was upon them, of dwindling funds and the anxious search for work that would not come. And on Ethel lay long, vacant, lonely hours in dull surroundings. Differences arose from the most indifferent things ; one night Lewisham lay awake in unfathomable amazement because she had convinced him she did not care a rap for the Welfare of Humanity, and deemed his Socialism a fancy and an indiscretion. And one Sunday afternoon they started for a walk under the pleasantest auspices, and returned flushed and angry, satire and retort flying free—on the score of the social conventions in Ethel's novelettes. For some inexplicable reason Lewisham saw fit to hate her novelettes very bitterly. These encounters indeed were mere skirmishes for the most part, and the silences and embarrassments that followed ended sooner or later in a " making up," tacit or definite, though once or twice this making up only re-opened the healing wound. And always each skirmish left its scar, effaced from yet another line of their lives the lingering tints of romantic colour.

There came no work, no added income for either of them, saving two trifles, for five long months. Once Lewisham won twelve shillings in the prize competition of a penny weekly, and three times came infinitesimal portions of typewriting from a poet who had apparently seen the *Athenæum* advertisement. His name was Edwin Peak Baynes and his hand-

writing was sprawling and unformed. He sent her several
short lyrics on scraps of paper with instructions that he
desired "three copies of each written beautifully in different
styles" and " *not* fastened with metal fasteners but with silk
thread of an appropriate colour." Both of our young people
were greatly exercised by these instructions. One fragment
was called "Bird Song," one "Cloud Shadows," and one
"Eryngium," but Lewisham thought they might be spoken
of collectively as Bosh. By way of payment, this poet sent,
in contravention of the postal regulations, half a sovereign
stuck into a card, asking her to keep the balance against
future occasions. In a little while, greatly altered copies of
these lyrics were returned by the poet in person, with this
enigmatical instruction written across the cover of each:
"This style I like, only if possible more so."

Lewisham was out, but Ethel opened the door, so this
endorsement was unnecessary. "He's really only a boy,"
said Ethel, describing the interview to Lewisham, who was
curious. They both felt that the youthfulness of Edwin Peak
Baynes detracted something from the reality of this
employment.

From his marriage until the final examination in June,
Lewisham's life had an odd amphibious quality. At home
were Ethel and the perpetual aching pursuit of employment,
the pelting irritations of Madam Gadow's persistent overcharges, and so forth, and amid such things he felt extraordinarily grown up; but intercalated with these experiences
were those intervals at Kensington, scraps of his adolescence,
as it were, lying amidst the new matter of his manhood,
intervals during which he was simply an insubordinate and
disappointing student with an increasing disposition to gossip.
At South Kensington he dwelt with theories and ideals as a
student should; at the little rooms in Chelsea—they grew
very stuffy as the summer came on, and the accumulation of
the penny novelettes Ethel favoured made a litter—there
was his particular private concrete situation, and ideals gave
place to the real.

It was a strangely narrow world, he perceived dimly, in
which his manhood opened. The only visitors were the
Chafferys. Chaffery would come to share their supper, and
won upon Lewisham in spite of his roguery by his incessantly
entertaining monologue and by his expressed respect for and
envy of Lewisham's scientific attainments. Moreover, as
time went on, Lewisham found himself more and more in
sympathy with Chaffery's bitterness against those who order
the world. It was good to hear him on bishops and that sort
of people. He said what Lewisham wanted to say, beautifully.
Mrs. Chaffery was perpetually flitting out of the house as
Lewisham came home, a dim, black, nervous, untidy little
figure. She came because Ethel, in spite of her expressed

belief that love was " all in all," found married life a little dull and lonely while Lewisham was away. And she went hastily when he came, because of a certain irritability that the struggle against the world was developing. He told no one at Kensington about his marriage, at first because it was such a delicious secret and then for quite other reasons. So there was no overlapping. The two worlds began and ended sharply at the wrought-iron gates. But the day came when Lewisham passed those gates for the last time and his adolescence ended altogether.

In the final examination of the biological course, the examination that signalised the end of his income of a weekly guinea, he knew well enough that he had done badly. The evening of the last day's practical work found him belated, hot-headed, beaten, with ruffled hair and red ears. He sat to the last moment doggedly struggling to keep cool and to mount the ciliated funnel of an earthworm's nephridium. But ciliated funnels come not to those who have shirked the laboratory practice. He rose, surrendered his paper to the morose elderly young assistant demonstrator who had welcomed him so flatteringly eight months before, and walked down the laboratory to the door where the rest of his fellow-students clustered.

Smithers was talking loudly about the " twistiness " of the identification, and the youngster with the big ears was listening attentively.

" Here's Lewisham ! How did *you* get on, Lewisham ? " asked Smithers, not concealing his assurance.

" Horribly," said Lewisham shortly, and pushed past.

" Did you spot D ? " clamoured Smithers.

Lewisham pretended not to hear.

Miss Heydinger stood with her hat in her hand and looked at Lewisham's hot eyes. He was for walking past her, but something in her face penetrated even his disturbance. He stopped.

" Did you get out the nephridium ? " he said as graciously as he could.

She shook her head. " Are you going downstairs ? " she asked.

" Rather," said Lewisham, with a vague intimation in his manner of the offence Smithers gave him.

He opened the glass door from the passage to the staircase. They went down one tier of that square spiral in silence.

" Are you coming up again next year ? " asked Miss Heydinger.

" No," said Lewisham. " No, I shall not come here again. Ever."

Pause. " What will you do ? " she asked.

" I don't know. I have to get a living somehow. It's been bothering me all the session."

" I thought——" She stopped. " Will you go down to your uncle's again ? " she said.

" No. I shall stop in London. It's no good going out of things into the country. And besides—I've quarrelled rather with my uncle."

" What do you think of doing ?—teaching ? "

" I suppose it will be teaching. I'm not sure. Anything that turns up."

" I see," she said.

They went on down in silence for a time.

" I suppose you will come up again ? " he asked.

" I may try the botanical again—if they can find room. And, I was thinking—sometimes one hears of things. What is your address ? So that if I heard of anything——"

Lewisham stopped on the staircase and thought. " Of course," he said. He made no effort to give her the address, and she demanded it again at the foot of the stairs.

" That confounded nephridium—— ! " he said. " It has put everything out of my head."

They exchanged addresses on leaflets torn from Miss Hey-dinger's little notebook.

She waited at the Book in the hall while he signed his name. At the iron gates of the Schools she said : " I am going through Kensington Gardens."

He was now feeling irritated about the addresses, and he would not see the implicit invitation. " I am going towards Chelsea."

She hesitated a moment, looking at him—puzzled. " Good-bye then," she said.

" Good-bye," he answered, lifting his hat.

He crossed the Exhibition Road slowly with his packed glazed bag, now seamed with cracks, in his hand. He went thoughtfully down to the corner of the Cromwell Road and turned along that to the right so that he could see the red pile of the Science Schools rising fair and tall across the gardens of the Natural History Museum. He looked back towards it regretfully.

He was quite sure that he had failed in this last examina-tion. He knew that any career as a scientific man was now closed to him for ever. And he remembered now how he had come along this very road to that great building for the first time in his life, and all the hopes and resolves that had swelled within him as he had drawn near. That dream of incessant unswerving work ! Where might he have reached if only he had had singleness of purpose to make it a reality ? . . .

And in these gardens it was that he and Smithers and Parkson had sat on a seat hard by the fossil tree and dis-coursed of Socialism together before the great paper was read. . . .

"Yes," he said, speaking aloud to himself; "yes—*that's* all over too. Everything's over."

Presently the corner of the Natural History Museum came between him and his receding Alma Mater. He sighed and turned his face towards the stuffy little rooms at Chelsea, and the still unconquered world.

# CHAPTER TWENTY-SEVEN

## CONCERNING A QUARREL

IT was late in September that this particular quarrel occurred. Almost all the roseate tints seemed gone by this time, for the Lewishams had been married six months. Their financial affairs had changed from the catastrophic to the sordid ; Lewisham had found work. An army crammer named Captain Vigours wanted some one energetic for his mathematical duffers, and to teach geometrical drawing and what he was pleased to call " Sandhurst Science." He paid no less than two shillings an hour for his uncertain demands on Lewisham's time. Moreover, there was a class in lower mathematics beginning at Walham Green where Lewisham was to show his quality. Fifty shillings a week or more seemed credible—more might be hoped for. It was now merely a case of tiding over the interval until Vigours paid. And meanwhile the freshness of Ethel's blouses departed, and Lewisham refrained from the repair of his boot, which had cracked across the toe.

The beginning of the quarrel was trivial enough. But by the end they got to generalities. Lewisham had begun the day in a bad temper and under the cloud of an overnight passage of arms—and a little incident that had nothing to do with their ostensible difference lent it a warmth of emotion quite beyond its merits. As he emerged through the folding-doors he saw a letter lying among the sketchily laid breakfast things, and Ethel's attitude suggested the recoil of a quick movement ; the letter suddenly dropped. Her eyes met his and she flushed. He sat down and took the letter—a trifle awkwardly perhaps. It was from Miss Heydinger. He hesitated with it half-way to his pocket, then decided to open it. It displayed an ample amount of reading, and he read. On the whole he thought it rather a dull sort of letter, but he did not allow this to appear. When it was read he put it carefully in his pocket.

That formally had nothing to do with the quarrel. The breakfast was already over when the quarrel began. Lewisham's morning was vacant, and he proposed to occupy it in the revision of certain notes bearing upon " Sandhurst Science." Unhappily the search for his notebook brought him into collision with the accumulation of Ethel's novelettes.

" These things are everywhere," he said after a gust of vehement handling. " I *wish* you'd tidy them up sometimes."

" They were tidy enough till you began to throw them about," Ethel pointed out.

" Confounded muck ! it's only fit to be burnt," Lewisham

remarked to the universe, and pitched one viciously into the corner.

"Well, you tried to write one, anyhow," said Ethel, recalling a certain "Mammoth" packet of note-paper that had come on an evil end before Lewisham found his industrial level. This reminiscence always irritated him exceedingly.

"Eh?" he said sharply.

"You tried to write one," repeated Ethel—a little unwillingly.

"You don't mean me to forget that."

"It's you reminded me."

He stared hostility for a space.

"Well, the things make a beastly litter anyhow, there isn't a tidy corner anywhere in the room. There never is."

"That's just the sort of thing you always say."

"Well—is there?"

"Yes, there is."

"Where?"

Ethel professed not to hear. But a devil had possession of Lewisham for a time. "It isn't as though you had anything else to do," he remarked, wounding dishonourably.

Ethel turned. "If I put those things away," she said with tremendous emphasis on the "put," "you'd only say I'd hidden them. What is the good of trying to please you?"

The spirit of perversity suggested to Lewisham, "None apparently."

Ethel's cheeks glowed and her eyes were bright with unshed tears. Abruptly she abandoned the defensive and blurted out the thing that had been latent so long between them. Her voice took a note of passion. "Nothing I can do ever does please you, since that Miss Heydinger began to write to you."

There was a pause, a gap. Something like astonishment took them both. Hitherto it had been a convention that she knew nothing of the existence of Miss Heydinger. He saw a light. "How did you know?" he began, and perceived that line was impossible. He took the way of the natural man; he ejaculated an "Ugh!" of vast disgust, he raised his voice. "You are unreasonable!" he cried in angry remonstrance. "Fancy saying that! As though you ever tried to please me! Just as though it wasn't all the other way about!" He stopped—struck by a momentary perception of injustice. He plunged at the point he had shirked. "How did you know it was Miss Heydinger——?"

Ethel's voice took upon itself the quality of tears. "I wasn't meant to know, was I?" she said.

"But how?"

"I suppose you think it doesn't concern me? I suppose you think I'm made of stone."

"You mean—you think——?"

" Yes—I *do*."

For a brief interval Lewisham stared at the issue she had laid bare. He sought some crushing proposition, some line of convincing reasoning, with which to overwhelm and hide this new aspect of things. It would not come. He found himself fenced in on every side. A surging, irrational rage seized upon him.

" Jealousy ! " he cried. " Jealousy ! Just as though—— Can't I have letters about things you don't understand—that you *won't* understand ? If I asked you to read them you wouldn't—— It's just because——"

" You never give me a *chance* to understand."

" Don't I ? "

" No ! "

" Why !—at first I was always trying. Socialism, religion—all those things. But you don't care—you won't care. You won't have that I've thought over these things at all, that I care for these things ! It wasn't any *good* to argue. You just care for me in a way—and all the rest of me—doesn't matter ! And because I've got a friend . . .''

" Friend ! "

" Yes—*friend* ! "

" Why !—you hide her letters ! ''

" Because I tell you you wouldn't understand what they are about. But, pah ! I won't argue. I *won't* ! You're jealous and there's the end of the matter ! ''

" Well, who *wouldn't* be jealous ? ''

He stared at her as if he found the question hard to see. The theme was difficult—invincibly difficult. He surveyed the room for a diversion. The notebook he had disinterred from her novelettes lay upon the table and reminded him of his grievance of ruined hours. His rage exploded. He struck out abruptly towards fundamental things. He gesticulated forcibly. " This can't go on ! " he cried, " this can't go on ! How can I work ? How can I do anything ? ''

He made three steps and stood in a clear space.

" I won't *stand* it—I won't go on at this ! Quarrels—bickerings—discomfort. Look there ! I meant to work this morning. I meant to look up notes ! Instead of which you start a quarrel——''

The gross injustice raised Ethel's voice to an outcry. " *I* didn't start the quarrel——''

The only response to this was to shout, and Lewisham shouted. " You start a quarrel ! " he repeated. " You make a shindy ! You spring a dispute—jealousy !—on me ! How can I do anything ? How can one stop in a house like this ? I shall go out. Look here !—I shall go out. I shall go to Kensington and work there ! ''

He perceived himself wordless, and Ethel was about to speak. He glared about him, seeking a prompt climax.

Instant action was necessary. He perceived Huxley's *Vertebrata* upon the side-table. He clutched it, swaying it through a momentous arc, and hurled it violently into the empty fireplace.

For a second he seemed to be seeking some other missile. He perceived his hat on the chest of drawers, seized it and strode tragically from the room.

He hesitated with the door half closed, then opened it wide and slammed it vehemently. Thereby the world was warned of the justice of his rage, and so he passed with credit into the street.

He went striding heedless of his direction through the streets dotted with intent people hurrying to work, and presently habit turned his feet towards the Brompton Road. The eastward trend of the morning traffic caught him. For a time, save for a rebellious ingredient of wonder at the back of his mind, he kept his anger white and pure. Why had he married her? was the text to which he clung. Why in the name of destiny had he married her? But anyhow he had said the decisive thing. He would not stand it! It must end. Things were intolerable and they must end. He meditated devastating things that he might presently say to her in pursuance of this resolution. He contemplated acts of cruelty. In such ways he would demonstrate clearly that he would not stand it. He was very careful to avoid inquiring what it was he would not stand.

How in the name of destiny had he come to marry her? The quality of his surroundings mingled in some way with the quality of his thoughts. The huge distended buildings of corrugated iron in which the Art Museum (of all places!) culminates, the truncated Oratory all askew to the street, seemed to have a similar quarrel with fate. How in the name of destiny? After such high prolusions!

He found that his thoughts had carried him past the lodge of the museum. He turned back irritably and went through the turnstile. He entered the museum and passed beneath the gallery of Old Iron on his way to the Education Library. The vacant array of tables, the bays of attendant books had a quality of refuge. . . .

So much for Lewisham in the morning. Long before midday all the vigour of his wrath was gone, all his passionate conviction of Ethel's unworthiness. Over a pile of neglected geological works he presented a face of gloom. His memory presented a picture of himself as noisy, overbearing, and unfair. What on earth had it all been about?

By two o'clock he was on his way to Vigours', and his mood was acute remorse. Of the transition there can be no telling in words, for thoughts are more subtle than words and emotions infinitely vaguer. But one thing at least is definite, that a memory returned.

It drifted in to him, through the glass roof of the Library far above. He did not perceive it as a memory at first, but as an irritating obstacle to attention. He struck the open pages of the book before him with his flat hand. " Damn that infernal hurdy-gurdy ! " he whispered.

Presently he made a fretful movement and put his hands over his ears.

Then he thrust his books from him, got up, and wandered about the Library. The organ came to an abrupt end in the middle of a bar, and vanished in the circumambient silence of space.

Lewisham standing in a bay closed a book with a snap and returned to his seat.

Presently he found himself humming a languid tune, and thinking again of the quarrel that he had imagined banished from his mind. What in the name of destiny had it all been about ? He had a curious sense that something had got loose, was sliding about in his mind. And as if by way of answer emerged a vision of Whortley—a singularly vivid vision. It was moonlight and a hillside, the little town lay lit and warm below, and the scene was set to music, a lugubriously senti- mental air. For some reason this music had the quality of a barrel organ—though he knew that properly it came from a band—and it associated with itself a mystical formula of words, drawling words :

" Sweet dreamland fa—ces passing to and fro,
    Bring back to mem'ry, days of long ago—oh ! "

This air not only reproduced the picture with graphic vividness, but it trailed after it an enormous cloud of irrational emotion, emotion that had but a moment before seemed gone for ever from his being.

He recalled it all ! He had come down that hillside and Ethel had been with him. . . .

Had he really felt like that about her ?

" Pah ! " he said suddenly and reverted to his books.

But the tune and the memory had won their footing, they were with him through his meagre lunch of milk and scones— he had resolved at the outset he would not go back to her for the midday meal—and on his way to Vigours' they insisted on attention. It may be that lunching on scone and milk does in itself make for milder ways of thinking. A sense of extra- ordinary contradiction, of infinite perplexity, came to him.

" But then," he asked, " how the devil did we get to *this* ? "

Which is indeed one of the fundamental questions of matrimony.

The morning tumults had given place to an almost scientific calm. Very soon he was grappling manfully with the question. There was no disputing it, they had quarrelled. Not once but several times lately they had quarrelled. It was real quarrelling—they had stood up against one another, striking, watching to strike, seeking to wound. He tried to recall just how things had gone—what he had said and what she had replied. He could not do it. He had forgotten phrases and connections. It stood in his memory not as a sequence of events but as a collection of disconnected static sayings ; each saying blunt, permanent, inconsecutive like a graven inscription. And of the scene there came only one picture— Ethel with a burning face and her eyes shining with tears.

The traffic of a cross street engaged him for a space. He emerged on the farther side full of the vivid contrast of their changed relations. He made a last effort to indict her, to show that she was entirely to blame for the transition. She had quarrelled with him, she had quarrelled deliberately because she was jealous. She was jealous of Miss Heydinger because she was stupid. But now these accusations faded like smoke as he put them forth. But the picture of two little figures back there in the moonlit past did not fade. It was in the narrows of Kensington High Street that he abandoned her arraignment. It was beyond the Town Hall that he made the new step. Was it, after all, just possible that in some degree he himself rather was the chief person to blame ?

It was instantly as if he had been aware of that all the time. Once he had made that step, he moved swiftly. Not a hundred paces before the struggle was over, and he had plunged headlong into the blue abyss of remorse. And all these things that had been so dramatic and forcible, all the vivid brutal things he had said, stood no longer graven inscriptions but in letters of accusing flame. He tried to imagine he had not said them, that his memory played him a trick, tried to suppose he had said something similar perhaps but much less forcible. He attempted with almost equal futility to minimise his own wounds. His endeavour served only to measure the magnitude of his fall.

He had recovered everything now, he saw it all. He recalled Ethel sunlit in the avenue, Ethel white in the moonlight before they parted outside the Frobisher house, Ethel as she would come out of Lagune's house greeting him for their nightly walk, Ethel new wedded, as she came to him through the folding-doors radiant in the splendour his emotions threw about her. And at last Ethel angry, dishevelled and tear-stained in that ill-lit, untidy little room. All to the cadence of a hurdy-gurdy tune ! From that to this ! How had it been possible to get from such an opalescent dawning to such a dismal day ? What was it had gone ? He and she were the same two persons who walked so brightly in awakened memory; he and she who had lived so bitterly through the last few weeks of misery !

His mood sank for a space to the quality of groaning. He

implicated her now at most as his partner in their failure—
" What a mess we have made of things ! " was his new motif.
" What a mess ! "

He knew love now for what it was, knew it for something
more ancient and more imperative than reason. He knew
now that he loved her, and his recent rage, his hostility, his
condemnation of her seemed to him the reign of some exterior
influence in his mind. He thought incredulously of the long
decline in tenderness that had followed the first days of their
delight in each other, the diminution of endearment, the first
yielding to irritability, the evenings he had spent doggedly
working, resisting all his sense of her presence. " One cannot
always be love-making," he had said, and so—they were
slipping apart. Then in countless little things he had not
been patient, he had not been fair. He had wounded her by
harshness, by unsympathetic criticism, above all by his absurd
secrecy about Miss Heydinger's letters. Why on earth had
he kept those letters from her ? as though there was something
to hide ! What was there to hide ? What possible antagonism
could there be ? Yet it was by such little things that their
love was now like some once valued possession that had been
in brutal hands, it was scratched and chipped and tarnished,
it was on its way to being altogether destroyed. Her manner
had changed towards him, a gulf was opening that he might
never be able to close again.

" No, it *shall* not be ! " he said, " it shall not be ! "

But how to get back to the old footing ? how to efface the
things he had said, the things that had been done ?

Could they get back ?

For a moment he faced a new possibility. Suppose they
could not get back ! Suppose the mischief was done ! Suppose that when he slammed the door behind him it locked,
and was locked against him for ever ! .

" But we *must* ! " said Lewisham, " we must ! "

He perceived clearly that this was no business of reasoned
apologies. He must begin again, he must get back to emotion,
he must thrust back the overwhelming pressure of everyday
stresses and necessities that was crushing all the warmth and
colour from their lives. But how ? How ?

He must make love to her again. But how to begin—how
to mark the change ? There had been making-up before,
sullen concessions and treaties. But this was different. He
tried to imagine something he might say, some appeal that he
might make. Everything he thought of was cold and hard,
or pitiful and undignified, or theatrical and foolish. Suppose
the door *was* closed ! If already it was too late ! In every
direction he was confronted by the bristling memories of harsh
things. He had a glimpse of how he must have changed in her
eyes, and things became intolerable for him. For now he
was assured he loved her still with all his heart.

And suddenly came a florist's window, and in the centre of it a glorious heap of roses.

They caught his eye before they caught his mind.  He saw white roses, virginal white, roses of cream and pink and crimson, the tints of flesh and pearl, rich, a mass of scented colour, visible odours, and in the midst of them a note of sullen red.  It was as it were the very colour of his emotion. He stopped abruptly.  He turned back to the window and stared frankly.  It was gorgeous, he saw, but why so particularly did it appeal to him ?

Then he perceived as though it was altogether self-evident what he had to do.  This was what he wanted.  This was the note he had to strike.  Among other things because it would repudiate the accursed worship of pinching self-restraint that was one of the incessant stresses between them.  They would come to her with a pure unexpectedness, they would flame upon her.

Then, after the roses, he would return.

Suddenly the grey trouble passed from his mind ; he saw the world full of colour again.  He saw the scene he desired bright and clear, saw Ethel no longer bitter and weeping, but glad as once she had always seemed glad.  His heart-beats quickened.  It was giving had been needed, and he would give.

Some weak voice of indiscreet discretion squeaked and vanished.  He had, he knew, a sovereign in his pocket. He went in.

He found himself in front of a formidable young lady in black, and unprepared with any formula.  He had never bought flowers before.  He looked about him for an inspiration.  He pointed at the roses.  " I want those roses," he said. . . .

He emerged again with only a few small silver coins remaining out of the sovereign he had changed.  The roses were to go to Ethel, properly packed ; they were to be delivered according to his express direction at six o'clock.

" Six o'clock," Lewisham had reiterated very earnestly.

" We quite understand," the young lady in black had said, and had pretended to be unable to conceal a smile.  " We're *quite* accustomed to sending out flowers."

# CHAPTER TWENTY-EIGHT

THE COMING OF THE ROSES

AND the roses miscarried !
When Lewisham returned from Vigours' it was already nearly seven. He entered the house with a beating heart. He had expected to find Ethel excited, the roses displayed. But her face was white and jaded. He was so surprised by this that the greeting upon his lips died away. He was balked ! He went into the sitting-room and there were no roses to be seen. Ethel came past him and stood with her back to him looking out of the window. The suspense was suddenly painful. . . .

He was obliged to ask, though he was certain of the answer, " Has nothing come ? "

Ethel looked at him. " What did you think had come ? "

" Oh ! nothing."

She looked out of the window again. " No," she said slowly, " nothing has come."

He tried to think of something to say that might bridge the distance between them, but he could think of nothing. He must wait until the roses came. He took out his books and a gaunt hour passed to supper-time. Supper was a chilly ceremonial set with necessary over-polite remarks. Disappointment and exasperation darkened Lewisham's soul. He began to feel angry with everything—even with her—he perceived she still judged him angry and that made him angry with her. He was resuming his books and she was helping Madam Gadow's servant to clear away, when they heard a rapping at the street door. " They have come at last," he said to himself brightening, and hesitated whether he should bolt or witness her reception of them. The servant was a nuisance. Then he heard Chaffery's voice, and whispered a soft " damn ! " to himself.

The only thing to do now if the roses came was to slip out into the passage, intercept them and carry them into the bedroom by the door between that and the passage. It would be undesirable for Chaffery to witness that phase of sentiment. He might flash some dart of ridicule that would stick in their memory for ever.

Lewisham tried to show that he did not want a visitor. But Chaffery was in high spirits and could have warmed a dozen cold welcomes. He sat down without any express invitation in the chair that he preferred.

Before Mr. and Mrs. Chaffery the Lewishams veiled whatever trouble might be between them beneath an insincere cordiality, and Chaffery was soon talking freely, unsuspicious of their crisis. He produced two cigars. " I had a wild moment," he said. "'For once,' said I, 'the honest shall smoke the admirable—or the admirable shall smoke the honest,' whichever you like best. Try one ? No ? Those austere principles of yours ! There will be more pleasure then. But really, I would as soon you smoked it as I. For to-night I radiate benevolence."

He cut the cigar with care, he lit it with ceremony, waiting until nothing but honest wood was burning on the match, and for fully a minute he was silent, evolving huge puffs of smoke. And then he spoke again, punctuating his words by varied and beautiful spirals. "So far," he said, "I have only trifled with knavery."

As Lewisham said nothing he resumed after a pause.

"There are three sorts of men in the world, my boy, three and no more—and of women only one. There are happy men and there are knaves and fools. Hybrids I don't count. And to my mind knaves and fools are very much alike."

He paused again.

"I suppose they are," said Lewisham flatly, and frowned at the fireplace.

Chaffery eyed him. "I am talking wisdom. To-night I am talking a particular brand of wisdom. I am broaching some of my oldest and finest, because—as you will find one day—this is a special occasion. And you are distrait ! "

Lewisham looked up. "Birthday ? " he said.

"You will see. But I was making golden observations about knaves and fools. I was early convinced of the absolute necessity of righteousness if a man is to be happy. I know it as surely as there is a sun in the heavens. Does that surprise you ? "

"Well, it hardly squares——"

"No. I know. I will explain all that. But let me tell you the happy life. Let me give you that, as if I lay on my deathbed and this was a parting gift. In the first place, mental integrity. Prove all things, hold fast to that which is right. Let the world have no illusions for you, no surprises. Nature is full of cruel catastrophes, man is a physically degenerate ape, every appetite, every instinct, needs the curb ; salvation is not in the nature of things but whatever salvation there may be is in the nature of man ; face all these painful things. I hope you follow that ? "

"Go on," said Lewisham, with the debating-society taste for a thesis prevailing for a minute over that matter of the roses.

"In youth, exercise and learning ; in adolescence, ambition, and in early manhood, love—no footlight passion." Chaffery was very solemn and insistent, with a lean extended finger, upon this point.

"Then marriage, young and decent, and then children and stout honest work for them, work too for the State in which they live ; a life of self-devotion, indeed, and for sunset a decent pride—that is the happy life. Rest assured that is the happy life ; the life Natural Selection has been shaping for man since life began. So a man may go happy from the cradle to the grave—at least—passably happy. And to do this needs just three things—a sound body, a sound intelligence, and a sound will. . . . A sound will."

Chaffery paused on the repetition.

" No other happiness endures. And when all men are wise, all men will seek that life. Fame ! Wealth ! Art !—the Red Indians worship lunatics, and we are still by way of respecting the milder sorts. But I say that all men who do not lead that happy life are knaves and fools. The physical cripple, you know, poor devil, I count a sort of bodily fool."

" Yes," weighed Lewisham, " I suppose he is."

" Now a fool fails of happiness because of his insufficient mind, he miscalculates, he stumbles and hobbles, some cant or claptrap whirls him away ; he gets passion out of a book and wife out of the stews, or he quarrels on a petty score ; threats frighten him, vanity beguiles him, he fails by blindness. But the knave who is not a fool fails against the light. Many knaves are fools also—*most* are—but some are not. I know— I am a knave but no fool. The essence of your knave is that he lacks the will, the motive capacity to seek his own greater good. The knave abhors persistence. Strait is the way and narrow the gate ; the knave cannot keep to it and the fool cannot find it."

Lewisham lost something of what Chaffery was saying by reason of a rap outside. He rose, but Ethel was before him. He concealed his anxiety as well as he could, and was relieved when he heard the front door close again and her footsteps pass into the bedroom by the passage door. He reverted to Chaffery.

" Has it ever occurred to you," asked Chaffery, apparently apropos of nothing, " that intellectual conviction is no motive at all ? Any more than a railway map will run a train a mile."

" Eh ? " said Lewisham. " Map—run a train a mile—of course, yes. No, it won't."

" That is precisely my case," said Chaffery. " That is the case of your pure knave everywhere. We are not fools— because we know. But yonder runs the highway, windy, hard and austere, a sort of dry happiness that will endure ; and here is the pleasant by-way—lush, my boy, lush, as the poets have it, and with its certain man-trap among the flowers. . . ."

Ethel returned through the folding-doors. She glanced at Lewisham, remained standing for a while, sat down in the basket chair as if to resume some domestic needlework that lay upon the table, then rose and went back into the bedroom.

Chaffery proceeded to expatiate on the transitory nature of passion and all glorious and acute experiences. Whole passages of that discourse Lewisham did not hear, so intent was he upon those roses. Why had Ethel gone back into the bedroom ? Was it possible—— ? Presently she returned, but she sat down so that he could not see her face.

" If there is one thing to set against the wholesome life it is adventure," Chaffery was saying. " But let every adventurer pray for an early death, for with adventures come wounds, and with wounds come sickness, and—except in romances—sickness affects the nervous system. Your nerve goes. Where are you then, my boy ? "

" Ssh ! what's that ? " said Lewisham.

It was a rap at the house door. Heedless of the flow of golden wisdom, he went out at once and admitted a gentleman friend of Madam Gadow, who passed along the passage and vanished down the staircase. When he returned Chaffery was standing to go.

" I could have talked with you longer," he said, " but you have something on your mind, I see. I will not worry you by guessing what. Some day you will remember. . . ." He said no more but laid his hand on Lewisham's shoulder.

One might almost fancy he was offended at something.

At any other time Lewisham might have been propitiatory, but now he offered no apology. Chaffery turned to Ethel and looked at her curiously for a moment. " Good-bye," he said, holding out his hand to her.

On the doorstep Chaffery regarded Lewisham with the same curious look, and seemed to weigh some remark. " Good-bye," he said at last with something in his manner that kept Lewisham at the door for a moment looking after his stepfather's receding figure. But immediately the roses were uppermost again.

When he re-entered the living-room he found Ethel sitting idly at her typewriter, playing with the keys. She got up at his return and sat down in the armchair with a novelette that hid her face. He stared at her, full of questions. After all, then, they had not come. He was intensely disappointed now, he was intensely angry with the ineffable young shopwoman in black. He looked at his watch and then again, he took a book and pretended to read and found himself composing a scathing speech of remonstrance to be delivered on the morrow at the flower-shop. He put his book down, went to his black bag, opened and closed it aimlessly. He glanced covertly at Ethel and found her looking covertly at him. He could not quite understand her expression.

He fidgeted into the bedroom and stopped as dead as a pointer.

He felt an extraordinary persuasion of the scent of roses. So strong did it seem that he glanced outside the room door, expecting to find a box there, mysteriously arrived. But there was no scent of roses in the passage.

Then he saw close by his foot an enigmatical pale object, and stooping, picked up the creamy petal of a rose. He stood with it in his hand, perplexed beyond measure. He perceived a slight disorder of the valance of the dressing-table and linked it with this petal by a swift intuition.

He made two steps, lifted the valance, and behold ! there lay his roses crushed together !

He gasped like a man who plunges suddenly into cold water. He remained stooping with the valance raised.

Ethel appeared in the half doorway and her expression was unfamiliar. He stared at her white face.

" Why on earth did you put my roses here ? " he asked.

She stared back at him. Her face reflected his astonishment.

" Why did you put my roses here ? " he asked again.

" Your roses ! " she cried. " What ! Did *you* send those roses ? "

# CHAPTER TWENTY-NINE

### THORNS AND ROSE PETALS

HE remained stooping and staring up at her, realising the implication of her words only very slowly.

Then it grew clear to him.

As she saw understanding dawning in his face, she uttered a cry of consternation. She came forward and sat down upon the little bedroom chair. She turned to him and began a sentence. " I," she said and stopped, with an impatient gesture of her hands. " *Oh !* "

He straightened himself and stood regarding her. The basket of roses lay overturned between them.

" You thought these came from some one else ? " he said, trying to grasp this inversion of the universe.

She turned her eyes. " I did not know," she panted. " A trap. . . . Was it likely—they came from you ? "

" You thought they came from some one else," he said.

" Yes," she said, " I did."

" Who ? "

" Mr. Baynes."

" That boy ! "

" Yes—that boy."

" Well ! "

Lewisham looked about him—a man in the presence of the inconceivable.

" You mean to say you have been carrying on with that youngster behind my back ? " he asked.

She opened her lips to speak and had no words to say.

His pallor increased until every tinge of colour had left his face. He laughed and then set his teeth. Husband and wife looked at one another.

" I never dreamt," he said in even tones.

He sat down on the bed, thrusting his feet among the scattered roses with a sort of grim satisfaction. " I never dreamt," he repeated, and the flimsy basket kicked by his swinging foot hopped indignantly through the folding-doors into the living-room and left a trail of blood-red petals.

They sat for perhaps two minutes and when he spoke again his voice was hoarse. He reverted to former formula. " Look here," he said, and cleared his throat, " I don't know whether you think I'm going to stand this, but I'm not."

He looked at her. She sat staring in front of her, making no attempt to cope with disaster.

" When I say I'm not going to stand it," explained Lewisham, " I don't mean having a row or anything of that sort. One can quarrel and be disappointed over—other things—and still go on. But this is a different thing altogether.

" Of all dreams and illusions ! . . . Think what I have los<sup>t</sup> in this accursed marriage. And *now* . . . You don't unde r-stand—you won't understand."

" Nor you," said Ethel, weeping but neither looking at him nor moving her hands from her lap where they lay helplessly. " *You* don't understand."

" I'm beginning to."

He sat in silence gathering force. " In one year," he said, " all my hopes, all my ambitions have gone. I know I have been cross and irritable—I know that. I've been pulled two ways. But . . . I bought you these roses."

She looked at the roses, and then at his white face, made an imperceptible movement towards him, and became impassive again.

" I do think one thing. I have found out you are shallow, you don't think, you can't feel things that I think and feel. I have been getting over that. But I did think you were loyal——"

" I *am* loyal," she cried.

" And you think—— Bah !—you poke my roses under the table ! "

Another portentous silence. Ethel stirred and he turned his eyes to watch what she was about to do. She produced her handkerchief and began to wipe her dry eyes rapidly, first one and then the other. Then she began sobbing. " I'm . . . as loyal as you . . . anyhow," she said.

For a moment Lewisham was aghast. Then he perceived he must ignore that argument.

" I would have stood it—I would have stood anything if you had been loyal—if I could have been sure of you. I am a fool, I know, but I would have stood the interruption of my work, the loss of any hope of a Career, if I had been sure you were loyal. I . . . I cared for you a great deal."

He stopped. He had suddenly perceived the pathetic. He took refuge in anger.

" And you have deceived me ! How long, how much, I don't care. You have deceived me. And I tell you "—he began to gesticulate—" I'm not so much your slave and fool as to stand that ! No woman shall make me *that* sort of fool, whatever else—— So far as I am concerned, this ends things. This ends things. We are married—but I don't care if we were married five hundred times. I won't stop with a woman who takes flowers from another man——"

" I *didn't*," said Ethel.

Lewisham gave way to a transport of anger. He caught up a handful of roses and extended them, trembling. " What's *this* ? " he asked. His finger bled from a thorn, as once it had bled from a blackthorn spray.

" I *didn't* take them," said Ethel. " I couldn't help it if they were sent."

"Ugh!" said Lewisham. "But what is the good of argument and denial? You took them in, you had them. You may have been cunning, but you have given yourself away. And our life and all this"—he waved an inclusive hand at Madam Gadow's furniture—"is at an end."

He looked at her and repeated with bitter satisfaction, "At an end."

She glanced at his face and his expression was remorseless. "I will not go on living with you," he said, lest there should be any mistake. "Our life is at an end."

Her eyes went from his face to the scattered roses. She remained staring at these. She was no longer weeping, and her face, save about the eyes, was white.

He presented it in another form. "I shall go away.

"We never ought to have married," he reflected. "But . . . I never expected *this*!"

"I didn't know," she cried out, lifting up her voice. "I *didn't* know. How could *I* help! *Oh!*"

She stopped and stared at him with hands clenched, her eyes haggard with despair.

Lewisham remained impenetrably malignant.

"I don't *want* to know," he said, answering her dumb appeal. "That settles everything. *That!*" He indicated the scattered flowers. "What does it matter to me what has happened or hasn't happened? Anyhow—oh! I don't mind. I'm glad. See? It settles things.

"The sooner we part the better. I shan't stop with you another night. I shall take my box and my portmanteau into that room and pack. I shall stop in there to-night, sleep in a chair or *think*. And to-morrow I shall settle up with Madam Gadow and go. You can go back . . . to your cheating."

He stopped for some seconds. She was deadly still. "You wanted to, and now you may. You wanted to, before I got work. You remember? You know your place is still open at Lagune's. I don't care. I tell you I don't care *that*. Not that! You may go your own way—and I shall go mine. See? And all this rot—this sham of living together when neither cares for the other—I don't care for you *now*, you know, so you needn't think it—will be over and done with. As for marriage —I don't care *that* for marriage—it can't make a sham and a blunder anything but a sham.

"It's a sham, and shams have to end, and that's the end of the matter."

He stood up resolutely. He kicked the scattered roses out of his way and dived beneath the bed for his portmanteau. Ethel neither spoke nor moved, but remained watching his movements. For a time the portmanteau refused to emerge, and he marred his stern resolution by a half audible "Come here —damn you!" He swung it into the living-room and returned for his box. He proposed to pack in that room.

When he had taken all his personal possessions out of the bedroom, he closed the folding-doors with an air of finality. He knew from the sounds that followed that she flung herself upon the bed, and that filled him with grim satisfaction.

He stood listening for a space, then set about packing methodically. The first rage of discovery had abated, he knew quite clearly that he was inflicting grievous punishment and that gratified him. There was also indeed a curious pleasure in the determination of a long and painful period of vague misunderstanding by this unexpected crisis. He was acutely conscious of the silence on the other side of the folding-doors, he kept up a succession of deliberate little noises, beat books together and brushed clothes, to intimate the resolute prosecution of his preparations.

That was about nine o'clock. At eleven he was still busy. . . .

Darkness came suddenly upon him. It was Madam Gadow's economical habit to turn off all her gas at that hour unless she chanced to be entertaining friends.

He felt in his pocket for matches and he had none. He whispered curses. Against such emergencies he had bought a brass lamp and in the bedroom there were candles. Ethel had a candle alight, he could see the bright yellow line that appeared between the folding-doors. He felt his way presently towards the mantel, receiving a blow in the ribs from a chair on the way, and went carefully amidst Madam Gadow's once amusing ornaments.

There were no matches on the mantel. Going to the chest of drawers he almost fell over his open portmanteau. He had a silent ecstasy of rage. Then he kicked against the basket in which the roses had come. He could find no matches on the chest of drawers.

Ethel must have the matches in the bedroom, but that was absolutely impossible. He might even have to ask her for them, for at times she pocketed matches. . . . There was nothing for it but to stop packing. Not a sound came from the other room.

He decided he would sit down in the armchair and go to sleep. He crept very carefully to the chair and sat down. Another interval of listening and he closed his eyes and composed himself for slumber.

He began to think over his plans for the morrow. He imagined the scene with Madam Gadow, and then his departure to find bachelor lodgings once more. He debated in what direction he should go to get suitable lodgings. Possible difficulties with his luggage, possible annoyances of the search loomed gigantic. He felt greatly irritated at these minor difficulties. He wondered if Ethel also was packing. What particularly would she do ? He listened but he could hear nothing. She was very still. She was really very still !

What could she be doing ?    He forgot the bothers of the morrow in his new interest.    Presently he rose very softly and listened.    Then he sat down again impatiently.    He tried to dismiss his curiosity about the silence by recapitulating the story of his wrongs.

He had some difficulty in fixing his mind upon this theme, but presently his memories were flowing freely.    Only it was not wrongs now that he could recall.    He was pestered by an absurd idea that he had again behaved unjustly to Ethel, that he had been headlong and malignant.    He made strenuous efforts to recover his first heat of jealousy—in vain.    Her remark that she had been as loyal as he, became an obstinate headline in his mind.    Something arose within him that insisted upon Ethel's possible fate if he should leave her.    What particularly would she do ?    He knew how much her character leant upon his.    Good Heavens !    What might she not do ?

By an effort he succeeded in fixing his mind on Baynes. That helped him back to the harsher footing.    However hard things might be for her she deserved them.    She deserved them !

Yet presently he slipped again, slipped back to the remorse and regrets of the morning time.    He clutched at Baynes as a drowning man clutches at a rope, and recovered himself. For a time he meditated on Baynes.    He had never seen the poet, so his imagination had scope.    It appeared to him as an exasperating obstacle to a tragic avenging of his honour that Baynes was a mere boy—possibly even younger than himself.

The question, " What will become of Ethel ? " rose to the surface again.    He struggled against its possibilities.    No ! That was not it !    That was her affair.

He felt inexorably kept to the path he had chosen, for all the waning of his rage.    He had put his hand to the plough.    " If you condone this," he told himself, " you might condone anything.    There are things one *must* not stand."    He tried to keep to that point of view—assuming for the most part out of his imagination what it was he was not standing.    A dim sense came to him of how much he was assuming.    At any rate she must have flirted ! . . . He resisted this reviving perception of justice as though it was some unspeakably disgraceful craving.    He tried to imagine her with Baynes.

He determined he would go to sleep.

But his was a waking weariness.    He tried counting.    He tried to distract his thoughts from her by going over the atomic weights of the elements. . . .

He shivered, and realised that he was cold and sitting cramped on an uncomfortable horsehair chair.    He had dozed. He glanced for the yellow line between the folding-doors.    It was still there but it seemed to quiver.    He judged the candle must be flaring.    He wondered why everything was so still.

Now why should he suddenly feel afraid ?

He sat for a long time trying to hear some movement, his head craning forward in the darkness. . . .

A grotesque idea came into his head that all that had happened a very long time ago. He dismissed that. He contested an unreasonable persuasion that some irrevocable thing had passed. But why was everything so still ?

He was invaded by a prevision of unendurable calamity.

Presently he rose and crept very slowly and with infinite precautions against noise, towards the folding-doors. He stood listening with his ear near the yellow chink.

He could hear nothing, not even the measured breathing of a sleeper.

He perceived that the doors were not shut but slightly ajar. He pushed against the inner one very gently and opened it silently. Still there was no sound of Ethel. He opened the door still wider and peered into the room. The candle had burnt down and was flaring in its socket. Ethel was lying half undressed upon the bed, and in her hand and close to her face was a rose.

He stood watching her, fearing to move. He listened hard and his face was very white. Even now he could not hear her breathing.

After all, it was probably all right. She was just asleep. He would slip back before she woke. If she found him——

He looked at her again. There was something in her face——

He came nearer, no longer heeding the sounds he made. He bent over her. Even now she did not seem to breathe.

He saw that her eyelashes were still wet, the pillow by her cheek was wet. Her white, tear-stained face hurt him. . . .

She was intolerably pitiful to him. He forgot everything but that and how he had wounded her that day. And then she stirred and murmured indistinctly a foolish name she had given him.

He forgot that they were going to part for ever. He felt nothing but a great joy that she could stir and speak. His jealousy flashed out of being. He dropped upon his knees.

" Dear," he whispered. " Is it all right ?   I . . . I could not hear you breathing. I could not hear you breathing."

She started and was awake.

" I was in the other room," said Lewisham in a voice full of emotion. " Everything was so quiet. I was afraid—I did not know what had happened. Dear—Ethel dear. Is it all right ? "

She sat up quickly and scrutinised his face. " Oh ! let me tell you," she wailed. " Do let me tell you. It's nothing. It's nothing. You wouldn't hear me. You wouldn't hear me. It wasn't fair—before you had heard me. . . ."

His arms tightened about her.    " Dear," he said, " I knew it was nothing. I knew. I knew."

She spoke in sobbing sentences. "It was so simple. Mr. Baynes . . . something in his manner . . . I knew he might be silly. . . . Only I did so want to help you." She paused. Just for one instant she saw one untellable indiscretion as it were in a lightning flash. A chance meeting it was, a " silly " thing or so said, a panic, retreat. She would have told it—had she known how. But she could not do it. She hesitated. She abolished it—untold. She went on : "And then, I thought he had sent the roses and I was frightened. . . . I was frightened."

" Dear one," said Lewisham. " Dear one ! I have been cruel to you. I have been unjust. I understand. I *do* understand. Forgive me. Dearest—forgive me."

" I did so want to do something for you. It was all I could do—that little money. And then you were angry. I thought you didn't love me any more because I did not understand your work. . . . And that Miss Heydinger—— Oh ! it was hard."

" Dear one," said Lewisham, " I do not care your little finger for Miss Heydinger."

" I know how I hamper you. But if you will help me. Oh ! I would work, I would study. I would do all I could to understand."

" Dear," whispered Lewisham. " *Dear.*"

" And to have *her*——"

" Dear," he vowed, " I have been a brute. I will end all that. I will end all that."

He took her suddenly into his arms and kissed her.

" Oh, I *know* I'm stupid," she said.

" You're not. It's I have been stupid. I have been unkind, unreasonable. All to-day . . . I've been thinking about it. Dear ! I don't care for anything—— It's *you*. If I have you nothing else matters. . . . Only I get hurried and cross. It's the work and being poor. Dear one, we *must* hold to each other. All to-day—— It's been dreadful. . . ."

He stopped. They sat clinging to one another.

" I do love you," she said presently with her arms about him. " Oh ! I do—*do*—love you."

He drew her closer to him.

He kissed her neck. She pressed him to her.

Their lips met.

The expiring candle streamed up into a tall flame, flickered, and was suddenly extinguished. The air was heavy with the scent of roses.

# CHAPTER THIRTEEN

## A WITHDRAWAL

ON Tuesday Lewisham returned from Vigours' at five—at half-past six he would go on to his science class at Walham Green—and discovered Mrs. Chaffery and Ethel in tears. He was fagged and rather anxious for some tea, but the news they had for him drove tea out of his head altogether.

"He's gone," said Ethel.

"Who's gone? What! Not Chaffery?"

Mrs. Chaffery, with a keen eye to Lewisham's behaviour, nodded tearfully over an experienced handkerchief.

Lewisham grasped the essentials of the situation forthwith, and trembled on the brink of an expletive. Ethel handed him a letter.

For a moment Lewisham held this in his hand asking questions. Mrs. Chaffery had come upon it in the case of her eight-day clock when the time to wind it came round. Chaffery, it seemed, had not been home since Saturday night. The letter was an open one addressed to Lewisham, a long rambling would-be clever letter, oddly inferior in style to Chaffery's conversation. It had been written some hours before Chaffery's last visit; his talk then had been perhaps a sort of codicil.

"The inordinate stupidity of that man Lagune is driving me out of the country," Lewisham saw. "It has been at last a definite stumbling-block—even a legal stumbling-block, I fear. I am off. I skedaddle. I break ties. I shall miss our long refreshing chats—you had found me out and I could open my mind. I am sorry to part from Ethel also, but thank Heaven she has you to look to! And indeed they both have you to look to, though the 'both' may be a new light to you."

Lewisham growled, went from page 1 to page 3—conscious of their both looking to him now—even intensely—and discovered Chaffery in a practical vein.

"There is but little light and portable property in that house in Clapham that has escaped my lamentable improvidence, but there are one or two things; the iron-bound chest, the bureau with a broken hinge, and the large air pump, distinctly pawnable if only you can contrive to get them to a pawnshop. You have more Will power than I—I never could get the confounded things downstairs. That iron-bound box was originally mine, before I married your mother-in-law, so that I am not altogether regardless of your welfare and the necessity of giving some equivalent. Don't judge me too harshly."

Lewisham turned over sharply without finishing that page.

"My life at Clapham," continued the letter, "has irked me for some time, and to tell you the truth, the spectacle of your vigorous young happiness—you are having a very good time, you know, fighting the world—reminded me of the passing years. To be frank in self-criticism, there is more than a touch of the New Woman about me, and I feel I have still to live my own life. What a beautiful phrase that is—to live one's own life !—redolent of honest scorn for moral plagiarism. No *Imitatio Christi* in that. . . . I long to see more of men and cities. . . . I begin late, I know, to live my own life, bald as I am, and grey-whiskered ; but better late than never. Why should the educated girl have the monopoly of the game ?  And after all, the whiskers will dye. . . .

"There are things—I touch upon them lightly—that will presently astonish Lagune." Lewisham became more attentive. "I marvel at that man, grubbing hungry for marvels amidst the almost incredibly marvellous. What can be the nature of a man who gapes after Poltergeists with the miracle of his own silly existence (inconsequent, reasonless, unfathomably weird) nearer to him than breathing and closer than hands and feet. What is *he* for, that he should wonder at Poltergeists ?  I am astonished these by no means flimsy psychic phenomena do not turn upon their investigators, and that a Research Society of eminent illusions and hallucinations does not pursue Lagune with sceptical inquiries. Take his house—expose the alleged man of Chelsea !  *A priori* they might argue that a thing so vain, so unmeaning, so strongly beset by cackle, could only be the diseased imagining of some hysterical phantom. Do *you* believe that such a thing as Lagune exists ?  I must own to the gravest doubts. But happily his banker is of a more credulous type than I. . . . Of all that Lagune will tell you soon enough."

Lewisham read no more. "I suppose he thought himself clever when he wrote that rot," said Lewisham bitterly, throwing the sheets forcibly athwart the table. "The simple fact is, he's stolen, or forged, or something—and bolted."

There was a pause. "What will become of Mother ? " said Ethel.

Lewisham looked at Mother and thought for a moment. Then he glanced at Ethel.

"We're all in the same boat," said Lewisham.

"I don't want to give any trouble to a single human being," said Mrs. Chaffery.

"I think you might get a man his tea, Ethel," said Lewisham, sitting down suddenly ; "anyhow." He drummed on the table with his fingers. "I have to get to Walham Green by a quarter to seven."

"We're all in the same boat," he repeated after an interval, and continued drumming. He was chiefly occupied by the curious fact that they were all in the same boat. What an extraordinary faculty he had for acquiring responsibility ! He looked up suddenly and caught Mrs. Chaffery's tearful eye directed to Ethel and full of distressful interrogation, and his perplexity was suddenly changed to pity. "It's all right, Mother," he said. "I'm not going to be unreasonable. I'll stand by you."

"Ah !" said Mrs. Chaffery. "As if I didn't know !" and Ethel came and kissed him.

He seemed in imminent danger of universal embraces.

"I wish you'd let me have my tea," he said. And while he had his tea he asked Mrs. Chaffery questions and tried to get the new situation into focus.

But even at ten o'clock when he was returning hot and jaded from Walham Green he was still trying to get the situation into focus. There were vague ends and blank walls of interrogation in the matter, that perplexed him.

He knew that his supper would be only the prelude to an interminable "talking over," and indeed he did not get to bed until nearly two. By that time a course of action was already agreed upon. Mrs. Chaffery was tied to the house in Clapham by a long lease and thither they must go. The ground floor and first floor were let unfurnished, and the rent of these practically paid the rent of the house. The Chafferys occupied basement and second floor. There was a bedroom on the second floor formerly let to the first floor tenants, that he and Ethel could occupy, and in this an old toilet-table could be put for such studies as were to be prosecuted at home. Ethel could have her typewriter in the subterranean breakfast-room. Mrs. Chaffery and Ethel must do the catering and the bulk of the housework, and as soon as possible, since letting lodgings would not square with Lewisham's professional pride, they must get rid of the lease that bound them and take some smaller and more suburban residence. If they did that without leaving any address it might save their feelings from any return of the prodigal Chaffery.

Mrs. Chaffery's frequent and pathetic acknowledgments of Lewisham's goodness only partly relieved his disposition to a philosophical bitterness. And the practical issues were complicated by excursions upon the subject of Chaffery, what he might have done, and where he might have gone, and whether by any chance he might not return.

When at last Mrs. Chaffery, after a violent and tearful kissing and blessing of them both—they were "good dear children," she said—had departed, Mr. and Mrs. Lewisham returned into their sitting-room. Mrs. Lewisham's little face was enthusiastic. "You're a Trump," she said, extending the willing arms that were his reward. "I know," she said, "I know, and all to-night I have been loving you. Dear ! Dear ! Dear. . . ."

The next day Lewisham was too full of engagements to communicate with Lagune, but the following morning he called and found the psychic investigator busy with the proofs of *Hesperus*. He welcomed the young man cordially neverthe-less, conceiving him charged with the questions that had been promised long ago—it was evident he knew nothing of Lewisham's marriage. Lewisham stated his case with some bluntness.

" He was last here on Saturday," said Lagune. " You have always been inclined to suspicion about him. Have you any grounds ? "

" You'd better read this," said Lewisham, repressing a grim smile, and he handed Lagune Chaffery's letter.

He glanced at the little man ever and again to see if he had come to the personal portion, and for the rest of the time occupied himself with an envious inventory of the writing appointments about him. No doubt the boy with the big ears had had the same sort of thing. . . .

When Lagune came to the question of his real identity he blew out his cheeks in the most astonishing way but made no other sign.

" Dear, dear ! " he said at last. " My bankers ! "

He looked at Lewisham with the exaggerated mildness of his spectacled eye. " What do you think it means ? " he asked. " Has he gone mad ? We have been conducting some experiments involving—considerable mental strain. He and I and a lady. Hypnotic——"

" I should look at my cheque-book if I were you."

Lagune produced some keys and got out his cheque-book. He turned over the counterfoils. " There's nothing wrong here," he said, and handed the book to Lewisham.

" Um," said Lewisham. " I suppose this—— I say, *is this* right ? "

He handed back the book to Lagune, open at the blank counterfoil of a cheque that had been removed. Lagune stared and passed his hand over his forehead in a confused way. " I can't see this," he said.

Lewisham had never heard of post hypnotic suggestion and he stood incredulous. " You can't see that ? " he said. " What nonsense ! "

" I can't see it," repeated Lagune.

For some seconds Lewisham could not get away from stupid repetitions of his inquiry. Then he hit upon a collateral proof. " But look here ! Can you see *this* counterfoil ? "

" Plainly," said Lagune.

" Can you read the number ? "

" Five thousand two hundred and seventy-nine."

" Well, and this ? "

" Five thousand two hundred and eighty-one."

" Well—where's five thousand two hundred and eighty ? "

Lagune began to look uncomfortable. " Surely," he said, " he has not—— Will you read it out—the cheque, the counterfoil I mean, that I am unable to see."

" It's blank," said Lewisham with an irresistible grin.

" Surely," said Lagune, and the discomfort of his expression deepened. " Do you mind if I call in a servant to confirm—— ? "

Lewisham did not mind, and the same girl who had admitted him to the séance appeared. When she had given her evidence she went again. As she left the room by the door behind Lagune her eyes met Lewisham's, and she lifted her eyebrows, depressed her mouth and glanced at Lagune with a meaning expression.

" I'm afraid," said Lagune, " that I have been shabbily treated. Mr. Chaffery is a man of indisputable powers— indisputable powers ; but I am afraid—I am very much afraid he has abused the conditions of the experiment. All this—and his insults—touch me rather nearly."

He paused. Lewisham rose. " Do you mind if you come again ? " asked Lagune with gentle politeness.

Lewisham was surprised to find himself sorry.

" He was a man of extraordinary gifts," said Lagune. " I had come to rely upon him. . . . My cash balance has been rather heavy lately. How he came to know of that I am unable to say. Without supposing, that is, that he had very remarkable gifts."

When Lewisham saw Lagune again he learnt the particulars of Chaffery's misdeed and the additional fact that the " lady " had also disappeared. " That's a good job," he remarked selfishly. " There's no chance of *his* coming back." He spent a moment trying to imagine the " lady " ; he realised more vividly than he had ever done before the narrow range of his experience, the bounds of his imagination. These people also—with grey hair and truncated honour—had their emotions ! Even it may be glowing ! He came back to facts. Chaffery had induced Lagune when hypnotised to sign a blank cheque as an " autograph." " The strange thing is," explained Lagune, " it's doubtful if he's legally account-able. The law is so peculiar about hypnotism, and I certainly signed the cheque, you know."

The little man, in spite of his losses, was now almost cheerful again on account of a curious side issue. " You may say it is coincidence," he said, " you may call it a fluke, but I prefer to look for some other interpretation. Consider this. The amount of my balance is a secret between me and my bankers. He never had it from *me*, for I did not know it— I hadn't looked at my pass-book for months. But he drew it all in one cheque, within seventeen and sixpence of the total. And the total was over five hundred pounds ! "

He seemed quite bright again as he culminated.

" Within seventeen and sixpence," he said. " Now how do you account for that, eh ? Give me a materialistic explanation that will explain away all that. You can't. Neither can I."

" I think I can," said Lewisham.

" Well—what is it ? "

Lewisham nodded towards a little drawer of the bureau. " Don't you think—perhaps "—a little ripple of laughter passed across his mind—" he had a skeleton key ? "

Lagune's face lingered amusingly in Lewisham's mind as he returned to Clapham. But after a time that amusement passed away. He declined upon the extraordinary fact that Chaffery was his father-in-law, Mrs. Chaffery his mother-in-law, that these two and Ethel constituted his family, his clan, and that grimy graceless house up the Clapham hillside was to be his home. Home ! His connection with these things as a point of worldly departure was as inexorable now as though he had been born to it. And a year ago, except for a fading reminiscence of Ethel, none of these people had existed for him. The ways of Destiny ! The happenings of the last few months, foreshortened in perspective, seemed to have almost a pantomimic rapidity. The thing took him suddenly as being laughable ; and he laughed.

His laugh marked an epoch. Never before had Lewisham laughed at any fix in which he had found himself. The enormous seriousness of adolescence was coming to an end ; the days of his growing were numbered. It was a laugh of infinite admissions.

# CHAPTER THIRTY-ONE

## IN BATTERSEA PARK

Now although Lewisham had promised to bring things to a conclusion with Miss Heydinger, he did nothing in the matter for five weeks, he merely left that crucial letter of hers unanswered. In that time their removal from Madam Gadow's into the gaunt house at Clapham was accomplished—not without polyglot controversy—and the young couple settled themselves into the little room on the second floor even as they had arranged. And there it was that suddenly the world was changed—was astonishingly transfigured—by a whisper.

It was a whisper between sobs and tears, with Ethel's arms about him and Ethel's hair streaming down so that it hid her face from him. And he too had whispered, dismayed perhaps a little, and yet feeling a strange pride, a strange novel emotion, feeling altogether different from the things he had fancied he might feel when this thing that he had dreaded should come. Suddenly he perceived finality, the advent of the solution, the reconciliation of the conflict that had been waged so long. Hesitations were at an end—he took his line.

Next day he wrote a note and two mornings later he started for his mathematical duffers an hour before it was absolutely necessary, and instead of going directly to Vigours', went over the bridge to Battersea Park. There waiting for him by a seat where once they had met before, he found Miss Heydinger pacing. They walked up and down side by side, speaking for a little while about indifferent topics, and then they came upon a pause. . . .

"You have something to tell me?" said Miss Heydinger abruptly.

Lewisham changed colour a little. "Oh yes," he said; "the fact is——" He affected ease. "Did I ever tell you I was married?"

"*Married?*"

"Yes."

"Married!"

"Yes," a little testily.

For a moment neither spoke. Lewisham stood without dignity staring at the dahlias of the London County Council, and Miss Heydinger stood regarding him.

"And that is what you have to tell me?"

Mr. Lewisham turned and met her eyes. "Yes!" he said. "That is what I have to tell you."

Pause. "Do you mind if I sit down," asked Miss Heydinger in an indifferent tone.

"There is a seat yonder," said Lewisham, "under the tree."

They walked to the seat in silence.

"Now," said Miss Heydinger, quietly. "Tell me whom you have married."

Lewisham answered sketchily. She asked him another question and another. He felt stupid and answered with a halting truthfulness.

"I might have known," she said, "I might have known. Only I would not know. Tell me some more. Tell me about her."

Lewisham did. The whole thing was abominably disagreeable to him, but it had to be done, he had promised Ethel it should be done. Presently Miss Heydinger knew the main outline of his story, knew all his story except the emotion that made it credible. "And you were married—before the second examination?" she repeated.

"Yes," said Lewisham.

"But why did you not tell me of this before?" asked Miss Heydinger.

"I don't know," said Lewisham. "I wanted to—that day, in Kensington Gardens. But I didn't. I suppose I ought to have done so."

"I think you ought to have done so."

"Yes, I suppose I ought. . . . But I didn't. Somehow—it has been hard. I didn't know what you would say. The thing seemed so rash, you know, and all that."

He paused blankly.

"I suppose you had to do it," said Miss Heydinger presently, with her eyes on his profile.

Lewisham began the second and more difficult part of his explanation. "There's been a difficulty," he said, "all the way along—I mean—about you, that is. It's a little difficult—— The fact is, my wife, you know—— She looks at things differently from what we do."

"We?"

"Yes—it's odd, of course. But she has seen your letters——"

"You didn't show her——?"

"No. But, I mean, she knows you write to me, and she knows you write about Socialism and Literature and—things we have in common—things she hasn't."

"You mean to say she doesn't understand these things?"

"She's not thought about them. I suppose there's a sort of difference in education——"

"And she objects—— ?"

"No," said Lewisham, lying promptly. "She doesn't object . . ."

"Well?" said Miss Heydinger, and her face was white.

"She feels that—— She feels—she does not say, of

course, but I know she feels that it is something she ought
to share. I know—how she cares for me. And it shames
her—it reminds her—— Don't you see how it hurts her ? "

" Yes. I see. So that even that little——" Miss Heydinger's breath seemed to catch and she was abruptly silent.

She spoke at last with an effort. " That it hurts *me*," she
said, and grimaced and stopped again.

" No," said Lewisham, " that is not it." He hesitated.

" I *knew* this would hurt you."

" You love her. You can sacrifice——"

" No. It is not that. But there is a difference. Hurting
*her*—she would not understand. But you—somehow it seems
a natural thing for me to come to you. I seem to look to
you—— For her I am always making allowances——"

" You love her."

" I wonder if it *is* that makes the difference. Things are
so complex. Love means anything—or nothing. I know
you better than I do her, you know me better than she will
ever do. I could tell you things I could not tell her. I
could put all myself before you—almost—and know you
would understand—— Only——"

" You love her."

" Yes," said Lewisham lamely and pulling at his moustache.
" I suppose . . . that must be it."

For a space neither spoke. Then Miss Heydinger said
" *Oh !* " with extraordinary emphasis.

" To think of this end to it all ! That all your promise . . . .
What is it she gives that I could not have given ?

" Even now ! Why should I give up that much of you
that is mine ? If she could take it—— But she cannot
take it. If I let you go—you will do nothing. All this
ambition, all these interests will dwindle and die, and she
will not mind. She will not understand. She will think that
she still has you. Why should she covet what she cannot
possess ? Why should she be given the thing that is mine
—to throw aside ? "

She did not look at Lewisham, but before her, her face a
white misery.

" In a way—I had come to think of you as something
belonging to me . . . I shall—still."

" There is one thing," said Lewisham after a pause ; " it is a
thing that has come to me once or twice lately. Don't you
think that perhaps you over-estimate the things I might
have done ? I know we've talked of great things to do.
But I've been struggling for half a year and more to get the
sort of living almost any one seems able to get. It has taken
me all my time. One can't help thinking after that, perhaps
the world is a stiffer sort of affair . . ."

" No," she said decisively. " You could have done great
things.

"Even now," she said, "you may do great things——
If only I might see you sometimes, write to you sometimes.
You are so capable and—weak. You must have somebody—
That is your weakness. You fail in your belief. You must
have support and belief—unstinted support and belief. Why
could I not be that to you ? It is all I want to be. At least
—all I want to be now. Why need she know ? It robs her
of nothing. I want nothing—she has. But I know of my
own strength too I can do nothing. I know that with you . . . .
It is only knowing hurts her. Why should she know ? "

Mr. Lewisham looked at her doubtfully. That phantom
greatness of his, it was that lit her eyes. In that instant at
least he had no doubts of the possibility of his Career. But
he knew that in some way the secret of his greatness and this
admiration went together. Conceivably they were one and
indivisible. Why indeed need Ethel know ? His imagination
ran over the things that might be done, the things that might
happen, and touched swiftly upon complication, confusion,
discovery.

"The thing is, I must simplify my life. I shall do nothing
unless I simplify my life. Only people who are well off can
be—complex. It is one thing or the other——"

He hesitated and suddenly had a vision of Ethel weeping
as once he had seen her weep with the light on the tears in
her eyes.

"No," he said almost brutally. "No. It's like this—
I can't do anything underhand. I mean—I'm not so amazingly honest—now. But I've not that sort of mind. She
would find me out. It would do no good and she would find
me out. My life's too complex. I can't manage it and go
straight. I—you've overrated me. And besides—— Things
have happened. Something——" He hesitated and then
snatched at his resolve. "I've got to simplify—and that's
the plain fact of the case. I'm sorry, but it is so."

Miss Heydinger made no answer. Her silence astonished
him. For nearly twenty seconds perhaps they sat without
speaking. With a quick motion she stood up and at once
he stood up before her. Her face was flushed, her eyes
downcast.

"Good-bye," she said suddenly in a low tone and held
out her hand.

"But," said Lewisham and stopped. Miss Heydinger's
colour left her.

"Good-bye," she said, looking him suddenly in the eyes
and smiling awry. "There is no more to say, is there ?
Good-bye."

He took her hand. "I hope I didn't——"

"Good-bye," she said impatiently, and suddenly disengaged her hand and turned away from him. He made a
step after her.

" Miss Heydinger," he said, but she did not stop. " Miss Heydinger." He realised that she did not want to answer him again. . . .

He remained motionless, watching her retreating figure. An extraordinary sense of loss came into his mind, a vague impulse to pursue her and pour out vague passionate protestations. . . .

Not once did she look back. She was already remote when he began hurrying after her. Once he was in motion he quickened his pace and gained upon her. He was within thirty yards of her as she drew near the gates.

His pace slackened. Suddenly he was afraid she might look back. She passed out of the gates, out of his sight. He stopped, looking where she had disappeared. He sighed and took the pathway to his left that led back to the bridge and Vigours.

Half-way across this bridge came another crisis of indecision. He stopped, hesitating. An impertinent thought obtruded. He looked at his watch and saw that he must hurry if he would catch the train for Earl's Court and Vigours. He said Vigours might go to the devil.

But in the end he caught his train.

# CHAPTER THIRTY-TWO

THAT night about seven Ethel came into their room with a waste-paper basket she had bought for him, and found him sitting at the little toilet-table at which he was to " write." The outlook was, for a London outlook, spacious, down a long slope of roofs towards the Junction, a huge sky of blue passing upward to the darkling zenith and downward into a hazy bristling mystery of roofs and chimneys, from which emerged signal lights and steam puffs, gliding chains of lit window carriages and the vague vistas of streets. She showed him the basket and put it beside him, and then her eye caught the yellow document in his hand. " What is that you have there ? "

He held it out to her, " I found it—lining my yellow box. I had it at Whortley."

She took it and perceived a chronological scheme. It was headed " SCHEMA," there were memoranda in the margin, and all the dates had been altered by a hasty hand.

" Hasn't it got yellow ? " she said.

That seemed to him the wrong thing for her to say. He stared at the document with a sudden accession of sympathy. There was an interval. He became aware of her hand upon his shoulder, that she was bending over him. " Dear," she whispered, with a strange change in the quality of her voice. He knew she was seeking to say something that was difficult to say.

" Yes ? " he said presently.

" You are not grieving ? "

" What about ? "

" *This.*"

" No ! "

" You are not—you are not even sorry ? " she said.

" No—not even sorry."

" I can't understand that. It's so much——"

" I'm glad," he proclaimed. " *Glad.*"

" But—the trouble—the expense—everything—and your work ? "

" Yes," he said, " that's just it."

She looked at him doubtfully. He glanced up at her, and she questioned his eyes. He put his arm about her, and presently and almost absent-mindedly she obeyed his pressure and bent down and kissed him.

" It settles things," he said holding her. " It joins us. Don't you see ? Before . . . But now it's different. It's something we have between us. It's something that . . . . It's the link we needed. It will hold us together, cement us together. It will be our life. This will be my work now. The other . . ."

He faced a truth. " It was just . . . vanity ! "

There was still a shade of doubt in her face, a wistfulness. Presently she spoke.

" Dear," she said.

" Yes ? "

She knitted her brows. " No ! " she said. " I can't say it."

In the interval she came into a sitting position on his knees.

He kissed her hand, but her face remained grave, and she looked out upon the twilight. " I know I'm' stupid," she said. " The things I say . . . aren't the things I feel."

He waited for her to say more.

" It's no good," she said.

He felt the onus of expression lay on him. He too found it a little difficult to put into words. " I think I understand," he said, and wrestled with the impalpable. The pause seemed long and yet not altogether vacant. She lapsed abruptly into the prosaic. She started from him.

" If I don't go down, Mother will get supper . . ."

At the door she stopped and turned a twilight face to him. For a moment they scrutinised one another. To her he was no more than a dim outline. Impulsively he held out his arms. . . .

Then at the sound of a movement downstairs she freed herself and hurried out. He heard her call " Mother ! You're not to lay supper. You're to rest."

He listened to her footsteps until the kitchen had swallowed them up. Then he turned his eyes to the Schema again and for a moment it seemed but a little thing.

He picked it up in both hands and looked at it as if it was the writing of another man, and indeed it was the writing of another man. " Pamphlets in the Liberal Interest," he read, and smiled.

Presently a train of thought carried him off. His attitude relaxed a little, the Schema became for a time a mere symbol, a point of departure, and he stared out of the window at the darkling night. For a long time he sat pursuing thoughts that were half emotions, emotions that took upon themselves the shape and substance of ideas. The deepening current stirred at last among the roots of speech.

" Yes, it was vanity," he said. " A boy's vanity. For me—anyhow. I'm too two-sided. . . . Two-sided ? . . . Commonplace ! "

" Dreams like mine—abilities like mine. Yes—any man ! And yet . . . The things I meant to do ! "

His thoughts went to his Socialism, to his red-hot ambition of world mending. He marvelled at the vistas he had discovered since those days.

" Not for us—— Not for us.

" We must perish in the wilderness—some day. Somewhen. But not for us. . . .

" Come to think, it is all the Child. The future is the
Child. The Future. What are we—any of us—but servants
or traitors to that ? . . .

" Natural Selection—it follows . . . this way is happiness
. . . must be. There can be no other."

He sighed. " To last a lifetime, that is."

" And yet—it is almost as if Life had played me a trick
—promised so much—given so little ! . . .

" No ! One must not look at it in that way. That will
not do ! That will *not* do.

" Career ! In itself it is a career—the most important
career in the world. Father ! Why should I want more ?

" And . . . Ethel ! No wonder she seemed shallow. . . .
She has been shallow. No wonder she was restless. Un-
fulfilled . . . What had she to do ? She was drudge, she
was toy . . .

" Yes. This is life. This alone is life ! For this we were
made and born. All these other things—all other things—
they are only a sort of play . . .

" Play ! "

His eyes came back to the Schema. His hands shifted to
the opposite corner and he hesitated. The vision of that
arranged Career, that ordered sequence of work and successes,
distinction and yet further distinctions, rose brightly from
the symbol. Then he compressed his lips and tore the yellow
sheet in half, tearing very deliberately. He doubled the
halves and tore again, doubled again very carefully and neatly
until the Schema was torn into numberless little pieces. With
it he seemed to be tearing his past self.

" Play," he whispered after a long silence.

" It is the end of adolescence," he said ; " the end of empty
dreams. . . ."

He became very still, his hands resting on the table, his
eyes staring out of the blue oblong of the window. The
dwindling light gathered itself together and became a star.

He found he was still holding the torn fragments. He
stretched out his hand and dropped them into that new waste-
paper basket Ethel had bought for him.

Two pieces fell outside the basket. He stooped, picked
them up and put them carefully with their fellows.

**THE END**

# MARRIAGE

" And the Poor Dears haven't the shadow of a doubt they will live happily ever afterwards."—*From a Private Letter*.

# CONTENTS

## Book One
## *Marjorie Marries*

## Book Two
## *Marjorie Married*

## Book Three
## *Marjorie at Lonely Hut*

*Book One*
*Marjorie Marries*

# CHAPTER ONE

## A DAY WITH THE POPES

### § 1

A<small>N</small> extremely pretty girl occupied a second-class compartment in one of those trains which percolate through the rural tranquillities of middle England from Ganford in Oxfordshire to Rumbold Junction in Kent. She was going to join her family at Buryhamstreet after a visit to some Gloucestershire friends. Her father, Mr. Pope, once a leader in the coach-building world and now by retirement a gentleman, had taken the Buryhamstreet vicarage furnished for two months (beginning on the fifteenth of July) at his maximum summer rental of seven guineas a week. His daughter was on her way to this retreat.

At first she had been an animated traveller, erect and keenly regardful of every detail upon the platforms of the stations at which her conveyance lingered, but the tedium of the journey and the warmth of the sunny afternoon had relaxed her pose by imperceptible degrees, and she sat now comfortably in the corner, with her neat toes upon the seat before her, ready to drop them primly at the first sign of a fellow-traveller. Her expression lapsed more and more towards an almost somnolent reverie. She wished she had not taken a second-class ticket, because then she might have afforded a cup of tea at Reading and so fortified herself against this insinuating indolence.

She was travelling second class, instead of third as she ought to have done, through one of those lapses so inevitable to young people in her position. The two Carmel boys and a cousin, two greyhounds and a chow had come to see her off; they had made a brilliant and prosperous group on the platform and extorted the manifest admiration of two youthful porters, and it had been altogether too much for Marjorie Pope to admit it was the family custom, except when her father's nerves had to be considered, to go third class. So she had made a hasty calculation—she knew her balance to a penny because of the recent tipping—and found it would just run to it. Fourpence remained—and there would be a porter at Buryhamstreet !

Her mother had said : " You will have Ample." Well, opinions of amplitude vary. With numerous details fresh in her mind, Marjorie decided it would be wiser to avoid financial discussion during her first few days at Buryhamstreet.

There was much in Marjorie's equipment in the key of travelling second class at the sacrifice of afternoon tea. There was, for example, a certain quiet goodness of style about her

clothes, though the skirt betrayed age, and an entire absence
of style about her luggage, which was all in the compartment
with her.   It consisted of a distended hold-all, a very
good tennis racquet in a stretcher, a portmanteau of cheap
white basketwork held together by straps, and a very new,
expensive-looking and meretricious dressing-bag of imitation
morocco which had been one of her chief financial errors at
Oxbridge.   The collection was eloquent indeed of incompatible
standards. . . .

Marjorie had a chin that was small in size if resolute in
form, and a mouth that was not noticeably soft and weak
because it was conspicuously soft and pretty.   Her nose was
delicately aquiline and very subtly and finely modelled, and
she looked out upon the world with steady, grey-blue eyes
beneath broad, level brows that contradicted in a large
measure the hint of weakness below.   Her abundance of
copper-red hair flowed back very prettily from her broad
low forehead and over her delicate ears, and she had that
warm-tinted clear skin that goes so well with reddish hair.
She had a very dainty neck, and the long slender lines of her
body were full of the promise of a riper beauty.   She had the
good open shoulders of a tennis-player and a swimmer.   Some
day she was to be a tall, ruddy, beautiful woman.   She wore
simple clothes of silvery-grey and soft green, and about her
waist was a belt of grey leather in which there now wilted two
creamy-petalled roses.

That was the visible Marjorie.   Somewhere out of time and
space was an invisible Marjorie who looked out on the world
with those steady eyes, and smiled or drooped with the soft
red lips, and dreamt and wondered and desired.

§ 2

What a queer thing the invisible human being would appear
if, by some discovery as yet inconceivable, some spiritual
X-ray photography, we could flash it into sight !   Long ago
I read a book called *Soul Shapes* that was full of ingenious
ideas, but I doubt very much if the thing so revealed would
have any shape, any abiding solid outline at all.   It is something more fluctuating and discursive than that—at any rate
for every one young enough not to have set and hardened.
Things come into it and become it, things drift out of it and
cease to be it, things turn upside down in it and change and
colour and dissolve, and grow and eddy about and blend into
each other.   One might figure it, I suppose, as a preposterous
jumble animated by a will ;  a floundering disconnectedness
through which an old hump of impulse rises and thrusts
unaccountably ;  a river beast of purpose wallowing in a black
eddy of mud and weeds and floating objects and creatures
drowned.   Now the sunshine of gladness makes it all vivid,
now it is sombre and grimly insistent under the sky of some

darkling mood, now an emotional gale sweeps across it and
it is one confused agitation. . . .

And surely these invisible selves of men were never so
jumbled, so crowded, complicated, and stirred about as they
are at the present time.  Once I am told they had a sort of
order, were sphered in religious beliefs, crystal clear, were
arranged in a cosmogony that fitted them as hand fits glove,
were separated by definite standards of right and wrong
which presented life as planned in all its essential aspects from
the cradle to the grave.  Things are so no longer.  That
sphere is broken for most of us ;  even if it is tied about and
mended again, it is burst like a seed case ;  things have fallen
out and things have fallen in. . . .

Can I convey in any measure how it was with Marjorie ?

What was her religion ?

In college forms and returns and such-like documents, she
would describe herself as " Church of England."  She had
been baptized according to the usages of that body, but she
had hitherto evaded confirmation into it, and although it is a
large, wealthy, and powerful organisation with many minds
to serve it, it had never succeeded in getting into her quick
and apprehensive intelligence any lucid and persuasive conception of what it considered God and the universe were up
to with her.  It had failed to catch her attention and state
itself to her.  A number of humorous and other writers, and
the general trend of talk around her, and perhaps her own
shrewd little observation of superficial things, had, on the
other hand, created a fairly definite belief in her that it wasn't
as a matter of fact up to very much at all, that what it said
wasn't said with that absolute honesty which is a logical
necessity in every religious authority, and that its hierarchy
had all sorts of political and social considerations confusing its
treatment of her immortal soul. . . .

Marjorie followed her father in abstaining from church.
He too professed himself " Church of England," but he was,
if we are to set aside merely superficial classifications, an
irascible atheist with a respect for usage and Good Taste,
and an abject fear of the disapproval of other gentlemen of his
class.  For the rest he secretly disliked clergymen on account
of the peculiarity of their collars, and a certain influence they
had with women.  When Marjorie at the age of fourteen had
displayed a hankering after ecclesiastical ceremony and
emotional religion, he had declared :  " We don't want any of
*that* nonsense," and sent her into the country to a farm where
there were young calves and a bottle-fed lamb and kittens.
At times her mother went to church and displayed considerable
orthodoxy and punctilio, at times the good lady didn't, and
at times she thought in a broad-minded way that there was a
Lot in Christian Science, and subjected herself to the ministrations of an American named Silas Root.  But his ministrations

were too expensive for continuous use, and so the old faith did not lose its hold upon the family altogether. . . .

At school Marjorie had been taught what I may best describe as Muffled Christianity—a temperate and discreet system designed primarily not to irritate parents, in which the painful symbol of the crucifixion and the riddle of what Salvation was to save her from, and, indeed, the coarser aspects of religion generally, were entirely subordinate to images of amiable perambulations, and a rich mist of finer feelings. She had been shielded not only from arguments against her religion, but from arguments for it—the two things go together—and I do not think it was particularly her fault that she was now growing up like the great majority of respectable English people, with her religious faculty as it were artificially faded, and an acquired disposition to regard any speculation of why she was, and whence and whither, as rather foolish, not very important, and in the very worst possible taste.

And so, the crystal globe being broken which once held souls together, you may expect to find her a little dispersed and inconsistent in her motives, and with none of that assurance a simpler age possessed of the exact specification of goodness or badness, the exact delimitation of right and wrong. Indeed, she did not live in a world of right and wrong, or anything so stern ; " horrid " and " jolly " had replaced these archaic orientations. In a world where a mercantile gentility has conquered passion and God is neither blasphemed nor adored, there necessarily arises this generation of young people, a little perplexed, indeed, and with a sense of something missing, but feeling their way inevitably at last to the great releasing question, " Then why shouldn't we have a good time ? "

Yet there was something in Marjorie, as in most human beings, that demanded some general idea, some aim, to hold her life together. A girl upon the borders of her set at college was fond of the phrase " living for the moment," and Marjorie associated with it the speaker's lax mouth, sloe-like eyes, soft, quick-flushing, boneless face, and a habit of squawking and bouncing in a forced and graceless manner. Marjorie's natural disposition was to deal with life in a steadier spirit than that. Yet all sorts of powers and forces were at work in her, some exalted, some elvish, some vulgar, some subtle. She felt keenly and desired strongly, and in effect she came perhaps nearer the realisation of that offending phrase than its original exponent. She had a clean intensity of feeling that made her delight in a thousand various things, in sunlight and textures and the vividly quick, accurate acts of animals, in landscape and the beauty of other girls, in wit and people's voices, and good strong reasoning, and the desire and skill of art. She had a clear, rapid memory that made her excel perhaps a little too easily at school and college, an eagerness of sympathetic interest that won people very quickly and led to disappointments, and a very strong sense of the primary importance of Miss Marjorie Pope in the world. And when any very definite dream of what she would like to be and what she would like to do, such as being the principal of a ladies' college, or the first woman member of Parliament, or the wife of a barbaric chief in Borneo, or a great explorer, or the wife of a million-aire and a great social leader, or George Sand, or Saint Teresa, had had possession of her imagination for a few weeks, an entirely contrasted and equally attractive dream would presently arise beside it and compete with it and replace it. It wasn't so much that she turned against the old one as that she was attracted by the new ; and she forgot the old dream rather than abandoned it, simply because she was only one person and hadn't therefore the possibility of realising both.

In certain types Marjorie's impressionability aroused a passion of proselytism. People of the most diverse kinds sought to influence her, and they invariably did so. Quite a number of people, including her mother and the principal of her college, believed themselves to be the leading influence in her life. And this was particularly the case with her Aunt Plessington. Her Aunt Plessington was devoted to social and political work of an austere and aggressive sort (in which Mr. Plessington participated) ; she was childless, and had a Movement of her own, the Good Habits Movement, a pro-gressive movement of the utmost scope and benevolence which aimed at extensive interferences with the food and domestic intimacies of the more defenceless lower classes by means ultimately of legislation ; and she had Marjorie up to see her, took her for long walks while she influenced with earnestness and vigour, and at times had an air of bequeathing her mantle, movement and everything, quite definitely to her " little Madge." She spoke of training her niece to succeed her, and bought all the novels of Mrs. Humphry Ward for her as they appeared, in the hope of quickening in her that flame of politico-social ambition, that insatiable craving for dinner-parties with important guests, which is so distinctive of the more influential variety of English womanhood. It was due rather to her own habit of monologue than to any reserve on the part of Marjorie that she entertained the belief that her niece was entirely acquiescent in these projects. They went into Marjorie's mind and passed. For nearly a week, it is true, she had dramatised herself as the angel and inspiration of some great modern statesman, but this had been ousted by a far more insistent dream, begotten by a picture she had seen in some exhibition, of a life of careless savagery, whose central and constantly recurrent incident was the riding of bare-backed horses out of deep-shadowed forest into a foamy sunlit sea—in a costume that would certainly have struck Aunt Plessington as a mistake.

If you could have seen Marjorie in her railway compartment,

with the sunshine, sunshine mottled by the dirty window, tangled in her hair and creeping to and fro over her face as the train followed the curves of the line, you would certainly have agreed with me that she was pretty, and you might even have thought her beautiful. But it was necessary to fall in love with Marjorie before you could find her absolutely beautiful. You might have speculated just what business was going on behind those drowsily thoughtful eyes. If you are—as people say—" Victorian," you might even have whispered " Day Dreams " at the sight of her. . . .

She *was* dreaming, and in a sense she was thinking of beautiful things. But only mediately. She was thinking how very much she would enjoy spending freely and vigorously, quite a considerable amount of money—Heaps of money.

You see the Carmels, with whom she had just been staying, were shockingly well off. They had two motor-cars with them in the country, and the boys had the use of the second one as though it was just an old bicycle. Marjorie had had a cheap white dinner-dress, made the year before by a Chelsea French girl, a happy find of her mother's, and it was shapely and simple and not at all bad, and she had worn her green beads and her Egyptian necklace of jade ; but Kitty Carmel and her sister had had a new costume nearly every night, and pretty bracelets, and rubies, big pearls, and woven gold, and half a score of delightful and precious things for neck and hair. Everything in the place was bright and good and abundant, the servants were easy and well-mannered, without a trace of hurry or resentment, and one didn't have to be sharp about the eggs and things at breakfast in the morning, or go without. All through the day, and even when they had gone to bathe from the smart little white and green shed on the upper lake, Marjorie had been made to feel the insufficiency of her equipment. Kitty Carmel, being twenty-one, possessed her own cheque-book and had accounts running at half a dozen West-end shops ; and both sisters had furnished their own rooms according to their taste, with a sense of obvious effect that had set Marjorie speculating just how a room might be done by a girl with a real eye for colour and a real brain behind it. . . .

The train slowed down for the seventeenth time. Marjorie looked up and read " Buryhamstreet."

### § 3

Her reverie vanished, and by a complex but almost instantaneous movement she had her basket off the rack and the carriage door open. She became teeming anticipations. There, advancing in a string, were Daffy, her elder sister, Theodore, her younger brother, and the dog Toupee. Sydney and Rom hadn't come. Daffy was not copper-red like her sister, but really quite coarsely red-haired ; she was bigger

than Marjorie, and with irregular teeth instead of Marjorie's
neat row; she confessed them in a broad simple smile of
welcome. Theodore was hatless, rustily fuzzy-headed, and
now a wealth of quasi-humorous gesture. The dog Toupee
was straining at a leash, and doing its best, in a yapping,
confused manner, to welcome the wrong people by getting
its lead round their legs.

"Toupee!" cried Marjorie, waving the basket. "Toupee!"

They all called it Toupee because it was like one, but the
name was forbidden in her father's hearing. Her father had
decided that the proper name for a family dog in England is
Towser, and did his utmost to suppress a sobriquet that was
at once unprecedented and not in the best possible taste.
Which was why the whole family, with the exception of Mrs.
Pope of course, stuck to Toupee. . . .

Marjorie flashed a second's contrast with the Carmel
splendours.

"Hullo, old Daffy. What's it like?" she asked, handing
out the basket as her sister came up.

"It's a lark," said Daffy. "Where's the dressing-bag?"

"Thoddy," said Marjorie, following up the dressing-bag
with the hold-all. "Lend a hand."

"Stow it, Toupee," said Theodore, and caught the hold-all
in time.

In another moment Marjorie was out of the train, had done
the swift kissing proper to the occasion, and rolled a hand over
Toupee's head—Toupee, who, after a passionate lunge at a
particularly savoury drover from the next compartment, was
now frantically trying to indicate that Marjorie was the one
human being he had ever cared for. Brother and sister were
both sketching out the state of affairs at Buryhamstreet
Vicarage in rapid competitive jerks, each eager to tell things
first—and the whole party moved confusedly towards the
station exit. Things pelted into Marjorie's mind.

"We've got an old donkey-cart. I thought we shouldn't
get here—ever. . . . Madge, we can go up the church tower
whenever we like, only old Daffy won't let me shin up the
flagstaff. It's *perfectly* safe—you couldn't fall off if you
tried. . . . Had positively to get out at the level crossing and
*pull* him over. . . . There's a sort of moat in the garden. . . .
You never saw such furniture, Madge! And the study! It's
hung with texts, and stuffed with books about the Scarlet
Woman. . . . Piano's rather good, it's a Broadwood. . . .
The dad's got a war on about the tennis net. Oh, frightful!
You'll see. It won't keep up. He's had a letter kept waiting
by *The Times* for a fortnight, and it's a terror at breakfast.
Says the motor people have used influence to silence him.
Says that's a game two can play at. . . . Old Sid got herself
upset stuffing windfalls. Rather a sell for old Sid, considering
how refined she's getting. . . ."

There was a brief lull as the party got into the waiting governess-cart. Toupee, after a preliminary refusal to enter, made a determined attempt on the best seat, from which he would be able to bark in a persistent, official manner at anything that passed. That suppressed, and Theodore's proposal to drive refused, they were able to start, and attention was concentrated upon Daffy's negotiation of the station approach. Marjorie turned on her brother with a smile of warm affection.

" How are you, old Theodore ? "

" I'm all right, old Madge."

" Mummy ? "

" Every one's all right," said Theodore ; " if it wasn't for that damned infernal net——"

" Ssssh ! " cried both sisters together.

" *He* says it," said Theodore.

Both sisters conveyed a grave and relentless disapproval.

" Pretty bit of road," said Marjorie. " I like that little house at the corner."

A pause and the eyes of the sisters met.

" *He's* here," said Daffy.

Marjorie affected ignorance.

" Who's here ? "

" *Il vostro senior Miraculoso.*"

" Just as though a fellow couldn't understand your kiddy little Italian," said Theodore, pulling Toupee's ear.

" Oh well, I thought he might be," said Marjorie, regardless of her brother.

" Oh ! " said Daffy. " I didn't know——"

Both sisters looked at each other, and then both glanced at Theodore. He met Marjorie's eyes with a grimace of profound solemnity.

" Little brothers," he said, " shouldn't know. Just as though they didn't ! Rot ! But let's change the subject, my dears, all the same. Lemme see. There are a new sort of flea on Toupee, Madge, that he gets from the hens."

" *Is* a new sort," corrected Daffy. " He's horrider than ever, Madge. He leaves his soap in soak now to make us think he has used it. This is the village High Street. Isn't it jolly ? "

" Corners don't *bite* people," said Theodore, with a critical eye to the driving.

Marjorie surveyed the High Street, while Daffy devoted a few moments to Theodore.

The particular success of the village was its brace of chestnut trees which, with that noble disregard of triteness which is one of the charms of villages the whole world over, shadowed the village smithy. On either side of the roadway between it and the paths was a careless width of vivid grass protected by white posts, which gave way to admit a generous access on either hand to a jolly public-house, leering over red blinds, and swinging a painted sign against its competitor. Several of the cottages had real thatch and most had porches ; they had creepers nailed to their faces, and their gardens, crowded now with flowers, marigolds, begonias, snapdragon, delphiniums, white foxgloves, and monkshood, seemed almost too good to be true. The doctor's house was pleasantly Georgian, and the village shop, which was also a post and telegraph office, lay back with a slight air of repletion, keeping its bulging double shop-windows wide open in a manifest attempt not to fall asleep. Two-score of shock-headed boys and pinafored girls were drilling upon a bald space of ground before the village school, and near by, the national emotion at the ever-memorable Diamond Jubilee of Queen Victoria had evoked an artistic drinking-fountain of grey stone. Beyond the subsequent green—there were the correctest geese thereon——the village narrowed almost to a normal road again, and then, recalling itself with a start, lifted a little to the church-yard wall about the grey and ample church. " It's just like all the villages that ever were," said Marjorie, and gave a cry of delight when Daffy, pointing to the white gate between two elm trees that led to the vicarage, remarked : " That's us."

In confirmation of which statement, Sydney and Rom, the two sisters next in succession to Marjorie, and with a strong tendency to be twins in spite of the year between them, appeared in a state of vociferous incivility opening the way for the donkey-carriage. Sydney was Sydney, and Rom was just short for Romola—one of her mother's favourite heroines in fiction.

" Old Madge," they said ; and then throwing respect to the winds, " Old Gargoo ! " which was Marjorie's forbidden nickname, and short for gargoyle (though surely only Victorian Gothic ever produced a gargoyle that had the remotest right to be associated with the neat brightness of Marjorie's face).

She overlooked the offence, and the pseudo-twins boarded the cart from behind, whereupon the already overburthened donkey, being old and in a manner wise, quickened his pace for the house to get the whole thing over.

" It's really an avenue," said Daffy ; but Marjorie, with her mind strung up to the Carmel standards, couldn't agree. It was like calling a row of boy-scouts Potsdam grenadiers. The trees were at irregular distances, of various ages, and mostly on one side. Still it was a shady, pleasant approach.

And the vicarage was truly very interesting and amusing. To these Londoners accustomed to live in a state of compression, elbows practically touching, in a tall, narrow fore-and-aft stucco house, all window and staircase, in a despondent Brompton square, there was an effect of maundering freedom about the place, of enlargement almost to the pitch of adventure, and sunlight to the pitch of intoxication. The house itself was long and low, as if a London house holidaying in the country had flung itself asprawl ; it had two disconnected and roomy staircases, and when it had exhausted itself completely as a house, it turned to the right and began again as rambling, empty stables, coach house, cart sheds, men's bedrooms up ladders, and outhouses of the most various kinds. On one hand was a neglected orchard, in the front of the house was a bald, worried-looking lawn area capable of simultaneous tennis and croquet, and at the other side a copious and confused vegetable and flower garden full of roses, honesty, hollyhocks, and such-like herbaceous biennials and perennials, lapsed at last into shrubbery, where a sickle-shaped, weedy lagoon of uncertain aims, which had evidently, as a rustic bridge and a weeping willow confessed, aspired to be an " ornamental water," declined at last to ducks. And there was access to the church and the key of the church tower, and one went across the corner of the lawn and by a little iron gate into the churchyard to decipher inscriptions, as if the tombs of all Buryhamstreet were no more than a part of the accommodation relinquished by the vicar's household.

Marjorie was hurried over the chief points of all this at a breakneck pace by Sydney and Rom, and when Sydney was called away to the horrors of practice—for Sydney in spite of considerable reluctance was destined by her father to be " the musical one "—Rom developed a copious affection, due apparently to some occult æsthetic influence in Marjorie's silvery-grey and green, and led her into the unlocked vestry, and there prayed in a whisper that she might be given " one good hug, just *one* "—and so they came out with their arms about each other very affectionately to visit the lagoon again. And then Rom remembered that Marjorie hadn't seen either the walnut tree in the orchard, or the hen with nine chicks. . . .

Somewhere among all these interests came tea and Mrs. Pope.

Mrs. Pope kissed her daughter with an air of having really wanted to kiss her half an hour ago, but of having been distracted since. She was a fine-featured, anxious-looking little woman with a close resemblance to all her children, in spite of the fact that they were markedly dissimilar one to the other except only that they took their ruddy colouring from their father. She was dressed in a neat blue dress that had perhaps been hurriedly chosen, and her method of doing her hair was a manifest compromise between duty and pleasure. She embarked at once upon an exposition of the bedroom arrangements, which evidently involved difficult issues. Marjorie was to share a room with Daffy—that was the gist of it—as the only other available apartment, originally promised to Marjorie, had been secured by Mr. Pope for what he called his " matutinal ablutions, *videlicet* tub."

" Then, when your Aunt Plessington comes, you won't have

to move," said Mrs. Pope with an air of a special concession. " Your father's looking forward to seeing you, but he mustn't be disturbed just yet. He's in the vicar's study. He's had his tea in there. He's writing a letter to *The Times*, answering something they said in a leader, and also a private note calling attention to their delay in printing his previous communication, and he wants to be delicately ironical without being in any way offensive. He wants to hint without actually threatening that very probably he will go over to the *Spectator* altogether if they do not become more attentive. *The Times* used to print his letters punctually, but latterly these automobile people seem to have got hold of it. . . . He has the window on the lawn open, so that I think, perhaps, we'd better not stay out here—for fear our voices might disturb him."

" Better get right round the other side of the church," said Daffy.

" He'd hear far less of us if we went indoors," said Mrs. Pope.

§ 4

The vicarage seemed tight packed with human interest for Marjorie and her mother and sisters. Going over houses is one of the amusements proper to her sex, and she and all three sisters and her mother, as soon as they had finished an inaudible tea, went to see the bedroom she was to share with Daffy, and then examined, carefully and in order, the furniture and decoration of the other bedrooms, went through the rooms downstairs, always excepting and avoiding very carefully and closing as many doors as possible on, and hushing their voices whenever they approached, the study in which her father was being delicately ironical without being offensive to *The Times*. None of them had seen any of the vicarage people at all—Mr. Pope had come on a bicycle and managed all the negotiations—and it was curious to speculate about the individuals whose personalities pervaded the worn and faded furnishings of the place.

The Popes' keen-eyed inspection came at times, I think, dangerously near prying. The ideals of decoration and interests of the vanished family were so absolutely dissimilar to their London standards as to arouse a sort of astonished wonder in their minds. Some of the things they decided were perfectly hideous, some quaint, some were simply and weakly silly. Everything was different from Hartstone Square. Daffy was perhaps more inclined to contempt, and Mrs. Pope to refined amusement and witty appreciation than Marjorie. Marjorie felt there was something in these people that she didn't begin to understand, she needed some missing clue that would unlock the secret of their confused peculiarity. She was one of those who have an almost instinctive turn for

decoration in costume and furniture ; she had already had a
taste of how to do things in arranging her rooms at Bennett
College, Oxbridge, where also she was in great demand among
the richer girls as an adviser.  She knew what it was to try
and fail as well as to try and succeed, and these people, she
felt, hadn't tried for anything she comprehended.  She
couldn't quite see why it was that there was at the same time
an attempt at ornament and a disregard of beauty, she couldn't
quite do as her mother did and dismiss it as an absurdity and
have done with it.  She couldn't understand, too, why everything should be as if it were faded and weakened from something originally bright and clear.

All the rooms were thick with queer little objects that
indicated a quite beaver-like industry in the production of
" work."  There were embroidered covers for nearly every
article on the washhand-stand, and mats of wool and crochet
wherever anything stood on anything ; there were " tidies "
everywhere, and odd little brackets covered with gilded and
varnished fir cones and bearing framed photographs and small
jars and all sorts of colourless, dusty little objects, and every
where on the walls tacks sustained crossed fans with badly
painted flowers or transfer pictures.  There was a jar on the
bedroom mantel covered with varnished postage-stamps and
containing grey-haired dried grasses.  There seemed to be a
moral element in all this, for in the room Sydney shared with
Rom there was a decorative piece of lettering which declared
that—

> " Something attempted, something done,
>    Has earned a night's repose."

There were a great number of texts that set Marjorie's
mind stirring dimly with intimations of a missed significance.
Over her own bed, within the lattice of an Oxford frame, was
the photograph of a picture of an extremely composed young
woman in a trailing robe, clinging to the Rock of Ages in the
midst of histrionically aggressive waves, and she had a feeling,
rather than a thought, that perhaps for all the oddity of the
presentation it did convey something acutely desirable, that
she herself had had moods when she would have found something very comforting in just such an impassioned grip.
And in a framed, floriferous card, these incomprehensible
words :

THY GRACE IS SUFFICIENT FOR ME

seemed to be saying something to her tantalisingly just
outside her range of apprehension.

Did all these things light up somehow to those dispossessed
people—from some angle she didn't attain ?  Were they

living and moving realities when those others were at home again ?

The drawing-room had no texts ; it was altogether more pretentious and less haunted by the faint and faded flavour of religion that pervaded the bedrooms. It had, however, evidences of travel in Switzerland and the Mediterranean. There was a piano in black and gold, a little out of tune, and surmounted by a Benares brass jar enveloping a scarlet geranium in a pot. There was a Japanese screen of gold wrought upon black, that screened nothing. There was a framed chromo-lithograph of Jerusalem hot in the sunset, and another of Jerusalem cold under a sub-tropical moon, and there were gourds, roses of Jericho, sandalwood rosaries and kindred trash from the Holy Land in profusion upon a what-not. Such books as the room contained had been arranged as symmetrically as possible about a large, pink-shaded lamp upon the claret-coloured cloth of a round table, and were to be replaced, Mrs. Pope said, at their departure. At present they were piled on a side-table. The girls had been through them all, and were ready with the choicer morsels for Marjorie's amusement. There was *Black Beauty*, the sympathetic story of a soundly Anglican horse, and a large Bible extra-illustrated with photographs of every well-known scriptural picture from Michael Angelo to Doré, and a book of injunctions to young ladies upon their behaviour and deportment that Rom and Sydney found particularly entertaining. Marjorie discovered that Sydney had picked up a new favourite phrase. " I'm afraid we're all dreadfully cynical," said Sydney, several times.

A more advanced note was struck by a copy of *Aurora Leigh*, richly underlined in pencil, but with exclamation marks at some of the bolder passages. . . .

And presently, still avoiding the open study window very elaborately, this little group of twentieth-century people went again into the church—the church whose foundations were laid in A.D. 912—foundations of rubble and cement that included flat Roman bricks from a still remoter basilica. Their voices dropped instinctively, as they came into its shaded quiet from the exterior sunshine. Marjorie went apart and sat in a pew that gave her a glimpse of the one good stained-glass window. Rom followed her, and perceiving her mood to be restful, sat a yard away. Syd began a whispered dispute with her mother whether it wasn't possible to try the organ, and whether Theodore might not be bribed to blow. Daffy discovered relics of a lepers' squint and a holy-water stoup, and then went to scrutinise the lettering of the ten commandments of the Mosaic law that shone black and red on gold on either side of the IHS monogram behind the white-clothed communion table that had once been the altar. Upon a notice-board hung about the waist

of the portly pulpit were the numbers of hymns that had
been sung three days ago.  The sound Protestantism of the
vicar had banished superfluous crosses from the building ;
the Bible reposed upon the wings of a great brass eagle ;
shining blue and crimson in the window, Saint Christopher
carried his Lord.  What a harmonised synthesis of conflicts
a country church presents !  What invisible mysteries of
filiation spread between these ancient ornaments and symbols
and the new young minds from the whirlpool of the town that
looked upon them now with such bright, keen eyes, wondering
a little, feeling a little, missing so much ?

It was all so very cool and quiet now—with something of
the immobile serenity of death.

§ 5

When Mr. Pope had finished his letter to *The Times*, he
got out of the window of the study, treading on a flower-bed
as he did so—he was the sort of man who treads on flower-
beds—partly with the purpose of reading his composition
aloud to as many members of his family as he could assemble
for the purpose, and so giving them a chance of appreciating
the nuances of his irony more fully than if they saw it just
in cold print without the advantage of his intonation, and
partly with the belated idea of welcoming Marjorie.  The
lawn presented a rather discouraging desolation.  Then he
became aware that the church tower frothed with his daughters.
In view of his need of an audience, he decided after a brief
doubt that their presence there was unobjectionable, and
waved his MS. amiably.  Marjorie flapped a handkerchief
in reply. . . .

The subsequent hour was just the sort of hour that gave
Mr. Pope an almost meteorological importance to his family.
He began with an amiability that had no fault except, perhaps,
that it was slightly forced after the epistolary strain in the
study, and his welcome to Marjorie was more than cordial.
" Well, little Madge-cat ! " he said, giving her an affectionate
but sound and heavy thump on the left shoulder-blade,
" got a kiss for the old daddy ? "

Marjorie submitted a cheek.

" That's right," said Mr. Pope ;  " and now I just want
you all to advise me——"

He led the way to a group of wicker garden chairs.  " You're
coming, Mummy ? " he said, and seated himself comfortably
and drew out a spectacle case, while his family grouped itself
dutifully.  It made a charming little picture of a Man and
his Womankind.  " I don't often flatter myself," he said,
" but this time I think I've been neat—neat's the word for it."

He cleared his throat, put on his spectacles, and emitted
a long, flat preliminary note, rather like the sound of a child's
trumpet.  " Er—' Dear Sir ! ' "

" Rom," said Mrs. Pope, " don't creak your chair."

" It's Daffy, Mother," said Rom.

" Oh, *Rom !* " said Daffy.

Mr. Pope paused, and looked with a warning eye over his left spectacle-glass at Rom.

" Don't creak your chair, Rom," he said, " when your mother tells you."

" I was *not* creaking my chair," said Rom.

" I heard it," said Mr. Pope suavely.

" It was Daffy."

" Your mother does not think so," said Mr. Pope.

" Oh, all right ! I'll sit on the ground," said Rom, crimson to the roots of her hair.

" Me too," said Daffy. " I'd rather."

Mr. Pope watched the transfer gravely. Then he re-adjusted his glasses, cleared his throat again, trumpeted, and began. " Er—' Dear Sir ' ! "

" Oughtn't it to be simply ' Sir,' father, for an editor ? " said Marjorie.

" Perhaps I didn't explain, Marjorie," said her father with the calm of great self-restraint, and dabbing his left hand on the manuscript in his right, " that this is a *private* letter—a private letter."

" I didn't understand," said Marjorie.

" It would have been evident as I went on," said Mr. Pope, and prepared to read again.

This time he was allowed to proceed, but the interruptions had ruffled him, and the gentle stresses that should have lifted the subtleties of his irony into prominence missed the words, and he had to go back and do his sentences again. Then Rom suddenly, horribly, uncontrollably, was seized with hiccups. At the second hiccup Mr. Pope paused, and looked very hard at his daughter with magnified eyes ; as he was about to resume, the third burst its way through the unhappy child's utmost effort.

Mr. Pope rose with an awful resignation. "That's enough," he said. He regarded the pseudo-twin vindictively. "You haven't the self-control of a child of six," he said. Then very touchingly to Mrs. Pope : " Mummy, shall we try a game of tennis with the New Generation ? "

" Can't you read it after supper ? " asked Mrs. Pope.

" It must go by the eight o'clock post," said Mr. Pope, putting the masterpiece into his breast pocket, the little masterpiece that would now perhaps never be read aloud to any human being. " Daffy, dear, do you mind going in for the racquets and balls ? "

The social atmosphere was now sultry and overcast, and Mr. Pope's decision to spend the interval before Daffy returned in seeing whether he couldn't do something to the net, which was certainly very unsatisfactory, did not improve

matters. Then, unhappily, Marjorie who had got rather
keen upon tennis at the Carmels', claimed her father first
two services as faults, contrary to the etiquette of the family.
It happened that Mr. Pope had a really very good, hard,
difficult, smart-looking serve, whose only defect was that it
always went either too far or else into the net, and so a feeling
had been fostered and established by his wife that, on the
whole, it was advisable to regard the former variety as a
legitimate extension of a father's authority. Naturally,
therefore, Mr. Pope was nettled at Marjorie's ruling, and his
irritation increased when his next two services to Daffy
perished in the net. (" Damn that net ! Puts one's eye
out.") Then Marjorie gave him an unexpected soft return
which he somehow muffed, and then Daffy just dropped a
return over the top of the net. (Love-game.) It was then
Marjorie's turn to serve, which she did with a new twist
acquired from the eldest Carmel boy that struck Mr. Pope
as un-English. " Go on," he said concisely. " Fifteen-love."

She was gentle with her mother and they got their first
rally, and when it was over Mr. Pope had to explain to
Marjorie that if she returned right up into his corner of the
court he would have to run backwards very fast and might
fall over down the silly slope at that end. She would have
to consider him and the court. One didn't get everything
out of a game by playing merely to win. She said " All
right, Daddy," rather off-handedly, and immediately served
to him again, and he, taken a little unawares, hit the ball
with the edge of his racquet and sent it out, and then he
changed racquets with Daffy—it seemed he had known all
along she had taken his, but he had preferred to say nothing
—uttered a word of advice to his wife just on her stroke,
and she, failing to grasp his intention as quickly as she ought
to have done, left the score forty-fifteen. He felt better when
he returned Marjorie's serve, and then before she could
control herself she repeated her new unpleasant trick of
playing into the corner again, whereupon, leaping back with
an agility that would have shamed many a younger man,
Mr. Pope came upon disaster. He went spinning down the
treacherous slope behind, twisted his ankle painfully and
collapsed against the iron railings of the shrubbery. It was
too much, and he lost control of himself. His daughters
had one instant's glimpse of the linguistic possibilities of a
strong man's agony. " I told her," he went on as if he had
said nothing. " Tennis ! "

For a second perhaps he seemed to hesitate upon a course
of action. Then as if by a great effort he took his coat from
the net post and addressed himself houseward incarnate
Grand Dudgeon—limping.

" Had enough of it, Mummy," he said, and added some
happily inaudible comment on Marjorie's new style of play.

The evening's exercise was at an end.

The three ladies regarded one another in silence for some moments.

" I will take in the racquets, dear," said Mrs. Pope.

" I think the other ball is at your end," said Daffy. . . .

The apparatus put away, Marjorie and her sister strolled thoughtfully away from the house.

" There's croquet here too," said Daffy. " We've not had the things out yet ! " . . .

" He'll play, I suppose."

" He wants to play." . . .

" Of course," said Marjorie after a long pause, " there's no *reasoning* with dad ! "

## § 6

Character is one of England's noblest and most deliberate products, but some Englishmen have it to excess. Mr. Pope had.

He was one of that large and representative class which imparts a dignity to national commerce by inheriting big businesses from its ancestors. He was a coach-builder by birth, and a gentleman by education and training. He had been to City Merchant's and Cambridge.

Throughout the earlier half of the nineteenth century the Popes had been the princes of the coach-building world. Mr. Pope's great-grandfather had been a North London wheel-wright of conspicuous dexterity and integrity, who had founded the family business ; his son, Mr. Pope's grandfather, had made that business the occupation of his life and brought it to the pinnacle of pre-eminence ; his son, who was Marjorie's grandfather, had displayed a lesser enthusiasm, left the house at the works for a home ten miles away and sent a second son into the Church. It was in the days of the third Pope that the business ceased to expand, and began to suffer severely from the competition of an enterprising person who had originally supplied the firm with varnish, gradually picked up the trade in most other materials and accessories needed in coach-building, and passed on by almost imperceptible stages to delivering the article complete—dispensing at last altogether with the intervention of Pope and Son—to the customer. Marjorie's father had succeeded in the fulness of time to the inheritance this insurgent had damaged.

Mr. Pope was a man of firm and resentful temper, with an admiration for Cato, Brutus, Cincinnatus, Cromwell, Washington, and the sterner heroes generally, and by nature a little ill-used and offended at things. He suffered from indigestion and extreme irritability. He found himself in control of a business where more flexible virtues were needed. The Popes based their fame on a heavy, proud type of vehicle, which the increasing luxury and triviality of the age tended

to replace by lighter forms of carriage, carriages with diminu-
tive and apologetic names. As these lighter forms were not
only lighter but less expensive, Mr. Pope with a pathetic
confidence in the loyalty of the better class of West End
customer, determined to " make a stand " against them. He
was the sort of man to whom making a stand is in itself a
sombre joy. If he had had to choose his pose for a portrait,
he would certainly have decided to have one foot advanced,
the other planted like a British oak behind, the arms folded
and the brows corrugated—making a stand.

Unahppily the stars in their courses and the general improvement of roads throughout the country fought against
him. The lighter carriages, and especially the lighter
carriages of that varnish-selling firm, which was now absorb-
ing businesses right and left, prevailed over Mr. Pope's
resistance. For crossing a mountain pass or fording a river,
for driving over the scene of a recent earthquake or following
a retreating army, for being run away with by frantic horses
or crushing a personal enemy, there can be no doubt the Pope
carriages remained to the very last the best possible ones and
fully worth the inflexible price demanded. Unhappily all
carriages in a civilisation essentially decadent are not subjected to these tests, and the manufactures of his rivals were
not only much cheaper, but had a sort of meretricious smart-
ness, a disingenuous elasticity, above all a levity, hateful
indeed to the spirit of Mr. Pope yet attractive to the wanton
customer. Business dwindled. Nevertheless the habitual
element in the good-class customer did keep things going,
albeit on a shrinking scale, until Mr. Pope came to the un-
fortunate decision that he would make a stand against automobiles. He regarded them as an intrusive nuisance which
had to be seen only to be disowned by the landed gentry of
England. Rather than build a car he said he would go out
of business. He went out of business. Within five years of
this determination he sold out the name, goodwill, and other
vestiges of his concern to a mysterious buyer who turned
out to be no more than an agent for those persistently expand-
ing varnish-makers, and he retired with a genuine grievance
upon the family accumulations—chiefly in Consols and Home
Railways.

He refused however to regard his defeat as final, put great
faith in the approaching exhaustion of the petrol supply, and
talked in a manner that should have made the Automobile
Association uneasy, of devoting the rest of his days to the
purification of England from these aggressive mechanisms.
" It was a mistake," he said, " to let them in." He became
more frequent at his excellent West End Club, and directed a
certain portion of his capital to largely indecisive but on the
whole unprofitable speculations in South African and South
American enterprises. He mingled a little in affairs. He was

a tough conventional speaker, rich in established phrases and never abashed by hearing himself say commonplace things, and in addition to his campaign against automobiles he found time to engage also in quasi-political activities, taking chairs, saying a few words and so on, cherishing a fluctuating hope that his eloquence might ultimately win him an invitation to contest a constituency in the interests of reaction and the sounder elements in the Liberal party.

He had a public-spirited side, and he was particularly attracted by that mass of modern legislative proposals which aims at a more systematic control of the lives of lower-class persons for their own good by their betters.  Indeed, in the first enthusiasm of his proprietorship of the Pope works at East Purblow, he had organised one of those benevolent industrial experiments that are now so common.  He felt strongly against the drink evil—that is to say the unrestricted liberty of common people to drink what they prefer, and he was acutely impressed by the fact that working-class families do not spend their money in the way that seems most desirable to upper middle-class critics.  Accordingly he did his best to replace the dangerous freedoms of money by that ideal of the social reformer, Payment in Kind.  To use his invariable phrase, the East Purblow experiment did " no mean service " to the cause of social reform.  Unhappily it came to an end through a prosecution under the Truck Act, that blot upon the Statute Book, designed, it would appear, even deliberately to vitiate man's benevolent control of his fellow-man.  The lessons to be drawn from that experience, however, grew if anything with the years.  He rarely spoke without an allusion to it, and it was quite remarkable how readily it could be adapted to illuminate a hundred different issues in the hospitable columns of the *Spectator*. . . .

## § 7

At seven o'clock Marjorie found herself upstairs changing into her apple-green frock.  She had had a good refreshing wash in cold soft water, and it was pleasant to put on thinner silk stockings and dainty satin slippers and let down and at last brush her hair and dress loiteringly after the fatigues of her journey and the activities of her arrival.  She looked out on the big church and the big trees behind it against the golden quiet of a summer evening with extreme approval.

" I suppose those birds are rooks," she said.

But Daffy had gone to see that the pseudo-twins had done themselves justice in their muslin frocks and pink sashes ; they were apt to be a little sketchy with their less accessible buttons.

Marjorie became aware of two gentlemen with her mother on the lawn below.

One was her almost affianced lover, Will Magnet, the humorous writer. She had been doing her best not to think about him all day, but now he became an unavoidable central fact. She regarded him with an almost perplexed scrutiny, and wondered vividly why she had been so excited and pleased by his attentions during the previous summer.

Mr. Magnet was one of those quiet, deliberately unassuming people who do not even attempt to be beautiful. Not for him was it to pretend, but to prick the bladder of pretence. He was a fairish man of forty, pale, with a large, protuberant, observant grey eye—I speak particularly of the left—and a face of quiet animation warily alert for the wit's opportunity. His nose and chin were pointed, and his lips thin and quaintly pressed together. He was dressed in grey, with a low-collared silken shirt showing a thin neck, and a flowing black tie, and he carried a grey felt hat in his joined hands behind his back. She could hear the insinuating cadences of his voice as he talked in her mother's ear. The other gentleman, silent on her mother's right, must, she knew, be Mr. Wintersloan, whom Mr. Magnet had proposed to bring over. His dress betrayed that modest gaiety of disposition becoming in an artist, and indeed he was one of Mr. Magnet's favourite illustrators. He was in a dark bluish-grey suit ; a black tie that was quite unusually broad went twice around his neck before succumbing to the bow, and his waistcoat appeared to be of some gaily patterned orange silk. Marjorie's eyes returned to Mr. Magnet. Hitherto she had never had an opportunity of remarking that his hair was more than a little attenuated towards the crown. It was funny how his tie came out under his chin to the right.

What an odd thing men's dress had become ! she thought. Why did they wear those ridiculous collars and ties ? Why didn't they always dress in flannels and look as fine and slender and active as the elder Carmel boy, for example ? Mr. Magnet couldn't be such an ill-shaped man. Why didn't every one dress to be just as beautiful and splendid as possible ?—instead of wearing queer things !

" Coming down ? " said Daffy, a vision of sulphur-yellow, appearing in the doorway.

" Let *them* go first," said Marjorie, with a finer sense of effect. " And Theodore. We don't want to make part of a comic entry with Theodore, Daffy."

Accordingly the two sisters watched discreetly—they had to be wary on account of Mr. Magnet's increasingly frequent glances at the windows—and when at last all the rest of the family had appeared below, they decided their cue had come. Mr. Pope strolled into the group, with no trace of his recent *débâcle* except a slight limp. He was wearing a jacket of damson-coloured velvet which he affected in the country, and all traces of his Grand Dudgeon were gone. But then he rarely had Grand Dudgeon except in the sanctities of family life, and hardly ever when any other man was about.

" Well," his daughters heard him say, with a witty allusiveness that was difficult to follow, " so the Magnet has come to the Mountain again—eh ? "

" Come on, Madge," said Daffy, and the two sisters emerged harmoniously together from the house.

It would have been manifest to a meaner capacity than any present that evening that Mr. Magnet regarded Marjorie with a distinguished significance. He had two eyes, but he had that mysterious quality so frequently associated with a bluish-grey iris which gives the effect of looking hard with one large orb, a sort of grey searchlight effect, and he now used this eye ray to convey a respectful but firm admiration in the most unequivocal manner. He saluted Daffy courteously, and then allowed himself to retain Marjorie's hand for just a second longer than was necessary as he said—very simply— " I am very pleased indeed to meet you again—very."

A slight embarrassment fell between them.

" You are staying near here, Mr. Magnet ? "

" At the inn," said Mr. Magnet, and then, " I chose it because it would be near you."

His eye pressed upon her again for a moment.

" Is it comfortable ? " said Marjorie.

" So charmingly simple," said Mr. Magnet. " I love it."

A tinkling bell announced the preparedness of supper, and roused the others to the consciousness that they were silently watching Mr. Magnet and Marjorie.

" It's quite a simple farmhouse supper," said Mrs. Pope.

### § 8

There were ducks, green peas, and adolescent new potatoes for supper, and afterwards stewed fruit and cream and junket and cheese, bottled beer, Gilbey's Burgundy, and home-made lemonade. Mrs. Pope carved because Mr. Pope splashed too much, and bones upset him and made him want to show up chicken in *The Times*. So he sat at the other end and rallied his guests while Mrs. Pope distributed the viands. He showed not a trace of his recent umbrage. Theodore sat between Daffy and his mother because of his table manners, and Marjorie was on her father's right hand and next to Mr. Wintersloan, while Mr. Magnet was in the middle of the table on the opposite side in a position convenient for looking at her. Both maids waited.

The presence of Magnet invariably stirred the latent humorist in Mr. Pope. He felt that he who talks to humorists should himself be humorous, and it was his private persuasion that with more attention he might have been, to use a favourite form of expression, " no mean jester." Quite a lot of little things of his were cherished as " Good " both by himself and,

with occasional inaccuracies, by Mrs. Pope. He opened out
now in a strain of rich allusiveness.

"What will you drink, Mr. Wintersloan ? " he said. " Wine
of the country, yclept beer, red wine from France, or my wife's
potent brew from the golden lemon ? "

Mr. Wintersloan thought he would take Burgundy. Mr.
Magnet preferred beer.

> "I've heard there's iron in the Beer,
> And I believe it,"

misquoted Mr. Pope, and nodded as it were to the marker to
score. "Daffy and Marjorie are still in the lemonade stage.
Will you take a little Burgundy to-night, Mummy ? "

Mrs. Pope decided she would, and was inspired to ask
Mr. Wintersloan if he had been in that part of the country
before. Topography ensued. Mr. Wintersloan had a style
of his own, and spoke of the Buryhamstreet district as a
" pooty little country—pooty little hills, with a swirl in them."
This pleased Daffy and Marjorie, and their eyes met for a
moment.

Then Mr. Magnet, with a ray full on Marjorie, said he had
always been fond of Surrey. "I think if ever I made a home
in the country I should like it to be here."

Mr. Wintersloan said Surrey would tire him, it was too
bossy and curly, too flocculent ; he would prefer to look on
broader, simpler lines, with just a sudden catch in the breath
in them—if you understand me ?

Marjorie did, and said so.

"A sob—such as you get at the break of a pinewood on a
hill."

This baffled Mr. Pope, but Marjorie took it. "Or the short
dry cough of a cliff," she said.

"Exactly," said Mr. Wintersloan, and having turned a little
deliberate close-lipped smile on her for a moment, resumed his
wing.

"So long as a landscape doesn't *sneeze*," said Mr. Magnet
in that irresistible dry way of his, and Rom and Sydney, at
any rate, choked.

"Now is the hour when landscapes yawn," mused Mr. Pope,
coming in all right at the end.

Then Mrs. Pope asked Mr. Wintersloan about his route to
Buryhamstreet, and then Mr. Pope asked Mr. Magnet whether
he was playing at a new work or working at a new play.

Mr. Magnet said he was dreaming over a play. He wanted
to bring out the more serious side of his humour, go a little
deeper into things than he had hitherto done.

"Mingling smiles and tears," said Mr. Pope approvingly.

Mr. Magnet said very quietly that all true humour did that.

Then Mrs. Pope asked what the play was to be about, and
Mr. Magnet, who seemed disinclined to give an answer, turned

the subject by saying he had to prepare an address on humour for the next dinner of the *Literati*. "It's to be a humorist's dinner, and they've made me the guest of the evening—by way of a joke to begin with," he said with that dry smile again.

Mrs. Pope said he shouldn't say things like that. She then said "Syd!" quietly but sharply to Sydney, who was making a disdainful, squinting face at Theodore, and told the parlour-maid to clear away the plates for sweets. Mr. Magnet professed great horror of public speaking. He said that whenever he rose to make an after-dinner speech all the ices he had ever eaten seemed to come out of the past, and sit on his back-bone.

The talk centred for a while on Mr. Magnet's address, and apropos of Tests of Humour, Mr. Pope, who in his way was "no mean raconteur," related the story of the man who took the salad dressing with his hand, and when his host asked why he did that, replied: "Oh, I thought it was spinach!"

"Many people," added Mr. Pope, "wouldn't see the point of that. And if they don't see the point they can't—and the more they try the less they do."

All four girls hoped secretly and not too confidently that their laughter had not sounded hollow.

And then for a time the men told stories as they came into their heads in an easy, irresponsible way. Mr. Magnet spoke of the humour of the omnibus-driver who always dangled and twiddled his badge "by way of a joke" when he passed the conductor whose father had been hanged, and Mr. Pope, perhaps a little irrelevantly, told the story of the small boy who was asked his father's last words, and said "mother was with him to the end," which particularly amused Mrs. Pope. Mr. Wintersloan gave the story of the woman who was taking her son to the hospital with his head jammed into a saucepan, and explained to the other people in the omnibus: "You see, what makes it so annoying, it's me only saucepan!" Then they came back to the Sense of Humour with the dentist who shouted with laughter, and when asked the reason by his patient, choked out: "Wrong tooth!" and then Mr. Pope reminded them of the heartless husband who, suddenly informed that his mother-in-law was dead, exclaimed: "Oh, don't make me laugh, please, I've got a split lip. . . ."

§ 9

The conversation assumed a less anecdotal quality with the removal to the drawing-room. On Mr. Magnet's initiative the gentlemen followed the ladies almost immediately, and it was Mr. Magnet who remembered that Marjorie could sing.

Both the elder sisters indeed had sweet clear voices, and they had learned a number of those jolly songs the English made before the dull Hanoverians came. Syd accompanied, and Rom sat back in the low chair in the corner and fell deeply in love with Mr. Wintersloan. The three musicians in their

green and sulphur-yellow and white made a pretty group in
the light of the shaded lamp against the black-and-gold
Broadwood, the tawdry screen, its pattern thin glittering upon
darkness, and the deep shadows behind. Marjorie loved
singing, and forgot herself as she sang.

> " I love, and he loves me again,
>     Yet dare I not tell who ;
> For if the nymphs should know my swain,
>     I fear they'd love him too "

she sang, and Mr. Magnet could not conceal the intensity of
his admiration.

Mr. Pope had fallen into a pleasant musing ; several other
ripe old yarns, dear delicious old things, had come into his
mind that he felt he might presently recall when this unavoidable display of accomplishments was overpast, and it was
with one of them almost on his lips that he glanced across at
his guest. He was surprised to see Mr. Magnet's face trans-
figured. He was sitting forward, looking up at Marjorie,
and he had caught something of the expression of those blessed
boys who foam about the feet of an Assumption. For an
instant Mr. Pope did not understand.

Then he understood. It was Marjorie ! He had a twinge
of surprise, and glanced at his daughter as though he had
never seen her before. He perceived in a flash for the first
time that this troublesome, clever, disrespectful child was tall
and shapely and sweet and indeed quite a beautiful young
woman. He forgot his anecdotes. His being was suffused
with pride and responsibility and the sense of virtue rewarded.
He did not reflect for a moment that Marjorie embodied in
almost equal proportions the very best points in his mother
and his mother-in-law, and avoided his own more salient
characteristics with so neat a dexterity that from top to toe,
except for the one matter of colour, not only did she not
resemble him but she scarcely even alluded to him. He
thought simply that she was his daughter, that she derived
from him, that her beauty was his. She was the outcome of
his meritorious preparations. He recalled all the moments
when he had been kind and indulgent to her, all the bills he
had paid for her ; all the stresses and trials of the coach-
building collapse, all the fluctuations of his speculative adventures, became things he had faced patiently and valiantly
for her sake. He forgot the endless times when he had been
viciously cross with her, all the times when he had pished
and tushed and sworn in her hearing. He had on provocation and in spite of her mother's protests slapped her pretty
vigorously, but such things are better forgotten ; nor did he
recall how bitterly he had opposed the college education
which had made her now so clear in eye and thought, nor the

frightful shindy, only three months since, about that identical
green dress in which she now stood delightful. He forgot
these petty details, as an idealist should. There she was,
his daughter. An immense benevolence irradiated his soul—
for Marjorie—for Magnet. His eyes were suffused with a not
ignoble tenderness. The man, he knew, was worth at least
thirty-five thousand pounds, a discussion of investments had
made that clear, and he must be making at least five thousand
a year ! A beautiful girl, a worthy man ! A good fellow,
a sound good fellow, a careful fellow too—as these fellows
went !

Old daddy would lose his treasure of course.

Well, a father must learn resignation, and he for one would
not stand in the way of his girl's happiness. A day would
come when, very beautifully and tenderly, he would hand
her over to Magnet, his favourite daughter to his trusted
friend. " Well, my boy, there's no one in all the world——"
he would begin.

It would be a touching parting. " Don't forget your old
father, Maggots," he would say. At such a moment that
quaint nickname would surely not be resented. . . .

He reflected how much he had always preferred Marjorie
to Daffy. She was brighter—more like him. Daffy was
unresponsive, with a touch of bitterness under her tongue. . . .

He was already dreaming he was a widower, rather infirm,
the object of Magnet's and Marjorie's devoted care, when
the song ceased, and the wife he had for the purpose of reverie
just consigned so carelessly to the cemetery proposed that
they should have a little game that every one could play at.
A number of pencils and slips of paper appeared in her hands.
She did not want the girls to exhaust their repertory on this
first occasion—and besides, Mr. Pope liked games in which
one did things with pencils and strips of paper. Mr. Magnet
wished the singing to go on, he said, but he was overruled.

So for a time every one played a game in which Mr. Pope
was particularly proficient. Indeed, it was rare that any
one won but Mr. Pope. It was called " The Great Departed,"
and it had such considerable educational value that all the
children had to play at it whenever he wished.

It was played in this manner : one the of pseudo-twins
opened a book and dabbed a finger on the page, and read
out the letter immediately at the tip of her finger, then they
all began to write as hard as they could, writing down the
names of every great person they could think of, whose name
began with that letter. At the end of five minutes Mr. Pope
said Stop ! and then began to read his list out, beginning
with the first name. Everybody who had that name crossed
it out and scored one, and after his list was exhausted all the
surviving names on the next list were read over in the same
way, and so on. The names had to be the names of dead

celebrated people, only one monarch of the same name of
the same dynasty was allowed, and Mr. Pope adjudicated on all
doubtful cases. It was great fun.

The first two games were won as usual by Mr. Pope, and
then Mr. Wintersloan, who had been a little distraught in his
manner, brightened up and scribbled furiously.

The letter was *D*, and after Mr. Pope had rehearsed a tale
of nine-and-twenty names, Mr. Wintersloan read out his list
in that curious voice of his which suggested nothing so much
as some mobile drink glucking out of the neck of a bottle
held upside down.

" Dahl," he began.

" Who was Dahl ? " asked Mr. Pope.

" 'Vented dahlias," said Mr. Wintersloan, with a sigh.
" Danton."

" Forgot him," said Mr. Pope.

" Davis."

" Davis ? "

" Davis Straits. Doe."

" Who ? "

" John Doe, Richard Roe."

" Legal fiction, I'm afraid," said Mr. Pope.

" Dam," said Mr. Wintersloan, and added after a slight
pause : " Antony van."

Mr. Pope made an interrogative noise.

" Painter—eighteenth century—Dutch. Dam, Jan van,
his son. Dam, Frederick van. Dam, Wilhelm van. Dam,
Diedrich van. Dam, Wilhelmina, wood-engraver, gifted
woman. Diehl."

" Who ? "

" Painter — dead — famous. See Düsseldorf. It's all
painters now—all guaranteed dead, all good men. Deeds of
Norfolk, the aquarellist, Denton, Dibbs."

" Er ? " said Mr. Pope.

" The Warwick Claude, *you* know. Died 1823."

" Dickson, Dunting, John Dickery. Peter Dickery, William
Dock—I beg your pardon ? "

Mr. Pope was making a protesting gesture, but Mr. Winters-
sloan's bearing was invincible, and he proceeded.

In the end he emerged triumphant with forty-nine names,
mostly painters for whose fame he answered, but whose
reputations were certainly new to every one else present.
" I can go on like that," said Mr. Wintersloan, " with any
letter," and turned that hard little smile full on Marjorie.
" I didn't see how to do it at first. I just cast about. But I
know a frightful lot of painters. No end. Shall we try
again ? "

Marjorie glanced at her father. Mr. Wintersloan's methods
were all too evident to her. A curious feeling pervaded the
room that Mr. Pope didn't think Mr. Wintersloan's conduct

honourable, and that he might even go some way towards
saying so.

So Mrs. Pope became very brisk and stirring, and said she
thought that now perhaps a charade would be more amusing.
It didn't do to keep on at a game too long.   She asked Rom
and Daphne and Theodore and Mr. Wintersloan to go out,
and they all agreed readily, particularly Rom.   " Come on ! "
said Rom to Mr. Wintersloan.   Everybody else shifted into
an audience-like group between the piano and the what-not.
Mr. Magnet sat at Marjorie's feet, while Syd played a kind of
voluntary, and Mr. Pope leaned back in his chair, with his
brows knit and lips moving, trying to remember something.

The charade *was* very amusing.   The word was Catarrh,
and Mr. Wintersloan, as the patient in the last act being given
gruel, surpassed even the children's very high expectations.
Rom, as his nurse, couldn't keep her hands off him.   Then
the younger people kissed round and were packed off to bed,
and the rest of the party went to the door upon the lawn
and admired the night.   It was a glorious summer night,
deep blue, and rimmed warmly by the afterglow, moonless,
and with a few big lamp-like stars above the black still shapes
of trees.

Mrs. Pope said they would all accompany their guests to the
gate at the end of the avenue—in spite of the cockchafers.

Mr. Pope's ankle, however, excused him ; the cordiality of
his parting from Mr. Wintersloan seemed a trifle forced, and
he limped thoughtfully and a little sombrely towards the
study to see if he could find an encyclopædia or some such
book of reference that would give the names of the lesser
lights of Dutch, Italian, and English painting during the last
two centuries.

He felt that Mr. Wintersloan had established an extraordinarily bad precedent.

§ 10

Marjorie discovered that she and Mr. Magnet had fallen a
little behind the others.   She would have quickened her pace,
but Mr. Magnet stopped short and said :   " Marjorie !

" When I saw you standing there and singing," said Mr.
Magnet, and was short of breath for a moment.

Marjorie's natural gift for interruption failed her altogether.

" I felt I would rather be able to call you mine—than win
an empire."

The pause seemed to lengthen between them, and Marjorie's
remark when she made it at last struck her even as she made
it as being but poorly conceived.   She had some weak idea
of being self-depreciatory.

" I think you had better win an empire, Mr. Magnet," she
said meekly.

Then, before anything more was possible, they had come

up to Daffy and Mr. Wintersloan and her mother at the gate. . . .

As they returned Mrs. Pope was loud in the praises of Will Magnet. She had a little clear-cut voice, very carefully and very skilfully controlled, and she dilated on his modesty, his quiet helpfulness at table, his ready presence of mind. She pointed out instances of those admirable traits, incidents small in themselves but charming in their implications. When somebody wanted junket, he had made no fuss, he had just helped them to junket. " So modest and unassuming," sang Mrs. Pope. " You'd never dream he was quite rich and famous. Yet every book he writes is translated into Russian and German and all sorts of languages. I suppose he's almost the greatest humorist we have. That play of his ; what is it called ?—*Our Owd Woman*—has been performed nearly twelve hundred times ! I think that is the most wonderful of gifts. Think of the people it has made happy."

The conversation was mainly monologue. Both Marjorie and Daffy were unusually thoughtful.

### § 11

Marjorie ended the long day in a worldly mood.

" Penny for your thoughts," said Daffy abruptly, brushing the long firelit rapids of her hair.

" Not for sale," said Marjorie, and roused herself. " I've had a long day.

" It's always just the time I particularly wish I was a man," she remarked after a brief return to meditation. " Fancy, no hairpins, no brushing, no tie-up to get lost about, no strings. I suppose they haven't strings ? "

" They haven't," said Daffy with conviction.

She met Marjorie's interrogative eye. " Father would swear at them," she explained. " He'd naturally tie himself up—and we should hear of it."

" I didn't think of that," said Marjorie, and stuck out her chin upon her fists. " Sound induction."

She forgot this transitory curiosity.

" Suppose one had a maid, Daffy—a real maid . . . a maid who mended your things . . . did your hair while you read. . . .

" Oh ! " here goes," and she stood up and grappled with the task of undressing.

# CHAPTER TWO

## THE TWO PROPOSALS OF MR. MAGNET

### § I

IT was presently quite evident to Marjorie that Mr. Magnet intended to propose marriage to her, and she did not even know whether she wanted him to do so.

She had met him first the previous summer while she had been staying with the Petley-Cresthams at High Windower, and it had been evident that he found her extremely attractive. She had never had a real grown man at her feet before, and she had found it amazingly entertaining. She had gone for a walk with him the morning before she came away—a frank and ingenuous proceeding that made Mrs. Petley-Crestham say the girl knew what she was about, and she had certainly coquetted with him in an extraordinary manner at golf-croquet. After that Oxbridge had swallowed her up, and though he had called once on her mother while Marjorie was in London during the Christmas vacation, he hadn't seen her again. He had written—which was exciting—a long friendly humorous letter about nothing in particular, with an air of its being quite the correct thing for him to do, and she had answered, and there had been other exchanges. But all sorts of things had happened in the interval, and Marjorie had let him get into quite a back place in her thoughts—the fact that he was a member of her father's club had seemed somehow to remove him from a great range of possibilities —until a drift in her mother's talk towards him and a letter from him with an indefinable change in tone towards intimacy, had restored him to importance. Now here he was in the foreground of her world again, evidently more ardent than ever, and with a portentous air of being about to do something decisive at the very first opportunity. What was he going to do ? What had her mother been hinting at ? And what, in fact, did the whole thing amount to ?

Marjorie was beginning to realise that this was going to be a very serious affair indeed for her—and that she was totally unprepared to meet it.

It had been very amusing, very amusing indeed, at the Petley-Cresthams', but there were moments now when she felt towards Mr. Magnet exactly as she would have felt if he had been one of the Oxbridge tradesmen hovering about her with a " little account," full of apparently exaggerated items. . . .

Her thoughts and feelings about this business were all in confusion. Her mind was full of scraps, every sort of idea, every sort of attitude contributed something to that Twentieth-

Century jumble. For example, and so far as its value went among motives, it was by no means a trivial consideration ; she wanted to be proposed to for its own sake. Daffy had had a proposal last year, and although it wasn't any sort of eligible proposal, still there it was, and she had given herself tremendous airs. But Marjorie would certainly have preferred some lighter kind of proposal than that which now threatened her. She felt that behind Mr. Magnet were sanctions ; that she wasn't free to deal with this proposal as she liked. He was at Buryhamstreet almost with the air of being her parents' guest.

Less clear and more instinctive than her desire for a proposal was her inclination to see just all that Mr. Magnet was disposed to do, and hear all that he was disposed to say. She was curious. He didn't behave in the least as she had expected a lover to behave. But then none of the boys, the " others " with whom she had at times stretched a hand towards the hem of emotion, had ever done that. She had an obscure feeling that perhaps presently Mr. Magnet must light up, be stirred and stirring. Even now his voice changed very interestingly when he was alone with her. His breath seemed to go—as though something had pricked his lung. If it hadn't been for that new, disconcerting realisation of an official pressure behind him, I think she would have been quite ready to experiment extensively with his emotions. . . .

But she perceived as she lay awake next morning that she wasn't free for experiments any longer. What she might say or do now would be taken up very conclusively. And she had no idea what she wanted to say or do.

Marriage regarded in the abstract—that is to say, with Mr. Magnet out of focus—was by no means an unattractive proposal to her. It was very much at the back of Marjorie's mind that after Oxbridge, unless she was prepared to face a very serious row indeed and go to teach in a school—and she didn't feel any call whatever to teach in a school—she would probably have to return to Hartstone Square and share Daffy's room again, and assist in the old collective, wearisome task of propitiating her father. The freedoms of Oxbridge had enlarged her imagination until that seemed an almost unendurably irksome prospect. She had tasted life as it could be in her father's absence, and she was beginning to realise just what an impossible person he was. Marriage was escape from all that ; it meant not only respectful parents but a house of her very own, furniture of her choice, great freedom of movement, an authority, an importance. She had seen what it meant to be a prosperously married young woman in the person of one or two resplendent old girls revisiting Bennett College, scattering invitations, offering protections and opportunities. . . .

Of course there is love.

Marjorie told herself, as she had been trained to tell herself, to be sensible, but something within her repeated : *there is love.*

Of course she liked Mr. Magnet. She really did like Mr. Magnet very much. She had had her girlish dreams, had fallen in love with pictures of men and actors and a music-master and a man who used to ride by as she went to school ; but wasn't this desolating desire for self-abandonment rather silly ?—something that one left behind with much else when it came to putting up one's hair and sensible living, something to blush secretly about and hide from every eye ?

Among other discrepant views that lived together in her mind as cats and rats and parrots and squirrels and so forth used to live together in those Happy Family cages unseemly men in less well-regulated days were wont to steer about our streets, was one instilled by quite a large proportion of the novels she had read, that a girl was a sort of self-giving prize for high moral worth. Mr. Magnet she knew was good, was kind, was brave with that truer courage, moral courage, which goes with his type of physique ; he was modest, unassuming, well off and famous, and very much in love with her. His True Self, as Mrs. Pope had pointed out several times, must be really very beautiful, and in some odd way a line of Shakespeare had washed up in her consciousness as being somehow effectual on his behalf :

" Love looks not with the eye but with the mind."

She felt she ought to look with the mind. Nice people surely never looked in any other way. It seemed from this angle almost her duty to love him. . . .

Perhaps she did love him, and mistook the symptoms. She did her best to mistake the symptoms. But if she did truly love him, would it seem so queer and important and antagonising as it did that his hair was rather thin upon the crown of his head ?

She wished she hadn't looked down on him. . . .

Poor Marjorie ! She was doing her best to be sensible, and she felt herself adrift above a clamorous abyss of feared and forbidden thoughts. Down there she knew well enough it wasn't thus that love must come. Deep in her soul, the richest thing in her life indeed and the best thing she had to give humanity, was a craving for beauty that at times became almost intolerable, a craving for something other than beauty and yet inseparably allied with it, a craving for deep excitement, for a sort of glory in adventure, for passion—for things akin to great music and heroic poems and bannered traditions of romance. She had hidden away in her an immense tumultuous appetite for life, an immense tumultuous capacity for living. To be loved beautifully was surely the crown and climax of her being.

She did not dare to listen to these deeps, yet these insurgent voices filled her. Even while she drove her little crocodile of primly sensible thoughts to their sane appointed conclusion, her blood and nerves and all her being were protesting that Mr. Magnet would not do, that whatever other worthiness was in him, regarded as a lover he was preposterous and flat and foolish and middle-aged, and that it were better never to have lived than to put the treasure of her life to his meagre lips and into his hungry, unattractive arms. " The ugliness of it ! The spiritless horror of it ! " so dumbly and formlessly the rebel voices urged.

" One has to be sensible," said Marjorie to herself, suddenly putting down Shaw's book on Municipal Trading, which she imagined she had been reading. . . .

Perhaps all marriage was horrid, and one had to get over it. That was rather what her mother had conveyed to her.

§ 2

Mr. Magnet made his first proposal in form three days later, after coming twice to tea and staying on to supper. He had played croquet with Mr. Pope, he had been beaten twelve times in spite of twinges in the sprained ankle—heroically borne—had had three victories lucidly explained away, and heard all the particulars of the East Purblow experiment three times over, first in relation to the new Labour Exchanges, then regarded at rather a different angle in relation to female betting, tally-men, and the sanctities of the home generally, and finally in a more exhaustive style, to show its full importance from every side and more particularly as demonstrating the gross injustice done to Mr. Pope by the neglect of its lessons, a neglect too systematic to be accidental, in the social reform literature of the time. Moreover, Mr. Magnet had been made to understand thoroughly how several later quasi-charitable attempts of a similar character had already become, or must inevitably become, unsatisfactory through their failure to follow exactly in the lines laid down by Mr. Pope.

Mr. Pope was really very anxious to be pleasant and agreeable to Mr. Magnet, and he could think of no surer way of doing so than by giving him an unrestrained intimacy of conversation that prevented anything more than momentary intercourse between his daughter and her admirer. And not only did Mr. Magnet find it difficult to get away from Mr. Pope without offence, but whenever by any chance Mr. Pope was detached for a moment Mr. Magnet discovered that Marjorie either wasn't to be seen, or if she was she wasn't to be isolated by any device he could contrive, before the unappeasable return of Mr. Pope.

Mr. Magnet did not get his chance therefore until Lady Petchworth's little gathering at Summerhay Park.

Lady Petchworth was Mrs. Pope's oldest friend, and one of those brighter influences which save our English country-side from lassitude. She had been more fortunate than Mrs. Pope, for while Mr. Pope with that aptitude for disadvantage natural to his temperament had, he said, been tied to a business that never gave him a chance, Lady Petchworth's husband had been a reckless investor of exceptional good luck. In particular, led by a dream, he had put most of his money into a series of nitrate deposits in caves in Saghalien hounted by benevolent penguins, and had been rewarded beyond the dreams of avarice. His foresight had received the fitting reward of a knighthood, and Sir Thomas, after restoring the Parish Church at Summerhay in a costly and destructive manner, spent his declining years in an enviable contentment with Lady Petchworth and the world at large, and died long before infirmity made him really troublesome.

Good fortune had brought out Lady Petchworth's social aptitudes. Summerhay Park was everything that a clever woman, inspired by that gardening literature which has been so abundant in the opening years of the twentieth century, could make it. It had rosaries and rock gardens, sun-dials and yew hedges, pools and ponds, lead figures and stone urns, box borderings and wilderness corners and hundreds and hundreds of feet of prematurely aged red-brick wall with broad herbaceous borders; the walks had primroses, primulas, and cowslips in a quite disingenuous abundance, and in spring the whole extent of the park was gay, here with thousands of this sort of daffodil just bursting out and here with thousands of that sort of narcissus just past its prime, and every patch ready to pass itself off in its naturalised way as the accidental native flower of the field, if only it hadn't been for all the other different varieties coming on or wilting off in adjacent patches. . . .

Her garden was only the beginning of Lady Petchworth's activities. She had a model dairy, and all her poultry was white, and so far as she was able to manage it she made Summer-hay a model village. She overflowed with activities, it was astonishing in one so plump and blonde, and meeting followed meeting in the artistic little red-brick and green-stained timber village hall she had erected. Now it was the National Theatre and now it was the National Mourning ; now it was the Break-Up of the Poor Law, and now the Majority Report, now the Mothers' Union, and now Socialism, and now Indi-vidualism, but always something progressive and beneficial. She did her best to revive the old village life, and brought her very considerable powers of compulsion to make the men dance in simple old Morris dances, dressed up in costumes they secretly abominated, and to induce the mothers to dress their children in art-coloured smocks instead of the prints and blue serge frocks they preferred. She did not despair, she said, of creating a spontaneous peasant art movement in the district, springing from the people and expressing the people, but so far it had been necessary to import not only instructors and material, but workers to keep the thing going, so sluggish had the spontaneity of our English country-side become.

Her little gatherings were quite distinctive of her. They were a sort of garden-party extending from midday to six or seven ; there would be a nucleus of house guests, and the highways and byways on every hand would be raided to supply persons and interests. She had told her friend to " bring the girls over for the day," and flung an invitation to Mr. Pope, who had at once excused himself on the score of his ankle. Mr. Pope was one of those men who shun social gatherings—ostensibly because of a sterling simplicity of taste, but really because his intolerable egotism made him feel slighted and neglected on these occasions. He told his wife he would be far happier with a book at home, exhorted her not to be late, and was seen composing himself to read the *Vicar of Wakefield*—whenever they published a new book Mr. Pope pretended to read an old one—as the hired waggonette took the rest of his family—Theodore very unhappy in buff silk and a wide Stuart collar—down the avenue.

They found a long lunch-table laid on the lawn beneath the chestnuts, and in full view of the poppies and forget-me-nots around the stone obelisk, a butler and three men-servants with brass buttons and red-and-white-striped waistcoats gave dignity to the scene, and beyond, on the terrace, amidst abundance of deck-chairs, cane chairs, rugs, and cushions, a miscellaneous and increasing company seethed under Lady Petchworth's plump but entertaining hand. There were, of course, Mr. Magnet and his friend Mr. Wintersloan—Lady Petchworth had been given to understand how the land lay ; and there was Mr. Bunford Paradise the musician, who was doing his best to teach a sullen holiday class in the village schoolroom to sing again the artless old folk-songs of Surrey, in spite of the invincible persuasion of everybody in the class that the songs were rather indelicate and extremely silly ; there were the Rev. Jopling Baynes, and two Cambridge undergraduates in flannels, and a Doctor something or other from London. There was also the Hon. Charles Muskett, Lord Pottinger's cousin and estate agent, in tweeds and very helpful. The ladies included Mrs. Raff, the well-known fashion writer, in a wonderful costume, the anonymous doctor's wife, three or four neighbouring mothers with an undistinguished daughter or so, and two quiet-mannered middle-aged ladies, whose names Marjorie could not catch, and whom Lady Petchworth, in that well-controlled voice of hers, addressed as Kate and Julia, and seemed on the whole disposed to treat as humorous. There was also Fräulein Schmidt in charge of Lady Petchworth's three tall and already abundant children, Prunella

Prudence, and Mary, and a young, newly married couple of cousins, who addressed each other in soft undertones and sat apart. These were the chief items that became distinctive in Marjorie's survey ; but there were a number of other people who seemed to come and go, split up, fuse, change their appearance slightly, and behave in the way inadequately apprehended people do behave on these occasions.

Marjorie very speedily found her disposition to take a detached and amused view of the entertainment in conflict with more urgent demands. From the outset Mr. Magnet loomed upon her—he loomed nearer and nearer. He turned his eye upon her as she came up to the wealthy expanse of Lady Petchworth's presence, like some sort of obsolescent iron-clad turning a dull-grey, respectful, loving searchlight upon a fugitive torpedo-boat, and thereafter he seemed to her to be looking at her without intermission, relentlessly, and urging himself towards her. She wished he wouldn't. She hadn't at all thought he would on this occasion.

At first she relied upon her natural powers of evasion, and the presence of a large company. Then gradually it became apparent that Lady Petchworth and her mother, yes—and the party generally, and the gardens and the weather and the stars in their courses were of a mind to co-operate in giving opportunity for Mr. Magnet's unmistakable intentions.

And Marjorie, with that instability of her sex which has been a theme for masculine humour in all ages, suddenly and with an extraordinary violence didn't want to make up her mind about Mr. Magnet. She didn't want to accept him ; and as distinctly she didn't want to refuse him. She didn't even want to be thought about as making up her mind about him—which was, so to speak, an enlargement of her previous indisposition. She didn't even want to seem to avoid him, or to be thinking about him, or aware of his existence.

After the greeting of Lady Petchworth she had succeeded very clumsily in not seeing Mr. Magnet, and had addressed herself to Mr. Wintersloan, who was standing a little apart, looking under his hand, with one eye shut, at the view between the tree stems towards Buryhamstreet. He told her that he thought he had found something " pooty " that hadn't been done, and she did her best to share his artistic interests with a vivid sense of Mr. Magnet's tentative incessant approach behind her.

He joined them, and she made a desperate attempt to entangle Mr. Wintersloan in a three-cornered talk, in vain. He turned away at the first possible opportunity, and left her to an embarrassed and eloquently silent *tête-à-tête*. Mr. Magnet's professional wit had deserted him. " It's nice to see you again," he said after an immense interval. " Shall we go and look at the aviary ? "

" I hate to see birds in cages," said Marjorie, " and it's

frightfully jolly just here. Do you think Mr. Wintersloan
will paint this ? He does paint, doesn't he ? "

" I know him best in black and white," said Mr. Magnet.

Marjorie embarked on entirely insincere praises of Mr.
Wintersloan's manner and personal effect ; Magnet replied
tepidly, with an air of reserving himself to grapple with the
first conversational opportunity.

" It's a splendid day for tennis," said Marjorie. " I think
I shall play tennis all the afternoon."

" I don't play well enough for this publicity."

" It's glorious exercise," said Marjorie. " Almost as good
as dancing," and she decided to stick to that resolution. " I
never lose a chance of tennis if I can help it."

She glanced round and detected a widening space between
themselves and the next adjacent group.

" They're looking at the goldfish," she said. " Let us
join them."

Every one moved away as they came up to the little round
pond, but then Marjorie had luck, and captured Prunella,
and got her to hold hands and talk, until Fräulein Schmidt
called the child away. And then Marjorie forced Mr. Magnet
to introduce her to Mr. Bunford Paradise. She had a bright
idea of sitting between Prunella and Mary at the lunch-table,
but a higher providence had assigned her to a seat at the end
between Julia—or was it Kate ?—and Mr. Magnet. However, one of the undergraduates was opposite, and she saved
herself from undertones by talking across to him boldly about
Newnham, though she hadn't an idea of his name or college.
From that she came to tennis. To her inflamed imagination
he behaved as if she was under a Taboo, but she was desperate,
and had pledged him and his friend to a foursome before the
meal was over.

" Don't *you* play ? " said the undergraduate to Mr. Magnet.

" Very little," said Mr. Magnet. " Very little——"

At the end of an hour she was conspicuously and publicly
shepherded from the tennis court by Mrs. Pope.

" Other people want to play," said her mother in a clear
little undertone.

Mr. Magnet fielded her neatly as she came off the court.

" You play tennis like—a wild bird," he said, taking
possession of her.

Only Marjorie's entire freedom from Irish blood saved him
from a vindictive repartee.

§ 3

" Shall we go and look at the aviary ? " said Mr. Magnet,
reverting to a favourite idea of his, and then remembered
she did not like to see caged birds.

" Perhaps we might see the Water Garden ? " he said.

'The Water Garden is really very delightful indeed—anyhow. You ought to see that."

On the spur of the moment, Marjorie could think of no objection to the Water Garden, and he led her off.

"I often think of that jolly walk we had last summer," said Mr. Magnet, "and how you talked about your work at Oxbridge."

Marjorie fell into a sudden rapture of admiration for a butterfly.

Twice more was Mr. Magnet baffled, and then they came to the little pool of water-lilies with its miniature cascade of escape at the head and source of the Water Garden. "One of Lady Petchworth's great successes," said Mr. Magnet.

"I suppose the lotus is like the water-lily," said Marjorie, with no hope of staving off the inevitable.

She stood very still by the little pool, and in spite of her pensive regard of the floating blossoms, stiffly and intensely aware of his relentless regard.

"Marjorie," came his voice at last, strangely softened. "There is something I want to say to you."

She made no reply.

"Ever since we met last summer——"

A clear cold little resolution not to stand this had established itself in Marjorie's mind. If she must decide, she *would* decide. He had brought it upon himself.

"Marjorie," said Mr. Magnet, "I love you."

She lifted a clear unhesitating eye to his face. "I'm sorry Mr. Magnet," she said.

"I wanted to ask you to marry me," he said.

"I'm sorry, Mr. Magnet," she repeated.

They looked at one another. She felt a sort of scared exultation at having done it ; her mother might say what she liked.

"I love you very much," he said, at a loss.

"I'm sorry," she repeated obstinately.

"I thought you cared for me a little."

She left that unanswered. She had a curious feeling that there was no getting away from this splashing, babbling pool, that she was fixed there until Mr. Magnet chose to release her, and that he didn't mean to release her yet. In which case she would go on refusing.

"I'm disappointed," he said.

Marjorie could only think that she was sorry again, but as she had already said that three times, she remained awkwardly silent.

"Is it because——" he began and stopped.

"It isn't because of anything. Please let's go back to the others, Mr. Magnet. I'm sorry if I'm disappointing."

And by a great effort she turned about.

Mr. Magnet remained regarding her—I can only compare

it to the searching preliminary gaze of an artistic photographer.
For a crucial minute in his life Marjorie hated him. " I don't
understand," he said at last.

Then with a sort of naturalness that ought to have touched
her he said : " Is it possible, Marjorie—that I might hope ?
—that I have been inopportune ? "

She answered at once with absolute conviction.

" I don't think so, Mr. Magnet."

" I'm sorry," he said, " to have bothered you."

" *I'm* sorry," said Marjorie.

A long silence followed.

" I'm sorry too," he said.

They said no more, but began to retrace their steps. It
was over. Abruptly, Mr. Magnet's bearing had become
despondent—conspicuously despondent. " I had hoped," he
said, and sighed.

With a thrill of horror Marjorie perceived he meant to *look*
rejected, let every one see he had been rejected—after
encouragement.

What would they think ?   How would they look ?   What
conceivably might they not say ?   Something of the importance of the thing she had done, became manifest to her.
She felt first intimations of regret.   They would all be watching, Mother, Daffy, Lady Petchworth.   She would reappear
with this victim visibly suffering beside her.   What could
she say to straighten his back and lift his chin ?   She could
think of nothing.   Ahead at the end of the shaded path she
could see the copious white form, the agitated fair wig and
red sunshade of Lady Petchworth——

### § 4

Mrs. Pope's eye was relentless ; nothing seemed hidden
from it ; nothing indeed was hidden from it ; Mr. Magnet's
back was diagrammatic.   Marjorie was a little flushed and
bright-eyed, and professed herself eager, with an unnatural
enthusiasm, to play golf-croquet.   It was eloquently significant that Mr. Magnet did not share her eagerness, declined
to play, and yet when she had started with the Rev. Jopling
Baynes as partner, stood regarding the game with a sort of
tender melancholy from the shade of the big chestnut tree.

Mrs. Pope joined him unobtrusively.

" You're not playing, Mr. Magnet," she remarked.

" I'm a looker-on this time," he said with a sigh.

" Marjorie's winning, I think," said Mrs. Pope.

He made no answer for some seconds.

" She looks so charming in that blue dress," he remarked
at last, and sighed from the lowest deeps.

" That bird's-egg blue suits her," said Mrs. Pope, ignoring
the sigh.   " She's clever in her girlish way, she chooses all
her own dresses—colours, material, everything."

(And also, though Mrs. Pope had not remarked it, she concealed her bills.)

There came a still longer interval, which Mrs. Pope ended with the slightest of shivers. She perceived Mr. Magnet was heavy for sympathy and ripe to confide. " I think," she said, " it's a little cool here. Shall we walk to the Water Garden, and see if there are any white lilies ? "

" There are," said Mr. Magnet sorrowfully, " and they are very beautiful—*quite* beautiful."

He turned to the path along which he had so recently led Marjorie.

He glanced back as they went along between Lady Petch-worth's herbaceous border and the poppy beds. " She's so full of life," he said, with a sigh in his voice.

Mrs. Pope knew she must keep silent.

" I asked her to marry me this afternoon," Mr. Magnet blurted out. " I couldn't help it."

Mrs. Pope made her silence very impressive.

" I know I ought not to have done so without consulting you "—he went on lamely ; " I'm very much in love with her. It's—it's done no harm."

Mrs. Pope's voice was soft and low. " I had no idea, Mr. Magnet. . . . You know she is very young. Twenty. A mother——"

" I know," said Magnet. " I can quite understand. But I've done no harm. She refused me. I shall go away to-morrow. Go right away for ever. . . . I'm sorry."

Another long silence.

" To me, of course, she's just a child," Mrs. Pope said at last. " She *is* only a child, Mr. Magnet. She could have had no idea that anything of the sort was in your mind——"

Her words floated away into the stillness.

For a time they said no more. The lilies came into sight, dreaming under a rich green shade on a limpid pool of brown water, water that slept and brimmed over as it were un-consciously into a cool splash and ripple of escape. " How beautiful ! " cried Mrs. Pope, for a moment genuine.

" I spoke to her here," said Mr. Magnet.

The fountains of his confidence were unloosed.

" Now I've spoken to you about it, Mrs. Pope," he said, " I can tell you just how I—oh, it's the only word—adore her. She seems so sweet and easy—so graceful——"

Mrs. Pope turned on him abruptly, and grasped his hands ; she was deeply moved. " I can't tell you," she said, " what it means to a mother to hear such things——"

Words failed her, and for some moments they engaged in a mutual pressure.

" Ah ! " said Mr. Magnet, and had a queer wish it was the mother he had to deal with.

" Are you sure, Mr. Magnet," Mrs. Pope went on as their

emotions subsided, "that she really meant what she said Girls are very strange creatures——"

"She seems so clear and positive."

"Her manner is always clear and positive."

"Yes. I know."

"I know she *has* cared for you."

"No ! "

"A mother sees. When your name used to be mentioned—— But these are not things to talk about. There is something —something sacred——"

"Yes," he said. "Yes. Only—— Of course, one thing——"

Mrs. Pope seemed lost in the contemplation of water-lilies.

"I wondered," said Mr. Magnet, and paused again. Then, almost breathlessly, "I wondered if there should be perhaps —some one else ? "

She shook her head slowly. "I should know," she said.

"Are you sure ? "

"I know I should know."

"Perhaps recently ? "

"I am sure I should know. A mother's intuition——"

Memories possessed her for a while. "A girl of twenty is a mass of contradictions. I can remember myself as if it was yesterday. Often one says no, or yes—out of sheer nervousness. . . . I am sure there is no other attachment——"

It occurred to her that she had said enough. "What a dignity that old goldfish has ! " she remarked. "He waves his tail—as if he were a beadle waving little boys out of church."

## § 5

Mrs. Pope astonished Marjorie by saying nothing about the all too obvious event of the day for some time, but her manner to her second daughter on their way home was strangely gentle. It was as if she had realised for the first time that regret and unhappiness might come into that young life. After supper, however, she spoke. They had all gone out to look for the new moon just before the children went to bed ; Daffy was showing the pseudo-twins the old moon in the new moon's arms, and Marjorie found herself standing by her mother's side. "I hope, dear," said Mrs. Pope, "that it's all for the best—and that you've done wisely, dear."

Marjorie was astonished and moved by her mother's tone.

"It's so difficult to know what *is* for the best," Mrs. Pope went on.

"I had to do—as I did," said Marjorie.

"I only hope you may never find you have made a Great Mistake, dear. He cares for you very, very much."

"Oh ! we see it now ! " cried Rom, "we see it now ! Mummy, have you seen it ? Like a little old round ghost being nursed ! "

When Marjorie said " Good-night," Mrs. Pope kissed her with an unaccustomed effusion.

It occurred to Marjorie that after all her mother had no selfish end to serve in this affair.

## § 6

The idea that perhaps after all she had made a Great Mistake, the Mistake of her Life it might be, was quite firmly established in its place among all the other ideas in Marjorie's mind by the time she had dressed next morning. Sub-sequent events greatly intensified this persuasion. A pair of new stockings she had trusted sprang a bad hole as she put them on. She found two unmistakable bills from Oxbridge beside her plate, and her father was " horrid " at breakfast.

Her father, it appeared, had bought the ordinary shares of a Cuban railway very extensively, on the distinct under-standing that they would improve. In a decent universe, with a proper respect for meritorious gentlemen, these shares would have improved accordingly, but the weather had seen fit to shatter the wisdom of Mr. Pope altogether. The sugar crop had collapsed, the bears were at work, and every morning now saw his nominal capital diminished by a dozen pounds or so. I do not know what Mr. Pope would have done if he had not had his family to help him bear his trouble. As it was he relieved his tension by sending Theodore from the table for dropping a knife, telling Rom when she turned the plate round to pick the largest banana that she hadn't the self-respect of a child of five, and remarking sharply from behind *The Times* when Daffy asked Marjorie if she was going to sketch : " Oh, for God's sake don't *whisper* ! " Then when Mrs. Pope came round the table and tried to take his coffee-cup softly to refill it without troubling him, he snatched at it, wrenched it roughly out of her hand, and said with his mouth full, and strangely in the manner of a snarling beast : " No' ready yet. Half foo'."

Marjorie wanted to know why every one didn't get up and leave the room. She glanced at her mother and came near to speaking.

And very soon she would have to come home and live in the midst of this again—indefinitely !

After breakfast she went to the tumble-down summer-house by the duck pond, and contemplated the bills she had not dared to open at table. One was boots, nearly three pounds, the other books, over seven. " I *know* that's wrong," said Marjorie, and rested her chin on her hand, knitted her brows and tried to remember the details of orders and deliveries. . . .

Marjorie had fallen into the net prepared for our sons and daughters by the delicate modesty of the Oxbridge authorities in money matters, and she was, for her circumstances, rather heavily in debt. But I must admit that in Marjorie's nature the Oxbridge conditions had found an eager and adventurous streak that rendered her particularly apt to these temptations.

I doubt if reticence is really a virtue in a teacher. But this is a fearful world, and the majority of those who instruct our youth have the painful sensitiveness of the cloistered soul to this spirit of terror in things. The young need particularly to be told truthfully and fully all we know of three fundamental things ; the first of which is God, the next their duty towards their neighbours in the matter of work and money, and the third Sex. These things, and the adequate why of them, and some sort of adequate how, make all that matters in education. But all three are obscure and deeply moving topics, topics for which the donnish mind has a kind of special ineptitude, and which it evades with the utmost skill and delicacy. The middle part of this evaded triad was now being taken up in Marjorie's case by the Oxbridge tradespeople.

The Oxbridge shopkeeper is peculiar among shopkeepers in the fact that he has to do very largely with shy and immature customers with an extreme and distinctive ignorance of most commercial things. They are for the most part short of cash, but with vague and often large probabilities of credit behind them, for most people, even quite straightened people, will pull their sons and daughters out of altogether unreasonable debts at the end of their university career ; and so the Oxbridge shopkeeper becomes a sort of propagandist of the charms and advantages of insolvency. Alone among retailers he dislikes the sight of cash, declines it, affects to regard it as a coarse ignorant truncation of a budding relationship, begs to be permitted to wait. So the youngster just up from home discovers that money may stay in the pocket, be used for cab and train fares and light refreshments ; all the rest may be had for the asking. Marjorie, with her innate hunger for good fine things, with her quite insufficient pocket-money, and the irregular habits of expenditure a spasmodically financed, hard-up home is apt to engender, fell very readily into this new, delightful custom of having it put down (whatever it happened to be). She had all sorts of things put down. She and the elder Carmel girl used to go shopping together, having things put down. She brightened her rooms with colour-prints and engravings, got herself pretty and becoming clothes, acquired a fitted dressing-bag already noted in this story, and one or two other trifles of the sort, revised her footwear, created a very nice little bookshelf, and although at times she felt a little astonished and scared at herself, resolutely refused to estimate the total of accumulated debt she had attained. Indeed until the bills came in it was impossible to do that, because, following the splendid example of the Carmel girl, she hadn't even inquired the price of quite a number of things. . . .

She didn't dare think now of the total. She lied even to herself about that. She had fixed on fifty pounds as the unendurable maximum. " It is less than fifty pounds," she said, and added : " *must* be." But something in her below the threshold of consciousness knew that it was more.

And now she was in her third year, and the Oxbridge tradesman, generally satisfied with the dimensions of her account, and no longer anxious to see it grow, was displaying the less obsequious side of his character. He wrote remarks at the bottom of his account, remarks about settlement, about having a bill to meet, about having something to go on with. He asked her to give the matter her " early attention." She had a disagreeable persuasion that if she wanted many more things anywhere she would have to pay ready money for them. She was particularly short of stockings. She had overlooked stockings recently.

Daffy, unfortunately, was also short of stockings.

And now, back with her family again, everything conspired to remind Marjorie of the old stringent habits from which she had had so delightful an interlude. She saw Daffy eye her possessions, reflect. This morning something of the awfulness of her position came to her. . . .

At Oxbridge she had made rather a joke of her debts.

" I'd *swear* I haven't had three pairs of house shoes," said Marjorie. " But what can one do ? "

And about the whole position the question was, " What can one do ? "

She proceeded with tense nervous movements to tear these two distasteful demands into very minute pieces. Then she collected them all together in the hollow of her hand, and buried them in the loose mould in a corner of the summer-house.

" Madge," said Theodore, appearing in the sunshine of the doorway, " Aunt Plessington's coming ! She's sent a wire. Some one's got to meet her by the twelve-forty train."

### § 7

Aunt Plessington's descent was due to her sudden discovery that Buryhamstreet was in close proximity to Summerhay Park, indeed only three miles away. She had promised a lecture on her movements for Lady Petchworth's village room in Summerhay, and she found that with a slight readjustment of dates she could combine this engagement with her promised visit to her husband's sister, and an evening or so of influence for her little Madge. So she had sent Hubert to telegraph at once, and " here," she said triumphantly on the platform, after a hard kiss at Marjorie's cheek, " we are again."

There, at any rate, she was, and Uncle Hubert was up the platform seeing after the luggage, in his small, anxious way.

Aunt Plessington was a tall, lean woman, with firm features, a high colour and a bright eye, who wore hats to show she despised them, and carefully dishevelled hair. Her dress was always good, but extremely old and grubby, and she commanded respect chiefly by her voice. Her voice was the true governing-class voice, a strangulated contralto, abundant and authoritative ; it made everything she said clear and important, so that if she said it was a fine morning it was like leaded print in *The Times*, and she had over her large front teeth lips that closed quietly and with a slight effort after her speeches, as if the words she spoke tasted well and left a peaceful, secure sensation in the mouth.

Uncle Hubert was a less distinguished figure, and just a little reminiscent of the small attached husbands one finds among the lower crustacea ; he was much shorter and rounder than his wife, and if he had been left to himself, he would probably have been comfortably fat in his quiet little way. But Aunt Plessington had made him a Haigite, which is one of the fiercer kinds of hygienist, just in the nick of time. He had round shoulders, a large nose, and glasses that made him look astonished—and she said he had a great gift for practical things, and made him see after everything in that line while she did the lecturing. His directions to the porter finished, he came up to his niece. " Hello, Marjorie ! " he said, in a peculiar voice that sounded as though his mouth was full (though, of course, poor dear, it wasn't), " how's the First Class ? "

" A second's good enough for me, Uncle Hubert," said Marjorie, and asked if they would rather walk or go in the donkey-cart, which was waiting outside with Daffy. Aunt Plessington, with an air of great *bonhomie*, said she'd ride in the donkey-cart, and they did. But no pseudo-twins or Theodore came to meet this arrival, as both uncle and aunt had a way of asking how the lessons were getting on that they found extremely disagreeable. Also their aunt measured them, and incited them with loud encouraging noises to grow one against the other in an urgent, disturbing fashion.

Aunt Plessington's being was consumed by thoughts of getting on. She was like Bernard Shaw's life force, and she really did not seem to think there was anything in existence but shoving. She had no idea what a lark life can be, and occasionally how beautiful it can be, when you do not shove, if only, which becomes increasingly hard each year, you can get away from the shovers. She was one of an energetic family of eight sisters who from the cradle had maintained themselves against a mutual pressure by the use of their elbows. They had all married against each other, all sorts of people ; two had driven their husbands into bishoprics and made quite typical bishop's wives, one got a leading barrister, one a high War Office official, and one a rich Jew, and Aunt Plessington, after spending some years in just missing a rich and only slightly demented baronet, had pounced—it's the only word for it—on Uncle Hubert. "A woman is nothing without a husband," she said, and took him. He was in his furtive way a fairly comfortable Oxford don, and bringing him out and using him as a basis, she specialised in intellectual philanthropy and evolved her Movement. It was quite remarkable how rapidly she overhauled her sisters again.

What the Movement was, varied considerably from time to time, but it was always aggressively beneficial towards the lower strata of the community. Among its central ideas was her belief that these lower strata can no more be trusted to eat than they can to drink, and that the licensing monopoly which has made the poor man's beer thick, lukewarm and discreditable, and so greatly minimised its consumption, should be extended to the solid side of his dietary. She wanted to place considerable restrictions upon the sale of all sorts of meat, upon groceries and the less hygienic and more palatable forms of bread (which do not sufficiently stimulate the coatings of the stomach), to increase the present difficulties in the way of tobacco purchasers, and to put an end to that wanton and deleterious consumption of sweets which has so bad an effect upon the enamel of the teeth of the younger generation. Closely interwoven with these proposals was an adoption of the principle of the East Purblow Experiment, the principle of Payment in Kind. She was quite in agreement with Mr. Pope that poor people, when they had money, frittered it away, and so she proposed very extensive changes in the Truck Act, which could enable employers, under suitable safeguards, and with the advice of a small body of spinster inspectors, to supply hygienic housing, approved clothing of a moral and wholesome sort, various forms of insurance, edifying rations, cuisine, medical aid and educational facilities as circumstances seemed to justify in lieu of the wages the employees handled so ill. . . .

As no people in England will ever admit they belong to the lower strata of society, Aunt Plessington's Movement attracted adherents from every class in the community.

She now, as they drove slowly to the vicarage, recounted to Marjorie—she had the utmost contempt for Daffy because of her irregular teeth and a general lack of progressive activity —the steady growth of the Movement, and the increasing respect shown for her and Hubert in the world of politico-social reform. Some of the meetings she had addressed had been quite full, various people had made various remarks about her, hostile for the most part and yet insidiously flattering, and everybody seemed quite glad to come to the little dinners she gave in order, she said, to gather social support for her reforms. She had been staying with the Mastersteins, who were keenly interested, and after she had polished off Lady Petchworth she was to visit Lady Rosenbaum. It was all

going on swimmingly, these newer English gentry were eager
to learn all she had to teach in the art of breaking in the Anglo-
Saxon villagers, and now, how was Marjorie going on, and
what was *she* going to do in the world ?

Marjorie said she was working for her final.

" And what then ? " asked Aunt Plessington.

" Not very clear, Aunt, yet."

" Looking round for something to take up ? "

" Yes, Aunt."

" Well, you've time yet. And it's just as well to see how
the land lies before you begin. It saves going back. You'll
have to come up to London with me for a little while, and see
things, and be seen a little."

" I should love to."

" I'll give you a good time," said Aunt Plessington, nodding
promisingly. " Theodore getting on at school ? "

" He's had his remove."

" And how's Sydney getting on with the music ? "

" Excellently."

" And Rom. Rom getting on ? "

Marjorie indicated a more restrained success.

" And what's Daffy doing ? "

" Oh ! *get* on ! " said Daffy, and suddenly whacked the
donkey rather hard. " I beg your pardon, Aunt ? "

" I asked what *you* were up to, Daffy ? "

" Dusting, Aunt—and the virtues," said Daffy.

" You ought to find something better than that."

" Father tells me a lot about the East Purblow Experiment,"
said Daffy after a perceptible interval.

" Ah ! " cried Aunt Plessington with a loud encouraging
note, but evidently making the best of it, " *that's* better.
Sociological observation."

" Yes, Aunt," said Daffy, and negotiated a corner with
exceptional care.

### § 8

Mrs. Pope, who had an instinctive disposition to pad when
Aunt Plessington was about, had secured the presence at lunch
of Mr. Magnet (who was after all staying on in Buryhamstreet)
and the Rev. Jopling Baynes. Aunt Plessington liked to meet
the clergy, and would always if she could win them over to
an interest in the Movement. She opened the meal with a
brisk attack upon him. " Come, Mr. Baynes," she said,
" what do your people eat here ? Hubert and I are making a
study of the gluttonous side of village life, and we find that
no one knows so much of that as the vicar—not even the
doctor."

The Rev. Jopling Baynes was a clergyman of the evasive
type with a quite distinguished voice. He pursed his lips
and made his eyes round. " Well, Mrs. Plessington," he said

and fingered his glass, " it's the usual dietary.  The usual dietary."

" Too much and too rich, badly cooked and eaten too fast," said Aunt Plessington.  " And what do you think is the remedy ? "

" We make an Effort," said the Rev. Jopling Baynes, " we make an Effort.  A Hint here, a Word there."

" Nothing organised ? "

" Nu," said the Rev. Jopling Baynes, and shook his head with a kind of resignation.

" We are going to alter all that," said Aunt Plessington briskly, and went on to expound the Movement and the diverse way in which it might be possible to control and improve the domestic expenditure of the working classes.

The Rev. Jopling Baynes listened sympathetically across the table and tried to satisfy a healthy appetite with as abstemious an air as possible while he did so.  Aunt Plessington passed rapidly from general principles to a sketch of the success of the Movement, and Hubert, who had hitherto been busy with his lunch, became audible from behind the exceptionally large floral trophy that concealed him from his wife, bubbling confirmatory details.  She was very bright and convincing as she told of this prominent man met and subdued, that leading antagonist confuted, and how the Bishops were coming in.  She made it clear in her swift way that an intelligent cleric resolved to get on in this world *en route* for a better one hereafter, might do worse than take up her Movement.  And this touched in, she turned her mind to Mr. Magnet.

(That floral trophy, I should explain, by the by, was exceptionally large because of Mrs. Pope's firm conviction that Aunt Plessington starved her husband.  Accordingly she masked him, and so was able to heap second and third helpings upon his plate without Aunt Plessington discovering his lapse.  The avidity with which Hubert ate confirmed her worst suspicions and evinced, so far as anything ever did evince, his gratitude.)

" Well, Mr. Magnet," she said, " I wish I had your sense of humour."

" I wish you had," said Mr. Magnet.

" I should write tracts," said Aunt Plessington.

" I knew it was good for something," said Mr. Magnet, and Daffy laughed in a tentative way.

" I mean it," said Aunt Plessington brightly.  " Think if we had a Dickens—and you are the nearest man alive to Dickens—on the side of social reform to-day ! "

Mr. Magnet's light manner deserted him.  " We do what we can, Mrs. Plessington," he said.

" How much more might be done," said Aunt Plessington, " if humour could be organised."

" Hear, hear ! " said Mr. Pope.

"If all the humorists of England could be induced to laugh at something together."

"They do—at times," said Mr. Magnet, but the atmosphere was too serious for his light touch.

"They could laugh it out of existence," said Aunt Plessington.

It was evident Mr. Magnet was struck by the idea.

"Of course," he said, "in *Punch*, to which I happen to be an obscure occasional contributor——"

Mrs. Pope was understood to protest that he should not say such things.

"We *do* remember just what we can do either in the way of advertising or injury. I don't think you'll find us up against any really *solid* institutions."

"But do you think, Mr. Magnet, you are sufficiently kind to the New ?" Aunt Plessington persisted.

"I think we are all grateful to *Punch*," said the Rev. Jopling Baynes suddenly and sonorously, "for its steady determination to direct our mirth into the proper channels. I do not think that any one can accuse its editor of being unmindful of his great responsibilities——"

Marjorie found it a very interesting conversation.

She always met her aunt again with a renewal of a kind of admiration. That loud authoritative rudeness, that bold thrusting forward of the Movement until it became the sole criterion of worth or success, this annihilation by disregard of all that Aunt Plessington wasn't and didn't and couldn't, always in the intervals seemed too good to be true. Of course this really was the way people got on and made a mark, but she felt it must be almost as trying to the nerves as aeronautics. Suppose, somewhere up there your engine stopped ! How Aunt Plessington dominated the table ! Marjorie tried not to catch Daffy's eye. Daffy was unostentatiously keeping things going, watching the mustard, rescuing the butter, restraining Theodore, and I am afraid not listening very carefully to Aunt Plessington. The children were marvellously silent and jumpily well-behaved, and Mr. Pope, in a very unusual state of subdued amiability, sat at the end of the table with the East Purblow Experiment on the tip of his tongue. He liked Aunt Plessington, and she was good for him. They had the same inherent distrust of the intelligence and good intentions of their fellow creatures, and she had the knack of making him feel that he too was getting on, that she was saying things on his behalf in influential quarters, and in spite of the almost universal conspiracy (based on jealousy) to ignore his stern old-world virtues, he might still be able to battle his way to the floor of the House of Commons and there deliver himself before he died of a few sorely needed home-truths about motor-cars, decadence and frivolity generally. . . .

§ 9

After lunch Aunt Plessington took her little Madge for an
energetic walk, and showed herself far more observant than
the egotism of her conversation at that meal might have
led one to suppose.  Or perhaps she was only better informed.
Aunt Plessington loved a good hard walk in the afternoon ;
and if she could get any one else to accompany her, then
Hubert stayed at home, and curled up into a ball on a sofa
somewhere, and took a little siesta that made him all the
brighter for the intellectual activities of the evening.  The
thought of a young life, new, untarnished, just at the outset,
just addressing itself to the task of getting on, always stimulated her mind extremely, and she talked to Marjorie with a
very real and effectual desire to help her to the utmost of
her ability.

She talked of a start in life, and the sort of start she had
had.  She showed how many people who began with great
advantages did not shove sufficiently, and so dropped out of
things and weren't seen and mentioned.  She defended
herself for marrying Hubert, and showed what a clever
shoving thing it had been to do.  It startled people a little,
and made them realise that here was a woman who wanted
something more in a man than a handsome organ-grinder.
She made it clear that she thought a clever marriage, if not
a startlingly brilliant one, the first duty of a girl.  It was a
girl's normal gambit.  She branched off to the things single
women might do, in order to justify this view.  She did not
think single women could do very much.  They might perhaps
shove as suffragettes, but even there a husband helped
tremendously—if only by refusing to bail you out.  She ran
over the cases of a number of prominent single women.

" And what," said Aunt Plessington, " do they all amount
to ?  A girl is so hampered and an old maid is so neglected,"
said Aunt Plessington.

She paused.

" Why don't you up and marry Mr. Magnet, Marjorie ? "
she said, with her most brilliant flash.

" It takes two to make a marriage, Aunt," said Marjorie
after a slight hesitation.

" My dear child !  he worships the ground you tread on ! "
said Aunt Plessington.

" He's rather—grown up," said Marjorie.

" Not a bit of it.  He's not forty.  He's just the age."

" I'm afraid it's a little impossible."

" Impossible ? "

" You see I've refused him, Aunt."

" Naturally—the first time !  But I wouldn't send him
packing the second."

There was an interval.

than a quarter of the time.  Rom, who had already got up early and read through about a third of *Aurora Leigh*, now set herself with dogged determination to finish that great poem.  Syd practised an extra ten minutes—for Aunt Plessington didn't mind practice so long as there wasn't a tune.  Mrs. Pope went into the kitchen and made a long-needed fuss about the waste of rice.  Mr. Pope began the pamphlet he had had in contemplation for some time upon the advantages to public order of Payment in Kind.  Theodore, who had washed behind his ears and laced his boots in all the holes, went into the yard before breakfast and hit a tennis ball against the wall and back, five hundred and twenty-two times—a record.  He would have resumed this after breakfast, but his father came round the corner of the house with a pen in his mouth, and asked him indistinctly, but fiercely, what the *devil* he was doing.  So he went away, and after a fretful interval set himself to revise his Latin irregular verbs.  By twelve he had done wonders.

Later in the day the widening circle of aggressive urgency reached the kitchen, and at two the cook gave notice in order, she said, to better herself.

Lunch, unconscious of this impending shadow, was characterised by a virtuous cheerfulness, and Aunt Plessington told in detail how her seven-and-twenty nephews and nieces, the children of her various sisters, were all getting on.  On the whole, they were not getting on so brilliantly as they might have done (which indeed is apt to be the case with the children of people who have loved not well but too wisely), and it was borne in upon the mind of the respectfully listening Marjorie that, to borrow an easy colloquialism of her aunt's, she might " take the shine out of the lot of them " with a very little zeal and effort—and of course Mr. Magnet.

The lecture in the evening at Summerhay was a great success.

The chair was taken by the Rev. Jopling Baynes, Lady Petchworth was enthroned behind the table, Hubert was in charge of his wife's notes—if notes should be needed—and Mr. Pope, expectant of an invitation at the end to say a few words about the East Purblow Experiment, also occupied a chair on the platform.  Lady Petchworth, with her abundant soft blond hair, brightly blond still in spite of her fifty-five years, her delicate features, her plump hands, her numerous chins and her entirely inaudible voice, made a pleasing contrast with Aunt Plessington's resolute personality.  She had perhaps an even greater assurance of authority, but it was a quiet assurance ; you felt that she knew that if she spoke in her sleep she would be obeyed, that it was quite unnecessary to make herself heard.  The two women, indeed, the one so assertive, the other so established, were at the opposite poles of authoritative British womanhood, and harmonised charmingly. The little room struck the note of a well-regulated brightness at every point. It had been decorated in a Keltic but entirely respectful style by one of Lady Petchworth's artistic discoveries, it was lit by paraffin lamps that smelled hardly at all, and it was gay with colour prints illustrating the growth of the British Empire from the battle of Ethandune to the surrender of Cronje. The hall was fairly full. Few could afford to absent themselves from these brightening occasions, but there was a tendency on the part of the younger and the less thoughtful section of the village manhood to accumulate at the extreme back and rumble in what appeared to be a slightly ironical spirit, so far as it had any spirit, with its feet.

The Rev. Jopling Baynes opened proceedings with a few well-chosen remarks, in which he complimented every one present either singly or collectively according to their rank and importance, and then Aunt Plessington came forward to the centre of the platform amidst a hectic flush of applause, and said " Haw ! " in a loud clear ringing tone.

She spoke without resorting to the notes in Hubert's little fist, very freely and easily. Her strangulated contralto went into every corner of the room and positively seemed to look for and challenge inattentive auditors. She had come over, she said, and she had been very glad to come over and talk to them that night, because it meant not only seeing them but meeting her very dear delightful friend Lady Petchworth (loud applause) and staying for a day or so with her brother-in-law Mr. Pope (unsupported outburst of applause from Mr. Magnet), to whom she and social reform generally owed so much. She had come to talk to them that night about the National Good Habits Movement, which was attracting so much attention and which bore so closely on our National Life and Character ; she happened to be—here Aunt Plessington smiled as she spoke—a humble person connected with that movement, just a mere woman connected with it ; she was going to explain to them as well as she could in her womanly way and in the time at her disposal just what it was and just what it was for, and just what means it adopted and just what ends it had in view. Well, they all knew what Habits were, and that there were Good Habits and Bad Habits, and she supposed that the difference between a good man and a bad man was just that the good man had good habits and the bad one had bad habits. Everybody she supposed wanted to get on. If a man had good habits he got on, and if he had bad habits he didn't get on, and she supposed it was the same with a country, if its people had good habits they got on, and if its people had bad habits they didn't get on. For her own part she and her husband (Hubert gave a little self-conscious jump) had always cultivated good habits, and she had to thank him with all her heart for his help in doing so. (Applause from

the front seats.)  Now, the whole idea of her movement was
to ask, how can we raise the standard of the national habits ?
how can we get rid of bad habits and cultivate good ones ?  . . .
(Here there was a slight interruption due to some one being
suddenly pushed off the end of a form at the back, and coming
to the floor with audible violence, after which a choked and
obstructed tittering continued intermittently for some time.)

Some of her audience, she remarked, had not yet acquired
the habit of sitting still.

(Laughter, and a coarse vulgar voice :  " Good old Billy
Punt ! ")

Well, to resume, she and her husband had made a special
and careful study of habits ; they had consulted all sorts of
people and collected all sorts of statistics, in fact they had
devoted themselves to this question, and the conclusion to
which they came was this, that Good Habits were acquired by
Training and Bad Habits came from neglect and carelessness
and leaving people, who weren't fit for such freedom, to run
about and do just whatever they liked.  And so, she went on
with a note of complete demonstration, the problem resolved
itself into the question of how far they could get more Training into the national life, and how they could check extravagant
and unruly and wasteful and unwise ways of living.  (Hear,
hear ! from Mr. Pope.)  And this was the problem she and her
husband had set themselves to solve.

(Scuffle, and a boy's voice at the back, saying :  " Oh, *shut*
it, Nuts !  SHUT it ! ")

Well, she and her husband had worked the thing out, and
they had come to the conclusion that what was the matter
with the great mass of English people was first that they had
rather too much loose money, and secondly that they had rather
too much loose time.  (A voice :  " What O ! " and the Rev.
Jopling Baynes suddenly extended his neck, knitted his
brows, and became observant of the interrupter.)  She did not
say they had too much money (a second voice :  " Not 'Arf ! "),
but too much *loose* money.  She did not say they had too much
time, but too much loose time, that is to say, they had money
and time they did not know how to spend properly.  And so
they got into mischief.  A great number of people in this
country, she maintained, and this was especially true of the
lower classes, did not know how to spend either money or
time ; they bought themselves wasteful things and injurious
things, and they frittered away their hours in all sorts of
foolish, unprofitable ways.  And, after the most careful and
scientific study of this problem, she and her husband had come
to the conclusion that two main principles must underlie any
remedial measures that were attempted, the first of which
was the Principle of Payment in Kind, which had already had
so interesting a trial at the great carriage works of East
Purblow, and the second, the Principle of Continuous Occupa-

tion, which had been recognised long ago in popular wisdom by that admirable proverb—or rather quotation—she believed it was a quotation, though she gave, she feared, very little time to poetry (" Better employed," from Mr. Pope)—

> " Satan finds some mischief still
> For idle hands to do."

(Irrepressible outbreak of wild and sustained applause from the back seats, and in a sudden lull a female voice asking in a flattened, thwarted tone : " Ain't there to be no lantern then ? ")

The lecturer went on to explain what was meant by either member of what perhaps they would permit her to call this double-barrelled social remedy.

It was an admirable piece of lucid exposition. Slowly the picture of a better, happier, more disciplined England grew upon the minds of the meeting. First she showed the new sort of employer her movement would evoke, an employer paternal, philanthropic, vaguely responsible for the social order of all his dependents. (Lady Petchworth was seen to nod her head slowly at this.) Only in the last resort, and when he was satisfied that his worker and his worker's family were properly housed, hygienically clothed and fed, attending suitable courses of instruction and free from any vicious inclinations, would he pay wages in cash. In the discharge of the duties of payment he would have the assistance of expert advice, and the stimulus of voluntary inspectors of his own class. He would be the natural clan master, the captain and leader, adviser and caretaker of his banded employees. Responsibility would stimulate him, and if responsibility did not stimulate him, inspectors (both men and women inspectors) would. The worker, on the other hand, would be enormously more healthy and efficient under the new régime. His home, designed by qualified and officially recognised architects, would be prettier as well as more convenient and elevating to his taste, his children admirably trained and dressed in the new and more beautiful clothing with which Lady Petchworth (applause) had done so much to make them familiar, his vital statistics compared with current results would be astonishingly good, his mind free from any anxiety but the proper anxiety of a man in his position, to get his work done properly and earn recognition from those competent and duly authorised to judge it. Of all this she spoke with the inspiring note of absolute conviction. All this would follow Payment in Kind and Continuous Occupation as the day follows sunrise. And there would always—and here Aunt Plessington's voice seemed to brighten—be something for the worker to get on with, something for him to do : lectures, classes, reading-rooms, improving entertainments. His time would be filled. The proper authorities would see that it was filled—and filled in the right

way. Never for a moment need he be bored. He would
never have an excuse for being bored. That was the second
great idea, the complementary idea to the first. " And here
it is," she said, turning a large encouraging smile on Lady
Petchworth, " that the work of a National Theatre, instructive,
stimulating, well regulated, and morally sustaining, would
come in." He wouldn't, of course, be *compelled* to go, but
there would be his seat, part of his payment in kind, and with
the public-house shut, most other temptations would be
removed. . . .

The lecture reached its end at last with only one other
interruption. Some would-be humorist suddenly inquired,
apropos of nothing : " What's the fare to America, Billy ? "
and a voice, presumably Billy's, answered him : " Mor'n
*you'll* ev 'av in *you'* pocket."

The Rev. Jopling Baynes, before he called upon Mr. Pope
for his promised utterance about East Purblow, could not
refrain from pointing out how silly " in every sense of the
word " these wanton interruptions were. What, he asked,
had English social reform to do with the fare to America ?—
and having roused the meeting to an alert silence by the
length of his pause, answered in a voice of ringing contempt :
" Nothing—*whatsoever.*" Then Mr. Pope made his few
remarks about East Purblow with the ease and finish that
come from long practice ; much, he said, had to be omitted
" in view of " the restricted time at his disposal, but he did
not grudge that, the time had been better filled. (" No, no,"
from Aunt Plessington.) Yes, yes—by the lucid and delightful
lecture they had all enjoyed, and he not least among them.
(Applause.) . . .

§ 11

They came out into a luminous blue night, with a crescent
young moon high overhead. It was so fine that the Popes
and the Plessingtons and Mr. Magnet declined Lady Petchworth's proffered car, and walked back to Buryhamstreet
across the park through a sleeping pallid cornfield, and along
by the edge of the pine woods. Mr. Pope would have liked
to walk with Mr. Magnet and explain all that the pressure
on his time had caused him to omit from his speech, and why
it was he had seen fit to omit this part and include that. Some
occult power, however, baffled this intention, and he found
himself going home in the company of his brother-in-law and
Daffy, with Aunt Plessington and his wife like a barrier between
him and his desire. Marjorie, on the other hand, found Mr.
Magnet's proximity inevitable. They fell a little behind and
were together again for the first time since her refusal.

He behaved, she thought, with very great restraint, and
indeed he left her a little doubtful on that occasion whether
he had not decided to take her decision as final. He talked

chiefly about the lecture, which had impressed him very deeply. Mrs. Plessington, he said, was so splendid—made him feel trivial. He felt stirred up by her, wanted to help in this social work, this picking up of helpless people from the muddle in which they wallowed.

He seemed not only extraordinarily modest but extraordinarily gentle that night, and the warm moonshine gave his face a shadowed earnestness it lacked in more emphatic lights. She felt the profound change in her feelings that had followed her rejection of him. It had cleared away the oppression from him. She had no longer any sense of entanglement and pursuit, and all the virtues his courtship had obscured shone clear again. He was kindly, he was patient—and she felt something about him a woman is said always to respect, he gave her an impression of ability. After all, he could with a movement of his little finger banish the trouble that crushed and overwhelmed her. Of all her load of debt he could earn the payment in a day.

" Your aunt goes to-morrow ? " he said.

Marjorie admitted it.

" I wish I could talk to her more. She's so inspiring."

" You know of our little excursion for Friday ? " he asked after a pause.

She had not heard. Friday was Theodore's birthday ; she knew it only too well because she had had to part with her stamp collection—which very luckily had chanced to get packed and come to Buryhamstreet—to meet its demand. Mr. Magnet explained he had thought it might be fun to give a picnic in honour of the anniversary.

" How jolly of you ! " said Marjorie.

" There's a pretty bit of river between Wamping and Friston Hanger—I've wanted you to see it for a long time, and Friston Hanger church has the prettiest view. The tower gets the bend of the river."

He told her all he meant to do as if he submitted his plans for her approval. They would drive to Wamping and get a very comfortable steam launch one could hire there. Wintersloan was coming down again ; an idle day of this kind just suited his temperament. Theodore would like it, wouldn't he ?

" Theodore will think he is King of Surrey ! "

" I'll have a rod and line if he wants to fish. I don't want to forget anything. I want it to be *his* day really and truly."

The slightest touch upon the pathetic note ? She could not tell.

But that evening brought Marjorie nearer to loving Magnet than she had ever been. Before she went to sleep that night she had decided he was quite a tolerable person again ; she had been too nervous and unjust with him. After all, his urgency and awkwardness had been just a part of his sincerity.

Perhaps the faint doubt whether he would make his request again gave the zest of uncertainty to his devotion. Of course, she told herself, he would ask again. And then the blissful air of limitless means she might breathe. The blessed release. . . .

She was suddenly fast asleep.

### § 12

Friday was after all not so much Theodore's day as Mr. Magnet's.

Until she found herself committed there was no shadow of doubt in Marjorie's mind of what she meant to do. " Before I see you again," said Aunt Plessington at the parting kiss, " I hope you'll have something to tell me." She might have been Hymen thinly disguised as an aunt, waving from the departing train. She continued by vigorous gestures and unstinted display of teeth and a fluttering handkerchief to encourage Marjorie to marry Mr. Magnet, until the curve of the cutting hid her from view. . . .

Fortune favoured Mr. Magnet with a beautiful day, and the excursion was bright and successful from the outset. It was well done, and what perhaps was more calculated to impress Marjorie, it was done with lavish generosity. From the outset she turned a smiling countenance upon her host. She did her utmost to suppress a reviving irrational qualm in her being, to maintain clearly and simply her overnight decision, that he should propose again and that she should accept him.

Yet the festival was just a little dream-like in its quality to her perceptions. She found she could not focus clearly on its details.

Two waggonettes came from Wamping ; there was room for everybody and to spare, and Wamping revealed itself a pleasant small country town with stocks under the market hall, and just that tint of green paint and that loafing touch the presence of a boating river gives.

The launch was brilliantly smart with abundant crimson cushions and a tasselled awning, and away to the left was a fine old bridge that dated in its essentials from Plantagenet times.

They started with much whistling and circling, and went away up-river under overhanging trees that sometimes swished the funnel, splashing the meadow path and making the reeds and bulrushes dance with their wash. They went through a reluctant lock, steamed up a long reach, they passed the queerly painted Potwell Inn with its picturesque group of poplars and its absurd new notice-board of " Omlets." . . . Theodore was five stone of active happiness ; he and the pseudo-twins, strictly under his orders as the universal etiquette of birthdays prescribes, clambered round and round the boat, clutching the awning rail and hanging over the water in an entirely secure and perilous-looking manner. No one, unless his father happened to be upset by something, would check him, he knew, on this auspicious day. Mr. Magnet sat with the grey eye on Marjorie and listened a little abstractedly to Mr. Pope, who was telling very fully what he would say if the Liberal party were to ask his advice at the present juncture. Mrs. Pope attended discreetly, and Daffy and Marjorie with a less restrained interest, to Mr. Wintersloan, who showed them how to make faces out of a fist tied up in a pocket-hand-kerchief, how to ventriloquise, how to conjure with halfpence—which he did very amusingly—and what the buttons on a man's sleeve were for ; Theodore clambering at his back discovered what he was at, and by right of birthday made him do all the faces and tricks over again. Then Mr. Wintersloan told stories of all the rivers along which, he said, he had travelled in steamboats ; the Rhine, the Danube, the Hoogly and the Fall River, and particularly how he had been bitten by a very young crocodile. " It's the smell of the oil brings it all back to me," he said. " And the kind of sway it gives you."

He made sinuous movements of his hand, and looked at Marjorie with that wooden yet expressive smile.

Friston Hanger proved to be even better than Wamping. It had a character of its own because it was built very largely of a warm buff-coloured local rock instead of the usual brick, and the outhouses at least of the little inn at which they landed were thatched. Most of the cottages had casement windows with diamond panes, and the streets were cobbled and very up and down hill. The place ran to high walls richly suggestive of hidden gardens, overhung by big trees and pierced by secretive important-looking doors. And over it all rose an unusually big church, with a tall buttressed tower surmounted by a lantern of pierced stone.

" We'll go through the town and look at the ruins of the old castle beyond the church," said Mr. Magnet to Marjorie, " and then I want you to see the view from the church tower."

And as they went through the street, he called her attention again to the church tower in a voice that seemed to her to be inexplicably charged with significance. " I want you to go up there," he said.

" How about something to eat, Mr. Magnet ? " remarked Theodore suddenly, and everybody felt surprised when Mr. Magnet answered : " Who wants things to eat on your birth-day, Theodore ? "

But they saw the joke of that when they reached the castle ruins and found in the old tilting yard, with its ivy-covered arch framing a view of the town and stream, a table spread with a white cloth that shone in the sunshine, glittering with glass and silver and gay with a bowl of salad and flowers and

cold pies and a jug of claret-cup and an ice pail—a silver pail !
containing two promising-looking bottles—in the charge of
two real live waiters, in evening-dress as waiters should be,
but with straw hats to protect them from the sun and weather.
" Oh ! " cried Mrs. Pope, " what a *splendid* idea, Mr. Magnet,"
when the destination of the feast was perfectly clear, and even
Theodore seemed slightly overawed—almost as if he felt his
birthday was being carried too far and might provoke a
judgment later. Manifestly Mr. Magnet must have ordered
this in London, and have had it sent down, waiters and all !
Theodore knew he was a very wonderful little boy in spite
of the acute criticism of four devoted sisters, and Mr. Magnet
had noticed him before at times, but this was, well, rather
immense ! " Look at the pie-crusts, old man ! " And on
the pie-crusts, and on the icing of the cake, their munificent
host had caused to be done in raised letters of dough and
chocolate the word " Theodore."

" Oh, *Mr.* Magnet ! " said Marjorie—his eye so obviously
invited her to say something. Mr. Pope tried a nebulous joke
about " groaning boards of Frisky Hanger," and only Mr.
Wintersloan restrained his astonishment and admiration.
" You could have got those chaps in livery," he said—unheeded. The lunch was as a matter of fact his idea ; he had
refused to come unless it was provided, and he had somehow
counted on blue coats, brass buttons, and yellow waistcoats—
but everybody else of course ascribed the whole invention to
Mr. Magnet.

" Well," said Mr. Pope with a fine air of epigram, " the only
thing I can say is—to eat it," and prepared to sit down.

" Melon," cried Mr. Magnet to the waiters, " we'll begin
with the melon. Have you ever tried melon with pepper and
salt, Mrs. Pope ? "

" You put salt in everything," admired Mr. Pope. " Salt
from those attics of yours—Attic salt."

" Or there's ginger ! " said Mr. Magnet, after a whisper from
the waiter.

Mr. Pope said something classical about " ginger hot in the
mouth."

" Some of these days," said Mr. Wintersloan, " when I have
exhausted all other sensations, I mean to try melon and
mustard."

Rom made a wonderful face at him.

" I can think of worse things than that," said Mr. Wintersloan with a hard brightness.

" Not till after lunch, Mr. Wintersloan ! " said Rom heartily.

" The claret-cup's all right for Theodore, Mrs. Pope," said
Magnet. " It's a special twelve-year-old brand." (He
thought of everything !)

" Mummy," said Mr. Pope, " you'd better carve this pie,
I think."

" I want very much," said Mr. Magnet in Marjorie's ear and very confidentially, " to show you the view from the church tower.  I think—it will appeal to you."

" Rom ! " said Theodore, uncontrollably, in a tremendous stage whisper, "there's peaches ! . . . *There* ! on the hamper ! "

" Champagne, ma'am ? " said the waiter suddenly in Mrs. Pope's ear, wiping ice-water from the bottle.

(But what could it have cost him ?)

### § 13

Marjorie would have preferred that Mr. Magnet should not have decided with such relentless determination to make his second proposal on the church tower.  His purpose was luminously clear to her from the beginning of lunch onward, and she could feel her nerves going under the strain of that long expectation.  She tried to pull herself together, tried not to think about it, tried to be amused by the high spirits and nonsense of Mr. Wintersloan and Syd and Rom and Theodore ; but Mr. Magnet was very pervasive, and her mother didn't ever look at her, looked past her and away from her and all round her, in a profoundly observant manner.  Marjorie felt chiefly anxious to get to the top of that predestinate tower and have the whole thing over, and it was with a start that she was just able to prevent one of the assiduous waiters filling her glass with champagne for the third time.

There was a little awkwardness in dispersing after lunch.  Mr. Pope, his heart warmed by the champagne and mellowed by a subsequent excellent cigar, wanted very much to crack what he called a " post-prandial jest " or so with the great humorist, while Theodore also, deeply impressed with the discovery that there was more in Mr. Magnet than he had supposed, displayed a strong disposition to attach himself more closely than he had hitherto done to this remarkable person, and study his quiet but enormous possibilities with greater attention.  Mrs. Pope with a still alertness did her best to get people adjusted, but Syd and Rom had conceived a base and unnatural desire to subjugate the affections of the youngest waiter, and wouldn't listen to her proposal that they should take Theodore away into the town ;  Mr. Wintersloan displayed extraordinary cunning and resource in evading a *tête-à-tête* with Mr. Pope that would have released Mr. Magnet.  Now Mrs. Pope came to think of it, Mr. Wintersloan never had had the delights of a good talk with Mr. Pope, he knew practically nothing about the East Purblow Experiment except for what Mr. Magnet might have retailed to him, and she was very greatly puzzled to account for his almost manifest reluctance to go into things thoroughly.  Daffy remained on hand, available but useless, and Mrs. Pope, smiling at the landscape and a prey to Management within, was suddenly inspired to take her eldest daughter into her confidence.

"Daffy," she said, with a guileful finger extended and pointing to the lower sky as though she was pointing out the less obvious and more atmospheric beauties of Surrey, "get Theodore away from Mr. Magnet if you can. He wants to talk to Marjorie."

Daffy looked round. "Shall I call him ? " she said.

"No," said Mrs. Pope, "do it—just—quietly."

"I'll try," said Daffy and stared at her task, and Mrs. Pope, feeling that this might or might not succeed but that anyhow she had done what she could, strolled across to her husband and laid a connubial touch upon his shoulder. "All the young people," she said, "are burning to climb the church tower. I never *can* understand this activity after lunch."

"Not me," said Mr. Pope. "Eh, Magnet ? "

"*I'm* game," said Theodore. "Come along, Mr. Magnet."

"I think," said Mr. Magnet, looking at Marjorie, "I shall go up. I want to show Marjorie the view."

"We'll stay here, Mummy, eh ? " said Mr. Pope, with a quite unusual geniality, and suddenly put his arm round Mrs. Pope's waist. Her motherly eye sought Daffy's, and indicated her mission. "I'll come with you, Theodore," said Daffy. "There isn't room for every one at once up that tower."

"I'll go with Mr. Magnet," said Theodore, relying firmly on the privileges of the day. . . .

For a time they played for position, with the intentions of Mr. Magnet showing more and more starkly through the moves of the game. At last Theodore was lured down a side street by the sight of a huge dummy fish dangling outside a tackle-and-bait shop, and Mr. Magnet and Marjorie, already with a dreadful feeling of complicity, made a movement so rapid it seemed to her almost a bolt for the church tower. Whatever Mr. Magnet desired to say, and whatever elasticity his mind had once possessed with regard to it, there can be no doubt that it had now become so rigid as to be sayable only in that one precise position, and in the exact order he had determined upon. But when at last they got to that high serenity, Mr. Magnet was far too hot and far too much out of breath to say anything at all for a time except an almost explosive gust or so of approbation of the scenery. "Shor'breath ! " he said, "win'ey stairs always—that 'fect on me—buful sceny—Suwy—like it always."

Marjorie found herself violently disposed to laugh ; indeed she had never before been so near the verge of hysterics.

"It's a perfectly lovely view," she said. "No wonder you wanted me to see it."

"Naturally," said Mr. Magnet, "wanted you to see it."

Marjorie, with a skill her mother might have envied, wriggled into a half-sitting position in an embrasure and concentrated herself upon the broad wooded undulations that went about the horizon, and Mr. Magnet mopped his face with surreptitious gestures, and took deep restoring breaths.

" I've always wanted to bring you here," he said, " ever since I found it in the spring."

" It was very kind of you, Mr. Magnet," said Marjorie.

" You see," he explained, " whenever I see anything fine or rich or splendid or beautiful now, I seem to want it for you." His voice quickened as though he were repeating something that had been long in his mind. " I wish I could give you all this country. I wish I could put all that is beautiful in the world at your feet."

He watched the effect of this upon her for a moment.

" Marjorie," he said, " did you really mean what you told me the other day, that there was indeed no hope for me ? I have a sort of feeling I bothered you that day, that perhaps you didn't mean all——"

He stopped short.

" I don't think I knew what I meant," said Marjorie, and Magnet gave a queer sound of relief at her words. " I don't think I know what I mean now. I don't think I can say I love you, Mr. Magnet. I would if I could. I like you very much indeed, I think you are awfully kind, you're more kind and generous than any one I have ever known. . . ."

Saying he was kind and generous made her through some obscure association of ideas feel that he must have understanding. She had an impulse to put her whole case before him frankly. " I wonder," she said, " if you can understand what it is to be a girl ? "

Then she saw the absurdity of her idea, of any such miracle of sympathy. He was entirely concentrated upon the appeal he had come prepared to make.

" Marjorie," he said, " I don't ask you to love me yet. All I ask is that you shouldn't decide *not* to love me."

Marjorie became aware of Theodore, hotly followed by Daffy, in the churchyard below. " I *know* he's up there," Theodore was manifestly saying.

Marjorie faced her lover gravely.

" Mr. Magnet," she said, " I will certainly promise you that."

" I would rather be your servant, rather live for your happiness, than do anything else in all the world," said Mr. Magnet. " If you would trust your life to me, if you would deign——" He paused to recover his thread. " If you would deign to let me make life what it should be for you, take every care from your shoulders, face every responsibility——"

Marjorie felt she had to hurry. She could almost feel the feet of Theodore coming up that tower.

" Mr. Magnet," she said, " you don't understand. You don't realise what I am. You don't know how unworthy I am —what a mere ignorant child——"

" Let me be judge of that ! " cried Mr. Magnet.

They paused almost like two actors who listen for the prompter. It was only too obvious that both were aware of a little medley of imperfectly subdued noises below. Theodore had got to the ladder that made the last part of the ascent, and there Daffy had collared him. " *My* birthday," said Theodore. " Come down ! You *shan't* go up there ! " said Daffy. " You *mustn't,* Theodore ! " " Why not ? " There was something like a scuffle, and whispers. Then it would seem Theodore went—reluctantly and with protests. But the conflict receded.

" Marjorie ! " said Mr. Magnet, as though there had been no pause, " if you would consent only to make an experiment, if you would try to love me. Suppose you *tried* an engagement. I do not care how long I waited. . . ."

He paused. " Will you try ? " he urged upon her distressed silence.

She felt as though she forced the word. " *Yes* ! " she said in a very low voice.

Then it seemed to her that Mr. Magnet leaped upon her. She felt herself pulled almost roughly from the embrasure, and he had kissed her. She struggled in his embrace. " Mr. Magnet ! " she said. He lifted her face and kissed her lips. " Marjorie ! " he said, and she had partly released herself.

" Oh, *don't* kiss me," she cried, " don't kiss me yet ! "

" But a kiss ! "

" I don't like it."

" I beg your pardon ! " he said. " I forgot—— But you. . . . You. . . . I couldn't help it."

She was suddenly wildly sorry for what she had done. She felt she was going to cry, to behave absurdly.

" I want to go down," she said.

" Marjorie, you have made me the happiest of men ! All my life, all my strength I will spend in showing you that you have made no mistake in trusting me——"

" Yes," she said, " yes," and wondered what she could say or do. It seemed to him that her shrinking pose was the most tenderly modest thing he had ever seen.

" Oh, my dear ! " he said, and restrained himself and took her passive hand and kissed it.

" I want to go down to them ! " she insisted.

He paused on the topmost rung of the ladder, looking unspeakable things at her. Then he turned to go down, and for the second time in her life she saw that incipient thinness. . . .

" I am sure you will never be sorry," he said. . . .

They found Mr. and Mrs. Pope in the churchyard. Mr. Pope was reading with amusement for the third time an epitaph that had caught his fancy—

> " Lands ever bright, days ever fair,
>     And yet we weep that *he* is there "

he read. " You know, that's really Good. That ought to be printed somewhere."

Mrs. Pope glanced sharply at her daughter's white face, and found an enigma. Then she looked at Mr. Magnet.

There was no mistake about Mr. Magnet. Marjorie had accepted him, whatever else she had felt or done.

§ 14

Marjorie's feelings for the rest of the day are only to be accounted for on the supposition that she was overwrought. She had a preposterous reaction. She had done this thing with her eyes open after days of deliberation, and now she felt as though she was caught in a trap. The clearest thing in her mind was that Mr. Magnet had taken hold of her and kissed her, kissed her on the lips, and that presently he would do it again. And also she was asking herself with futile reiteration why she had got into debt at Oxbridge ? Why had she got into debt ? For such silly little things too !

Nothing definite was said in her hearing about the engagement, but everybody seemed to understand. Mr. Pope was the most demonstrative, he took occasion to rap her hard upon the back, his face crinkled with a resolute kindliness. " Ah ! " he said, " sly Maggots ! "

He also administered several resounding blows to Magnet's shoulder-blades, and irradiated the party with a glow of benevolent waggery. Marjorie submitted without an answer to these paternal intimations. Mrs. Pope did no more than watch her daughter. Invisible but overwhelming forces were busy in bringing Marjorie and her glowing lover alone together again. It happened at last, as he was departing ; she was almost to her inflamed imagination thrust out upon him, had to take him to the gate ; and there in the shadow of the trees he kissed her " good night " with passionate effusion.

" Madge," he said, " Madge ! "

She made no answer. She submitted passively to his embrace, and then suddenly and dexterously disengaged herself from him, ran in, and without saying good-night to any one went to her room and to bed.

Mr. Pope was greatly amused by this departure from the customary routine of life, and noted it archly.

When Daffy came up, Marjorie was ostentatiously going to sleep. . . .

As she herself was dropping off, Daffy became aware of an odd sound, somehow familiar, and yet surprising and disconcerting.

Suddenly, wide awake again, she started up. Yes, there was no mistake about it ! And yet it was very odd.

" Madge, what's up ? "

No answer.

" I say ! you aren't crying, Madge, are you ? "

Then after a long interval : " *Madge !* "

An answer came in a muffled voice, almost as if Marjorie had something in her mouth.   " Oh, shut it, old Daffy."

" But, Madge ? " said Daffy after reflection.

" Shut it.   *Do* shut it !  Leave me alone, I say !   Can't you leave me alone ?   Oh ! "—and for a moment she let her sobs have way with her—" Daffy, don't worry me.   Old Daffy !   *Please !* "

Daffy sat up for a long time in the stifled silence that ensued, and then like a sensible sister gave it up, and composed herself again to slumber. . . .

Outside, watching the window in a state of nebulous ecstasy, was Mr. Magnet, moonlit and dewy.   It was a high serene night with a growing moon and a scattered company of major stars, and if no choir of nightingales sang there was at least a very active nightjar.   " More than I hoped," whispered Mr. Magnet, " more than I dared to hope."   He was very sleepy, but it seemed to him improper to go to bed on such a night— on such an occasion.

# CHAPTER THREE

## THE MAN WHO FELL OUT OF THE SKY

### § 1

FOR the next week Marjorie became more nearly intro-
spective than she had ever been in her life before.
She began to doubt her hitherto unshaken conviction
that she was a single, consistent human being. She found
such discords and discrepancies between mood and mood,
between the conviction of this hour and the feeling of that,
that it seemed to her she was rather a collection of samples
of emotion and attitude than anything so simple as an
individual.

For example, there can be no denying there was one Marjorie
in the bundle who was immensely set up by the fact that she
was engaged, and going to be at no very remote date mistress
of a London house. She was profoundly Plessingtonian, and
quite the vulgarest of the lot. The new status she had
attained and the possibly beautiful house and the probably
successful dinner-parties and the arrangement and importance
of it was the substance of this creature's thought. She
designed some queenly dresses. This was the Marjorie most
in evidence when it came to talking with her mother and
Daphne. I am afraid she patronised Daphne, and ignored the
fact that Daphne, who had begun with a resolute magna-
nimity, was becoming annoyed and resentful.

And she thought of things she might buy, and the jolly
feeling of putting them about and making fine effects with
them. One thing, she told Daphne, she had clearly resolved
upon : the house should be always full and brimming over
with beautiful flowers. " I've always wished mother would
have more flowers—and not keep them so long when she has
them. . . ."

Another Marjorie in the confusion of her mind was doing
her sincerest, narrow best to appreciate and feel grateful for
and return the devotion of Mr. Magnet. This Marjorie
accepted and even elaborated his views, laid stress on his
voluntary subjection, harped upon his goodness, brought her
to kiss him.

" I don't deserve all this love," this side of Marjorie told
Magnet. " But I mean to learn to love you———"

" My dear one ! " cried Magnet, and pressed her hand. . . .

A third Marjorie among the many was an altogether acuter
and less agreeable person. She was a sprite of pure criticism,
and in spite of the utmost efforts to suppress her, she declared
night and day in the inner confidences of Marjorie's soul that
she did not believe in Mr. Magnet's old devotion at all. She

was anti-Magnet, a persistent insurgent. She was dreadfully
unsettling. It was surely this Marjorie that wouldn't let the
fact of his baldness alone, and who discovered and insisted
upon a curious unbeautiful flatness in his voice whenever he
was doing his best to speak from the heart. And as for this
devotion, what did it amount to ? A persistent, unimagina-
tive besetting of Marjorie, a growing air of ownership, an
expansive, undulgent, smiling disposition to thwart and
control. And he was always touching her ! Whenever he
came near her she would wince at the freedoms a large, kind
hand might take with her elbow or wrist, at a possible sudden
clumsy pat at some erring strand of hair.

Then there was an appraising satisfaction in his eye.

On the third day of their engagement he began, quite
abruptly, to call her " Magsy." " We'll end this scandal of
a Girl Pope," he said. " Magsy Magnet, you'll be—M.M.
No women M.P.s for *us*, Magsy. . . ."

She became acutely critical of his intellectual quality. She
listened with a new alertness to the conversations at the dinner-
table, the bouts of wit with her father. She carried off utter-
ances and witticisms for maturer reflection. She was amazed
to find how little they could withstand the tests and acids
of her mind. So many things, such wide and interesting
fields, he did not so much think about as cover with a large
enveloping shallowness. . . .

He came strolling round the vicarage into the garden one
morning about eleven, though she had not expected him until
lunch-time ; and she was sitting with her feet tucked up
on the aged but still practicable garden-seat reading Shaw's
*Common Sense of Municipal Trading*. He came and leaned
over the back of the seat, and she looked up, said " Good
morning. Isn't it perfectly lovely ? " and indicated by a
book still open that her interest in it remained alive.

" What's the book, Magsy ? " he asked, took it out of
her slightly resisting hand, closed it and read the title. " Um,"
he said ; " isn't this a bit stiff for little women's brains ? "

All the rebel Marjories were up in arms at that.

" Dreadful word, ' Municipal.' I *don't* like it." He shook
his head with a grimace of humorous distaste.

" I suppose women have as good brains as men," said
Marjorie, " if it comes to that."

" Better," said Magnet. " That's why they shouldn't
trouble about horrid things like Municipal and Trading. . . .
On a day like this ! "

" Don't you think this sort of thing is interesting ? "

" Oh ! " he said, and flourished the book. " Come ! And
besides—*Shaw* ! "

" He makes a very good case."

" But he's such a—mountebank."

" Does that matter ? He isn't a mountebank there."

"He's not sincere. I doubt if you had a serious book on Municipal Trading, Magsy, whether you'd make head or tail of it. It's a stiff subject. Shaw just gets his chance for a smart thing or so. . . . I'd rather you read a good novel."

He really had the air of taking her reading in hand.

"You think I ought not to read an intelligent book."

"I think we ought to leave those things to the people who understand."

"But we ought to understand."

He smiled wisely. "There's a lot of things *you* have to understand," he said, "nearer home than this."

Marjorie was ablaze now. "What a silly thing to say !" she cried, with an undergraduate's freedom. "Really, you are talking nonsense ! I read that book because it interests me. If I didn't, I should read something else. Do you mean to suggest that I'm reading like a child, who holds a book upside down ?"

She was so plainly angry that he was taken aback. "I don't mean to suggest——" he began, and turned to greet the welcome presence, the interrogative eye of Mrs. Pope.

"Here we are !" he said, "having a quarrel !"

"Marjorie !" said Mrs. Pope.

"Oh, it's serious !" said Mr. Magnet, and added with a gleam : "It's about Municipal Trading !"

Mrs. Pope knew the wicked flicker in Marjorie's eye better than Mr. Magnet. She had known it from the nursery, and yet she had never quite mastered its meaning. She had never yet realised it was Marjorie, she had always regarded it as something other Marjorie, some other Marjorie, ought to keep under control. So now she adopted a pacificatory tone.

"Oh ! lovers' quarrels," she said, floating over the occasion. "Lovers' quarrels. You mustn't ask *me* to interfere !"

Marjorie, already ashamed of her heat, thought for an instant she ought to stand that, and then decided abruptly with a return to choler that she would not do so. She stood up, and held out her hand for her book.

"Mr. Magnet," she said to her mother with remarkable force and freedom as she took it, "has been talking unutterable nonsense. I don't call that a lovers' quarrel—anyhow."

Then, confronted with a double astonishment, and having no more to say, she picked up her skirt quite unnecessarily, and walked with a heavenward chin indoors.

"I'm afraid," explained Mr. Magnet, "I was rather too free with one of Magsy's favourite authors."

"Which is the favourite author now ?" asked Mrs. Pope, after a reflective pause, with a mother's indulgent smile.

"Shaw." He raised amused eyebrows. "It's just the age, I suppose."

"She's frightfully loyal while it lasts," said Mrs. Pope. "No one dare say a word against them."

" I think it's adorable of her," said Mr. Magnet—with an
answering loyalty and gusto.

§ 2

The aviation accident occurred while Mrs. Pope, her two
eldest daughters, and Mr. Magnet were playing golf-croquet
upon the vicarage lawn. It was a serene, hot afternoon,
much too hot to take a game seriously, and the four little
figures moved slowly over the green and grouped and dispersed
as the game required. Mr. Magnet was very fond of golf-
croquet, he displayed a whimsical humour and much invention
at this game, it was not too exacting physically ; and he could
make his ball jump into the air in the absurdest manner.
Occasionally he won a laugh from Marjorie or Daffy. No one
else was in sight ; the pseudo-twins and Theodore and Toupee
were in the barn, and Mr. Pope was six miles away at Wamping,
lying prone, nibbling grass blades and watching a county
cricket match, as every good Englishman, who knows what is
expected of him, loves to do. . . . Click went ball and mallet,
and then after a long interval, click. It seemed incredible
that anything could possibly happen before tea.

But this is no longer the world it was. Suddenly this
tranquil scene was slashed and rent by the sound and vision of
a monoplane tearing across the heavens.

A purring and popping arrested Mr. Magnet in mid-jest,
and the monster came sliding up the sky over the trees beside
the church to the east, already near enough to look big, a great
stiff shape, big buff sails stayed with glittering wire, and with
two wheels beneath its body. It drove up the sky, rising with
a sort of upward heaving, until the croquet players could see
the driver and a passenger perched behind him quite clearly.
It passed to the right of the church tower and only a few yards
above the level of the flagstaff, there wasn't fifty feet of clear-
ance altogether, and as it did so Marjorie could see both driver
and passenger making hasty movements. It became immense
and overshadowing, and every one stood rigid as it swept
across the sun above the vicarage chimneys. Then it seemed
to drop twenty feet or so abruptly, and then both the men
cried out as it drove straight for the line of poplars between
the shrubbery and the meadow. " Oh, oh, OH ! " cried
Mrs. Pope and Daffy. Evidently the aviator was trying to
turn sharply ; the huge thing banked, but not enough, and
came about and slipped away until its wing was slashing into
the tree tops with a thrilling swish of leaves and the snapping of
branches and stays.

" Run ! " cried Magnet, and danced about the lawn, and
the three ladies rushed sideways as the whole affair slouched
down on them. It came on its edge, hesitated whether to
turn over as a whole, then crumpled, and amidst a volley of
smashing and snapping came to rest amidst ploughed-up

turf, a clamorous stench of petrol, and a cloud of dust and blue smoke within twenty yards of them. The two men had jumped to clear the engine, had fallen headlong, and were now both covered by the fabric of the shattered wing.

It was all too spectacular for word or speech until the thing lay still. Even then the croquet players stood passive for a while, waiting for something to happen. It took some seconds to reconcile their minds to this sudden loss of initiative in a monster that had been so recently and threateningly full of go. It seemed quite a long time before it came into Marjorie's head that she ought perhaps to act in some way. She saw a tall young man wriggling on all-fours from underneath the wreckage of fabric. He stared at her rather blankly. She went forward with a vague idea of helping him. He stood up, swayed doubtfully on his legs, turned, and became energetic, struggling mysteriously with the edge of the left wing. He gasped and turned fierce blue eyes over his shoulder.

" Help me to hold the confounded thing up ! " he cried, with a touch of irritation in his voice at her attitude.

Marjorie at once seized the edge of the plane and pushed. The second man, in a peculiar button-shaped head-dress, was lying crumpled up underneath, his ear and cheek were bright with blood, and there was a streak of blood on the ground near his head.

" That's right. Can you hold it if I use only one hand ? "

Marjorie gasped " Yes," with a terrific weight as it seemed suddenly on her wrists.

" Righto," and the tall young man had thrust himself backward under the plane until it rested on his back, and collared the prostrate man. " Keep it up ! " he said fiercely when Marjorie threatened to give way. He seemed to assume that she was there to obey orders, and with much grunting and effort he had dragged his companion clear of the wreckage.

The man's face was a mass of blood, and he was sickeningly inert to his companion's lugging.

" Let it go," said the tall young man, and Marjorie thanked heaven as the broken wing flapped down again.

She came helpfully to his side, and became aware of Daffy and her mother a few paces off. Magnet—it astonished her— was retreating hastily. But he had to go away because the sight of blood upset him—so much that it was always wiser for him to go away.

" Is he hurt ? " cried Mrs. Pope.

" We both are," said the tall young man, and then, as though these other people didn't matter and he and Marjorie were old friends, he said : " Can we turn him over ? "

" I think so," said Marjorie, grasped the damaged man's shoulder and got him over skilfully.

" Will you get some water ? " said the tall young man to Daffy and Mrs. Pope, in a way that sent Daffy off at once for a pail.

"He wants water," she said to the parlour-maid who was hurrying out of the house.

The tall young man had gone down on his knees by his companion, releasing his neck, and making a hasty first examination of his condition. "The pneumatic cap must have saved his head," he said, throwing the thing aside. "Lucky he had it. He can't be badly hurt. Just rubbed his face along the ground. Silly thing to have come as we did."

He felt the heart, and tried the flexibility of an arm.

"*That's* all right," he said.

He became judicial and absorbed over the problems of his friend's side. "Um," he remarked. He knelt back and regarded Marjorie for the first time. "Thundering smash," he said. His face relaxed into an agreeable smile. "He only bought it last week."

"Is he hurt?"

"Rib, I think—or two ribs perhaps. Stunned rather. All *this*—just his nose."

He regarded Marjorie and Marjorie him for a brief space. He became aware of Mrs. Pope on his right hand. Then at a clank behind, he turned round to see Daphne advancing with a pail of water. The two servants were now on the spot, and the odd-job man, and the old lady who did out the church, and Magnet hovered doubtfully in the distance. Suddenly with shouts and barks of sympathetic glee the pseudo-twins, Theodore and Toupee, shot out of the house. New thoughts were stirring in the young aviator. He rose, wincing as he did so. "I'm afraid I'm a little rude," he said.

"I do hope your friend isn't hurt," said Mrs. Pope, feeling the duty of a hostess.

"He's not hurt *much*—so far as I can see. Haven't we made rather a mess of your lawn?"

"Oh, not at all!" said Mrs. Pope.

"We have. If that is your gardener over there, it would be nice if he kept back the people who seem to be hesitating beyond those trees. There will be more presently. I'm afraid I must throw myself on your hands." He broke into a chuckle for a moment. "I have, you know. Is it possible to get a doctor? My friend's not hurt so very much, but still he wants expert handling. He's Sir Rupert Solomonson, from "—he jerked his head back—"over beyond Tunbridge Wells. My name's Trafford."

"I'm Mrs. Pope, and these are my daughters."

Trafford bowed. "We just took the thing out for a lark," he said.

Marjorie had been regarding the prostrate man. His mouth was open, and he showed beautiful teeth. Apart from the dry blood upon him he was not an ill-looking man. He was manifestly a Jew, a square-rigged Jew (you have remarked of course that there are square-rigged Jews, whose noses are within bounds, and fore-and-aft Jews, whose noses aren't), with not so much a bullet-head as a round-shot, cropped like the head of a Capuchin monkey. Suddenly she was down and had his head on her knee, with a quick movement that caught Trafford's eye. " He's better," she said. " His eyelids flickered. Daffy, bring the water."

She had felt a queer repugnance at first with this helpless man, but now that professional nurse who lurks in the composition of so many women, was uppermost. " Give me your handkerchief," she said to Trafford, and with Daffy kneeling beside her and also interested, and Mrs. Pope a belated but more experienced and authoritative third, Sir Rupert was soon getting the best of attention.

" Wathall . . ." said Sir Rupert suddenly, and tried again : " Wathall." A third effort gave " Wathall about, eh ? "

" If we could get him into the shade," said Marjorie.

" Woosh," cried Sir Rupert. " Weeeooo ! "

" That's all right," said Trafford. " It's only a rib or two."

" Eeeeeyoooo ! " said Sir Rupert.

" Exactly. We're going to carry you out of the glare."

" Don't touch me," said Sir Rupert. " Gooo."

It took some persuasion before Sir Rupert would consent to be moved, and even then he was for a time—oh ! crusty. But presently Trafford and the two girls had got him into the shade of a large bush close to where in a circle of rugs and cushions the tea-things lay prepared. There they camped. The helpful odd-job man was ordered to stave off intruders from the village ; water, towels, pillows were forthcoming. Mr. Magnet reappeared as tentative assistance, and Solomonson became articulate and brave and said he'd nothing but a stitch in his side. In his present position he wasn't at all uncomfortable. Only he didn't want any one near him. He enforced that by an appealing smile. The twins, invited to fetch the doctor, declined, proffering Theodore. They had conceived juvenile passions for the tall young man, and did not want to leave him. He certainly had a very nice face. So Theodore, after walking twice round the wreckage, tore himself away and departed on Rom's bicycle. Inquiry centred on Solomonson for a time. His face, hair and neck were wet but no longer bloody, and he professed perfect comfort so long as he wasn't moved, and no one came too near him. He was very clear about that, though scrupulously polite, and scrutinised their faces to see if they were equally clear. Satisfied upon this point he closed his eyes and spoke no more. He looked then like a Capuchin monkey lost in pride. There came a pause. Every one was conscious of having risen to an emergency and behaved well under unusual circumstances. The young man's eye rested on the adjacent tea-things, lacking nothing but the coronation of the teapot.

" Why not," he remarked, " have tea ? "

"If you think your friend——" began Mrs. Pope.

"Oh! *he's* all right. Aren't you, Solomonson? There's nothing more now until the doctor."

"Only want to be left alone," said Solomonson, and closed his heavy eyelids again.

Mrs. Pope told the maids, with an air of dismissal, to get tea.

"We can keep an eye on him," said Trafford.

Marjorie surveyed her first patient with a pretty unconscious mixture of maternal gravity and girlish interest, and the twins, to avoid too openly gloating upon the good looks of Trafford, chose places and secured cushions round the tea-things, calculating to the best of their ability how they might secure the closest proximity to him. Mr. Magnet and Toupee had gone to stare at the monoplane; they were presently joined by the odd-job man in an interrogative mood. "Pretty complete smash, sir!" said the odd-job man, and then perceiving heads over the hedge by the churchyard, turned back to his duty of sentinel. Daffy thought of the need of more cups and plates and went in to get them, and Mrs. Pope remarked that she did hope Sir Rupert was not badly hurt. . . .

"Extraordinary all this is," remarked Mr. Trafford. "Now, here we were after lunch, twenty miles away—smoking cigars and with no more idea of having tea with you than—I was going to say—flying. But that's out of date now. Then we just thought we'd try the thing. . . . Like a dream."

He addressed himself to Marjorie: "I never feel that life is quite real until about three days after things have happened. Never. Two hours ago I had not the slightest intention of ever flying again."

"But haven't you flown before?" asked Mrs. Pope.

"Not much. I did a little at Sheppey, but it's so hard for a poor man to get his hands on a machine. And here was Solomonson, with this thing in his hangar, eating its head off. 'Let's take it out,' I said, 'and go once round the park.' And here we are. . . . I thought it wasn't wise for him to come. . . ."

Sir Rupert, without opening his eyes, was understood to assent.

"Do you know," said Trafford, "the sight of your tea makes me feel frightfully hungry."

"I don't think the engine's damaged," he said cheerfully, "do you?" as Magnet joined them. "The ailerons are in splinters, and the left wing's not much better. But that's about all except the wheels. One falls so much lighter than you might suppose—from the smash. . . . Lucky it didn't turn over. Then, you know, the engine comes on the top of you, and you're done."

§ 3

The doctor arrived after tea, with a bag and a stethoscope in a small coffin-like box, and the Popes and Mr. Magnet

withdrew while Sir Rupert was carefully sounded, tested,
scrutinised, questioned, watched and examined in every way
known to medical science. The outcome of the conference
was presently communicated to the Popes by Mr. Trafford
and the doctor. Sir Rupert was not very seriously injured,
but he was suffering from concussion and shock, two of his
ribs were broken and his wrist sprained, unless perhaps one
of the small bones was displaced. He ought to be bandaged
up and put to bed. . . .

   " Couldn't we——" said Mrs. Pope, but the doctor assured
her his own house was quite the best place. There Sir Rupert
could stay for some days. At present the cross-country
journey over the Downs or by the South-Eastern Railway
would be needlessly trying and painful. He would with the
Popes' permission lie quietly where he was for an hour or so,
and then the doctor would come with a couple of men and a
carrying bed he had, and take him off to his own house.
There he would be, as Mr. Trafford said, " as right as nine-
pence," and Mr. Trafford could put up either at the Red Lion
with Mr. Magnet or in the little cottage next door to the
doctor. (Mr. Trafford elected for the latter as closer to his
friend.) As for the smashed aeroplane, telegrams would be
sent at once to Sir Rupert's engineers at Chesilbury, and
they would have all that cleared away by midday to-
morrow. . . .

   The doctor departed ; Sir Rupert, after stimulants, closed
his eyes, and Mr. Trafford seated himself at the tea-things
for some more cake, as though introduction by aeroplane
was the most regular thing in the world.

   He had pleasant and easy manners, an entire absence of
self-consciousness, and a quick talkative disposition that
made him very rapidly at home with everybody. He described all the sensations of flight, his early lessons and experiments, and in the utmost detail the events of the afternoon
that had led to this disastrous adventure. He made his
suggestion of " trying the thing " seem the most natural
impulse in the world. The bulk of the conversation fell on
him ; Mr. Magnet, save for the intervention of one or two
jests, was quietly observant ; the rest were well disposed to
listen. And as Mr. Trafford talked his eye rested ever and
again on Marjorie with the faintest touch of scrutiny and
perplexity, and she, too, found a curious persuasion growing
up in her mind that somewhere, somehow, she and he had met
and had talked rather earnestly. But how and where eluded
her altogether. . . .

   They had sat for an hour—the men from the doctor's
seemed never coming—when Mr. Pope returned unexpectedly
from his cricket match, which had ended prematurely in a
rot on an overdry wicket. He was full of particulars of the
day's play, and how Wiper had got a most amazing catch

and held it, though he fell; how Jenks had deliberately
bow cd at a man's head, he believed, and Gibbs thrown a man
out from slip. He was burning to tell all this in the utmost
detail to Magnet and his family, so that they might at least
share the retrospect of his pleasure. He had thought out
rather a good pun on Wiper, and he was naturally thwarted
to find all this good, rich talk crowded out by a more en-
grossing topic.

At the sight of a stranger grouped in a popular manner
beside the tea-things, he displayed a slight acerbity, which
was if anything increased by the discovery of a prostrate
person with large brown eyes and an expression of Oriental
patience and disdain, in the shade of a bush near by. At
first he seemed scarcely to grasp Mrs. Pope's explanations,
and regarded Sir Rupert with an expression that bordered
on malevolence. Then, when his attention was directed to
the smashed machine upon the lawn, he broke out into a loud
indignant : " Good God ! What next ? "

He walked towards the wreckage, disregarding Mr. Trafford
beside him. " A man can't go away from his house for an
hour ! " he complained.

" I can assure you we did all we could to prevent it," said
Trafford.

" Ought never to have had it to prevent," said Mr. Pope.
" Is your friend hurt ? "

" A rib—and shock," said Trafford.

" Well—he deserves it," said Mr. Pope. " Rather than
launch myself into the air in one of those infernal things, I'd
be stood against a wall and shot."

" Tastes differ, of course," said Trafford, with unruffled
urbanity.

" You'll have all this cleared away," said Mr. Pope.

" Mechanics—oh ! a complete breakdown party—are
speeding to us in fast motors," said Trafford. " Thanks to
the kindness of your domestic in taking a telegram for me."

" Hope they won't kill any one," said Mr. Pope, and just
for a moment the conversation hung fire. " And your
friend ? " he asked.

" He goes in the next ten minutes—well, whenever the
litter comes from the doctor's. Poor old Solomonson ! "

" Solomonson ? "

" Sir Rupert."

" Oh ! " said Mr. Pope. " Is that the Pigmentation
Solomonson ? "

" I believe he does do some beastly company of that sort,"
said Trafford. " Isn't it amazing we didn't smash our engine ? "

Sir Rupert Solomonson was indeed a familiar name to
Mr. Pope. He had organised the exploitation of a number of
pigment and by-product patents, and the ordinary and
deferred shares of his syndicate had risen to so high a price

as to fill Mr. Pope with the utmost confidence in their future ;
indeed he had bought considerably, withdrawing capital to
do so from an Argentine railway whose stock had awakened
his distaste and a sort of moral aversion by slumping heavily
after a bad wheat and linseed harvest.   This discovery did
much to mitigate his first asperity, his next remark to Trafford
was almost neutral, and he was even asking Sir Rupert
whether he could do anything to make him comfortable, when
the doctor returned with a litter, borne by four hastily
compiled bearers.

### § 4

Some brightness seemed to vanish when the buoyant Mr.
Trafford, still undauntedly cheerful, limped off after his
more injured friend, and disappeared through the gate.
Marjorie found herself in a world whose remaining manhood
declined to see anything but extreme annoyance in this gay,
exciting rupture of the afternoon.   " Good God ! " said Mr.
Pope.   " What next ?   What next ? "

" Registration, I hope," said Mr. Magnet—" and relegation
to the desert of Sahara."

" One good thing about it," said Mr. Pope—" it all wastes
petrol.   And when the petrol supply gives out—they're done."

" Certainly we might all have been killed ! " said Mrs.
Pope, feeling she had to bear her witness against their visitors,
and added :   " If we hadn't moved out of the way, that is."

There was a simultaneous movement towards the shattered
apparatus, about which a small contingent of villagers, who
had availed themselves of the withdrawal of the sentinel, had
now assembled.

" Look at it ! " said Mr. Pope, with bitter hostility.   " Look
at it ! "

Every one had anticipated his command.

" They'll never come to anything," said Mr. Pope, after a
pause of silent hatred.

" But they *have* come to something," said Marjorie.

" They've come to smash ! " said Mr. Magnet, with the
true humorist's air.

" But consider the impudence of this invasion, the wild—
objectionableness of it ! "

" They're nasty things," said Mr. Magnet.   " Nasty things ! "

A curious spirit of opposition stirred in Marjorie.   It
seemed to her that men who play golf-croquet and watch
cricket matches have no business to contemn men who risk
their lives in the air.   She sought for some controversial
opening.

" Isn't the engine rather wonderful ? " she remarked.

Mr. Magnet regarded the engine with his head a little on
one side.   " It's the usual sort," he said.

" There weren't engines like that twenty years ago."

" There weren't people like *you* twenty years ago," said
Mr. Magnet, smiling wisely and kindly, and turned his back
on the thing.

Mr. Pope followed suit. He was filled with the bitter
thought that he would never now be able to tell the history
of the remarkable match he had witnessed. It was all spoiled
for him—spoiled for ever. Everything was disturbed and
put out.

" They've left us our tennis lawn," he said, with a not
unnatural resentment passing to invitation. " What do you
say, Magnet ? Now you've begun the game you must keep
it up ? "

" If Marjorie, or Mrs. Pope, or Daffy . . . ? " said Magnet.

Mrs. Pope declared the house required her. And so with
the gravest apprehensions, and an insincere compliment to
their father's energy, Daffy and Marjorie made up a foursome
for that healthy and invigorating game. But that evening
Mr. Pope got his serve well into the bay of the sagging net
almost at once, and with Marjorie in the background taking
anything he left her, he won quite easily, and everything
became pleasant again. Magnet gloated upon Marjorie and
served to her like a missionary giving Bibles to heathen
children, he seemed always looking at her instead of the ball,
and except for a slight disposition on the part of Daffy to
slash, nothing could have been more delightful. And at
supper Mr. Pope, rather crushing his wife's attempt to re-
capitulate the more characteristic sayings and doings of Sir
Rupert and his friend, did after all succeed in giving every
one a very good idea indeed of the more remarkable incidents
of the cricket match at Wamping, and made the pun upon
the name of Wiper he had had in mind all the afternoon. A
general talk about cricket and the Immense Good of cricket
followed. Mr. Pope said he would make cricket-playing
compulsory for every English boy.

Every one, it seemed to Marjorie, was forgetting that dark
shape athwart the lawn, and all the immense implication of its
presence, with a deliberate and irrational skill, and she noted
that the usual move towards the garden at the end of the
evening was not made.

### § 5

In the night-time Marjorie had a dream that she was flying
about in the world on a monoplane with Mr. Trafford as a
passenger.

Then Mr. Trafford disappeared, and she was flying about
alone with a curious uneasy feeling that in a minute or so
she would be unable any longer to manage the machine.

Then her father and Mr. Magnet appeared very far below,
walking about and disapproving of her. Mr. Magnet was
shaking his head very, very sagely, and saying : " Rather a

stiff job for little Marjorie," and her father was saying she
would be steadier when she married. And then, she wasn't
clear how, the engine refused to work until her bills were paid,
and she began to fall, and fall, and fall towards Mr. Magnet.
She tried frantically to pay her bills. She was falling down the
fronts of skyscrapers and precipices—and Mr. Magnet was
waiting for her below with a quiet kindly smile that grew
wider and wider and wider. . . .

She woke up palpitating.

### § 6

Next morning a curious restlessness came upon Marjorie.
Conceivably it was due to the absence of Magnet, who had
gone to London to deliver his long promised address on "The
Characteristics of English Humour" to the *Literati* Club. Conceivably she missed his attentions. But it crystallised out in
the early afternoon into the oddest form, a powerful craving to
go to the little town of Pensting, five miles off, on the other
side of Buryhamstreet, to buy silk shoe-laces.

She decided to go in the donkey-cart. She communicated her intention to her mother, but she did not communicate an equally definite intention to be reminded suddenly
of Sir Rupert Solomonson as she was passing the surgery,
and make an inquiry on the spur of the moment—it wouldn't
surely be anything but a kindly and justifiable impulse to do
that. She might see Mr. Trafford perhaps, but there was no
particular harm in that.

It is also to be remarked that finding Theodore disposed to
encumber her vehicle with his presence she expressed her
delight at being released from the need of going, and abandoned the whole expedition to him—knowing as she did perfectly well that if Theodore hated anything more than navi-
gating the donkey-cart alone, it was going unprotected into a
shop to buy articles of feminine apparel—until he chucked the
whole project and went fishing—if one can call it fishing when
there are no fish and the fisherman knows it—in the decadent
ornamental water.

And it is also to be remarked that as Marjorie approached
the surgery she was seized with an absurd and powerful
shyness, so that not only did she not call at the surgery, she
did not even look at the surgery, she gazed almost rigidly
straight ahead, telling herself, however, that she merely deferred that kindly impulse until she had bought her laces.
And so it happened that about half a mile beyond the end of
Buryhamstreet she came round a corner upon Trafford, and
by a singular fatality he also was driving a donkey, or, rather,
was tracing a fan-like pattern on the road with a donkey's
hoofs. It was a very similar donkey to Marjorie's but the
vehicle was a governess-cart, and much smarter than Marjorie's
turn-out. His ingenuous face displayed great animation at

the sight of her, and as she drew alongside he hailed her with an almost unnatural ease of manner.

" Hullo ! " he cried.   " I'm taking the air.   You seem to be able to drive donkeys forward.   How do you do it ?   I can't. Never done anything so dangerous in my life before.   I've just been missed by two motor-cars, and hung for a terrible minute with my left wheel on the very verge of an unfathomable ditch.   I could hear the little ducklings far, far below, and bits of mould dropping.   I tried to count before the splash. Aren't you—*white* ? "

" But why are you doing it ? "

" One must do something.   I'm bandaged up and can't walk.   It hurt my leg more than I knew—your doctor says. Solomonson won't talk of anything but how he feels, and *I* don't care a rap how he feels.   So I got this thing and came out with it."

Marjorie made her inquiries.   There came a little pause.

" Some day no one will believe that men were ever so foolish as to trust themselves to draught animals," he remarked. " Hullo !   Look out !   The horror of it ! "

A large oil van—a huge drum on wheels—motor-driven, had come round the corner, and after a preliminary and quite insufficient hoot, bore down upon them, and, missing Trafford as it seemed by a miracle, swept past.   Both drivers did wonderful things with whips and reins, and found themselves alone in the road again, with their wheels locked and an indefinite future.

" I leave the situation to you," said Trafford.   " Or shall we just sit and talk until the next motor-car kills us ? "

" We ought to make an effort," said Marjorie, cheerfully, and descended to lead the two beasts.

Assisted by an elderly hedger, who had been taking a disregarded interest in them for some time, she separated the wheels and got the two donkeys abreast.   The old hedger's opinion of their safety on the king's highway was expressed by his action rather than his words ; he directed the beasts towards a shady lane that opened at right angles to the road.   He stood by their bridles while Marjorie resumed her seat.

" It seems to me clearly a case for compromise," said Trafford.   " You want to go that way, I want to go that way. Let us both go *this* way.   It is by such arrangements that civilisation becomes possible."

He dismissed the hedger generously, and resumed his reins.

" Shall we race ? " he asked.

" With your leg ? " she inquired.

"No, with the donkeys.   I say, this *is* rather a lark.   At first I thought it was both dangerous and dull.   But things have changed.   I am in beastly high spirits.   I feel there will be a cry before night ; but still, I am——   I wanted the companionship of an unbroken person.   It's so jolly to meet you again."

" Again ? "

" After the year before last."

" After the year before last ? "

" You didn't know," said Trafford, " I had met you before ? How aggressive I must have seemed ! Well, *I* wasn't quite clear. I spent the greater part of last night—my ankle being foolish in the small hours—in trying to remember how and where."

" I don't remember," said Marjorie.

" I remembered you very distinctly, and some things I thought about you, but not where it had happened. Then in the night I got it. It *is* a puzzle, isn't it ? You see, I was wearing a black gown, and I had been out of the sunlight for some months—and my eye, I remember it acutely, was bandaged. I'm usually bandaged somewhere.

> ' I was a King in Babylon
>   And you were a Christian slave

—I mean a candidate."

Marjorie remembered suddenly. " You're Professor Trafford."

" Not in this atmosphere. But I am at the Romeike College. And as soon as I recalled examining you I remembered it—minutely. You were intelligent, though unsound—about cryo-hydrates it was. Ah, you remember me now. As most young women are correct by rote and unintelligent in such questions, and as it doesn't matter a rap about anything of that sort, whether you are correct or not, as long as the mental gesture is right——" He paused for a moment as though tired of his sentence. " I remembered you."

He proceeded in his easy and detached manner, that seemed to make every topic possible, to tell her his first impressions of her, and show how very distinctly indeed he remembered her.

" You set me philosophising. I'd never examined a girls' school before, and I was suddenly struck by the spectacle of the fifty of you. What's going to become of them all ?

" I thought," he went on, " how bright you were, and how keen and eager you were—*you*, I mean, in particular—and just how certain it was your brightness and eagerness would be swallowed up by some silly ordinariness or other—stuffy marriage or stuffy domestic duties. The old, old story—done over again with a sort of threadbare baldness. (Nothing to say against it if it's done well.) I got quite sentimental and pathetic about life's breach of faith with women. Odd, isn't it, how one's mind runs on ? But that's what I thought. It's all come back to me."

Marjorie's bright, clear eye came round to him. ." I don't see very much wrong with the lot of women," she reflected. " Things are different nowadays. Anyhow——"

She paused.

" You don't want to be a man ? "

" *No* ! "

She was emphatic.

" Some of us cut more sharply at life than you think," he said, plumbing her unspoken sense.

She had never met a man before who understood just how a girl can feel the slow obtuseness of his sex. It was almost as if he had found her out at something.

"Oh," she said, "perhaps you do," and looked at him with an increased interest.

" I'm half feminine, I believe," he said. " For instance, I've got just a woman's joy in textures and significant shapes. I know how you feel about that. I can spend hours, even now, in crystal gazing—I don't mean to see some silly revelation of some silly person's proceedings somewhere, but just for the things themselves. I wonder if you have ever been in the Natural History Museum at South Kensington, and looked at Ruskin's crystal collection ? I saw it when I was a boy, and it became—I can't help the word—an obsession. The inclusions like moss and like trees, and all sorts of fantastic things, and the cleavages and enclosures with little bubbles, and the lights and shimmer—— What were we talking about ? Oh, about the keen way your feminine perceptions cut into things. And yet somehow I was throwing contempt on the feminine intelligence. I don't do justice to the order of my thoughts. Never mind. We've lost the thread. But I wish you knew my mother."

He went on while Marjorie was still considering the proper response to this.

" You see, I'm her only son and she brought me up, and we know each other—oh ! very well. She helps with my work. She understands nearly all of it. She makes suggestions. And to this day I don't know if she's the most original or the most parasitic of creatures. And that's the way with all women and girls, it seems to me. You're as critical as light, and as undiscriminating. . . . I say, do I strike you as talking nonsense ? "

" Not a bit," said Marjorie. " But you do go rather fast."

" I know," he admitted. " But somehow you excite me. I've been with Solomonson a week, and he's dull at all times. It was that made me take out that monoplane of his. But it did him no good."

He paused.

" They told me after the exam.," said Marjorie, "you knew more about crystallography—than any one."

" Does that strike you as a dull subject ? "

" No," said Marjorie, in a tone that invited justifications.

" It isn't. I think—naturally, that the world one goes into when one studies molecular physics is quite the most beautiful of Wonderlands. . . . I can assure you I work sometimes like a man who is exploring a magic palace. . . . Do you know anything of molecular physics ? "

" You examined me," said Marjorie.

" The sense one has of exquisite and wonderful rhythms—just beyond sound and sight ! And there's a taunting suggestion of its being all there, displayed and confessed, if only one were quick enough to see it. Why, for instance, when you change the composition of a felspar almost imperceptibly, do the angles change ? What's the correspondence between the altered angle and the substituted atom ? Why does this bit of clear stuff swing the ray of light so much out of its path, and that swing it more ? Then what happens when crystals gutter down and go into solution. The endless launching of innumerable little craft. Think what a clear solution must be if only one had ultramicroscopic eyes and could see into it, see the extraordinary patternings, the swimming circling constellations. And then the path of a ray of polarised light beating through it ! It takes me like music. Do you know anything of the effects of polarised light, the sight of a slice of olivine-gabbro for instance between crossed Nicols ? "

" I've seen some rock sections," said Marjorie. " I forget the names of the rocks."

" The colours ? "

" Oh yes, the colours."

" Is there anything else so rich and beautiful in all the world ? And every different mineral and every variety of that mineral has a different palette of colours, a different scheme of harmonies—and is telling you something."

" If only you understood."

" Exactly. All the ordinary stuff of life—you know—the carts and motor-cars and dusty roads and cinder sifting—seems so blank to me—with that persuasion of swing and subtlety beneath it all. As if the whole world was fire and crystal and aquiver—with some sort of cotton wrappers thrown over it. . . ."

" Dust sheets," said Marjorie. " I know."

" Or like a diamond painted over ! "

" With that sort of grey paint, very full of body—that lasts."

" Yes." He smiled at her. " I can't help apologetics. Most people think a professor of science is just——"

" A professor of science."

" Yes. Something all pedantries and phrases. I want to clear my character. As though it is foolish to follow a vortex ring into a vacuum, and wise to whack at a dirty golf ball on a suburban railway bank. Oh, their golf ! Under high heaven ! . . . You don't play golf, do you, by any chance ? "

" Only the woman's part," said Marjorie.

" And they despise us," he said. " Solomonson can hardly hide how he despises us. Nothing is more wonderful than the

way these people go on despising us who do research, who have
this fever of curiosity, who won't be content with—what did
you call those wrappers ? "

"Dust sheets."

"Yes, dust sheets. What a life ! Swaddling bands, dust
sheets and a shroud ! You know, research and discovery
aren't nearly so difficult as people think—if only you have the
courage to say a thing or try a thing now and then that it
isn't usual to say or try. And after all "—he went off at a
tangent—"these confounded ordinary people aren't justified
in their contempt. We keep on throwing them things over
our shoulders, electric bells, telephones, Marconigrams. Look
at the beautiful electric trams that come towering down the
London streets at nightfall, ships of light in full sail ! Twenty
years ago they were as impossible as immortality. We
conquer the seas for these—golfers, put arms into their hands
that will certainly blow them all to bits if ever the idiots go
to war with them, come sailing out of the air on them——"

He caught Marjorie's eye and stopped.

"*Falling* out of the air on them," corrected Marjorie very
softly.

"That was only an accident," said Mr. Trafford. . . .

So they began a conversation in the lane where the trees
met overhead that went on and went on like a devious path
in a shady wood, and touched upon all manner of things. . . .

### § 7

In the end quite a number of people were aggrieved by this
dialogue, in the lane that led nowhither. . . .

Sir Rupert Solomonson was the first to complain. Trafford
had been away "three mortal hours." No one had come
near him, not a soul, and there hadn't been even a passing car
to cheer his ear.

Sir Rupert admitted he had to be quiet. "But not so
*damned* quiet."

"I'd have been glad," said Sir Rupert, "if a hen had laid
an egg and clucked a bit. You might have thought there
had been a Resurrection or somethin', and cleared off everybody. Lord ! it was deadly. I'd have sung out myself if it
hadn't been for these infernal ribs. . . ."

Mrs. Pope came upon the affair quite by accident.

"Well, Marjorie," she said as she poured tea for the family,
"did you get your laces ? "

"Never got there, Mummy," said Marjorie, and paused
fatally.

"Didn't get there ! " said Mrs. Pope. "That's worse
than Theodore ! Wouldn't the donkey go, poor dear ? "

There was nothing to colour about, and yet Marjorie felt
the warm flow in neck and cheek and brow. She threw extraordinary quantities of candour into her manner. "I had a

romantic adventure," she said rather quietly.   " I was going to tell you."

(Sensation.)

" You see, it was like this," said Marjorie.   " I ran against Mr. Trafford. . . ."

She drank tea, and pulled herself together for a lively description of the wheel-locking and the subsequent conversation, a bright ridiculous account which made the affair happen by implication on the high road and not in a byway, and was adorned with every facetious ornament that seemed likely to get a laugh from the children.   But she talked rather fast, and she felt she forced the fun a little.   However, it amused the children all right, and Theodore created a diversion by choking with his tea.   From first to last Marjorie was extremely careful to avoid the affectionate scrutiny of her mother's eye.   And had this lasted the *whole* afternoon ? asked Mrs. Pope.   Oh, they'd talked for half an hour, said Marjorie, or more, and had driven back very slowly together. " He did all the talking.   You saw what he was yesterday. And the donkeys seemed too happy together to tear them away."

" But what was it all about ? " asked Daffy, curious.

" He asked after you, Daffy, most affectionately," said Marjorie, and added, " several times."   (Though Trafford had as a matter of fact displayed a quite remarkable disregard of all her family.)

" And," she went on, getting a plausible idea at last, " he explained all about aeroplanes.   And all that sort of thing. Has daddy gone to Wamping for some more cricket ? . . ."

(But none of this was lost on Mrs. Pope.)

§ 8

Mr. Magnet's return next day was heralded by nearly two-thirds of a column in *The Times*.

The Lecture on the " Characteristics of Humour " had evidently been quite a serious affair, and a very imposing list of humorists and of prominent people associated with their industry had accepted the hospitality of the *Literati*.

Marjorie ran her eyes over the Chairman's flattering introduction, then with a queer faint flavour of hostility she reached her destined husband's utterance.   She seemed to hear the flat full tones of his voice as she read, and automatically the desiccated sentences of the reporter filled out again into those rich, quietly deliberate unfoldings of sound that were already too familiar to her ear.

Mr. Magnet had begun with modest disavowals.   " There was a story, he said "—so the report began—" whose hallowed antiquity ought to protect it from further exploitation, but he was tempted to repeat it because it offered certain analogies to the present situation.   There were three characters in the story, a bluebottle and two Scotsmen.   (Laughter.)   The bluebottle buzzed on the pane, otherwise a profound silence reigned. This was broken by one of the Scotsmen trying to locate the bluebottle with zoological exactitude. Said this Scotsman : ' Sandy, I am thinking if yon fly is a birdie or a beastie.' The other replied : ' Man, don't spoil good whisky with religious conversation.' (Laughter.) He was tempted, Mr. Magnet resumed, to ask himself and them why it was that they should spoil the after-effects of a most excellent and admirably served dinner by an academic discussion on British humour. At first he was pained by the thought that they proposed to temper their hospitality with a demand for a speech. A closer inspection showed that he was to introduce a debate and that others were to speak, and that was a new element in their hospitality. Further, he was permitted to choose the subject so that he could bring their speeches within the range of his comprehension. (Laughter.) His was an easy task. He could make it easier ; the best thing to do would be to say nothing at all. (Laughter.) "

For a space the reporter seemed to have omitted largely—perhaps he was changing places with his relief—and the next sentence showed Mr. Magnet engaged as it were in revising a *hortus siccus* of jokes. " There was the humour of facts and situations," he was saying, " or that humour of expression for which there was no human responsibility, as in the case of Irish humour ; he spoke of the humour of the soil which found its noblest utterance in the bull. Humour depended largely on contrast. There was a humour of form and expression which had many local varieties. American humour had been characterised by exaggeration, the suppression of some link in the chain of argument or narrative, and a wealth of simile and metaphor which had been justly defined as the poetry of a pioneer race. . . ."

Marjorie's attention slipped its anchor, and caught lower down upon : " In England there was a near kinship between laughter and tears ; their mental relations were as close as their physical. Abroad this did not appear to be the case. It was different in France. But perhaps on the whole it would be better to leave the humour of France and what some people still unhappily chose to regard as matters open to controversy—he referred to choice of subject—out of their discussion altogether. (' Hear, hear,' and cheers.) " . . .

Attention wandered again. Then she remarked — it reminded her in some mysterious way of a dropped hairpin— " It was noticeable that the pun to a great extent had become *démodé*. . . ."

At this point the flight of Marjorie's eyes down the column was arrested by her father's hand gently but firmly taking possession of *The Times*. She yielded it without reluctance, turned to the breakfast-table, and never resumed her study of the social relaxations of humorists. . . .

Indeed she forgot it. Her mind was in a state of extreme perplexity. She didn't know what to make of herself or anything or anybody. Her mind was full of Trafford and all that he had said and done and all that he might have said and done, and it was entirely characteristic that she could not think of Magnet in any way at all except as a bar-like shadow that lay across all her memories and all the bright possibilities of this engaging person.

She thought particularly of the mobile animation of his face, the keen flash of enthusiasm in his thoughts and expressions. . . .

It was perhaps more characteristic of her time than of her that she did not think she was dealing so much with a moral problem as an embarrassment, and that she hadn't as yet felt the first stirrings of self-reproach for the series of disingenuous proceedings that had rendered the yesterday's encounter possible. But she was restless, wildly restless as a bird whose nest is taken. She could abide nowhere. She fretted through the morning, avoided Daffy in a marked manner, and inflicted a stinging and only partially merited rebuke upon Theodore for slouching, humping and—of all trite grievances !—not washing behind his ears. As if any chap washed behind his ears ! She thought tennis with the pseudo-twins might assuage her, but she broke off after losing two sets ; and then she went into the garden to get fresh flowers, and picked a large bunch and left them on the piano until her mother reminded her of them. She tried a little Shaw. She struggled with an insane wish to walk through the wood behind the village and have an accidental meeting with some one who couldn't possibly appear but whom it would be quite adorable to meet. Anyhow, she conquered that.

She had a curious and rather morbid indisposition to go after lunch to the station and meet Mr. Magnet as her mother wished her to do, in order to bring him straight to the vicarage to early tea, but here again reason prevailed and she went.

Mr. Magnet arrived by the 2.27, and to Marjorie's eye his alighting presence had an effect of being not so much covered with laurels as distended by them. His face seemed whiter and larger than ever. He waved a great handful of newspapers.

" Hullo, Magsy ! " he said. " They've given me a thumping Press. I'm nearer swelled head than I've ever been, so mind how you touch me ! "

" We'll take it down at croquet," said Marjorie.

" They've cleared that thing away ? "

" And made up the lawn like a billiard-table," she said.

" That makes for skill," he said waggishly. " I shall save my head after all."

For a moment he seemed to bloom towards kissing her, but she averted this danger by a business-like concern for his bag.

He intrusted this to a porter, and reverted to the triumph
of over-night so soon as they were clear of the station. He
was overflowing with kindliness towards his fellow-humorists,
who had appeared in force and very generously at the banquet,
and had said the most charming things—some of which were
in one report and some in another, and some the reporters had
missed altogether—some of the kindliest.

"It's a pleasant feeling to think that a lot of good fellows
think you are a good fellow," said Mr. Magnet.

He became solicitous for her. How had she got on while
he was away? She asked him how one was likely to get on
at Buryhamstreet ; monoplanes didn't fall every day, and
as she said that it occurred to her she was behaving meanly.
But he was going on to his next topic before she could qualify.

"I've got something in my pocket," he remarked, and play-
fully : "Guess."

She did, but she wouldn't. She had a curious sinking of the
heart.

"I want you to see it before any one else," he said. "Then
if you don't like it, it can go back. It's a sapphire."

He was feeling nervously in his pockets, and then the little
box was in her hand.

She hesitated to open it. It made everything so dreadfully
concrete. And this time the sense of meanness was altogether
acuter. He'd bought this in London ; he'd brought it down,
hoping for her approval. Yes, it was—horrid. But what
was she to do ?

"It's—awfully pretty," she said, with the glittering symbol
in her hand, and indeed he had gone to one of those artistic
women who are reviving and improving upon the rich old
Roman designs. "It's so beautifully made."

"I'm so glad you like it. You really *do* like it ? "

"I don't deserve it."

"Oh ! But you *do* like it ? "

"Enormously."

"Ah ! I spent an hour in choosing it."

She could see him. She felt as though she had picked his
pocket.

"Only I don't deserve it, Mr. Magnet. Indeed I don't.
I feel I am taking it on false pretences."

"Nonsense, Magsy. Nonsense ! Slip it on your finger, girl."

"But I don't," she insisted.

He took the box from her, pocketed it and seized her hand.
She drew it away from him.

"No ! " she said. "I feel like a cheat. You know, I
don't—I'm sure I don't love——"

"I'll love enough for two," he said, and got her hand again.
"No ! " he said at her gesture, "you'll wear it. Why shouldn't
you ? "

And so Marjorie came back along the vicarage avenue with

his ring upon her hand. And Mr. Pope was evidently very glad to see him. . . .

The family was still seated at tea upon rugs and wraps, and still discussing humorists at play, when Professor Trafford appeared, leaning on a large stick and limping, but resolute, by the church gate. " Pish ! " said Mr. Pope. Marjorie tried not to reveal a certain dismay, there was dumb, rich approval in Daphne's eyes, and the pleasure of Theodore and the pseudo-twins was only too scandalously evident. " Hoo-Ray ! " said Theodore, with ill-concealed relief.

Mrs. Pope was the incarnate invocation of tact as Trafford drew near.

" I hope," he said, with obvious insincerity, " I don't invade you. But Solomonson is frightfully concerned and anxious about your lawn, and whether his men cleared it up properly and put things right." His eye went about the party and rested on Marjorie. " How are you ? " he said, in a friendly voice.

" Well, we seem to have got our croquet lawn back," said Mr. Pope. "And our nerves are recovering. How is Sir Rupert ? "

" A little fractious," said Trafford, with the ghost of a smile.

" You'll take some tea ? " said Mrs. Pope in the pause that followed.

" Thank you," said Trafford, and sat down instantly.

" I saw your jolly address in the *Standard*," he said to Magnet. "I haven't read anything so amusing for some time."

" Rom, dear," said Mrs. Pope, " will you take the pot in and get some fresh tea ? "

Mr. Trafford addressed himself to the flattery of Magnet with considerable skill. He had detected a lurking hostility in the eyes of the two gentlemen that counselled him to propitiate them if he meant to maintain his footing in the vicarage, and now he talked to them almost exclusively and ignored the ladies modestly but politely in the way that seems natural and proper in a British middle-class house of the better sort. But as he talked chiefly of the improvement of motor machinery that had recently been shown at the Engineering Exhibition, he did not make that headway with Marjorie's father that he had perhaps anticipated. Mr. Pope fumed quietly for a time, and then suddenly spoke out.

" I'm no lover of machines," he said abruptly, slashing across Mr. Trafford's description. " All our troubles began with villainous saltpetre. I'm an old-fashioned man with a nose—and a neck, and I don't want the one offended or the other broken. No, don't ask me to be interested in your valves and cylinders. What do you say, Magnet ? It starts machinery in my head to hear about them. . . ."

On such occasions as this when Mr. Pope spoke out, his horror of an anti-climax or any sort of contradiction was apt to bring the utterance to a culmination not always to be distinguished from a flight. And now he rose to his feet as he delivered himself.

" Who's for a game of tennis ? " he said, " in this last uncontaminated patch of air ? I and Marjorie will give you a match, Daffy—if Magnet isn't too tired to join you."

Daffy looked at Marjorie for an instant.

" We'll want you, Theodore, to look after the balls in the potatoes," said Mr. Pope, lest that ingenuous mind should be corrupted behind his back. . . .

Mrs. Pope found herself left to entertain a slightly disgruntled Trafford. Rom and Syd hovered on the off-chance of notice, at the corner of the croquet lawn nearest the tea-things. Mrs. Pope had already determined to make certain matters clearer than they appeared to be to this agreeable but superfluous person, and she was greatly assisted by his opening upon the subject of her daughters. " Jolly tennis looks," he said.

" Don't they ? " said Mrs. Pope. " I think it is such a graceful game for a girl."

Mr. Trafford glanced at Mrs. Pope's face, but her expression was impenetrable.

" They both like it and play it so well," she said. " Their father is so skilful and interested in games. Marjorie tells me you were her examiner a year or so ago."

" Yes. She stuck in my memory—her work stood out."

" Of course she is clever," said Mrs. Pope, " or we shouldn't have sent her to Oxbridge. There she's doing quite well— quite well. Every one says so. I don't know, of course, if Mr. Magnet will let her finish there."

" Mr. Magnet ? "

" She's just engaged to him. Of course she's frightfully excited about it, and naturally he wants her to come away and marry. There's very little excuse for a long engagement. No."

Her voice died in a musical note, and she seemed to be scrutinising the tennis with an absorbed interest. " They've got new balls," she said, as if to herself.

Trafford had rolled over, and she fancied she detected a change in his voice when it came. " Isn't it rather a waste not to finish a university career ? " he said.

" Oh, it wouldn't be wasted. Of course a girl like that will be hand and glove with her husband. She'll be able to help him with the scientific side of his jokes and all that. I sometimes wish it had been Daffy who had gone to college, though. I sometimes think we've sacrificed Daffy. She's not the bright quickness of Marjorie, but there's something quietly solid about her mind—something *stable*. Perhaps I didn't want her to go away from me. . . . Mr. Magnet is doing wonders at the net. He's just begun to play—to please Marjorie. Don't you think he's a dreadfully amusing man, Mr. Trafford ? He says such *quiet* things."

§ 9

The effect of this *éclaircissement* upon Mr. Trafford was not
what it should have been.    Properly he ought to have realised
at once that Marjorie was for ever beyond his aspirations,
and if he found it too difficult to regard her with equanimity,
then he ought to have shunned her presence.    But instead,
after his first shock of incredulous astonishment, his spirit
rose in a rebellion against arranged facts that was as un-
English as it was ungentlemanly.    He went back to Solomonson with a mood of thoughtful depression giving place to a
growing passion of indignation.    He presented it to himself
in a generalised and altruistic form.    " What the deuce is
the good of all this talk of Eugenics," he asked himself aloud,
" if they are going to hand over that shining girl to that
beastly little area sneak ? "

He called Mr. Magnet a " beastly little area sneak ! "

Nothing could show more clearly just how much he had
contrived to fall in love with Marjorie during his brief sojourn
in Buryhamstreet and the acuteness of his disappointment,
and nothing could be more eloquent of his forcible and undisciplined temperament.    And out of the ten thousand possible
abusive epithets with which his mind was no doubt stored,
this one, I think, had come into his head because of the alert
watchfulness with which Mr. Magnet followed a conversation,
as he waited his chance for some neat but brilliant flash of
comment. . . .

Trafford, like Marjorie, was another of those undisciplined
young people our age has produced in such significant quantity.
He was just six-and-twenty, but the facts that he was big of
build, had as an only child associated much with grown-up
people, had given him the self-reliance and assurance of a
much older man.    He had still to come his croppers and
learn most of the important lessons in life, and, so far, he
wasn't aware of it.    He was naturally clean-minded, very
busy and interested in his work, and on remarkably friendly
and confidential terms with his mother who kept house for
him, and though he had had several small love disturbances,
this was the first occasion that anything of the kind had
ploughed deep into his feelings and desires.

The situation perplexed him.    Marjorie perplexed him.
It was, had he known it, the beginning for him of a lifetime
of problems and perplexities.    He was absolutely certain she
didn't love Magnet.    Why, then, had she agreed to marry him ?
Such pressures and temptations as he could see about her
seemed light to him in comparison with such an undertaking.

Were they greater than he supposed ?

His method of coming to the issue of that problem was
entirely original.    He presented himself next afternoon with
the air of an invited guest, drove Mr. Pope, who was suffering

from liver, to expostulatory sulking in the study, and expressed a passionate craving for golf-croquet, in spite of Mrs. Pope's extreme solicitude for his still bandaged ankle. He was partnered with Daffy, and for a long time he sought speech with Marjorie in vain. At last she was isolated in a corner of the lawn, and with the thinnest pretence of inadvertence, in spite of Daffy's despairing cry of " She plays next ! " he laid up within two yards of her. He walked across to her as she addressed herself to her ball, and speaking in an incredulous tone and with the air of a comment on the game, he said : " I say, are you engaged to that chap Magnet ? "

Marjorie was amazed, but remarkably not offended. Something in his tone set her trembling. She forgot to play, and stood with her mallet hanging in her hand.

" Punish him ! " came the voice of Magnet from afar.

" Yes," she said faintly.

His remark came low and clear. It had a note of angry protest. " *Why ?* "

Marjorie, by way of answer, hit her ball so that it jumped and missed his, ricochetted across the lawn and out of the ground on the farther side.

" I'm sorry if I've annoyed you," said Trafford, as Marjorie went after her ball, and Daffy thanked heaven aloud for the respite.

They came together no more for a time, and Trafford, observant with every sense, found no clue to the riddle of her grave, intent bearing. She played very badly, and with unusual care and deliberation. He felt he had made a mess of things altogether, and suddenly found his leg was too painful to go on. " Partner," he asked, " will you play out my ball for me ? I can't go on. I shall have to go."

Marjorie surveyed him, while Daffy and Magnet expressed solicitude. He turned to go, mallet in hand, and found Marjorie following him.

" Is that the heavier mallet ? " she asked, and stood before him looking into his eyes and weighing a mallet in either hand.

" Mr. Trafford, you're one of the worst examiners I've ever met," she said.

He looked puzzled.

" I don't know *why*," said Marjorie, " I wonder as much as you. But I am " ; and seeing the light dawning in his eyes, she turned about, and went back to the *débâcle* of her game.

## § 10

After that Mr. Trafford had one clear desire in his being which ruled all his other desires. He wanted a long, frank, unembarrassed and uninterrupted conversation with Marjorie. He had a very strong impression that Marjorie wanted exactly the same thing. For a week he besieged the situation in vain. After the fourth day Solomonson was only kept in

Buryhamstreet by sheer will-power, exerted with a brutality that threatened to end that friendship abruptly. He went home on the sixth day in his largest car, but Trafford stayed on beyond the limits of decency to perform some incomprehensible service that he spoke of as " clearing up."

" I want," he said, " to clear up."

" But what *is* there to clear up, my dear boy ? "

" Solomonson, you're a pampered plutocrat," said Trafford, as though everything was explained.

" I don't see any sense in it at all," said Solomonson, and regarded his friend aslant with thick, black eyebrows raised.

" I'm going to stay," said Trafford.

And Solomonson said one of those unhappy and entirely disregarded things that ought never to be said.

" There's some girl in this," said Solomonson.

" Your bedroom's always waiting for you at Riplings," he said, when at last he was going off. . . .

It was Trafford's conviction that Marjorie also wanted, with an almost equal eagerness, the same opportunity for speech and explanations that he desired, and this sustained him in a series of unjustifiable intrusions upon the seclusion of the Popes. But although the manner of Mr. and Mrs. Pope did change considerably for the better after his next visit, it was extraordinary how impossible it seemed for him and Marjorie to achieve their common end of an encounter.

Always something intervened.

In the first place, Mrs. Pope's disposition to optimism had got the better of her earlier discretions, and a casual glance at Daphne's face when their visitor reappeared started quite a new thread of interpretations in her mind. She had taken the opportunity of hinting at this when Mr. Pope asked over his shirt-stud that night, " What the devil that—that chauffeur chap meant by always calling in the afternoon."

" Now that Will Magnet monopolises Marjorie," she said, after a pause and a rustle or so, " I don't see why Daffy shouldn't have a little company of her own age."

Mr. Pope turned round and stared at her. " I didn't think of that," he said. " But, anyhow, I don't like the fellow."

" He seems to be rather clever," said Mrs. Pope, " though he certainly talks too much. And after all, it was Sir Rupert's aeroplane. *He* was only driving it to oblige."

" He'll think twice before he drives another," said Mr. Pope, wrenching off his collar. . . .

Once Mrs. Pope had turned her imagination in this more and more agreeable direction, she was rather disposed, I am afraid, to let it bolt with her. And it was a deflection that certainly fell in very harmoniously with certain secret speculations of Daphne's. Trafford, too, being quite unused to any sort of social furtiveness, did perhaps, in order to divert

attention from his preoccupation with Marjorie, attend more
markedly to Daphne than he would otherwise have done.
And so presently he found Daphne almost continuously on
his hands. So far as she was concerned, he might have told
her the entire history of his life, and every secret he had in
the world, without let or hindrance. Mrs. Pope, too, showed
a growing appreciation of his company, became sympathetic
and confidential in a way that invited confidence, and threw
a lot of light on her family history and Daffy's character.
She had found Daffy a wonderful study, she said. Mr. Pope,
too, seemed partly reconciled to him. The idea that, after
all, both motor-cars and monoplane were Sir Rupert's, and
not Trafford's, had produced a reaction in the latter gentleman's favour. Moreover, it had occurred to him that
Trafford's accident had perhaps disposed him towards a more
thoughtful view of mechanical traction, and that this tendency
would be greatly helped by a little genial chaff. So that he
ceased to go indoors when Trafford was there, and hung
about meditating and delivering sly digs at this new victim
of his ripe, old-fashioned humour.

Nor did it help Trafford in his quest for Marjorie and a
free, outspoken delivery that the pseudo-twins considered
him a person of very considerable charm, and that Theodore,
though indisposed to " suck up " to him publicly—I write
here in Theodorese—did so desire intimate and solitary
communion with him, more particularly in view of the
chances that seemed to hang about him of an adventitious
aeroplane ride, as to stalk him persistently, hovering on the
verge of groups, playing a waiting game with a tennis ball
and an old racquet, strolling artlessly towards the gate of the
avenue when the time seemed ripening for his appearance
or departure.

On the other hand, Marjorie was greatly entangled by
Magnet.

Magnet was naturally an attentive lover ; he was full of
small encumbering services, and it made him none the less
assiduous to perceive that Marjorie seemed to find no sort of
pleasure in all the little things he did. He seemed to think
that if picking the very best rose he could find for her did
not cause a very perceptible brightening in her, then it was
all the more necessary quietly to force her racquet from her
hand and carry it for her, or help her ineffectually to cross a
foot-wide ditch, or offer to read her in a rich, abundant, well-
modulated voice, some choice passage from *The Forest Lovers*
of Mr. Maurice Hewlett. And behind these devotions there
was a streak of jealousy. He knew as if by instinct that it
was not wise to leave these two handsome young people
together ; he had a queer little disagreeable sensation whenever they spoke to one another or looked at one another
Whenever Trafford and Marjorie found themselves in a group

there was Magnet in the midst of them.   He knew the value of his Marjorie, and did not mean to lose her. . . .

Being jointly baffled in this way was oddly stimulating to Marjorie's and Trafford's mutual predisposition.   If you really want to throw people together, the thing to do—thank God for Ireland !—is to keep them apart.   By the fourth day of this emotional incubation, Marjorie was thinking of Trafford to the exclusion of all her reading ; and Trafford was lying awake at nights—oh, for half an hour and more—thinking of bold, decisive ways of getting at Marjorie, and bold, decisive things to say to her when he did.

(But why she should be engaged to Magnet continued, nevertheless, to puzzle him extremely.   It was a puzzle to which no complete solution was ever to be forthcoming. . . .)

### § 11

At last that opportunity came.   Marjorie had come with her mother into the village, and while Mrs. Pope made some purchases at the general shop she walked on to speak to Mrs. Blythe the washerwoman.   Trafford suddenly emerged from the Red Lion with a soda syphon under each arm. She came forward smiling.

" I say," he said forthwith, " I want to talk with you—badly."

" And I," she said unhesitatingly, " with you."

" How can we ? "

" There's always people about.   It's absurd."

" We'll have to meet."

" Yes."

" I have to go away to-morrow.   I ought to have gone two days ago.   Where *can* we meet ? "

She had it all prepared.

" Listen," she said.   " There is a path runs from our shrubbery through a little wood to a stile on the main road." He nodded.   " Either I will be there at three or about half-past five or—there's one more chance.   While father and Mr. Magnet are smoking at nine. . . . I might get away."

" Couldn't I write ? "

" No.   Impossible."

" I've no end of things to say. . . ."

Mrs. Pope appeared outside her shop, and Trafford gesticulated a greeting with the syphons.   " All right," he said to Marjorie.   " I'm shopping," he cried as Mrs. Pope approached.

### § 12

All through the day Marjorie desired to go to Trafford and could not do so.   It was some minutes past nine when at last with a swift rustle of skirts that sounded louder than all the world to her, she crossed the dimly-lit hall between dining-room and drawing-room and came into the dreamland of

moonlight upon the lawn. She had told her mother she was
going upstairs ; at any moment she might be missed, but she
would have fled now to Trafford if an army pursued her.
Her heart seemed beating in her throat, and every fibre of
her being was aquiver. She flitted past the dining-room
window like a ghost, she did not dare to glance aside at the
smokers within, and round the lawn to the shrubbery, and
so under a blackness of trees to the gate where he stood
waiting. And there he was, dim and mysterious and wonderful, holding the gate open for her, and she was breathless, and
speechless, and near sobbing. She stood before him for a
moment, her face moonlit and laced with the shadows of
little twigs, and then his arms came out to her.

"My darling," he said, "oh, my darling ! "

They had no doubt of one another or of anything in the
world. They clung together ; their lips came together fresh
and untainted as those first lovers' in the garden.

"I will die for you," he said ; "I will give all the world
for you. . . ."

They had thought all through the day of a hundred statements and explanations they would make when this moment
came, and never a word of it all was uttered. All their
anticipations of a highly strung eventful conversation vanished,
phrases of the most striking sort went like phantom leaves
before a gale. He held her and she clung to him between
laughing and sobbing, and both were swiftly and conclusively
assured their lives must never separate again.

§ 13

Marjorie never knew whether it was a moment or an age
before her father came upon them. He had decided to take a
turn in the garden when Magnet could no longer restrain
himself from joining the ladies, and he chanced to be stick in
hand because that was his habit after twilight. So it was he
found them. She heard his voice falling through love and
moonlight like something that comes out of an immense
distance.

"Good God ! " he cried, "what next ! "

But he still hadn't realised the worst.

"Daffy," he said, "what in the name of goodness—— ? "

Marjorie put her hands before her face too late.

"Good Lord ! " he cried with a rising inflection, "it's
Madge ! "

Trafford found the situation difficult. "I should explain——"

But Mr. Pope was giving himself up to a towering rage.
"You damned scoundrel ! " he said. "What the devil are
you doing ? " He seized Marjorie by the arm and drew her
towards him. "My poor misguided girl ! " he said, and
suddenly she was tensely alive, a little cry of horror in her

throat, for her father, at a loss for words and full of heroic rage, had suddenly swung his stick with passionate force, and struck at Trafford's face. She heard the thud, saw Trafford wince and stiffen. For a perfectly horrible moment it seemed to her these men, their faces queerly distorted by the shadows of the branches in the slanting moonlight, might fight. Then she heard Trafford's voice, sounding cool and hard, and she knew that he would do nothing of the kind. In that instant if there had remained anything to win in Marjorie it was altogether won. " I asked your daughter to meet me here," he said.

" Be off with you, sir ! " cried Mr. Pope. " Don't tempt me further, sir," and swung his stick again. But now the force had gone out of him. Trafford stood with a hand out ready for him, and watched his face.

" I asked your daughter to meet me here, and she came. I am prepared to give you any explanation———"

" If you come near this place again———"

For some moments Marjorie's heart had been held still, now it was beating violently. She felt this scene must end. " Mr. Trafford," she said, " will you go ? Go now. Nothing shall keep us apart ! "

Mr. Pope turned on her. " Silence, girl ! " he said.

" I shall come to you to-morrow," said Trafford.

" Yes," said Marjorie, " to-morrow."

" Marjorie ! " said Mr. Pope, " *will* you go indoors."

" I have done nothing———"

" Be off, sir."

" I have done nothing———"

" Will you be off, sir ? And you, Marjorie—will you go indoors ? "

He came round upon her, and after one still moment of regard for Trafford—and she looked very beautiful in the moonlight with her hair a little disordered and her face alight— she turned to precede her father through the shrubbery.

Mr. Pope hesitated whether he should remain with Trafford. A perfectly motionless man is very disconcerting.

" Be off, sir," he said over his shoulder, lowered through a threatening second, and followed her.

But Trafford remained stiffly with a tingling temple down which a thread of blood was running, until their retreating footsteps had died down into that confused stirring of little sounds which makes the stillness of an English wood at night.

Then he roused himself with a profound sigh, and put a hand to his cut and bruised cheek.

" *Well* ! " he said.

# CHAPTER FOUR

## CRISIS

### § 1

CRISIS prevailed in Buryhamstreet that night. On half a dozen sleepless pillows souls communed with the darkness, and two at least of those pillows were wet with tears.

Not one of those wakeful heads was perfectly clear about the origins and bearings of the trouble ; not even Mr. Pope felt absolutely sure of himself. It had come as things come to people nowadays, because they will not think things out, much less talk things out, and are therefore in a hopeless tangle of values that tightens sooner or later to a knot. . . .

What an uncharted perplexity, for example, was the mind of that excellent woman Mrs. Pope !

Poor lady ! she hadn't a stable thing in her head. It is remarkable that some queer streak in her composition sympathised with Marjorie's passion for Trafford. But she thought it such a pity ! She fought that sympathy down as if it were a wicked thing. And she fought too against other ideas that rose out of the deeps and did not so much come into her mind as cluster at the threshold, the idea that Marjorie was in effect grown up, a dozen queer criticisms of Magnet, and a dozen subtle doubts whether after all Marjorie was going to be happy with him as she assured herself the girl would be. (So far as any one knew Trafford might be an excellent match !) And behind these would-be invaders of her guarded mind prowled even worse ones, doubts, horrible disloyal doubts, about the wisdom and kindness of Mr. Pope.

Quite early in life Mrs. Pope had realised that it is necessary to be very careful with one's thoughts. They lead to trouble. She had clipped the wings of her own mind therefore so successfully that all her conclusions had become evasions, all her decisions compromises. Her profoundest working convictions was a belief that nothing in the world was of value but " tact," and that the art of living was to " tide things over." But here it seemed almost beyond her strength to achieve any sort of tiding over. . . .

(Why *couldn't* Mr. Pope lie quiet ?)

Whatever she said or did had to be fitted to the exigencies of Mr. Pope.

Availing himself of the privileges of matrimony, her husband, so soon as Mr. Magnet had gone and they were upstairs together, had explained the situation with vivid simplicity, and had gone on at considerable length and with great vivacity to enlarge upon his daughter's behaviour. He ascribed this moral disaster—he presented it as a moral disaster of absolutely calamitous dimensions—entirely to Mrs. Pope's faults and negligences. Warming with his theme he had employed a number of homely expressions rarely heard by decent women except in these sacred intimacies, to express the deep indignation of a strong man moved to unbridled speech by the wickedness of those near and dear to him. Still warming, he raised his voice and at last shouted out his more forcible meanings, until she feared the servants and children might hear, waved a clenched fist at imaginary Traffords and scoundrels generally, and at last, giving way to his outraged virtue, smote and kicked blameless articles of furniture in a manner deeply impressive to the feminine intelligence.

Finally he sat down in the little armchair between her and the cupboard where she was accustomed to hang up her clothes, stuck out his legs very stiffly across the room, and despaired of his family in an obtrusive and impregnable silence for an enormous time.

All of which awakened a deep sense of guilt and unworthiness in Mrs. Pope's mind, and prevented her going to bed, but did not help her in the slightest degree to grasp the difficulties of the situation. . . .

She would have lain awake anyhow, but she was greatly helped in this by Mr. Pope's restlessness. He was now turning over from left to right or from right to left at intervals of from four to seven minutes, and such remarks as " Damned scoundrel ! Get out of this ! " or " *My* daughter and degrade yourself in this way ! " or " Never let me see your face again ! " " Plight your troth to one man, and fling yourself shamelessly —I repeat it, Marjorie, shamelessly—into the arms of another ! " kept Mrs. Pope closely in touch with the general trend of his thoughts.

She tried to get together her plans and perceptions rather as though she swept up dead leaves on a gusty day. She knew that the management of the whole situation rested finally on her, and that whatever she did or did not do, or whatever arose to thwart her arrangements, its entire tale of responsibility would ultimately fall upon her shoulders. She wondered what was to be done with Marjorie, with Mr. Magnet ? Need he know ? Could that situation be saved ? Everything at present was raw in her mind. Except for her husband's informal communications she did not even know what had appeared, what Daffy had seen, what Magnet thought of Marjorie's failure to bid him good-night. For example, had Mr. Magnet noticed Mr. Pope's profound disturbance ? She had to be ready to put a face on things before morning, and it seemed impossible she could do so. In times of crisis, as every woman knows, it is always necessary to misrepresent everything to everybody, but how she was to dovetail her misrepresentations, get the best effect from them, extract a working system of rights and wrongs from them, she could not imagine. . . .

(Oh ! she did so wish Mr. Pope would lie quiet.)

But he had no doubts of what became *him*. He had to maintain a splendid and irrational rage—at any cost—to anybody.

### § 2

A few yards away, a wakeful Marjorie confronted a joyless universe. She had a baffling realisation that her life was in a hopeless mess, that she really had behaved disgracefully, and that she couldn't for a moment understand how it had happened. She had intended to make quite sure of Trafford—and then put things straight.

Only her father had spoiled everything.

She regarded her father that night with a want of natural affection terrible to record. Why had he come just when he had, just as he had ? Why had he been so violent, so impossible ?

Of course she had had no business to be there. . . .

She examined her character with a new unprecedented detachment. Wasn't she, after all, rather a mean human being ? It had never occurred to her before to ask such a question. Now she asked it with only too clear a sense of the answer. She tried to trace how these multiplying threads of meanness had first come into the fabric of a life she had supposed herself to be weaving in extremely bright, honourable and adventurous colours. She ought, of course, never to have accepted Magnet. . . .

She faced the disagreeable word ; was she a liar ?

At any rate, she told lies.

And she'd behaved with extraordinary meanness to Daphne. She realised that now. She had known, as precisely as if she had been told, how Daphne felt about Trafford, and she'd never given her an inkling of her own relations. She hadn't for a moment thought of Daphne. No wonder Daffy was sombre and bitter. Whatever she knew, she knew enough. She had heard Trafford's name in urgent whispers on the landing. " I suppose you couldn't leave him alone," Daffy had said, after a long, hostile silence. That was all. Just a sentence without prelude or answer flung across the bedroom, revealing a perfect understanding—deeps of angry disillusionment. Marjorie had stared and gasped, and made no answer.

Would she ever see him again ? After this horror of rowdy intervention ? She didn't deserve to ; she didn't deserve anything. . . . Oh, the tangle of it all ! The tangle of it all ! And those bills at Oxbridge ! She was just dragging Trafford down into her own miserable morass of a life.

Her thoughts would take a new turn. " I love him," she whispered soundlessly. " I would die for him. I would like to lie under his feet—and him not know it."

Her mind hung on that for a long time.  " Not know it until afterwards," she corrected.

She liked to be exact, even in despair. . . .

And then in her memory he was struck again, and stood stiff and still.  She wanted to kneel to him, imagined herself kneeling. . . .

And so on, quite inconclusively, round and round through the interminable night hours.

### § 3

The young man in the village was, if possible, more perplexed, round-eyed and generally inconclusive than any one else in this series of nocturnal disturbances.  He spent long intervals sitting on his window-sill regarding a world that was scented with nightstock, and seemed to be woven of moonshine and gossamer.  Being an inexpert and infrequent soliloquist, his only audible comment on his difficulties was the repetition in varying intonations of his fervent, unalterable conviction that he was damned.  But behind this simple verbal mask was a great fury of mental activity.

He had something of Marjorie's amazement at the position of affairs.

He had never properly realised that it was possible for any one to regard Marjorie as a daughter, to order her about and resent the research for her society as criminal.  It was a new light in his world.  Some day he was to learn the meaning of fatherhood, but in these night watches he regarded it as a hideous survival of mediæval darknesses.

" Of course," he said, entirely ignoring the actual quality of their conversation, " she had to explain about the Magnet affair.  Can't one—converse ? "

He reflected through great intervals.

" I *will* see her !  Why on earth shouldn't I see her ?

" I suppose they can't lock her up ! "

For a time he contemplated a writ of Habeas Corpus.  He saw reason to regret the gaps in his legal knowledge.

" Can any one get a writ of Habeas Corpus for any one—it doesn't matter whom "—more especially if you are a young man of six-and-twenty, anxious to exchange a few richly-charged words with a girl of twenty who is engaged to some one else ?

The night had no answer.

It was nearly dawn when he came to the entirely inadvisable conclusion—I use his own words—to go and have it out with the old ruffian.  He would sit down and ask him what he meant by it all—and reason with him.  If he started flourishing that stick again, it would have to be taken away.

And having composed a peroration upon the institution of the family of a character which he fondly supposed to be extraordinarily tolerant, reasonable and convincing, but which was indeed calculated to madden Mr. Pope to frenzy, Mr. Trafford went very peacefully to sleep.

## § 4

Came dawn, with a noise of birds and afterwards a little sleep, and then day, and heavy eyes opened again, and the sound of frying and the smell of coffee recalled our actors to the stage. Mrs. Pope was past her worst despair ; always the morning brings courage and a clearer grasp of things, and she could face the world with plans shaped subconsciously during those last healing moments of slumber.

Breakfast was difficult, but not impossible. Mr. Pope loomed like a thundercloud, but Marjorie very wisely pleaded a headache, and was taken a sympathetic cup of tea. The pseudo-twins scented trouble, but Theodore was heedless and overfull of an entertaining noise made by a moorhen as it dived in the ornamental water that morning. You could make it practically *sotto voce,* and it amused Syd. He seemed to think *The Times* opaque to such small sounds, and learned better only to be dismissed underfed and ignominiously from the table to meditate upon the imperfections of his soul in the schoolroom. There for a time he was silent, and then presently became audible again, playing with a ball and, presumably, Marjorie's tennis racquet.

Directly she could disentangle herself from breakfast, Mrs. Pope, with all her plans acute, went up to the girls' room. She found her daughter dressing in a leisurely and meditative manner. She shut the door almost confidentially. " Marjorie," she said, " I want you to tell me all about this."

" I thought I heard father telling you," said Marjorie.

" He was too indignant," said Mrs. Pope, " to explain clearly. You see, Marjorie "—she paused before her effort—" he knows things—about this Professor Trafford."

" What things ? " asked Marjorie, turning sharply.

" I don't know, my dear—and I can't imagine."

She looked out of the window, aware of Marjorie's entirely distrustful scrutiny.

" I don't believe it," said Marjorie.

" Don't believe what, dear ? "

" Whatever he says."

" I wish I didn't," said Mrs. Pope, and turned. " Oh, Madge," she cried, " you cannot imagine how all this distresses me ! I cannot—I cannot conceive how you came to be in such a position ! Surely honour——•! Think of Mr. Magnet, how good and patient he has been ! You don't know that man. You don't know all he is, and all that it means to a girl. He is good and honourable and—pure. He is kindness itself. It seemed to me that you were to be so happy —rich, honoured."

She was overcome by a rush of emotion ; she turned to the bed and sat down.

" *There* ! " she said desolately. " It's all ruined, shattered, gone."

Marjorie tried not to feel that her mother was right.

"If father hadn't interfered," she said weakly.

"Oh don't, my dear, speak so coldly of your father! You don't know what he has to put up with. You don't know his troubles and anxieties—all this wretched business." She paused, and her face became portentous. "Marjorie, do you know if these railways go on as they are going he may have to *eat into his capital* this year. Just think of that, and the worry he has! And this last shame and anxiety!"

Her voice broke again. Marjorie listened with an expression that was almost sullen.

"But what is it," she said, "that father knows about Mr. Trafford?"

"I don't know, dear. I don't know. But it's something that matters—that makes it all different."

"Well, may I speak to Mr. Trafford before he leaves Buryhamstreet?"

"My dear! Never see him, dear—never think of him again!" Your father would not dream—— Some day, Marjorie, you will rejoice—you will want to thank your father on your bended knees that he saved you from the clutches of this man. . . ."

"I won't believe anything about Mr. Trafford," she said slowly, "until I know——"

She left the sentence incomplete.

She made her declaration abruptly. "I love Mr. Trafford," she said, with a catch in her voice, "and I don't love Mr. Magnet."

Mrs. Pope received this like one who is suddenly stabbed. She sat still as if overwhelmed, one hand pressed to her side and her eyes closed. Then she said, as if she gasped involuntarily—

"It's too dreadful! Marjorie," she said. "I want to ask you to do something. After all, a mother has *some* claim. Will you wait just a little? Will you promise me to do nothing—nothing, I mean, to commit you—until your father has been able to make inquiries? Don't *see* him for a little while. Very soon you'll be one-and-twenty, and then perhaps things may be different. If he cares for you, and you for him, a little separation won't matter. . . . Until your father has inquired. . . ."

"Mother," said Marjorie, "I can't——"

Mrs. Pope drew in the air sharply between her teeth, as if in agony.

"But, mother—— Mother, I *must* let Mr. Trafford know that I'm not to see him. I *can't* suddenly cease. . . . If I could see him once——"

"Don't!" said Mrs. Pope, in a hollow voice.

Marjorie began weeping. "He'd not understand," she said. "If I might just speak to him!"

"Not alone, Marjorie."

Marjorie stood still. "Well—before you."

Mrs. Pope conceded the point. " And then, Marjorie——" she said.

" I'd keep my word, mother," said Marjorie, and began to sob in a manner she felt to be absurdly childish—" until—until I am one-and-twenty. I'd promise that."

Mrs. Pope did a brief calculation. " Marjorie," she said, " it's only your happiness I think of."

" I know," said Marjorie, and added in a low voice, " and father."

" My dear, you don't understand your father. . . . I believe—I do firmly believe—if anything happened to any of you girls—anything bad—he would kill himself. . . . And I know he means that you aren't to go about so much as you used to do, unless we have the most definite promises. Of course, your father's ideas aren't always my ideas, Marjorie ; but it's your duty—— You know how hasty he is and—quick. Just as you know how good and generous and kind he is "—she caught Marjorie's eye, and added a little lamely —" at bottom." . . . She thought. " I think I could get him to let you say just one word with Mr. Trafford. It would be very difficult, but——"

She paused for a few seconds, and seemed to be thinking deeply.

" Marjorie," she said, " Mr. Magnet must never know anything of this."

" But, mother—— ! "

" Nothing ! "

" I can't go on with my engagement ! "

Mrs. Pope shook her head inscrutably.

" But how *can* I, mother ? "

" You need not tell him *why*, Marjorie."

" But——"

" Just think how it would humiliate and distress him ! You *can't*, Marjorie. You must find some excuse—oh, any excuse ! But not the truth—not the truth, Marjorie. It would be too dreadful."

Marjorie thought. " Look here, mother, I *may* see Mr. Trafford again ? I *may* really speak to him ? "

" Haven't I promised ? "

" Then I'll do as you say," said Marjorie.

## § 5

Mrs. Pope found her husband seated at the desk in the ultra-Protestant study, meditating gloomily.

" I've been talking to her," she said. " She's in a state of terrible distress."

" She ought to be," said Mr. Pope.

" Philip, you don't understand Marjorie."

" I don't."

" You think she was kissing that man."

" Well, she was."

" You can think *that* of her ! "

Mr. Pope turned his chair to her.   " But I *saw !* "

Mrs. Pope shook her head.   " She wasn't ; she was strug-gling to get away from him.   She told me so herself.   I've been into it with her.   You don't understand, Philip.   A man like that has a sort of fascination for a girl.   He dazzles her.   It's the way with girls.   But you're quite mistaken. . . . Quite.   It's a sort of hypnotism.   She'll grow out of it.   Of course, she *loves* Mr. Magnet.   She does indeed.   I've not a doubt of it.   But——"

" You're *sure* she wasn't kissing him ? "

" Positive."

" Then why didn't she say so ? "

" A girl's so complex.   You didn't give her a chance.   She's fearfully ashamed of herself—fearfully ; but it's just because she *is* ashamed that she won't admit it."

" I'll make her admit it."

" You ought to have had all boys," said Mrs. Pope.   " Oh ! she'll admit it some day—readily enough.   But I believe a girl of her spirit would rather *die* than begin explaining.   You can't expect it of her.   Really you can't."

He grunted and shook his head slowly from side to side.

She sat down in the armchair beside the desk.

" I want to know just exactly what we are to do about the girl, Philip.   I can't bear to think of her—up there."

" How ? " he asked.   " Up there ? "

" Yes," she answered with that skilful inconsecutiveness of hers, and let a brief silence touch his imagination.   " Do you think that man means to come here again ? " she asked.

" Chuck him out if he does," said Mr. Pope, grimly.

She pressed her lips together firmly.   She seemed to be weighing things painfully.   " I wouldn't," she said at last.

" What do you mean ? " asked Mr. Pope.

" I do not want you to make an open quarrel with Mr. Trafford."

" *Not* quarrel ! "

" Not an open one," said Mrs. Pope.   " Of course, I know how nice it would be if you *could* use a horsewhip, dear.   There's such a lot of things—if we could only just slash.   But —it won't help.   Get him to go away.   She's consented never to see him again—practically.   She's ready to tell him so herself.   Part them against their will—oh ! and the thing may go on for no end of time.   But treat it as it ought to be treated——   She'll be very tragic for a week or so, and then she'll forget him like a dream.   He *is* a dream—a girl's dream. . . . If only we leave it alone, she'll leave it alone."

§ 6

Things were getting straight, Mrs. Pope felt.   She had now merely to add a few touches to the tranquillisation of Daphne,

and the misdirection of the twins' curiosity. These touches
accomplished, it seemed that everything was done. After a
brief reflection, she dismissed the idea of putting things to
Theodore. She ran over the possibilities of the servants
eavesdropping, and found them negligible. Yes, everything
was done—everything. And yet . . .

The queer string in her nature between religiosity and superstition began to vibrate. She hesitated. Then she slipped
upstairs, fastened the door, fell on her knees beside the bed
and put the whole thing as acceptably as possible to Heaven
in a silent, simple, but lucidly explanatory prayer. . . .

She came out of her chamber brighter and braver than she
had been for eighteen long hours. She could now, she felt,
await the developments that threatened with the serenity
of one who is prepared at every point. She went almost
happily to the kitchen, only about forty-five minutes behind
her usual time, to order the day's meals and see with her own
eyes that economies prevailed. And it seemed to her on the
whole consoling, and at any rate a distraction, when the cook
informed her that after all she *had* meant to give notice on the
day of Aunt Plessington's visit.

### § 7

The unsuspecting Magnet, fatigued but happy—for three
hours of solid humorous writing (omitting every unpleasant
suggestion and mingling in the most acceptable and saleable
proportions smiles and tears) had added its quota to the intellectual heritage of England, made a simple light lunch
cooked in homely village-inn fashion, lit a well-merited
cigar, and turned his steps towards the vicarage. He was
preceded at some distance along the avenuesque drive by the
back of Mr. Trafford, which he made no attempt to overtake.

Mr. Trafford was admitted and disappeared, and a minute
afterwards Magnet reached the door.

Mrs. Pope appeared radiant—about the weather. A rather
tiresome man had just called upon Mr. Pope about business
matters, she said, and he might be detained five or ten minutes.
Marjorie and Daffy were upstairs—resting. They had been
disturbed by bats in the night.

" Isn't it charmingly rural ? " said Mrs. Pope. " *Bats !* "

She talked about bats and the fear she had of their getting
in her hair, and as she talked she led the way brightly but
firmly as far as possible out of earshot of the windows of the
ultra-Protestant study in which Mr. Pope was now (she did so
hope temperately) interviewing Mr. Trafford.

### § 8

Directly Mr. Trafford had reached the front door it had
opened for him, and closed behind him at once. He had found
himself with Mrs. Pope. " You wish to see my husband ? "

she had said, and had led him to the study forthwith. She had returned at once to intercept Mr. Magnet. . . .

Trafford found Mr. Pope seated sternly at the centre of the writing-desk, regarding him with a threatening brow.

" Well, sir," said Mr. Pope, breaking the silence, " you have come to offer some explanation——"

While awaiting this encounter Mr. Pope had not been insensitive to the tactical and scenic possibilities of the occasion. In fact, he had spent the latter half of the morning in intermittent preparations, arranging desk, books, hassocks in advantageous positions, and not even neglecting such small details as the stamp tray, the articles of interest from Jerusalem, and the rock-crystal cenotaph, which he had exhibited in such a manner as was most calculated to damp, chill and subjugate an antagonist in the exposed area towards the window. He had also arranged the chairs in a highly favourable pattern.

Mr. Trafford was greatly taken aback by Mr. Pope's juridical manner and by this form of address, and he was further put out by Mr. Pope saying with a regal gesture to the best illuminated and most isolated chair :  " Be seated, sir."

Mr. Trafford's exordium vanished from his mind, he was at a loss for words until spurred to speech by Mr. Pope's almost truculent :  " Well ? "

" I am in love, sir, with your daughter."

" I am not aware of it," said Mr. Pope, and lifted and dropped the paper-weight.  " My daughter, sir, is engaged to marry Mr. Magnet.  If you had approached me in a proper fashion before presuming to attempt—to attempt "—— his voice thickened with indignation—" liberties with her, you would have been duly informed of her position—and every one would have been saved "—he lifted the paper-weight— " everything that has happened."  (Bump.)

Mr. Trafford had to adjust himself to the unexpected elements in this encounter.  " Oh ! " he said.

" Yes," said Mr. Pope, and there was a distinct interval.

" Is your daughter in love with Mr. Magnet ? " asked Mr. Trafford in an almost colloquial tone.

Mr. Pope smiled gravely.  " I presume so, sir."

" She never gave me that impression, anyhow," said the young man.

" It was neither her duty to give nor yours to receive that impression," said Mr. Pope.

Again Mr. Trafford was at a loss.

" Have you come here, sir, merely to bandy words ? " asked Mr. Pope, drumming with ten fingers on the table.

Mr. Trafford thrust his hands into his pockets and assumed a fictitious pose of ease.  He had never found any one in his life before quite so provocative of colloquialism as Mr. Pope.

" Look here, sir, this is all very well," he began, " but why can't I fall in love with your daughter ?  I'm a Doctor of

Science and all that sort of thing. I've a perfectly decent outlook. My father was rather a swell in his science. I'm an entirely decent and respectable person."

" I beg to differ," said Mr. Pope.

" But I am."

" Again,' said Mr. Pope, with great patience, and a slight forward bowing of the head, " I beg to differ."

" Well—differ. But all the same——"

He paused and began again, and for a time they argued to no purpose. They generalised about the position of an engaged girl and the rights and privileges of a father. Then Mr. Pope, " to cut all this short," told him frankly he wasn't wanted, his daughter did not want him, nobody wanted him ; he was an invader, he had to be got rid of—" if possible by peaceful means." Trafford disputed these propositions and asked to see Marjorie. Mr. Pope had been leading up to this, and at once closed with that request.

" She is as anxious as any one to end this intolerable siege," he said. He went to the door and called for Marjorie, who appeared with conspicuous promptitude. She was in a dress of green linen that made her seem to Trafford very cool as well as very dignified ; she was tense with restrained excitement, and either—for these things shade into each other— entirely without a disposition to act her part or acting with consummate ability. Trafford rose at the sight of her, and remained standing. " Mr. Pope closed the door and walked back to the desk. " Mr Trafford has to be told," he said, " that you don't want him in Buryhamstreet." He arrested Marjorie's forward movement towards Trafford by a gesture of the hand, seated himself, and resumed his drumming on the table. " Well ? " he said.

" I don't think you ought to stay in Buryhamstreet, Mr. Trafford," said Marjorie.

" You don't want me to ? "

" It will only cause trouble—and scenes."

" You want me to go ? "

" Away from here."

" You really mean that ? "

Marjorie did not answer for a little time ; she seemed to be weighing the exact force of all she was going to say.

" Mr. Trafford," she answered, " everything I've ever said to you—everything—I've *meant*, more than I've ever meant anything. Everything ! "

A little flush of colour came into Trafford's cheeks. He regarded Marjorie with a brightening eye.

" Oh well," he said, " I don't understand. But I'm entirely in your hands, of course."

Marjorie's pose and expression altered. For an instant she was a miracle of instinctive expression, she shone at him, she conveyed herself to him, she assured him. Her

eyes met his, she stood warmly flushed and quite unconquered
—visibly, magnificently *his*.  She poured into him just that
riotous pride and admiration that gives a man altogether to
a woman. . . . Then it seemed as if a light passed, and she
was just an everyday Marjorie standing there.

" I'll do anything you want me to," said Trafford.

" Then I want you to go."

" Ah ! " said Mr. Pope.

" Yes," said Trafford, with his eyes on her self-possession.

" I've promised not to write or send to you, or—think
more than I can help of you, until I'm twenty-one—nearly
two months from now."

" And then ? "

" I don't know.  How can I ? "

" You hear, sir ? " from Mr. Pope, in the pause of mutual
scrutiny that followed.

" One question," said Mr. Trafford.

" You've surely asked enough, sir," said Mr. Pope.

" Are you still engaged to Magnet ? "

" Sir ! "

" Please, father ! " said Marjorie, with unusual daring and
in her mother's voice.  " Mr. Trafford, after what I've told
you—you must leave that to me."

" She *is* engaged to Mr. Magnet," said Mr. Pope.  " Tell
him outright, Marjorie.  Make it clear."

" I think I understand," said Trafford, with his eyes on
Marjorie.

" I've not seen Mr. Magnet since last night," said Marjorie.
" And so—naturally—I'm still engaged to him."

" Precisely ! " said Mr. Pope, and turned with a face of
harsh interrogation to his importunate caller.  Mr. Trafford
seemed disposed for further questions.  " I don't think we
need detain you, Madge," said Mr. Pope, over his shoulder.

The two young people stood facing one another for a
moment, and I am afraid that they were both extremely
happy and satisfied with each other.  It was all right, they
were quite sure—all right.  Their lips were almost smiling.
Then Marjorie made an entirely dignified exit.  She closed
the door very softly, and Mr. Pope turned to his visitor again
with a bleak politeness.  " I hope that satisfies you," he said.

" There is nothing more to be said at present, I admit,"
said Mr. Trafford.

" Nothing," said Mr. Pope.

Both gentlemen bowed.  Mr. Pope rose ceremoniously, and
Mr. Trafford walked doorward.  He had a sense of latent
absurdities in these tremendous attitudes.  They passed
through the hall—processionally.  But just at the end some
lower strain in Mr. Trafford's nature touched the fine dignity
of the occasion with an inappropriate remark.

" Good-bye, sir," said Mr. Pope, holding the house door wide.

" Good-bye, sir," said Mr. Trafford, and then added with
a note of untimely intimacy in his voice, and an inexcusable
levity upon his lips : " You know—there's nobody—no man
in the world—I'd sooner have for a father-in-law than you."

Mr. Pope, caught unprepared on the spur of the moment,
bowed in a cold and distant manner, and then almost immediately closed the door to save himself from violence. . . .

From first to last neither gentleman had made the slightest
allusion to a considerable bruise upon Mr. Trafford's left
cheek, and a large abrasion above his ear.

### § 9

That afternoon Marjorie began her difficult task of getting
disengaged from Mr. Magnet. It was difficult because she
was pledged not to tell him of the one thing that made this
line of action not only explicable, but necessary. Magnet,
perplexed and disconcerted, and secretly sustained by her
mother's glancing sidelights on the feminine character and
the instability of "girlish whims," remained at Buryhamstreet until the family returned to Hartstone Square. The
engagement was ended—formally—but in such a manner
that Magnet was left a rather pathetic and invincibly assiduous
besieger. He lavished presents upon both sisters, he devised
treats for the entire family, he enriched Theodore beyond
the dreams of avarice, and he discussed his love and admiration for Marjorie, and the perplexities and delicacies of the
situation not only with Mrs. Pope, but with Daphne. At
first he had thought very little of Daphne, but now he was
beginning to experience the subtle pleasures of a confidential
friendship. She understood, he felt ; it was quite wonderful
how she understood. He found Daffy much richer in response
than Marjorie, and far less disconcerting in reply. . . .

Mr. Pope, for all Marjorie's submission to his wishes, developed a Grand Dudgeon of exceptionally fine proportions
when he heard of the breach of the engagement. He ceased
to speak to his daughter or admit himself aware of her existence, and the Grand Dudgeon's blighting shadow threw a chill
over the life of every one in the house. He made it clear
that the Grand Dudgeon would only be lifted by Marjorie's
re-engagement to Magnet, and that whatever blight or inconvenience fell on the others was due entirely to Marjorie's
wicked obstinacy. Using Mrs. Pope as an intermediary, he
also conveyed to Marjorie his decision to be no longer burthened
with the charges of her education at Oxbridge, and he made
it seem extremely doubtful whether he should remember her
approaching twenty-first birthday.

Marjorie received the news of her severance from Oxbridge,
Mrs. Pope thought, with a certain hardness.

" I thought he would do that," said Marjorie. " He's
always wanted to do that," and said no more.

# CHAPTER FIVE

## A TELEPHONE CALL

### § 1

TRAFFORD went back to Solomonson for a day or so, and then to London, to resume the experimental work of the research he had in hand. But he was so much in love with Marjorie that for some days it was a very dazed mind that fumbled with the apparatus—arranged it and rearranged it, and fell into day-dreams that gave the utmost concern to Durgan the bottle-washer.

"He's not going straight at things," said Durgan the bottle-washer to his wife. "He usually goes so straight at things it's a pleasure to watch it. He told me he was going down into Kent to think everything out." Mr. Durgan paused impressively, and spoke with a sigh of perplexity. "He hasn't. . . ."

But later Durgan was able to report that Trafford had pulled himself together. The work was moving.

"I was worried for a bit," said Mr. Durgan. "But I *think* it's all right again. I *believe* it's all right again."

### § 2

Trafford was one of those rare scientific men who really ought to be engaged in scientific research.

He could never leave an accepted formula alone. His mind was like some insatiable corrosive, that ate into all the hidden inequalities and plastered weaknesses of accepted theories, and bit its way through every plausibility of appearance. He was extraordinarily fertile in exasperating alternative hypotheses. His invention of destructive test experiments was as happy as the respectful irony with which he brought them into contact with the generalisations they doomed. He was already, at six-and-twenty, hated, abused, obstructed, and respected. He was still outside the Royal Society, of course, and the editors of the scientific periodicals admired his papers greatly, and delayed publication ; but it was fairly certain that that pressure of foreign criticism and competition which prevents English scientific men of good family and social position from maintaining any such national standards as we are able to do in art, literature, and politics, would finally carry him in. And since he had a small professorship worth three hundred a year, which gave him the command of a sufficient research laboratory and the services of Mr. Durgan, a private income of nearly three hundred more, a devoted mother to keep house for him, and an invincible faith in Truth, he had every prospect of winning in his particular struggle to inflict more Truth, new lucidities, and fresh powers upon this fractious and unreasonable universe.

In the world of science now, even more than in the world of literature and political thought, the thing that is alive struggles, half suffocated, amidst a copious production of things born dead. The endowment of research, the organisation of scientific progress, the creation of salaried posts, and the assignment of honours, has attracted to this field just that type of man which is least gifted to penetrate and discover, and least able to admit its own defect or the quality of a superior. Such men are producing great bulky masses of imitative research, futile inquiries, and monstrous entanglements of technicality about their subjects ; and it is to their instinctive antagonism to the idea of a " gift " in such things that we owe the preposterous conception of a training for research, the manufacture of mental blinkers that is to say, to avoid what is the very soul of brilliant inquiry— applicable discursiveness. The trained investigator is quite the absurdest figure in the farce of contemporary intellectual life ; he is like a bath-chair perpetually starting to cross the Himalayas by virtue of a licence to do so. For such enterprises one must have wings. Organisation and genius are antipathetic. The vivid and creative mind, by virtue of its qualities, is a spasmodic and adventurous mind ; it resents blinkers, and the mere implication that it can be driven in harness to the unexpected. It demands freedom. It resents regular attendance from ten to four and punctualities in general and all those paralysing minor tests of conduct that are vitally important to the imagination of the authoritative dull. Consequently, it is being eliminated from its legitimate field, and it is only here and there among the younger men that such a figure as Trafford gives any promise of a renewal of that enthusiasm, that intellectual enterprise, which were distinctive of the great age of scientific advance.

Trafford was the only son of his parents. His father had been a young surgeon, more attracted by knowledge than practice, who had been killed by a scratch of the scalpel in an investigation upon ulcerative processes, at the age of twenty-nine. Trafford at that time was three years old, so that he had not the least memory of his father ; but his mother, by a thousand almost unpremeditated touches, had built up a figure for him and a tradition that was shaping his life. She had loved her husband passionately, and when he died her love burned up like a flame released, and made a god of the good she had known with him. She was then a very beautiful and active-minded woman of thirty, and she did her best to reconstruct her life ; but she could find nothing so living in the world as the clear courage, the essential simplicity, and tender memories of the man she had lost. And she was the more devoted to him that he had had little weaknesses of temper and bearing, and that an outrageous campaign had been waged against him that did not cease with his death. He had, in some medical periodical, published drawings of a dead dog clamped to display a deformity, and these had been seized upon by a group of anti-vivisection fanatics as the representation of a vivisection. A libel action had been pending when he died ; but there is no protection of the dead from libel. That monstrous lie met her on pamphlet cover, on hoardings, in sensational appeals ; it seemed immortal, and she would have suffered the pains of a dozen suttees, if she could have done so, to show the world how the power and tenderness of this alleged tormentor of helpless beasts had gripped one woman's heart. It counted enormously in her decision to remain a widow and concentrate her life upon her son.

She watched his growth with a care and passionate subtlety that even at six-and-twenty he was still far from suspecting. She dreaded his becoming a mother's pet, she sent him away to school and fretted through long terms alone, that he might be made into a man. She interested herself in literary work and social affairs lest she should press upon him unduly. She listened for the crude expression of growing thought in him with an intensity that was almost anguish. She was too intelligent to dream of forming his mind, he browsed on every doctrine to find his own, but she did desire most passionately, she prayed, she prayed in the darkness of sleepless nights, that the views, the breadths, the spacious emotions which had ennobled her husband in her eyes should rise again in him.

There were years of doubt and waiting. He was a good boy and a bad boy, now brilliant, now touching, now disappointing, now gloriously reassuring, and now heartrending as only the children of our blood can be. He had errors and bad moments, lapses into sheer naughtiness, phases of indolence, attacks of contagious vulgarity. But more and more surely she saw him for his father's son ; she traced the same great curiosities, the same keen dauntless questioning ; whatever incidents might disturb and perplex her, his intellectual growth went on strong and clear and increasing like some sacred flame that is carried in procession, halting perhaps and swaying but keeping on, over the heads of a tumultuous crowd.

He went from his school to the Royal College of Science, thence to successes at Cambridge, and thence to Berlin. He travelled in Asia Minor and Persia, had a journey to America, and then came back to her and London, sunburned, moustached, manly, and a little strange. When he had been a boy she had thought his very soul pellucid ; it had clouded opaquely against her scrutiny as he passed into adolescence. Then through the period of visits and departures, travel together, separations, he grew into something detached and admirable, a man curiously reminiscent of his father, un-

expectedly different.    She ceased to feel what he was feeling
in his mind, had to watch him, infer, guess, speculate about
him.    She desired for him and dreaded for him with an undying
tenderness, but she no longer had any assurance that she
could interfere to help him.    He had his father's trick of
falling into thought.    Her brown eyes would watch him
across the flowers and delicate glass and silver of her dinner-
table when he dined at home with her.    Sometimes he seemed
to forget she existed, sometimes he delighted in her, talked
to amuse her, petted her ;  sometimes, and then it was she
was happiest, he talked of plays and books with her, discussed general questions, spoke even of that broadly conceived
scheme of work which engaged so much of his imagination.
She knew that it was distinguished and powerful work.    Old
friends of her husband spoke of it to her, praised its inspired
directness, its beautiful simplicity.    Since the days of Wollas-
ton, they said, no one had been so witty an experimenter,
no one had got more out of mere scraps of apparatus or
contrived more ingenious simplifications.

When he had accepted the minor Professorship which gave
him a footing in the world of responsible scientific men, she
had taken a house in a quiet street in Chelsea which necessi-
tated a daily walk to his laboratory.    It was a little old Georgian
house with worn and graceful rooms, a dignified front door
and a fine gateway of Sussex ironwork much painted and
eaten away.    She arranged it with great care ;  she had kept
most of her furniture, and his study had his father's bureau,
and the selfsame agate paper-weight that had pressed the unfinished paper he left when he died.    She was a woman of
persistent friendships, and there came to her, old connections
of those early times trailing fresher and younger people in
their wake, sons, daughters, nephews, disciples ;  her son
brought home all sorts of interesting men, and it was remarkable to her that amidst the talk and discussion at her table,
she discovered aspects of her son and often quite intimate
aspects she would never have seen with him alone.

She would not let herself believe that this Indian summer of
her life could last for ever.    He was no passionless devotee
of research, for all his silence and restraints.    She had seen him
kindle with anger at obstacles and absurdities, and quicken
in the presence of beauty.    She knew how readily and richly
he responded to beauty.    Things happened to have run
smoothly with him so far, that was all.    " Of course," she said,
" he must fall in love.    It cannot be long before he falls in
love."

Once or twice that had seemed to happen, and then it had
come to nothing. . . .

She knew that sooner or later this completion of his possibilities must come, that the present steadfastness of purpose
was a phase in which forces gathered, that love must sweep into

his life as a deep and passionate disturbance. She wondered where it would take him, whether it would leave him enriched or devastated. She saw at times how young he was ; she had, as I suppose most older people have about their juniors, the profoundest doubt whether he was wise enough yet to be trusted with a thing so good as himself. He had flashes of high-spirited indiscretion, and at times a wildfire of humour flared in his talk. So far that had done no worse for him than make an enemy or so in scientific circles. But she had no idea of the limits of his excitability. She would watch him and fear for him—she knew the wreckage love can make—and also she desired that he should lose nothing that life and his nature could give him.

## § 3

In the two months of separation that ensued before Marjorie was one-and-twenty, Trafford's mind went through some remarkable phases. At first the excitement of his passion for Marjorie obscured everything else, then with his return to London and his laboratory the immense inertia of habit and slowly developed purposes, the complex yet convergent system of ideas and problems to which so much of his life had been given, began to reassert itself. His love was vivid and intense, a light in his imagination, a fever in his blood ; but it was a new thing ; it had not crept into the flesh and bones of his being, it was away there in Surrey ; the streets of London, his home, the white-walled chambers in which his apparatus was arranged, with its skylight and high windows and charts of constants, had no suggestion of her. She was outside—an adventure—a perplexing incommensurable with all these things.

He had left Buryhamstreet with Marjorie riotously in possession of his mind. In the train he could think of nothing but Marjorie, and how she had shone at him in the study, and how her voice had sounded when she spoke, and how she stood and moved, and the shape and sensation of her hands, and how it had felt to hold her for those brief moments in the wood and press lips and body to his, and how her face had gleamed in the laced shadows of the moonlight, soft and wonderful.

In fact, he thought of Marjorie.

He thought she was splendid, courageous, wise by instinct. He had no doubt of her or that she was to be his—when the weeks of waiting had passed by. She was his, and he was Marjorie's ; that had been settled from the beginning of the world. It didn't occur to him that anything had happened to alter his life or any of his arrangements in any way, except that they were altogether altered—as the world is altered without displacement when the sun pours up in the east. He was glorified—and everything was glorified.

He wondered how they would meet again, and dreamt a

thousand impossible and stirring dreams, but he dreamt them as dreams.

At first, to Durgan's infinite distress, he thought of her all day; and then, as the old familiar interests grappled him again, he thought of her in the morning and the evening and as he walked between his home and the laboratory and at all sorts of incidental times—and even when the close-locked riddles of his research held the foreground and focus of his thoughts he still seemed to be thinking of her as a radiant background to ions and molecules and atoms and interwoven systems of eddies and quivering oscillations deep down in the very heart of matter.

And always he thought of her as something of the summer. The rich decays of autumn came, the Chelsea roads were littered with variegated leaves that were presently wet and dirty and slippery, the twilight crept down into the day towards five o'clock and four, but in his memory of her the leaves were green, the evenings were long, the warm quiet of rural Surrey in high August filled the air. So that it was with a kind of amazement he found her in London and in November close at hand. He was called to the college telephone one day from a conversation with a proposed research student. It was a middle-aged woman bachelor anxious for the D.Sc., who wished to occupy the farther bench in the laboratory; but she had no mental fire, and his mind was busy with excuses and discouragements.

He had no thought of Marjorie when she answered, and for an instant he did not recognise her voice.

" Yes, I'm Mr. Trafford." . . .

" Who is it ? " he reiterated with a note of irascibility. " Who ? "

The little voice laughed. " Why ! I'm Marjorie ! " it said.

Then she was back in his life like a lantern suddenly become visible in a wood at midnight.

It was like meeting her as a china figure, neat and perfect and two inches high. It was her voice, very clear and very bright and quite characteristic, as though he was hearing it through the wrong end of a telescope. It was her voice, clear as a bell ; confident without a shadow.

" It's *me* ! Marjorie !   I'm twenty-one to-day ! "

It was like a little arrow of exquisite light shot into the very heart of his life.

He laughed back.   " Are you for meeting me then, Marjorie ? "

§ 4

They met in Kensington Gardens with an air of being clandestine and defiant. It was one of those days of amber sunlight, soft air, and tender beauty with which London relieves the tragic glooms of the year's decline. There was still a residue of warm-tinted leaves in puffs and clusters upon the tree branches, a boat or two ruffled the blue Serpentine, and the waterfowl gave colour and animation to the selvage of the water. The sedges were still a greenish yellow.

The two met shyly. They were both a little unfamiliar to each other. Trafford was black-coated, silk-hatted, umbrella-d, a decorous young professor in the place of the cheerful areonaut who had fallen so gaily out of the sky. Marjorie had a new tailor-made dress of russet-green, and a little cloth toque ruled and disciplined the hair he had known as a ruddy confusion. . . . They had dreamt, I think, of extended arms and a wild rush to embrace one another. Instead, they shook hands.

" And so," said Trafford, " we meet again ! "

" I don't see why we shouldn't meet ! " said Marjorie.

There was a slight pause.

" Let's have two of those jolly little green chairs," said Trafford. . . .

They walked across the grass towards the chairs he had indicated, and both were full of the momentous things they were finding it impossible to say.

" There ought to be squirrels here, as there are in New York," he said at last.

They sat down. There was a moment's silence, and then Trafford's spirit rose in rebellion and he plunged at this—this stranger beside him.

" Look here," he said, " do you still love me, Marjorie ? "

She looked up into his face with eyes in which surprise and scrutiny passed into something altogether beautiful. " I love you—altogether," she said in a steady, low voice.

And suddenly she was no longer a stranger, but the girl who had flitted to his arms breathless, unhesitating, through the dusk. His blood quickened. He made an awkward gesture as though he arrested an impulse to touch her. " My sweetheart," he said. " My dear one ! "

Marjorie's face flashed responses. " It's you," he said.

" Me," she answered.

" Do you remember ? "

" Everything ! "

" My dear ! "

" I want to tell you things," said Marjorie. " What are we to do ? " . . .

He tried afterwards to retrace that conversation. He was chiefly ashamed of his scientific preoccupations during that London interval. He had thought of a thousand things ; Marjorie had thought of nothing else but love and him. Her happy assurance, her absolute confidence that his desires would march with hers, reproached and confuted every adverse thought in him as though it was a treachery to love. He had

that sense which I suppose comes at times to every man, of
entire unworthiness for the straight, unhesitating decision,
the clear simplicity of a woman's passion.  He had dreamt
vaguely, unsubstantially, the while he had arranged his
pressures and temperatures and infinitesimal ingredients, and
worked with goniometer and trial models and the new calculating machine he had contrived for his research.  But she
had thought clearly, definitely, fully—of nothing but coming
to him.  She had thought out everything that bore upon
that ; reasons for precipitance, reasons for delay, she had
weighed the rewards of conformity against the glamour of
romance.  It became more and more clear to him as they
talked, that she was determined to elope with him, to go to
Italy, and there have an extraordinarily picturesque and
beautiful time.  Her definiteness shamed his poverty of
anticipation.  Her enthusiasm carried him with her.  Of
course it was so that things must be done. . . .

When at last they parted under the multiplying lamps of
the November twilight, he turned his face eastward.  He was
afraid of his mother's eyes—he scarcely knew why.  He
walked along Kensington Gore, and the clustering confused
lights of street and house, white and golden and orange and
pale lilac, the moving lamps and shining glitter of the traffic,
the luminous interiors of omnibuses, the reflection of carriage
and hoarding, the fading daylight overhead, the phantom
trees to the left, the deepening shadows and blacknesses
among the houses on his right, the bobbing heads of way-
farers, were just for him the stir and hue and texture of fairyland.  All the world was fairyland.  He went to his club and
dined there, and divided the evening between geography, as
it is condensed in Baedeker and Murray on North Italy, Italian
Switzerland and the Italian Riviera, and a study of the
marriage laws as they are expounded in *Whitaker's Almanack*,
the *Encyclopædia Britannica*, and other convenient works of
reference.  He replaced the books as he used them, and went
at last from the library into the smoking-room, but seeing a
man who might talk to him there, he went out at once into
the streets, and fetched a wide compass by Baker Street,
Oxford Street, and Hyde Park, home.

He was a little astonished at himself and everything.

But it was going to be—splendid.

(What poor things words can be !)

§ 5

He found his mother still up.  She had been re-reading
*The Old Wives' Tale*, and she sat before a ruddy fire in the
shadow beyond the lit circle of a green-shaded electric light
thinking, with the book put aside.  In the dimness above was
his father's portrait.  "Time you were in bed, mother," he
said reprovingly, and kissed her eyebrow and stood above

her. " What's the book ? " he asked, and picked it up and put it down, forgotten. Their eyes met. She perceived he had something to say ; she did not know what. " Where have you been ? " she asked.

He told her, and they lapsed into silence. She asked another question and he answered her, and the indifferent conversation ended again. The silence lengthened. Then he plunged : " I wonder, mother, if it would put you out very much if I brought home a wife to you ? "

So it had come to this—and she had not seen it coming. She looked into the glowing recesses of the fire before her and controlled her voice by an effort. " I'd be glad for you to do it, dear—if you loved her," she said very quietly. He stared down at her for a moment ; then he knelt down beside her and took her hand and kissed it. " *My dear*," she whispered softly, stroking his head, and her tears came streaming. For a time they said no more.

Presently he put coal on the fire, and then sitting on the hearthrug at her feet and looking away from her into the flames—in an attitude that took her back to his boyhood— he began to tell her brokenly and awkwardly of Marjorie.

" It's so hard, mother, to explain these things," he began. " One doesn't half understand the things that are happening to one. I want to make you in love with her, dear, just as I am. And I don't see how I can."

" Perhaps I shall understand, my dear. Perhaps I shall understand better than you think."

" She's such a beautiful thing—with something about her—— You know those steel blades you can bend back to the hilt—and they're steel ! And she's tender. It's as if some one had taken tears, mother, and made a spirit out of them——"

She caressed and stroked his hand. " My dear," she said, " I know."

" And a sort of dancing daring in her eyes."

" Yes," she said. " But tell me where she comes from, and how you met her—and all the circumstantial things that a sensible old woman can understand."

He kissed her hand and sat down beside her, with his shoulder against the arm of her chair, his fingers interlaced about his knee. She could not keep her touch from his hair, and she tried to force back the thought in her mind that all these talks must end, that very soon indeed they would end. And she was glad, full of pride and joy too that her son was a lover after her heart, a clean and simple lover as his father had been before him. He loved this unknown Marjorie, finely, sweetly, bravely, even as she herself could have desired to have been loved. She told herself she did not care very greatly even if this Marjorie should prove unworthy. So long as her son was not unworthy.

He pieced his story together.  He gave her a picture of the Popes, Marjorie in her family like a jewel in an ugly setting, so it seemed to him, and the queer dull rage of her father and all that they meant to do.  She tried to grasp his perplexities and advise, but chiefly she was filled with the thought that he was in love.  If he wanted a girl he should have her, and if he had to take her by force, well, wasn't it his right ?  She set small store upon the Popes that night—or any circumstances.  And since she herself had married on the slightest of security, she was concerned very little that this great adventure was to be attempted on an income of a few hundreds a year.  It was outside her philosophy that a wife should be anything but glad to tramp the roads if need be with the man who loved her.  He sketched out valiant plans, was for taking Marjorie away in the teeth of all opposition and bringing her back to London.  It would have to be done decently, of course, but it would have, he thought, to be done.  Mrs. Trafford found the prospect perfect ; never before had he sounded and looked so like that dim figure which hung still and sympathetic above them.  Ever and again she glanced up at her husband's quiet face. . . .

On one point she was very clear with him.

" You'll live with us, mother ? " he said abruptly.

" Not with you.  As near as you like.  But one house, one woman. . . . I'll have a little flat of my own—for you both to come to me."

" Oh, nonsense, mother !  You'll have to be with us. Living alone, indeed ! "

" My dear, I'd *prefer* a flat of my own.  You don't understand—everything.  It will be better for all of us like that."

There came a little pause between them, and then her hand was on his head again.  " Oh, my dear," she said, " I want you to be happy.  And life can be difficult.  I won't give a chance—for things to go wrong.  You're hers, dear, and you've got to be hers—be each other's altogether.  I've watched so many people.  And that's the best, the very best you can have.  There's just the lovers—the real enduring lovers ; and the uncompleted people who've failed to find it." . . .

§ 6

Trafford's second meeting with Marjorie, which, by the bye, happened on the afternoon of the following day, brought them near to conclusive decisions.  The stiffness of their first encounter in London had altogether vanished.  She was at her prettiest and in the highest spirits—and she didn't care for anything else in the world.  A gauzy silk scarf which she had bought and not paid for that day, floated atmospherically about her straight trim body ;  her hair had caught the infection of insurrection and was waving rebelliously about

her ears. As he drew near her his grave discretion passed
from him as clouds pass from a hillside. She smiled radiantly.
He held out both his hands for both of hers, and never did a
maiden come so near and yet not get a public and shameless
kissing.

One could as soon describe music as tell their conversation.
It was a matter of tones and feelings. But the idea of flight
together, of the bright awakening in unfamiliar sunshine
with none to come between them, had gripped them both. A
certain sober gravity of discussion only masked that deeper
inebriety. It would be easy for them to get away ; he had no
lectures until February ; he could, he said, make arrangements, leave his research. She dreaded disputation. She was
for a simple disappearance, notes on pincushions and defiantly
apologetic letters from Boulogne, but his mother's atmosphere
had been a gentler one than her home's, with a more powerful
disposition to dignity. He still couldn't understand that the
cantankerous egotism of Pope was indeed the essential man ;
it seemed to him a crust of bad manners that reason ought to
pierce.

The difference in their atmospheres came out in their talk,
in his desire for a handsome and dignified wedding—though
the very heavens protested—and her resolve to cut clear of
every one, to achieve a sort of gaol delivery of her life, make a
new beginning altogether with the minimum of friction and the
maximum of surprise. Unused to fighting, he was magnificently prepared to fight ; she, with her intimate knowledge
of chronic domestic conflict, was for the evasion of all the
bickerings, scoldings, and misrepresentations his challenge
would occasion. He thought in his innocence a case could
be stated and discussed ; but no family discussion she had
ever heard had even touched the realities of the issue that
occasioned it.

" I don't like this underhand preparation," he said.

" Nor I," she echoed. " But what can one do ? "

" Well, oughtn't I to go to your father and give him a
chance ? Why shouldn't I ? It's—the dignified way."

" It won't be dignified for father," said Marjorie, " anyhow."

" But what right has he to object ? "

" He isn't going to discuss his rights with you. He *will*
object."

" But *why* ? "

" Oh ! because he's started that way. He hit you. I
haven't forgotten it. Well, if he goes back on that now——
He'd rather die than go back on it. You see, he's ashamed in
his heart. It would be like confessing himself wrong not to
keep it up that you're the sort of man one hits. He just hates
you because he hit you. I haven't been his daughter for
twenty-one years for nothing."

" I'm thinking of us," said Trafford. " I don't see we oughtn't to go to him just because he's likely to be—unreasonable."

" My dear, do as you please. He'll forbid and shout, and hit tables until things break. Suppose he locks me up ! "

" Oh, Habeas Corpus, and my strong right arm ! He's much more likely to turn you out-of-doors."

" Not if he thinks the other will annoy you more. I'll have to bear a storm."

" Not for long."

" He'll bully mother till she cries over me. But do as you please. She'll come and she'll beg me—— Do as you please. Perhaps I'm a coward. I'd far rather I could slip away."

Trafford thought for a moment. " I'd far rather you could," he answered, in a voice that spoke of inflexible determinations.

They turned to the things they meant to do. " *Italy* ! " she whispered. " *Italy* ! " Her face was alight with her burning expectation of beauty, of love, of the new heaven and the new earth that lay before them. The intensity of that desire blazing through her seemed to shame his dull discretions. He had to cling to his resolution, lest it should vanish in that contagious intoxication.

" You understand I shall come to your father," he said, as they drew near the gate where it seemed discreet for them to part.

" It will make it harder to get away," she said, with no apparent despondency. " It won't stop us. Oh ! do as you please."

She seemed to dismiss the question, and stood hand-in-hand with him in a state of glowing gravity. She wouldn't see him again for four-and-twenty hours. Then a thought came into her head—a point of great practical moment.

" Oh ! " she said, " of course, you won't tell father you've seen me."

She met his eye. " Really you mustn't," she said. " You see—he'll make a row with mother for not having watched me better. I don't know what he isn't likely to do. It isn't myself—— This is a confidential communication—all this. No one in this world knows I am meeting you. If you *must* go to him, go to him."

" For myself ? "

She nodded, with her open eyes on his—eyes that looked now very blue and very grave, and her lips a little apart.

She surprised him a little, but even this sudden weakness seemed adorable.

" All right," he said.

" You don't think that I'm shirking—— ? " she asked, a little too eagerly.

"You know your father best," he answered. "I'll tell you all he says and all the terror of him here to-morrow afternoon."

## § 7

In the stillness of the night Trafford found himself thinking over Marjorie ; it was a new form of mental exercise which was destined to play a large part in his existence for many subsequent years. There had come a shadow on his confidence in her. She was a glorious person ; she had a kind of fire behind her and in her—shining through her, like the lights in a fire-opal, but—— He wished she had not made him promise to conceal their meeting and their close co-operation from her father. Why did she do that ? It would spoil his case with her father, and it could forward things for them in no conceivable way. And from that, in some manner too subtle to trace, he found his mind wandering to another problem, which was destined to reappear with a slowly dwindling importance very often in this procedure of thinking over Marjorie in the small hours. It was the riddle—it never came to him in the daytime, but only in those intercalary and detachedly critical periods of thought—why exactly had she engaged herself to Magnet ? Why had she ? He couldn't imagine himself, in Marjorie's position, doing anything of the sort. Marjorie had ways of her own ; she was different. . . . Well, anyhow, she was splendid and loving and full of courage. . . . He had got no further than this when at last he fell asleep.

## § 8

Trafford's little attempt to regularise his position was as creditable to him as it was inevitably futile. He sought out 29 Hartstone Square in the morning on his way to his laboratory, and he found it one of a great row of stucco houses each with a portico and a dining-room window on the ground floor, and each with a railed area from which troglodytic servants peeped. Collectively the terrace might claim a certain ugly dignity of restraint, there was none of your Queen Anne nonsense of art or beauty about it, and the narrow height, the subterranean kitchens of each constituent house, told of a steep relentless staircase and the days before the pampering of the lower classes began. The houses formed a square, as if the British square so famous at Waterloo for its dogged resistance to all the forces of the universe had immortalised itself in buildings, and they stared upon a severely railed garden of hardy shrubs and gravel to which the tenants had the inestimable privilege of access. They did not use it much, that was their affair, but at any rate they had keys and a nice sense of rights assured, and at least other people were kept out.

Trafford turned out of a busy high-road full of the mixed exhilarating traffic of our time, and came along a quiet street into this place, and it seemed to him he had come into a corner of defence and retreat, into an atmosphere of obstinate and unteachable resistances. But this illusion of conservativism in its last ditch was dispelled altogether in Mr. Pope's portico. Youth flashed out of these solemnities like a dart shot from a cave. Trafford was raising his hand to the solid brass knocker when abruptly it was snatched from his fingers, the door was flung open, and a small boy with a number of dirty books in a strap flew out and hit him with projectile violence.

" Blow ! " said the young gentleman, recoiling, and Trafford recovering said : " Hullo, Theodore ! "

" Lord ! " said Theodore, breathless, " it's you ! *What* a lark ! Your name's never mentioned—nohow. What *did* you do ? . . . Wish I could stop and see it ! I'm ten minutes late. *Ave atque vale.* So long ! "

He vanished with incredible velocity. And Mr. Trafford was alone in possession of the open doorway except for Toupee, who after a violent outbreak of hostility altered his mind and cringed to his feet in abject and affectionate propitiation. A pseudo-twin appeared, said " Hello ! " and vanished, and then he had an instant's vision of Mr. Pope, newspaper in hand, appearing from the dining-room. His expression of surprise changed to malevolence, and he darted back into the room from which he had emerged. Trafford decided to take the advice of a small brass plate on his left hand, and " ring also."

A housemaid came out of the bowels of the earth very promptly and ushered him up two flights of stairs into what was manifestly Mr. Pope's study.

It was a narrow, rather dark room lit by two crimson curtained windows, and with a gas fire before which Mr. Pope's walking boots were warming for the day. The apartment revealed to Trafford's cursory inspection many of the stigmata of an Englishman of active intelligence and literary tastes. There in the bookcase were the collected works of Scott, a good large illustrated *Shakespeare* in numerous volumes, and a complete set of bound *Punches* from the beginning. A pile of back numbers of *The Times* stood on a cane stool in a corner, and in a little bookcase handy for the occupier of the desk were *Whitaker, Wisden* and an old peerage. The desk bore traces of recent epistolary activity, and was littered with the printed matter of Aunt Plessington's movements. Two or three recent issues of *The Financial Review of Reviews* were also visible. About the room hung steel engravings apparently of defunct judges or at any rate of exceedingly grim individuals, and over the mantel were trophies of athletic prowess, a bat witnessing that Mr. Pope had once captained the second eleven at Harrogby.

Mr. Pope entered with a stern expression and a sentence prepared. " Well, sir," he said with a note of ironical affability, " to what may I ascribe this—intrusion ? "

Mr. Trafford was about to reply when Mr. Pope interrupted. " Will you be seated ? " he said, and turned his desk chair about for himself, and occupying it, crossed his legs and pressed the finger-tips of his two hands together. " Well, sir ? " he said.

Trafford remained standing astraddle over the boots before the gas fire.

" Look here, sir," he said ; " I am in love with your daughter. She's one-and-twenty, and I want to see her—and in fact——" He found it hard to express himself. He could think only of a phrase that sounded ridiculous. " I want—in fact—to pay my addresses to her."

" Well, sir, I don't want you to do so. That is too mild. I object strongly—very strongly. My daughter has been engaged to a very distinguished and able man, and I hope very shortly to hear that that engagement—— Practically it is still going on. I don't want you to intrude upon my daughter further."

" But look here, sir. There's a certain justice—I mean a certain reasonableness——"

Mr. Pope held out an arresting hand. " I don't wish it. Let that be enough."

" Of course it isn't enough. I'm in love with her—and she with me. I'm an entirely reputable and decent person——"

" May I be allowed to judge what is or is not suitable companionship for my daughter ?—and what may or may not be the present state of her affections ? "

" Well, that's rather the point we are discussing. After all, Marjorie isn't a baby. I want to do all this—this affair, openly and properly if I can, but, you know, I mean to marry Marjorie—anyhow."

" There are two people to consult in that matter."

" I'll take the risk of that."

" Permit me to differ."

A feeling of helplessness came over Trafford. The curious irritation Mr. Pope always roused in him began to get the better of him. His face flushed hotly. " Oh really ! really ! this is—this is nonsense ! " he cried. " I never heard anything so childish and pointless as your objection——"

" Be careful, sir ! " cried Mr. Pope, " be careful ! "

" I'm going to marry Marjorie."

" If she marries you, sir, she shall never darken my doors again ! "

" If you had a thing against me ! "

" *Haven't* I ! "

" What have you ? "

There was a quite perceptible pause before Pope fired his shot.

" Does any decent man want the name of Trafford associated with his daughter. Trafford ! Look at the hoardings, sir ! "

A sudden blaze of anger lit Trafford. " My God ! " he cried, and clenched his fists and seemed for a moment ready to fall upon the man before him. Then he controlled himself by a violent effort. " You believe in that libel on my dead father ? " he said, with white lips.

" Has it ever been answered ? "

" A hundred times. And anyhow !—Confound it ! I don't believe—*you* believe it. You've raked it up—as an excuse ! You want an excuse for your infernal domestic tyranny ! That's the truth of it. You can't bear a creature in your household to have a will or preference of her own. I tell you, sir, you are intolerable—intolerable ! "

He was shouting, and Pope was standing now and shouting too. " Leave my house, sir. Get out of my house, sir. You come here to insult me, sir ! "

A sudden horror of himself and Pope seized the younger man. He stiffened and became silent. Never in his life before had he been in a bawling quarrel. He was amazed and ashamed.

" Leave my house ! " cried Pope, with an imperious gesture towards the door.

Trafford made an absurd effort to save the situation. " I am sorry, sir, I lost my temper. I had no business to abuse you——"

" You've said enough."

" I apologise for that. I've done what I could to manage things decently."

" Will you go, sir ? " threatened Mr. Pope.

" I'm sorry I came," said Trafford.

Mr. Pope took his stand with folded arms and an expression of weary patience.

" I did what I could," said Trafford at the door.

The staircase and passage were deserted. The whole house seemed to have caught from Mr. Pope that same quality of seeing him out. . . .

" Confound it ! " said Trafford in the street. " How on earth did all this happen ? " . . .

He turned eastward, and then realised that work would be impossible that day. He changed his direction for Kensington Gardens, and in the flower-bordered walk near the Albert Memorial he sat down on a chair, and lugged at his moustache and wondered. He was extraordinarily perplexed, as well as ashamed and enraged by this uproar. How had it begun ? Of course, he had been stupidly abusive, but the insult to his father had been unendurable. Did a man of Pope's sort quite honestly believe that stuff ? If he didn't, he deserved kicking. If he did, of course he was entitled to have it cleared up. But then he wouldn't listen ! Was there any case for the man at all ? Had he, Trafford, really put the thing so that Pope would listen ? He couldn't remember. What was it he had said in reply to Pope ? What was it exactly that Pope had said ?

It was already vague ; it was a confused memory of headlong words and answers ; what wasn't vague, what rang in his ears still, was the hoarse discord of two shouting voices.

Could Marjorie have heard ?

## § 9

So Marjorie carried her point. She wasn't to be married tamely after the common fashion which trails home and all one's beginnings into the new life. She was to be eloped with, romantically and splendidly, into a glorious new world. She walked on shining clouds, and if she felt some remorse, it was a very tender and satisfactory remorse, and with a clear conviction below it that in the end she would be forgiven.

They made all their arrangements elaborately and carefully. Trafford got a licence to marry her ; she was to have a new outfit from top to toe to go away with on that eventful day. It accumulated in the shop, and they marked the clothes *M. T.* She was watched, she imagined, but as her father did not know she had seen Trafford, nothing had been said to her, and no attempt was made to prohibit her going out and coming in. Trafford entered into the conspiracy with a keen interest, a certain amusement, and a queer little feeling of distaste. He hated to hide any act of his from any human being. The very soul of scientific work, you see, is publication. But Marjorie seemed to justify all things, and when his soul turned against furtiveness, he reminded it that the alternative was bawling.

One eventful afternoon he went to the college, and Marjorie slipped round by his arrangement to have tea with Mrs. Trafford. . . .

He returned about seven in a state of nervous apprehension ; came upstairs two steps at a time, and stopped breathless on the landing. He gulped as he came in, and his eyes were painfully eager. " She's been ? " he asked.

But Marjorie had won Mrs. Trafford.

" She's been," she answered. " Yes, she's all right, my dear."

" Oh, mother ! " he said.

" She's a beautiful creature, dear—and such a child ! Oh ! such a child ! And God bless you, dear. God bless you. . . .

" I think all young people are children. I want to take you both in my arms and save you. . . . I'm talking nonsense, dear."

He kissed her, and she clung to him as if he were something too precious to release.

## § 10

The elopement was a little complicated by a surprise manœuvre of Mrs. Pope's. She was more alive to the quality of the situation, poor lady ! than her daughter suspected ; she was watching, dreading, perhaps even furtively sympathising and trying to arrange—oh ! trying dreadfully to arrange. She had an instinctive understanding of the deep blue quiet in Marjorie's eyes, and the girl's unusual tenderness with Daffy and the children. She peeped under the blind as Marjorie went out, noted the care in her dress, watched her face as she returned, never plumbed her with a question for fear of the answer. She did not dare to breathe a hint of her suspicions to her husband, but she felt things were adrift in swift, smooth water, and her soul cried out for delay. So presently there came a letter from Cousin Susan Pendexter at Plymouth. The weather was beautiful, Marjorie must come at once, pack up and come and snatch the last best glow of the dying autumn away there in the west. Marjorie's jerry-built excuses, her manifest chagrin and reluctance, confirmed her mother's worst suspicions.

She submitted and went, and Mrs. Pope and Syd saw her off.

I do not like to tell how, a week later, Marjorie explained herself and her dressing-bag and a few small articles back to London from Plymouth. Suffice it that she lied desperately and elaborately. Her mother had never achieved such miracles of mis-statement, and she added a vigour that was all her own. It is easier to sympathise with her than exonerate her. She was in a state of intense impatience, and—what is strange—extraordinarily afraid that something would separate her from her lover if she did not secure him. She was in a fever of determination. She could not eat or sleep or attend to anything whatever ; she was occupied altogether with the thought of assuring herself to Trafford. He towered in her waking vision over town and land and sea.

He didn't hear the lies she told ; he only knew she was magnificently coming back to him. He met her at Paddington, a white-faced, tired, splendidly resolute girl, and they went to the waiting registrar's forthwith.

She bore herself with the intentness and dignity of one who is taking the cardinal step in life. They kissed as though it was a symbol, and were keenly business-like about cabs and luggage and trains. At last they were alone in the train together. They stared at one another.

" We've done it, Mrs. Trafford ! " said Trafford.

She snapped like an over-taut string, crumpled, clung to him, and without a word was weeping passionately in his arms.

It surprised him that she could weep as she did, and still

more to see her as she walked by his side along the Folkestone pier, altogether recovered, erect, a little flushed and excited like a child. She seemed to miss nothing. " Oh, smell the sea ! " she said. " Look at the lights ! Listen to the swish of the water below." She watched the luggage spinning on the wire rope of the giant crane, and he watched her face and thought how beautiful she was. He wondered why her eyes could sometimes be so blue and sometimes dark as night.

The boat cleared the pier and turned about and headed for France. They walked the upper deck together and stood side by side, she very close to him.

" I've never crossed the sea before," she said.

" Old England," she whispered. " It's like leaving a nest. A little row of lights and that's all the world I've ever known, shrunken to that already."

Presently they went forward and peered into the night.

" Look ! " she said. " *Italy* ! There's sunshine and all sorts of beautiful things ahead. Warm sunshine, wonderful old ruins, green lizards. . . ." She paused and whispered almost noiselessly : *love*——"

They pressed against each other.

" And yet isn't it strange ? All you can see is darkness, and clouds—and big waves that hiss as they come near. . . ."

§ 11

Italy gave all her best to welcome them. It was a late year, a golden autumn, with skies of such blue as Marjorie had never seen before. They stayed at first in a pretty little Italian hotel with a garden on the lake, and later they walked over Salvatore to Morcote and by boat to Ponte Tresa, and thence they had the most wonderful and beautiful tramp in the world to Luino, over the hills by Castelrotto. To the left of them all day was a broad valley with low-lying villages swimming in a luminous mist, to the right were purple mountains. They passed through paved streets with houses the colour of flesh and ivory, with balconies hung with corn and gourds, with tall church campaniles rising high, and great archways giving upon the blue lowlands ; they tramped along avenues of sweet chestnut and between stretches of exuberant vineyard, in which men and women were gathering grapes—purple grapes, a hatful for a soldo, that rasped the tongue. Everything was strange and wonderful to Marjorie's eyes ; now it would be a wayside shrine and now a yoke of soft-going, dewlapped oxen, now a chapel hung about with *ex votos*, and now some unfamiliar cultivation, or a gipsy-eyed child, or a scorpion that scuttled in the dust. The very names of the villages were like jewels to her, Varasca, Croglio, Ronca, Sesia, Monteggio. They walked, or sat by the wayside and talked, or rested at the friendly table of some kindly albergo. A woman as beautiful as Ceres, with a white neck all open, made them an omelette, and then fetched her baby from its cradle to nurse it while she talked to them as they made their meal. And afterwards she filled their pockets with roasted chestnuts, and sent them with melodious good wishes upon their way. And always high over all against the translucent blue hung the white shape of Monte Rosa, that warmed in colour as the evening came.

Marjorie's head was swimming with happiness and beauty, and with every fresh delight she recurred again to the crowning marvel of this clean-limbed man beside her, who smiled and carried all her luggage in a huge rucksack that did not seem to exist for him, and watched her and caressed her — and was hers, *hers* !

At Baveno there were letters. They sat at a little table outside a café and read them, suddenly mindful of England again. Incipient forgiveness showed through Mrs. Pope's reproaches, and there was also a simple, tender love-letter (there is no other word for it) from old Mrs. Trafford to her son.

From Baveno they set off up Monte Mottarone—whence one may see the Alps from Visto to Ortler Spitz—trusting to find the inn still open, and if it was closed to get down to Orta somehow before night. Or at the worst sleep upon the mountain-side.

(Monte Mottarone ! Just for a moment taste the sweet Italian name upon your lips.) Those were the days before the funicular from Stresa, when one trudged up a rude path through the chestnuts and walnuts.

As they ascended the long windings through the woods, they met an old poet and his wife, coming down from sunset and sunrise. There was a word or two about the inn, and they went upon their way. The old man turned ever and again to look at them.

" Adorable young people," he said. " Adorable happy young people. . . .

" Did you notice, dear, how she held that dainty little chin of hers ? . . .

" Pride is such a good thing, my dear, clear, straight pride like theirs—and they were both so proud ! . . .

" Isn't it good, dear, to think that once you and I may have looked like that to some passer-by. I wish I could bless them—sweet, swift young things ! I wish, dear, it was possible for old men to bless young people without seeming to set up for saints. . . ."

# CHAPTER ONE

## SETTLING DOWN

### § 1

IT was in a boat among the reeds upon the lake of Orta that Trafford first became familiarised with the idea that Marjorie was capable of debt.

"Oh, I ought to have told you," she began, apropos of nothing.

Her explanation was airy ; she had let the thing slip out of her mind for a time. But there were various debts to Oxbridge tradespeople. How much ? Well, rather a lot. Of course, the tradespeople were rather enticing when first one went up—— How much, anyhow ?

" Oh, about fifty pounds," said Marjorie, after her manner. " Not *more*. I've not kept all the bills ; and some haven't come in. You know how slow they are."

" These things *will* happen," said Trafford, though, as a matter of fact, nothing of the sort had happened in his case. " However, you'll be able to pay as soon as you get home, and get them all off your mind."

" I think fifty pounds will clear me," said Marjorie, clinging to her long-established total, " if you'll let me have that."

" Oh, we don't do things like that," said Trafford. " I'm arranging that my current account will be a sort of joint account, and your signature will be as good as mine—for the purpose of drawing, at least. You'll have your own cheque-book——"

" I don't understand, quite," said Marjorie.

" You'll have your own cheque-book and write cheques as you want them. That seems the simplest way to me."

" Of course," said Marjorie. " But isn't this—rather unusual ? Father always used to allowance mother."

" It's the only decent way according to my ideas," said Trafford. " A man shouldn't marry when he can't trust."

" Of course not," said Marjorie. Something between fear and compunction wrung her. " Do you think you'd better ? " she asked, very earnestly.

" Better ? "

" Do this."

" Why not ? "

" It's—it's so generous."

He didn't answer. He took up an oar and began to push out from among the reeds with something of the shy awkwardness of a boy who becomes apprehensive of thanks. He stole a glance at her presently and caught her expression—there was something very solemn and intent in her eyes—and he thought what a grave, fine thing his Marjorie could be.

313

But, indeed, her state of mind was quite exceptionally confused. She was disconcerted—and horribly afraid of herself.

"Do you mean that I can spend what I like ?" asked Marjorie.

"Just as I may," he said.

"I wonder," said Marjorie again, "if I'd better ?"

She was tingling with delight at this freedom, and she
knew she was not fit for its responsibility. She just came
short of a passionate refusal of his proposal. He was still
so new to her, and things were so wonderful, or I think she
would have made that refusal.

"You've got to," said Trafford, and ended the matter.

So Marjorie was silent—making good resolutions.

§ 2

Perhaps some day it may be possible to tell in English
again, in the language of Shakespeare and Herrick, of the
passion, the tenderness, the beauty, and the delightful
familiarisations of a happy honeymoon ; suffice it now, in
this delicate period, to record only how our two young lovers
found one day that neither had a name for the other. He
said she could be nothing better than Marjorie to him ; and
she, after a number of unsuccessful experiments, settled down
to the old schoolboy nickname made out of his initials, R. A. G.

"Dick," she said, "is too bird-like and boy-like. Andrew
I can't abide. Godwin gives one no chances for current use.
Rag you must be. Mag and Rag—poor innocents ! Old rag !"

"Mag," he said, "has its drawbacks. The street-boy in
London says, ' Shut your mug.' No, I think I shall stick to
Marjorie. . . ."

All honeymoons must end at last, so back they came to
London, still very bright and happy. And then Marjorie,
whose eyes had changed from flashing stones to darkly shining
pools of blue, but whose soul had still perhaps to find its depths,
set herself to the business of decorating and furnishing the
little house Mrs. Trafford had found for them within ten
minutes of her own. Meanwhile they lived in lodgings.

There can be no denying that Marjorie began her furnishing
with severely virtuous intentions. She was very particular
to ask Trafford several times what he thought she might
spend upon the enterprise. He had already a bedroom and a
study equipped, and he threw out three hundred pounds as
his conception of an acceptable figure. "Very well," said
Marjorie, with a note of great precision, "now I shall know,"
and straightway that sum took a place in her imagination
that was at once definitive and protective, just as her estimate
of fifty pounds for her Oxbridge debts had always been. She
assured herself she was going to do things, and she assured
herself she was doing things, on three hundred pounds. At
times the astonishment of two or three school friends, who
joined her in her shopping, stirred her to a momentary surprise

at the way she was managing to keep things within that limit, and following a financial method that had, after all, in spite of some momentary and already nearly forgotten distresses, worked very well at Oxbridge, she refrained from any additions until all the accounts had come to hand.

It was an immense excitement, shopping to make a home. There was in her composition a strain of constructive artistry with such concrete things, a strain that had hitherto famished. She was making a beautiful, secure little home for Trafford, for herself, for possibilities—remote perhaps, but already touching her imagination with the anticipation of warm, new, wonderful delights. There should be simplicity indeed in this home, but no bareness, no harshness, never an ugliness nor a discord. She had always loved colour in the skies, in the landscape, in the texture of stuffs and garments ; now out of the chaotic skein of countless shops she could choose and pick and mingle her threads in a glow of feminine self-expression.

On three hundred pounds, that is to say—as a maximum.

The house she had to deal with was, like Mrs. Trafford's, old and rather small ; it was partly to its lack of bedroom accommodation, but much more to the invasion of the street by the back premises of Messrs. Siddons & Thrale, the great Chelsea outfitters, that was due the lowness of the rent which brought it within the means of Trafford. Marjorie knew very clearly that her father would say her husband had taken her to live in a noisy slum, and that made her all the keener to insure that every good point in the interior told to its utmost, and that whatever was to be accessible to her family should glow with a refined but warm prosperity. The room downstairs was shapely, and in ripping off the papered canvas of the previous occupier, some very dilapidated but admirably proportioned panelling was brought to light. The dining-room and study door on the ground floor, by a happy accident, were of mahogany, with really very beautiful brass furnishings ; and the dining-room window upon the minute but by no means offensive paved garden behind, was curved and had a little shallow balcony of ironwork, half covered by a devitalised but leafy grape-vine. Moreover, the previous occupier had equipped the place with electric light and a bathroom of almost American splendour on the landing, glass-shelved, white-tiled, and white painted, so that it was a delight to go into.

Marjorie's mind leaped very rapidly to the possibilities of this little establishment. The panelling must be done and done well, anyhow ; that would be no more than a wise economy, seeing it might at any time help them to re-let ; it would be painted white, of course, and thus set the key for a clean brightness of colour throughout. The furniture would stand out against the softly shining white, and its line and proportions must be therefore the primary qualities to consider as she bought it. The study was much narrower than the dining-room, and so the passage, which the agent called the hall, was much broader and more commodious behind the happily wide staircase than in front, and she was able to banish out of the sight of the chance visitor all that litter of hat-stand and umbrella-stand, letters, boxes arriving and parcels to post, which had always offended her eye at home. At home there had been often the most unsightly things visible, one of Theo's awful caps, or his school books, and not infrequently her father's well-worn and all too fatally comfortable house slippers. A good effect at first is half the victory of a well-done house, and Marjorie accomplished another of her real economies here by carpeting hall and stair-case with a fine-toned, rich-feeling and rather high-priced blue carpet, held down by very thick brass stair-rods. She hung up four well-chosen steel engravings, put a single Chippendale chair in the hall, and a dark old Dutch clock that had turned out to be only five pounds when she had expected the shop-man to say eleven or twelve, on the half-landing. That was all. Round the corner by the study door was a mahogany slab, and the litter all went upon a capacious but very simple dark-stained hat-stand and table that were out of the picture entirely until you reached the stairs.

Her dining-room was difficult for some time. She had equipped that with a dark oak Welsh dresser made very bright with a dessert service that was, in view of its extremely decorative quality, remarkably cheap, and with some very pretty silver-topped glass bottles and flasks. This dresser and a number of simple but shapely facsimiles of old chairs, stood out against a nearly primrose paper, very faintly patterned, and a dark blue carpet with a margin of dead black stained wood. Over the mantel was a German colour-print of waves full of sunlight breaking under cliffs, and between this and the window were dark bookshelves, and a few bright-coloured books. On the wall, black-framed, were four very good Japanese prints, rich in greenish-blues and blueish-greys that answered the floor, and the window curtains took up some of the colours of the German print. But something was needed towards the window, she felt, to balance the warmly shining plates upon the dresser. The deep rose-red of the cherries that adorned them was too isolated, usurped too dominating a value. And while this was weighing upon her mind she saw in a window in Regent Street a number of Bokhara hangings very nobly displayed. They were splendid pieces of needlework, particularly glorious in their crimsons and reds, and suddenly it came to her that it was just one of these, one that had great ruby flowers upon it with dead-blue interlacings, that was needed to weld her gay-coloured scheme together. She hesitated, went half-way to Piccadilly Circus, turned back and asked the prices. The prices were towering prices, ten, fifteen, eighteen guineas, and when at last the

shopmen produced one with all the charm of colour she sought
at eight, it seemed like ten guineas snatched back as they
dropped from her hands. And still hesitating, she had three
that pleased her most sent home, " on approval," before she
decided finally to purchase one of them. But the trial was
conclusive. And then, struck with a sudden idea, she carried
off a long narrow one she had had no idea of buying before
into the little study behind. Suppose, she thought, instead of
hanging two curtains as anybody else would do in that window,
she ran this glory of rich colour across from one side on a great
rod of brass.

She was giving the study the very best of her attention.
After she had lapsed in some other part of the house from the
standards of rigid economy she had set up, she would as it were
restore the balance by adding something to the gracefully
dignified arrangement of this den he was to use. And the
brass rod of the Bokhara hanging that was to do instead of
curtains released her mind somehow to the purchase of certain
old candlesticks she had hitherto resisted. They were to
stand, bored to carry candle electric lights, on either corner of
the low bookcase that faced the window. They were very
heavy, very shapely candlesticks, and they cost thirty-five
shillings. They looked remarkably well when they were put
up, except that a sort of hollowness appeared between them
and clamoured for a delightful old brass-footed workbox she
had seen in a shop in Baker Street. Inquiry confirmed her
quick impression that this was a genuine piece (of quite exceptional genuineness) and that the price—they asked five
pounds ten and came down to five guineas—was in accordance
with this. It was a little difficult (in spite of the silent hunger
between the candlesticks) to reconcile this particular article
with her dominating idea of an austerely restrained expenditure, until she hit on the device of calling it a *hors d'œuvre,* and
regarding it not as furniture but as a present from herself to
Trafford that happened to fall in very agreeably with the process of house furnishing. She decided she would some day
economise its cost out of her dress allowance. The bookcase
on which it stood was a happy discovery in Kensington, just
five feet high, and with beautiful oval glass fronts, and its
capacity was supplemented and any excess in its price at least
morally compensated by a very tall, narrow, distinguished-
looking set of open shelves that had been made for some
special corner in another house, and which anyhow were really
and truly dirt cheap. The desk combined grace and good
proportions to an admirable extent, the fender of pierced brass
looked as if it had always lived in immediate contact with
the shapely old white marble fireplace, and the two armchairs
were marvels of dignified comfort. By the fireplace were a
banner-shaped needlework firescreen, a white sheepskin
hearthrug, a little patch and powder table adapted to carry

LML—M                                                      L

books, and a green-shaded lamp, grouped in a common inaudible demand for a reader in slippers.   Trafford, when at
last the apartment was ready for his inspection, surveyed these
arrangements with a kind of dazzled admiration.

" By Jove ! " he said.   " How little people know of the
homes of the Poor ! "

Marjorie was so delighted with his approval that she determined to show Mrs. Trafford next day how prettily at least
her son was going to live.   The good lady came and admired
everything, and particularly the Bokhara hangings.   She did
not seem to appraise, but something set Marjorie talking
rather nervously of a bargain-hunter's good fortune.   Mrs.
Trafford glanced at the candlesticks and the low bookcase, and
returned to the glowing piece of needlework that formed the
symmetrical window curtain in the study.   She took it in her
hand, and whispered, " Beautiful ! "

" But aren't these rather good ? " asked Mrs. Trafford.

Marjorie answered, after a little pause.   " They're not too
good for *him*," she said.

### § 3

And now these young people had to resume life in London
in earnest.   The orchestral accompaniment of the world at
large began to mingle with their hitherto unsustained duet.
It had been inaudible in Italy.   In Chelsea it had sounded,
faintly perhaps but distinctly, from their very first inspection of the little house.   A drawing-room speaks of callers, a
dining-room of lunches and dinners.   It had swayed Marjorie
from the front door inward.

During their honeymoon they had been gloriously unconscious of comment.   Now Marjorie began to show herself
keenly sensitive to the advent of a score of personalities, and
very anxious to show just how completely successful in every
sense her romantic disobedience had been.   She knew she had
been approved of, admired, condemned, sneered at, thoroughly
discussed.   She felt it her first duty to Trafford, to all who had
approved of her flight, to every one, herself included, to make
this marriage obviously, indisputably, a success, a success
not only by her own standards but by the standards of any one
soever who chose to sit in judgment on her.

There was Trafford.   She felt she had to extort the admission from every one that he was the handsomest, finest, ablest,
most promising and most delightful man a prominent
humorist was ever jilted for.   She wanted them to understand clearly just all that Trafford was—and that involved,
she speedily found in practice, making them believe a very
great deal that as yet Trafford wasn't.   She found it practically
impossible not to anticipate his election to the Royal Society
and the probability of a more important professorship.   She
felt that anyhow he was an F.R.S. in the sight of God. . . .

It was almost equally difficult not to indicate a larger income than facts justified.

It was entirely in Marjorie's vein in those early days that she would want to win on every score and by every standard of reckoning. If Marjorie had been a general she would have counted no victory complete if the struggle was not sustained and desperate, and if it left the enemy with a single gun or flag, or herself with so much as a man killed or wounded. The people she wanted to impress varied very widely. She wanted to impress the Carmel girls, and the Carmel girls, with their racial trick of acute appraisement, were only to be won by the very highest quality all round. They had, she knew, two standards of quality, cost and distinction. As far as possible, she would give them distinction. But whenever she hesitated over something on the verge of cheapness the thought of those impending judgments tipped the balance. The Carmel girls were just two influential representatives of a host. She wanted to impress quite a number of other school and college friends. There were various shy, plastic-spirited, emotional creatures, of course, for the most part with no confidence in their own appearance, who would be impressed quite adequately enough by Trafford's good looks and witty manner and easy temper. They might perhaps fall in love with him and become slavish to her after the way of their kind, and anyhow they would be provided for, but there were plenty of others of a harder texture whose tests would be more difficult to satisfy. There were girls who were the daughters of prominent men, who must be made to understand that Trafford was prominent, girls who were well connected, who must be made to realise the subtle excellence of Trafford's blood. As she thought of Constance Graham, for example, or Ottiline Winchelsea, she felt the strongest disposition to thicken the by no means well-authenticated strands that linked Trafford with the Traffords of Trafford-over-Lea. She went about the house dreaming a little apprehensively of these coming calls, and the pitiless light of criticism they would bring to bear, not indeed upon her happiness—that was assured—but upon her success.

The social side of the position would have to be strained to the utmost, Marjorie felt, with Aunt Plessington. The thought of Aunt Plessington made her peculiarly apprehensive. Aunt Plessington had to the fullest extent that contempt for merely artistic or scientific people which sits so gracefully upon the administrative English. You see, people of that sort do not get on in the sense that a young lawyer or barrister gets on. They do not make steps ; they boast and quarrel and are jealous perhaps, but that steady patient shove upward seems beyond their intelligence. The energies God manifestly gave them for shoving, they dissipate in the creation of weak beautiful things and unremunerative theories, or in the establishment of views sometimes diametrically opposed to the ideas of influential people. And they are " queer "—socially. They just moon about doing this so-called " work " of theirs, and even when the judgment of eccentric people forces a kind of reputation upon them—Heaven knows why !—they make no public or social use of it. It seemed to Aunt Plessington that the artist and the scientific man were dealt with very neatly and justly in the Parable of the Buried Talent. Moreover, their private lives were often scandalous, they married for love instead of interest, often quite disadvantageously, and their relationships had all the instability that is natural upon such a foundation. And, after all, what good were they ? She had never met an artist or a prominent imaginative writer or scientific man that she had not been able to subdue in a minute or so by flat contradiction, and if necessary slightly raising her voice. They had little or no influence even upon their own public appointments. . . .

The thought of the invasion of her agreeable little back-street establishment by this Britannic system of judgments filled Marjorie's heart with secret terrors. She felt she had to grapple with and overcome Aunt Plessington, or be for ever fallen—at least, so far as that amiable lady's report went, and she knew it went pretty far. She wandered about the house trying to imagine herself Aunt Plessington.

Immediately she felt the gravest doubts whether the whole thing wasn't too graceful and pretty. A rich and rather massive ugliness, of course, would have been the thing to fetch Aunt Plessington. Happily, it was Aunt Plessington's habit to veil her eyes with her voice. She might not see very much.

The subjugation of Aunt Plessington was difficult, but not altogether hopeless, Marjorie felt, provided her rejection of Magnet had not been taken as an act of personal ingratitude. There was a case on her side. She was discovering, for example, that Trafford had a really very considerable range of acquaintance among quite distinguished people ; big figures like Evesham and MacHaldo, for example, were intelligently interested in the trend of his work. She felt this gave her a basis for Plessingtonian justifications. She could produce those people—as one shows one's loot. She could imply, " Oh, Love and all that nonsense ! Certainly not ! *This* is what I did it for." With skill and care and good luck, and a word here and there in edgeways, she believed she might be able to represent the whole adventure as the well-calculated opening of a campaign on soundly Plessingtonian lines. Her marriage to Trafford, she tried to persuade herself, might be presented as something almost as brilliant and startling as her aunt's swoop upon her undistinguished uncle.

She might pretend that all along she had seen her way to things, to coveted dinner-tables and the familiarity of coveted guests, to bringing people together and contriving arrange-

ments, to influence and prominence, to culminations and
intrigues impossible in the comparatively specialised world
of a successful humorist and playwright, and so at last to those
high freedoms of authoritative and if necessary offensive
utterance in a strangulated contralto, and from a position of
secure eminence, which is the goal of all virtuously ambitious
Englishwomen of the governing classes—that is to say, of all
virtuously ambitious Englishwomen. . . .

§ 4

And while such turbid solicitudes as these were flowing in
again from the London world to which she had returned, and
fouling the bright, romantic clearness of Marjorie's life, Trafford,
in his ampler, less detailed way was also troubled about their
coming re-entry into society. He, too, had his old associations.

For example, he was by no means confident of the favourable
judgments of his mother upon Marjorie's circle of school and
college friends, whom he gathered from Marjorie's talk were
destined to play a large part in this new phase of his life. She
had given him very ample particulars of some of them ; and
he found them interesting rather than richly attractive personalities. It is to be noted that while he thought always of
Marjorie as a beautiful, grown-up woman, and his mate and
equal, he was still disposed to regard her intimate friends as
schoolgirls of an advanced and aggressive type. . . .

Then that large circle of distinguished acquaintances which
Marjorie saw so easily and amply utilised for the subjugation
of Aunt Plessington didn't present itself quite in that sense
to Trafford's private thoughts. He hadn't that certitude of
command over them, nor that confidence in their unhesitating
approval of all he said and did. Just as Marjorie wished him
to shine in the heavens over all her people, so, in regard to his
associates, he was extraordinarily anxious that they should
realise, and realise from the outset without qualification or
hesitation, how beautiful, brave and delightful she was. And
you know he had already begun to be aware of an evasive
feeling in his mind that at times she did not altogether do
herself justice—he scarcely knew as yet how or why. . . .

She was very young. . . .

One or two individuals stood out in his imagination, representatives and symbols of the rest. Particularly there was
that old giant, Sir Roderick Dover, who had been, until
recently, the Professor of Physics in the great Oxford laboratories. Dover and Trafford had one of those warm friendships
which spring up at times between a rich-minded man whose
greatness is assured and a young man of brilliant promise. It
was all the more affectionate because Dover had been a friend
of Trafford's father. These two and a group of other careless-
minded, able, distinguished and uninfluential men at the

Winton Club affected the end of the smoking-room near the
conservatory in the hours after lunch, and shared the joys of
good talk and fine jesting about the big fireplace there.  Under
Dover's broad influence they talked more ideas and less gossip
than is usual with English club men.   Twaddle about appointments, about reputations, topics from the morning's papers,
London architecture, and the commerce in " good stories "
took refuge at the other end in the window bays or by the
farther fireplace.   Trafford only began to realise on his return
to London how large a share this intermittent perennial conversation had contributed to the atmosphere of his existence.
Amidst the romantic circumstances of his flight with Marjorie
he had forgotten the part these men played in his life and
thoughts.   Now he was enormously exercised in the search for a
reconciliation between these, he felt, incommensurable factors.

He was afraid of what might be Sir Roderick's unspoken
judgment on Marjorie and the house she had made—though
what was there to be afraid of ?   He was still more afraid—
and this was even more remarkable—of the clear little judgments—hard as loose, small diamonds in a bed—that he
thought Marjorie might pronounce on Sir Roderick.   He had
never disguised from himself that Sir Roderick was fat—
nobody who came within a hundred yards of him could be
under any illusion about that—and that he drank a good deal,
ate with a cosmic spaciousness, loved a cigar, and talked and
laughed with a freedom that sometimes drove delicate-minded
new members into the corners remotest from the historical
fireplace.   Trafford knew himself quite definitely that there
was a joy in Dover's laugh and voice, a beauty in his face
(that was somehow mixed up with his healthy corpulence),
and a breadth, a charity, a leonine courage in his mind (that
was somehow mixed up with his careless freedom of speech)
that made him an altogether satisfactory person.

But supposing Marjorie didn't see any of that !

Still, he was on the verge of bringing Sir Roderick home when
a talk at the club one day postponed that introduction of the two
extremes of Trafford's existence for quite a considerable time.

Those were the days of the first enthusiasms of the militant
suffrage movement, and the occasional smashing of a Downing
Street window or an assault upon a minister kept the question
of woman's distinctive intelligence and character persistently
before the public.   Godley Buzard, the feminist novelist, had
been the guest of some member to lunch, and the occasion
was too provocative for any one about Dover's fireplace to
avoid the topic.   Buzard's presence, perhaps, drove Dover
into an extreme position on the other side ;  he forgot Trafford's
new-wedded condition, and handled this great argument, an
argument which has scarcely progressed since its beginning
in the days of Plato and Aristophanes, with the freedoms of an
ancient Greek and the explicitness of a modern scientific man.

He opened almost apropos of nothing. "Women," he said, "are inferior—and you can't get away from it."

"You can deny it," said Buzard.

"In the face of the facts," said Sir Roderick. "To begin with, they're several inches shorter, several pounds lighter ; they've less physical strength in foot-pounds."

"More endurance," said Buzard.

"Less sensitiveness merely. All those are demonstrable things—amenable to figures and apparatus. Then they stand nervous tensions worse, the breaking-point comes sooner. They have weaker inhibitions, and inhibition is the test of a creature's position in the mental scale."

He maintained that in the face of Buzard's animated protest. Buzard glanced at their moral qualities. "More moral ! " cried Dover, " more self-restraint ! Not a bit of it ! Their desires and passions are weaker even than their controls ; that's all. Weaken restraints and they show their quality. A drunken woman is far worse than a drunken man. And as for their biological significance——"

"They are the species," said Buzard, "and we are the accidents."

"They are the stolon and we are the individualised branches. They are the stem and we are the fruits. Surely it's better to exist than just transmit existence. And that's a woman's business, though we've fooled and petted most of 'em into forgetting it. . . ."

He proceeded to an attack on the intellectual quality of women. He scoffed at the woman artist, at feminine research, at what he called the joke of feminine philosophy. Buzard broke in with some sentences of reply. He alleged the lack of feminine opportunity, inferior education.

"You don't or won't understand me," said Dover. "It isn't a matter of education or opportunity, or simply that they're of inferior capacity ; it lies deeper than that. They don't *want* to do these things. They're different."

"Precisely," ejaculated Buzard, as if he claimed a score.

"They don't care for these things. They don't care for art or philosophy, or literature or anything except the things that touch them directly. That's their peculiar difference. Hunger they understand, and comfort, and personal vanity and desire, furs and chocolate and husbands, and the extreme importance conferred upon them by having babies at infrequent intervals. But philosophy or beauty for its own sake, or dreams ! Lord ! no ! The Mahometans know they haven't souls, and they say it. We know, and keep it up that they have. Haven't all we scientific men had 'em in our laboratories working ; don't we know the papers they turn out ? Every sane man of five-and-forty knows something of the disillusionment of the feminine dream, but we who've had the beautiful creatures under us, weighing rather badly,

handling rather weakly, invariably missing every fine detail
and all the implications of our researches, never flashing,
never leaping, never being even thoroughly bad—we're
specialists in the subject.  At the present time there are far
more educated young women than educated young men
available for research work—and who wants them ?  Oh, the
young professors who've still got ideals perhaps.  And in they
come, and if they're dull, they just voluminously do nothing,
and if they're bright, they either marry your demonstrator
or get him into a mess.  And the work—— ?  It's nothing
to them.  No woman ever painted for the love of painting,
or sang for the sounds she made, or philosophised for the sake
of wisdom as men do——"

Buzard intervened with instances.  Dover would have none
of them.  He displayed astonishing and distinctive knowledge.
" Madame Curie," clamoured Buzard, " Madame Curie."

" There was Curie," said Dover.  " No woman alone has
done such things.  I don't say women aren't clever," he insisted.
" They're too clever.  Give them a man's track or a man's intention marked and defined, they'll ape him to the life——"

Buzard renewed his protests, talking at the same time as
Dover, and was understood to say that women had to care
for something greater than art or philosophy.  They were
custodians of life, the future of the race——

" And that's my crowning disappointment," cried Dover.
" If there was one thing in which you might think women
would show a sense of some divine purpose in life, it is in the
matter of children—and they show about as much care in
that matter, oh !—as rabbits.  Yes, rabbits !  I stick to it.
Look at the things a nice girl will marry ; look at the men's
children she'll consent to bring into the world.  Cheerfully !
Proudly !  For the sake of the home and the clothes.  Nasty
little beasts they'll breed without turning a hair.  All about
us we see girls and women marrying ugly men, dull and stupid
men, ill-tempered dyspeptic wrecks, sickly young fools, human
rats—*rats* ! "

" No, no ! " cried Trafford to Dover.

Buzard's voice clamoured that all would be different when
women had the vote.

" If ever we get a decent care for Eugenics, it will come
from men," said a white-faced little man on the sofa beside
Trafford, in the confidential tone of one who tells a secret.

" Doing it cheerfully ! " insisted Dover.

Trafford in mid-protests was suddenly stricken into silence
by a memory.  It was as if the past had thrown a stone at the
back of his head and hit it smartly.  He nipped his sentence
in the bud.  He left the case for women to Buzard. . . .

He revived that memory again on his way home.  It had
been in his mind overlaid by a multitude of newer, fresher
things, but now he took it out and looked at it.  It was queer,

it was really very queer, to think that once upon a time, not so very long ago, Marjorie had been prepared to marry Magnet. Of course she had hated it, but still—— . . .

There is much to be discovered about life, even by a brilliant and rising young Professor of Physics. . . .

Presently Dover, fingering the little glass of yellow chartreuse he had hitherto forgotten in the heat of controversy, took a more personal turn.

" Don't we know," he said, and made the limpid amber vanish in his pause—" don't we know we've got to manage and control 'em—just as we've got to keep 'em and stand the racket of their misbehaviour ? Don't our instincts tell us ? Doesn't something tell us all that if we let a woman loose with our honour and trust, some other man will get hold of her ? We've tried it long enough now, this theory that a woman's a partner and an equal ; we've tried it long enough to see some of the results, and does it work ? Does it ? A woman's a prize, a possession, a responsibility, something to take care of and be careful about. . . . You chaps, if you'll forgive me, you advanced chaps, seem to want to have the women take care of you. You seem always to want to force decisions on them, make them answerable for things that you ought to decide and answer for. . . . If one could, if one could ! If ! . . . But they're not helps—that's a dream—they're dis-tractions, gratifications, anxieties, dangers, undertakings. . . ."

Buzard got in his one effective blow at this point. " That's why you've never married, Sir Roderick ? " he threw out.

The big man was checked for a moment. Trafford won-dered what memory lit that instant's pause. " I've had my science," said Dover.

§ 5

Mrs. Pope was of course among the first to visit the new home so soon as it was open to inspection. She arrived, looking very bright and neat in a new bonnet and some new black furs that suited her, bearing up bravely but obviously in a state of dispersed and miscellaneous emotion. . . .

In many ways Marjorie's marriage had been a great relief to her mother. Particularly it had been a financial relief. Marjorie had been the most expensive child of her family, and her cessation had led to increments both of Mrs. Pope's and Daphne's all too restricted allowances. Mrs. Pope had been able therefore to relapse from the orthodox Anglicanism into which poverty had driven her, and indulge for an hour weekly in the consolations of Higher Thought. These exer-cises in emancipated religiosity occurred at the house of Mr. Silas Root, and were greatly valued by a large circle of clients. Essentially they were orgies of vacuity, and they cost six guineas for seven hours. They did her no end of good. All through the precious weekly hour she sat with him in a silent twilight, very, very still and feeling—oh! "higher" than anything, and when she came out she wore an inane smile on her face and was prepared not to worry, to lie with facility, and to take the easiest way in every eventuality in an entirely satisfactory and exalted manner. Moreover he was "treating" her investments. Acting upon his advice, and doing the whole thing quietly with the idea of preparing a pleasant surprise for her husband, she had sold out of certain Home Railway debentures and invested in a company for working the auriferous waste which is so abundant in the drainage of Philadelphia, a company whose shareholders were chiefly higher-thought disciples, and whose profits therefore would inevitably be greatly enhanced by their concerted mental action. It was to the prospective profits in this that she owed the new black furs she was wearing.

The furs and the bonnet and the treatment she had had on the previous day, all helped to brace her up on Marjorie's doorstep for a complex and difficult situation, and to carry her through the first tensions of her call. She was so much to pieces as it was that she could not help feeling how much more to pieces she might have been—but for the grace of Silas Root. She knew she ought to have very strong feelings about Trafford, though it was not really clear to her what feelings she ought to have. On the whole she was inclined to believe she was experiencing moral disapproval mixed up with a pathetic and rather hopeless appeal for the welfare of the tender life that had entrusted itself so recklessly to these brutal and discreditable hands, though indeed if she had really dared to look inside her mind her chief discovery would have been a keenly jealous appreciation of Trafford's good looks and generous temper, and a feeling of injustice as between her own lot and Marjorie's. However, going on her assumed basis she managed to be very pale, concise, and tight-lipped at any mention of her son-in-law, and to put a fervour of helpless devotion into her embraces of her daughter. She surveyed the house with a pained constrained expression, as though she tried in vain to conceal from herself that it was all slightly improper, and even such objects as the Bokhara hangings failed to extort more than an insincere, "Oh, very nice, dear—*very* nice."

In the bedroom, she spoke about Mr. Pope. "He was dreadfully upset," she said. "His first thought was to come after you both with a pistol. If—if *he* hadn't married you——"

"But, dear Mummy, of *course* we meant to marry! We married right away."

"Yes, dear, of course. But if he hadn't——"

She paused, and Marjorie, with a momentary flush of indignation in her cheeks, did not urge her to conclude her explanation.

"He's *wounded*," said Mrs. Pope. "Some day perhaps he'll come round—you were always his favourite daughter."

"I know," said Marjorie concisely, with a faint flavour of cynicism in her voice.

"I'm afraid, dear, at present—he will do nothing for you."

"I don't think Rag would like him to," said Marjorie with an unreal serenity ; "*ever*."

"For a time I'm afraid he'll refuse to see you. He just wants to forget—everything."

"Poor old dad ! I wish he wouldn't put himself out like this. Still, I won't bother him, Mummy, if you mean that."

Then suddenly into Mrs. Pope's unsystematic unstable mind, started perhaps by the ring in her daughter's voice, there came a wave of affectionate feeling. That she had somehow to be hostile and unsympathetic to Marjorie, that she had to pretend that Trafford was wicked and disgusting, and not be happy in the jolly hope and happiness of this bright little house, cut her with a keen swift pain. She didn't know clearly why she was taking this coldly hostile attitude, or why she went on doing so, but the sense of that necessity hurt her none the less. She put out her hands upon her daughter's shoulders and whimpered : "Oh, my dear ! I do wish things weren't so difficult—so very difficult."

The whimper changed by some inner force of its own to honest sobs and tears.

Marjorie passed through a flash of amazement to a sudden understanding of her mother's case. "Poor dear Mummy," she said. "Oh ! poor dear Mummy. It's a shame of us ! "

She put her arms about her mother and held her for a while.

"It *is* a shame," said her mother in a muffled voice, trying to keep hold of this elusive thing that had somehow both wounded her and won her daughter back. But her poor grasp slipped again. "I knew you'd come to see it," she said, dabbing with her handkerchief at her eyes. "I knew you would." And then with the habitual loyalty of years resuming its sway : "He's always been so good to you." . . .

But Mrs. Pope had something more definite to say to Marjorie, and came to it at last with a tactful offhandedness. Marjorie communicated it to Trafford about an hour later on his return from the laboratory. "I say," she said, "old Daffy's engaged to Magnet ! "

She paused, and added with just the faintest trace of resentment in her voice, "She can have him, as far as I'm concerned."

"He didn't wait long," said Trafford tactlessly.

"No," said Marjorie ; "he didn't wait long. . . . Of course she got him on the rebound." . . .

## § 6

Mrs. Pope was only a day or so ahead of a cloud of callers. The Carmel girls followed close upon her, tall figures of black fur, with costly-looking muffs and a rich glitter at neck and wrist. Marjorie displayed her house, talking fluently about

other things, and watching for effects. The Carmel girls ran
their swift dark eyes over her appointments, glanced quickly
from side to side of her rooms, saw only too certainly that the
house was narrow and small—— But did they see that it
was clever ? They saw at any rate that she meant it to be
clever, and with true Oriental politeness said as much urgently
and extravagantly. Then there were the Rambord girls
and their mother, an unobservant lot who chattered about
the ice at Prince's ; then Constance Graham came with a
thoroughbred but very dirty aunt ; and then Ottiline Winchelsea with an American minor poet, who wanted a view of
mountains from the windows at the back, and said the bathroom ought to be done in pink. Then Lady Solomonson
came ; an extremely expensive-looking fair lady with an
affectation of cynicism, a keen intelligence, acutely apt conversation, and a queer effect of thinking of something else
all the time she was talking. She missed nothing. . . .

Hardly anybody failed to appreciate the charm and decision
of Marjorie's use of those Bokhara embroideries.

They would have been cheap at double the price.

### § 7

And then our two young people went out to their first
dinner-parties together. They began with Trafford's rich
friend Solomonson, who had played so large and so passive
a part in their first meeting. He had behaved with a sort
of magnanimous triumph over the marriage. He made it
almost his personal affair, as though he had brought it about.
" I knew there was a girl in it," he insisted, " and you told
me there wasn't. O-a-ah ! And you kept me in that smell
of disinfectant and things—what a chap that doctor was for
spilling stuff !—for six blessed days ! . . ."

Marjorie achieved a dress at once simple and good with
great facility by not asking the price until it was all over.
(There is no half-success with dinner-dresses, either the thing
is a success and inestimable, or not worth having at any price
at all.) It was blue with a thread of gold, and she had a
necklace of blueish moonstones, gold-set, and her hair ceased
to be copper and became golden, and her eyes unfathomable
blue. She was radiant with health and happiness, no one else
there had her clear freshness, and her manner was as restrained
and dignified and ready as a proud young wife's can be.
Every one seemed to like her and respect her and be interested
in her, and Trafford kissed her flushed cheek in the hansom
as they came home again and crowned her happiness. It
had been quite a large party, and really much more splendid
and brilliant than anything she had ever seen before. There
had been one old gentleman with a coloured button and
another with a ribbon ; there had been a countess with
historical pearls, and half a dozen other people one might

fairly call distinguished. The house was tremendous in its way, spacious, rich, glowing with lights, abounding in vistas and fine remote backgrounds. In the midst of it all she had a sudden thrill at the memory that less than a year ago she had been ignominiously dismissed from the dinner-table by her father for a hiccup. . . .

A few days after Aunt Plessington suddenly asked the Traffords to one of her less important but still interesting gatherings ; not one of those that swayed the world perhaps, but one which Marjorie was given to understand achieved important subordinate wagging. Aunt Plessington had not called, she explained in her note, because of the urgent demands the Movement made upon her time ; it was her wonderful hard-breathing way never to call on any one, and it added tremendously to her reputation ; none the less it appeared—though here the scrawl became illegible—she meant to shove and steer her dear niece upward at a tremendous pace. They were even asked to come a little early so that she might make Trafford's acquaintance.

The dress was duly admired, and then Aunt Plessington —assuming the hearthrug and forgetting the little matter of their career—explained quite Napoleonic and wonderful things she was going to do with her Movement, fresh principles, fresh applications, a big committee of all the " names "— they were easy to get if you didn't bother them to do things —a new and more attractive title, " Payment in Kind " was to give way to " Reality of Reward," and she herself was going to have her hair bleached bright white (which would set off her eyes and colour and the general geniality of appearance due to her projecting teeth), and so greatly increase her " platform efficiency." Hubert, she said, was toiling away hard at the detail of these new endeavours. He would be down in a few minutes' time. Marjorie, she said, ought to speak at their meetings. It would help both the Traffords to get on if Marjorie cut a dash at the outset, and there was no such dash to be cut as speaking at Aunt Plessington's meetings. It was catching on ; all next season it was sure to be the thing. So many promising girls allowed themselves to be submerged altogether in marriage for a time, and when they emerged every one had forgotten the promise of their début. She had an air of rescuing Marjorie from an impending fate by disabusing Trafford from injurious prepossessions. . . .

Presently the guests began to drop in, a vegetarian health specialist, a rising young woman factory inspector, a phrenologist who was being induced to put great talents to better uses under Aunt Plessington's influence, his dumb, obscure, but inevitable wife, a colonial bishop, a baroness with a taste rather than a capacity for intellectual society, a wealthy jam and pickle manufacturer and his wife, who had subscribed largely to the funds of the Movement and wanted to meet the lady of title, and the editor of the Movement's organ, *Upward and On*, a young gentleman of abundant hair and cadaverous silences, whom Aunt Plessington patted on the shoulder and spoke of as "one of our discoveries." And then Uncle Hubert came down, looking ruffled and over-worked, with his ready-made dress-tie—he was one of those men who can never master the art of tying a bow—very much askew. The conversation turned chiefly on the Move-ment ; if it strayed Aunt Plessington reached out her voice after it and brought it back in a masterful manner.

Through soup and fish Marjorie occupied herself with the inflexible rigour of the young editor, who had brought her down. When she could give her attention to the general conversation she discovered her husband a little flushed and tackling her aunt with an expression of quiet determination. The phrenologist and the vegetarian health specialist were regarding him with amazement, the jam and pickle manu-facturer's wife was evidently deeply shocked. He was refusing to believe in the value of the Movement, and Aunt Plessington was manifestly losing her temper.

" I don't see, Mrs. Plessington," he was saying, "that all this amounts to more than a kind of Glorified District Visiting. That is how I see it. You want to attack people in their homes—before they cry out to you. You want to compel them by this Payment in Kind of yours to do what you want them to do instead of trying to make them want to do it. Now, I think your business is to make them want to do it. You may perhaps increase the amount of milk in babies, and the amount of whitewash in cottages and slums by your methods—I don't dispute the promise of your statistics—but you're going to do it at a cost of human self-respect that's out of all proportion——"

Uncle Hubert's voice, with that thick utterance that always suggested a mouthful of plums, came booming down the table. " All these arguments," he said, " have been answered long ago."

" No doubt," said Trafford with a faint asperity. " But tell me the answers."

" It's ridiculous," said Aunt Plessington, " to talk of the self-respect of the kind of people—oh ! the very dregs ! "

" It's just because the plant is delicate that you've got to handle it carefully," said Trafford.

" Here's Miss Gant," said Aunt Plessington, " *she* knows the strata we are discussing. She'll tell you they have positively *no* self-respect—none at all."

" *My* people," said Miss Gant, as if in conclusive testimony, " actually conspire with their employers to defeat me."

" I don't see the absence of self-respect in that," said Trafford.

" But all their interests——"

" I'm thinking of their pride." . . .

The discussion lasted to the end of dinner and made no headway. As soon as the ladies were in the drawing-room,

Aunt Plessington, still warm from the conflict, turned on Marjorie and said, " I *like* your husband. He's wrong-headed, but he's young and he's certainly spirited. He *ought* to get on if he wants to. Does he do nothing but his researches ? "

" He lectures in the Spring Term," said Marjorie.

" Ah ! " said Aunt Plessington with a triumphant note, " you must alter all that. You must interest him in wider things. You must bring him out of his shell, and let him see what it is to deal with Affairs. Then he wouldn't talk such nonsense about our Work."

Marjorie was at a momentary loss for a reply, and in the instant's respite Aunt Plessington turned to the jam and pickle lady and asked in a bright, encouraging note : " Well ! And how's the Village Club getting on ? " . . .

She had another lunge at Trafford as he took his leave. " You must come again soon," she said. " I *love* a good wrangle, and Hubert and I never want to talk about our Movement to any one but unbelievers. You don't know the beginnings of it yet. Only I warn you they have a way of getting converted. I warn you." . . .

On this occasion there was no kissing in the cab. Trafford was exasperated.

" Of all the intolerable women ! " he said, and was silent for a time.

" The astounding part of it is," he burst out, " that this sort of thing, this Movement and all the rest of it, does really give the quality of English public affairs. It's like a sample —dredged. The—the *cheapness* of it ! Raised voices, rash assertions, sham investigations, meetings and committees and meetings, that's the stuff of it, and politicians really have to attend to it, and silly, ineffective, irritating bills really get drafted and messed about with and passed on the strength of it. Public affairs are still in the Dark Ages. Nobody now would think of getting together a scratch committee of rich old women and miscellaneous conspicuous people to design an electric tram, and jabbering and jabbering and jabbering, and if any one objects "—a note of personal bitterness came into his voice—" jabbering faster ; but nobody thinks it ridiculous to attempt the organisation of poor people's affairs in that sort of way. This project of the super-session of Wages by Payment in Kind—oh ! it's childish. If it wasn't it would be outrageous and indecent. Your uncle and aunt haven't thought for a moment of any single one of the necessary consequences of these things they say their con-founded Movement aims at, effects upon the race, upon public spirit, upon people's habits and motives. They've just a queer craving to feel powerful and influential, which they think they can best satisfy by upsetting the lives of no end of harmless poor people—the only people they dare upset—and that's about as far as they go. . . . Your aunt's detestable, Marjorie."

Marjorie had never seen him so deeply affected by anything but herself. It seemed to her he was needlessly disturbed by a trivial matter. He sulked for a space, and then broke out again.

"That confounded woman talks of my physical science," he said, "as if research were an amiable weakness, like collecting postage-stamps. And it's changed human conditions more in the last ten years than all the parliamentary wire-pullers and legislators and administrative experts have done in two centuries. And for all that, there's more clerks in White-hall than professors of physics in the whole of England." . . .

"I suppose it's the way that sort of thing gets done," said Marjorie, after an interval.

"That sort of thing doesn't get done," snapped Trafford. "All these people burble about with their movements and jobs, and lectures and stuff—and *things happen*. Like some one getting squashed to death in a crowd. Nobody did it, but anybody in the muddle can claim to have done it—if only they've got the cheek of your Aunt Plessington."

He seemed to have finished.

"*Done*!" he suddenly broke out again. "Why! people like your Aunt Plessington don't even know where the handle is. If they ventured to look for it, they'd give the whole show away! Done, indeed!"

"Here we are!" said Marjorie, a little relieved to find the hansom turning out of King's Road into their own side street. . . .

And then Marjorie wore the blue dress with great success at the Carmels'. The girls came and looked at it and admired it—it was no mere politeness. They admitted there was style about it, a quality—there was no explaining. "You're *wonderful*, Madge!" cried the younger Carmel girl.

The Carmel boy, seizing the opportunity of a momentary seclusion in a corner, ended a short but rather portentous silence with "I say, you *do* look ripping," in a voice that implied the keenest regret for the slacknesses of a summer that was now infinitely remote to Marjorie. It was ridiculous that the Carmel boy should have such emotions—he was six years younger than Trafford and only a year older than Marjorie, and yet she was pleased by his manifest wound. . . .

There was only one little thing at the back of her mind that alloyed her sense of happy and complete living that night, and that was the ghost of an addition sum. At home, in her pretty bureau, a gathering pile of bills, as yet unpaid, and an empty cheque-book with appealing counterfoils, awaited her attention.

Marjorie had still to master the fact that all the fine braveries and interests and delights of life that offer themselves so amply to the favoured children of civilisation, trail and, since the fall of man at any rate, have trailed after them something—something, the justification of morality, the despair of all easy, happy souls, the unavoidable drop of bitterness in the cup of pleasure—the Reckoning.

# CHAPTER TWO

## THE CHILD OF THE AGES

### § I

WHEN the intellectual history of this time comes to be written, nothing I think will stand out more strikingly than the empty gulf in quality between the superb and richly fruitful scientific investigations that are going on and the general thought of other educated sections of the community. I do not mean that the scientific men are as a whole a class of supermen, dealing with and thinking about everything in a way altogether better than the common run of humanity, but that in their own field they think and work with an intensity, an integrity, a breadth, boldness, patience, thoroughness and faithfulness that (excepting only a few artists) puts their work out of all comparison with any other human activity. Often the field in which the work is done is very narrow, and almost universally the underlying philosophy is felt rather than apprehended. A scientific man may be large and deep-minded, deliberate and personally detached in his work, and hasty, commonplace and superficial in every other relation of life. Nevertheless it is true that in these particular directions the human mind has achieved a new and higher quality of attitude and gesture, a veracity, self-detachment and self-abnegating vigour of criticism that tend to spread out and must ultimately spread out to every other human affair. In these uncontroversial issues at least mankind has learned the rich rewards that ensue from patience and infinite pains.

The peculiar circumstances of Trafford's birth and upbringing had accentuated his natural disposition toward this new thoroughness of intellectual treatment which has always distinguished the great artist, and which to-day is also the essential quality of the scientific method. He had lived apart from any urgency to produce and compete in the common business of the world ; his natural curiosities, fed and encouraged by his natural gifts, had grown into a steady passion for clarity and knowledge. But with him there was no specialisation. He brought out from his laboratory into the everyday affairs of the world the same sceptical restraint of judgment which is the touchstone of scientific truth. This made him a tepid and indeed rather a scornful spectator of political and social life. Party formulæ, international rivalries, social customs, and very much of the ordinary law of our state impressed him as a kind of fungoid growth out of a fundamental intellectual muddle. It all maintained itself hazardously, changing and adapting itself unintelligently to unseen conditions. He saw no ultimate truth in this seething welter of human efforts, no tragedy as yet in its defeats, no value in its victories. It had to go on, he believed, until the spreading certitudes of the scientific method pierced its unsubstantial thickets, burst its delusive films, drained away its folly. Aunt Plessington's talk of order and progress and the influence of her Movement impressed his mind very much as the cackle of some larger kind of hen—which cackles because it must. Only Aunt Plessington being human simply imagined the egg. She laid—on the plane of the ideal. When the great nonsensical issues between liberal and conservative, between socialist and individualist, between " Anglo-Saxon " and " Teuton," between the " white race " and the " yellow race " arose in Trafford's company, he would if he felt cheerful take one side or the other as chance or his amusement with his interlocutors determined, and jest and gibe at the opponent's inconsistencies, and if on the other hand he chanced to be irritable he would lose his temper at this " chewing of mesembryanthemum " and sulk into silence. " Chewing mesembryanthemum " was one of Trafford's favourite images—no doubt the reader knows that abundant fleshy Mediterranean weed and the weakly unpleasant wateriness of its substance. After such discussions he went back to his laboratory and his proper work with a feeling of escape, as if he shut a door upon a dirty and undisciplined market-place crowded with mental defectives. Yet even before he met and married Marjorie, there was a queer little undertow of thought in his mind which insisted that this business could not end with door-slamming, that he didn't altogether leave the social confusion outside his panels when he stood alone before his apparatus, and that sooner or later that babble of voices would force his defences and overcome his disdain.

His particular work upon the intimate constitution of matter had broadened very rapidly in his hands. The drift of his work had been to identify all colloids as liquid solutions of variable degrees of viscosity, and to treat crystalline bodies as the only solids. He had dealt with oscillating processes in colloid bodies with especial reference to living matter. He had passed from a study of the melting and toughening of glass to the molecular structure of a number of elastic bodies, and so, by a characteristic leap into botanical physiology, to the states of resinous and gummy substances at the moment of secretion. He worked at first upon a false start, and then resumed to discover a growing illumination. He found himself in the presence of phenomena that seemed to him to lie near the still undiscovered threshold of the secret processes of living protoplasm. He was, as it were, breaking into biology by way of molecular physics. He spent many long nights of deep excitement, calculating and arranging the development of these seductive intimations. It was this work which his marriage had interrupted, and to which he was now returning.

He was surprised to find how difficult it was to take it up again. He had been only two months away from it, and yet already it had not a little of the feeling of a relic taken from a drawer. Something had faded. It was at first as if a film had come over his eyes, so that he could no longer see these things clearly and subtly and closely. His senses, his emotions, had been living in a stirring and vivid illumination. Now in this cool quietude bright clouds of coloured memory-stuff swam distractingly before his eyes. Phantom kisses on his lips, the memory of touches and the echoing vibrations of an adorable voice, the thought of a gay delightful fireside and the fresh recollection of a companion intensely felt beside him, effaced the delicate profundities of this dim place. Durgan hovered about him, helpful and a mute reproach. Trafford had to force his attention daily for the better part of two weeks before he had fully recovered the fine enchanting interest of that suspended work.

### § 2

At last one day he had the happiness of possession again. He had exactly the sensation one gets when some hitherto intractable piece of a machine one is putting together, clicks neatly and beyond all hoping, into its place. He found himself working in the old style, with the hours slipping by disregarded. He sent out Durgan to get him tobacco and tea and smoked-salmon sandwiches, and he stayed in the laboratory all night. He went home about half-past five, and found a white-faced, red-eyed Marjorie still dressed, wrapped in a travelling-rug, and crumpled and asleep in his study armchair beside the grey ashes of an extinct fire.

In the instant before she awoke he could see what a fragile and pitiful being a healthy and happy young wife can appear. Her pose revealed an unsuspected slender weakness of body, her face something infantile and wistful he had still to reckon with. She awoke with a start and stared at him for a moment, and at the room about her. " Oh, where have you been ? " she asked almost querulously. " Where *have* you been ? "

" But, my dear ! " he said, as one might speak to a child " why aren't you in bed ? It's just dawn."

" Oh," she said, " I waited and I waited. It seemed you *must* come. I read a book. And then I fell asleep." And then with a sob of feeble self-pity, " And here I am ! " She rubbed the back of her hand into one eye and shivered. " I'm cold," she said, " and I want some tea."

" Let's make some," said Trafford.

" It's been horrible waiting," said Marjorie, without moving ; " horrible ! Where have you been ? "

" I've been working. I got excited by my work. I've been

at the laboratory. I've had the best spell of work I've ever had since our marriage."

"But I have been up all night ! " she cried, with her face and voice softening to tears. " How *could* you ? How *could* you ? "

He was surprised by her weeping. He was still more surprised by the self-abandonment that allowed her to continue. " I've been working," he repeated, and then looked about with a man's helplessness for the tea apparatus. One must have hot water and a teapot and a kettle ; he would find those in the kitchen. He strolled thoughtfully out of the room, thinking out the further details of tea-making all mixed up with amazement at Marjorie, while she sat wiping her eyes with a crumpled pocket-handkerchief. Presently she followed him down with the rug about her like a shawl, and stood watching him as he lit a fire of wood and paper among the ashes in the kitchen fireplace. " It's been dreadful," she said, not offering to help.

" You see," he said, on his knees, " I'd really got hold of my work at last."

" But you should have sent——"

" I was thinking of my work. I clean forgot."

" Forgot ? "

" Absolutely."

" Forgot—*me* ! "

" Of course," said Trafford, with a slightly puzzled air ; " you don't see it as I do."

The kettle engaged him for a time. Then he threw out a suggestion. " We'll have to have a telephone."

" I couldn't imagine where you were. I thought of all sorts of things. I almost came round—but I was so horribly afraid I mightn't find you."

He renewed his suggestion of a telephone.

" So that if I really want you——" said Marjorie. " Or if I just want to feel you're there."

" Yes," said Trafford slowly, jabbing a piece of firewood into the glow ; but it was chiefly present in his mind that much of that elaborate experimenting of his wasn't at all a thing to be cut athwart by the exasperating gusts of a telephone bell clamouring for attention. Hitherto the laboratory telephone had been in the habit of disconnecting itself early in the afternoon.

And yet after all it was this instrument, the same twisted wire and little quivering tympanum, that had brought back Marjorie into his life.

## § 3

And now Trafford fell into a great perplexity of mind. His banker had called his attention to the fact that his account was overdrawn to the extent of three hundred and thirteen pounds, and he had been under that vague sort of impression one always has about one's current account that he was a hundred and fifty or so to the good. His first impression was that those hitherto infallible beings, those unseen gnomes of the pass-book whose lucid figures, neat tickings, and unrelenting additions constituted banks to his imagination, must have made a mistake ; his second that some one had tampered with a cheque. His third thought pointed to Marjorie and the easy circumstances of his home. For a fortnight now she had been obviously ailing, oddly irritable ; he did not understand the change in her, but it sufficed to prevent his taking the thing to her at once and going into it with her as he would have done earlier. Instead he had sent for his pass-book, and in the presence of its neat columns realised for the first time the meaning of Marjorie's " three hundred pounds." Including half a dozen cheques to Oxbridge tradesmen for her old debts, she had spent, he discovered, nearly seven hundred and fifty.

He sat before the little bundle of crumpled strips of pink and white, perforated, purple stamped and effaced, in a state of extreme astonishment. It was no small factor in his amazement to note how very carelessly some of those cheques of Marjorie's had been written. Several she had not even crossed. The effect of it all was that she'd just spent his money—freely—with an utter disregard of the consequences.

Up to that moment it had never occurred to Trafford that anybody one really cared for could be anything but punctilious about money. Now here, with an arithmetical exactitude of demonstration, he perceived that Marjorie wasn't.

It was so tremendous a discovery for him, so disconcerting and startling, that he didn't for two days say a word to her about it. He couldn't think of a word to say. He felt that even to put these facts before her amounted to an accusation of disloyalty and selfishness that he hadn't the courage to make. His work stopped altogether. He struggled hourly with that accusation. Did she realise—— ? There seemed no escape from his dilemma ; either she didn't care or she didn't understand !

His thoughts went back to the lake of Orta, when he had put all his money at her disposal. She had been surprised, and now he perceived she had also been a little frightened. The chief excuse he could find for her was that she was inexperienced —absolutely inexperienced.

Even now, of course, she was drawing fresh cheques. . . .

He would have to pull himself together, and go into the whole thing—for all its infinite disagreeableness—with her. . . .

But it was Marjorie who broached the subject.

He had found work at the laboratory unsatisfactory, and after lunching at his club he had come home and gone to his study in order to think out the discussion he contemplated

with her.    She came in to him as he sat at his desk.    " Busy ? "
she said.    " Not very," he answered ; and she came up to
him, kissed his head, and stood beside him with her hand on his
shoulder.

" Pass-book ? " she asked.

He nodded.

" I've been overrunning."

" No end."

The matter was opened.    What would she say ?

She bent to his ear and whispered, " I'm going to overrun
some more."

His voice was resentful.    " You *can't,*" he said compactly
without looking at her.    " You've spent—enough."

" There's—things."

" What things ? "

Her answer took some time in coming.    " We'll have to
give a wedding present to Daffy. . . . I shall want—some
more furniture."

Well, he had to go into it now.    " I don't think you can
have it," he said, and then as she remained silent, " Marjorie,
do you know how much money I've got ? "

" Six thousand."

" I *had.*    But we've spent nearly a thousand pounds.    Yes
—one thousand pounds—over and above income.    We meant
to spent four hundred.    And now, we've got—hardly anything over five."

" Five thousand," said Marjorie.

" Five thousand."

" And there's your salary."

" Yes, but at this pace——"

" Dear," said Marjorie, and her hands came about his neck,
" dear—there's something——"

She broke off.    An unfamiliar quality in her voice struck
into him.    He turned his head to see her face, rose to his feet
staring at her.

This remarkable young woman had become soft and wonderful as April hills across which clouds are sweeping.    Her
face was as if he had never seen it before ; her eyes bright with
tears.

" Oh ! don't let's spoil things by thinking of money," she
said.    " I've got something——"    Her voice fell to a whisper.
" Don't let's spoil things by thinking of money. . . . It's too
good, dear, to be true.    It's too good to be true.    It makes
everything perfect. . . . We'll have to furnish that little
room.    I didn't dare to hope it—somehow.    I've been so
excited and afraid.    But we've got to furnish that little room
there—that empty little room upstairs, dear, that we left
over. . . . Oh, my *dear !* my *dear* ! "

§ 4

The world of Trafford and Marjorie was filled and trans-figured by the advent of their child.

For two days of abundant silences he had been preparing a statement of his case for her, he had been full of the danger to his research and all the waste of his life that her extrava-gance threatened. He wanted to tell her just all that his science meant to him, explain how his income and life had all been arranged to leave him, mind and time and energy, free for these commanding investigations. His life was to him the service of knowledge—or futility. He had perceived that she did not understand this in him ; that for her, life was a blaze of eagerly sought experiences and gratifications. So far he had thought out things, and had them ready for her. But now all this impending discussion vanished out of his world. Their love was to be crowned by the miracle of parentage. This fact flooded his outlook and submerged every other consideration.

This manifest probability came to him as if it were an unforeseen marvel. It was as if he had never thought of such a thing before, as though a fact entirely novel in the order of the universe had come into existence. Marjorie became again magical and wonderful for him, but in a manner new and strange ; she was grave, solemn, significant. He was filled with a passionate solicitude for her welfare, and a passionate desire to serve her. It seemed impossible to him that only a day or so ago he should have been accusing her in his heart of disloyalty, and searching for excuses and mitigations. . . .

All the freshness of his first love for Marjorie returned, his keen sense of the sweet gallantry of her voice and bearing, his admiration for the swift, falcon-like swoop of her decisions, for the grace and poise of her body, and the steady frankness of her eyes ; but now it was all charged with his sense of this new joint life germinating at the heart of her slender vigour, spreading throughout her being to change it altogether into womanhood for ever. In this new light his passion for research and all the scheme of his life appeared faded and unworthy, as much egotism as if he had been devoted to hunting or golf or any such aimless preoccupation. Father-hood gripped him and faced him about. It was manifestly a monstrous thing that he should ever have expected Marjorie to become a mere undisturbing accessory to the selfish intel-lectualism of his career, to slave and limit herself to a mere bachelor income, and play no part of her own in the movement of the world. He knew better now. Research must fall into its proper place, and for his immediate business he must set to work to supplement his manifestly inadequate resources.

At first he could form no plan at all for doing that. He determined that research must still have his morning hours until lunch-time, and, he privately resolved, some part of the night. The rest of his day, he thought, he would set aside for a time to money-making. But he was altogether inexperienced in the methods of money-making ; it was a new problem, and a new sort of problem to him altogether. He discovered himself helpless and rather silly in the matter. The more obvious possibilities seemed to be that he might lecture upon his science or write. He communicated with a couple of lecture agencies, and was amazed at their scepticism : no doubt he knew his science, on that point they were compli-mentary in a profuse, unconvincing manner, but could he interest like X—and here they named a notorious quack—could he *draw* ? He offered Science Notes to a weekly periodical ; the editor answered that for the purposes of his publication he preferred, as between professors and journalists, journalists. " You real scientific men," he said, " are no doubt a thousand times more accurate and novel and all that, but as no one seems able to understand you——" He went to his old fellow-student, Gwenn, who was editing *The Scientific Review*, and through him he secured some semi-popular lectures, which involved, he found, travelling about twenty-nine miles weekly at the rate of four-and-sixpence a mile—counting nothing for the lectures. Afterwards Gwenn arranged for some regular notes on physics and micro-chemistry. Trafford made out a weekly time-table, on whose white of dignity, leisure, and the honourable pursuit of know-ledge, a diaper of red marked the claims of domestic necessity.

§ 5

It was astonishing how completely this coming child domin-ated the whole atmosphere and all the circumstances of the Traffords. It became their central fact, to which everything else turned and pointed. Its effect on Marjorie's circle of school and college friends was prodigious. She was the first of their company to cross the mysterious boundaries of a woman's life. She became to them a heroine mingled with something of the priestess. They called upon her more abundantly and sat with her, noted the change in her eyes and voice and bearing, talking with a kind of awe and a faint diffidence of the promised new life.

Many of them had been deeply tinged by the woman's suffrage movement, the feminist note was strong among them, and when one afternoon Ottiline Winchelsea brought round Agatha Alimony, the novelist, and Agatha said in that deep-ringing voice of hers : " I hope it will be a girl, so that presently she may fight the battle of her sex," there was the profoundest emotion. But when Marjorie conveyed that to Trafford he was lacking in response.

" I want a boy," he said, and, being pressed for a reason, explained : " Oh, one likes to have a boy. I want him with

just your quick eyes and ears, my dear, and just my own safe
and certain hands."

Mrs. Pope received the news with that depth and aimless
complexity of emotion which had now become her habitual
method with Marjorie. She kissed and clasped her daughter,
and thought confusedly over her shoulder, and said : " Of
course, dear—— Oh, I *do* so hope it won't annoy your
father." Daffy was " nice," but vague, and sufficiently
feminist to wish it a daughter, and the pseudo-twins said
" *Hoo*-ray ! " and changed the subject at the earliest possible
opportunity. But Theodore was deeply moved at the prospect
of becoming an uncle, and went apart and mused deeply and
darkly thereon for some time. It was difficult to tell just
what Trafford's mother thought ; she was complex and subtle,
and evidently did not show Marjorie all that was in her mind ;
but at any rate it was clear the prospect of a grandchild pleased
and interested her. And about Aunt Plessington's views there
was no manner of doubt at all. She thought, and remarked
judicially, as one might criticise a game of billiards, that on the
whole it was just a little bit too soon.

§ 6

Marjorie kept well throughout March and April, and then
suddenly she grew unutterably weary and uncomfortable in
London. The end of April came hot and close and dry—so
hot that it might have been July—the scrap of garden wilted,
and the streets were irritating with fine dust and blown scraps
of paper and drifting straws. She could think of nothing
but the shade of trees, and cornfields under sunlight and the
shadows of passing clouds. So Trafford took out an old
bicycle and wandered over the home counties for three days,
and at last hit upon a little country cottage near Great
Missenden, a cottage a couple of girl artists had furnished and
now wanted to let. It had a long, untidy vegetable garden
and a small orchard and drying-ground, with an old, super-
annuated humbug of a pear-tree near the centre surrounded
by a green seat, and high hedges with the promise of honeysuckle and dog-roses, and gaps that opened into hospitable
beech woods—woods not so thick but that there were glades
of bluebells, bracken and, to be exact, in places embattled
stinging-nettles. He took it and engaged a minute, active,
interested, philoprogenitive servant girl for it, and took
Marjorie thither in a taxi-cab. She went out, wrapped in a
shawl, and sat under the pear-tree and cried quietly with
weakness and sentiment and the tenderness of afternoon sunshine, and forthwith began to pick up wonderfully, and was
presently writing to Trafford to buy her a dog to go for walks
with, while he was away in London.

Trafford was still struggling along with his research in spite
of a constant gravitation to the cottage and Marjorie's side,

but he was also doing his best to grapple with the difficulties of his financial situation. His Science Notes, which were very uncongenial and troublesome to do, and his lecturing, still left his income far behind his expenditure, and the problem of minimising the invitable fresh inroads on his capital was insistent and distracting. He discovered that he could manage his notes more easily and write a more popular article if he dictated to a typist instead of writing out the stuff in his own manuscript. Dictating made his sentences more copious and open, and the effect of the young lady's by no means acquiescent back was to make him far more explicit than he tended to be pen in hand. With a pen and alone he felt the boredom of the job unendurably, and, to be through with it, became more and more terse, allusive, and compactly technical, after the style of his original papers. One or two articles by him were accepted and published by the monthly magazines, but as he took what the editors sent him, he did not find this led to any excessive opulence. . . .

But his heart was very much with Marjorie through all this time. Hitherto he had taken her health and vigour and companionship for granted, and it changed his attitudes profoundly to find her now an ailing thing, making an invincible appeal for restraint and consideration and help. She changed marvellously, she gained a new dignity, and her complexion took upon itself a fresh, soft beauty. He would spend three or four days out of a week at the cottage, and long hours of that would be at her side, paper and notes of some forthcoming lecture at hand neglected, talking to her consolingly and dreamingly. His thoughts were full of ideas about education ; he was obsessed, as are most intelligent young parents of the modern type, by the enormous possibilities of human improvement that might be achieved—if only one could begin with a baby from the outset, on the best lines, with the best methods, training and preparing it—presumably for a cleaned and chastened world. Indeed, he made all the usual discoveries of intelligent modern young parents very rapidly, fully and completely, and overlooked in quite the normal fashion most of those practical difficulties that finally reduce them to human dimensions again.

" I sit and muse sometimes when I ought to be computing," he said. " Old Durgan watches me and grunts. But think, if we take reasonable care, watch its phases, stand ready with a kindergarten toy directly it stretches out its hand—think what we can make of it ! " . . .

" We will make it the most wonderful child in the world," said Marjorie. " Indeed, what else can it be ? "

" Your eyes," said Trafford, " and my hands."

" A girl."

" A boy."

He kissed her white and passive wrist.

## § 7

The child was born a little before expectation at the cottage throughout a long summer's night and day in early September. Its coming into the world was a long and painful struggle ; the general practitioner who had seemed two days before a competent and worthy person enough, revealed himself as hesitating, old-fashioned, and ill-equipped. He had a lingering theological objection to the use of chloroform, and the nurse from London sulked under his directions and came and discussed his methods scornfully with Trafford. From sundown until daylight Trafford chafed in the little sitting-room and tried to sleep, and hovered listening at the foot of the narrow staircase to the room above. He lived through interminable hours of moaning and suspense. . . .

The dawn and sunrise came with a quality of beautiful horror. For years afterwards that memory stood out among other memories as something peculiarly strange and dreadful. Day followed an interminable night and broke slowly. Things crept out of darkness, awoke as it were out of mysteries and reclothed themselves in unsubstantial shadows and faint-hued forms. All through that slow infiltration of the world with light and then with colour, the universe it seemed was moaning and endeavouring, and a weak and terrible struggle went on and kept on in that forbidden room whose windows opened upon the lightening world, dying to a sobbing silence, rising again to agonising cries, fluctuating, a perpetual obstinate failure to achieve a tormenting end. He went out, and behold the sky was a wonder of pink-flushed level clouds and golden hope, and nearly every star except the morning star had gone, the supine moon was pale and half-dissolved in blue, and the grass which had been grey and wet, was green again, and the bushes and trees were green. He returned and hovered in the passage, washed his face, listened outside the door for age-long moments, and then went out again to listen under the window. . . . He went to his room and shaved, sat for a long time thinking, and then suddenly knelt by his bed and prayed. He had never prayed before in all his life. . . .

He returned to the garden, and there neglected and wet with dew was the camp-chair Marjorie had sat on the evening before, the shawl she had been wearing, the novel she had been reading. He brought these things in as if they were precious treasures. . . .

Light was pouring into the world again now. He noticed with an extreme particularity the detailed dewy delicacy of grass and twig, the silver edges to the leaves of briar and nettle, the soft clearness of the moss on bank and wall. He noted the woods with the first warmth of autumn tinting their green, the clear, calm sky, with just a wisp or so of purple cloud waning to a luminous pink on the brightening east, the exquisite freshness of the air. And still through the open window, incessant, unbearable, came this sound of Marjorie moaning, now dying away, now reviving, now weakening again. . . .

Was she dying ? Were they murdering her ? It was incredible this torture could go on. Somehow it must end. Chiefly he wanted to go in and kill the doctor. But it would do no good to kill the doctor !

At last the nurse came out, looking scared, to ask him to cycle three miles away and borrow some special sort of needle that the fool of a doctor had forgotten. He went, outwardly meek, and returning was met by the little interested servant, very alert and excited and rather superior—for here was something no man can do—with the news that he had a beautiful daughter, and that all was well with Marjorie.

He said "Thank God, thank God!" several times, and then went out into the kitchen and began to eat some flabby toast and drink some lukewarm tea he found there. He was horribly fatigued. "Is she all right ?" he asked over his shoulder, hearing the doctor's footsteps on the stairs. . . .

They were very pontifical and official with him.

Presently they brought out a strange, wizened little animal, wailing very stoutly, with a face like a very, very old woman, and reddish skin, and hair—it had quite a lot of wet blackish hair of an incredible delicacy of texture. It kicked with a stumpy monkey's legs and inturned feet. He held it ; his heart went out to it. He pitied it beyond measure, it was so weak and ugly. He was astonished and distressed by the fact of its extreme endearing ugliness. He had expected something strikingly pretty. It clenched a fist, and he perceived it had all its complement of fingers, and ridiculous, pretentious little finger-nails. Inside that fist it squeezed his heart. . . . He did not want to give it back to them. He wanted to protect it. He felt they could not understand it or forgive, as he could forgive, its unjustifiable ugliness and feebleness. . . .

Later, for just a moment, he was permitted to see Marjorie —Marjorie so spent, so unspeakably weary, and yet so re-assuringly vital and living, so full of gentle pride and gentler courage amidst the litter of surgical precaution, that the tears came streaming down his face and he sobbed shamelessly as he kissed her. "Little daughter," she whispered and smiled—just as she had always smiled—that sweet, dear smile of hers !—and closed her eyes and said no more. . . .

Afterwards as he walked up and down the garden he remembered their former dispute, and thought how charac-teristic of Marjorie it was to have a daughter in spite of all his wishes.

§ 8

For weeks and weeks this astonishing and unprecedented being filled the Traffords' earth and sky. Very speedily its minute quaintness passed, and it became a vigorous delightful baby that was, as the nurse explained repeatedly and very explicitly, not only quite exceptional and distinguished, but exactly everything that a baby should be. Its weight became of supreme importance ; there was a splendid week when it put on nine ounces, and an indifferent one when it added only one. And then came a terrible crisis. It was ill ; some sort of infection had reached it, an infantile cholera. Its temperature mounted to a hundred and three and a half. It became a flushed misery, wailing with a pathetic feeble voice. Then it ceased to wail. Marjorie became white-lipped and heavy-eyed from want of sleep, and it seemed to Trafford that perhaps his child might die. It seemed to him that the spirit of the universe must be a monstrous Caliban, since children had to die. He went for a long walk through the October beech-woods, under a windy sky and in a drift of falling leaves, wondering with a renewed freshness at the haunting futilities of life. Life was not futile—anything but that, but futility seemed to be stalking it, waiting for it. . . . When he returned the child was already better, and in a few days it was well again—but very light and thin.

When they were sure of its safety, Marjorie and he confessed the extremity of their fears to one another. They had not dared to speak before, and even now they spoke in undertones of the shadow that had hovered and passed over the dearest thing in their lives.

# CHAPTER THREE

## § 1

IN the course of the next six months the child of the ages became an almost ordinary healthy baby, and Trafford began to think consecutively about his scientific work again—in the intervals of effort of a more immediately practical sort.

The return of molecular physics and particularly of the internal condition of colloids to something like their old importance in his life was greatly accelerated by the fact that a young Oxford don named Behrens was showing extraordinary energy in what had been for a time Trafford's distinctive and undisputed field. Behrens was one of those vividly clever energetic people who are the despair of originative men. He had begun as Trafford's pupil and sedulous ape ; he had gone on to work that imitated Trafford's in everything except its continual freshness, and now he was ransacking every scrap of suggestion to be found in Trafford's work, and developing it with an intensity of uninspired intelligence that most marvellously simulated originality. He was already being noted as an authority ; sometimes in an article his name would be quoted and Trafford's omitted in relation to Trafford's ideas, and in every way his emergence and the manner of his emergence threatened and stimulated his model and master. A great effort had to be made. Trafford revived the drooping spirits of Durgan by a renewed punctuality in the laboratory. He began to stay away from home at night and work late again, now, however, under no imperative inspiration, but simply because it was only by such an invasion of the evening and night that it would be possible to make headway against Behren's unremitting industry. And this new demand upon Trafford's already strained mental and nervous equipment began very speedily to have its effect upon his domestic life.

It is only in romantic fiction that a man can work strenuously to the limit of his power and come home to be sweet, sunny, and entertaining. Trafford's preoccupation involved a certain negligence of Marjorie, a certain indisposition to be amused or interested by trifling things, a certain irritability. . . .

## § 2

And now, indeed, the Traffords were coming to the most difficult and fatal phase in marriage. They had had that taste of defiant adventure which is the crown of a spirited love affair, they had known the sweetness of a maiden passion for a maid, and they had felt all those rich and solemn emotions, those splendid fears and terrible hopes that weave themselves about the great partnership in parentage. And now, so far as sex was concerned, there might be much joy and delight still, but no more wonder, no fresh discoveries of incredible new worlds and unsuspected stars. Love, which had been a new garden, an unknown land, a sunlit sea to launch upon, was now a rich treasure-house of memories. And memories, although they afford a perpetually increasing enrichment to emotion, are not sufficient in themselves for the daily needs of life.

For this, indeed, is the truth of passionate love, that it works out its purpose and comes to an end. A day arrives in every marriage when the lovers must face each other, disillusioned, stripped of the last shred of excitement—undisguisedly themselves. And our two were married ; they had bound themselves together under a penalty of scandalous disgrace, to take the life-long consequences of their passionate association.

It was upon Trafford that this exhaustion of the sustaining magic of love pressed most severely, because it was he who had made the greatest adaptations to the exigencies of their union. He had crippled, he perceived more and more clearly, the research work upon which his whole being had once been set, and his hours were full of tiresome and trivial duties and his mind engaged and worried by growing financial anxieties. He had made these abandonments in a phase of exalted passion for the one woman in the world and her unprecedented child, and now he saw, in spite of all his desire not to see, that she was just a weak human being among human beings, and neither she nor little Margharita so very marvellous.

But while Marjorie shrank to the dimensions of reality, research remained still a luminous and commanding dream. In love one fails or one wins home, but the lure of research is for ever beyond the hills, every victory is a new desire. Science has inexhaustibly fresh worlds to conquer. . . .

He was beginning now to realise the dilemma of his life, the reality of the opposition between Marjorie and child and home on the one hand and on the other this big wider thing, this remoter, severer demand upon his being. He had long perceived these were distinct and different things, but now it appeared more and more inevitable that they should be antagonistic and mutually disregardful things. Each claimed him altogether, it seemed, and suffered compromise impatiently. And this is where the particular stress of his situation came in. Hitherto he had believed that nothing of any importance was secret or inexplicable between himself and Marjorie. His ideal of his relationship had assumed a complete sympathy of feeling, an almost instinctive identity of outlook. And now it was manifest they were living in a state of inadequate understanding, that she knew only in the most general and opaque form the things that interested him so profoundly,

and had but the most superficial interest in his impassioned
curiosities. And missing as she did the strength of his intellectual purpose she missed too, she had no inkling of, the
way in which her careless expansiveness pressed upon him.
She was unaware that she was destroying an essential thing
in his life.

He could not tell how far this antagonism was due to
inalterable discords of character, how far it might not be an
ineradicable sex difference, a necessary aspect of marriage.
The talk of old Sir Roderick Dover at the Winton Club ger-
minated in his mind, a branching and permeating suggestion.
And then would come a phase of keen sympathy with
Marjorie ; she would say brilliant and penetrating things,
display a swift cleverness that drove all these intimations of
incurable divergence clean out of his head again. Then he
would find explanations in the differences in his and Marjorie's
training and early associations. He perceived his own upbringing had had a steadfastness and consistency that had
been altogether lacking in hers. He had had the rare advantage of perfect honesty in the teaching and tradition of his
home. There had never been any shams or sentimentalities
for him to find out and abandon. From boyhood his mother's
hand had pointed steadily to the search for truth as the
supreme ennobling fact in life. She had never preached this
to him, never delivered discourses upon his father's virtues,
but all her conversation and life was saturated with this
idea. Compared with this atmosphere of high and sustained
direction, the intellectual and moral quality of the Popes,
he saw, was the quality of an agitated rag-bag. They had
thought nothing out, joined nothing together, they seemed
to believe everything and nothing, they were neither religious
nor irreligious, neither moral nor adventurous. In the place
of a religion, and tainting their entire atmosphere, they had
the decaying remains of a dead Anglicanism ; it was clear
they did not believe in its creed, and as clear that they did
not want to get rid of it ; it afforded them no guidance, but
only vague pretensions, and the dismal exercises of Silas
Root flourished in its shadows, a fungus, a post-mortem
activity of the soul. None of them had any idea of what
they were for or what their lives as a whole might mean ;
they had no standards, but only instincts and an instinctive
fear of instincts ; Pope wanted to be tremendously respected
and complimented by everybody and get six per cent. for
his money ; Mrs. Pope wanted things to go smoothly ; the
young people had a general indisposition to do anything that
might " look bad," and otherwise " have a good time."
But neither Marjorie nor any of them had any test for a
good time, and so they fluctuated in their conceptions of
what they wanted from day to day. Now it was Plessingtonian standards, now Carmel standards, now the standards

of Agatha Alimony ; now it was a stimulating novel, now a gleam of æsthetic imaginativeness come, Heaven knows whence, that dominated her mood. He was beginning to understand all this at last, and to see the need of coherence in Marjorie's mood.

He realised the unfairness of keeping his thoughts to himself, the need of putting his case before her, and making her realise their fatal and widening divergence. He wanted to infect her with his scientific passion, to give her his sense of the gravity of their practical difficulties. He would sit amidst his neglected work in his laboratory framing explanatory phrases. He would prepare the most lucid and complete statements, and go about with these in his mind for days waiting for an opportunity of saying what he felt so urgently had to be said.

But the things that seemed so luminous and effective in the laboratory had a curious way of fading and shrinking beside the bright colours of Marjorie's Bokhara hangings, in the presence of little Margharita pink and warm and entertaining in her bath, or amidst the fluttering rustle of the afternoon tea-parties that were now becoming frequent in his house. And when he was alone with her he discovered they didn't talk now any more—except in terms of a constrained and formal affection.

What had happened to them ? What was the matter between himself and Marjorie that he couldn't even intimate his sense of their divergence ? He would have liked to discuss the whole thing with his mother, but somehow that seemed disloyal to Marjorie. . . .

One day they quarrelled.

He came in about six in the afternoon, jaded from the delivery of a suburban lecture and the consequent tedium of suburban travel, and discovered Marjorie examining the effect of a new picture which had replaced the German print of sunlit waves over the dining-room mantelpiece. It was a painting in the post-impressionist manner, and it had arrived after the close of the exhibition in Weldon Street at which Marjorie had bought it. She had bought it in obedience to a sudden impulse, and its imminence had long weighed upon her conscience. She had gone to the show with Sydney Flor and old Mrs. Flor, Sydney's mother, and a kind of excitement had come upon them at the idea of possessing this particular picture. Mrs. Flor had already bought three Herbins, and her daughter wanted to dissuade her from more. " But they're so delightful," said Mrs. Flor. " You're overrunning your allowance," said Sydney. Disputing the point, they made inquiries for the price, and learned that this bright epigram in colour was going begging—was even offered at a reduction from the catalogue price. A reduced price always had a strong appeal nowadays to Marjorie's mind. " If you don't get it," she said abruptly, " I shall."

The transition from that attitude to ownership was amazingly rapid. Then nothing remained but to wait for the picture. She had dreaded a mistake, a blundering discord, but now with the thing hung she could see her quick eye had not betrayed her. It was a mass of reds, browns, purples, and vivid greens and greys ; an effect of roof and brick house facing upon a Dutch canal, and it lit up the room and was echoed and reflected by all the rest of her courageous colour scheme, like a coal-fire amidst mahogany and metal. It justified itself to her completely, and she faced her husband with a certain confidence.

" Hullo ! " he cried.

" A new picture," she said.   " What do you think of it ? "

" What is it ? "

" A town or something—never mind.   Look at the colour. It heartens everything."

Trafford looked at the painting with a reluctant admiration.

" It's brilliant—and impudent.   He's an artist—whoever he is.   He hits the thing.   But—I say—how did you get it ? "

" I bought it."

" Bought it !   Good Lord !   How much ? "

" Oh !  ten guineas," said Marjorie, with an affectation of ease ;  " it will be worth thirty in ten years' time."

Trafford's reply was to repeat :  " Ten guineas ! "

Their eyes met, and there was singularly little tenderness in their eyes.

" It was priced at thirteen," said Marjorie, ending a pause, and with a sinking heart.

Trafford had left her side.   He walked to the window and sat down in a chair.

" I think this is too much," he said, and his voice had disagreeable notes in it she had never heard before.   " I have just been earning two guineas at Croydon, of all places, administering comminuted science to fools—and here I find—this exploit !   Ten guineas' worth of picture.   To say we can't afford it is just to waste a mild expression.   It's—mad extravagance.   It's waste of money—it's—oh !—monstrous disloyalty.   Disloyalty ! "   He stared resentful at the cheerful, unhesitating daubs of the picture for a moment.   Its affected carelessness goaded him to fresh words.   He spoke in a tone of absolute hostility.   " I think this winds me up to something," he said.   " You'll have to give up your cheque-book, Marjorie."

" Give up my cheque-book ! "

He looked up at her and nodded.   There was a warm flush in her cheeks, her lips panted apart, and tears of disappointment and vexation were shining beautifully in her eyes. She mingled the quality of an indignant woman with the distress and unreasonable resentment of a child.

" Because I've bought this picture ? "

" Can we go on like this ? " he asked, and felt how miserably

he had bungled in opening this question that had been in his
mind so long.

" But it's *beautiful* ! " she said.

He disregarded that. He felt now that he had to go on with
these long-premeditated expostulations. He was tired and
dusty from his third-class carriage, his spirit was tired and
dusty, and he said what he had to say without either breadth
or power, an undignified statement of personal grievances, a
mere complaint of the burthen of work that falls upon a man.
That she missed the high aim in him, and all sense of the
greatness they were losing had vanished from his thoughts.
He had too heavy a share of the common burthen, and she
pressed upon him unthinkingly ; that was all he could say. He
girded at her with a bitter and loveless truth ; it was none the
less cruel that in her heart she knew the things he said were
true. But he went beyond justice—as every quarrelling
human being does ; he called the things she had bought and
the harmonies she had created, " this litter and rubbish for
which I am wasting my life." That stabbed into her pride
acutely and deeply. She knew anyhow that it wasn't so
simple and crude as that. It was not mere witlessness she
contributed to their trouble. She tried to indicate her sense
of that. But she had no power of ordered reasoning, she made
futile interruptions, she was inexpressive of anything but
emotion, she felt gagged against this flow of indignant, hostile
words. They blistered her.

Suddenly she went to her little desk in the corner, unlocked
it with trembling hands, snatched her cheque-book out of a heap
of still unsettled bills, and having locked that anti-climax safe
away again, turned upon him. " Here it is," she said, and stood
poised for a moment. Then she flung down the little narrow grey
cover—nearly empty, it was, of cheques, on the floor before him.

" Take it," she cried, " take it. I never asked you to give
it me."

A memory of Orta and its reeds and sunshine and love rose
like a luminous mist between them. . . .

She ran weeping from the room.

He leaped to his feet as the door closed. " Marjorie ! " he cried.
But she did not hear him. . . .

### § 3

The disillusionment about marriage which had discovered
Trafford a thwarted, overworked, and worried man, had
revealed Marjorie with time on her hands, superabundant
imaginative energy, and no clear intimation of any occupation.
With them, as with thousands of young couples in London
to-day, the bread-winner was overworked, and the spending
partner's duty was chiefly the negative one of not spending.
You cannot consume your energies merely in not spending
money. Do what she could, Marjorie could not contrive to

make house and child fill the waking hours. She was far too active and irritable a being to be beneficial company all day for genial, bubble-blowing little Margharita ; she could play with that young lady and lead her into ecstasies of excitement and delight, and she could see with an almost instinctive certainty when anything was going wrong ; but for the rest that little life reposed far more beneficially upon the passive acquiescence of May, her pink and wholesome nurse. And the household generally was in the hands of a trustworthy cook-general, who maintained a tolerable routine. Marjorie did not dare to have an idea about food or domestic arrangements ; if she touched that routine so much as with her little finger it sent up the bills. She could knock off butcher and green-grocer and do every scrap of household work that she could touch, in a couple of hours a day. She tried to find some work to fill her leisure ; she suggested to Trafford that she might help him by writing up his Science Notes from rough pencil memoranda, but when it became clear that the first step to her doing this would be the purchase of a Remington typewriter and a special low table to carry it, he became bluntly discouraging. She thought of literary work, and sat down one day to write a short story and earn guineas, and was surprised to find that she knew nothing of any sort of human being about whom she could invent a story. She tried a cheap subscription at Mudie's and novels, and they filled her with a thirst for events ; she tried needlework, and found her best efforts æsthetically feeble and despicable, and that her mind prowled above the silks and colours like a hungry wolf.

The early afternoons were the worst time, from two to four, before calling began. The devil was given great power over Marjorie's early afternoon. She could even envy her former home life then, and reflect that there, at any rate, one had a chance of a game or a quarrel with Daffy or Syd or Rom or Theodore. She would pull herself together and go out for a walk, and whichever way she went there were shops and shops and shops, a glittering array of tempting opportunities for spending money. Sometimes she would give way to spending exactly as a struggling drunkard decides to tipple. She would fix on some object, some object trivial and a little rare and not too costly, as being needed—when she knew perfectly well it wasn't needed—and choose the remotest shops and display the exactest insistence upon her requirements. Sometimes she would get home from these raids without buying at all. After four the worst of the day was over ; one could call on people or people might telephone and follow up with a call ; and there was a chance of Trafford coming home. . . .

One day at the Carmels' she found herself engaged in a vigorous flirtation with young Carmel. She hadn't noticed it coming on, but there she was in a window-seat talking quite closely to him. He said he was writing a play, a wonderful

passionate play about St. Francis, and only she could inspire
and advise him. Wasn't there some afternoon in the week
when she sat and sewed, so that he might come and sit by her
and read to her and talk to her ? He made his request with a
certain confidence, but it filled her with a righteous panic ;
she pulled him up with an abruptness that was almost in-
artistic. On her way home she was acutely ashamed of herself ; this was the first time she had let any man but Trafford
think he might be interesting to her, but once or twice on
former occasions she had been on the verge of such provocative
intimations. This sort of thing anyhow mustn't happen.

But if she didn't dress with any distinction—because of
the cost—and didn't flirt and trail men in her wake, what was
she to do at the afternoon gatherings which were now her chief
form of social contact ? What was going to bring people to her
house ? She knew that she was more than ordinarily beautiful
and that she could talk well, but that does not count for much
if you are rather dowdy, and quite uneventfully virtuous.

It became the refrain of all her thoughts that she must find
something to do.

There remained " Movements."

She might take up a Movement. She was a rather exceptionally good public speaker. Only her elopement and
marriage had prevented her being president of her college
Debating Society. If she devoted herself to some Movement
she would be free to devise an ostentatiously simple dress for
herself and stick to it, and she would be able to give her little
house a significance of its own, and present herself publicly
against what is perhaps quite the best of all backgrounds for a
good-looking, clear-voiced, self-possessed woman, a platform.
Yes ; she had to go in for a Movement.

She reviewed the chief contemporary Movements much as
she might have turned over dress fabrics in a draper's shop,
weighing the advantages and disadvantages of each. . . .

London, of course, is always full of Movements. Essentially
they are absorbents of superfluous feminine energy. They
have a common flavour of progress and revolutionary purpose,
and common features in abundant meetings, officials, and
organisation generally. Few are expensive, and still fewer
produce any tangible results in the world. They direct themselves at the most various ends ; the Poor, that favourite
butt, either as a whole or in such typical sections as the indigent invalid or the indigent aged, the young, public health,
the woman's cause, the prevention of animal food, anti-
vivisection, the gratuitous advertisement of Shakespeare
(that neglected poet), novel but genteel modifications of medical
or religious practice, dress reform, the politer aspects of
socialism, the encouragement of aeronautics, universal military
service, garden suburbs, domestic arts, proportional representation, duodecimal arithmetic, and the liberation of the drama.

They range in size and importance from campaigns on a
Plessingtonian scale to sober little intellectual Beckingham
things that arrange to meet half-yearly, and die quietly before
the second assembly.  If Heaven by some miracle suddenly
gave every Movement in London all it professed to want, our
world would be standing on its head and everything would be
extremely unfamiliar and disconcerting.  But, as Mr. Roose-
velt once remarked, the justifying thing about life is the effort
and not the goal, and few Movements involve any real and
impassioned struggle to get to the ostensible object.  They
exist as an occupation ;  they exercise the intellectual and
moral activities without undue disturbance of the normal
routines of life.  In the days when everybody was bicycling,
an ingenious mechanism called Hacker's Home Bicycle used
to be advertised.  Hacker's Home Bicycle was a stand bearing
small rubber wheels upon which one placed one's bicycle
(properly equipped with a cyclometer) in such a way that it
could be mounted and ridden without any sensible forward
movement whatever.  In bad weather, or when the state of
the roads made cycling abroad disagreeable, Hacker's Home
Bicycle could be placed in front of an open window and ridden
furiously for any length of time.  Whenever the rider tired,
he could descend—comfortably at home again—and examine
the cyclometer to see how far he had been.  In exactly the
same way the ordinary London Movement gives scope for
the restless and progressive impulse in human nature without the risk of personal entanglements or any inconvenient
disturbance of the milieu.

Marjorie considered the Movements about her.  She surveyed the accessible aspects of socialism, but that old treasure-
house of constructive suggestion had an effect like a rich
château which has been stormed and looted by a mob.  For a
time the proposition that " we are all Socialists nowadays "
had prevailed.  The blackened and discredited frame remained, the contents were scattered ;  Aunt Plessington had a
few pieces, the Tory Democrats had taken freely, the Liberals
were in possession of a hastily compiled collection.  There
wasn't, she perceived, and there never had been a Socialist
Movement ;  the socialist idea which had now become part of
the general consciousness, had always been too big for polite
domestication.  She weighed Aunt Plessington, too, in the
balance, and found her not so much wanting indeed as excessive.  She felt that a Movement with Aunt Plessington in it
couldn't possibly offer even elbow-room for anybody else.
Philanthrophy generally she shunned.  The Movements that
aim at getting poor people into rooms and shouting at
them in an improving, authoritative way, aroused an instinctive dislike in her.  Her sense of humour, again, would
not let her patronise Shakespeare or the stage, or raise the
artistic level of the country by means of green-dyed deal,

and the influence of Trafford on her mind debarred her from attempting the physical and moral regeneration of humanity by means of beans and nut butter. It was indeed rather by the elimination of competing Movements than by any positive preference that she found herself declining at last towards Agatha Alimony's section of the suffrage movement. . . . It was one of the less militant sections, but it held more meetings and passed more resolutions than any two others.

One day Trafford, returning from an afternoon of forced and disappointing work in his laboratory—his mind had been steadfastly sluggish and inelastic—discovered Marjorie's dining-room crowded with hats and all the rustle and colour which plays so large a part in constituting contemporary feminine personality. Buzard, the feminist writer, and a young man just down from Cambridge who had written a decadent poem, were the only men present. The chairs were arranged meeting-fashion, but a little irregularly to suggest informality ; the post-impressionist picture was a rosy benediction on the gathering, and at a table in the window sat Mrs. Pope in the chair, looking quietly tactful in an unusually becoming bonnet, supported by her daughter and Agatha Alimony. Marjorie was in a simple gown of bluish-grey, hatless amidst a froth of foolish bows and feathers, and she looked not only beautiful and dignified but deliberately and conscientiously patient until she perceived the new arrival. Then he noted she was a little concerned for him, and made some futile sign he did not comprehend. The meeting was debating the behaviour of women at the approaching census, and a small, earnest, pale-faced lady with glasses was standing against the fireplace with a crumpled envelope covered with pencilled notes in her hand, and making a speech. Trafford wanted his tea badly, but he had not the wit to realise that his study had been converted into a refreshment room for the occasion ; he hesitated, and seated himself near the doorway, and so he was caught ; he couldn't, he felt, get away and seem to slight a woman who was giving herself the pains of addressing him.

The small lady in glasses was giving a fancy picture of the mind of Mr. Asquith and its attitude to the suffrage movement, and telling with a sort of inspired intimacy just how Mr. Asquith had hoped to " bully women down," and just how their various attempts to bring home to him the eminent reasonableness of their sex by breaking his windows, interrupting his meetings, booing at him in the streets and threatening his life, had time after time baffled this arrogant hope. There had been many signs lately that Mr. Asquith's heart was failing him. Now here was a new thing to fill him with despair. When Mr. Asquith learned that women refused to be counted in the census, then at least she was convinced he must give in. When he gave in it would not be long—she had her information upon good authority—before they got the Vote. So what they had to do was not to be counted in the census. That was their paramount duty at the present time. The women of England had to say quietly but firmly to the census man when he came round : " No, we don't count in an election, and we won't count now. Thank you." No one could force a woman to fill in a census paper she didn't want to, and for her own part, said the little woman with the glasses, she'd starve first. (Applause.) For her own part she was a householder with a census paper of her own, and across that she was going to write quite plainly and simply what she thought of Mr. Asquith. Some of those present wouldn't have census papers to fill up ; they would be sent to the man, the so-called Head of the House. But the W.S.B.U. had foreseen that. Each householder had to write down the particulars of the people who slept in his house on Sunday night, or who arrived home before midday on Monday ; the reply of the women of England must be not to sleep in a house that night where census papers were properly filled, and not to go home until the following afternoon. All through that night the women of England must be abroad. She herself was prepared, and her house would be ready. There would be coffee and refreshments enough for an unlimited number of refugees, there would be twenty or thirty sofas and mattresses and piles of blankets for those who chose to sleep safe from all counting. In every quarter of London there would be houses of refuge like hers. And so they would make Mr. Asquith's census fail, as it deserved to fail, as every census would fail until women managed these affairs in a sensible way. For she supposed they were all agreed that only women could manage these things in a sensible way. That was *her* contribution to this great and important question. (Applause, amidst which the small lady with the glasses resumed her seat.)

Trafford glanced doorward, but before he could move another speaker was in possession of the room. This was a very young, tall, fair, round-shouldered girl who held herself with an unnatural rigidity, fixed her eyes on the floor just in front of the chairwoman, and spoke with knitted brows and an effect of extreme strain. She remarked that some people did not approve of this proposed boycott of the census. She hung silent for a moment, as if ransacking her mind for something mislaid, and then proceeded to remark that she proposed to occupy a few moments in answering that objection—if it could be called an objection. They said that spoiling the census was an illegitimate extension of the woman movement. Well, she objected—she objected fiercely—to every word of that phrase. Nothing was an illegitimate extension of the woman movement. Nothing could be. (Applause.) That was the very principle they had been fighting for all along. So that, examined in this way, this so-called objection resolved

itself into a mere question-begging phrase. Nothing more.
And her reply therefore to those who made it was that they
were begging the question, and however well that might do for
men, it would certainly not do, they would find, for women.
(Applause.) For the freshly awakened consciousness of women.
(Further applause.) This was a war in which quarter was
neither asked nor given ; if it were not so things might be
different. She remained silent after that for the space of
twenty seconds perhaps, and then remarked that that seemed to
be all she had to say, and sat down amidst loud encouragement.

Then with a certain dismay Trafford saw his wife upon her
feet. He was afraid of the effect upon himself of what she was
going to say, but he need have had no reason for his fear.
Marjorie was a seasoned debater, self-possessed, with a voice
very well controlled and a complete mastery of that elaborate
appearance of reasonableness which is so essential to good
public speaking. She could speak far better than she could
talk. And she startled the meeting in her opening sentence
by declaring that she meant to stay at home on the census
night, and supply her husband with every scrap of information he hadn't got already that might be needed to make the
return an entirely perfect return. (Marked absence of applause.)

She proceeded to avow her passionate interest in the
feminist movement of which this agitation for the vote was
merely the symbol. (A voice : " No ! ") No one could be
more aware of the falsity of woman's position at the present
time than she was—she seemed to be speaking right across
the room to Trafford—they were neither pets nor partners,
but something between the two ; now indulged like spoiled
children, now blamed like defaulting partners ; constantly
provoked to use the arts of their sex, constantly mischievous
because of that provocation. She caught her breath and
stopped for a moment, as if she had suddenly remembered the
meeting intervening between herself and Trafford. No, she
said, there was no more ardent feminist and suffragist than
herself in the room. She wanted the vote and everything it
implied with all her heart. With all her heart. But every
way to get a thing wasn't the right way, and she felt with every
fibre of her being that this petulant hostility to the census was
a wrong way and an inconsistent way, and likely to be an
unsuccessful way—one that would lose them the sympathy
and help of just that class of men they should look to for
support, the cultivated and scientific men. (A voice : " Do
we want them ? ") What was the commonest charge made
by the man in the street against women ?—that they were
unreasonable and unmanageable, that it was their way to get
things by crying and making an irrelevant fuss. And here
they were, as a body, doing that very thing ! Let them think
what the census and all that modern organisation of vital
statistics of which it was the central feature stood for. It

stood for order, for the replacement of guesses and emotional generalisation by a clear knowledge of facts, for the replacement of instinctive and violent methods, by which women had everything to lose (a voice : " No ! "), by reason and knowledge and self-restraint, by which women had everything to gain. To her the advancement of science, the progress of civilisation, and the emancipation of womanhood were nearly synonymous terms. At any rate, they were different phases of one thing. They were different aspects of one wider purpose. When they struck at the census, she felt, they struck at themselves. She glanced at Trafford as if she would convince him that this was the real voice of the suffrage movement, and sat down amidst a brief, polite applause, that warmed to rapture as Agatha Alimony, the deep-voiced, stirring Agatha, rose to reply.

Miss Alimony, who was wearing an enormous hat with three nodding ostrich feathers, a purple bow, a gold buckle and numerous minor ornaments of various origin and substance, said they had all of them listened with the greatest appreciation and sympathy to the speech of their hostess. Their hostess was a newcomer to the movement, she knew she might say this without offence, and was passing through a phase, an early phase, through which many of them had passed. This was the phase of trying to take a reasonable view of an unreasonable situation. (Applause.) Their hostess had spoken of science, and no doubt science was a great thing ; but there was something greater than science, and that was the ideal. It was woman's place to idealise. Sooner or later their hostess would discover, as they had all discovered, that it was not to science but the ideal that women must look for freedom. Consider, she said, the scientific men of to-day. Consider, for example, Sir James Crichton-Browne, the physiologist. Was he on their side ? On the contrary, he said the most unpleasant things about them on every occasion. He went out of his way to say them. Or consider Sir Almroth Wright, did he speak well of women ? Or Sir Ray Lankester, the biologist, who was the chief ornament of the Anti-Suffrage Society. Or Sir Roderick Dover, the physicist, who—forgetting Madame Curie, a far more celebrated physicist than himself, she ventured to say—had recently gone outside his province altogether to abuse feminine research. There were your scientific men. Mrs. Trafford had said their anti-census campaign would annoy scientific men ; well, under the circumstances, she wanted to annoy scientific men. (Applause.) She wanted to annoy everybody. Until women got the vote (loud applause) the more annoying they were the better. When the whole world was impressed by the idea that voteless women were an intolerable nuisance, then there would cease to be voteless women. (Enthusiasm.) Mr. Asquith had said—

And so on for quite a long time. . . .

Buzard rose out of waves of subsiding emotion. Buzard
was a slender, long-necked, stalk-shaped man with gilt glasses,
uneasy movements and a hypersensitive manner. He didn't
so much speak as thrill with thought vibrations; he spoke
like an entranced but still quite gentlemanly sibyl. After
Agatha's deep trumpet calls, he sounded like a solo on the
piccolo. He picked out all his more important words with a
little stress as though he gave them capitals. He said their
hostess's remarks had set him thinking. He thought it was
possible to stew the Scientific Argument in its own Juice.
There was something he might call the Factuarial Estimate of
Values. Well, it was a High Factuarial Value on their side,
in his opinion at any rate, when Anthropologists came and
told him that the Primitive Human Society was a Matriarchate.
(" But it wasn't ! " said Trafford to himself.) It had a
High Factuarial Value when they assured him that Every One
of the Great Primitive Inventions was made by a Woman,
and that it was to Women they owed Fire and the early Epics
and Sagas. (" Good Lord ! " said Trafford.) It had a High
Factuarial Value when they not only asserted but proved
that for Thousands of Years, and perhaps for Hundreds of
Thousands of Years, Women had been in possession of Articulate Speech before men rose to that Level of Intelligence. . . .

It occurred suddenly to Trafford that he could go now ;
that it would be better to go ; that indeed he *must* go ; it was
no doubt necessary that his mind should have to work in the
same world as Buzard's mental processes, but at any rate those
two sets of unsympathetic functions need not go on in the same
room. Something might give way. He got up, and with those
elaborate efforts to be silent that lead to the violent upsetting
of chairs, got himself out of the room and into the passage, and
was at once rescued by the sympathetic cook-general, in her
most generalised form, and given fresh tea in his study—which
impressed him as being catastrophically disarranged. . . .

§ 4

When Marjorie was at last alone with him she found him
in a state of extreme mental stimulation. " Your speech,"
he said, " was all right. I didn't know you could speak like
that, Marjorie. But it soared like the dove above the waters.
Waters ! I never heard such a flood of rubbish. . . . You
know, it's a mistake to *mass* women. It brings out something
silly. . . . It affected Buzard as badly as any one. The
extraordinary thing is they have a case, if only they'd be
quiet. Why did you get them together ? "

" It's our local branch."

" Yes, but *why* ? "

" Well, if they talk about things—Discussions like this
clear up their minds."

" Discussion ! It wasn't discussion."

" Oh ! it was a beginning."

" Chatter of that sort isn't the beginning of discussion, it's the end. It's the death-rattle. Nobody was meeting the thoughts of any one. I admit Buzard, who's a man, talked the worst rubbish of all. That Primitive Matriarchate of his ! So it isn't sex. I've noticed before that the men in this movement of yours are worse than the women. It isn't sex. It's something else. It's a foolishness. It's a sort of irresponsible looseness." He turned on her gravely. " You ought not to get all these people here. It's contagious. Before you know it you'll find your own mind liquefy and become enthusiastic and slip about. You'll begin to talk monomania about Mr. Asquith."

" But it's a great movement, Rag, even if incidentally they say and do silly things ! "

" My dear ! aren't I feminist ? Don't I want women fine and sane and responsible ! Don't I want them to have education, to handle things, to vote like men and bear themselves with the gravity of men ? And these meetings—all hat and flutter ! These displays of weak, untrained, hysterical vehemence ! These gatherings of open-mouthed impressionable young girls to be trained in incoherence ! You can't go on with it ! "

Marjorie regarded him quietly for a moment. " I must go on with something," she said.

" Well, not this."

" Then *what* ? "

" Something sane."

" Tell me what."

" It must come out of yourself."

Marjorie thought sullenly for a moment. " Nothing comes out of myself," she said.

" I don't think you realise a bit what my life has become," she went on ; " how much I'm like some one who's been put in a pleasant, high-class prison."

" This house ! It's your own ! "

" It doesn't give me an hour's mental occupation in the day. It's all very well to say I might do more in it. I can't—without absurdity. Or expenditure. I can't send the girl away and start scrubbing. I can't make jam or do ornamental needlework. The shops do it better and cheaper, and I haven't been trained to it. I've been trained *not* to do it. I've been brought up on games and school-books, and fed on mixed ideas. I can't sit down and pacify myself with a needle as women used to do. Besides, I not only detest doing needlework but I hate it—the sort of thing a woman of my kind does anyhow—when it's done. I'm no artist. I'm not sufficiently interested in outside things to spend my time in serious systematic reading, and after four or five novels—oh, these meetings are better than that ! You see, you've got a life—too much of it—*I* haven't got enough. I wish almost I

could sleep away half the day.   Oh !   I want something *real*,
Rag ;  something more than I've got."   A sudden inspiration
came to her.    " Will you let me come to your laboratory and
work with you ? "

She stopped abruptly.   She caught up her own chance question
and pointed it at him, a vitally important challenge.    " Will
you let me come to your laboratory and work ? " she repeated.

Trafford thought.   " No," he said.

" Why not ? "

" Because I'm in love with you.   I can't think of my work
when you're about. . . . And you're too much behind.   Oh,
my dear !  don't you see how you're behind ? "   He paused.
" I've been soaking in this stuff of mine for ten long years."

" Yes," assented Marjorie flatly.

He watched her downcast face, and then it lifted to him
with a helpless appeal in her eyes, and lift in her voice.    " But
look here, Rag ! " she cried—" what on earth am I to *DO* ? "

§ 5

At least there came out of these discussions one thing, a
phrase, a purpose, which was to rule the lives of the Traffords
for some years.   It expressed their realisation that instinct
and impulse had so far played them false, that life for all its
rich gifts of mutual happiness wasn't adjusted between them.
" We've got," they said, " to talk all this out between us.
We've got to work this out."   They didn't mean to leave
things at a misfit, and that was certainly their present relation.
They were already at the problem of their joint lives, like a
tailor with his pins and chalk.   Marjorie hadn't rejected a
humorist and all his works in order to decline at last to the
humorous view of life, that rather stupid, rather pathetic,
grin-and-bear-it attitude compounded in incalculable proportions of goodwill, evasion, indolence, slovenliness, and
(nevertheless) spite (masquerading indeed as jesting comment),
which supplies the fabric of everyday life for untold thousands
of educated middle-class people.   She hated the misfit.   She
didn't for a moment propose to pretend that the ungainly
twisted sleeve, the puckered back, was extremely jolly and
funny.   She had married with a passionate anticipation of
things fitting and fine, and it was her nature, in great matters
as in small, to get what she wanted strenuously before she
counted the cost.   About both their minds there was something sharp and unrelenting, and if Marjorie had been disposed
to take refuge from facts in swathings of æsthetic romanticism,
whatever covering she contrived would have been torn to rags
very speedily by that fierce and steely veracity which swung
down out of the laboratory into her home.

One may want to talk things out long before one hits upon
the phrases that will open up the matter.

There were two chief facts in the case between them, and

so far they had looked only one in the face—the fact that
Marjorie was unemployed to a troublesome and distressing
extent, and that there was nothing in her nature or training
to supply, and something in their circumstances and relations
to prevent, any adequate use of her energies. With the
second fact neither of them cared to come to close quarters
as yet, and neither as yet saw very distinctly how it was
linked to the first, and that was the steady excess of her
expenditure over their restricted means. She was secretly
surprised at her own weakness. Week by week and month
by month, they were spending all his income and eating into
that little accumulation of capital that had once seemed so
sufficient against the world. . . .

And here it has to be told that although Trafford knew
that Marjorie had been spending too much money, he still
had no idea of just how much money she had spent. She
was doing her utmost to come to an understanding with him,
and at the same time—I don't explain it, I don't excuse it—
she was keeping back her bills from him, keeping back urgent
second and third and fourth demands, that she had no cheque-
book now to stave off even by the most partial satisfaction.
It kept her awake at nights, that catastrophic explanation,
that all unsuspected by Trafford hung over their attempts
at mutual elucidation ; it kept her awake but she could not
bring it to the speaking point, and she clung, in spite of her
own intelligence, to a persuasion that *after* they had got
something really settled and defined then it would be time
enough to broach the particulars of this second divergence. . . .

Talking one's relations over isn't particularly easy between
husband and wife at any time ; we are none of us so sure of
one another as to risk loose phrases or make experiments in
expression in matters so vital ; there is inevitably an excessive
caution on the one hand and an abnormal sensitiveness to
hints and implications on the other. Marjorie's bills were
only an extreme instance of these unavoidable suppressions
that always occur. Moreover, when two people are continuously together, it is amazingly hard to know when and
where to begin ; where intercourse is unbroken it is as a
matter of routine being constantly interrupted. You cannot
broach these broad personalities while you are getting up in
the morning, or over the breakfast-table while you make
the coffee, or when you meet again after a multitude of small
events at tea, or in the evening when one is rather tired and
trivial after the work of the day. Then Miss Margharita
Trafford permitted no sustained analysis of life in her presence.
She synthesised things fallaciously, but for the time con-
vincingly ; she insisted that life wasn't a thing you discussed,
but pink and soft and jolly, which you crowed at and laughed
at and addressed as " Goo." Even without Margharita there
were occasions when the Traffords were a forgetfulness to

one another. After an ear has been pinched or a hand has
been run through a man's hair, or a pretty bare shoulder
kissed, all sorts of broader interests lapse into a temporary
oblivion. They found discussion much more possible when
they walked together. A walk seemed to take them out of
the everyday sequence, isolated them from their household,
abstracted them a little from one another. They set out
one extravagant spring Sunday to Great Missenden, and once
in spring also they discovered the Waterlow Park. On each
occasion they seemed to get through an enormous amount
of talking. But the Great Missenden walk was all mixed up
with a sweet keen wind, and beech-woods just shot with
spring green and bursting hedges and the extreme earliness
of honeysuckle, which Trafford noted for the first time, and
a clamorous rejoicing of birds. And in the Waterlow Park
there was a great discussion of why the yellow crocus comes
before white and purple, and the closest examination of the
manner in which daffodils and narcissi thrust their green
noses out of the garden beds. Also they found the ugly,
ill-served, aggressively propagandist non-alcoholic refreshment-room in that gracious old house a scandal and disappointment, and Trafford scolded at the stupidity of
officialdom that can control so fine a thing so ill.

Though they talked on these walks they were still curiously
evasive. Indeed, they were afraid of each other. They
kept falling away from their private thoughts and intentions.
They generalised, they discussed Marriage and George Gissing
and Bernard Shaw and the suffrage movement and the
agitation for the reform of the divorce laws. They pursued
imaginary cases into distant thickets of contingency remotely
far from the personal issues between them. . . .

§ 6

One day came an incident that Marjorie found wonderfully
illuminating. Trafford had a fit of rage. Stung by an
unexpected irritation, he forgot himself, as people say, and
swore, and was almost physically violent, and the curious
thing was that so he lit up things for her as no premeditated
attempt of his had ever done.

A copy of the *Scientific Bulletin* fired the explosion. He
sat down at the breakfast-table with the heaviness of a rather
overworked and worried man, tasted his coffee, tore open a
letter and crumpled it with his hand, turned to the *Bulletin*,
regarded its list of contents with a start, opened it, read for
a minute, and expressed himself with an extraordinary heat
of manner in these amazing and unprecedented words :

" Oh ! Damnation and damnation ! "

Then he shied the paper into the corner of the room and
pushed his plate from him.

" Damn the whole scheme of things ! " he said, and met the blank amazement of Marjorie's eye.

" Behrens ! " he said with an air of explanation.

" Behrens ? " she echoed with a note of inquiry.

" He's doing my stuff ! "

He sat darkling for a time, and then hit the table with his fist so hard that the breakfast-things seemed to jump together— to Marjorie's infinite amazement. " I can't *stand* it ! " he said.

She waited some moments. " I don't understand," she began. " What has he done ? "

" Oh ! " was Trafford's answer. He got up, recovered the crumpled paper and stood reading. " Fool and thief," he said. Marjorie was amazed beyond measure. She felt as though she had been effaced from Trafford's life. " Ugh ! " he cried, and slapped back the *Bulletin* into the corner with quite needless violence. He became aware of Marjorie again.

" He's doing my work," he said.

And then as if he completed the explanation : " And I've got to be in Croydon by half-past ten to lecture to a pack of spinsters and duffers, because they're too stupid to get the stuff from books. It's all in books—every bit of it."

He paused and went on in tones of unendurable wrong. " It isn't as though he was doing it right. He isn't. He can't. He's a fool. He's a clever, greedy, dishonest fool with a twist. Oh ! the pile, the big Pile of silly muddled technicalities he's invented already ! The solemn mess he's making of it ! And there he is, I can't get ahead of him, I can't get at him. I've got no time. I've got no room or leisure to swing my mind in ! Oh, curse these engagements, curse all these silly fretting entanglements of lecture and article ! I never get the time, I can't get the time, I can't get my mind clear ! I'm worried ! I'm badgered ! And meanwhile Behrens——! "

" Is he discovering what you want to discover ? "

" Behrens ! *No !* He's going through the breaches I made. He's guessing out what I meant to do. And he's getting it set out all wrong—misleading terminology— distinctions made in the wrong place. Oh, the fool he is ! "

" But afterwards—— "

" Afterwards I may spend my life—removing the obstacles he's made. He'll be established and I shan't. You don't know anything of these things. You don't understand."

She didn't. Her next question showed as much. " Will it affect your F.R.S. ? " she asked.

" Oh ! *that's* safe enough, and it doesn't matter anyhow. The F.R.S. ! Confound the silly little F.R.S. As if that mattered. It's seeing all my great openings—misused. It's seeing all I might be doing. This brings it all home to me. Don't you understand, Marjorie ? Will you never understand ? I'm getting away from all *that* ! I'm being hustled away by all this work, this silly everyday work to get money.

Don't you see that unless I can have time for thought and research, life is just darkness to me ? I've made myself master of that stuff. I had, at any rate. No one can do what I can do there. And when I find myself—oh, shut out, shut out ! I come near raving. As I think of it I want to rave again." He paused. Then with a swift transition : "I suppose I'd better eat some breakfast. Is that egg boiled ? "

She gave him an egg, brought him coffee, put things before him, seated herself at the table. For a little while he ate in silence. Then he cursed Behrens.

"Look here ! " she said. "Bad as I am, you've got to reason with me, Rag. I didn't know all this. I didn't understand. . . . I don't know what to do."

"What *is* there to do ? "

"I've got to do something. I'm beginning to see things. It's just as though everything had become clear suddenly." She was weeping. "Oh, my dear ! I want to help you. I have so wanted to help you. Always. And it's come to this ! "

"But it's not *your* fault. I didn't mean that. It's—it's in the nature of things."

"It's my fault."

"It's not your fault."

"It is."

"Confound it, Marjorie. When I swear at Behrens I'm not swearing at you."

"It's my fault. All this is my fault. I'm eating you up. What's the good of your pretending, Rag ? You know it is. Oh ! when I married you I meant to make you happy, I had no thought but to make you happy, to give myself to you, my body, my brains, everything, to make life beautiful for you——"

"Well, *haven't* you ? " He thrust out a hand she did not take.

"I've broken your back," she said.

An unwonted resolution came into her face. Her lips whitened. "Don't you know, Rag," she said, forcing herself to speak— "don't you guess ? You don't know half ! In that bureau there—— In there ! It's stuffed with bills. Unpaid bills."

She was weeping, with no attempt to wipe the streaming tears away ; terror made the expression of her wet face almost fierce. "Bills," she repeated. "More than a hundred pounds still. Yes ! Now. *Now !* "

He drew back, stared at her, and with no trace of personal animus, like one who hears of a common disaster, remarked with a quiet emphasis : "Oh, *damn* ! "

"I know," she said, "Damn ! " and met his eyes. There was a long silence between them. She produced a handkerchief and wiped her eyes. "That's what I amount to," she said.

"It's your silly upbringing," he said after a long pause.

"And my silly self."

She stood up, unlocked and opened her littered desk, turned and held out the key to him.

individuality quite distinctly their own, and she was now beginning to converse with startling enterprise and intelligence.

"Big, big, bog," she said at the sight of Daffy.

"Remembers you," said Marjorie.

"Bog! Go ta-ta!" said Margharita.

"There!" said Marjorie, and May, the nurse in the background, smiled unlimited appreciation.

"Bably," said Margharita.

"That's herself!" said Marjorie, falling on her knees.
"She talks like this all day. Oh de sweetums, den! *Was* it?"
Daffy made amiable gestures and canary-like noises with
her lips, and Margharita responded jovially.

"You darling!" cried Marjorie, "you delight of life,"
kneeling by the cot and giving the crowing, healthy little mite
a passionate hug.

"It's really the nicest of babies," Daffy conceded, and
reflected. . . .

"I don't know what I should do with a kiddy," said Daffy,
as the infant worship came to an end; "I'm really glad we
haven't one—yet. He'd love it, I know. But it would be a
burthen in some ways. They *are* a tie. As he says, the next
few years means so much for him. Of course, here his reputation is immense, and he's known in Germany, and there
are translations into Russian; but he's still got to conquer
America, and he isn't really well known yet in France. They
read him, of course, and buy him in America, but they're—
*restive.* Oh! I do so wish they'd give him the Nobel prize,
Madge, and have done with it! It would settle everything.
Still, as he says, we mustn't think of that—yet, anyhow. He
isn't—venerable enough. It's doubtful, he thinks, that they
would give the Nobel prize to any humorist now that Mark
Twain is dead. Mark Twain was different, you see, because
of the German Enperor and all that white hair and everything."

At this point Margharita discovered that the conversation
had drifted away from herself, and it was only when they got
downstairs again that Daffy could resume the thread of
Magnet's career, which had evidently become the predominant
interest in her life. She brought out all the worst elements of
Marjorie's nature and their sisterly relationship. There were
moments when it became nakedly apparent that she was
magnifying Magnet to belittle Trafford. Marjorie did her
best to counter-brag. She played her chief card in the F.R.S.

"They always ask Will to the Royal Society Dinner," threw
out Daffy; "but of course he can't always go. He's asked
to so many things."

Five years earlier Marjorie would have kicked her shins for
that.

Instead she asked pointedly, offensively, if Magnet was any
balder.

"He's not really bald," said Daffy unruffled, and went on to discuss the advisability of a second motor-car—purely for town use. " I tell him I don't want it," said Daffy, " but he's frightfully keen upon getting one."

### § 8

When Daffy had at last gone, Marjorie went back into Trafford's study and stood on the hearthrug regarding its appointments, with something of the air of one who awakens from a dream. She had developed a new, appalling thought. Was Daffy really a better wife than herself ? It was dawning upon Marjorie that she hadn't been doing the right thing by her husband, and she was as surprised as if it had been suddenly brought home to her that she was neglecting Margharita. This was her husband's study—and it showed just a little dusty in the afternoon sunshine, and everything about it denied the pretensions of serene sustained work that she had always made to herself. Here were the crumpled galley-proofs of his Science Notes ; here were unanswered letters. There—she dare not touch them—were computations, under a glass paper-weight. What did they amount to now ? On the table under the window were back numbers of the *Scientific Bulletin* in a rather untidy pile, and on the footstool by the armchair she had been accustomed to sit at his feet when he stayed at home to work, and look into the fire, and watch him furtively, and sometimes give way to an overmastering tenderness and make love to him. The thought of Magnet, pampered, fenced around, revered in his industrious tiresome repetitions, variations, dramatisations and so forth of the half-dozen dry little old jokes which the British public accepted as his characteristic offering and rewarded him for so highly, contrasted vividly with her new realisation of Trafford's thankless work and worried face.

And she loved him, she loved him—*so*. She told herself in the presence of all these facts, and without a shadow of doubt in her mind that all she wanted in the world was to make him happy.

It occurred to her as a rather drastic means to this end that she might commit suicide.

She had already gone some way in the composition of a touching letter of farewell to him, containing a luminous analysis of her own defects, before her common sense swept away this imaginative exercise.

Meanwhile, as if it had been working at her problem all the time that this exciting farewell epistle had occupied the foreground of her thoughts, her natural lucidity emerged with the manifest conclusion that she had to alter her way of living. She had been extraordinarily regardless of him, she only began to see that, and now she had to take up the problem of his necessities. Her self-examination, now that it had begun, was thorough. She had always told herself before that she had made a most wonderful and beautiful little home for him. But had

she made it for him ?    Had he as a matter of fact ever wanted
it, except that he was glad to have it through her ?    No doubt
it had given him delight and happiness, it had been a marvellous little casket of love for them, but how far did that out-
weigh the burthen and limitation it had imposed upon him ?
She had always assumed he was beyond measure grateful to
her for his home, in spite of all her bills, but was he ?    It was
like sticking a knife into herself to ask that, but she was now
in a phase heroic enough for the task—was he ?    She had
always seen herself as the giver of bounties ; greatest bounty
of all was Margharita.    She had faced pains and terrors and
the shadow of death to give him Margharita.    Now with
Daffy's illuminating conversation in her mind, she could turn
the light upon a haunting doubt that had been lurking in the
darkness for a long time.    Had he really so greatly wanted
Margharita ?    Had she ever troubled to get to the bottom
of that before ?    Hadn't she as a matter of fact wanted
Margharita ten thousand times more than he had done ?
Hadn't she in effect imposed Margharita upon him, as she had
imposed her distinctive and delightful home upon him, re-
gardlessly, because these things were the natural and legitimate
developments of herself ?

These things were not his ends.

Had she hitherto ever really cared what his ends might be ?

A phrase she had heard abundantly enough in current
feminist discussion recurred to her mind, " the economic
dependence of women," and now for the first time it was
charged with meaning.    She had imposed these things upon
him not because she loved him, but because these things that
were the expansions and consequences of her love for him were
only obtainable through him.    A woman gives herself to a
man out of love, and remains clinging parasitically to him out
of necessity.    Was there no way of evading that necessity ?

For a time she entertained dreams of marvellous social
reconstructions.    Suppose the community kept all its women,
suppose all property in homes and furnishings and children
vested in them !    That was Marjorie's version of that idea
of the Endowment of Womanhood which has been creeping
into contemporary thought during the last two decades.    Then
every woman would be a Princess to the man she loved. . . .
She became more definitely personal.    Suppose she herself
was rich, then she could play the Princess to Trafford ; she
could have him free, unencumbered, happy, and her lover !
Then, indeed, her gifts would be gifts, and all her instincts and
motives would but crown his unhampered life !    She could not
go on from that idea, she lapsed into a golden reverie, from
which she was roused by the clock striking five.

In half an hour perhaps Trafford would be home again.
She could at least be so much of a princess as to make his home
sweet for his home-coming.    There should be tea in here,

where callers did not trouble. She glanced at an empty copper vase. It ached. There was no light in the room. There would be just time to dash out into the High Street and buy some flowers for it before he came. . . .

§ 9

Spring and a renewed and deepened love for her husband were in Marjorie's blood. Her mind worked rapidly during the next few days, and presently she found herself clearly decided upon her course of action. She had to pull herself together and help him, and if that meant a Spartan and strenuous way of living, then manifestly she must be Spartan and strenuous. She must put an end once for all to her recurrent domestic deficits, and since this could only be done by getting rid of May, she must get rid of May and mind the child herself. (Every day, thank Heaven ! Margharita became more intelligent, more manageable, and more interesting.) Then she must also make a far more systematic and thorough study of domestic economy than she had hitherto done, and run the shopping and housekeeping on severer lines ; she bought fruit carelessly, they had far too many joints ; she never seemed able to restrain herself when it came to flowers. And in the evenings, which would necessarily be very frequently lonely evenings if Trafford's researches were to go on, she would type-write, and either acquire great speed at that or learn shorthand, and so save Trafford his present expenditure on a typist. That unfortunately would mean buying a typewriter. . . .

She found one afternoon in a twopenny book-box, with which she was trying to allay her craving for purchases, a tattered little pamphlet entitled : " Proposals for the Establishment of an Order of Samurai," which fell in very exactly with her mood. The title " dated " ; it carried her mind back to her middle girlhood and the defeats of Kuropatkin and the futile earnest phase in English thought which followed the Boer War. The order was to be a sort of self-appointed nobility serving the world. It shone with the light of a generous dawn, but cast, I fear, the shadow of the prig. Its end was the Agenda Club. . . . She read and ceased to read—and dreamt.

The project unfolded the picture of a new method of conduct to her, austere, yet picturesque and richly noble. These Samurai, it was intimated, were to lead lives of hard discipline and high effort, under self-imposed rule and restraint. They were to stand a little apart from the excitements and temptations of everyday life, to eat sparingly, drink water, resort greatly to self-criticism and self-examination, and harden their spirits by severe and dangerous exercises. They were to dress simply, work hard, and be the conscious and deliberate salt of the world. They were to walk among mountains. Incidentally, great power was to be given them. Such systematic effort and self-control as this seemed to

Marjorie to give just all she wasn't and needed to be, to save
her life and Trafford's from a common disaster. . . .

It particularly appealed to her that they were to walk
among mountains. . . .

But it is hard to make a change in the colour of one's life
amidst the routine one has already established about oneself,
in the house that is grooved by one's weaknesses, amidst
hangings and ornaments living and breathing with the life
of an antagonistic and yet insidiously congenial ideal. A great
desire came upon Marjorie to go away with Trafford for a
time, out of their everyday life into strange and cool and
spacious surroundings. She wanted to leave London and its
shops, and the home and the movements and the callers and
rivalries, and even dimpled little Margharita's insistent claims,
and get free and think. It was the first invasion of their lives
by this conception, a conception that was never afterwards
to leave them altogether, of retreat and reconstruction. She
knelt upon the white sheepskin hearthrug at Trafford's feet
one night, and told him of her desire. He, too, was tired of
his work and his vexations, and ripe for this suggestion of an
altered life. The Easter holidays was approaching, and nearly
twenty unencumbered days. Mrs. Trafford, they knew, would
come into the house, meanwhile, and care for Margharita.
They would go away somewhere together and walk, no luggage
but a couple of knapsacks, no hotel but some homely village
inn. They would be in the air all day, until they were saturated with sweet air and the spirit of clean restraints. They
would plan out their new rule, concentrate their aims. "And
I could think," said Trafford, "of this new work I can't begin
here. I might make some notes." Presently came the question of where the great walk should be. Manifestly it must
be among mountains, manifestly, and Marjorie's eye saw
those mountains with snow upon their summits and cold
glaciers on their flanks. Could they get to Switzerland ? If
they travelled second class throughout, and took the cheaper
way, as Samurai should ? . . .

§ 10

That holiday seemed to Marjorie as if they had found a lost
and forgotten piece of honeymoon. She had that same sense
of fresh beginnings that had made their first walk in Italian
Switzerland so unforgettable. She was filled with the happiness of recovering Trafford when he had seemed to be slipping
from her. All day they talked of their outlook, and how they
might economise away the need of his extra work, and so
release him for his research again. For the first time he talked
of his work to her, and gave her some intimation of its scope
and quality. He became enthusiastic with the sudden invention of experimental devices, so that it seemed to her almost
worth while if instead of going on they bolted back, he to his

laboratory and she to her nursery, and so at once inaugurate
the new régime. But they went on, to finish the holiday out.
And the delight of being together again, with unfettered hours
of association ! They rediscovered each other, the same—and
a little changed. If their emotions were less bright and intense, their interest was far wider and deeper.

The season was too early for high passes, and the weather
was changeable. They started from Fribourg and walked to
Thun and then back to Bulle, and so to Bultigen, Saanen,
Montbovon and the Lake of Geneva. They had rain several
days, the sweet, soft, windless mountain rain that seems so
tolerable to those who are accustomed to the hard and driven
downpours of England, and in places they found mud and
receding snow ; the inns were at their homeliest, and none the
worse for that, and there were days of spring sunshine when a
multitude of minute and delightful flowers came out as it
seemed to meet them—it was impossible to suppose so great a
concourse universal—and spread in a scented carpet before
their straying feet. The fruit-trees in the valleys were pow-
dered with blossom, and the new grass seemed rather green-
tinted sunlight than merely green. And they walked with a
sort of stout leisureliness, knapsacks well hung and cloaks
about them, with their faces fresh and bright under the bracing
weather, and their lungs deep charged with mountain air,
talking of the new austerer life that was now beginning. With
great snow-capped mountains in the background, streaming
precipices overhead, and a sward of flowers to go upon, that
strenuous prospect was altogether delightful. They went as it
pleased them, making detours into valleys, coming back upon
their steps. The interludes of hot, bright April sunshine made
them indolent, and they would loiter and halt where some
rock or wall invited, and sit basking like happy animals,
talking very little, for long hours together. Trafford seemed
to have forgotten all the strain and disappointment of the
past two years, to be amazed but in no wise incredulous at this
enormous change in her and in their outlook ; it filled her with
a passion of pride and high resolve to think that so she could
recover and uplift him.

He was now very deeply in love with her again. He talked
indeed of his research, but so that it might interest her, and
when he thought alone, he thought not of it but of her, making
again the old discoveries, his intense delight in the quality of
her voice, his joy in a certain indescribable gallantry in her
bearing. He pitied all men whose wives could not carry
themselves, and whose voices failed and broke under the
things they had to say. And then again there was the way
she moved her arms, the way her hands took hold of things,
the alert lucidity of her eyes, and then that faint, soft shadow
of a smile upon her lips when she walked thinking or observant,
all unaware that he was watching her.

It rained in the morning of their eleventh day, and then gave way to warmth and sunshine, so that they arrived at Les Avants in the afternoon a little muddy and rather hot. At one of the tables under the trees outside the Grand Hotel was a small group of people dressed in the remarkable and imposing costume which still in those days distinguished the motorist.   They turned from their tea to a more or less frank inspection of the Traffords, and suddenly broke out into cries of recognition and welcome.   Solomonson—for the most part brown leather—emerged with extended hands, and behind him, nestling in the midst of immense and costly furs, appeared the kindly salience and brightness of his Lady's face.   " Good luck ! " cried Solomonson.   " Good luck !   Come and have tea with us !   But this is a happy encounter ! "

" We're dirty—but so healthy ! " cried Marjorie, saluting Lady Solomonson.

" You look, oh !—splendidly well," that lady responded.

" We've been walking."

" With just that knapsack ! "

" It's been glorious."

" But the courage ! " said Lady Solomonson, and did not add, " the tragic hardship ! " though her tone conveyed it. She had all the unquestioning belief of her race in the sanity of comfort.   She had ingrained in her the most definite ideas of man's position and woman's, and that any one, man or woman, should walk in mud except under dire necessity, was outside the range of her philosophy.   She thought Marjorie's thick boots and short skirts quite the most appalling feminine costume she had ever seen.   She saw only a ruined complexion and damaged womanhood in Marjorie's rain-washed, sun-bit cheek.   Her benevolent heart rebelled at the spectacle.   It was dreadful, she thought, that nice young people like the Traffords should have come to this.

The rest of the party were now informally introduced. They were all very splendid and disconcertingly free from mud.   One was Christabel Morrison, the actress, a graceful figure in a green baize coat and brown fur, who looked ever so much more charming than her innumerable postcards and illustrated-paper portraits would have led one to expect ; her neighbour was Solomonson's cousin Lee, the organiser of the Theatre Syndicate, a brown-eyed, attenuated, quick-minded little man with an accent that struck Trafford as being on the whole rather Dutch, and the third lady was Lady Solomonson's sister, Mrs. Lee.   It appeared they were all staying at Lee's villa above Vevey, part of an amusing assembly of people who were either vividly rich or even more vividly clever, an accumulation which the Traffords in the course of the next twenty minutes were three times invited, with an increasing appreciation and earnestness, to join.

From the first our two young people were not indisposed

to do so. For eleven days they had maintained their duologue at the very highest level, seven days remained to them before they must go back to begin the hard new life in England, and there was something very attractive—they did not for a moment seek to discover the elements of that attractiveness—in this proposal of five or six days of luxurious indolence above the lake, a sort of farewell to the worldly side of worldly things, before they set forth upon the high and narrow path they had resolved to tread.

"But we've got no clothes," cried Marjorie, "no clothes at all! We've these hobnail boots and a pair each of heelless slippers."

"My dear!" cried Lady Solomonson in real distress, and as much aside as circumstances permitted, "my dear! My sister can manage all that!" Her voice fell to earnest undertones. "We can really manage all that. The house is packed with things. We'll come to dinner in fancy dress. And Scott, my maid, is so clever."

"But really!" said Marjorie.

"My dear!" said Lady Solomonson. "Everything." And she changed places with Lee in order to be perfectly confidential and explicit. "Rachel!" she cried, and summoned her sister for confirmatory assurances. . . .

"But my husband!" Marjorie became audible.

"We've long Persian robes," said Mrs. Lee, with a glance of undisguised appraisement. "He'll be splendid. He'll look like a Soldan. . . ."

The rest of the company forced a hectic conversation in order not to seem to listen, and presently Lady Solomonson and her sister were triumphant. They packed Marjorie into the motor-car, and Trafford and Solomonson returned to Vevey by the train and thence up to the villa by a hired automobile.

§ 11

They didn't go outside the magic confines of the Lees' villa for three days, and when they did they were still surrounded by their host's service and possessions ; they made an excursion to Chillon in his motor-cars, and went in his motor-boat to lunch with the Maynards in their lake-side villa close to Geneva. During all that time they seemed lifted off the common earth into a world of fine fabrics, agreeable sounds, noiseless unlimited service, and ample untroubled living. It had an effect of enchantment, and the long healthy arduous journey thither seemed a tale of incredible effort amidst these sunny excesses. The weather had the whim to be serenely fine, sunshine-like summer and the bluest of skies shone above the white wall and the ilex thickets and cypresses that bounded them in from the great world of crowded homes and sous and small necessities. And through the texture of it all for Trafford ran a thread of curious new suggestion. An intermittent discussion of economics and socialism was going on between himself and Solomonson and an agreeable little stammering man in brown named Minter, who walked up in the afternoon from Vevey—he professed to be writing a novel during the earlier half of the day. Minter displayed the keenest appreciation of everything in his entertainment, and blinked cheerfully and expressed opinions of the extremest socialistic and anarchistic flavour to an accompaniment of grateful self-indulgence. "Your port-wine is wonderful, Lee," he would say, sipping it. "A terrible retribution will fall upon you some day for all this."

The villa had been designed by Lee to please his wife, and if it was neither very beautiful nor very dignified, it was at any rate very pretty and amusing. It might have been built by a Parisian dressmaker—in the châteauesque style. It was of greyish-white stone, with a roof of tiles. It had little balconies and acutely roofed turrets, and almost burlesque buttresses, pierced by doors and gates ; and sun-trap loggias, as pleasantly casual as the bows and embroideries of a woman's dress ; and its central hall, with an impluvium that had nothing to do with rain-water, and its dining-room, to which one ascended from this hall between pillars up five broad steps, were entirely irrelevant to all its exterior features. Unobtrusive men-servants in grey with scarlet facings hovered serviceably.

From the little terrace, all set with orange-trees in tubs, one could see, through the branches and steps of evergreens and over a foreground of budding, starting vineyard, the clustering roofs of Vevey below, an agglomeration veiled ever so thinly in the mornings by a cobweb of wood smoke, against the blue background of lake with its winged sailing-boats and sombre Alpine distances. Minter made it all significant by a wave of the hand. "All this," he said, and of the crowded work-a-day life below, "all that."

"All this," with its rich litter of stuffs and ornaments, its fine profusion, its delicacies of flower and food and furniture, its frequent inconsecutive pleasures, its noiseless, ready service, was remarkably novel and yet remarkably familiar to Trafford. For a time he could not understand this undertone of familiarity, and then a sunlit group of hangings in one of the small rooms that looked out upon the lake took his mind back to his own dining-room, and the little, inadequate, but decidedly good, Bokhara embroidery that dominated it like a flag, that lit it, and now lit his understanding, like a confessed desire. Of course, Mrs. Lee—happy woman !—was doing just everything that Marjorie would have loved to do. Marjorie had never confessed as much, perhaps she had never understood as much, but now in the presence of Mrs. Lee's æsthetic exuberances, Trafford at least understood. He surveyed the little room, whose harmonies he had at first simply taken for granted, noted the lustre-ware that answered to the gleaming Persian tiles, the inspiration of a metallic thread in the hangings, and the exquisite choice of the deadened paint upon the woodwork, and realised for the first time how little aimless extravagance can be, and all the timid, obstinately insurgent artistry that troubled his wife. He stepped through the open window into a loggia, and stared unseeingly over glittering, dark-green leaves to the mysteries of distance in the great masses above St. Gingolph, and it seemed for the first time that perhaps in his thoughts he had done his wife a wrong. He had judged her fickle, impulsive, erratic, perhaps merely because her mind followed a different process from his, because while he went upon the lines of constructive truth, her guide was a more immediate and instinctive sense of beauty.

He was very much alive to her now, and deeply in love with her. He had reached Les Avants with all his sense of their discordance clean washed and walked out of his mind by rain and sun and a flow of high resolutions, and the brotherly swing of their strides together. They had come to the Lees' villa, mud-splashed, air-sweet comrades, all unaware of the subtle differences of atmosphere they had to encounter. They had no suspicion that it was only about half of each other that had fraternised. Now here they were in a company that was not only altogether alien to their former mood, but extremely interesting and exciting and closely akin to the latent factors in Marjorie's composition. Their hostess and her sister had the keen, quick æsthetic sensibilities of their race, with all that freedom of reading and enfranchisement of mind which is the lot of Western women. Lee had an immense indulgent affection for his wife ; he regarded her arrangements and exploits with an admiration that was almost American. And Mrs. Lee's imagination had run loose in pursuit of beautiful and remarkable people and splendours rather than harmonies of line and colour. Lee, like Solomonson, had that inexplicable alchemy of mind which distils gold from the commerce of the world (" All this," said Minter to Trafford, " is an exhalation from all that ") ; he accumulated wealth as one grows a beard, and found his interest in his uxorious satisfactions, and so Mrs. Lee, with her bright watchful eyes, quick impulsive movements, and instinctive command had the utmost freedom to realise her ideals.

In the world at large Lee and Solomonson seemed both a little short and a little stout, and a little too black and bright for their entirely conventional clothing, but for the dinner and evening of the villa they were now, out of consideration for Trafford, at their ease, and far more dignified in Oriental robes. Trafford was accommodated with a long, black, delicately embroidered garment that reached to his feet, and suited something upstanding and fine in his bearing ; Minter, who had stayed on from an afternoon call, was gorgeous in Chinese embroidery. The rest of the men clung boldly or bashfully to evening dress. . . .

On the evening of his arrival Trafford, bathed and robed, found the rest of the men assembling about an open wood fire in the smaller hall at the foot of the main staircase. Lee was still upstairs, and Solomonson, with a new grace of gesture begotten by his costume, made the necessary introductions ; a little man with fine-cut features and a Galway accent was Rex the playwright ; a tall, grey-haired, clean-shaven man was Bright from the New York Central Museum; and a bearded giant with a roof of red hair and a remote eye was Radlett Barns, the great portrait-painter, who consents to paint your portrait for posterity as the King confers a knighthood. These were presently joined by Lee and Pacey, the blond-haired musician, and Mottersham, whose patents and inventions control electric lighting and heating all over the world. And then, with the men duly gathered and expectant, the women came down the wide staircase.

The staircase had been planned and lit for these effects, and Mrs. Lee meant to make the most of her new discovery. Her voice could be heard in the unseen corridor above arranging the descent : " You go first, dear. Will you go with Christabel ? " The conversation about the fire checked and ceased with the sound of voices above and the faint rustle of skirts. Then came Christabel Morrison, her slender grace beautifully contrasted with the fuller beauties of that great lady of the stage, Marion Rufus. Lady Solomonson descended confidentially in a group of three, with Lady Mottersham and sharp-tongued little Mrs. Rex, all very rich and splendid. After a brief interval their hostess preceded Marjorie, and was so much of an artist that she had dressed herself merely as a foil to this new creation. She wore black and scarlet, that made the white face and bright eyes under her sombre hair seem the face of an inspiring spirit. A step behind her and to the right of her came Marjorie, tall and wonderful, as if she were the queen of earth and sunshine, swathed barbarically in gold and ruddy brown, and with her abundant hair bound back by a fillet of bloodstones and gold. Radlett Barns exclaimed at the sight of her. She was full of the manifest consciousness of dignity as she descended, quite conscious and quite unembarrassed ; two borrowed golden circlets glittered on her shining arm, and a thin chain of gold and garnets broke the contrast of the warm, sun-touched neck above, with the unsullied skin below.

She sought and met her husband's astonishment with the faintest, remotest of smiles. It seemed to him that never before had he appreciated her beauty. His daily companion had become this splendour in the sky. She came close by him with hand extended to greet Sir Philip Mottersham. He was sensible of the glow of her, as it were of a scented aura about her. He had a first full intimation of the cult and worship of woman and the magnificence of women, old as the Mediterranean and its goddesses, and altogether novel to his mind. . . .

Christabel Morrison found him a pleasant but not very entertaining or exciting neighbour at the dinner-table, and was relieved when the time came for her to turn an ear to the artistic compliments of Radlett Barns. But Trafford was too interested and amused by the general effect of the dinner to devote himself to the rather heavy business of really exhilarating Christabel. He didn't give his mind to her. He found the transformation of Sir Rupert into a turbanned Oriental who might have come out of a picture by Carpaccio, gently stimulating and altogether delightful His attention returned again and again to that genial swarthiness. Mrs. Lee on his left lived in her eyes, and didn't so much talk to him as rattle her mind at him almost absent-mindedly, as one might dangle keys at a baby while one talked to its mother. Yet it was evident she liked the look of him. Her glance went from his face to his robe, and up and down the table, at the bright dresses, the shining arms, the glass and light and silver. She asked him to tell her just where he had tramped and just what he had seen, and he had scarcely begun answering her question before her thoughts flew off to three trophies of china and silver, struggling groups of china boys bearing up great silver shells of fruit and flowers that stood down the centre of the table. "What do you think of my chubby boys ? " she asked. " They're German work. They came from a show at Düsseldorf last week. Ben saw I liked them, and sent back for them secretly, and here they are ! I thought they might be too colourless. But are they ? "

"No," said Trafford ; "they're just cool. Under that glow of fruit. Is this salt-cellar English cut glass ? "

"Old Dutch," said Mrs. Lee. "Isn't it jolly ? " She embarked with a roving eye upon the story of her Dutch glass, which was abundant and admirable, and broke off abruptly to say, "Your wife is wonderful.

"Her hair goes back," she said, "like music. You know what I mean—a sort of easy rhythm. You don't mind my praising your wife ? "

Trafford said he didn't.

"And there's a sort of dignity about her. All my life, Mr. Trafford, I've wanted to be tall. It stopped my growth."

She glanced off at a tangent. "Tell me, Mr. Trafford," she asked, "was your wife beautiful like this when you married her ? I mean—of course she was a beautiful girl and adorable and all that ; but wasn't she just a slender thing ? "

She paused, but if she had a habit of asking disconcerting questions she did not at any rate insist upon answers, and she went on to confess that she believed she would be a happier woman poor than rich—" not that Ben isn't all he should be " —but that then she would have been a fashionable dressmaker. "People want help," she said, "so much more help than they get. They go about with themselves—what was it Mr. Radlett

Barns said the other night ?—oh ! like people leading horses they
daren't ride. I think he says such good things at times, don't
you ? So wonderful to be clever in two ways like that. Just
look *now* at your wife—now, I mean, that they've drawn that
peacock-coloured curtain behind her. My brother-in-law has
been telling me you keep the most wonderful and precious secrets
locked up in your breast ; that you know how to make gold and
diamonds and all sorts of things. If I did—I should make them."

She pounced suddenly upon Rex at her left with questions
about the Keltic Renascence, was it still going on—or what ?
and Trafford was at liberty for a time to enjoy the bright
effects about him, the shadowed profile and black hair of
Christabel to the right of him, and the coruscating refractions
and reflections of Lady Solomonson across the white and silver
and ivory and blossom of the table. Then Mrs. Lee dragged
him into a sudden conflict with Rex, by saying abruptly—

" Of course, Mr. Trafford wouldn't believe that."

He looked perhaps a little lost.

" I was telling Mrs. Lee," said Rex, " that I don't believe
there's any economy of human toil in machinery whatever.
I mean that the machine itself really embodies all the toil it
seems to save, toil that went to the making of it and preparing
of it and getting coal for it. . . ."

§ 12

Next morning they found their hostess at breakfast in the
dining-room, and now the sun was streaming through a high
triple window that had been curtained overnight, and they
looked out through clean, bright plate-glass upon mountains
half dissolved in a luminous mist, and a mist-veiled lake below.
Great stone jars upon the terrace bore a blaze of urged and
early blossom, and beyond were cypresses. Their hostess
presided at one of two round tables, at a side table various
breakfast dishes kept warm over spirit-lamps, and two men-
servants dispensed tea and coffee. In the bay of the window
was a fruit-table, with piled fruit-plates and finger-bowls.

Mrs. Lee waved a welcoming hand, and drew Marjorie to
a seat beside her. Rex was consuming trout and Christabel
peaches, and Solomonson, all his overnight Orientalism abandoned, was in outspoken tweeds and quite under the impression that he was interested in golf. Trafford got frizzled
bacon for Marjorie and himself, and dropped into a desultory
conversation, chiefly sustained by Christabel, about the
peculiarly exalting effect of beautiful scenery on Christabel's
mind. Mrs. Lee was as usual distraught, and kept glancing
towards the steps that led up from the hall. Lady Solomonson appeared with a rustle in a wrapper of pink Chinese silk.
" I came down after all," she said. " I lay in bed weighing rolls
and coffee and relaxed muscles against your English breakfast
downstairs. And suddenly I remembered your little sausages ! "

She sat down with a distribution of handkerchief, bag, letters, a gold fountain-pen and such-like equipments, and Trafford got her some of the coveted delicacies. Mrs. Lee suddenly cried out, " *Here* they come ! *Here* they come ! " and simultaneously the hall resonated with children's voices and the yapping of a Skye terrier.

Then a gay little procession appeared ascending the steps. First came a small but princely little boy of three, with a ruddy face and curly black hair, behind him was a slender, rather awkward girl of perhaps eleven, and a sturdier daughter of Israel of nine. A nurse in artistic purple followed, listening inattentively to some private whisperings of a knickerbockered young man of five, and then came another purple-robed nurse against contingencies, and then a nurse of a different, white-clad, and more elaborately costumed sort, carrying a sumptuous baby of eight or nine months. " Ah ! the *darlings* ! " cried Christabel, springing up quite beautifully, and Lady Solomon-son echoed the cry. The procession broke against the tables and split about the breakfast-party. The small boy in petti-coats made a confident rush for Marjorie, Christabel set herself to fascinate his elder brother, the young woman of eleven scrutin-ised Trafford with speculative interest and edged towards him coyly, and Mrs. Lee interviewed her youngest born. The amiable inanities suitable to the occasion had scarcely begun before a violent clapping of hands announced the appearance of Lee.

It was Lee's custom, Mrs. Lee told Marjorie over her massively robed baby, to get up very early and work on rolls and coffee ; he never breakfasted nor joined them until the children came. All of them rushed to him for their morning kiss, and it seemed to Trafford that Lee at least was an alto-gether happy creature as he accepted the demonstrative salu-tations of this struggling, elbowing armful of offspring, and emerged at last like a man from a dive, flushed and ruffled and smiling, to wish his adult guests good morning.

" Come upstairs with us, Daddy," cried the children, tugging at him. " Come upstairs ! "

Mrs. Lee ran her eye about her table and rose. " It's the children's hour," she said to Marjorie. " You don't, I hope, mind children ? "

" But," said Trafford incredulous, and with a friendly arm about his admirer, " is this tall young woman yours ? "

The child shot him a glance of passionate appreciation for this scrap of flattery.

" We began young," said Mrs. Lee, with eyes of uncritical pride for the ungainly one, and smiled at her husband.

" Upstairs," cried the boy of five and the girl of nine. " Upstairs ! "

" May we come ? " asked Marjorie.

" May we all come ? " asked Christabel, determined to be in the movement.

Rex strolled towards the cigars, with disentanglement obviously in his mind.

" Do you really care ? " asked Mrs. Lee. " You know, I'm so proud of their nursery. Would you care—— ? Always I go up at this time."

" I've my little nursery too," said Marjorie.

" Of course ! " cried Mrs. Lee. " I forgot. Of course " ; and overwhelmed Marjorie with inquiries as she followed her husband. Every one joined the nurseryward procession except Rex, who left himself behind with an air of inadvertency, and escaped to the terrace and a cigar. . . .

It was a wonderful nursery, a suite of three bedrooms, a green-and-white, well-lit schoolroom, and a vast playroom, and hovering about the passage Trafford remarked a third purple nurse and a very efficient and serious-looking Swiss governess. The schoolroom and the nursery displayed a triumph of judicious shopping and arrangement, the best of German and French and English things had been blended into a harmony at once hygienic and pedagogic and humanly charming. For once Marjorie had to admire the spending of another woman, and admit to herself that even she could not have done better with the money.

There were clever little desks for the elder children to work at, adjustable desks scientifically lit so that they benefited hands and shoulders and eyes ; there were artistically coloured and artistically arranged pictures, and a little library held all the best of Lang and Lucas, rare good things like *Uncle Lubin*, Maurice Baring's story of *Forget-me-not*, *Johnny Crow's Garden*, *The Bad Child's Book of Beasts*, animal books and bird books, costume books and story books, colour books and rhyme books, abundant, yet every one intelligently chosen, no costly meretricious printed rubbish such as silly Gentile mothers buy. Then in the great nursery, with its cork carpet on which any toy would stand or run, was an abundance of admirable possessions and shelving for everything, and great fat cloth elephants to ride, and go-carts, and hooks for a swing. Marjorie's quick eye saw, and she admired effusively and envied secretly, and Mrs. Lee appreciated her appreciation. A skirmishing romp of the middle children and Lee went on about the two of them, and Trafford was led off by his admirer into a cubby-house in one corner (with real glass windows made to open) and the muslin curtains were drawn while he was shown a secret under vows. Lady Solomonson discovered some soldiers, and was presently on her knees in a corner with the five-year-old boy.

" These are like my Teddy's," she was saying. " My Billy has some of these."

Trafford emerged from the cubby-house, which was perhaps a little cramped for him, and surveyed the room, with his admirer lugging at his arm unheeded, and whispering : " Come back with me."

Of course this was the clue to Lee and Solomonson. How extremely happy Lee appeared to be ! Enormous vistas of dark philoprogenitive parents and healthy little Jews and Jewesses seemed to open out to Trafford, hygienically reared, exquisitely trained and educated. And he and Marjorie had just one little daughter—with a much poorer educational outlook. She had no cloth elephant to ride, no elaborate cubby-house to get into, only a half-dozen picture-books or so, and later she wouldn't when she needed it get that linguistic Swiss.

He wasn't above the normal human vanity of esteeming his own race and type the best, and certain vulgar aspects of what nowadays one calls Eugenics crossed his mind.

§ 13

During those few crowded days of unfamiliar living Trafford accumulated a vast confused mass of thoughts and impressions. He realised acutely the enormous gulf between his attitudes towards women and those of his host and Solomonson—and indeed of all the other men. It had never occurred to him before that there was any other relationship possible between a modern woman and a modern man but a frank comradeship and perfect knowledge, helpfulness, and honesty. That had been the continual implication of his mother's life, and of all that he had respected in the thought and writing of his time. But not one of these men in their place—with the possible exception of Minter, who remained brilliant but ambiguous—believed anything of the sort. It necessarily involved in practice a share of hardship for women, and it seemed fundamental to them that women should have no hardship. He sought for a word, and hung between chivalry and Orientalism. He inclined towards chivalry. Their women were lifted a little off the cold ground of responsibility. Charm was their obligation. " A beautiful woman should be beautifully dressed," said Radlett Barns in the course of the discussion of a contemporary portrait-painter. Lee nodded to indorse an obvious truth. " But she ought to dress herself," said Barns. " It ought to be herself to the points of the old lace—chosen and assimilated. It's just through not being that, that so many rich women are —detestable. Heaps of acquisition. Caddis-women. . . ."

Trafford ceased to listen, he helped himself to a cigar and pinched its end and lit it, while his mind went off to gnaw at : " A beautiful woman should be beautifully dressed," as a dog retires with a bone. He couldn't escape from its shining truth, and withal it was devastating to all the purposes of his life.

He rejected the word " Orientalism " ; what he was dealing with here was chivalry. " All this " was indeed, under the thinnest of disguises, the castle and the pavilion, and Lee and Solomonson were valiant knights, who entered the lists not indeed with spear and shield but with prospectus and ingenious enterprise, who drew cheques instead of swords for

their ladies' honour, who held " all that " in fee and subjection that these exquisite and wonderful beings should flower
in rich perfection.   All these women lived in a magic security
and abundance, far above the mire and adventure of the
world ;  their knights went upon quests for them and returned
with villas and pictures and diamonds and historical pearls.
And not one of them all was so beautiful a being as his Marjorie,
whom he made his squaw, whom he expected to aid and
follow him, and suffer uncomplainingly the rough services
of the common life.   Not one was half so beautiful as Marjorie,
nor half so sweet and wonderful. . . .

If such thoughts came in Lee's villa, they returned with
redoubled force when Trafford found himself packed painfully
with Marjorie in the night train to Paris.   His head ached
with the rattle and suffocation of the train, and he knew hers
must ache more.   The windows of the compartment and the
door were all closed, the litigious little commercial traveller
in shiny grey had insisted upon that, there was no corner
seat either for Marjorie or himself, the dim big package over
her head swayed threateningly.   The green shade over the
light kept opening with the vibration of the train, the pallid
old gentleman with the beard had twisted himself into a
ghastly resemblance to a broken-necked corpse, and pressed
his knees hard and stiffly against Trafford, and the small,
sniffing, bow-legged little boy beside the rusty widow woman
in the corner smelled mysteriously and penetratingly of
Roquefort cheese.   For the seventeenth time the little
commercial traveller jumped up with an unbecoming expletive, and pulled the shade over the light, and the silent young
man in the fourth corner stirred and readjusted his legs.

For a time, until the crack of light overhead had widened
again, every one became a dark head-dangling outline. . . .

He watched the dim shape before him and noted the weary
droop of her pose.   He wished he had brought water.   He
was intolerably thirsty, and his thirst gave him the measure
of hers.   This jolting fœtid compartment was a horrible place
for her, an intolerably horrible place.   And she was standing
it, for all her manifest suffering, with infinite gallantry and
patience.   What a gallant soul indeed she was !   Whatever
else she did she never failed to rise to a challenge.   Her very
extravagance that had tried their lives so sorely was perhaps
just one aspect of that same quality.   It is so easy to be
saving if one is timid ;  so hard if one is unaccustomed to fear.
How beautiful she had shone at times in the lights and glitter
of that house behind there !   and now she was back in her
weather-stained tweeds again, like a shining sword thrust
back into a rusty old sheath.

Was it fair that she should come back into the sheath because
of this passion of his for a vast inexhaustible research ?

He had never asked himself before if it was fair to assume

she would follow his purpose and his fortunes. He had taken
that for granted. And she too had taken that for granted,
which was so generously splendid of her. All her disloyalties
had been unintentional, indeed almost instinctive, breaches
of her subordination to this aim which was his alone. These
breaches he realised had been the reality of her nature fighting
against her profoundest resolutions.

He wondered what Lee must think of this sort of married life.
How ugly and selfish it must seem from that point of view !

He perceived for the first time the fundamental incongruity
of Marjorie's position ; she was made to shine, elaborately
prepared and trained to shine, desiring keenly to shine, and
then imprisoned and hidden in the faded obscurity of a small
poor home. How conspicuously, how extremely he must be
wanting in just that sort of chivalry in which Lee excelled !
Those business men lived for their women to an extent he had
hitherto scarcely dreamt of doing. . . .

His want of chivalry was beyond dispute. And was there
not also an extraordinary egotism in this concentration upon
his own purposes, a self-esteem, a vanity ? Had her life no
rights ? Suppose now he were to give her—two years, three
years perhaps of his life—altogether. Or even four. Was it
too much to grudge her four ? Solomonson had been at his
old theme with him, a theme the little man had never relinquished since their friendship first began years ago, possibilities
of a business alliance and the application of a mind of exceptional freshness and penetration to industrial development.
Why shouldn't that be tried ? Why not " make money " for
a brief strenuous time, and then come back, when Marjorie's
pride and comfort were secured ? . . .

(Poor dear, how weary she looked !)

He wondered how much more remained of this appalling
night. It would have made so little difference if they had
taken the day train and travelled first-class. Wasn't she indeed entitled to travel first-class ? Pictures of the immense
spaciousness, the softness, cleanliness, and dignity of first-class
compartments appeared in his mind. . . .

He would have looked at his watch, but to get at it would
mean disturbing the silent young man on his left.

Outside in the corridor there broke out a noisy dispute
about a missing coupon, a dispute in that wonderful language
that is known to the facetious as *entente cordiale*, between an
Englishman and the conductor of the train. . . .

§ 14

In Paris there was a dispute with an extortionate cabman,
and the crossing from Dieppe to Newhaven was rough and
bitterly cold. They were both ill. They reached home very
dirty and weary, and among the pile of letters and papers on
Trafford's desk was a big bundle of Science Note proofs, and

two letters from Croydon and Pinner to alter the hours of his lectures for various plausible and irritating reasons.

The little passage looked very small and rather bare as the door shut behind them, and the worn places that had begun to be conspicuous during the last six months, and which they had forgotten during the Swiss holiday, reasserted themselves. The dining-room, after spacious rooms flooded with sunshine, betrayed how dark it was, and how small. Those Bokhara embroideries that had once shone so splendid, now, after Mrs. Lee's rich and unlimited harmonies, seemed skimpy and insufficient, mere loin-cloths for the artistic nakedness of the home. They felt, too, they were beginning to find out their post-impressionist picture. They had not remembered it as nearly so crude as it now appeared. The hole a flying coal had burned in the unevenly faded dark-blue carpet looked larger than it had ever done before, and was indeed the only thing that didn't appear faded and shrunken.

§ 15

The atmosphere of the Lees' villa had disturbed Marjorie's feelings and ideas even more than it had Trafford's. She came back struggling to recover those high resolves that had seemed so secure when they had walked down to Les Avants. There was a curiously tormenting memory of that vast, admirable nursery, and the princely procession of children that would not leave her mind. No effort of her reason could reconcile her to the inferiority of Margharita's equipment. She had a detestable craving for a uniform for May. But May was going. . . .

But indeed she was not so sure that May was going.

She was no longer buoyantly well, she was full of indefinable apprehensions of weakness and failure. She struggled to control an insurgence of emotions that rose out of the deeps of her being. She had now, she knew, to take on her share of the burden, to become one of the Samurai, to show her love no longer as a demand but as a service. Yet from day to day she procrastinated under the shadow of apprehended things ; she forbore to dismiss May, to buy that second-hand type-writer she needed, to take any irrevocable step towards the realisation of the new way of living. She tried to think away her fears, but they would not leave her. She felt that Trafford watched her pale face with a furtive solicitude and wondered at her hesitations ; she tried in vain to seem cheerful and careless in his presence, with an anxiety, with premonitions that grew daily. There was no need to worry him unduly. . . .

But soon the matter was beyond all doubting. One night she gathered her courage together suddenly, and came down into his study in her dressing-gown with her hair about her shoulders. She opened the door, and her heart failed her.

" Rag," she whispered.

" Yes," he said busily from his desk, without looking round.

" I want to speak to you," she answered, and came slowly, and stood beside him silently.

" Well, old Marjorie ? " he said presently, drawing a little intricate pattern in the corner of his blotting paper, and wondering whether this was a matter of five pounds or ten.

" I meant so well," she said, and caught herself back into silence again.

He started at a thought, at a depth and meaning in her voice, turned his chair about to look at her, and discovered she was weeping and choking noiselessly. He stood up close to her, moving very slowly and silently, his eyes full of this new surmise, and now without word or gesture from her he knew his thought was right. " My dear," he whispered.

She turned her face from him. " I meant so well," she sobbed. " My dear ! I meant so well." Still with an averted face her arms came out to him in a desperate unreasoning appeal for love. He took her and held her close to him. " Never mind, dear," he said. " Don't mind." Her passion now was unconstrained. " I thought——" he began, and left the thing unsaid.

" But your work," she said, " your research ? "

" I must give up research," he said.

" Oh, my dearest ! "

" I must give up research," he repeated. " I've been seeing it for days. Clearer and clearer. *This*, dear, just settles things. Even—as we were coming home in that train—I was making up my mind. At Vevey I was talking to Solomonson."

" My dear," she whispered, clinging to him.

" I talked to Solomonson. He had ideas—a proposal."

" No," she said.

" Yes," he said. " I've left the thing too long."

He repeated. " I must give up research—for years. I ought to have done it long before."

" I had meant so well," she said. " I meant to work. I meant to deny myself. . . ."

" I'm glad," he whispered. " Glad ! Why should you weep ? " It seemed nothing to him then, that so he should take a long farewell to the rare, sweet air of that wonderland his mind had loved so dearly. All he remembered was that Marjorie was very dear to him, very dear to him, and that all her being was now calling out for him and his strength. " I had thought anyhow of giving up research," he repeated. " This merely decides. It happens to decide. I love you, dear. I put my research at your feet. Gladly. This is the end, and I do not care, my dear, at all. I do not care at all—seeing I have you. . . ."

He stood beside her for a moment, and then sat down again, sideways, upon his chair.

" It isn't you, my dear, or me," he said, " but life that beats us—that beautiful, irrational mother. . . . Life does not care for research or knowledge, but only for life. Oh ! the world has

to go on yet for tens of thousands of years before—before we
are free for that.  I've got to fight—as other men fight. . . ."

He thought in silence for a time, oddly regardless of her.
" But if it was not you," he said, staring at the fireplace with
knitted brows, " if I did not love you. . . . Thank God, I
love you, dear !  Thank God, our children are love children !
I want to live—to my finger-tips, but if I didn't love you—
oh ! love you ! then I think now—I'd be glad—I'd be glad, I
think, to cheat life of her victory."

" Oh, my dear ! " she cried, and clung weeping to him, and
caught at him and sat herself upon his knees, and put her arms
about his head, and kissed him passionately with tear-salt
lips, with her hair falling about his face.

" My dear," she whispered. . . .

### § 16

So soon as Trafford could spare an afternoon amidst his
crowded engagements he went to talk to Solomonson, who
was now back in London.  " Solomonson," he said, " you
were talking about rubber at Vevey."

" I remember," said Solomonson with a note of welcome.

" I've thought it over."

" I *thought* you would."

" I've thought things over.  I'm going to give up my professorship—and science generally, and come into business—
if that is what you are meaning."

Solomonson turned his paper-weight round very carefully
before replying.  Then he said :  " You mustn't give up your
professorship yet, Trafford.  For the rest—I'm glad."

He reflected, and then his bright eyes glanced up at Trafford.
" I knew," he said, " you would."

" I didn't," said Trafford.  " Things have happened since."

" Something was bound to happen.  You're too good—for
what it gave you.  I didn't talk to you out there for nothing.
I saw things. . . . Let's go into the other room, and smoke
and talk it over."  He stood up as he spoke.

" I thought you would," he repeated, leading the way.  " I
knew you would.  You see—one *has* to.  You can't get out of it.

" It was all very well before you were married," said Solomonson, stopping short to say it, " but when a man's married
he's got to think.  He can't go on devoting himself to his art
and his science and all that—not if he's married anything worth
having.  No.  Oh, I understand.  He'd got to look about
him, and forget the distant prospect for a bit.  I saw you'd
come to it.  *I* came to it.  Had to.  I had ambitions—just
as you have.  I've always had an inclination to do a bit of
research on my own.  I *like* it, you know.  Oh ! I could have
done things.  I'm sure I could have done things.  I'm not a
born money-maker.  But——"  He became very close and
confidential.  " It's—*them*.  You said good-bye to science for

a bit when you flopped me down on that old croquet-lawn, Trafford." He went off to reminiscences. "Lord, how we went over ! No more aviation for me, Trafford ! "

He arranged chairs, and produced cigars. "After all—this of course—it's interesting. Once you get into the movement of it, it takes hold of you. It's a game."

"I've thought over all you said," Trafford began, using premeditated phrases. "Bluntly—I want three thousand a year, and I don't make eight hundred. It's come home to me. I'm going to have another child."

Solomonson gesticulated a congratulation.

"All the same, I hate dropping research. It's stuff I'm made to do. About that, Solomonson, I'm almost super-stitious. I could say I had a call. . . . It's the maddest state of affairs ! Now that I'm doing absolutely my best work for mankind, work I firmly believe no one else can do, I just manage to get six hundred—nearly two hundred of my eight hundred is my own. What does the world think I could do better—that would be worth four times as much."

"The world doesn't think anything at all about it," said Solomonson.

"Suppose it did ! "

The thought struck Sir Rupert. He knitted his brows and looked hard obliquely at the smoke of his cigar. "Oh, it won't," he said, rejecting a disagreeable idea. "There isn't any world —not in that sense. That's the mistake you make, Trafford."

"It's not what your work is worth," he explained. "It's what your advantages can get for you. People are always going about supposing—just what you suppose—that people ought to get paid in proportion to the good they do. It's forgetting what the world is, to do that. Very likely some day civilisation will get to that, but it hasn't got to it yet. It isn't going to get to it for hundreds and hundreds of years."

His manner became confidential. "Civilisation's just a fight, Trafford—just as savagery is a fight, and being a wild beast is a fight—only you have padded gloves on and there's more rules. We aren't out for everybody, we're out for ourselves—and a few friends perhaps—within limits. It's no good hurrying ahead and pretending civilisation's something else when it isn't. That's where all these Socialists and people come a howler. Oh, *I* know the Socialists. I see 'em at my wife's At Homes. They come along with the literary people and the artists' wives and the actors and actresses, and none of them take much account of me because I'm just a business man and rather dark and short, and so I get a chance of looking at them from the side that isn't on show while the other's turned to the women, and they're just as fighting as the rest of us, only they humbug more and they don't seem to me to have a decent respect for any of the common rules. And that's about what it all comes to, Trafford."

Sir Rupert paused, and Trafford was about to speak when the former resumed again, his voice very earnest, his eyes shining with purpose. He liked Trafford, and he was doing his utmost to make a convincing confession of the faith that was in him. "It's when it comes to the women," said Sir Rupert, "that one finds it out. That's where *you've* found it out. You say, I'm going to devote my life to the service of Humanity in general. You'll find Humanity in particular, in the shape of all the fine, beautiful, delightful, and desirable women you come across, preferring a narrower turn of devotion. See ? That's all. *Caeteris paribus*, of course. That's what I found out, and that's what you've found out, and that's what everybody with any sense in his head finds out, and there you are !"

"You put it—graphically," said Trafford.

"I feel it graphically. I may be all sorts of things, but I do know a fact when I see it. I'm here with a few things I want and a woman or so I have and want to keep, and the kids upstairs, bless 'em ! and I'm in league with all the others who want the same sort of things. Against any one or anything that upsets us. We stand by the law and each other, and that's what it all amounts to. That's as far as my patch of Humanity goes. Humanity at large ! Humanity be blowed ! *Look* at it ! It isn't that I'm hostile to Humanity, mind you, but that I'm not disposed to go under as I should do if I didn't say that. So I say it. And that's about all it is, and there you are !"

He regarded Trafford over his cigar, drawing fiercely at it for some moments. Then seeing Trafford on the point of speaking, he snatched it from his lips, demanded silence by waving it at his hearer, and went on.

"I say all this in order to dispose of any idea that you can keep up the open-minded tell-everybody-everything scientific attitude if you come into business. You can't. Put business in two words and what is it ? Keeping something from somebody else, and making him pay for it——"

"Oh, look here !" protested Trafford. "That's not the whole of business."

"There's making him want it, of course, advertisement and all that, but that falls under making him pay for it, really."

"But a business man organises public services, consolidates, economises."

Sir Rupert made his mouth look very wide by sucking in the corners. "Incidentally," he said, and added after a judicious pause : "Sometimes. . . . I thought we were talking of making money."

"Go on," said Trafford.

"You set me thinking," said Solomonson. "It's the thing I always like about you. I tell you, Trafford, I don't believe that the majority of people who make money help civilisation forward any more than the smoke that comes out of the engine helps the train forward. If you put it to me, I don't. I've got no illusions of that sort. They're about as much help as—fat. They accumulate because things happen to be arranged so."

" Things will be arranged better some day."

" They aren't arranged better now. Grip that ! *Now*, it's a sort of paradox. If you've got big gifts and you choose to help forward the world, if you choose to tell all you know, and give away everything you can do in the way of work, you've got to give up the ideas of wealth and security, and that means fine women and children. You've got to be a *deprived* sort of man. ' All right,' you say, ' That's me ! ' But how about your wife being a deprived sort of woman ? Eh ? That's where it gets you ! And meanwhile, you know, while *you* make your sacrifices and do your researches, there'll be little mean sharp active beasts making money all over you like maggots on a cheese. And if everybody who'd got gifts and altruistic ideas gave themselves up to it, then evidently only the mean and greedy lot would breed and have the glory. They'd get everything. Every blessed thing. There wouldn't be an option they didn't hold. And the other chaps would produce the art and the science and the literature, as far as the men who'd got hold of things would let 'em, and perish out of the earth altogether. . . . There you are ! Still, that's how things are made. . . .

" But it isn't worth it. It isn't worth extinguishing oneself in order to make a world for those others, anyhow. Them and their children. Is it ? Eh ? It's like building a temple for flies to buzz in. . . . There is such a thing as a personal side to Eugenics, you know."

Solomonson reflected over the end of his cigar. " It isn't good enough," he concluded.

" You're infernally right," said Trafford.

" Very well," said Solomonson, " and now we can get to business."

§ 17

The immediate business was the systematic exploitation of the fact that Trafford had worked out the problem of synthesising indiarubber. He had done so with an entire indifference to the commercial possibilities of the case, because he had been irritated by the enormous publicity given to Behrens' assertion that he had achieved this long-sought end. Of course the production of artificial rubbers and rubber-like substances had been one of the activities of the synthetic chemist for many years, from the appearance of Tilden's isoprene rubber onward, and there was already a formidable list of collaterals, dimethybutadiene, and so forth, by which the coveted goal could be approached. Behrens had boldly added to this list as his own a number of variations upon a theme of Trafford's originally designed to settle certain curiosities about

elasticity. Behrens' products were not only more massively
rubber-like than anything that had gone before them, but also
extremely cheap to produce, and his bold announcement of
success had produced a check in rubber sales and widespread
depression in the quiveringly sensitive market of plantation
shares. Solomonson had consulted Trafford about this
matter at Vevey, and had heard with infinite astonishment
that Trafford had already roughly prepared and was proposing
to complete and publish, unpatented and absolutely unprotected, first a smashing demonstration of the unsoundness of
Behrens' claim, and then a lucid exposition of just what had
to be done and what could be done to make an indiarubber
absolutely indistinguishable from the natural product. The
business man could not believe his ears.

" My dear chap, positively—you mustn't," Solomonson
had screamed, and he had opened his fingers and humped his
shoulders and for all his public school and university training
lapsed undisguisedly into the Oriental. " Don't you *see* all
you are throwing away ? " he squealed.

" I suppose it's our quality to throw such things away,"
said Trafford, when at last Solomonson's point of view became
clear to him. They had embarked upon a long rambling discussion of that issue of publication, a discussion they were now
taking up again. " When men dropped that idea of concealing
knowledge, alchemist gave place to chemist," said Trafford,
" and all that is worth having in modern life, all that makes
it better and safer and more hopeful than the ancient life, began."

" My dear fellow," said Solomonson, " I know, I know.
But to give away the synthesis of rubber ! To just shove it
out of the window into the street ! *Gare l'eau !* Oh ! And
when you could do with so much too ! " . . .

Now they resumed the divergent threads of that Vevey talk.

Solomonson had always entertained the warmest friendship
and admiration for Trafford, and it was no new thing that he
should desire a business co-operation. He had been working
for that in the old days at Riplings ; he had never altogether
let the possibility drop out of sight between them in spite of
Trafford's repudiations. He believed himself to be a scientific
man turned to business, but indeed his whole passion was for
organisation and finance. He knew he could do everything
but originate, and in Trafford he recognised just that rare
combination of an obstinate and penetrating simplicity with
constructive power which is the essential blend in the making
of great intellectual initiatives. To Trafford belonged the
secret of novel and unsuspected solutions ; what were fixed
barriers and unsurmountable conditions to trained investigators and commonplace minds, would yield to his gift of
magic inquiry. He could startle the accepted error into self-
betrayal. Other men might play the game of business infinitely better than he—Solomonson knew, indeed, quite well

that he himself could play the game infinitely better than
Trafford—but it rested with Trafford by right divine of genius
to alter the rules. If only he could be induced to alter the
rules secretly, unostentatiously, on a business footing, instead
of making catastrophic plunges into publicity! And everything that had made Trafford up to the day of his marriage
was antagonistic to such strategic reservations. The servant
of science has as such no concern with personal consequences ;
his business is the steady, relentless clarification of knowledge.
The human affairs he changes, the wealth he makes or destroys,
are no concern of his ; once these things weigh with him,
become primary, he has lost his honour as a scientific man.

"But you *must* think of consequences," Solomonson had cried
during those intermittent talks at Vevey. "Here you are,
shying this cheap synthetic rubber of yours into the world
—for it's bound to be cheap ! any one can see that—like a
bomb into a market-place. What's the good of saying you
don't care about the market-place, that *your* business is just to
make bombs and drop them out of the window ? You smash
up things just the same. Why ! you'll ruin hundreds and thousands of people, people living on rubber shares, people working
in plantations, old, inadaptable workers in rubber works. . . ."

Sir Rupert was now still a little incredulous of Trafford's
change of purpose, and for a time argued conceded points.
Then slowly he came to the conditions and methods of the
new relationship. He sketched out a scheme of co-operation
and understandings between his firm and Trafford, between
them both and his associated group in the city.

Behrens was to have rope and produce his slump in plantation shares, then Trafford was to publish his criticism of
Behrens, reserving only that catalytic process which was his
own originality, the process that was to convert the inert,
theoretically correct synthetic rubber, with a mysterious
difference in the quality of its phases, into the real right thing.
With Behrens exploded, plantation shares would recover, and
while their friends in the city manipulated that, Trafford
would resign his professorship and engage himself to an ostentatious promotion syndicate for the investigation of synthetic
rubber. His discovery would follow immediately the group
had cleared itself of plantation shares ; indeed he could begin
planning the necessary works forthwith ; the large scale operations in the process were to be protected as far as possible
by patents, but its essential feature, the addition of a specific
catalytic agent, could be safely dealt with as a secret process.

"I hate secrecy," said Trafford.

"Business," interjected Solomonson, and went on with his
exposition of the relative advantages of secrecy and patent
rights. It was all a matter of just how many people you had
to trust. As that number increased, the more and more
advisable did it become to put your cards on the table and

risk the complex uncertain protection of the patent law. They went into elaborate calculations, clerks were called upon to hunt up facts and prices, and the table was presently littered with waste arithmetic.

" I believe we can do the stuff at tenpence a pound," said Solomonson, leaning back in his chair at last and rattling his fountain-pen between his teeth, " so soon, that is, as we deal in quantity. Tenpence ! We can lower the price and spread the market, sixpence by sixpence. In the end—there won't be any more plantations. Have to grow tea. . . . I say, let's have an invalid dinner of chicken and champagne, and go on with this. It's fascinating. You can telephone."

They dined together, and Solomonson on champagne rather than chicken. His mind, which had never shown an instant's fatigue, began to glow and sparkle. This enterprise, he declared, was to be only the first of a series of vigorous exploitations. The whole thing warmed him. He would rather make ten thousand by such developments, than a hundred thousand by mere speculation. Trafford had but scratched the surface of his mine of knowledge. " Let's think of other things," said Sir Rupert Solomonson. " Diamonds ! No ! They've got too many tons stowed away already. A diamond now—it's an absolutely artificial value. At any time a new discovery and one wild proprietor might bust that show. Lord !—diamonds ! Metals ? Of course you've worked the colloids chiefly. I suppose there's been more done in metals and alloys than anywhere. There's a lot of other substances. Business has hardly begun to touch substances yet, you know, Trafford—flexible glass, for example, and things like that. So far we've always taken substances for granted. On our side, I mean. It's extraordinary how narrow the outlook of business and finance is—still. It never seems to lead to things, never thinks ahead. In this case of rubber, for example——"

" When men fight for their own hands and for profit and position in the next ten years or so, I suppose they tend to become narrow."

" I suppose they must." Sir Rupert's face glowed with a new idea, and his voice dropped a little lower. " But what a pull they get, Trafford, if perhaps—they don't, eh ? "

" No," said Trafford with a smile and a sigh, " the other sort gets the pull."

" Not *this* time," said Solomonson ; " not with you to spot processes and me to figure out the cost "—he waved his hands to the litter that had been removed to a side table—" and generally see how the business end of things is going. . . ."

*Book Three*

*Marjorie at Lonely Hut*

# CHAPTER ONE

## SUCCESSES

### § 1

I FIND it hard to trace the accumulation of moods and feelings that led Trafford and Marjorie at last to make their extraordinary raid upon Labrador. In a week more things happen in the thoughts of such a man as Trafford, changes, revocations, deflections, than one can chronicle in the longest of novels. I have already in an earlier passage of this story sought to give an image of the confused content of a modern human mind, but that pool was to represent a girl of twenty, and Trafford now was a man of nearly thirty-five, and touching life at a hundred points for one of the undergraduate Marjorie's. Perhaps that made him less confused, but it certainly made him fuller. Let me attempt therefore only the broad outline of his changes of purpose and activity until I come to the crucial mood that made these two lives a little worth telling about, amidst the many thousands of such lives that people are living to-day. . . .

It took him seven years from his conclusive agreement with Solomonson to become a rich and influential man. It took him only seven years, because already by the mere accident of intellectual interest he was in possession of knowledge of the very greatest economic importance, and because Solomonson was full of that practical loyalty and honesty that distinguishes his race. I think that in any case Trafford's vigour and subtlety of mind would have achieved the prosperity he had found necessary to himself, but it might have been, under less favourable auspices, a much longer and more tortuous struggle. Success and security were never so abundant nor so easily attained by men with capacity and a sense of proportion as they are in the varied and flexible world of to-day. We live in an affluent age with a nearly incredible continuous fresh increment of power pouring in from mechanical invention, and compared with our own most other periods have been meagre and anxious and hard-up times. Our problems are constantly less the problems of submission and consolation and continually more problems of opportunity. . . .

Trafford found the opening campaign, the operation with the plantation shares and his explosion of Behrens' pretensions, extremely uncongenial. It left upon his mind a confused series of memories of interviews and talks in offices for the most part dingy and slovenly, of bales of press-cuttings and blue-pencilled financial publications, of unpleasing encounters with a number of bright-eyed, flushed, excitable, and extremely cunning men, of having to be reserved and

limited in his talk upon all occasions, and of all the worst
aspects of Solomonson. All that part of the new treatment
of life that was to make him rich gave him sensations as though
he had ceased to wash himself mentally, until he regretted his
old life in his laboratory as a traveller in a crowded night train
among filthy people might regret the bathroom he had left
behind him. . . .

But the development of his manufacture of rubber was an
entirely different business, and for a time profoundly interesting. It took him into a new astonishing world, the world
of large-scale manufacture and industrial organisation. The
actual planning of the works was not in itself anything essentially new to him. So far as all that went it was scarcely more
than the problem of arranging an experiment upon a huge
and permanent scale, and all that quick ingenuity, that freshness and directness of mind that had made his purely scientific
work so admirable had ample and agreeable scope. Even the
importance of cost and economy at every point in the process
involved no system of considerations that was altogether
novel to him. The British investigator knows only too well
the necessity for husbanded material and inexpensive sub-
stitutes. But strange factors came in, a new region of interest
was opened with the fact that instead of one experimenter
working with the alert responsive assistance of Durgan, a
multitude of human beings—even in the first drafts of his
project they numbered already two hundred, before the
handling and packing could be considered—had to watch,
control, assist, or perform every stage in a long elaborate
synthesis. For the first time in his life Trafford encountered
the reality of Labour, as it is known to the modern producer.

It will be difficult in the future, when things now subtly
or widely separated have been brought together by the receding perspectives of time, for the historian to realise just how
completely out of the thoughts of such a young man as Trafford
the millions of people who live and die in organised productive
industry had been. That vast world of toil and weekly
anxiety, ill-trained and stupidly directed effort and mental
and moral feebleness, had been as much beyond the living
circle of his experience as the hosts of Genghis Khan or the
social life of the Forbidden City. Consider the limitations of
his world. In all his life hitherto he had never been beyond a
certain prescribed area of London's immensities, except by the
most casual and uninstructive straying. He knew Chelsea
and Kensington and the north bank and (as a boy) Battersea
Park, and all the strip between Kensington and Charing Cross,
with some scraps of the Strand as far as the Law Courts, a
shop or so in Tottenham Court Road and fragments about the
British Museum and Holborn and Regent's Park, a range up
Edgware Road to Maida Vale, the routes west and south-west
through Uxbridge and Putney to the country, and Wimbledon

Common and Putney Heath.  He had never been on Hampstead Heath nor visited the Botanical Gardens nor gone down the Thames below London Bridge, nor seen Sydenham nor Epping Forest nor the Victoria Park.  Take a map and blot all he knew and see how vast is the area left untouched.  All industrial London, all wholesale London, great oceans of human beings, fall into that excluded area.  The homes he knew were comfortable homes, the poor he knew were the parasitic and dependent poor of the West, the shops, good retail shops, the factories for the most part engaged in dressmaking.

Of course he had been informed about this vast rest of London.  He knew that as a matter of fact it existed, was populous, portentous, puzzling.  He had heard of " slums," read *Tales of Mean Streets*, and marvelled in a shallow transitory way at such wide wildernesses of life, apparently supported by nothing at all in a state of grey, darkling, but prolific discomfort.  Like the princess who wondered why the people having no bread did not eat cake, he could never clearly understand why the population remained there, did not migrate to more attractive surroundings.  He had discussed the problems of those wildernesses as young men do, rather confidently, very ignorantly, had dismissed them, recurred to them, and forgotten them amidst a press of other interests, but now it all suddenly became real to him with the intensity of a startling and intimate contact.  He discovered this limitless unknown greater London, this London of the majority, as if he had never thought of it before.  He went out to inspect favourable sites in regions whose very names were unfamiliar to him, travelled on dirty little intra-urban railway lines to hitherto unimagined railway stations, found parks, churches, workhouses, institutions, public-houses, canals, factories, gas-works, warehouses, foundries, and sidings, amidst a multitudinous dinginess of mean houses, shabby back yards, and ill-kept streets.  There seemed to be no limits to this threadbare side of London, it went on northward, eastward, and over the Thames southward, for mile after mile—endlessly.  The factories and so forth clustered in lines and banks upon the means of communication, the homes stretched between, an infinitude of parallelograms of grimy boxes with public-houses at the corners and churches and chapels in odd places, towering over which rose the Council schools, big, blunt, truncated-looking masses, the means to an education as blunt and truncated, born of tradition and confused purposes, achieving by accident what they achieve at all.

And about this sordid-looking wilderness went a population that seemed at first as sordid.  It was in no sense a tragic population.  But it saw little of the sun, felt the wind but rarely, and so had a white, dull skin that looked degenerate and ominous to a West End eye.  It was not naked nor barefooted, but it wore cheap clothes that were tawdry when new, and speedily became faded, discoloured, dusty, and draggled. It was slovenly and almost wilfully ugly in its speech and gestures. And the food it ate was rough and coarse if abundant, the eggs it consumed " tasted "—everything " tasted " ; its milk, its beer, its bread was degraded by base adulterations, its meat was hacked red stuff that hung in the dusty air until it was sold ; east of the city Trafford could find no place where by his standards he could get a tolerable meal tolerably served. The entertainment of this eastern London was jingle, its religion clap-trap, its reading feeble and sensational rubbish without kindliness or breadth. And if this great industrial multitude was neither tortured nor driven nor cruelly treated—as the slaves and common people of other days have been—yet it was universally anxious, perpetually anxious about urgent small necessities and petty dissatisfying things. . . .

That was the general effect of this new region in which he had sought out and found the fortunate site for his manufacture of rubber, and against this background it was that he had now to encounter a crowd of selected individuals, and weld them into a harmonious and successful " process." They came out from their millions to him, dingy, clumsy, and at first it seemed without any individuality. Insensibly they took on character, rounded off by unaccustomed methods into persons as marked and distinctive as any he had known.

There was Dowd, for instance, the technical assistant, whom he came to call in his private thoughts Dowd the Disinherited. Dowd had seemed a rather awkward, potentially insubordinate young man of unaccountably extensive and curiously limited attainments. He had begun his career in a crowded home behind and above a baker's shop in Hoxton, he had gone as a boy into the works of a Clerkenwell electric engineer, and there he had developed that craving for knowledge which is so common in poor men of the energetic type. He had gone to classes, read with a sort of fury, feeding his mind on the cheap and adulterated instruction of grant-earning crammers and on stale, meretricious, and ill-chosen books ; his mental food indeed was the exact parallel of the rough, abundant, cheap, and nasty groceries and meat that gave the East-ender his spots and dyspeptic complexion ; the cheap text-books were like canned meat and dangerous with intellectual ptomaines, the rascally encyclopædias like weak and whitened bread, and Dowd's mental complexion, too, was leaden and spotted. Yet essentially he wasn't, Trafford found, by any means bad stuff ; where his knowledge had had a chance of touching reality it became admirable, and he was full of energy in his work and a sort of honest zeal about the things of the mind. The two men grew from an acute mutual criticism into a mutual respect.

At first it seemed to Trafford that when he met Dowd he was only meeting Dowd, but a time came when it seemed to him that in meeting Dowd he was meeting all that vast ·new England outside the range of ruling-class dreams, that multitudinous greater England, cheaply treated, rather out of health, angry, energetic, and now becoming intelligent and critical, that England which organised industrialism has created. There were nights when he thought for hours about Dowd. Other figures grouped .themselves round him— Markham, the head clerk, the quintessence of East End respectability, with a house almost on the Victoria Park ; Casement, who saw to the packing ; Miss Peckover, an ex-·telegraph operator, a woman so entirely reliable and un-observant that the most betraying phase of the secret process could be confidently intrusted to her hands. Behind them were clerks, workmen, motor-van men, work-girls, a crowd of wage-earners, from amidst which some individual would assume temporary importance and interest by doing some-thing wrong, getting into trouble, becoming insubordinate, and having contributed a little vivid story to Trafford's gathering impressions of life, drop back again into undis-tinguished subordination.

Dowd became at last entirely representative.

When first Trafford looked Dowd in the eye, he met some-thing of the hostile interest one might encounter in a swords-man ready to begin a, duel. There was a watchfulness, an immense reserve. They discussed the work and the terms of their relationship, and all the while Trafford felt there was something almost threateningly not mentioned.

Presently he learned from a Silvertown employer what that concealed aspect was. Dowd was " the sort of man who makes trouble," disposed to strike rather than not upon a grievance, with a taste for open-air meetings, a member, obstinately adherent in spite of friendly remonstrance, of the Social Democratic party. This in spite of his clear duty to a wife and two small white knobby children. For a time he would not talk to Trafford of anything but business— Trafford was so manifestly the enemy, not to be trusted, the adventurous plutocrat, the exploiter—and when at last Dowd did open out he did so defiantly, throwing opinions at Trafford as a mob might hurl bricks at windows. At last they achieved a sort of friendship and understanding, an amiability as it were in hostility, but never from first to last would he talk to Trafford as one gentleman to another ; between them, and crossed only by flimsy temporary bridges, was his sense of incurable grievances and fundamental injustice. He seemed incapable of forgetting the disadvantages of his birth and upbringing, the inferiority and disorder of the house that sheltered him, the poor food that nourished him, the deadened air he breathed, the limited leisure, the inadequate books.

Implicit in his every word and act was the assurance that but for this handicap he could have filled Trafford's place, while Trafford would certainly have failed in his.

For all these things Dowd made Trafford responsible ; he held him to that inexorably.

" *You* sweat us," he said, speaking between his teeth ; " *you* limit us, *you* stifle us, and away there in the West End, *you* and the women you keep waste the plunder."

Trafford attempted palliation. " After all," he said, " it's not me so particularly——"

" But it is," said Dowd.

" It's the system things go upon."

" You're the responsible part of it. *You* have freedom, *you* have power and endless opportunity——"

Trafford shrugged his shoulders.

" It's because your sort wants too much," said Dowd, " that my sort hasn't enough."

" Tell me how to organise things better."

" Much you'd care. They'll organise themselves. Everything is drifting to class separation, the growing discontent, the growing hardship of the masses. . . . Then you'll see."

" Then what's going to happen ? "

" Overthrow. And social democracy."

" How is that going to work ? "

Dowd had been cornered by that before. " I don't care if it *doesn't* work," he snarled, " so long as we smash up this. We're getting too sick to care what comes after."

" Dowd," said Trafford abruptly, " *I'm* not so satisfied with things."

Dowd looked at him askance. " You'll get reconciled to it," he said. " It's ugly here—but it's all right there—at the spending end. . . . Your sort has got to grab, your sort has got to spend—until the thing works out and the social revolution makes an end of you."

" And then ? "

Dowd became busy with his work.

Trafford stuck his hands in his pockets and stared out of the dingy factory window.

" I don't object so much to your diagnosis," he said, " as to your remedy. It doesn't strike me as a remedy."

" It's an end," said Dowd, " anyhow. My God ! When I think of all the women and shirkers flaunting and frittering away there in the West, while here men and women toil and worry and starve. . . ." He stopped short like one who feels too full for controlled speech.

" Dowd," said Trafford after a fair pause, " what would you do if you were me ? "

" Do ! " said Dowd.

" Yes," said Trafford as one who reconsiders it, " what would you do ? "

" Now that's a curious question, Mr. Trafford," said Dowd, turning to regard him. " Meaning—if I were in your place ? "

" Yes," said Trafford. " What would you do in my place ? "

" I should sell out of this place jolly quick," he said.

" *Sell* ! " said Trafford softly.

" Yes—sell. And start a socialist daily right off. An absolutely independent, unbiased socialist daily."

" And what would that do ? "

" It would stir people up. Every day it would stir people up."

" But you see I can't edit. I haven't the money for half a year of a socialist daily. . . . And meanwhile people want rubber."

Dowd shook his head. " You mean that you and your wife want to have the spending of six or eight thousand a year," he said.

" I don't make half of that," said Trafford.

" Well—half of that," pressed Dowd. " It's all the same to me."

Trafford reflected. " The point where I don't agree with you," he said, " is in supposing that my scale of living— over there, is directly connected with the scale of living— about here."

" Well, isn't it ? "

" ' Directly,' I said. No. If we just stopped it—over there—there'd be no improvement here. In fact, for a time it would mean dislocations. It might mean permanent, hopeless, catastrophic dislocation. You know that as well as I do. Suppose the West End became—Tolstoyan ; the East would become chaos."

" Not much likelihood," sneered Dowd.

" That's another question. That we earn together here and that I spend alone over there, it's unjust and bad, but it isn't a thing that admits of any simple remedy. Where we differ, Dowd, is about that remedy. I admit the disease as fully as you do. I, as much as you, want to see the dawn of a great change in the ways of human living. But I don't think the diagnosis is complete and satisfactory ; our problem is an intricate muddle of disorders, not one simple disorder, and I don't see what treatment is indicated."

" Socialism," said Dowd, " is indicated."

" You might as well say that health is indicated," said Trafford with a note of impatience in his voice. " Does any one question that if we could have this socialist state in which every one is devoted and every one is free, in which there is no waste and no want, and beauty and brotherhood prevail universally, we wouldn't ? But—— You socialists have no scheme of government, no scheme of economic organisation, no intelligible guarantees of personal liberty, no method of progress, no ideas about marriage, no plan—except those little pickpocket plans of the Fabians that you despise as much as

I do—for making this order into that other order you've never yet taken the trouble to work out even in principle. Really you know, Dowd, what is the good of pointing at my wife's dresses and waving the red flag at me, and talking of human miseries——"

"It seems to wake you up a bit," said Dowd with characteristic irrelevance.

§ 2

The accusing finger of Dowd followed Trafford into his dreams. Behind it was his grey-toned, intelligent, resentful face, his smouldering eyes, his slightly frayed collar and vivid, ill-chosen tie. At times Trafford could almost hear his flat insistent voice, his measured h-less speech. Dowd was so penetratingly right—and so ignorant of certain essentials, so wrong in his forecasts and ultimates. It was true beyond disputing that Trafford as compared with Dowd had opportunity, power of a sort, the prospect and possibility of leisure. He admitted the liability that followed on that advantage. It expressed so entirely the spirit of his training that with Trafford the noble maxim of the older socialists : " from each according to his ability, to each according to his need," received an intuitive acquiescence. He had no more doubt than Dowd that Dowd was the victim of a subtle evasive injustice, innocently and helplessly underbred, underfed, cramped, and crippled, and that all his own surplus made him in a sense Dowd's debtor.

But Dowd's remedies !

Trafford made himself familiar with the socialist and labour newspapers, and he was as much impressed by their honest resentments and their enthusiastic hopefulness as he was repelled by their haste and ignorance, their cocksure confidence in untried reforms and impudent teachers, their indiscriminating progressiveness, their impulsive lapses into hatred, misrepresentation, and vehement personal abuse. He was in no mood for the humours of human character, and he found the ill-masked feuds and jealousies of the leaders, the sham statecraft of G. B. Magdeberg, M.P., the sham Machiavellism of Dorvil, the sham persistent good-heartedness of Will Pipes, discouraging and irritating. Altogether it seemed to him the conscious popular movement in politics, both in and out of Parliament, was a mere formless and indeterminate aspiration. It was a confused part of the general confusion, symptomatic perhaps, but exercising no controls and no direction.

His attention passed from the consideration of this completely revolutionary party to the general field of social reform. With the naïve directness of a scientific man, he got together the published literature of half a dozen flourishing agitations and philanthropies, interviewed prominent and rather embarrassed personages, attended meetings, and when he found the speeches too tiresome to follow watched the audience about him. He even looked up Aunt Plessington's Movement, and filled her with wild hopes and premature boastings about a promising convert. " Marjorie's brought him round at last ! " said Aunt Plessington. . " I knew I could trust my little Madge ! " His impression was not the cynic impression of these wide shallows of activity. Progress and social reform are not, he saw, mere cloaks of hypocrisy ; a wealth of good intention lies behind them in spite of their manifest futility. There is much dishonesty due to the blundering desire for consistency in people of hasty intention, much artless and a little calculated self-seeking, but far more vanity and amiable feebleness of mind in their general attainment of failure. The Plessingtons struck him as being after all very typical of the publicist at large, quite devoted, very industrious, extremely presumptuous and essentially thin-witted. They would cheat like ill-bred children, for example, on some petty point of reputation, but they could be trusted to expend, ineffectually indeed, but with the extremest technical integrity, whatever sums of money their adherents could get together. . . .

He emerged from this inquiry into the proposed remedies and palliatives for Dowd's wrongs with a better opinion of people's hearts and a worse one of their heads than he had hitherto entertained.

Pursuing this line of thought, he passed from the politicians and practical workers to the economists and sociologists. He spent the entire leisure of the second summer after the establishment of the factory upon sociological and economic literature. At the end of that bout of reading he attained a vivid realisation of the garrulous badness that rules in this field of work, and the prevailing slovenliness and negligence in regard to it. He chanced one day to look up the article on Socialism in the new *Encyclopædia Britannica*, and found in its entire failure to state the case for or against modern Socialism, to trace its origins, or to indicate any rational development in the movement, a symptom of the universal laxity of interest in these matters. Indeed, the writer did not appear to have heard of modern Socialism at all ; he discussed collective and individualist methods very much as a rather ill-read schoolgirl in a hurry for her college debating society might have done. Compared with the treatment of engineering or biological science in the same compilation, this article became almost symbolical of the prevailing habitual incompetence with which all this system of questions is still handled. The sciences were done scantily and carelessly enough, but they admitted at any rate the possibility of completeness. This did not even pretend to thoroughness.

One might think such things had no practical significance.

And at the back of it all was Dowd, remarkably more impatient
each year, confessing the failure of parliamentary methods, of
trades unionism, hinting more and more plainly at the advent
of a permanent guerilla war against capital, at the general
strike and sabotage.

" It's coming to that," said Dowd ; " it's coming to that.

" *What's the good of it ?* " he said, echoing Trafford's
words. " It's a sort of relief to the feelings. Why shouldn't
we ? "

§ 3

But you must not suppose that at any time these huge grey
problems of our social foundations and the riddle of intellectual
confusion one reaches through them, and the yet broader
riddles of human purpose that open beyond, constituted the
whole of Trafford's life during this time. When he came back
to Marjorie and his home, a curtain of unreality fell between
him and all these things. It was as if he stepped through such
boundaries as Alice passed to reach her Wonderland ; the other
world became a dream again ; as if he closed the pages of a
vivid book and turned to things about him. Or again it was
as if he drew down the blind of a window that gave upon a
landscape, grave, darkling, ominous, and faced the warm
realities of a brightly illuminated room. . . .

In a year or so he had the works so smoothly organised and
Dowd so reconciled, trained, and encouraged that his own
daily presence was unnecessary, and he would go three and
then only two mornings a week to conduct those secret phases
in the preparation of his catalytic that even Dowd could not
be trusted to know. He reverted more and more completely
to his own proper world.

And the first shock of discovering that greater London
which " isn't in it " passed away by imperceptible degrees.
Things that had been as vivid and startling as new wounds
became unstimulating and ineffective with repetition. He
got used to the change from Belgravia to East Ham from
East Ham to Belgravia. He fell in with the usual persuasion
in Belgravia, that, given a firm and prompt Home Secretary,
East Ham could be trusted to go on—for quite a long time
anyhow. One cannot sit down for all one's life in the face of
insoluble problems. He had a motor-car now that far out-
shone Magnet's, and he made the transit from west to east in
the minimum of time and with the minimum of friction. It
ceased to be more disconcerting that he should have workers
whom he could dismiss at a week's notice to want or prostitution than that he should have a servant waiting behind his
chair. Things were so. The main current of his life—and the
main current of his life flowed through Marjorie and his home—
carried him on. Rubber was his, but there were still limitless
worlds to conquer. He began to take up, working under

circumstances of considerable secrecy at Solomonson's
laboratories at Riplings, to which he would now go by motor-
car for two or three days at a time, the possibility of a cheap,
resilient, and very tough substance, rubber glass, that was
to be, Solomonson was assured, the road surface of the
future. . . .

§ 4

The confidence of Solomonson had made it possible for
Trafford to alter his style of living almost directly upon the
conclusion of their agreement. He went back to Marjorie
to broach a financially emancipated phase. They took a
furnished house at Shackleford, near Godalming in Surrey,
and there they lived for nearly a year—using their Chelsea
home only as a town apartment for Trafford when business
held him in London. And there it was, in the pretty Surrey
country, with the sweet air of pine and heather in Marjorie's
blood, that their second child was born. It was a sturdy little
boy, whose only danger in life seemed to be the superfluous
energy with which he resented its slightest disregard for his
small but important requirements.

When it was time for Marjorie to return to London, spring
had come round again, and Trafford's conceptions of life were
adapting themselves to the new scale upon which they were
now to do things. While he was busy creating his factory
in the East End, Marjorie was displaying an equal if a less
original constructive energy in Sussex Square, near Lancaster
Gate, for there it was the new home was to be established.
She set herself to furnish and arrange it so as to produce the
maximum of surprise and chagrin in Daphne, and she succeeded
admirably. The Magnets now occupied a flat in Whitehall
Court ; the furniture Magnet had insisted upon buying himself
with all the occult cunning of the humorist in these matters,
and not even Daphne could blind herself to the superiority
both in arrangement and detail of Marjorie's home. That
was very satisfactory, and so too was the inevitable exaggeration of Trafford's financial importance. " He can do what he
likes in the rubber world," said Marjorie. " In Mincing Lane,
where they deal in rubber shares, they used to call him and
Sir Rupert the Invaders ; now they call them the Conquering
Heroes. . . . Of course, it's mere child's play to Rag, but,
as he said, ' We want money.' It won't really interfere with
his more important interests. . . ."

I do not know why both those sisters were more vulgarly
competitive with each other than with any one else ; I have
merely to record the fact that they were so.

The effect upon the rest of Marjorie's family was equally
gratifying. Mr. Pope came to the house-warming as though
he had never had the slightest objection to Trafford's ante-
cedents, and told him casually after dinner that Marjorie had

always been his favourite daughter, and that from the first
he had expected great things of her. He told Magnet, who
was the third man of the party, that he only hoped Syd and
Rom would do as well as their elder sisters. Afterwards, in
the drawing-room, he whacked Marjorie suddenly and very
startlingly on the shoulder-blade—it was the first bruise he
had given her since Buryhamstreet days. " You've made a
man of him, Maggots," he said.

The quiet smile of the Christian Scientist was becoming
now the fixed expression of Mrs. Pope's face, and it scarcely
relaxed for a moment as she surveyed her daughter's splendours. She had triumphantly refused to worry over a rather
serious speculative disappointment, but her faith in her
prophet's spiritual power had been strengthened rather than
weakened by the manifest insufficiency of his financial pres-
tidigitations, and she was getting through life quite radiantly
now, smiling at (but not, of course, giving way to) beggars,
smiling at toothaches and headaches, both her own and other
people's, smiling away doubts, smiling away everything that
bows the spirit of those who are still in the bonds of the
flesh. . . .

Afterwards the children came round, Syd and Rom now
with skirts down and hair up, and rather stiff in the fine big
rooms, and Theodore in a high collar and very anxious to get
Trafford on his side in his ambition to chuck a proposed bank
clerkship and go in for professional aviation. . . .

It was pleasant to be respected by her family again, but the
mind of Marjorie was soon reaching out to the more novel
possibilities of her changed position. She need no longer
confine herself to teas and afternoons. She could now, delightful thought ! give dinners. Dinners are mere vulgarities
for the vulgar, but in the measure of your brains does a dinner
become a work of art. There is the happy blending of a
modern and distinguished simplicity with a choice of items
essentially good and delightful and just a little bit not what
was expected. There is the still more interesting and difficult
blending and arrangement of the diners. From the first
Marjorie resolved on a round table, and the achievement of
that rare and wonderful thing, general conversation. She had
a clear centre, with a circle of silver bowls filled with short cut
flowers and low shaded, old silver candlesticks adapted to the
electric light. The first dinner was a nervous experience for
her, but happily Trafford seemed unconscious of the importance of the occasion and talked very easily and well ; at last
she attained her old ambition to see Sir Roderick Dover in her
house ; and there was Remington, the editor of the *Blue
Weekly*, and his silent gracious wife ; Edward Crampton, the
historian, full of surprising new facts about Kosciusko ; the
Solomonsons and Mrs. Millingham, and Mary Gasthorne the
novelist. It was a good talking lot. Remington sparred agree-

ably with the old Toryism of Dover, flank attacks upon them both were delivered by Mrs. Millingham and Trafford, Crampton instanced Hungarian parallels, and was happily averted by Mary Gasthorne with travel experiences in the Carpathians ; the diamonds of Lady Solomonson and Mrs. Remington flashed and winked across the shining table as their wearers listened with unmistakable intelligence, and when the ladies had gone upstairs Sir Rupert Solomonson told all the men exactly what he thought of the policy of the *Blue Weekly*, a balanced, common-sense judgment. Upstairs Lady Solomonson betrayed a passion of admiration for Mrs. Remington, and Mrs. Millingham mumbled depreciation of the same lady's intelligence in Mary Gasthorne's unwilling ear. " She's *passive*," said Mrs. Millingham. " She bores him. . . ."

For a time Marjorie found dinner-giving delightful—it is like picking and arranging posies of human flowers—and fruits—and perhaps a little dried grass, and it was not long before she learned that she was esteemed a success as a hostess. She gathered her earlier bunches in the Carmel and Solomonson circle, with a stiffening from among the literary and scientific friends of Trafford and his mother, and one or two casual and undervalued blossoms from Aunt Plessington's active promiscuities. She had soon a gaily flowering garden of her own to pick from. Its strength and finest display lay in its increasing proportion of political intellectuals, men in and about the House who relaxed their minds from the tense detailed alertness needed in political intrigues by conversation that rose at times to the level of the smarter sort of article in the half-crown reviews. The women were more difficult than the men, and Marjorie found herself wishing at times that girl novelists and playwrights were more abundant, or women writers on the average younger. These talked generally well, and one or two capable women of her own type talked and listened with an effect of talking ; so many other women either chattered disturbingly, or else did not listen, with an effect of not talking at all, and so made gaps about the table. Many of these latter had to be asked because they belonged to the class of inevitable wives, *sine-qua-nons*, and through them she learned the value of that priceless variety of kindly unselfish men who can create the illusion of attentive conversation in the most uncomfortable and suspicious natures without producing backwater and eddy in the general flow of talk.

Indisputably Marjorie's dinners were successful. Of course, the abundance and æsthetic achievements of Mrs. Lee still seemed to her immeasurably out of reach, but it was already possible to show Aunt Plessington how the thing ought really to be done, Aunt Plessington with her narrow, lank, austerely served table, with a sort of quarter-deck at her own end and a subjugated forecastle round Hubert. And accordingly the Plessingtons were invited and shown, and to a party, too, that

restrained Aunt Plessington from her usual conversational
prominence. . . .

These opening years of Trafford's commercial phase were
full of an engaging activity for Marjorie as for him, and for her
far more completely than for him were the profounder solicitudes of life lost sight of in the bright succession of immediate
events.

Marjorie did not let her social development interfere with
her duty to society in the larger sense. Two years after the
vigorous and resentful Godwin came a second son, and a year
and a half later a third. "That's enough," said Marjorie,
"now we've got to rear them." The nursery at Sussex
Square had always been a show part of the house, but now it
became her crowning achievement. She had never forgotten
the Lee display at Vevey, the shining splendours of modern
maternity, the books, the apparatus, the space and light and
air. The whole second floor was altered to accommodate
these four triumphant beings, who absorbed the services of
two nurses, a Swiss nursery governess and two housemaids—
not to mention those several hundred obscure individuals who
were yielding a sustaining profit in the East End. At any
rate, they were very handsome and promising children, and
little Margharita could talk three languages with a childish
fluency, and invent and write a short fable in either French
or German—with only as much misspelling as any child of
eight may be permitted. . . .

Then there sprang up a competition between Marjorie
and the able, pretty wife of Halford Wallace, most promising
of under-secretaries. They gave dinners against each other,
they discovered young artists against each other, they went
to first-nights and dressed against each other. Marjorie was
ruddy and tall, Mrs. Halford Wallace dark and animated ;
Halford Wallace admired Marjorie, Trafford was insensible
to Mrs. Halford Wallace. They played for points so vague
that it was impossible for any one to say which was winning,
but none the less they played like artists, for all they were
worth. . . .

Trafford's rapid prosperity and his implicit promise of still
wider activities and successes brought him innumerable
acquaintances and many friends. He joined two or three
distinguished clubs, he derived an uncertain interest from a
series of week-end visits to ample, good-mannered households,
and for a time he found a distraction in little flashes of travel
to countries that caught at his imagination, Morocco, Mon-
tenegro, Southern Russia.

I do not know whether Marjorie might not have been
altogether happy during this early Sussex Square period, if
it had not been for an unconquerable uncertainty about
Trafford. But ever and again she became vaguely apprehensive of some perplexing unreality in her position. She had

never had any such profundity of discontent as he experienced. It was nothing clear, nothing that actually penetrated, distressing her. It was at most an uneasiness. For him the whole fabric of life was as it were torn and pierced by a provocative sense of depths unplumbed that robbed it of all its satisfactions. For her these glimpses were as yet rare, mere moments of doubt that passed again and left her active and assured.

§ 5

It was only after they had been married six or seven years that Trafford began to realise how widely his attitudes to Marjorie varied. He emerged slowly from a naïve unconsciousness of his fluctuations—a naïve unconsciousness of inconsistency that for most men and women remains throughout life. His ruling idea that she and he were friends, equals, confederates, knowing everything about each other, co-operating in everything, was very fixed and firm. But indeed that had become the remotest rendering of their relationship. Their lives were lives of intimate disengagement. They came nearest to fellowship in relation to their children ; there they shared an immense common pride. Beyond that was a less confident appreciation of their common house and their joint effect. And then they liked and loved each other tremendously. They could play upon each other and please each other in a hundred different ways, and they did so, quite consciously, observing each other with the completest externality. She was still in many ways for him the bright girl he had admired in the examination, still the mysterious dignified transfiguration of that delightful creature on the tragically tender verge of motherhood ; these memories were of more power with him than the present realities of her full-grown strength and capacity. He petted and played with the girl still ; he was still tender and solicitous for that early woman. He admired and co-operated also with the capable, narrowly ambitious, beautiful lady into which Marjorie had developed, but those remoter experiences it was that gave the deeper emotions to their relationship.

The conflict of aims that had at last brought Trafford from scientific investigation into business, had left it a little scar of hostility. He felt his sacrifice. He felt that he had given something for her that she had had no right to exact, that he had gone beyond the free mutualities of honest love and paid a price for her ; he had deflected the whole course of his life for her and he was entitled to repayments. Unconsciously he had become a slightly jealous husband. He resented inattentions and absences. He felt she ought to be with him and orient all her proceedings towards him. He did not like other people to show too marked an appreciation of her. She had a healthy love of admiration, and in addition her social ambitions made it almost inevitable that at times she should use her great personal charm to secure and retain adherents. He was ashamed to betray the resentments thus occasioned, and his silence widened the separation more than any protest could have done. . . .

For his own part he gave her no cause for a reciprocal jealousy. Other women did not excite his imagination very greatly, and he had none of the ready disposition to lapse to other comforters which is so frequent a characteristic of the husband out of touch with his life's companion. He was perhaps an exceptional man in his steadfast loyalty to his wife. He had come to her as new to love as she had been. He had never in his life taken that one decisive illicit step which changes all the aspects of sexual life for a man even more than for a woman. Love for him was a thing solemn, simple, and unspoiled. He perceived that it was not so for most other men, but that did little to modify his own private attitude. In his curious scrutiny of the people about him, he did not fail to note the drift of adventures and infidelities that glimmers along beneath the even surface of our social life. One or two of his intimate friends, Solomonson was one of them, passed through "affairs." Once or twice those dim proceedings splashed upward to the surface in an open scandal. There came Remington's startling elopement with Isabel Rivers, the writer, which took two brilliant and inspiring contemporaries suddenly and distressingly out of Trafford's world. Trafford felt none of that rage and forced and jealous contempt for the delinquents in these matters which is common in the ill-regulated, virtuous mind. Indeed, he was far more sympathetic with than hostile to the offenders. He had brains and imagination to appreciate the grim pathos of a process that begins as a hopeful quest, full of the suggestion of noble possibilities, full of the craving for missed intensities of fellowship and realisation, that loiters involuntarily towards beauties and delights, and ends at last too often, after the gratification of an appetite, in artificially hideous exposures, and the pelting misrepresentations of the timidly well-behaved vile. But the general effect of pitiful evasions, of unavoidable meannesses, of draggled heroics and tortuously insincere explanations confirmed him in his aversion from this labyrinthine trouble of extraneous love. . . .

But if Trafford was a faithful husband, he ceased to be a happy and confident one. There grew up in him a vast hinterland of thoughts and feelings, an accumulation of unspoken and largely of unformulated things in which his wife had no share. And it was in that hinterland that his essential self had its abiding-place. . . .

It came as a discovery, it remained for ever after a profoundly disturbing perplexity, that he had talked to Marjorie most carelessly, easily, and seriously, during their courtship and their honeymoon. He remembered their early intercourse now as an immense happy freedom in love. Then afterwards a curtain had fallen. That almost delirious sense of escaping from oneself, of having at last found some one from whom there need be no concealment, some one before whom one could stand naked-souled and assured of love as one stands before one's God, faded so that he scarce observed its passing, but only discovered at last that it had gone. He misunderstood and met misunderstanding. He found he could hurt her by the things he said, and be exquisitely hurt by her failure to apprehend the spirit of some ill-expressed intention. And it was so vitally important not to hurt, not to be hurt. At first he only perceived that he reserved himself ; then there came the intimation of the question, was she also perhaps in such another hinterland as his, keeping herself from him ?

He had perceived the cessation of that first bright outbreak of self-revelation, this relapse into the secrecies of individuality, quite early in their married life. I have already told of his first efforts to bridge their widening separation by walks and talks in the country, and by the long pilgrimage among the Alps that had ended so unexpectedly at Vevey. In the retrospect the years seemed punctuated with phases when " we must talk " dominated their intercourse, and each time the impulse of that recognised need passed away again by insensible degrees—with nothing said.

§ 6

Marjorie cherished an obstinate hope that Trafford would take up political questions and go into Parliament. It seemed to her that there was something about him altogether graver and wider than most of the active politicians she knew. She liked to think of those gravities assuming a practicable form, of Trafford very rapidly and easily coming forward into a position of cardinal significance. It gave her general expenditure a quality of concentration without involving any uncongenial limitation to suppose it aimed at the preparation of a statesman's circle whenever Trafford chose to need that. Little men in great positions came to her house and talked with opaque self-confidence at her table ; she measured them against her husband while she played the admiring female disciple to their half-confidential talk. She felt that he could take up these questions and measures that they reduced to trite twaddle, open the wide relevances behind them, and make them magically significant, sweep away the encrusting pettiness, the personalities and arbitrary prejudices. But why didn't he begin to do it ? She threw out hints he seemed blind towards, she exercised miracles of patience while he ignored her baits. She came near intrigue in her endeavour to entangle him in political affairs. For a time it seemed to her that she was succeeding—I have already told of his phase of inquiry and interest in socio-political work—and then he relapsed into a scornful restlessness, and her hopes weakened again.

But he could not concentrate his mind, he could not think where to begin. Day followed day, each with its attack upon his attention, its petty just claims, its attractive novelties of aspect. The telephone bell rang, the letters flopped into the hall, Malcolm the butler seemed always at hand with some distracting oblong on his salver. Dowd was developing ideas for a reconstructed organisation of the factory, Solomonson growing enthusiastic about rubber-glass, his house seemed full of women, Marjorie had an engagment for him to keep or the children were coming in to say good-night. To his irritated brain the whole scheme of his life presented itself at last as a tissue of interruptions which prevented his looking clearly at reality. More and more definitely he realised he wanted to get away and think. His former life of research became invested with an effect of immense dignity and of a steadfast singleness of purpose. . . .

But Trafford was following his own lights, upon his own lines. He was returning to that faith in the supreme importance of thought and knowledge, upon which he had turned his back when he left pure research behind him. To that familiar end he came by an unfamiliar route, after his long, unsatisfying examination of social reform movements and social and political theories. Immaturity, haste, and presumption vitiated all that region, and it seemed to him less and less disputable that the only escape for mankind from a continuing extravagant futility lay through the attainment of a quite unprecedented starkness and thoroughness of thinking about all these questions. This conception of a needed Renascence obsessed him more and more, and the persuasion, deeply felt if indistinctly apprehended, that somewhere in such an effort there was a part for him to play. . . .

Life is too great for us or too petty. It gives us no tolerable middle way between baseness and greatness. We must die daily on the levels of ignoble compromise or perish tragically among the precipices. On the one hand is a life—unsatisfying and secure, a plane of dulled gratifications, mean advantages, petty triumphs, adaptations, acquiescences, and submissions, and on the other a steep and terrible climb, set with sharp stones and bramble thickets and the possibilities of grotesque dislocations, and the snares of such temptation as come only to those whose minds have been quickened by high desire, and the challenge of insoluble problems and the intimations of issues so complex and great, demanding such a nobility of purpose, such a steadfastness, alertness, and openness of mind, that they fill the heart of man with despair. . . .

There were moods when Trafford would, as people say, pull himself together, and struggle with his gnawing discontent.

He would compare his lot with that of other men, reproach himself for a monstrous greed and ingratitude. He remonstrated with himself as one might remonstrate with a pampered child refusing to be entertained by a whole handsome nursery full of toys. Other men did their work in the world methodically and decently, did their duty by their friends and belongings, were manifestly patient through dulness, steadfastly cheerful, ready to meet vexations with a humorous smile, and grateful for orderly pleasures. Was he abnormal ? Or was he in some unsuspected way unhealthy ? Trafford neglected no possible explanations. Did he want this great Renascence of the human mind because he was suffering from some subtle form of indigestion ? He invoked, independently of each other, the aid of two distinguished specialists. They both told him in exactly the same voice and with exactly the same air of guineas well earned : " What you want, Mr. Trafford, is a change."

Trafford brought his mind to bear upon the instances of contentment about him. He developed an opinion that all men and many women were potentially at least as restless as himself. A huge proportion of the usage and education in modern life struck upon him now as being a training in contentment. Or rather in keeping quiet and not upsetting things. The serious and responsible life of an ordinary prosperous man fulfilling the requirements of our social organisation fatigues and neither completely satisfies nor completely occupies. Still less does the responsible part of the life of a woman of the prosperous classes engage all her energies or hold her imagination. And there has grown up a great informal organisation of employments, games, ceremonies, social routines, travel, to consume these surplus powers and excessive cravings, which might otherwise change or shatter the whole order of human living. He began to understand the forced preoccupation with cricket and golf, the shooting, visiting, and so forth, to which the young people of the economically free classes in the community are trained. He discovered a theory for hobbies and specialised interests. He began to see why people go to Scotland to get away from London, and come to London to get away from Scotland, why they crowd to and fro along the Riviera, swarm over Switzerland, shoot, yacht, hunt, and maintain an immense apparatus of racing and motoring. Because so they are able to remain reasonably contented with the world as it is. He perceived, too, that a man who has missed or broken through the training to this kind of life, does not again very readily subdue himself to the security of these systematised distractions. His own upbringing had been antipathetic to any such adaptations ; his years of research had given him the habit of naked intimacy with truth, filled him with a craving for reality and the destructive acids of a relentless critical method.

He began to understand something of the psychology of vice, to comprehend how small a part mere sensuality, how large a part the spirit of adventure and the craving for illegality, may play in the lives of those who are called evil livers. Mere animal impulses and curiosities it had always seemed possible to him to control, but now he was beginning to apprehend the power of that passion for escape, at any cost, in any way, from the petty, weakly stimulating, competitive motives of low-grade and law-abiding prosperity. . . .

For a time Trafford made an earnest effort to adjust himself to the position in which he found himself, and make a working compromise with his disturbing forces. He tried to pick up the scientific preoccupation of his earlier years. He made extensive schemes, to Solomonson's great concern, whereby he might to a large extent disentangle himself from business. He began to hunt out forgotten note-books and yellowing sheets of memoranda. He found the resumption of research much more difficult than he had ever supposed possible. He went so far as to plan a laboratory, and to make some inquiries as to site and the cost of building, to the great satisfaction not only of Marjorie but of his mother. Old Mrs. Trafford had never expressed her concern at his abandonment of molecular physics for money-making, but now in her appreciation of his return to pure investigation she betrayed her sense of his departure.

But in his heart he felt that this methodical establishment of virtue by limitation would not suffice for him. He said no word of this scepticism as it grew in his mind. Marjorie was still under the impression that he was returning to research, and that she was free to contrive the steady preparation for that happier day when he should assume his political inheritance. And then presently a queer little dispute sprang up between them. Suddenly, for the first time since he took to business, Trafford found himself limiting her again. She was disposed, partly through the natural growth of her circle and her setting and partly through a movement on the part of Mrs. Halford Wallace, to move from Sussex Square into a larger, more picturesquely built house in a more central position. She particularly desired a good staircase. He met her intimations of this development with a curious and unusual irritation. The idea of moving bothered him. He felt that exaggerated annoyance which is so often a concomitant of overwrought nerves. They had a dispute that was almost a quarrel, and though Marjorie dropped the matter for a time, he could feel she was still at work upon it.

# CHAPTER TWO

## TRAFFORD DECIDES TO GO

### § 1

A HAUNTING desire to go away into solitude grew upon Trafford very steadily. He wanted intensely to think, and London and Marjorie would not let him think. He wanted therefore to go away out of London and Marjorie's world. He wanted, he felt, to go away alone and face God, and clear things up in his mind. By imperceptible degrees this desire anticipated its realisation. His activities were affected more and more by intimations of a determined crisis. One eventful day it seemed to him that his mind passed quite suddenly from desire to resolve. He found himself with a project, already broadly definite. Hitherto he hadn't been at all clear where he could go. From the first almost he had felt that this change he needed, the change by which he was to get out of the thickets of work and perplexity and distraction that held him captive, must be a physical as well as a mental removal ; he must go somewhere, still and isolated, where sustained, detached thinking was possible. . . . His preference, if he had one, inclined him to some solitude among the Himalaya Mountains. That came perhaps from Kim and the precedent of the Hindoo's religious retreat from the world. But this retreat he contemplated was a retreat that aimed at a return, a clarified and strengthened resumption of the world. And then suddenly, as if he had always intended it, Labrador flashed through his thoughts, like a familiar name that had been for a time quite unaccountably forgotten.

The word "Labrador" drifted to him one day from an adjacent table as he sat alone at lunch in the Liberal Union Club. Some bore was reciting the substance of a lecture to a fellow-member. "Seems to be a remarkable country," said the speaker. "Mineral wealth hardly glanced at, you know. Furs and a few score Indians. And at our doors. Practically —at our doors."

Trafford ceased to listen. His mind was taking up this idea of Labrador. He wondered why he had not thought of Labrador before.

He had two or three streams of thought flowing in his mind, as a man who muses alone is apt to do. Marjorie's desire to move had reappeared ; a particular group of houses between Berkeley Square and Park Lane had taken hold of her fancy. She had urged the acquisition of one upon him that morning, and this kept coming up into consciousness like a wrong thread in a tapestry. Moreover, he was watching his fellow-members with a critical rather than a friendly eye. A half-speculative, half-hostile contemplation of his habitual associates was one of the queer aspects of this period of un-settlement. They exasperated him by their massive content-ment with the surface of things. They came in one after another patting their ties, or pulling at the lapels of their coats, and looked about them for vacant places with a con-scious ease of manner that irritated his nerves. No doubt they were all more or less successful and distinguished men, matter for conversation and food for anecdotes, but why did they trouble to give themselves the air of it? They halted or sat down by friends, enunciated vapid remarks in sonorous voices, and opened conversations in trite phrases, about London architecture, about the political situation or the morning's newspaper, conversations that ought, he felt, to have been thrown away unopened, so stale and needless they seemed to him. They were judges, lawyers of all sorts, bankers, company promoters, railway managers, stockbrokers, pressmen, politicians, men of leisure. He wondered if indeed they were as opaque as they seemed, wondered with the helpless wonder of a man of exceptional mental gifts whether any of them at any stage had had such thoughts as his, had wanted as acutely as he did now to get right out of the world. Did old Booch over there, for example, guzzling oysters, cry at times upon the unknown God in the vast silences of the night? But Booch, of course, was a member or something of the House of Laymen, and very sound on the Thirty-nine Articles —a man who ate oysters like that could swallow anything— and in the vast silences of the night he was probably heavily and noisily asleep. . . .

Blenkins, the gentlemanly colleague of Denton in the control of the *Old Country Gazette*, appeared on his way to the pay-desk, gesticulating amiably en route to any possible friend. Trafford returned his salutation, and pulled himself together immediately after in fear that he had scowled, for he hated to be churlish to any human being. Blenkins, too, it might be, had sorrow and remorse and periods of passionate self-distrust and self-examination; maybe Blenkins could weep salt tears, as Blenkins no doubt under suitable sword-play would reveal heart and viscera as quivering and oozy as any man's.

But to Trafford's jaundiced eye just then, it seemed that if you slashed Blenkins across, he would probably cut like a cheese. . . .

Now, in Labrador—— . . .

So soon as Blenkins had cleared, Trafford followed him to the pay-desk, and went on upstairs to the smoking-room, thinking of Labrador. Long ago he had read the story of Wallace and Hubbard in that wilderness.

There was much to be said for a winter in Labrador. It

was cold, it was clear, infinitely lonely, with a keen edge of danger and hardship and never a letter or a paper.

One could provision a hut and sit wrapped in furs, watching the Northern Lights. . . .

"I'm off to Labrador," said Trafford, and entered the smoking-room.

It was, after all, perfectly easy to go to Labrador. One had just to go. . . .

As he pinched the end of his cigar, he became aware of Blenkins, with a gleam of golden glasses and a flapping white cuff, beckoning across the room to him. With that probable scowl on his conscience Trafford was moved to respond with an unreal warmth, and strolled across to Blenkins and a group of three or four other people, including that vigorous young politician, Weston Massinghay, and Hart, K.C., about the farther fireplace. "We were talking of you," said Blenkins. "Come and sit down with us. Why don't you come into Parliament ? "

"I've just arranged to go for some months to Labrador."

"Industrial development ? " asked Blenkins, all alive.

"No. Holiday."

No Blenkins believes that sort of thing, but of course, if Trafford chose to keep his own counsel——

"Well, come into Parliament as soon as you get back."

Trafford had had that old conversation before. He pretended insensibility when Blenkins gestured to a vacant chair. "No," he said, still standing, "we settled all that. And now I'm up to my neck in—detail about Labrador. I shall be starting—before the month is out."

Blenkins and Hart simulated interest. "It's immoral," said Blenkins, "for a man of your standing to keep out of politics."

"It's more than immoral," said Hart ; "it's American."

"Solomonson comes in to represent the firm," smiled Trafford, signalled the waiter for coffee, and presently disentangled himself from their company.

For Blenkins Trafford concealed an exquisite dislike and contempt ; and Blenkins had a considerable admiration for Trafford, based on extensive misunderstandings. Blenkins admired Trafford because he was good-looking and well-dressed, with a beautiful and successful wife, because he had become reasonably rich very quickly and easily, was young and a Fellow of the Royal Society with a reputation that echoed in Berlin, and very perceptibly did not return Blenkins' admiration. All these things filled Blenkins with a desire for Trafford's intimacy, and to become the associate of the very promising political career that it seemed to him, in spite of Trafford's repudiations, was the natural next step in a deliberately and honourably planned life. He mistook Trafford's silences and detachment for the marks of a strong,

silent man, who was scheming the immense, vulgar, distin-
guished-looking achievements that appeal to the Blenkins'
mind. Blenkins was a sentimentally loyal party Liberal, and
as he said at times to Hart and Weston Massinghay : " If
those other fellows get hold of him—— ! "

Blenkins was the fine flower of Oxford Liberalism and the
Tennysonian days. He wanted to be like King Arthur and
Sir Galahad, with the merest touch of Launcelot, and to be
perfectly upright and splendid and very, very successful.
He was a fair, tenoring sort of person with an Arthurian
moustache and a disposition to long frock-coats. It had
been said of him that he didn't dress like a gentleman, but
that he dressed more like a gentleman than a gentleman ought
to dress. It might have been added that he didn't behave
like a gentleman, but that he behaved more like a gentleman
than a gentleman ought to behave. He didn't think, but he
talked and he wrote more thoughtfully in his leaders, and in
the little dialogues he wrote in imitation of Sir Arthur Helps,
than any other person who didn't think could possibly do.
He was an orthodox Churchman, but very, very broad ; he
held all the doctrines, a distinguished sort of thing to do in
an age of doubt, but there was a quality about them as he
held them—as though they had been run over by something
rather heavy. It was a flattened and slightly obliterated
breadth—nothing was assertive, but nothing, under examination, proved to be altogether gone. His profuse thoughtfulness was not confined to his journalistic and literary work, it
overflowed into Talks. He was a man for Great Talks,
interminable rambling floods of boyish observation, emotional
appreciation, and silly, sapient comment. He loved to discuss
"Who are the Best Talkers now Alive ? " He had written
an essay, " Talk in the Past." He boasted of week-ends
when the Talk had gone on from the moment of meeting in
the train to the moment of parting at Euston, or Paddington,
or Waterloo ; and one or two hostesses with embittered
memories could verify his boasting. He did his best to make
the club a Talking Club, and loved to summon men to a
growing circle of chairs. . . .

Trafford had been involved in Talks on one or two occasions,
and now, as he sat alone in the corridor and smoked and
drank his coffee, he could imagine the Talk he had escaped,
the Talk that was going on in the smoking-room—the platitudes, the sagacities, the digressions, the sudden revelation
of deep, irrational convictions. He reflected upon the various
Talks at which he had assisted. His chief impression of them
all was of an intolerable fluidity. Never once had he known
a Talk thicken to adequate discussion ; never had a new idea
or a new view come to him in a Talk. He wondered why
Blenkins and his like talked at all. Essentially they lived
for pose, not for expression ; they did not greatly desire to

discover, make, or be ; they wanted to seem and succeed.
Talking perhaps was part of their pose of great intellectual
activity, and Blenkins was fortunate to have an easy, unforced
running of the mind. . . .

Over his cigar Trafford became profoundly philosophical
about Talk. And after the manner of those who become
profoundly philosophical he spread out the word beyond its
original and proper intentions to all sorts of kindred and
parallel things. Blenkins and his miscellany of friends in
their circle of chairs were, after all, only a crude rendering of
very much of the intellectual activity of mankind. Men
talked so often as dogs bark. Those Talkers never came to
grips, fell away from topic to topic, pretended depth and
evaded the devastating horrors of sincerity. Listening was a
politeness amongst them that was presently rewarded with
utterance. Tremendously like dogs they were, in a dog-
fancying neighbourhood on a summer week-day afternoon.
Fluidity, excessive abundance, inconsecutiveness ; these were
the things that made Talk hateful to Trafford. . . .

Wasn't most literature in the same case ? Wasn't nearly
all present philosophical and sociological discussion in the
world merely a Blenkins circle on a colossal scale, with every
one looming forward to get in a deeply thoughtful word
edgeways at the first opportunity ? Imagine any one in
distress about his soul or about mankind, going to a professor
of economics or sociology or philosophy ! He thought of the
endless, big, expensive, fruitless books, the windy expansions
of industrious pedantry that mocked the spirit of inquiry.
The fields of physical and biological science alone had been
partially rescued from the floods of human inconsecutiveness.
There at least a man must, on the whole, join on to the work
of other men, stand a searching criticism, justify himself
Philosophically this was an age of relaxed schoolmen. He
thought of Doctor Codger at Cambridge, bubbling away with
his iridescent Hegelianism like a salted snail ; of Doctor
Quiller at Oxford, ignoring Bergson and fulminating a preposterous insular Pragmatism. Each contradicted the other
fundamentally upon matters of universal concern ; neither
ever joined issue with the other. Why in the name of humanity
didn't some one take hold of those two excellent gentlemen,
and bang their busy heads together hard and frequently until
they either compromised or cracked ?

§ 2

He forgot these rambling speculations as he came out into
the spring sunshine of Pall Mall, and halting for a moment
on the topmost step, regarded the tidy pavements, the rare
dignified shops, the waiting taxi-cabs, the pleasant, prosperous
passers-by. His mind lapsed back to the thought that he
meant to leave all this and go to Labrador. His mind went

a step further, and reflected that he would not only go to
Labrador, but—it was highly probable—come back again.

" And then ?

Why, after all, should he go to Labrador at all ? Why
shouldn't he make a supreme effort here ?

Something entirely irrational within him told him with
conclusive emphasis that he had to go to Labrador. . . .

He remembered there was this confounded business of the
proposed house in Mayfair to consider. . . .

§ 3

It occurred to him that he would go a little out of his way,
and look at the new great laboratories at the Romeike College,
of which his old bottle-washer Durgan was, he knew, extravagantly proud.  Romeike's widow was dead now and her will
executed, and her substance half turned already to bricks
and stone and glazed tiles and all those excesses of space and
appliance which the rich and authoritative imagine must
needs give us Science, however ill-selected and under-paid and
slighted the users of those opportunities may be.  The architects had had great fun with the bequest ;  a quarter of the
site was devoted to a huge square surrounded by dignified, if
functionless, colonnades, and adorned with those stone seats
of honour which are always so chill and unsatisfactory as
resting-places in our island climate.  The laboratories, except
that they were a little shaded by the colonnades, were everything a laboratory should be ;  the benches were miracles of
convenience, there wasn't anything the industrious investigator
might want, steam, high pressures, electric power, that he
couldn't get by pressing a button or turning a switch, unless
perhaps it was inspiring ideas.  And the new library at the
end, with its greys and greens, its logarithmic computators at
every table, was a miracle of mental convenience.

Durgan showed his old professor the marvels.

" If he *chooses* to do something here," said Durgan not too
hopefully, " a man can." . . .

" What's become of the little old room where we two used
to work ? " asked Trafford.

" They'll turn 'em all out presently," said Durgan, " when
this part is ready, but just at present it's very much as you
left it.   There's been precious little research done there since
you went away—not what *I* call research.  Females chiefly—
and boys.  Playing at it.  Making themselves into D.Sc.s by
a baby research instead of a man's examination.  It's like
broaching a thirty-two gallon cask full of Pap to think of it.
Lord, sir, the swill !  Research !  Counting and weighing
things !  Professor Lake's all right, I suppose, but his work
was mostly mathematical ; he didn't do much of it here.  No,
the old days ended, sir, when you . . ."

He arrested himself, and obviously changed his words. " Got busy with other things."

Trafford surveyed the place ; it seemed to him to have shrunken a little in the course of the three years that had intervened since he resigned his position.  On the wall at the back there still hung, fly-blown and a little crumpled, an old table of constants he had made for his elasticity researches. Lake had kept it there, for Lake was a man of generous appreciations, and rather proud to follow in the footsteps of an investigator of Trafford's subtlety and vigour.  The old sink in the corner where Trafford had once swilled his watch glasses and filled his beakers had been replaced by one of a more modern construction, and the combustion cupboard was unfamiliar until Durgan pointed out that it had been enlarged. The ground-glass window at the east end showed still the marks of an explosion that had banished a clumsy student from this sanctuary at the very beginning of Trafford's career.

" By Jove ! " he said after a silence, " but I did some good work here."

" You did, sir," said Durgan.

" I wonder—— I may take it up again presently."

" I doubt it, sir," said Durgan.

" Oh !  But suppose I come back ? "

" I don't think you would find yourself coming back, sir," said Durgan, after judicious consideration.

He adduced no shadow of a reason for his doubt, but some mysterious quality in his words carried conviction to Trafford's mind.  He knew that he would never do anything worth doing in molecular physics again.  He knew it now conclusively for the first time.

§ 4

He found himself presently in Bond Street.  The bright May day had brought out great quantities of people, so that he had to come down from altitudes of abstraction to pick his way among them.

He was struck by the prevailing interest and contentment in the faces he passed.  There was no sense of insecurity betrayed, no sense of the deeps and mysteries upon which our being floats like a film.  They looked solid, they looked satisfied ; surely never before in the history of the world has there been so great a multitude of secure-feeling, satisfied-looking, uninquiring people as there is to-day.  All the tragic great things of life seem stupendously remote from them ; pain is rare, death is out of sight, religion has shrunken to an inconsiderable, comfortable, reassuring appendage of the daily life.  And with the bright small things of immediacy they are so active and alert.  Never before has the world seen such multitudes, and a day must come when it will cease to see them for evermore.

As he shouldered his way through the throng before the Oxford Street shop windows he appreciated a queer effect, almost as it were of insanity, about all this rich and abundant and ultimately aimless life, this tremendous spawning and proliferation of uneventful humanity. These individual lives signified no doubt enormously to the individuals, but did all the shining, reflecting changing existence that went by like bubbles in a stream, signify collectively anything more than the leaping, glittering confusion of shoaling mackerel on a sun-lit afternoon ? The pretty girl looking into the window schemed picturesque achievements with lace and ribbon, the beggar at the curb was alert for any sympathetic eye, the chauffeur on the waiting taxi-cab watched the twopences ticking on with a quiet satisfaction ; each followed a keenly sought immediate end, but altogether ? Where were they going altogether ? Until he knew that, where was the sanity of state craft, the excuse of any impersonal effort, the significance of anything beyond a life of appetites and self-seeking instincts ?

He found that perplexing suspicion of priggishness affecting him again. Why couldn't he take the gift of life as it seemed these people took it ? Why was he continually lapsing into these sombre, dimly religious questionings and doubts ? Why after all should he concern himself with these riddles of some collective and ultimate meaning in things ? Was he, for all his ability and security, so afraid of the accidents of life that on that account he clung to this conception of a larger impersonal issue which the world in general seemed to have abandoned so cheerfully ? At any rate he did cling to it—and his sense of it made the abounding active life of this stirring, bristling thoroughfare an almost unendurable perplexity. . . .

By the Marble Arch a little crowd had gathered at the pavement edge. He remarked other little knots towards Paddington, and then still others, and inquiring, found the King was presently to pass. They promised themselves the gratification of seeing the King go by. They would see a carriage, they would see horses and coachmen, perhaps even they might catch sight of a raised hat and a bowing figure. And this would be a gratification to them, it would irradiate the day with a sense of experiences, exceptional and precious. For that some of them had already been standing about for two or three hours.

He thought of these waiting people for a time, and then he fell into a speculation about the King. He wondered if the King ever lay awake at three o'clock in the morning and faced the riddle of the eternities, or whether he did really take himself seriously and contentedly as being in himself the vital function of the State, performed his ceremonies, went hither and thither through a wilderness of gaping watchers, slept

well on it.  Was the man satisfied ?  Was he satisfied with
his empire as it was and himself as he was, or did some vision,
some high, ironical intimation of the latent and lost possibilities of his empire and of the world of Things Conceivable
that lies beyond the poor tawdry splendours of our present
loyalties, ever dawn upon him ?

Trafford's imagination conjured up a sleepless King Emperor
agonising for humanity. . . .

He turned to his right out of Lancaster Gate into Sussex
Square, and came to a stop at the pavement edge.

From across the road he surveyed the wide white front and
portals of the house that wasn't big enough for Marjorie.

## § 5

He let himself in with his latchkey.

Malcolm, his man, hovered at the foot of the staircase,
and came forward for his hat and gloves and stick.

" Mrs. Trafford in ? " asked Trafford.

" She said she would be in by four, sir."

Trafford glanced at his watch and went slowly upstairs.

On the landing there had been a rearrangement of the furniture, and he paused to survey it.  The alterations had been
made to accommodate a big cloisonné jar, that now glowed a
wonder of white and tinted whites and luminous blues upon
a dark, deep-shining stand.  He noted now the curtain of the
window had been changed from something—surely it had been
a reddish curtain !—to a sharp clear blue with a black border,
that reflected upon and sustained and encouraged the jar
tremendously.  And the wall behind——?  Yes.  Its deep
brown was darkened to an absolute black behind the jar, and
shaded up between the lacquer cabinets on either hand by
insensible degrees to the general hue.  It was wonderful,
perfectly harmonious, and so subtly planned that it seemed it
all might have grown, as flowers grow. . . .

He entered the drawing-room and surveyed its long and
handsome spaces.  Post-impressionism was over and gone ;
three long pictures by young Rogerson and one of Redwood's
gallant bronzes faced the tall windows between the white
marble fireplaces at either end.  There were two lean jars from
India, a young boy's head from Florence, and in a great bowl
in the remotest corner a radiant mass of azaleas. . . .

His mood of wondering at familiar things was still upon
him.  It came to him as a thing absurd and incongruous that
this should be his home.  It was all wonderfully arranged
into one dignified harmony, but he felt now that at a touch of
social earthquake, with a mere momentary lapse towards
disorder, it would degenerate altogether into litter, lie heaped
together confessed the loot it was.  He came to a stop opposite
one of the Rogerson's, a stiffly self-conscious shop-girl in her
Sunday clothes, a not unsuccessful emulation of Nicholson's

wonderful Mrs. Stafford of Paradise Row. Regarded as so
much brown and grey and amber-gold, it was coherent in
Marjorie's design, but regarded as a work of art, as a piece of
expression, how madly irrelevant was its humour and implications to that room and the purposes of that room ! Rogerson
wasn't perhaps trying to say much, but at any rate he was
trying to say something, and Redwood too was asserting freedom and adventure, and the thought of that Florentine of the
bust, and the patient, careful Indian potter, and every maker
of all the little casual articles about him, produced an effect
of muffled, stifled assertions. Against this subdued and disciplined background of muted, inarticulate cries—cries for
beauty, for delight, for freedom, Marjorie and her world
moved and rustled and chattered and competed—wearing
the skins of beasts, the love-plumage of birds, the woven
cocoon cases of little silkworms. . . .

" Preposterous," he whispered.

He went to the window and stared out ; turned about and
regarded the gracious variety of that long, well-lit room again,
then strolled thoughtfully upstairs. He reached the door of
his study, and a sound of voices from the schoolroom—it had
recently been promoted to this level from the rank of day
nursery—caught his mood. He changed his mind, crossed the
landing, and was welcomed with shouts.

The rogues had been dressing up. Margharita, that child
of the dreadful dawn, was now a sturdy and domineering girl
of eight, and she was attired in a gilt paper mitre and her
governess's white muslin blouse so tied at the wrists as to
suggest lawn sleeves, a broad crimson band doing duty as a
stole. She was Becket prepared for martyrdom at the foot
of the altar. Godwin, his eldest son, was a hot-tempered,
pretty-featured, pleasantly self-conscious boy of nearly seven,
and very happy now in a white dragoon's helmet and rude but
effective brown paper breastplate and greaves, as the party of
assassin knights. A small acolyte in what was in all human
probability one of the governess's more intimate linen garments assisted Becket, while the general congregation of
Canterbury was represented by Edward, aged two, and the
governess, disguised with a Union Jack tied over her head
after the well-known fashion of the middle ages. After the
children had welcomed their father and explained the bloody
work in hand, they returned to it with solemn earnestness,
while Trafford surveyed the tragedy. Godwin slew with
admirable gusto, and I doubt if the actual Thomas of Canterbury showed half the stately dignity of Margharita.

The scene finished, they went on to the penance of Henry
the Second ; and there was a tremendous readjustment of
costumes, with much consultation and secrecy. Trafford's
eyes went from his offspring to the long, white-painted room,
with its gay frieze of ships and gulls and its rug-variegated

cork carpet of plain brick-red. Everywhere it showed his
wife's quick cleverness, the clean, serviceable decorativeness
of it all, the pretty patterned window curtains, the writing-
desks, the little library, the flowers and bulbs in glasses, the
counting blocks and bricks and jolly toys, the blackboard on
which the children learned to draw in bold wide strokes, the
big, well-chosen German colour prints upon the walls. And
the children did credit to their casket ; they were not only full
of vitality but full of ideas, even Edward was already a person
of conversation. They were good stuff anyhow. . . .

It was fine in a sense, Trafford thought, to have given up his
own motives and curiosities to afford this airy pleasantness of
upbringing for them, and then came a qualifying thought.
Would they in their turn for the sake of another generation
have to give up fine occupations for mean occupations, deep
thoughts for shallow ? Would the world get them in turn ?
Would the girls be hustled and flattered into advantageous
marriages, that dinners and drawing-rooms might still prevail ? Would the boys, after this gracious beginning, presently have to swim submerged in another generation of
Blenkinses and their Talk, toil in arduous self-seeking, observe, respect, and manipulate shams, succeed or fail, and
succeeding, beget amidst hope and beautiful emotions yet
another generation doomed to insincerities and accommoda-
tions, and so die at last—as he must die ? . . .

He heard his wife's clear voice in the hall below, and went
down to meet her. She had gone into the drawing-room, and
he followed her in and through the folding-doors to the hinder
part of the room, where she stood ready to open a small
bureau. She turned at his approach, and smiled a pleasant,
habitual smile. . . .

She was no longer the slim, quick-moving girl who had come
out of the world to him when he crawled from beneath the
wreckage of Solomonson's plane, no longer the half-barbaric
young beauty who had been revealed to him on the staircase
of the Vevey villa. She was now a dignified, self-possessed
woman, controlling her house and her life with a skilful,
subtle appreciation of her every point and possibility. She
was wearing now a simple walking dress of brownish-fawn
colour, and her hat was touched with a steely blue that made
her blue eyes seem handsome and hard, and toned her hair to a
merely warm brown. She had, as it were, subdued her fine
colours into a sheath in order that she might presently draw
them again with more effect.

" Hullo, old man ! " she said, " you home ? "

He nodded. " The club bored me—and I couldn't work."

Her voice had something of a challenge and defiance in it.
" I've been looking at a house," she said. " Alice Carmel
told me of it. It isn't in Berkeley Square, but it's near it.
It's rather good."

He met her eye.   " That's—premature," he said.

" We can't go on living in this one."

" I won't go to another."

" But why ? "

" I just won't."

" It isn't the money ? "

" No," said Trafford, with sudden fierce resentment.
" I've overtaken you and beaten you there, Marjorie."

She stared at the harsh bitterness of his voice.  She was
about to speak when the door opened, and Malcolm ushered
in Aunt Plessington and Uncle Hubert.  Husband and wife
hung for a moment, and then realised their talk was at an
end. . . .

Marjorie went forward to greet her aunt, careless now of all
that once stupendous Influence might think of her.  She had
long ceased to feel even the triumph of victory in her big house,
her costly, dignified clothes, her assured and growing social
importance.  For five years Aunt Plessington had not even
ventured to advise ;  had once or twice admired.  All that
business of Magnet was—even elaborately—forgotten. . . .

Seven years of feverish self-assertion had left their mark
upon both the Plessingtons.  She was leaner, more gauntly
untidy, more aggressively ill-dressed.  She no longer dressed
carelessly, she defied the world with her clothes, waved her
tattered and dingy banners in its face.  Uncle Hubert was
no fatter, but in some queer way he had ceased to be thin.
Like so many people whose peripheries defy the manifest
quaint purpose of Providence, he was in a state of thwarted
adiposity, and with all the disconnectedness and weak irritability characteristic of this condition.  He had developed a
number of nervous movements, chin-strokings, cheek-scratch-
ings, and incredulous pawings at his more salient features.

" Isn't it a lark ? " began Aunt Plessington, with something
like a note of apprehension in her high-pitched voice, and
speaking almost from the doorway, " we're making a call
together.  I and Hubert !  It's an attack in force."

Uncle Hubert goggled in the rear and stroked his chin, and
tried to get together a sort of facial expression.

The Traffords made welcoming noises.

" We want you to do something for us," said Aunt Plessington, taking two hands with two hands. . . .

In the intervening years the Movement had had ups and
downs ;  it had had a boom, which had ended abruptly in a
complete loss of voice for Aunt Plessington—she had tried
to run it on a patent non-stimulating food and then it had
entangled itself with a new cult of philanthropic theosophy
from which it had been extracted with difficulty and in a
damaged condition.  It had never completely recovered from
that unhappy association.  Latterly Aunt Plessington had
lost her nerve, and she had taken to making calls upon people

with considerable and sometimes embarrassing demands for support, urging them to join committees, take chairs, stake reputations, speak and act as foils for her. If they refused she lost her temper very openly and frankly, and became industriously vindictive. She circulated scandals or created them. Her old assurance had deserted her ; the strangulated contralto was losing its magic power, she felt, in this degenerating England it had ruled so long. In the last year or so she had become extremely snappy with Uncle Hubert. She ascribed much of the Movement's futility to the decline of his administrative powers and the increasing awkwardness of his gestures, and she did her utmost to keep him up to the mark. Her only method of keeping him up to the mark was to jerk the bit. She had now come to compel Marjorie to address a meeting that was to inaugurate a new phase in the Movement's history, and she wanted Marjorie because she particularly wanted a daring, liberal, and spiritually amorous bishop, who had once told her with a note of profound conviction that Marjorie was a very, very beautiful woman. She was so intent upon her purpose that she scarcely noticed Trafford. He slipped from the room unobserved under cover of her playful preliminaries, and went to the untidy little apartment overhead which served in that house as his study. He sat down at the big desk, pushed his methodically arranged papers back, and drummed on the edge with his fingers.

" I'm damned if we have that bigger house," said Trafford.

§ 6

He felt he wanted to confirm and establish this new resolution, to go right away to Labrador for a year. He wanted to tell some one the thing definitely. He would have gone downstairs again to Marjorie, but she was submerged and swimming desperately against the voluble rapids of Aunt Plessington's purpose. It might be an hour before that attack withdrew. Presently there would be other callers. He decided to have tea with his mother and talk to her about this new break in the course of his life.

Except that her hair was now grey and her brown eyes by so much contrast brighter, Mrs. Trafford's appearance had altered very little in the nine years of her only son's marriage. Whatever fresh realisations of the inevitably widening separation between parent and child these years had brought her, she had kept to herself. She had watched her daughter-in-law sometimes with sympathy, sometimes with perplexity, always with a jealous resolve to let no shadow of jealousy fall between them. Marjorie had been sweet and friendly to her, but after the first outburst of enthusiastic affection, she had neither offered nor invited confidences. Old Mrs. Trafford had talked of Marjorie to her son guardedly, and had marked and respected a growing indisposition on his part to discuss

his wife. For a year or so after his marriage she had ached
at times with a sense of nearly intolerable loneliness, and then
the new interests she had found for herself had won their way
against this depression. The new insurrectionary movement of
women that had distinguished those years had attracted her
by its emotion and repelled her by its crudity, and she had
resolved, quite in the spirit of the man who had shaped her
life, to make a systematic study of all the contributory strands
that met in this difficult tangle. She tried to write, but she
found that the poetic gift, the gift of the creative and illuminating phrase which alone justifies writing, was denied to her, and
so she sought to make herself wise, to read and hear, and discuss and think over these things, and perhaps at last inspire
and encourage writings in others.

Her circle of intimates grew, and she presently remarked
with a curious interest that while she had lost the confidences
of her own son and his wife, she was becoming the confidante of
an increasing number of other people. They came to her, she
perceived, because she was receptive and sympathetic and
without a claim upon them or any interest to complicate the
freedoms of their speech with her. They came to her, because
she did not belong to them nor they to her. It is, indeed,
the defect of all formal and established relationship that it
embarrasses speech, and taints each phrase in intercourse with
the flavour of diplomacy. One can be far more easily outspoken to a casual stranger one may never see again than
to that inseparable other, who may misinterpret, who may
disapprove or misunderstand, and who will certainly in the
measure of that discord remember. . . .

It became at last a matter of rejoicing to Mrs. Trafford that
the ties of the old instinctive tenderness between herself and
her son, the memories of pain and tears and the passionate
conflict of childhood, were growing so thin and lax and inconsiderable that she could even hope some day to talk to him
again—almost as she talked to the young men and young
women who drifted out of the unknown to her and sat in her
little room and sought to express their perplexities and listened
to her advice. . . .

It seemed to her that afternoon the wished-for day had
come.

Trafford found her just returned from a walk in Kensington
Gardens and writing a note at her desk under the narrow
sunlit window that looked upon the High Street. " Finish
your letter, little mother," he said, and took possession of the
hearthrug.

When she had sealed and addressed her letter, she turned
her head and found him looking at his father's portrait.

" Done ? " he asked, becoming aware of her eyes.

She took her letter into the hall and returned to him, closing
the door behind her.

" I'm going away, little mother," he said with an unconvincing off-handedness. " I'm going to take a holiday."

" Alone ? "

" Yes. I want a change. I'm going off somewhere—untrodden ground as near as one can get it nowadays—Labrador."

Their eyes met for a moment.

" Is it for long ? "

" The best part of a year."

" I thought you were going on with your research work again."

" No." He paused. " I'm going to Labrador."

" Why ? " she asked.

" I'm going to think."

She found nothing to say for a moment. " It's good," she remarked, " to think." Then, lest she herself should seem to be thinking too enormously, she rang the bell to order the tea that was already on its way.

"It surprises a mother," she said, when the maid had come and gone, " when her son surprises her."

" You see," he repeated, as though it explained everything, " I want to think."

Then after a pause she asked some questions about Labrador ; wasn't it very cold, very desert, very dangerous and bitter ? and he answered informingly. How was he going to stay there ? He would go up the country with an expedition, build a hut and remain behind. Alone ? Yes—thinking. Her eyes rested on his face for a time. " It will be—lonely," she said after a pause.

She saw him as a little still speck against immense backgrounds of snowy wilderness.

The tea-things came before mother and son were back at essentials again. Then she asked abruptly : " Why are you going away like this ? "

" I'm tired of all this business and finance," he said after a pause.

" I thought you would be," she answered as deliberately.

" Yes. I've had enough of things. I want to get clear. And begin again somehow."

She felt they both hung away from the essential aspect. Either he or she must approach it. She decided that she would, that it was a less difficult thing for her than for him.

" And Marjorie ? " she asked.

He looked into his mother's eyes very quietly. " You see," he went on, deliberately disregarding her question, " I'm beached. I'm aground. I'm spoiled now for the old researches—spoiled altogether. And I don't like this life I'm leading. I detest it. While I was struggling it had a kind of interest. There was an excitement in piling up the first twenty thousand. But *now*—— ! It's empty, it's aimless, it's incessant."

He paused. She turned to the tea-things, and lit the spirit-lamp under the kettle. It seemed difficult to do, and her hand trembled. When she turned on him again it was with an effort.

" Does Marjorie like the life you are leading ? " she asked and pressed her lips together tightly.

He spoke with a bitterness in his voice that astonished her. " Oh, *she* likes it."

" Are you sure ? "

He nodded.

" She won't like it without you."

" Oh, that's too much ! It's her world. It's what she's done—what she's made. She can have it ; she can keep it, I've played my part and got it for her. But now—now I'm free to go. I will go. She's got everything else. I've done my half of the bargain. But my soul's my own. If I want to go away and think, I will. Not even Marjorie shall stand in the way of that."

She made no answer to this outburst for a couple of seconds. Then she threw out, " Why shouldn't Marjorie think, too ? "

He considered that for some moments. " She doesn't," he said, as though the words came from the roots of his being.

" But you two——"

" We don't talk. It's astonishing—how we don't. We don't. We can't. We try to, and we can't. And she goes her way, and now—I will go mine."

" And leave her ? "

He nodded.

" In London ? "

" With all the things she cares for."

" Except yourself."

" I'm only a means——"

She turned her quiet face to him. " You know," she said, " that isn't true." . . .

" No," she repeated to his silent contradiction.

" I've watched her," she went on. " You're *not* a means. I'd have spoken long ago if I had thought that. Haven't I watched ? Haven't I lain awake through long nights thinking about her and you, thinking over every casual mood, every little sign—longing to help—helpless." . . . She struggled with herself, for she was weeping. " *It has come to this,*" she said in a whisper, and choked back a flood of tears.

Trafford stood motionless, watching her. She became active. She moved round the table. She looked at the kettle, moved the cups needlessly, made tea, and stood waiting for a moment before she poured it out. " It's so hard to talk to you," she said, " and about all this. . . . I care so much. For her. And for you. . . . Words don't come, dear. . . . One says stupid things."

She poured out the tea, and left the cups steaming, and came and stood before him.

" You see," she said, " you're ill. You aren't just. You've come to an end. You don't know where you are and what you want to do. Neither does she, my dear. She's as aimless as you—and less able to help it. Ever so much less able."

" But she doesn't show it. She goes on. She wants things and wants things——"

" And you want to go away. It's the same thing. It's exactly the same thing. It's dissatisfaction. Life leaves you empty and craving—leaves you with nothing to do but little immediate things that turn to dust as you do them. It's her trouble, just as it's your trouble."

" But she doesn't show it."

" Women don't. Not so much. Perhaps even she doesn't know it. Half the women in our world don't know—and for a woman it's so much easier to go on—so many little things." . . .

Trafford tried to grasp the intention of this. " Mother," he said, " I mean to go away."

" But think of her ! "

" I've thought. Now I've got to think of myself."

" You can't—without her."

" I will. It's what I'm resolved to do."

" Go right away ? "

" Right away."

" And think ? "

He nodded.

" Find out—what it all means, my boy ? "

" Yes. So far as I'm concerned."

" And then—— ? "

" Come back, I suppose. I haven't thought."

" To her ? "

He didn't answer. She went and stood beside him, leaning upon the mantel. " Godwin," she said, " she'd only be further behind. . . . You've got to take her with you."

He stood still and silent.

" You've got to think things out with her. If you don't——"

" I can't."

" Then you ought to go away from her——" She stopped.

" For good ? " he asked.

" Yes."

They were both silent for a space. Then Mrs. Trafford gave her mind to the tea that was cooling in the cups, and added milk and sugar. She spoke again with the table between them.

" I've thought so much of these things," she said with the milk-jug in her hand. " It's not only you two, but others. And all the movement about us. . . . Marriage isn't what it was. It's become a different thing because women have

become human beings. Only—— You know, Godwin, all
these things are so difficult to express. Woman's come out of
being a slave, and yet she isn't an equal. . . . We've had a
sort of sham emancipation, and we haven't yet come to the
real one."

She put down the milk-jug on the tray with an air of grave
deliberation. "If you go away from her and make the most
wonderful discoveries about life and yourself, it's no good—
unless she makes them too. It's no good at all. . . . You
can't live without her in the end, any more than she can live
without you. You may think you can, but I've watched you.
You don't want to go away from her; you want to go away
from the world that's got hold of her, from the dresses and
parties and the competition and all this complicated flatness
we have to live in. . . . It wouldn't worry you a bit, if it
hadn't got hold of her. You don't want to get out of it for
your own sake. You *are* out of it. You are as much out of
it as any one can be. Only she holds you in it, because she
isn't out of it. Your going away will do nothing. She'll still
be in it—and still have her hold on you. . . . You've got to
take her away. Or else—if you go away—in the end it will
be just like a ship, Godwin, coming back to its moorings."

She watched his thoughtful face for some moments, then
arrested herself just in time in the act of putting a second
portion of sugar into each of the cups. She handed her son
his tea, and he took it mechanically. "You're a wise little
mother," he said. "I didn't see things in that light. . . . I
wonder if you're right?"

"I know I am," she said.

"I've thought more and more—it was Marjorie."

"It's the world."

"Women made the world. All the dress and display and
competition."

Mrs. Trafford thought. "Sex made the world. Neither
men nor women. But the world has got hold of the women
tighter than it has the men. They're deeper in." She looked
up into his face. "Take her with you," she said simply.

"She won't come," said Trafford, after considering it.

Mrs. Trafford reflected. "She'll come—if you make her,"
she said.

"She'll want to bring two housemaids."

"I don't think you know Marjorie as well as I do."

"But she can't——"

"She can. It's you—you'll want to take two housemaids
for her. Even you. . . . Men are not fair to women."

Trafford put his untasted tea upon the mantelshelf, and
confronted his mother with a question point blank. "Does
Marjorie care for me?" he asked.

"You're the sun of her world."

"But she goes her way."

" She's clever, she's full of life, full of activities, eager to make and arrange and order ; but there's nothing she is, nothing she makes, that doesn't centre on you."

" But if she cared, she'd understand ! "

" My dear, do *you* understand ? "

He stood musing. " I had everything clear," he said. " I saw my way to Labrador. . . ."

Her little clock pinged the hour. " Good God ! " he said, " I'm to be at dinner somewhere at seven. We're going to a first night. With the Bernards, I think. Then I suppose we'll have a supper. Always life is being slashed to tatters by these things. Always. One thinks in snatches of fifty minutes. It's dementia. . . ."

### § 7

They dined at the Loretto Restaurant with the Bernards and Richard Hampden and Mrs. Capes, the dark-eyed, quiet-mannered wife of the dramatist, a woman of impulsive speech and long silences, who had subsided from an early romance (Capes had been divorced for her while she was still a mere girl) into a markedly correct and exclusive mother of daughters. Through the dinner Marjorie was watching Trafford and noting the deep preoccupation of his manner. He talked a little to Mrs. Bernard until it was time for Hampden to entertain her, then finding Mrs. Capes was interested in Bernard, he lapsed into thought. Presently Marjorie discovered his eyes scrutinising herself.

She hoped the play would catch his mind, but the play seemed devised to intensify his sense of the tawdry unreality of contemporary life. Bernard filled the intervals with a conventional enthusiasm. Capes didn't appear.

" He doesn't seem to care to see his things," his wife explained.

" It's so brilliant," said Bernard.

" He has to do it," said Mrs. Capes slowly, her sombre eyes estimating the crowded stalls below. " It isn't what he cares to do."

The play was in fact an admirable piece of English stagecraft, and it dealt exclusively with that unreal other world of beings the English theatre has for its own purposes developed. Just as Greece through the ages evolved and polished and perfected the idealised life of its Homeric poems, so the British mind has evolved its Stage Land to embody its more honourable dreams, full of heroic virtues, incredible honour, genial worldliness, childish villainies, profound but amiable waiters and domestics, pathetic shepherds and preposterous crimes. Capes, needing an income, had mastered the habits and customs of this imagined world as one learns a language ; success endorsed his mastery ; he knew exactly how deeply to underline an irony and just when it is fit and

proper for a good man to call upon " God ! " or cry out
" Damn ! " In this play he had invented a situation in which
a charming and sympathetic lady had killed a gross and
drunken husband in self-defence, almost but not quite
accidentally, and had then appealed to the prodigious hero for
assistance in the resulting complications. At a great cost of
mental suffering to himself he had told his First and Only Lie
to shield her. Then years after he had returned to England
—the first act happened, of course, in India—to find her on the
eve of marrying, without any of the preliminary confidences
common among human beings, an old school friend of his.
(In plays all Gentlemen have been at school together, and
one has been the other's fag.) The audience had to be
interested in the problem of what the prodigious hero was to
do in this prodigious situation. Should he maintain a colossal
silence, continue his shielding, and let his friend marry the
murderess saved by his perjury, or—— ? . . . The dreadful
quandary ! Indeed, the absolute—inconvenience !

Marjorie watched Trafford in the corner of the box, as
he listened rather contemptuously to the statement of the
evening's Problem and then lapsed again into a brooding
quiet. She wished she understood his moods better. She
felt there was more in this than a mere resentment at her
persistence about the new house. . . .

Why didn't he go on with things ? . . .

This darkling mood of his had only become manifest to
her during the last three or four years of their life. Previously,
of course, he had been irritable at times.

Were they less happy now than they had been in the little
house in Chelsea ? It had really been a horrible little house.
And yet there had been a brightness then—a nearness. . . .

She found her mind wandering away upon a sort of stock-
taking expedition. How much of real happiness had she and
Trafford had together ? They ought by every standard to
be so happy. . . .

She declined the Bernards' invitation to a chafing-dish
supper, and began to talk so soon as she and Trafford had
settled into the car.

" Rag," she said, " something's the matter ? "

" Well—yes."

" The house ? "

" Yes—the house."

Marjorie considered through an interval.

" Old man, why are you so prejudiced against a bigger
house ? "

" Oh, because the one we have bores me, and the next one
will bore me more."

" But try it."

" I don't want to."

" Well," she said, and lapsed into silence.

" And then," he asked, " what are we going to do ? "

" Going to do—when ? "

" After the new house——"

" I'm going to open out," she said.

He made no answer.

" I want to open out. I want you to take your place in the world, the place you deserve."

" A four-footmen place ? "

" Oh ! the house is only a means."

He thought upon that. " A means," he asked, " to what ? Look here, Marjorie, what do you think you are up to with me and yourself ? What do you see me doing—in the years ahead ? "

She gave him a silent and thoughtful profile for a second or so.

" At first I suppose you are going on with your researches."

" Well ? "

" Then—— I must tell you what I think of you, Rag. Politics——"

" Good Lord ! "

" You've a sort of power. You could make things noble."

" And then ? Office ? "

" Why not ? Look at the little men they are."

" And then perhaps a still bigger house ? "

" You're not fair to me."

He pulled up the bearskin over his knees.

" Marjorie ! " he said. " You see—— We aren't going to do any of those things at all. . . . *No !* . . .

" I can't go on with my researches," he explained. " That's what you don't understand. I'm not able to get back to work. I shall never do any good research again. That's the real trouble, Marjorie, and it makes all the difference. As for politics—— I can't touch politics. I despise politics. I think this empire and the monarchy and Lords and Commons and patriotism and social reform and all the rest of it, silly, *silly* beyond words ; temporary, accidental, foolish, a mere stop-gap—like a gipsy's roundabout in a place where one will presently build a house. . . . You don't help make the house by riding on the roundabout. . . . There's no clear know-ledge—no clear purpose. . . . Only research matters—and expression perhaps—I suppose expression is a sort of research —until we get that—that sufficient knowledge. And you see, I can't take up my work again. I've lost something. . . ."

She waited.

" I've got into this stupid struggle for winning money," he went on, " and I feel like a woman must feel who's made a success of prostitution. I've been prostituted. I feel like ome one fallen and diseased. . . . Business and prostitution ; they're the same thing. All business is a sort of prostitution, all prostitution is a sort of business. Why should one sell one's brains any more than one sells one's body ? . . . It's so easy to succeed if one has good brains and cares to do it, and doesn't let one's attention or imagination wander—and it's so degrading. Hopelessly degrading. . . . I'm sick of this life, Marjorie. *I* don't want to buy things. I'm sick of buying. I'm at an end. I'm clean at an end. It's exactly as though suddenly in walking through a great house one came on a passage that ended abruptly in a door, which opened—on nothing ! Nothing ! "

" This is a mood," she whispered to his pause.

" It isn't a mood, it's a fact. . . . I've got nothing ahead, and I don't know how to get back. My life's no good to me any more. I've spent myself."

She looked at him with dismayed eyes. " But," she said, " this *is* a mood."

" No," he said, " no mood, but conviction. I *know*. . . ."

He started. The car had stopped at their house, and Malcolm was opening the door of the car. They descended silently, and went upstairs in silence.

He came into her room presently and sat down by her fireside. She had gone to her dressing-table and unfastened a necklace ; now with this winking and glittering in her hand she came and stood beside him.

" Rag," she said, " I don't know what to say. This isn't so much of a surprise. . . . I *felt* that somehow life was disappointing you, that I was disappointing you. I've felt it endless times, but more so lately. I haven't perhaps dared to let myself know just how much. . . . But isn't it what life is ? Doesn't every wife disappoint her husband ? We're none of us inexhaustible. After all, we've had a good time ; isn't it a little ungrateful to forget ? . . .

" Look here, Rag," she said. " I don't know what to do. If I did know, I would do it. . . . What are we to do ? "

" Think," he suggested.

" We've got to live as well as think."

" It's the immense troublesome futility of—everything," he said.

" Well, let us cease to be futile. Let us *do*. You say there is no grip for you in research, that you despise politics. . . . There's no end of trouble and suffering. Cannot we do social work, social reform, change the lives of others less fortunate than ourselves. . . ."

" Who are we that we should tamper with the lives of others ? "

" But one must do something."

He thought that over.

" No," he said, " that's the universal blunder nowadays. One must do the right thing. And we don't know the right thing, Marjorie. That's the very heart of the trouble. . . . Does this life satisfy *you* ? If it did would you always be so restless ? . . ."

" But," she said, " think of the good things in life ? "

" It's just the good, the exquisite things in life, that make me rebel against this life we are leading.  It's because I've seen the streaks of gold that I know the rest for dirt.  When I go cheating and scheming to my office, and come back to find you squandering yourself upon a horde of chattering, overdressed women, when I think that that is our substance and everyday and what we are, then it is I remember most the deep and beautiful things. . . . It is impossible, dear, it is intolerable that life was made beautiful for us—just for these vulgarities."

" Isn't there——" She hesitated.  " Love—still ? "

" But—— Has it been love ?  Love is a thing that grows.  But we took it—as people take flowers out of a garden, cut them off, put them in water. . . . How much of our daily life has been love ?  How much of it mere consequences of the love we've left behind us ? . . . We've just cohabited and ' made love '—you and I—and thought of a thousand other things. . . ."

He looked up at her.  " Oh, I love a thousand things about you," he said.  " But do I love *you*, Marjorie ?  Have I got you ?  Haven't I lost you—haven't we both lost something, the very heart of it all ?  Do you think that we were just cheated by instinct, that there wasn't something in it we felt and thought was there ?  And where is it now ?  Where is that brightness and wonder, Marjorie, and the pride and the immense unlimited hope ? "

She was still for a moment ; then knelt very swiftly before him and held out her arms.

" Oh, Rag ! " she said, with a face of tender beauty.  He took her finger-tips in his, dropped them and stood up above her.

" My dear," he cried, " my dear ! why do you always want to turn love into—touches ? . . . Stand up again. Stand up there, my dear ; don't think I've ceased to love you, but stand up there and let me talk to you as one man to another.  If we let this occasion slide to embraces . . ."

He stopped short.

She crouched before the fire at his feet.  " Go on," she said, " go on."

" I feel that all our lives, Marjorie—— . . . We have come to a crisis.  I feel that now—*now* is the time.  Either we shall save ourselves now or we shall never save ourselves. It is as if something had gathered and accumulated and could wait no longer.  If we do not seize this opportunity—— Then our lives will go on as they have gone on, will become more and more a matter of small excitements and elaborate comforts and distractions. . . ."

He stopped this halting speech and then broke out again.

" Oh ! why *should* the life of everyday conquer us ?  Why

should generation after generation of men have these fine beginnings, these splendid dreams of youth, attempt so much, achieve so much and then, then become—*this !* Look at this room, this litter of little satisfactions ! Look at your pretty books there, a hundred minds you have pecked at, bright things of the spirit that attracted you as jewels attract a jackdaw. Look at the glass and silver, and that silk from China ! And we are in the full tide of our years, Marjorie. Now is the very crown and best of our lives. And this is what we do, we sample, we accumulate. For this we loved, for this we hoped. Do you remember when we were young —that life seemed so splendid—it was intolerable we should ever die ? . . . The splendid dream ! The intimations of greatness ! . . . The miserable failure ! "

He raised clenched fists. " I won't stand it, Marjorie. I won't endure it. Somehow, in some way, I will get out of this life—and you with me. I have been brooding upon this and brooding, but now I know. . . ."

" But how ? " asked Marjorie, with her bare arms about her knees, staring into the fire. " *How ?* "

" We must get out of its constant interruptions, its incessant vivid, petty appeals. . . ."

" We might go away—to Switzerland."

" We *went* to Switzerland. Didn't we agree—it was our second honeymoon. It isn't a honeymoon we need. No, we'll have to go farther than that."

A sudden light broke upon Marjorie's mind. She realised he had a plan. She lifted a fire-lit face to him and looked at him with steady eyes and asked—

" Where ? "

" Ever so much farther."

" Where ? "

" I don't know."

" You do. You've planned something."

" I don't know, Marjorie. At least—I haven't made up my mind. Where it is very lonely. Cold and remote. Away from all this——" His mind stopped short, and he ended with a cry : " Oh ! God ! how I want to get out of all this ! "

He sat down in her armchair, and bowed his face on his hands.

Then abruptly he stood up and went out of the room.

### § 8

When in five minutes' time he came back into her room she was still upon her hearthrug before the fire, with her necklace in her hand, the red reflections of the flames glowing and wink-ing in her jewels and in her eyes. He came and sat again in her chair.

" I have been ranting," he said. " I feel I've been—elo-quent. You make me feel like an actor-manager, in a play by Capes. . . . You are the most difficult person for me to talk to in all the world—because you mean so much to me."

She moved impulsively and checked herself and crouched away from him. " I mustn't touch your hand," she whispered.

" I want to explain."

" You've got to explain."

" I've got quite a definite plan. . . . But a sort of terror seized me. It was like—shyness."

" I know. I knew you had a plan."

" You see. . . . I mean to go to Labrador."

He leaned forward with his elbows on his knees and his hands extended, explanatory. He wanted intensely that she should understand and agree, and his desire made him clumsy, now slow and awkward, now glibly and unsatisfyingly eloquent. But she comprehended his quality better than he knew. They were to go away to Labrador, this snowy desert of which she had scarcely heard, to camp in the very heart of the wilderness, two hundred miles or more from any human habitation——

" But how long ? " she asked abruptly.

" The better part of a year."

" And we are to talk ? "

" Yes," he said, " talk and think ourselves together—oh !—the old phrases carry it all—find God. . . ."

" It is what I dreamt of, Rag, years ago."

" Will you come," he cried, " out of all this ? "

She leaned across the hearthrug, and seized and kissed his hand. . . .

Then, with one of those swift changes of hers, she was in revolt. " But, Rag," she exclaimed, " this is dreaming. We are not free. There are the children, Rag ! We cannot leave the children ! "

" We can," he said. " We must."

" But, my dear !—our duty ! "

" *Is* it a mother's duty always to keep with her children ? They will be looked after, their lives are organised, there is my mother close at hand. . . . What is the good of having children at all—unless their world is to be better than our world ? . . . What are we doing to save them from the same bathos as this—to which we have come ? We give them food and health and pictures and lessons, that's all very well while they are just little children ; but we've got no religion to give them, no aim, no sense of a general purpose. What is the good of bread and health—and no worship ? . . . What can we say to them when they ask us why we brought them into the world ?—*We* happened—*you* happened. What are we to tell them when they demand the purpose of all this training, all these lessons ? When they ask what we are preparing them for ? Just that *you*, too, may have children ! Is that any answer ? Marjorie, it's common sense to try this over —to make this last supreme effort—just as it will be common sense to separate if we can't get the puzzle solved together."

" Separate ! "

" Separate. Why not ? We can afford it. Of course, we shall separate."

" But, Rag !—separate ! "

He faced her protest squarely. " Life is not worth living," he said, " unless it has more to hold it together than ours has now. If we cannot escape together, then—*I will go alone.*" . . .

§ 9

They parted that night resolved to go to Labrador together, with the broad outline of their subsequent journey already drawn. Each lay awake far into the small hours thinking of this purpose and of one another, with a strange sense of renewed association. Each woke to a morning of sunshine heavy-eyed. Each found that overnight decision remote and incredible. It was like something in a book or a play that had moved them very deeply. They came down to breakfast, and helped themselves after the wonted fashion of several years, Marjorie with a skilful eye to the large order of her household ; *The Times* had one or two characteristic letters which interested them both ; there was the usual picturesque irruption of the children and a distribution of early strawberries among them. Trafford had two notes in his correspondence which threw a new light upon the reconstruction of the Norton-Batsford company in which he was interested ; he formed a definite conclusion upon the situation, and went quite normally to his study and the telephone to act upon that.

It was only as the morning wore on that it became real to him that he and Marjorie had decided to leave the world. Then, with the Norton-Batsford business settled, he sat at his desk and mused. His apathy passed. His imagination began to present first one picture and then another of his retreat. He walked along Oxford Street to his Club thinking— " soon we shall be out of all this." By the time he was at lunch in his Club, Labrador had become again the magic refuge it had seemed the day before. After lunch he went to work in the library, finding out books about Labrador, and looking up the details of the journey.

But his sense of futility and hopeless oppression had vanished. He walked along the corridor and down the great staircase, and without a trace of the despairful hostility of the previous day, passed Blenkins, talking grey bosh with infinite thoughtfulness. He nodded easily to Blenkins. He was going out of it all, as a man might do who discovers after years of weary incarceration that the walls of his cell are made of thin paper. The time when Blenkins seemed part of a prison-house of routine and invincible stupidity seemed ten ages ago.

In Pall Mall Trafford remarked Lady Grampians and the

Countess of Claridge, two women of great influence, in a big
green car, on the way no doubt to create or sustain or destroy ;
and it seemed to him that it was limitless ages since these
poor old dears with their ridiculous hats and their ridiculous
airs, their luncheons and dinners and dirty aggressive old
minds, had sent tidal waves of competitive anxiety into his
home. . . .

He found himself jostling through the shopping crowd on the
sunny side of Regent Street. He felt now that he looked
over these swarming, preoccupied heads at distant things.
He and Marjorie were going out of it all, going clean out of it
all. They were going to escape from society and shopping,
and petty engagements and incessant triviality—as a bird flies
up out of weeds.

### § 10

But Marjorie fluctuated more than he did.

There were times when the expedition for which he was now
rapidly and methodically preparing, seemed to her the most
adventurously-beautiful thing that had ever come to her, and
times when it seemed the maddest and most hopeless of eccen-
tricities. There were times when she had devastating premonitions of filth, hunger, strain and fatigue, damp and cold,
when her whole being recoiled from the project, when she could
even think of staying secure in London and letting him go
alone. She developed complicated anxieties for the children ;
she found reasons for further inquiries, for delay. " Why
not," she suggested, " wait a year ? "

" No," he said, " I won't. I mean we are to do this, and do
it now, and nothing but sheer physical inability to do it will
prevent my carrying it out. . . . And you ? Of course you
are to come. I can't drag you shrieking all the way to
Labrador ; short of that I'm going to *make* you come with
me." . . .

She sat and looked up at him with dark lights in her upturned eyes, and a little added warmth in her cheek. " You've
never forced my will like this before," she said, in a low voice.
" Never."

He was too intent upon his own resolves to heed her tones.

" It hasn't seemed necessary somehow," he said, considering
her statement. " Now it does."

" This is something final," she said.

" It is final."

She found an old familiar phrasing running through her
head, as she sat crouched together, looking up at his rather
gaunt, very intent face, the speech of another woman echoing
to her across a vast space of years : " Whither thou goest I
will go——"

" In Labrador," he began . . .

# CHAPTER THREE

## THE PILGRIMAGE TO LONELY HUT

### § 1

MARJORIE was surprised to find how easy it was at last to part from her children and go with Trafford.

"I am not sorry," she said, "not a bit sorry—but I am fearfully afraid. I shall dream they are ill. . . . Apart from that, it's strange how you grip me—and they don't. . . ."

In the train to Liverpool she watched Trafford with the queer feeling which comes to all husbands and wives at times that that other partner is indeed an undiscovered stranger, just beginning to show perplexing traits—full of inconceivable possibilities.

For some reason his tearing her up by the roots in this fashion had fascinated her imagination. She felt a strange new wonder at him that had in it just a pleasant faint flavour of fear. Always before she had felt a curious aversion and contempt for those servile women who are said to seek a master, to want to be mastered, to be eager even for the physical subjugations of brute force. Now she could at least understand, sympathise even with them. Not only Trafford surprised her but herself. She found she was in an unwonted perplexing series of moods. All her feelings struck her now as being incorrect as well as unexpected; not only had life become suddenly full of novelty but she was making novel responses. She felt that she ought to be resentful and tragically sorry for her home and children. She felt this departure ought to have the quality of an immense sacrifice, a desperate and heroic undertaking for Trafford's sake. Instead she could detect little beyond an adventurous exhilaration when presently she walked the deck of the steamer that was to take her to St. John's. She had visited her cabin, seen her luggage stowed away, and now she surveyed the Mersey and its shipping with a renewed freshness of mind. She was reminded of the day, now nearly nine years ago, when she had crossed the sea for the first time—to Italy. Then, too, Trafford had seemed a being of infinitely wonderful possibilities. . . . What were the children doing?—that ought to have been her preoccupation. She didn't know; she didn't care! Trafford came and stood beside her, pointed out this and that upon the landing-stage, no longer heavily sullen, but alert, interested, almost gay. . . .

Neither of them could find any way to the great discussion they had set out upon, in this voyage to St. John's. But there was plenty of time before them. Plenty of time! They were

both the prey of that uneasy distraction which seems the inevitable quality of a passenger steamship. They surveyed
and criticised their fellow travellers, and prowled up and
down through the long swaying days and the cold dark nights.
They slept uneasily amidst fog-horn hootings and the startling
sounds of waves swirling against the ports. Marjorie had
never had a long sea voyage before ; for the first time in her
life she saw all the world, through a succession of days, as a
circle of endless blue waters, with the stars and planets and
sun and moon rising sharply from its rim. Until he has made
a voyage no one really understands that old Earth is a watery
globe. . . . They ran into thirty hours of storm, which subsided, and then came a slow time among icebergs, and a hoot-
ing, dreary passage through fog. The first three icebergs
were marvels, the rest bores ; a passing collier out of her course
and pitching heavily, a lonely black and dirty ship with a
manner almost derelict, filled their thoughts for half a day.
Their minds were in a state of tedious inactivity, eager for
such small interests and only capable of such small interests.
There was no hurry to talk, they agreed, no hurry at all, until
they were settled away ahead there among the snows. " There
we shall have plenty of time for everything. . . ."

Came the landfall and then St. John's, and they found
themselves side by side watching the town draw near. The
thought of landing and transference to another ship refreshed
them both. . . .

They were going, Trafford said, in search of God, but it was
far more like two children starting out upon a holiday.

§ 2

There was trouble and procrastination about the half-
breed guides that Trafford had arranged should meet them at
St. John's, and it was three weeks from their reaching New-
foundland before they got themselves and their guides and
equipment and general stores aboard the boat for Port Dupré.
Thence he had planned they should go in the Gibson schooner
to Manivikovik, the Marconi station at the mouth of the Green
River, and thence past the new pulp-mills up river to the
wilderness. There were delays and a few trivial, troublesome
complications in carrying out this scheme, but at last a day
came when Trafford could wave good-bye to the seven people
and eleven dogs which constituted the population of Peter
Hammond's, that last rude outpost of civilisation twenty miles
above the pulp-mill, and turn his face in good earnest towards
the wilderness.

Neither he nor Marjorie looked back at the headland for a
last glimpse of the little settlement they were leaving. Each
stared ahead over the broad, smooth sweep of water, broken
by one transverse bar of foaming shallows, and scanned the
low, tree-clad hills beyond that drew together at last in the

distant gorge out of which the river came. The morning was warm and full of the promise of a hot noon, so that the veils they wore against the assaults of sand-flies and mosquitoes were already a little inconvenient. It seemed incredible in this morning glow that the wooded slopes along the shore of the lake were the border of a land in which nearly half the inhabitants die of starvation. The deep-laden canoes swept almost noiselessly through the water with a rhythmic alternation of rush and pause as the dripping paddles drove and returned. Altogether there were four long canoes and five Indian breeds in their party, and when they came to pass through shallows both Marjorie and Trafford took a paddle.

They came to the throat of the gorge towards noon, and found strong flowing deep water between its high purple cliffs. All hands had to paddle again, and it was only when they came to rest in a pool to eat a midday meal and afterwards to land upon a mossy corner for a stretch and a smoke, that Marjorie discovered the peculiar beauty of the rock about them. On the dull purplish-grey surface splayed the most extraordinary mist of luminous iridescence. It fascinated her. Here was a land whose common substance had this gemlike opalescence. But her attention was very soon withdrawn from these glancing splendours.

She had had to put aside her veil to eat, and presently she felt the vividly painful stabs of the black-fly and discovered blood upon her face. A bigger fly, the size and something of the appearance of a small wasp, with an evil buzz, also assailed her and Trafford. It was a bad corner for flies ; the breeds even were slapping their wrists and swearing under the torment, and every one was glad to embark and push on up the winding gorge. It opened out for a time, and then the wooded shores crept in again, and in another half-hour they saw ahead of them among tumbled rocks a long rush of foaming waters that poured down from a brimming, splashing line of light against the sky. They crossed the river, ran the canoes into an eddy under the shelter of a big stone and began to unload. They had reached their first portage.

The rest of the first day was spent in packing and lugging first the cargoes and then the canoes up through thickets and over boulders and across stretches of reindeer moss for the better part of two miles to a camping ground about half-way up the rapids. Marjorie and Trafford tried to help with the carrying, but this evidently shocked and distressed the men too much, so they desisted and set to work cutting wood and gathering moss for the fires and bedding of the camp. When the iron stove was brought up, the man who had carried it showed them how to put it up on stakes and start a fire in it, and then Trafford went to the river to get water, and Marjorie made a kind of flour cake in the frying-pan in the manner an American woman from the wilderness had once shown her, and boiled water for tea. The twilight had deepened to night while the men were still stumbling up the trail with the last two canoes.

It gave Marjorie a curiously homeless feeling to stand there in the open with the sunset dying away below the black scrubby outlines of the treetops uphill to the north-west, and to realise the nearest roof was already a day's toilsome journey away. The cool night breeze blew upon her bare face and arms—for now the insects had ceased from troubling and she had cast aside gloves and veil and turned up her sleeves to cook—and the air was full of the tumult of the rapids tearing seaward over the rocks below. Struggling through the bushes towards her was an immense, headless quadruped with unsteady legs and hesitating paces, two of the men carrying the last canoe. Two others were now assisting Trafford to put up the little tent that was to shelter her, and the fifth was kneeling beside her, very solemnly and respectfully cutting slices of bacon for her to fry. The air was very sweet, and she wished she could sleep not in the tent but under the open sky.

It was queer, she thought, how much of the wrappings of civilisation had slipped from them already. Every day of the journey from London had released them or deprived them—she hardly knew which—of a multitude of petty comforts and easy accessibilities. The afternoon toil uphill intensified the effect of having clambered up out of things—to this loneliness, this twilight openness, this simplicity.

The men ate apart at a fire they made for themselves, and after Trafford and Marjorie had supped on damper, bacon, and tea, he smoked. They were both too healthily tired to talk very much. There was no moon, but a frosty brilliance of stars, the air which had been hot and sultry at midday grew keen and penetrating, and after she had made him tell her the names of constellations she had forgotten, she suddenly perceived the wisdom of the tent, went into it—it was sweet and wonderful with sprigs of the Labrador tea-shrub—undressed, and had hardly rolled herself up into a cocoon of blankets before she was fast asleep.

She was awakened by a blaze of sunshine pouring into the tent, a smell of fried bacon, and Trafford's voice telling her to get up. "They've gone on with the first loads," he said. "Get up, wrap yourself in a blanket, and come and bathe in the river. It's as cold as ice."

She blinked at him. "Aren't you stiff?" she asked.

"I was stiffer before I bathed," he said.

She took the tin he offered her. (They weren't to see china cups again for a year.) "It's woman's work getting tea," she said as she drank.

"You can't be a squaw all at once," said Trafford.

§ 3

After Marjorie had taken her dip, dried roughly behind a bush, twisted her hair into a pigtail and coiled it under her hat, she amused herself and Trafford as they clambered up through rocks and willows to the tent again by cataloguing her apparatus of bath and toilette at Sussex Square and tracing just when and how she had parted from each item on the way to this place.

"But I *say*!" she cried, with a sudden, sharp note of dismay, "we haven't soap! This is our last cake almost. I never thought of soap."

"Nor I," said Trafford.

He spoke again presently. "We don't turn back for soap," he said.

"We don't turn back for anything," said Marjorie. "Still—I didn't count on a soapless winter."

"I'll manage something," said Trafford, a little doubtfully. "Trust a chemist. . . ."

That day they finished the portage and came out upon a wide lake with sloping shores and a distant view of snow-topped mountains, a lake so shallow that at times their loaded canoes scraped on the glaciated rock below and they had to alter their course. They camped in a lurid sunset; the night was warm and mosquitoes were troublesome, and towards morning came a thunderstorm and wind and rain.

The dawn broke upon a tearing race of waves and a wild drift of slanting rain sweeping across the lake before a gale. Marjorie peered out at this as one peers out under the edge of an umbrella. It was manifestly impossible to go on, and they did nothing that day but run up a canvas shelter for the men and shift the tent behind a thicket of trees out of the full force of the wind. The men squatted stoically, and smoked and yarned. Everything got coldly wet, and for the most part the Traffords sat under the tent and stared blankly at this summer day in Labrador.

"Now," said Trafford, "we ought to begin talking."

"There's nothing much to do else," said Marjorie.

"Only one can't begin," said Trafford.

He was silent for a time. "We're getting out of things," he said. . . .

The next day began with a fine drizzle, through which the sun broke suddenly about ten o'clock. They made a start at once, and got a good dozen miles up the lake before it was necessary to camp again. Both Marjorie and Trafford felt stiff and weary and uncomfortable all day, and secretly a little doubtful now of their own endurance. They camped on an island on turf amidst slippery rocks, and the next day were in a foaming difficult river again, with glittering shallows that obliged every one to get out at times to wade and push.

All through the afternoon they were greatly beset by flies.
And so they worked their way on through a third day's
journey towards the silent inland of Labrador.

Day followed day of toilsome and often tedious travel ;
they fought rapids, they waited while the men stumbled up
long portages under vast loads, going and returning, they
camped and discussed difficulties and alternatives. The
flies sustained an unrelenting persecution, until faces were
scarred in spite of veils and smoke fires, until wrists and necks
were swollen and the blood in a fever. As they got higher and
higher towards the central plateau, the midday heat increased
and the nights grew colder, until they would find themselves
toiling, wet with perspiration, over rocks that sheltered a
fringe of ice beneath their shadows. The first fatigues and
lassitudes, the shrinking from cold water, the ache of muscular
effort, gave place to a tougher and tougher endurance ; skin
seemed to have lost half its capacity for pain without losing
a tithe of its discrimination, muscles attained a steely resilience ;
they were getting seasoned. " I don't feel philosophical,"
said Trafford, " but I feel well."

" We're getting out of things."

" Suppose we are getting out of our problems ! " . . .

One day as they paddled across a mile-long pool, they saw
three bears prowling in single file high up on the hillside.
" Look," said the man, and pointed with his paddle at the
big, soft, furry black shapes, magnified and startling in the
clear air. All the canoes rippled to a stop, the men, at first
still, whispered softly. One passed a gun to Trafford, who
hesitated and looked at Marjorie.

The air of tranquil assurance about these three huge loafing
monsters had a queer effect on Marjorie's mind. They made
her feel that they were at home and that she was an intruder.
She had never in her life seen any big wild animals except in a
menagerie. She had developed a sort of unconscious belief
that all big wild animals were in menageries nowadays, and
this spectacle of beasts entirely at large startled her. There
was never a bar between these creatures, she felt, and her
sleeping self. They might, she thought, do any desperate
thing to feeble men and women who came their way.

" Shall I take a shot ? " asked Trafford.

" No," said Marjorie, pervaded by the desire for mutual
toleration. " Let them be."

The big brutes disappeared in a gully, reappeared, came
out against the skyline one by one and vanished.

" Too long a shot," said Trafford, handing back the
gun. . . .

Their journey lasted altogether a month. Never once did
they come upon any human being save themselves, though
in one place they passed the poles—for the most part overthrown—of an old Indian encampment. But this desolation

was by no means lifeless. They saw great quantities of water-birds, geese, divers, Arctic partridge and the like, they became familiar with the banshee cry of the loon. They lived very largely on geese and partridge. Then for a time, about a string of lakes, the country was alive with migrating deer going south, and the men found traces of a wolf. They killed six caribou, and stayed to skin and cut them up and dry the meat to replace the bacon they had consumed, caught, fried, and ate great quantities of trout, and became accustomed to the mysterious dance of the Northern Lights as the sunset afterglow faded.

Everywhere, except in the river gorges, the country displayed the low hummocky lines and tarn-like pools of intensely glaciated land ; everywhere it was carpeted with reindeer moss growing upon peat and variegated by bushes of flowering, sweet-smelling Labrador tea. In places this was starred with little harebells and diversified by tussocks of heather and rough grass, and over the rocks trailed delicate dwarf shrubs and a very pretty and fragrant pink-flowered plant of which neither she nor Trafford knew the name. There was an astonishing amount of wild fruit, raspberries, cranberries, and a white kind of strawberry that was very delightful. The weather, after its first outbreak, remained brightly serene. . . .

And at last it seemed fit to Trafford to halt and choose his winter quarters. He chose a place on the side of a low, razor-backed rocky mountain ridge, about fifty feet above the river—which had now dwindled to a thirty-foot stream. His site was near a tributary rivulet that gave convenient water, in a kind of lap that sheltered between two rocky knees, each bearing thickets of willow and balsam. Not a dozen miles away from them now they reckoned was the Height of Land, the low watershed between the waters that go to the Atlantic and those that go to Hudson's Bay. Close beside the site he had chosen a shelf of rock ran out and gave a glimpse up the narrow rocky valley of the Green River's upper waters and a broad prospect of hill and tarn towards the south-east. North and north-east of them the country rose to a line of low crests, with here and there a yellowing patch of last year's snow, and across the valley were slopes covered in places by woods of stunted pine. It had an empty spaciousness of effect ; the one continually living thing seemed to be the Green River, hurrying headlong, noisily, perpetually, in an eternal flight from this high desolation. Birds were rare here, and the insects that buzzed and shrilled and tormented among the rocks and willows in the gorge came but sparingly up the slopes to them.

"Here presently," said Trafford, "we shall be in peace."

"It is very lonely," said Marjorie.

"The nearer to God."

"Think ! Not one of these hills has ever had a name."

"Well ? "

" It might be in some other planet."

" Oh !—we'll christen them.  That shall be Marjorie Ridge, and that Rag Valley.  This space shall be—oh !  Bayswater ! Before we've done with it, this place and every feature of it will be as familiar as Sussex Square.  More so—for half the houses there would be stranger to us, if we could see inside them, than anything in this wilderness. . . . As familiar, say—as your drawing-room.  That's better."

Marjorie made no answer, but her eyes went from the reindeer moss and scrub and thickets of the foreground to the low rocky ridges that bounded the view north and east of them.  The scattered boulders, the tangles of wood, the barren upper slopes, the dust-soiled survivals of the winter's snowfall, all contributed to an effect at once carelessly desert and hopelessly untidy.  She looked westward, and her memory was full of interminable streaming rapids, wastes of ice-striated rocks, tiresome struggles through woods and wild, wide stretches of tundra and tarn, trackless and treeless, infinitely desolate.  It seemed to her that the sea-coast was but a step from London and ten thousand miles away from her.

§ 4

The men had engaged to build the framework of hut and store shed before returning, and to this under Trafford's direction they now set themselves.  They were all half-breeds, mingling Indian with Scottish or French blood, sober and experienced men.  Three were named Mackenzie, two brothers and a cousin, and another, Raymond Noyes, was a relation and acquaintance of that George Elson who was with Wallace and Leonidas Hubbard, and afterwards guided Mrs. Hubbard in her crossing of Labrador.  The fifth was a boy of eighteen named Lean.  They were all familiar with the idea of summer travel in this country ;  quite a number, a score or so that is to say, of adventurous people, including three or four women, had ventured far in the wake of the Hubbards into these great wildernesses during the decade that followed that first tragic experiment in which Hubbard died.  But that any one not of Indian or Esquimaux blood should propose to face out the Labrador winter was a new thing to them.  They were really very sceptical at the outset whether these two highly civilised-looking people would ever get up to the Height of Land at all, and it was still with manifest incredulity that they set about the building of the hut and the construction of the sleeping-bunks for which they had brought up planking. A stream of speculative talk had flowed along beside Marjorie and Trafford ever since they had entered the Green River ; and it didn't so much come to an end as get cut off at last by the necessity of their departure.

Noyes would stand, holding a hammer and staring at the narrow little berth he was fixing together.

" You'll not sleep in this," he said.

" I will," replied Marjorie.

" You'll come back with us."

" Not me."

" There'll be wolves come and howl."

" Let 'em."

" They'll come right up to the door here. Winter makes 'em hidjus bold."

Marjorie shrugged her shoulders.

" It's that cold I've known a man have his nose froze while he lay in bed," said Noyes.

" Up here ? "

" Down the coast. But they say it's 'most as cold up here. Many's the man it's starved and froze." . . .

He and his companions told stories—very circumstantial and pitiful stories, of Indian disasters. They were all tales of weariness and starvation, of the cessation of food, because the fishing gave out, because the caribou did not migrate by the customary route, because the man of a family group broke his wrist, and then of the start of all or some of the party to the coast to get help and provisions, of the straining, starving fugitives caught by blizzards, losing the track, devouring small vermin raw, gnawing their own skin garments until they toiled half naked in the snow—becoming cannibals, becoming delirious, lying down to die. Once there was an epidemic of influenza, and three families of seven-and-twenty people just gave up and starved and died in their lodges, and were found, still partly frozen, a patient, pitiful company, by trappers in the spring. . . .

Such, they said, were the common things that happened in a Labrador winter. Did the Traffords wish to run such risks ?

A sort of propagandist enthusiasm grew up in the men. They felt it incumbent upon them to persuade the Traffords to return. They reasoned with them rather as one does with wilful children. They tried to remind them of the delights and securities of the world they were deserting. Noyes drew fancy pictures of the pleasures of London by way of contrast to the bitter days before them. " You've got everything there, everything. Suppose you feel a bit ill, you go out, and every block there's a drug store got everything—all the new rem'dies—p'raps twenty, thirty sorts of rem'dy Lit up, nice. And chaps in collars—like gentlemen. Or you feel a bit dull, and you go into the streets and there's people. Why ! when I was in New York I used to spend hours looking at the people. Hours ! And everything lit up, too. Sky signs ! Readin' everywhere. You can spend hours and hours in New York——"

" London," said Marjorie.

" Well, London—just going about and reading the things

they stick up. Every blamed sort of thing. Or you say, let's go out and be a bit lively. See? Up you get on a car and there you are! Great big restaurants, blazing with lights, and you can't think of a thing to eat they haven't got. Waiters all round you, dressed tremendous, fair asking you to have more. Or you say, let's go to a theatre. Very likely," said Noyes, letting his imagination soar, "you order up one of these automobillies."

"By telephone," helped Trafford.

"By telephone," confirmed Noyes. "When I was in New York there was a telephone in each room in the hotel. Each room. I didn't use it ever, except once when they didn't answer—but there it was. I know about telephones all right." . . .

Why had they come here? None of the men were clear about that. Marjorie and Trafford would overhear them discussing this question at their fire night after night; they seemed to talk of nothing else. They indulged in the boldest hypotheses, even in the theory that Trafford knew of deposits of diamonds and gold, and would trust no one but his wife with the secret. They seemed also attracted by the idea that our two young people had "done something." Lean, with memories of a tattered sixpenny novel that had drifted into his hands from England, had even notions of an elopement, of a pursuing husband or a vindictive wife. He was young and romantic, but it seemed incredible he should suggest that Marjorie was a royal princess. Yet there were moments when his manner betrayed a more than personal respect. . . .

One night after a hard day's portage Mackenzie was inspired by a brilliant idea. "They got no children," he said, in a hoarse, exceptionally audible whisper. "It worries them. Them as is Catholics goes pilgrimages, but these ain't Catholics. See?"

"I can't stand that," said Marjorie. "It touches my pride. I've stood a good deal. Mr. Mackenzie! . . . Mr. . . . Mackenzie."

The voice at the men's fire stopped and a black head turned round. "What is it, Mrs. Trafford?" asked Mackenzie.

She held up four fingers. "Four!" she said.

"Eh?"

"Three sons and a daughter," said Marjorie.

Mackenzie did not take it in until his younger brother had repeated her words.

"And you've come from them to this! . . . Sir, what have you come for?"

"We want to be here," shouted Trafford to their listening pause. Their silence was incredulous.

"We wanted to be alone together. There was too much —over there—too much everything."

Mackenzie, in silhouette against the fire, shook his head, entirely dissatisfied. He could not understand how there could be too much of anything. It was beyond a trapper's philosophy.

"Come back with us, sir," said Noyes. "You'll weary of it." . . .

Noyes clung to the idea of dissuasion to the end. "I don't care to leave ye," he said, and made a sort of byword of it that served when there was nothing else to say.

He made it almost his last words. He turned back for another handclasp as the others under their light returning packs went filing down the hill.

"I don't care to leave ye," he said.

"Good luck ! " said Trafford.

"You'll need it," said Noyes, and looked at Marjorie very gravely and intently before he turned about and marched off after his fellows. . .

Both Marjorie and Trafford felt a queer emotion, a sense of loss and desertion, a swelling in the throat, as that file of men receded over the rocky slopes, went down into a dip, reappeared presently small and remote cresting another spur, going on towards the little wood that hid the head of the rapids. They halted for a moment on the edge of the wood and looked back, then turned again one by one and melted stride by stride into the trees. Noyes was the last to go. He stood in an attitude that spoke as plainly as words. "I don't care to leave ye." Something white waved and flickered ; he had whipped out the letters they had given him for England, and he was waving them. Then as if by an effort he set himself to follow the others, and the two still watchers on the height above saw him no more.

# CHAPTER FOUR

§ 1

MARJORIE and Trafford walked slowly back to the hut. "There is much to do before the weather breaks," he said, ending a thoughtful silence. "Then we can sit inside there and talk about the things we need to talk about."

He added awkwardly : " Since we started, there has been so much to hold the attention. I remember a mood—an immense despair. I feel it's still somewhere at the back of things, waiting to be dealt with. It's our essential fact. But meanwhile we've been busy, looking at fresh things."

He paused. " Now it will be different perhaps. . . ."

For nearly four weeks indeed they were occupied very closely, and crept into their bunks at night as tired as wholesome animals who drop to sleep. At any time the weather might break ; already there had been two overcast days and a frowning conference of clouds in the north. When at last storms began they knew there would be nothing for it but to keep in the hut until the world froze up.

There was much to do to the hut. The absence of anything but stunted and impoverished timber and the limitation of time had forbidden a log hut, and their home was really only a double framework, rammed tight between inner and outer frame with a mixture of earth and boughs and twigs of willow, pine, and balsam. The floor was hammered earth carpeted with balsam twigs and a caribou-skin. Outside and within wall and roof were faced with coarse canvas— that was Trafford's idea—and their bunks occupied two sides of the hut. Heating was done by the sheet-iron stove they had brought with them, and the smoke was carried out to the roof by a thin sheet-iron pipe which had come up outside a roll of canvas. They had made the roof with about the pitch of a Swiss chålet, and it was covered with nailed waterproof canvas, held down by a large number of big lumps of stone. Much of the canvasing still remained to do when the men went down, and then the Traffords used every scrap of packing-paper and newspaper that had come up with them and was not needed for lining the bunks in covering any crack or join in the canvas wall.

Two decadent luxuries, a rubber bath and two rubber hot-water bottles, hung behind the door. They were almost the only luxuries. Kettles and pans and some provisions stood on a shelf over the stove ; there was also a sort of recess cupboard in the opposite corner, reserve clothes were in canvas trunks under the bunks, they kept their immediate supply of wood under the eaves just outside the door, and there was a big can of water between stove and door. When the winter came they would have to bring in ice from the stream.

This was their home. The tent that had sheltered Marjorie on the way up was erected close to this hut to serve as a rude scullery and outhouse, and they also made a long, roughly thatched roof with a canvas cover, supported on stakes, to shelter the rest of the stores. The stuff in tins and cases and jars they left on the ground under this ; the rest—the flour, candles, bacon, dried caribou beef, and so forth, they hung, as they hoped, out of the reach of any prowling beast. And finally and most important was the wood pile. This they accumulated to the north and east of the hut, and all day long with a sort of ant-like perseverance Trafford added to it from the thickets below. Once or twice, however, tempted by the appearance of birds, he went shooting, and one day he got five geese that they spent a day upon, plucking, cleaning, boiling, and putting up in all their store of empty cans, letting the fat float and solidify on the top to preserve this addition to their provision until the advent of the frost rendered all other preservatives unnecessary. They also tried to catch trout down in the river below, but though they saw many fish the catch was less than a dozen.

It was a discovery to both of them to find how companionable these occupations were, how much more side by side they could be amateurishly cleaning out a goose and disputing about its cooking, than they had ever contrived to be in Sussex Square.

" These things are so infernally interesting," said Trafford, surveying the row of miscellaneous cans upon the stove he had packed with disarticulated goose. " But we didn't come here to picnic. All this is eating us up. I have a memory of some immense tragic purpose——"

" That tin's *boiling* ! " screamed Marjorie sharply.

He resumed his thread after an active interlude.

" We'll keep the wolf from the door," he said.

" Don't talk of wolves ! " said Marjorie.

" Is it only when men have driven away the wolf from the door—oh ! altogether away, that they find despair in the sky ? I wonder——"

" What ? " asked Marjorie in his pause.

" I wonder if there is nothing really in life but this, the food hunt and the love hunt ? Is life just all hunger and need, and are we left with nothing—nothing at all—when these things are done ? . . . We're infernally uncomfortable here."

" Oh, nonsense ! " cried Marjorie.

" Think of your carpets at home ! Think of the great, warm, beautiful house that wasn't big enough !—And yet here, we're happy."

" We *are* happy," said Marjorie, struck by the thought. " Only——"

" Yes."

" I'm afraid. And I long for the children. And the wind *nips*."

" It may be those are good things for us. No ! This is just a lark as yet, Marjorie. It's still fresh, and full of distractions. The discomforts are amusing. Presently we'll get used to it. Then we'll talk out—what we have to talk out. . . . I say, wouldn't it keep and improve this goose of ours if we put in a little brandy ? "

§ 2

The weather broke at last. One might say it smashed itself over their heads. There came an afternoon darkness swift and sudden, a wild gale and an icy sleet that gave place in the night to snow, so that Trafford looked out next morning to see a maddening chaos of small white flakes, incredibly swift, against something that was neither darkness nor light. Even with the door but partly ajar a cruelty of cold put its claw within, set everything that was movable swaying and clattering, and made Marjorie hasten shuddering to heap fresh logs upon the fire. Once or twice Trafford went out to inspect tent and roof and store-shed, several times wrapped to the nose he battled his way for fresh wood, and for the rest of the blizzard they kept to the hut. It was slumberously stuffy, but comfortingly full of flavours of tobacco and food. There were two days of intermission and a day of gusts and icy sleet again, turning with one extraordinary clap of thunder to a wild downpour of dancing lumps of ice, and then a night when it seemed all Labrador, earth and sky together, was in hysterical protest against inconceivable wrongs.

And then the break was over ; the annual freezing-up was accomplished, winter had established itself, the snowfall moderated and ceased, and an icebound world shone white and sunlit under a cloudless sky.

§ 3

Through all that time they got no farther with the great discussion for which they had faced that solitude. They attempted beginnings.

" Where had we got to when we left England ? " tried Marjorie. " You couldn't work, you couldn't rest—you hated our life."

" Yes, I know. I had a violent hatred of the lives we were leading. I thought—we had to get away. To think. . . . But things don't leave us alone here."

He covered his face with his hands.

" Why did we come here ? " he asked.

" You wanted—to get out of things."

" Yes. But with you. . . . Have we, after all, got out of things at all ? I said coming up, perhaps we were leaving

our own problem behind. In exchange for other problems—
old problems men have had before. We've got nearer
necessity ; that's all. Things press on us just as much.
There's nothing more fundamental in wild nature, nothing
profounder—only something earlier. One doesn't get out of
life by going here or there. . . . But I wanted to get you away
—from all the things that had such a hold on you. . . .

"When one lies awake at nights, then one seems to get
down into things. . . ."

He went to the door, opened it, and stood looking out. Against
a wan daylight the snow was falling noiselessly and steadily.

"Everything goes on," he said. . . . "Relentlessly." . . .

§ 4

That was as far as they had got when the storms ceased
and they came out again into an air inexpressibly fresh and
sharp and sweet, and into a world blindingly clean and golden
white under the rays of the morning sun.

"We will build a fire out here," said Marjorie ; "make a
great pile. There is no reason at all why we shouldn't live
outside all through the day in such weather as this."

§ 5

One morning Trafford found the footmarks of some catlike
creature in the snow near the bushes where he was accustomed
to get firewood ; they led away very plainly up the hill, and
after breakfast he took his knife and rifle and snowshoes
and went after the lynx—for that he decided the animal
must be. There was no urgent reason why he should want
to kill a lynx, unless perhaps that killing it made the store
shed a trifle safer, but it was the first trail of any living thing
for many days ; it promised excitement ; some primordial
instinct perhaps urged him.

The morning was a little overcast, and very cold between
the gleams of wintry sunshine. "Good-bye, dear wife !"
he said, and then as she remembered afterwards came back a
dozen yards to kiss her. "I'll not be long," he said. "The
beast's prowling, and if it doesn't get wind of me I ought to
find it in an hour." He hesitated for a moment. "I'll not
be long," he repeated, and she had an instant's wonder whether
he hid from her the same dread of loneliness that she concealed.
Or perhaps he only knew her secret. Up among the tumbled
rocks he turned, and she was still watching him. "Good-bye !"
he cried and waved, and the willow thickets closed about him.

She forced herself to the petty duties of the day, made up
the fire from the pile he had left for her, set water to boil, put
the hut in order, brought out sheets and blankets to air, and
set herself to wash up. She wished she had been able to go
with him. The sky cleared presently, and the low December
sun lit all the world about her, but it left her spirit desolate.

She did not expect him to return until midday, and she sat herself down on a log before the fire to darn a pair of socks as well as she could. For a time this unusual occupation held her attention, and then her hands became slow and at last inactive, and she fell into a reverie. She thought at first of her children and what they might be doing ; in England across there to the east it would be about five hours later, four o'clock in the afternoon, and the children would be coming home through the warm muggy London sunshine with Fräulein Otto to tea. She wondered if they had the proper clothes, if they were well ; were they perhaps quarrelling or being naughty or skylarking gaily across the Park ? Of course Fräulein Otto was all right, quite to be trusted, absolutely trustworthy, and their grandmother would watch for a flushed face or an irrational petulance or any of the little signs that herald trouble with more than a mother's instinctive alertness. No need to worry about the children, no need whatever. . . . The world of London opened out behind these thoughts ; it was so queer to think that she was in almost the same latitude as the busy bright traffic of the autumn season in Kensington Gore ; that away there in ten thousand cleverly furnished drawing-rooms the ringing tea-things were being set out for the rustling advent of smart callers and the quick leaping gossip. And there would be all sorts of cakes and little things ; [for a while her mind ran on cakes and little things, and she thought in particular whether it wasn't time to begin cooking. . . . Not yet. What was it she had been thinking about ? Ah ! the Solomonsons and the Capeses and the Bernards and the Carmels and the Lees. Would they talk of her and Trafford ? It would be strange to go back to it all. Would they go back to it all ? She found herself thinking intently of Trafford.

What a fine human being he was ! And how touchingly human ! The thought of his moments of irritation, his baffled silences, filled her with a wild passion of tenderness. She had disappointed him ; all that life failed to satisfy him. Dear master of her life ! what was it he needed ? She too wasn't satisfied with life, but while she had been able to assuage herself with a perpetual series of petty excitements, theatres, new books and new people, meetings, movements, dinners, shows, he had grown to an immense discontent. He had most of the things men sought, wealth, respect, love, children. . . . So many men might have blunted their heart-ache with—adventures. There were pretty women, clever women, unoccupied women. She felt she wouldn't have minded—*much*—if it made him happy. . . . It was so wonderful he loved her still. . . . It wasn't that he lacked occupation ; on the whole he overworked. His business interests were big and wide. Ought he to go into politics ? Why was it that the researches that had held him once, could

hold him now no more ?   That was the real pity of it.   Was she
to blame for that ?   She couldn't state a case against herself,
and yet she felt she was to blame.   She had taken him away
from those things, forced him to make money. . . .

She sat chin on hand staring into the fire, the sock forgotten
on her knee.

She could not weigh justice between herself and him.   If
he was unhappy it was her fault.   She knew that with a
woman's irrational simplicity of conviction ; if he was unhappy it was no excuse that she had not known, had been
misled, had a right to her own instincts and purposes.   She
had got to make him happy.   But what was she to do, what
was there for her to do ? . . .

Only he could work out his own salvation, and until he had
light, all she could do was to stand by him, help him, cease to
irritate him, watch, wait.   Anyhow she could at least mend his
socks as well as possible, so that the threads would not chafe
him. . . .

She flashed to her feet.   What was that ?

It seemed to her she had heard the sound of a shot, and a
quick brief wake of echoes.   She looked across the icy waste of
the river, and then up the tangled slopes of the mountain.
Her heart was beating very fast.   It must have been up there,
and no doubt he had killed his beast.   Some shadow of doubt
she would not admit crossed that obvious suggestion.

This wilderness was making her as nervously responsive as
a creature of the wild.

Came a second shot ; this time there was no doubt of it.
Then the desolate silence closed about her again.

She stood for a long time staring at the shrubby slopes that
rose to the barren rock wilderness of the purple mountain
crest.   She sighed deeply at last, and set herself to make up
the fire and prepare for the midday meal.   Once far away
across the river she heard the howl of a wolf.

Time seemed to pass very slowly that day.   She found
herself going repeatedly to the space between the day tent
and the sleeping-hut from which she could see the stunted wood
that had swallowed him up, and after what seemed a long hour
her watch told her it was still only half-past twelve.   And the
fourth or fifth time that she went to look out she was set
atremble again by the sound of a third shot.   And then at
regular intervals out of that distant brown purple jumble of
thickets against the snow came two more shots.   " Something has happened," she said, " something has happened,"
and stood rigid.   Then she became active, seized the rifle
that was always at hand when she was alone, fired into the
sky and stood listening.

Prompt came an answering shot.

" He wants me," said Marjorie.   " Something—— Perhaps
he has killed something too big to bring ! "

She was for starting at once, and then remembered this was not the way of the wilderness.

She thought and moved very rapidly. Her mind catalogued possible requirements, rifle, hunting-knife, the oilskin bag with matches, and some chunks of dry paper, the rucksack—and he would be hungry. She took a saucepan and a huge chunk of cheese and biscuit. Then a brandy flask is sometimes handy —one never knows. Though nothing was wrong, of course. Needles and stout thread, and some cord. Snowshoes. A waterproof cloak could be easily carried. Her light hatchet for wood. She cast about to see if there was anything else. She had almost forgotten cartridges—and a revolver. Nothing more. She kicked a stray brand or so into the fire, put on some more wood, damped the fire with an armful of snow to make it last longer, and set out towards the willows into which he had vanished.

There was a rustling and snapping of branches as she pushed her way through the bushes, a stir that died insensibly into quiet again ; and then the camping-place became very still. . . .

Scarcely a sound occurred, except for the shuddering and stirring of the fire, and the reluctant infrequent drip from the icicles along the sunny edge of the log-hut roof. About one o'clock the amber sunshine faded out altogether, a veil of clouds thickened and became greyly ominous, and a little after two the first flakes of a snowstorm fell hissing into the fire. A wind rose and drove the multiplying snowflakes in whirls and eddies before it. The icicles ceased to drip, but one or two broke and fell with a weak tinkling. A deep soughing, a shuddering groaning of trees and shrubs, came ever and again out of the ravine, and the powdery snow blew like puffs of smoke from the branches.

By four the fire was out, and the snow was piling high in the darkling twilight against tent and hut. . . .

## § 6

Trafford's trail led Marjorie through the thicket of dwarf willows and down to the gully of the rivulet which they had called Marjorie Trickle ; it had long since become a trough of snow-covered ice ; the trail crossed this, and turning sharply uphill, went on until it was clear of shrubs and trees, and in the windy open of the upper slopes it crossed a ridge and came over the lip of a large desolate valley with slopes of ice and icy snow. Here she spent some time in following his loops back on the homeward trail before she saw what was manifestly the final trail running far away out across the snow, with the spoor of the lynx, a lightly-dotted line, to the right of it. She followed this suggestion of the trail, put on her snowshoes, and shuffled her way across this valley, which opened as she proceeded. She hoped that over the ridge she would find Trafford, and scanned the sky for the faintest discoloration of a fire, but there was none. That seemed odd to her, but the wind was in her face, and perhaps it beat the smoke down. Then as her eyes scanned the hummocky ridge ahead, she saw something, something very intent and still that brought her heart into her mouth. It was a big grey wolf, standing with back hunched and head down, watching and winding something beyond there, out of sight.

Marjorie had an instinctive fear of wild animals, and it still seemed dreadful to her that they should go at large, uncaged. She suddenly wanted Trafford violently, wanted him by her side. Also she thought of leaving the trail, going back to the bushes. She had to take herself in hand. In the wastes one did not fear wild beasts. One had no fear of them. But why not fire a shot to let him know she was near ?

The beast flashed round with an animal's instantaneous change of pose, and looked at her. For a couple of seconds, perhaps, woman and brute regarded one another across a quarter of a mile of snowy desolation.

Suppose it came towards her !

She would fire—and she would fire at it. She made a guess at the range and aimed very carefully. She saw the snow fly two yards ahead of the grisly shape, and then in an instant it had vanished over the crest.

She reloaded, and stood for a moment waiting for Trafford's answer. No answer came. "Queer !" she whispered, "queer !"—and suddenly such a horror of anticipation assailed her that she started running and floundering through the snow to escape it. Twice she called his name, and once she just stopped herself from firing a shot.

Over the ridge she would find him. Surely she would find him over the ridge.

She found herself among rocks, and there was a beaten and trampled place where Trafford must have waited and crouched. Then on and down a slope of tumbled boulders. There came a patch where he had either thrown himself down or fallen.

It seemed to her he must have been running. . . .

Suddenly, a hundred feet or so away, she saw a patch of violently disturbed snow—snow stained a dreadful colour, a snow of scarlet crystals ! Three strides, and Trafford was in sight.

She had a swift conviction he was dead. He was lying in a crumpled attitude on a patch of snow between convergent rocks, and the lynx, a mass of blood-smeared silvery fur, was in some way mixed up with him. She saw as she came nearer that the snow was disturbed round about them, and discoloured copiously, yellow widely, and in places bright red, with congealed and frozen blood. She felt no fear now, and no emotion ; all her mind was engaged with the clear, bleak perception of the fact before her. She did not care to call to him again. The lynx hid his head, it was as if he was burrowing underneath the creature ; his legs were twisted about each other in a queer, unnatural attitude.

Then, as she dropped off a boulder and came nearer, Trafford moved. A hand came out and gripped the rifle beside him ; he suddenly lifted a dreadful face, horribly scarred and torn, and crimson with frozen blood ; he pushed the grey beast aside, rose on an elbow, wiped his sleeve across his eyes, stared at her, grunted, and flopped forward. He had fainted.

She was now as clear-minded and as self-possessed as a woman in a shop. In another moment she was kneeling by his side. She saw, by the position of his knife and the huge rip in the beast's body, that he had stabbed the lynx to death as it clawed his head ; he must have shot and wounded it and then fallen upon it. His knitted cap was torn to ribbons, and hung upon his neck. Also his leg was manifestly injured ; how, she could not tell. It was chiefly evident he must freeze if he lay here. It seemed to her that perhaps he had pulled the dead brute over him to protect his torn skin from the extremity of cold. The lynx was already rigid, its clumsy paws asprawl—the torn skin and a clot upon Trafford's face were stiff as she put her hands about his head to raise him. She turned him over on his back—how heavy he seemed !— and forced brandy between his teeth. Then, after a moment's hesitation, she poured a little brandy on his wounds.

She glanced at his leg, which was surely broken, and back at his face. Then she gave him more brandy, and his eyelids flickered. He moved his hand weakly. "The blood," he said, "kept getting in my eyes."

She gave him brandy once again, wiping his face and glanced at his leg. Something ought to be done to that, she thought. But things must be done in order.

She stared up at the darkling sky with its grey promise of snow, and down the slopes of the mountain. Clearly they must stay the night here. They were too high for wood among these rocks, but three or four hundred yards below there were a number of dwarfed fir trees. She had brought her axe, so that a fire was possible. Should she go back to the camp and get the tent ?

Trafford was trying to speak again. "I got——" he said.

"Yes ? "

"Got my leg in that crack. Damn—damned nuisance."

Was he able to advise her ? She looked at him, and then perceived she must bind up his head and face. She knelt behind him and raised his head on her knee. She had a thick silk neck muffler, and this she supplemented by a band she cut and tore from her inner vest. She bound this, still warm from her body, about him, wrapped her cloak round him. The next thing was a fire. Five yards away, perhaps, a great mass of purple gabbro hung over a patch of nearly snowless moss. A hummock to the westward offered shelter from the weakly bitter wind, the icy draught, that was soughing down the valley. Always in Labrador, if you can, you camp against a rock surface ; it shelters you from the wind, reflects your fire, guards your back.

" Rag ! " she said.

" Rotten hole," said Trafford.

" What ? " she cried sharply.

" Got you in a rotten hole," he said. " Eh ? "

" Listen," she said, and shook his shoulder. " Look ! I want to get you up against that rock."

" Won't make much difference," said Trafford, and opened his eyes. " Where ? " he asked.

" There."

He remained quite quiet for a second perhaps. " Listen to me," he said. " Go back to camp."

" Yes," she said.

" Go back to camp. Make a pack of all the strongest food —strengthin'—strengthnin' food—you know ? " He seemed troubled to express himself.

" Yes," she said.

" Down the river. Down—down. Till you meet help."

" Leave you ? "

He nodded his head and winced.

" You're always plucky," he said. " Look facts in the face. Kiddies. Thought it over while you were coming." A tear oozed from his eye. " Not be a fool, Madge. Kiss me good-bye. Not be a fool. I'm done. Kids."

She stared at him, and her spirit was a luminous mist of tears. " You old *coward*," she said in his ear, and kissed the little patch of rough and bloody cheek beneath his eye. Then she knelt up beside him. " *I'm* boss now, old man," she said. " I want to get you to that place there under the rock. If I drag, can you help ? "

He answered obstinately : " You'd better go."

" I'll make you comfortable first," she answered, "anyhow."

He made an enormous effort, and then with her quick help and with his back to her knee, had raised himself on his elbows.

" And afterwards ? " he asked.

" Build a fire."

" Wood ? "

" Down there."

" Two bits of wood tied on my leg—splints. Then I can drag myself. See ? Like a blessed old walrus."

He smiled, and she kissed his bandaged face again.

" Else it hurts," he apologised, " more than I can stand."

She stood up again, thought, put his rifle and knife to his hand for fear of that lurking wolf, abandoning her own rifle with an effort, and went striding and leaping from rock to rock towards the trees below. She made the chips fly, and was presently towing three venerable pine dwarfs, bumping over rock and crevice, back to Trafford.    She flung them down, stood for a moment bright and breathless, then set herself to hack off the splints he needed from the biggest stem.    " Now," she said, coming to him.

" A fool," he remarked, " would have made the splints down there.    You're—*good*, Marjorie."

She lugged his leg out straight, put it into the natural and least painful pose, padded it with moss and her torn handkerchief, and bound it up.    As she did so a handful of snowflakes came whirling about them.    She was now braced up to every possibility.    " It never rains," she said grimly, " but it pours," and went on with her bone-setting.    He was badly weakened by pain and shock, and once he swore at her sharply.    " Sorry," he said.

She rolled him over on his chest, and left him to struggle to the shelter of the rock while she went for more wood.

The sky alarmed her.    The mountains up the valley were already hidden by driven rags of slaty snowstorm.    This time she found a longer but easier path for dragging her boughs and trees ; she determined she would not start the fire until nightfall, nor waste any time in preparing food until then.    There were dead boughs for kindling—more than enough.    It was snowing quite fast by the time she got up to him with her second load, and a premature twilight already obscured and exaggerated the rocks and mounds about her.    She gave some of her cheese to Trafford, and gnawed some herself on her way down to the wood again.    She regretted that she had brought neither candles nor lantern, because then she might have kept on until the cold of night stopped her, and she reproached herself bitterly because she had brought no tea.    She could forgive herself the lantern, she had never expected to be out after dark, but the tea was inexcusable.    She muttered self-reproaches while she worked like two men among the trees, panting puffs of mist that froze upon her lips and iced the knitted wool that covered her chin.    Why don't they teach a girl to handle an axe ? . . .

When at last the wolfish cold of the Labrador night had come, it found Trafford and Marjorie seated almost warmly on a bed of pine boughs between the sheltering dark rock behind and a big but well husbanded fire in front, drinking a queer-tasting but not unsavoury soup of lynx-flesh, that she had fortified with the remainder of the brandy.    Then they tried roast lynx and ate a little, and finished with some scraps of cheese and deep draughts of hot water.    Then—oh, Tyburnia and Chelsea and all that is becoming !—they smoked Trafford's pipe for alternate minutes, and Marjorie found great comfort in it.

The snowstorm poured incessantly out of the darkness to become flakes of burning fire in the light of the flames and then vanish magically, but it only reached them and wetted them in occasional gusts.    What did it matter for the moment

if the dim snow-heaps rose and rose about them ? A glorious
fatigue, an immense self-satisfaction possessed Marjorie ; she
felt that they had both done well.

" I am not afraid of to-morrow now," she said at last—a
thought matured. " No ! "

Trafford had the pipe and did not speak for a moment.
" Nor I," he said at last. " Very likely we'll get through with
it." He added after a pause : " I thought I was done for.
A man—loses heart. After a loss of blood."

" The leg's better ? "

" Hot as fire." His humour hadn't left him. " It's a
treat," he said. " The hottest thing in Labrador."

" I've been a good squaw this time, old man ? " she asked
suddenly.

He seemed not to hear her ; then his lips twitched and he made
a feeble movement for her hand. " I cursed you," he said. . . .

She slept, but on a spring as it were, lest the fire should fall.
She replenished it with boughs, tucked in the half-burned logs,
and went to sleep again. Then it seemed to her that some
invisible hand was pouring a thin spirit on the flames that
made them leap and crackle and spread north and south until
they filled the heavens. Her eyes were open and the snowstorm overpast, leaving the sky clear, and all the westward
heaven alight with the trailing, crackling, leaping curtains of
the Aurora, brighter than she had ever seen them before.
Quite clearly visible beyond the smoulder of the fire, a wintry
waste of rock and snow, boulder beyond boulder, passed into a
dun obscurity. The mountain to the right of them lay long
and white and stiff, a shrouded death. All earth was dead
and waste and nothing, and the sky alive and coldly marvellous, signalling and astir. She watched the changing,
shifting colours, and they made her think of the gathering
banners of inhuman hosts, the stir and marshalling of icy
giants for ends stupendous and indifferent to all the trivial
impertinence of man's existence. . . .

That night the whole world of man seemed small and shallow
and insecure to her, beyond comparison, One came, she
thought, but just a little way out of its warm and sociable
cities hither, and found this homeless wilderness ; one pricked
the thin appearances of life with microscope or telescope and
came to an equal strangeness. All the pride and hope of
human life goes to and fro in a little shell of air between this
ancient globe of rusty nickel-steel and the void of space ;
faint specks we are within a film ; we quiver between the
atom and the infinite, beings hardly more substantial than the
glow within an oily skin that drifts upon the water. The
wonder and the riddle of it ! Here she and Trafford were !
Phantasmal shapes of unsubstantial fluid thinly skinned
against evaporation and wrapped about with woven wool and
the skins of beasts, that yet reflected and perceived, suffered

and sought to understand ; that held a million memories, framed thoughts that plumbed the deeps of space and time— and another day of snow or icy wind might leave them just scattered bones and torn rags gnawed by a famishing wolf ! . . .

She felt a passionate desire to pray. . . .

She glanced at Trafford beside her, and found him awake and staring. His face was very pale and strange in that livid, flickering light. She would have spoken, and then she saw his lips were moving, and something, something she did not understand, held her back from doing so.

## § 7

The bleak, slow dawn found Marjorie intently busy. She had made up the fire, boiled water and washed and dressed Trafford's wounds, and made another soup of lynx. But Trafford had weakened in the night, the stuff nauseated him, he refused it and tried to smoke and was sick, and then sat back rather despairfully after a second attempt to persuade her to leave him there to die. This failure of his spirit distressed her and a little astonished her, but it only made her more resolute to go through with her work. She had awakened cold, stiff, and weary, but her fatigue vanished with movement ; she toiled for an hour replenishing her pile of fuel, made up the fire, put his gun ready to his hand, kissed him, abused him lovingly for the trouble he gave her until his poor torn face lit in response, and then parting on a note of cheerful confidence, set out to return to the hut. She found the way not altogether easy to make out, wind and snow had left scarcely a trace of their tracks, and her mind was full of the stores she must bring and the possibility of moving him nearer to the hut. She was startled to see by the fresh, deep spoor along the ridge how near the wolf had dared approach them in the darkness. . . .

Ever and again Marjorie had to halt and look back to get her direction right. As it was she came through the willow scrub nearly half a mile above the hut, and had to follow the steep bank of the frozen river down. At one place she nearly slipped upon an icy slope of rock.

One possibility she did not dare to think of during that time : a blizzard now would cut her off absolutely from any return to Trafford. Short of that she believed she could get through.

Her quick mind was full of all she had to do. At first she had thought chiefly of his immediate necessities, of food and some sort of shelter. She had got a list of things in her head— meat extract, bandages, corrosive sublimate by way of antiseptic, brandy, a tin of beef, some bread and so forth ; she went over that several times to be sure of it, and then for a time she puzzled about a tent. She thought she could manage a bale of blankets on her back, and that she could rig a sleeping-tent for herself and Trafford with one and some bent sticks. The big tent would be too much to strike and shift. And

then her mind went on to a bolder enterprise, which was to get
him home.    The nearer she could bring him to the log hut, the
nearer they would be to supplies.    She cast about for some sort
of sledge.    The snow was too soft and broken for runners,
especially among the trees, but if she could get a flat of smooth
wood she thought she might be able to drag him.    She decided
to try the side of her bunk.    She could easily get that off.    She
would have, of course, to run it edgewise through the thickets
and across the ravine, but after that she would have almost
clear going until she reached the steep place of broken rocks
within two hundred yards of him.    The idea of a sledge grew
upon her, and she planned to nail a rope along the edge and
make a kind of harness for herself.

She found the camping-place piled high with drifted snow,
which had invaded tent and hut, and that some beast, a
wolverine she guessed, had been into the hut, devoured every
candle-end and the uppers of Trafford's well-greased second
boots, and had then gone to the corner of the store shed and
clambered up to the stores.    She made no account of its
depredations there, but set herself to make a sledge and get her
supplies together.    There was a gleam of sunshine, but she
did not like the look of the sky, and she was horribly afraid
of what might be happening to Trafford.    She carried her stuff
through the wood and across the ravine, and returned for her
improvised sledge.    She was still struggling with that among
the trees when it began to snow again.

It was hard then not to be frantic in her efforts.    As it was,
she packed her stuff so loosely on the planking that she had to
repack it, and she started without putting on her snowshoes,
and floundered fifty yards before she discovered that omission.
The snow was now falling fast, darkling the sky and hiding
everything but objects close at hand  and she had to use all her
wits to determine her direction ; she knew she must go down
a long slope and then up to the ridge, and it came to her as a
happy inspiration that if she bore to the left she might strike
some recognisable vestige of her morning trail.    She had read
of people walking in circles when they have no light or guidance,
and that troubled her until she bethought herself of the little
compass on her watch-chain.    By that she kept her direction.
She wished very much she had timed herself across the waste,
so that she could tell when she approached the ridge.

Soon her back and shoulders were aching violently, and the
rope across her chest was tugging like some evil-tempered
thing.    But she did not dare to rest.    The snow was now
falling thick and fast, the flakes traced white spirals and made
her head spin, so that she was constantly falling away to the
south-westward and then correcting herself by the compass.
She tried to think how this zig-zagging might affect her course,
but the snow whirls confused her mind and a growing anxiety
would not let her pause to think.    She felt blinded ; it seemed

to be snowing inside her eyes, so that she wanted to rub them. Soon the ground must rise to the ridge, she told herself ; it must surely rise. Then the sledge came bumping at her heels and she perceived she was going downhill. She consulted the compass, and she found she was facing south. She turned sharply to the right again. The snowfall became a noiseless, pitiless torture to sight and mind.

The sledge behind her struggled to hold her back, and the snow balled under her snowshoes. She wanted to stop and rest, take thought, sit for a moment. She struggled with herself and kept on. She tried walking with shut eyes, and tripped and came near sprawling. " Oh God ! " she cried, " oh God ! " too stupefied for more articulate prayers.

Would the rise of the ground to the ribs of rock never come ?

A figure, black and erect, stood in front of her suddenly, and beyond appeared a group of black, straight antagonists. She staggered on towards them, gripping her rifle with some muddled idea of defence, and in another moment she was brushing against the branches of a stunted fir, which shed thick lumps of snow upon her feet. What trees are these ? Had she ever passed any trees ? No ! There were no trees on her way to Trafford. . . .

She began whimpering like a tormented child. But even as she wept she turned her sledge about to follow the edge of the wood. She was too much downhill, she thought, and she must bear up again.

She left the trees behind, made an angle uphill to the right, and was presently among trees again. Again she left them and again came back to them. She screamed with anger at them and twitched her sledge away. She wiped at the snowstorm with her arm as though she would wipe it away. She wanted to stamp on the universe. . . .

And she ached, she ached. . . .

Something caught her eye ahead, something that gleamed ; it was exactly like a long, bare, rather pinkish bone standing erect on the ground. Just because it was strange and queer she ran forward to it. Then as she came nearer she perceived it was a streak of barked trunk ; a branch had been torn off a pine tree and the bark stripped down to the root. And then her foot hit against a freshly hewn stump, and then came another, poking its pinkish wounds above the snow. And there were chips ! This filled her with wonder. Some one had been cutting wood ! There must be Indians or trappers near, she thought, and then realised the wood-cutter could be none other than herself.

She turned to the right and saw the rocks rising steeply close at hand. " Oh, Rag ! " she cried, and fired her rifle in the air.

Ten seconds, twenty seconds, and then so loud and near it amazed her, came his answering shot. It sounded like the hillside bursting.

In another moment she had discovered the trail she had made overnight and that morning by dragging firewood. It was now a shallow soft white trench. Instantly her despair and fatigue had gone from her. Should she take a load of wood with her ? she asked herself, in addition to the weight behind her, and had a better idea. She would unload and pile her stuff here, and bring him down on the sledge closer to the wood. She looked about and saw two rocks that diverged with a space between. She flashed schemes. She would trample the snow hard and flat, put her sledge on it, pile boughs and make a canopy of blanket overhead and behind. Then a fire in front.

She saw her camp admirable. She tossed her provisions down and ran up the broad windings of her pine-trail to Trafford, with the unloaded sledge bumping behind her. She ran as lightly as though she had done nothing that day.

She found him markedly recovered, weak and quiet, with snow drifting over his feet, his rifle across his knees, and his pipe alight. " Back already," he said, " but——"

He hesitated. " No grub ? "

She knelt over him, gave his rough unshaven cheek a swift kiss, and very rapidly explained her plan.

### § 8

In three days' time they were back at the hut, and the last two days they wore blue spectacles because of the midday glare of the sunlit snow.

It amazed Marjorie to discover as she lay awake in the camp on the edge of the ravine close to the hut to which she had lugged Trafford during the second day, that she was deeply happy. It was preposterous that she should be so, but those days of almost despairful stress were irradiated now by a new courage. She was doing this thing, against all Labrador and the snow-driving wind that blew from the polar wilderness, she was winning. It was a great discovery to her that hardship and effort almost to the breaking-point could ensue in so deep a satisfaction. She lay and thought how deep and rich life had become for her, as though in all this effort and struggle some unsuspected veil had been torn away. She perceived again, but now with no sense of desolation, that same infinite fragility of life which she had first perceived when she had watched the Aurora Borealis flickering up the sky. Beneath that realisation and carrying it, as a river flood may carry scum, was a sense of herself as something deeper, greater, more enduring than mountain or wilderness or sky, or any of those monstrous forms of Nature that had dwarfed her physical self to nothingness.

She had a persuasion of self-detachment and illumination, and withal of self-discovery. She saw her life of time and space for what it was. Away in London the children, with the coldest of noses and the gayest of spirits, would be scampering about their bedrooms in the mild morning sunlight of a London winter ; Elsie, the parlourmaid, would be whisking dexterous about the dining-room, the bacon would be cooking and the coffee-mill at work, the letters of the morning delivery perhaps just pattering into the letter-box, and all the bright little household she had made, with all the furniture she had arranged, all the characteristic decoration she had given it, all the clever convenient arrangements, would be getting itself into action for another day—and *it wasn't herself* ! It was the extremest of her superficiality.

She had come out of all that, and even so it seemed she had come out of herself ; this weary woman lying awake on the balsam boughs with a brain cleared by underfeeding and this continuous arduous bath of toil in snow-washed, frost-cleansed, starry air, this, too, was no more than a momentarily clarified window for her unknown and indefinable reality. What was that reality ? what was she herself ? She became interested in framing an answer to that, and slipped down from the peace of soul she had attained. Her serenity gave way to a reiteration of this question, reiterations increasing and at last oppressing like the snowflakes of a storm, perpetual whirling repetitions that at last confused her and hid the sky. . . .

She fell asleep.

### § 9

With their return to the hut, Marjorie had found herself encountering a new set of urgencies. In their absence that wretched little wolverine had found great plenty and happiness in the tent and store shed ; its traces were manifest nearly everywhere, and it had particularly assailed the candles, after a destructive time among the frozen caribou beef. It had clambered up on the packages of sardines and jumped thence on to a sloping pole that it could claw along into the frame of the roof. She rearranged the packages, but that was no good. She could not leave Trafford in order to track the brute down, and for a night or so she could not think of any way of checking its depredations. It came each night. . . . Trafford kept her close at home. She had expected that when he was back in his bunk, secure and warm, he would heal rapidly, but instead he suddenly developed all the symptoms of a severe feverish cold, and his scars, which had seemed healing, became flushed and ugly-looking. Moreover, there was something wrong with his leg, an ominous ache that troubled her mind. Every woman, she decided, ought to know how to set a bone. He was unable to sleep by reason of these miseries, though very desirous of doing so. He became distressingly weak and inert, he ceased to care for food, and presently he began to talk to himself with a complete disregard of her presence. Hourly she regretted her ignorance

of medicine that left her with no conceivable remedy for all
the aching and gnawing that worried and weakened him,
except bathing with antiseptics and a liberal use of quinine.

And his face became strange to her, for over his flushed and
sunken cheeks, under the raw spaces of the scar a blond beard
bristled and grew.  Presently Trafford was a bearded man.

Incidentally, however, she killed the wolverine by means
of a trap of her own contrivance, a loaded rifle with a bait of
what was nearly her last candles, rigged to the trigger.

But this loss of the candles brought home to them the
steady lengthening of the nights.  Scarcely seven hours of
day remained now in the black, cold grip of the darkness.
And through those seventeen hours of chill aggression they
had no light but the red glow of the stove.  She had to close
the door of the hut and bar every chink and cranny against
the icy air, that became at last a murderous, freezing wind.
Not only did she line the hut with every scrap of skin and
paper she could obtain, but she went out with the spade,
toiling for three laborious afternoons in piling and beating
snow against the outer frame.  And now it was that Trafford
talked at last, talked with something of the persistence of
delirium, and she sat and listened hour by hour, silently, for
he gave no heed to her or to anything she might say.  He
talked, it seemed, to God. . . .

§ 10

Darkness about a sullen glow of red, and a voice speaking.
The voice of a man, fevered and in pain, wounded and amidst
hardship and danger, struggling with the unrelenting riddle of
his being.  Ever and again when a flame leaped she would see
his face, haggard, bearded, changed, and yet infinitely familiar.

His voice varied, now high and clear, now mumbling, now
vexed and expostulating, now rich with deep feeling, now
fagged and slow ; his matter varied too ; now he talked like
one who is inspired, and now like one lost and confused,
stupidly repeating phrases, going back upon a misleading
argument, painfully, laboriously beginning over and over
again.  Marjorie sat before the stove watching it burn and
sink, replenishing it, preparing food, and outside the bitter
wind moaned and blew the powdery snow before it, and the
shortening interludes of pallid, diffused daylight which pass
for days in such weather, came and went.  Intense cold had
some now with leaden snowy days and starless nights.

Sometimes his speech filled her mind, seemed to fill all her
world ; sometimes she ceased to listen, following thoughts of
her own.  Sometimes she dozed ; sometimes she awakened
from sleep to find him talking.  But slowly she realised a
thread in his discourse, a progress and development.

Sometimes he talked of his early researches, and then he
would trace computations with his hands as if he were using

a blackboard, and became distressed to remember what he had written. Sometimes he would be under the claws of the lynx again, and fighting for his eyes. " Ugh ! " he said, " keep those hind legs still. Keep your hind legs still! Knife ? Ah ! got it. Gu—u—u, you *Beast* ! "

But the gist of his speech was determined by the purpose of his journey to Labrador. At last he was reviewing his life and hers, and all that their life might signify, even as he had determined to do. She began to perceive that whatever else drifted into his mind and talk, this recurred and grew, that he returned to the conclusion he had reached, and not to the beginning of the matter, and went on from that. . . .

" You see," he said, " our lives are nothing—nothing in themselves. I know that ; I've never had any doubts of that. We individuals just pick up a mixed lot of things out of the powers that begat us, and lay them down again presently a little altered, that's all—heredities, traditions, the finger-nails of my grandfather, a great-aunt's lips, the faith of a sect, the ideas of one's time. We live and then we die, and the threads run, dispersing this way and that. To make other people again. Whatever's immortal isn't that, our looks or our habits, our thoughts or our memories—just the shapes, these are, of one immortal stuff. . . . One immortal stuff." . . .

The voice died away as if he was baffled. Then it resumed.

" But we ought to *partake* of immortality ; that's my point. We ought to partake of immortality.

" I mean we're like the little elements in a magnet ; ought not to lie higgledy-piggledy, ought to point the same way, be polarised—— Something microcosmic, you know, ought to be found in a man.

" Analogies run away with one. Suppose the bar isn't magnetised yet ! Suppose purpose has to come ; suppose the immortal stuff isn't yet, isn't being but struggling to be. Struggling to be. . . . Gods ! that morning ! When the child was born ! And afterwards she was there—with a smile on her lips, and a little flushed and proud—as if nothing had happened so very much out of the way. Nothing so wonderful. And we had another life besides our own ! " . . .

Afterwards he came back to that. " That was a good image," he said, " something trying to exist, which isn't substance, doesn't belong to space or time, something stifled and enclosed, struggling to get through. Just confused birth cries, eyes that hardly see, deaf ears, poor little thrusting hands. A thing altogether blind at first, a twitching and thrusting of protoplasm under the waters, and then the plants creeping up the beaches, the insects and reptiles on the margins of the rivers, beasts with a flicker of light in their eyes answering the sun. And at last, out of the long interplay of desire and fear, an ape, an ape that stared and wondered and scratched queer pictures on a bone." . . .

He lapsed into silent thought for a time, and Marjorie glanced at his dim face in the shadows.

"I say nothing of ultimates," he said at last.

He repeated that twice before his thoughts would flow again.

"This is as much as I see, in time as I know it and space as I know it—*something struggling to exist.* It's true to the end of my limits. What can I say beyond that? It struggles to exist, becomes conscious, becomes now conscious of itself. That is where I come in, as a part of it. Above the beast in me is that—the desire to know better, to know—beautifully, and to transmit my knowledge. That's all there is in life for me beyond food and shelter and tidying up. This Being —opening its eyes, listening, trying to comprehend. Every good thing in man is that;—looking and making pictures, listening, and making songs, making philosophies and sciences, trying new powers, bridge and engine, spark and gun. At the bottom of my soul, *that.* We began with bone-scratching. We're still—near it. I am just a part of this beginning— mixed with other things. Every book, every art, every religion is that, the attempt to understand and express— mixed with other things. Nothing else matters, nothing whatever. I tell you—— Nothing whatever!

"I've always believed that. All my life I've believed that.

"Only I've forgotten.

"Every man with any brains believes that at the bottom of his heart. Only he gets busy and forgets. He goes shooting lynxes and breaks his leg. Odd, instinctive, brutal thing to do—to go tracking down a lynx to kill it. I grant you that, Marjorie. I grant you that."

"Grant me what?" she cried, startled beyond measure to hear herself addressed.

"Grant you that it is rather absurd to go hunting a lynx. And what big paws it has—disproportionately big! I wonder if that's an adaptation to snow? Tremendous paws they are. . . . But the real thing, I was saying, the real thing is to get knowledge and express it. All things lead up to that. Civilisation, social order, just for that. Except for that, all the life of man, all his affairs, his laws and police, his morals and manners—nonsense, nonsense, nonsense. Lynx hunts! Just ways of getting themselves mauled and clawed perhaps—into a state of understanding. Who knows?"

His voice became low and clear.

"Understanding spreading like a dawn. . . .

"Logic and language, clumsy implements, but rising to our needs, rising to our needs, thought clarified, enriched, reaching out to every man alive—some day—presently— touching every man alive, harmonising acts and plans, drawing men into gigantic co-operations, tremendous co-operations. . . .

"Until man shall stand upon this earth as upon a footstool and reach out his hand among the stars. . . .

" And then I went into the rubber market, and spent seven years of my life driving shares up and down and into a net ! . . . Queer game indeed ! Stupid ass Behrens was —at bottom. . . .

" There's a flaw in it somewhere." . . .

He came back to that several times before he seemed able to go on from it.

" There *is* a collective mind," he said, " a growing general consciousness—growing clearer. Something put me away from that, but I know it. My work, my thinking, was a part of that. That's why I was so mad about Behrens."

" Behrens ? "

" Of course. He'd got a twist, a wrong twist. It makes me angry now. It will take years, it will eat up some brilliant man to clean up after Behrens——

" Yes, but the point is "—his voice became acute—" why did I go making money and let Behrens in ? Why generally and in all sorts of things does Behrens come in ? . . .

He was silent for a long time, and then he began to answer himself. " Of course," he said, " I said it—or somebody said it—about this collective mind being mixed with other things. It's something arising out of life—not the common stuff of life. An exhalation. . . . It's like the little tongues of fire that came at Pentecost. . . . Queer how one comes drifting back to these images. Perhaps I shall die a Christian yet. . . . The other Christians won't like me if I do. What was I saying ? . . . It's what I reach up to, what I desire shall pervade me, not what I am. Just as far as I give myself purely to knowledge, to making feeling and thought clear in my mind and words, to the understanding and expression of the realities and relations of life, just so far do I achieve Salvation . . . Salvation ! . . .

" I wonder, is Salvation the same for every one ? Perhaps for one man Salvation is research and thought, and for another expression in art, and for another nursing lepers. Provided he does it in the spirit. He has to do it in the spirit." . . .

There came a silence as though some difficulty baffled him, and he was feeling back to get his argument again.

" This flame that arises out of life, that redeems life from purposeless triviality, *isn't* life. Let me get hold of that. That's a point. That's a very important point."

Something had come to him.

" I've never talked of this to Marjorie. I've lived with her nine years and more, and never talked of religion. Not once. That's so queer of us. Any other couple in any other time would have talked religion no end. . . . People ought to."

Then he stuck out an argumentative hand. " You see, Marjorie *is* life," he said.

" She took me."

He spoke slowly, as though he traced things carefully.

" Before I met her I suppose I wasn't half alive.  No !  Yet
I don't remember I felt particularly incomplete.  Women
were interesting, of course ; they excited me at times ; that girl
at Yonkers !—H'm.  I stuck to my work.  It was fine work ;
I forget half of it now, the half-concealed intimations I mean—
queer how one forgets !—but I know I felt my way to wide,
deep things.  It was like exploring caves—monstrous, limitless caves.  Such caves ! . . . Very still—underground.
Wonderful and beautiful. . . . They're lying there now for
other men to seek.  Other men will find them. . . . Then *she*
came, as though she was taking possession.  The beauty of
her, oh !  the life and bright eagerness, and the incompati-
bility !  That's the riddle !  I've loved her always.  When
she came to my arms it seemed to me the crown of life.  Caves
indeed !  Old caves !  Nothing else seemed to matter.  But
something did.  All sorts of things did.  I found that out
soon enough.  And when that first child was born.  That for
a time was supreme. . . . Yes—she's the quintessence of
life, the dear greed of her, the appetite, the clever appetite for
things.  She grabs.  She's so damned clever !  The light in
her eyes !  Her quick sure hands ! . . . Only my work was
crowded out of my life and ended, and she didn't seem to feel
it, she didn't seem to mind it.  There was a sort of disregard.
Disregard.  As though all that didn't really matter." . . .

" *My dear* ! " whispered Marjorie unheeded.  She wanted to
tell him it mattered now, mattered supremely, but she knew
he had no ears for her.

His voice flattened.  " It's perplexing," he said.  " The
two different things."

Then suddenly he cried out harshly :  " I ought never to have
married her—never, never !  I had my task.  I gave myself
to her.  Oh !  the high immensities, the great and terrible
things open to the mind of man !  And we breed children and
live in littered houses and play with our food and chatter,
chatter, chatter.  Oh, the chatter of my life !  The folly !
The women with their clothes.  I can hear them rustle now,
whiff the scent of it !  The scandals—as though the things
they did with themselves and each other mattered a rap ;  the
little sham impromptu clever things, the trying to keep young
—and underneath it all that continual cheating, cheating,
cheating, damning struggle for money ! . . .

" Marjorie, Marjorie, Marjorie !  Why is she so good and
no better ?  Why wasn't she worth it altogether ? . . .

" No !  I don't want to go on with it any more—ever.  I
want to go back.

" I want my life over again, and to go back.

" I want research, and the spirit of research that has died
in me, and that still, silent room of mine again, that room, as
quiet as a cell, and the toil that led to light.  Oh !  the coming
of that light, the uprush of discovery, the solemn joy as the

generalisation rises like a sun upon the facts—floods them with a common meaning. That is what I want. That is what I have always wanted. . . .

" Give me my time, oh God ! again ; I am sick of this life I have chosen. I am sick of it ! This—busy death ! Give me my time again. . . . Why did You make me, and then waste me like this ? Why are we made for folly upon folly ? Folly ! and brains made to scale high heaven, smeared into the dust ! Into the dust, into the dust. Dust ! "

He passed into weak, wandering repetitions of disconnected sentences, that died into whispers and silence, and Marjorie watched him and listened to him, and waited with a noiseless dexterity upon his every need.

## § 11

One day, she did not know what day, for she had lost count of the days, Marjorie set the kettle to boil and opened the door of the hut to look out, and the snow was ablaze with diamonds, and the air was sweet and still. It occurred to her that it would be well to take Trafford out into that brief brightness. She looked at him and found his eyes upon the sunlight, quiet and rather wondering eyes.

" Would you like to get out into that ? " she asked abruptly.

" Yes," he said, and seemed disposed to get up.

" You've got a broken leg," she cried, to arrest his movement, and he looked at her and answered : " Of course—I forgot."

She was all atremble that he should recognise her and speak to her. She pulled her rude old sledge alongside his bunk, and kissed him, and showed him how to shift and drop himself upon the plank. She took him in her arms and lowered him. He helped weakly but understandingly, and she wrapped him up warmly on the planks and lugged him out and built up a big fire at his feet, wondering, but as yet too fearful to rejoice, at the change that had come to him.

He said no more, but his eyes watched her move about with a kind of tired curiosity. He smiled for a time at the sun, and shut his eyes, and still faintly smiling, lay still. She had a curious fear that if she tried to talk to him this new lucidity would vanish again. She went about the business of the morning, glancing at him ever and again, until suddenly the calm of his upturned face smote her, and she ran to him and crouched down to him between hope and a terrible fear, and found that he was sleeping, and breathing very lightly, sleeping with the deep unconsciousness of a child. . . .

When he awakened the sun was red in the west. His eyes met hers, and he seemed a little puzzled.

" I've been sleeping, Madge ? " he said.

She nodded.

" And dreaming ? I've a vague sort of memory of preaching and preaching in a kind of black, empty place, where there

LML—M                                                          Q wasn't anything. . . . A fury of exposition . . . a kind of argument. . . . I say !—Is there such a thing in the world as a new-laid egg—and some bread-and-butter ? "

He seemed to reflect. " Of course," he said, " I broke my leg. Gollys ! I thought that beast was going to claw my eyes out. Lucky, Madge, it didn't get my eyes. It was just a chance it didn't."

He stared at her.

" I say," he said, " you've had a pretty rough time ! How long has this been going on ? "

He amazed her by raising himself on his elbow and sitting up.

" Your leg ! " she cried.

He put his hand down and felt it. " Pretty stiff," he said. " You get me some food—there *were* some eggs, Madge, frozen new-laid, anyhow—and then we'll take these splints off and feel it about a bit. Eh ! why not ? How did you get me out of that scrape, Madge ? I thought I'd got to be frozen as safe as eggs. (Those eggs ought to be all right, you know. If you put them on in a saucepan and wait until they boil.) I've a sort of muddled impression. . . . By Jove, Madge, you've had a time ! I say, you *have* had a time ! "

His eyes, full of a warmth of kindliness she had not seen for long weeks, scrutinised her face. " I say ! " he repeated, very softly.

All her strength went from her at his tenderness. " Oh, my dear," she wailed, kneeling at his side, " my dear, dear ! " and still regardful of his leg, she yet contrived to get herself weeping into his coveted arms.

He regarded her, he held her, he patted her back ! The infinite luxury to her ! He'd come back. He'd come back to her.

" How long has it been ? " he asked. " Poor dear ! Poor dear ! How long can it have been ? "

§ 12

From that hour Trafford mended. He remained clear-minded, helpful, sustaining. His face healed daily. Marjorie had had to cut away great fragments of gangrenous frozen flesh, and he was clearly destined to have a huge scar over forehead and cheek, but in that pure, clear air, once the healing had begun it progressed swiftly. His leg had set, a little shorter than its fellow and with a lump in the middle of the shin, but it promised to be a good serviceable leg none the less. They examined it by the light of the stove with their heads together, and discussed when it would be wise to try it. How do doctors tell when a man may stand on his broken leg ? She had a vague impression you must wait six weeks, but she could not remember why she fixed upon that time.

" It seems a decent interval," said Trafford. " We'll try it."

She had contrived a crutch for him against that momentous experiment, and he sat up in his bunk, pillowed up by a sack and her rugs, and whittled it smooth, and padded the fork with the skin of that slaughtered wolverine, poor victim of hunger !—while she knelt by the stove, feeding it with logs, and gave him an account of their position.

" We're somewhere in the middle of December," she said, " somewhere between the twelfth and the fourteenth—yes ! I'm as out as that !—and I've handled the stores pretty freely. So did that little beast until I got him." She nodded at the skin in his hand. " I don't see myself shooting much now, and so far I've not been able to break the ice to fish. It's too much for me. Even if it isn't too late to fish. This book we've got describes barks and mosses, and that will help, but if we stick here until the birds and things come, we're going to be precious short. We may have to last right into July. I've plans—but it may come to that. We ought to ration all the regular stuff, and trust to luck for a feast. The rations !—I don't know what they'll come to."

" Righto," said Trafford, admiring her capable gravity. " Let's ration."

" Marjorie," he asked abruptly, " are you sorry we came ? " Her answer came unhesitatingly. " *No !* "

" Nor I."

He paused. " I've found you out," he said. " Dear dirty living thing ! . . . You *are* dirty, you know."

" I've found myself," she answered, thinking. " I feel as if I've never loved you until this hut. I suppose I have in my way——"

" Lugano," he suggested. " Don't let's forget good things, Marjorie. " Oh ! And endless times ! "

" Oh, of course ! As for *that*—— ! But now—now you're in my bones. We were just two shallow, pretty, young things —loving. It was sweet, dear—sweet as youth—but not this. Unkempt and weary—then one understands love. I suppose I *am* dirty. Think of it ! I've lugged you through the snow till my shoulders chafed and bled. I cried with pain, and kept on lugging—— Oh, my dear ! my dear ! " He kissed her hair. " I've held you in my arms to keep you from freezing. (I'd have frozen myself first.) We've got to starve together perhaps before the end. . . . Dear, if I could make you, you should eat me. . . . I'm—I'm beginning to understand. I've had a light. I've begun to understand. I've begun to see what life has been for you, and how I've wasted—wasted."

" *We've* wasted ! "

" No," she said, " it was I."

She sat back on the floor and regarded him. " You don't remember things you said—when you were delirious ? "

" No," he answered. " What did I say ? "

" Nothing."

" Nothing clearly ? "

" It doesn't matter. No, indeed. Only you made me

understand. You'd never have told me. You've always been a little weak with me there. But it's plain to me why we didn't keep our happiness, why we were estranged. If we go back alive, we go back—all that settled for good and all."

" What ? "

" That discord. My dear, I've been a fool, selfish, ill-trained, and greedy. We've both been floundering about, but I've been the mischief of it. Yes, I've been the trouble. Oh, it's had to be so. What are we women—half savages, half pets, unemployed things of greed and desire—and suddenly we want all the rights and respect of souls ! I've had your life in my hands from the moment we met together. If I had known. . . . It isn't that we can make you or guide you— I'm not pretending to be an inspiration—but—but we can release you. We needn't press upon you ; we can save you from the instincts and passions that try to waste you alto-gether on us. . . . Yes, I'm beginning to understand. Oh, my child, my husband, my man ! You talked of your wasted life ! . . . I've been thinking—since first we left the Mersey. I've begun to see what it is to be a woman. For the first time in my life. We're the responsible sex. And we've forgotten it. We think we've done a wonder if we've borne men into the world and smiled a little, but indeed we've got to bear them all our lives. . . . A woman has to be steadier than a man and more self-sacrificing than a man, because when she plunges she does more harm than a man. . . . And what does she achieve if she does plunge ? Nothing—nothing worth counting. Dresses and carpets and hangings and pretty arrangements, excitements and satisfactions and competition and more excitements. We can't *do* things. We don't bring things off ! And you, you Monster ! you Dream ! you want to stick your hand out of all that is and make something that isn't, begin to be ! That's the man——"

" Dear old Madge ! " he said, " there's all sorts of women and all sorts of men."

" Well, our sort of women, then, and our sort of men."

" I doubt even that."

" I don't. I've found my place. I've been making my master my servant. We women—we've been looting all the good things in the world, and helping nothing. You've carried me on your back until you are loathing life. I've been making you fetch and carry for me, love me, dress me, keep me and my children, minister to my vanities and greeds. . . . No ; let me go on. I'm so penitent, my dear, so penitent I want to kneel down here and marry you all over again, heal up your broken life and begin again." . . .

She paused.

" One doesn't begin again," she said. " But I want to take a new turn. Dear, you're still only a young man ; we've thirty or forty years before us—forty years perhaps or more.

. . . What shall we do with our years ? We've loved, we've got children. What remains ? Here we can plan it out, work it out, day after day. What shall we do with our lives and life ? Tell me, make me your partner ; it's you who know, what are we doing with life ? "

§ 13

What are we doing with life ?

That question overtakes a reluctant and fugitive humanity. The Traffords were but two of a great scattered host of people, who, obeying all the urgencies of need and desire, struggling, loving, begetting, enjoying, do nevertheless find themselves at last unsatisfied. They have lived the round of experience, achieved all that living creatures have sought since the beginning of the world—security and gratification and offspring— and they find themselves still strong, unsatiated, with power in their hands and years before them, empty of purpose. What are they to do ?

The world presents such a spectacle of evasion as it has never seen before. Never was there such a boiling over and waste of vital energy. The Sphinx of our opportunity calls for the uttermost powers of heart and brain to read its riddle—the new, astonishing riddle of excessive power. A few give themselves to those honourable adventures that extend the range of man, they explore untravelled countries, climb remote mountains, conduct researches, risk life and limb in the fantastic experiments of flight, and a monstrous outpouring of labour and material goes on in the strenuous preparation for needless and improbable wars. The rest divert themselves with the dwarfish satisfactions of recognised vice, the meagre routine of pleasure, or still more timidly with sport and games— those new unscheduled perversions of the soul.

We are afraid of our new selves. The dawn of human opportunity appals us. Few of us dare look upon this strange light of freedom and limitless resources that breaks upon our world.

"Think," said Trafford, "while we sit here in this dark hut—think of the surplus life that wastes itself in the world for sheer lack of direction. Away there in England—I suppose that is westward "—he pointed—" there are thousands of men going out to-day to shoot. Think of the beautifully made guns, the perfected ammunition, the excellent clothes, the army of beaters, the carefully preserved woodland, the admirable science of it—all for that idiot massacre of half-tame birds ! Just because man once had need to be a hunter ! Think of the others again—golfing. Think of the big, elaborate houses from which they come, the furnishings, the service. And the women—dressing ! Perpetually dressing. *You*, Marjorie—you've done nothing but dress since we married. No, let me abuse you, dear ! It's insane, you know ! You dress your minds a little to talk amusingly, you spread your minds out to backgrounds, to households, picturesque and delightful gardens, nurseries. Those nurseries ! Think of our tremendously cherished and educated children ! And when they grow up what have we got for them ?   A feast of futility." . . .

## § 14

On the evening of the day when Trafford first tried to stand upon his leg, they talked far into the night.   It had been a great and eventful day for them, full of laughter and exultation. He had been at first ridiculously afraid ;  he had clung to her almost childishly, and she had held him about the body with his weight on her strong right arm and his right arm in her left hand, concealing her own dread of a collapse under a mask of taunting courage.   The crutch had proved admirable.   " It's my silly knees ! "  Trafford kept on saying.   " The leg's all right, but I get put out by my silly knees."

They made the day a feast, a dinner of two whole days' rations and a special soup instead of supper.   " The birds will come," they explained to each other, " ducks and geese, long before May.   May, you know, is the latest."

Marjorie confessed the habit of sharing his pipe was growing on her.   " What shall we do in Tyburnia ! " she said, and left it to the imagination.

" If ever we get back there," he said.

" I don't much fancy kicking a skirt before my shins again— and I'll be a black, coarse woman down to my neck at dinner for years to come ! " . . .

Then, as he lay back in his bunk and she crammed the stove with fresh boughs and twigs of balsam that filled the little space about them with warmth and with a faint, sweet smell of burning and with flitting red reflections, he took up a talk about religion they had begun some days before.

" You see," he said, " I've always believed in Salvation. I suppose a man's shy of saying so—even to his wife.   But I've always believed more or less distinctly that there was something up to which a life worked—always.   It's been rather vague, I'll admit.   I don't think I've ever believed in in-dividual salvation.   You see, I feel these are deep things, and the deeper one gets the less individual one becomes.   That's why one thinks of those things in darkness and loneliness— and finds them hard to tell.   One has an individual voice, or an individual birthmark, or an individualised old hat, but the soul—the soul's different. . . . It isn't me talking to you when it comes to that. . . . This question of what we are doing with life isn't a question to begin with for you and me as ourselves, but for you and me as mankind.   Am I spinning it too fine, Madge ? "

" No," she said, intent ;  " go on."

" You see, when we talk rations here, Marjorie, it's ourselves, but when we talk religion—it's mankind. You've either got to be Everyman in religion or leave it alone. That's my idea. It's no more presumptuous to think for the race than it is for a beggar to pray—though that means going right up to God and talking to Him. Salvation's a collective thing and a mystical thing—or there isn't any. Fancy the Almighty and me sitting up and keeping Eternity together! God and R. A. G. Trafford, F.R.S.—that's silly. Fancy a man in number seven boots, and a tailor-made suit in the nineteen-fourteen fashion, sitting before God! That's caricature. But God and Man! That's sense, Marjorie." . . .

He stopped and stared at her.

Marjorie sat red-lit, regarding him. "Queer things you say!" she said. "So much of this I've never thought out. I wonder why I've never done so. . . . Too busy with many things, I suppose. But go on and tell me more of these secrets you've kept from me!"

"Well, we've got to talk of these things as mankind—or just leave them alone, and shoot pheasants." . . .

"If I could shoot a pheasant now!" whispered Marjorie, involuntarily.

"And where do we stand? What do we need—I mean the whole race of us—kings and beggars together? You know, Marjorie, it's this—it's Understanding. That's what mankind has got to, the realisation that it doesn't understand, that it can't express, that it's purblind. We haven't got eyes for those greater things, but we've got the promise—the intimation of eyes. We've come out of an unsuspecting darkness, brute animal darkness, not into sight, that's been the mistake, but into a feeling of illumination, into a feeling of light shining through our opacity. . . .

"I feel that man has now before all things to know. That's his supreme duty, to feel, realise, see, understand, express himself to the utmost limits of his power."

He sat up, speaking very earnestly to her, and in that flickering light she realised for the first time how thin he had become, how bright and hollow his eyes; his hair was long over his eyes, and a rough beard flowed down to his chest. "All the religions," he said, "all the philosophies, have pretended to achieve too much. We've no language yet for religious truth or metaphysical truth; we've no basis yet broad enough and strong enough on which to build. Religion and philosophy have been impudent and quackish—quackish! They've been like the doctors, who have always pretended they could cure since the beginning of things, cure everything, and to this day even they haven't got more than the beginnings of knowledge on which to base a cure. They've lacked humility, they've lacked the honour to say they didn't know; the priests took things of wood and stone, the philosophers took little odd arrangements of poor battered words, metaphors, analogies,

abstractions, and said : ' That's it ! ' Think of their silly
old Absolute—ab-solutus, an untied parcel.   I heard Haldane
at the Aristotelian once, go on for an hour—no ! it was longer
than an hour—as glib and slick as a well-oiled sausage-
machine, about the different sorts of Absolute, and not a soul
of us laughed out at him !   The vanity of such profundities !
They've no faith, faith in patience, faith to wait for the coming
of God.   And since we don't know God, since we don't know
His will with us, isn't it plain that all our lives should be
a search for Him and it ?   Can anything else matter—after
we are free from necessity ?   That is the work now that is
before all mankind, to attempt understanding—by the perpetual fining of thought and the means of expression, by the
perpetual extension and refinement of science, by the research
that every artist makes for beauty and significance in his art,
by the perpetual testing and destruction and rebirth under
criticism of all these things, and by a perpetual extension of this
intensifying wisdom to more minds and more minds and more,
till all men share in it, and share in the making of it. . . .
There you have my creed, Marjorie ; there you have the very
marrow of me." . . .

He became silent.

" Will you go back to your work ? " she said abruptly.
" Go back to your laboratory ? "

He stared at her for a moment without speaking.   " Never,"
he said at last.

" But," she said, and the word dropped from her like a stone
that falls down a well. . . .

" My dear," he said, at last, " I've thought of that.   But
since I left that dear, dusty little laboratory, and all those
exquisite subtle things—I've lived.   I've left that man seven
long years behind me.   Some other man must go on—I think
some younger man—with the riddles I found to work on then.
I've grown—into something different.   It isn't how atoms
swing with one another, or why they build themselves up so
and not so, that matters any more to me.   I've got you and
all the world in which we live, and a new set of riddles filling
my mind, how thought swings about thought, how one man
attracts his fellows, how the waves of motive and conviction
sweep through a crowd and all the little drifting crystallisa-
tions of spirit with spirit and all the repulsions and eddies and
difficulties that one can catch in that turbulent confusion.
I want to do a new sort of work now altogether. . . . Life has
swamped me once, but I don't think it will get me under
again ;—I want to study men."

He paused, and she waited with a face aglow.

" I want to go back to watch and think—and I suppose
write.   I believe I shall write criticism.   But everything that
matters is criticism ! . . . I want to get into contact with the
men who are thinking.   I don't mean to meet them necessarily,

but to get into the souls of their books. Every writer who has anything to say, every artist who matters, is the stronger for every man or woman who responds to him. That's the great work—the Reality. I want to become a part of this stuttering attempt to express, I want at least to resonate, even if I do not help. . . . And you with me, Marjorie—you with me! Everything I write I want you to see and think about. I want you to read as I read. . . . Now after so long, now that—now that we've begun to talk, you know, to talk again——"

Something stopped his voice. Something choked them both into silence. He held out a lean hand, and she shuffled on her knees to take it. . . .

"Don't please make me," she stumbled through her thoughts, "one of those little parasitic, parroting wives— don't pretend too much about me—because you want me with you—— Don't forget a woman isn't a man."

"Old Madge," he said, "you and I have got to march together. Didn't I love you from the first, from that time when I was a boy examiner and you were a candidate girl—because your mind was clear?"

"And we will go back," she whispered, "with a work——"

"With a purpose," he said.

She disengaged herself from his arm, and sat close to him up on the floor. "I think I can see what you will do," she said. She mused. "For the first time I begin to see things as they may be for us. I begin to see a life ahead. For the very first time."

Queer ideas came drifting into her head. Suddenly she cried out sharply in that high note he loved. "Good heavens!" she said. "The absurdity! The infinite absurdity!"

"But what?"

"I might have married Will Magnet—— That's all."

She sprang to her feet. There came a sound of wind outside, a shifting of snow on the roof, and the door creaked. "Half-past eleven!" she exclaimed, looking at the watch that hung in the light of the stove door. "I don't want to sleep yet; do you? I'm going to brew some tea—make a convivial drink. And then we will go on talking. It's so good talking to you. So good! . . . I've an idea! Don't you think on this special day, it might run to a biscuit?" Her face was keenly anxious. He nodded. "One biscuit each," she said, trying to rob her voice of any note of criminality. "Just one, you know, won't matter."

She hovered for some moments close to the stove before she went into the arctic corner that contained the tin of tea. "If we can really live like that," she said "when we are home again!"

"Why not?" he answered.

She made no answer, but went across for the tea. . . .

He turned his head at the sound of the biscuit tin and
watched her put out the precious discs.

" I shall have another pipe," he proclaimed, with an agreeable note of excess. " Thank heaven for unstinted
tobacco." . . .

And now Marjorie's mind was teeming with thoughts of this
new conception of a life lived for understanding. As she went
about the preparation of the tea, her vividly concrete imagination was active with the realisation of the life they would lead
on their return. She could not see it otherwise than framed in
a tall, fine room, a study, a study in sombre tones, with high,
narrow, tall, dignified bookshelves and rich deep green curtains veiling its windows. There should be a fireplace of
white marble, very plain and well proportioned, with furnishings of old brass, and a big desk towards the window
beautifully lit by electric light, with abundant space for papers
to lie. And she wanted some touch of the wilderness about
it ; a skin perhaps. . . .

The tea was still infusing when she had determined upon an
enormous paper-weight of that iridescent Labradorite that
had been so astonishing a feature of the Green River Valley.
She would have it polished on one side only—the other should
be rough to show the felspar in its natural state. . . .

It wasn't that she didn't feel and understand quite fully
the intention and significance of all he had said, but that in
these symbols of texture and equipment her mind quite naturally clothed itself. And while this room was coming into
anticipatory being in her mind, she was making the tea very
deftly and listening to Trafford's every word.

§ 15

That talk marked an epoch for Marjorie. From that day
forth her imagination began to shape a new, ordered, and pur-
poseful life for Trafford and herself in London, a life not altogether divorced from their former life, but with a faith sustaining it and aims controlling it. She had always known of
the breadth and power of his mind, but now as he talked of
what he might do, what interests might converge and give
results through him, it seemed she really knew him for the
first time. In his former researches, so technical and withdrawn, she had seen little of his mind in action : now he was
dealing in his own fashion with things she could clearly understand. There were times when his talk affected her like that
joy of light one has in emerging into sunshine from a long and
tedious cave. He swept things together, flashed unsuspected
correlations upon her intelligence, smashed and scattered
absurd yet venerated conventions of thought, made undreamt-
of courses of action visible in a flare of luminous necessity.
And she could follow him and help him. Just as she had
hampered him and crippled him, so now she could release

him—she fondled that word. She found a preposterous image
in her mind that she hid like a disgraceful secret, that she tried
to forget, and yet its stupendous, its dream-like absurdity had
something in it that shaped her delight as nothing else could
do; she was, she told herself—hawking with an archangel! . . .

These were her moods of exaltation. And she was sure she
had never loved her man before, that this was indeed her beginning. It was as if she had just found him. . . .

Perhaps, she thought, true lovers keep on finding each other
all through their lives.

And he too had discovered her. All the host of Marjories
he had known, the shining, delightful, seductive, wilful, perplexing aspects that had so filled his life, gave place altogether
for a time to this steady-eyed woman, lean and warm-wrapped
with the valiant heart and frost-roughened skin. What a fine,
strong, ruddy thing she was ! How glad he was for this wild
adventure in the wilderness, if only because it had made him lie
among the rocks and think of her and wait for her and despair
of her life and God, and at last see her coming back to him,
flushed with effort and calling his name to him out of that
whirlwind of snow. . . . And there was at least one old
memory mixed up with all these new and overmastering impressions, the memory of her clear unhesitating voice as it had
stabbed into his life again long years ago, minute and bright in
the telephone : " *It's me, you know. It's Marjorie !* "

Perhaps after all she had not wasted a moment of his life,
perhaps every issue between them had been necessary, and
it was good altogether to be turned from the study of crystals
to the study of men and women. . . .

And now both their minds were Londonward, where all the
tides and driftage and currents of human thought still meet
and swirl together. They were full of what they would do
when they got back. Marjorie sketched that study to him—in
general terms and without the paper-weight—and began to
shape the world she would have about it. She meant to be
his squaw and body-servant first of all, and then—a mother.
Children, she said, are none the worse for being kept a little
out of focus. And he was rapidly planning out his approach
to the new questions to which he was now to devote his life.
" One wants something to hold the work together," he said, and
projected a book. " One cannot struggle at large for plain
statement and copious and free and courageous statement, one
needs a positive attack."

He designed a book, which he might write if only for the
definition it would give him and with no ultimate publication,
which was to be called: " The Limits of Language as a Means
of Expression." . . . It was to be a pragmatist essay, a
sustained attempt to undermine the confidence of all that
scholasticism and logic chopping which still lingers like the
*sequelæ* of a disease in our University philosophy. " Those

duffers sit in their studies and make a sort of tea of dry old words
—and think they're distilling the spirit of wisdom," he said.

He proliferated titles for a time, and settled at last on
" From Realism to Reality." He wanted to get at that at
once ; it fretted him to have to hang in the air, day by day,
for want of books to quote and opponents to lance and confute.
And he wanted to see pictures, too, and plays, read novels he
had heard of and never read, in order to verify or correct the
ideas that were seething in his mind about the qualities of
artistic expression. His thought had come out to a conviction
that the line to wider human understandings lies through a
huge criticism and cleaning up of the existing methods of
formulation, as a preliminary to the wider and freer discussion
of those religious and social issues our generation still shrinks
from. " It's grotesque," he said, " and utterly true that the
sanity and happiness of all the world lies in its habits of
generalisation." There was not even paper for him to make
notes or provisional drafts of the new work. He hobbled
about the camp fretting at these deprivations.

" Marjorie," he said, " we've done our job. Why should
we wait here on this frosty shelf outside the world ? My
leg's getting sounder—if it wasn't for that feeling of ice in it.
Why shouldn't we make another sledge from the other bunk
and start down——"

" To Hammond's ? "

" Why not ? "

" But the way ? "

" The valley would guide us. We could do four hours a
day before we had to camp. I'm not sure we couldn't try
the river. We could drag and carry all our food." . . .

She looked down the wide stretches of the valley. There
was the hill they had christened Marjorie Ridge. At least it
was familiar. Every night before nightfall if they started
there would be a fresh camping-place to seek among the snow-
drifts, a great heap of wood to cut to last the night. Suppose
his leg gave out—when they were already some days away, so
that he could no longer go on or she drag him back to the
stores ? Plainly there would be nothing for it then but to
lie down and die together. . . .

And a sort of weariness had come to her as a consequence
of two months of half-starved days, not perhaps a failure so
much as a reluctance of spirit.

" Of course," she said, with a new aspect drifting before her
mind, " then—we *could* eat. We *could* feed up before we
started. We could feast almost ! "

## § 16

" While you were asleep last night," Trafford began one
day as they sat spinning out their midday meal, " I was
thinking how badly I had expressed myself when I talked to

you the other day, and what a queer, thin affair I made of the plans I wanted to carry out. As a matter of fact, they're neither queer nor thin, but they are unreal in comparison with the common things of everyday life, hunger, anger, all the immediate desires. They must be. They only begin when those others are at peace. It's hard to set out these things; they're complicated and subtle, and one cannot simplify without falsehood. I don't want to simplify. The world has gone out of its way time after time through simplifications and short cuts. Save us from epigrams! And when one thinks over what one has said, at a little distance—one wants to go back to it, and say it all again. I seem to be not so much thinking things out as reviving and developing things I've had growing in my mind ever since we met. It's as though an immense reservoir of thought had filled up in my mind at last and was beginning to trickle over and break down the embankment between us. This conflict that has been going on between our life together and my—my intellectual life; it's only just growing clear in my own mind. Yet it's just as if one turned up a light on something that had always been there. . . .

"It's a most extraordinary thing to think out, Marjorie, that antagonism. Our love has kept us so close together, and always our purposes have been—like that." He spread divergent hands. "I've speculated again and again whether there isn't something incurably antagonistic between women (that's *you* generalised, Marjorie) and men (that's me) directly we pass beyond the conditions of the individualistic struggle. I believe every couple of lovers who've ever married have felt that strain. Yet it's not a difference in kind between us, but degree. The big conflict between us has a parallel in a little internal conflict that goes on; there's something of man in every woman and a touch of the feminine in every man. But you're nearer as woman to the immediate personal life of sense and reality than I am as man. It's been so ever since the men went hunting and fighting and the women kept hut, tended the children and gathered roots in the little cultivation close at hand. It's been so perhaps since the female carried and suckled her child and distinguished one male from another. It may be it will always be so. Men were released from that close, continuous touch with physical necessities long before women were. It's only now that women begin to be released. For ages now men have been wandering from field and home and city, over the hills and far away, in search of adventures and fresh ideas and the wells of mystery beyond the edge of the world, but it's only now that the woman comes with them too. Our difference isn't a difference in kind, old Marjorie; it's the difference between the old adventurer and the new feet upon the trail."

"We've got to come," said Marjorie.

"Oh! you've got to come. No good to be pioneers if the

race does not follow. The women are the backbone of the race ; the men are just the individuals. Into this Labrador and into all the wild and desolate places of thought and desire, if men come you women have to come too—and bring the race with you. Some day."

" A long day, mate of my heart."

" Who knows how long or how far ? Aren't you at any rate here, dear woman of mine ? . . . (*Surely you are here.*)"

He went off at a tangent. " There's all those words that seem to mean something and then don't seem to mean anything, that keep shifting to and fro from the deepest significance to the shallowest of clap-trap, Socialism, Christianity. . . . You know—they aren't anything really, as yet ; they are something trying to be. . . . Haven't I said that before, Marjorie ? "

She looked round at him. " You said something like that when you were delirious," she answered, after a little pause. " It's one of the ideas that you're struggling with. You go on, old man, and *talk*. We've months—for repetitions."

" Well, I mean that all these things are seeking after a sort of co-operation that's greater than our power even of imaginative realisation ; that's what I mean. The kingdom of Heaven, the communion of saints, the fellowship of men ; these are things like high peaks far out of the common life of every day, shining things that madden certain sorts of men to climb. Certain sorts of us ! I'm a religious man, I'm a socialistic man. These calls are more to me than my daily bread. I've got something in me more generalising than most men. I'm more so than many other men and most other women, I'm more socialistic than you. . . .

" You know, Marjorie, I've always felt you're a finer individual than me, I've never had a doubt of it. You're more beautiful by far than I, woman for my man. You've a keen appetite for things, a firmer grip on the substance of life. I love to see you do things, love to see you move, love to watch your hands ; you've cleverer hands than mine by far. . . . And yet—I'm a deeper and bigger thing than you. I reach up to something you don't reach up to. . . . You're in life—and I'm a little out of it. I'm like one of those fish that began to be amphibian, I go out into something where you don't follow—where you hardly begin to follow. . . .

" That's the real perplexity between thousands of men and women. . . .

" It seems to me that the primitive socialism of Christianity and all the stuff of modern socialism that matters is really aiming—almost unconsciously, I admit at times—at one simple end, at the release of the human spirit from the individualistic struggle——

" You used ' release ' the other day, Marjorie ? Of course, I remember. It's queer how I go on talking after you have understood."

"It was just a flash," said Marjorie. "We have intimations. Neither of us really understands. We're like people climbing a mountain in a mist, that thins out for a moment and shows valleys and cities, and then closes in again, before we can recognise them or make out where we are."

Trafford thought. "When I talk to you, I've always felt I mustn't be too vague. And the very essence of all this is a vague thing, something we shall never come nearer to in all our lives than to see it as a shadow and a glittering that escapes again into a mist. . . . And yet it's everything that matters, everything, the only thing that matters truly and for ever through the whole range of life. And we have to serve it with the keenest thought, the utmost patience, inordinate veracity. . . .

"The practical trouble between your sort and my sort, Marjorie, is the trouble between faith and realisation. You demand the outcome. Oh! and I hate to turn aside and realise. I've had to do it for seven years. Damnable years! Men of my sort want to understand. We want to understand, and you ask us to make. We want to understand atoms, ions, molecules, refractions. You ask us to make rubber and diamonds. I suppose it's right that incidentally we should make rubber and diamonds. Finally, I warn you, we will make rubber unnecessary and diamonds valueless. And again we want to understand how people react upon one another to produce social consequences, and you ask us to put it at once into a draft bill for the reform of something or other. I suppose life lies between us somewhere, we're the two poles of truth seeking and truth getting ; with me alone it would be nothing but a luminous dream, with you nothing but a scramble in which sooner or later all the lamps would be upset. . . . But it's ever too much of a scramble yet, and ever too little of a dream. All our world over there is full of the confusion and wreckage of premature realisations. There's no real faith in thought and knowledge yet. Old necessity has driven men so hard that they still rush with a wild urgency—though she goads no more. Greed and haste, and if, indeed, we seem to have a moment's breathing space, then the Gawdsaker tramples us under."

"My dear!" cried Marjorie, with a sharp note of amusement. "What is a Gawdsaker?"

"Oh," said Trafford, "haven't you heard that before? He's the person who gets excited by any deliberate discussion and gets up wringing his hands and screaming, 'For Gawd's sake, let's do something now!' I think they used it first for Pethick Lawrence, that man who did so much to run the old militant suffragettes and burke the proper discussion of woman's future. You know. You used to have 'em in Chelsea—with their hats. Oh! 'Gawdsaking' is the curse of all progress, the hectic consumption that kills a thousand

good beginnings. You see it in small things and in great.
You see it in my life ; Gawksaking turned my life-work to
cash and promotions, Gawdsaking—— Look at the way the
aviators took to flying for prizes and gate-money, the way pure
research is swamped by endowments for technical applications ! Then that poor ghost-giant of an idea the socialists
have ;—it's been treated like one of those unborn lambs they
kill for the fine skin of it, made into results before ever it was
alive. Could there be anything more pitiful ? The first great
dream and then the last phase ! when your Aunt Plessington
and the district visitors took and used it as a synonym for
Payment in Kind. . . . It's natural, I suppose, for people to
be eager for results, personal and immediate results—the last
lesson of life is patience. Naturally they want reality, naturally ! They want the individual life, something to handle and
feel and use and live by, something of their very own before
they die, and they want it now. But the thing that matters
for the race, Marjorie, is a very different thing : it is to get
the emerging thought process clear and to keep it clear—and
to let those other hungers go. We've got to go back to
England on the side of that delay, that arrest of interruption,
that detached, observant, synthesising process of the mind,
that solvent of difficulties and obsolescent institutions which
is the reality of collective human life. We've got to go back
on the side of pure science—literature untrammelled by the
preconceptions of the social schemers—art free from the
urgency of immediate utility—and a new, a regal, a god-like
sincerity in philosophy. And, above all, we've got to stop this
Jackdaw buying of yours, my dear, which is the essence of all
that is wrong with the world, this snatching at everything,
which loses everything worth having in life, this greedy confused realisation of our accumulated resources ! You're going
to be a non-shopping woman now. You've to come out of
Bond Street, you and your kind, like Israel leaving the
Egyptian flesh-pots. You're going to be my wife and my
mate. . . . Less of this service of things. Investments in
comfort, in security, in experience, yes ; but not just spending
any more." . . .

He broke off abruptly with : " I want to go back and
begin."

" Yes," said Marjorie, " we will go back," and saw minutely
and distantly, and yet as clearly and brightly as if she looked
into a concave mirror, that tall and dignified study, a very high
room indeed, with a man writing before a fine, long-curtained
window, and a great lump of rich-glowing Labradorite upon
his desk before him holding together an accumulation of
written sheets. . . .

She knew exactly the shop in Oxford Street where the stuff
for the curtains might be best obtained.

## § 17

One night Marjorie had been sitting musing before the stove for a long time, and suddenly she said : " I wonder if we shall fail ? I wonder if we shall get into a mess again when we are back in London ? . . . As big a mess and as utter a discontent as sent us here." . . .

Trafford was scraping out his pipe, and did not answer for some moments. Then he remarked : " What nonsense ! "

" But we shall," she said. " Everybody fails. To some extent, we are bound to fail. Because indeed nothing is clear ; nothing is a clear issue. . . . You know—I'm just the old Marjorie really, in spite of all these resolutions—the spend-thrift, the restless, the eager. I'm a born snatcher and shopper. We're just the same people really."

" No," he said, after thought. " You're all Labrador older."

" I always *have* failed," she considered, " when it came to any special temptations, Rag. I can't *stand* not having a thing ! "

He made no answer.

" And you're still the same old Rag, you know," she went on. " Who weakens into kindness if I cry. Who likes me well-dressed. Who couldn't endure to see me poor."

" Not a bit of it. No ! I'm a very different Rag with a very different Marjorie. Yes, indeed ! Things—are graver. Why !—I'm lame for life—and I've a scar. The very *look* of things is changed. . . ." He stared at her face and said : " You've hidden the looking-glass and you think I haven't noted it——"

" It keeps on healing," she interrupted. " And if it comes to that—where's my complexion ? " She laughed. " These are just the superficial aspects of the case."

" Nothing ever heals completely," he said, answering her first sentence, " and nothing ever goes back to the exact place it held before. We *are* different, you sun-bitten, frost-bitten wife of mine." . . .

" Character is character," said Marjorie, coming back to her point. " Don't exaggerate conversion, dear. It's not a bit of good pretending we shan't fall away, both of us. Each in our own manner. We shall. We shall, old man. London is still a tempting and confusing place, and you can't alter people fundamentally, not even by half-freezing and half-starving them. You only alter people fundamentally by killing them and replacing them. I shall be extravagant again and forget again, try as I may, and you will work again and fall away again and forgive me again. You know—— It's just as though we were each of us not one person, but a lot of persons, who sometimes meet and shout all together, and then disperse and forget and plot against each other." . . .

" Oh, things will happen again," said Trafford, in her pause. " But they will happen again with a difference—after this.

With a difference. That's the good of it all. . . . We've found something here—that makes everything different. . . . We've found each other, too, dear wife."

She thought intently.

"I am afraid," she whispered.

"But what is there to be afraid of ? "

"*Myself*."

She spoke after a little pause that seemed to hesitate. "At times I wish—oh, passionately !—that I could pray."

"Why don't you ? "

"I don't believe enough—in that. I wish I did."

Trafford thought. "People are always so exacting about prayer," he said.

"Exacting ? "

"You want to pray—and you can't make terms for a thing you want. I used to think I could. I wanted God to come and demonstrate a bit. . . . It's no good, Madge. . . . If God chooses to be silent—you must pray to the silence. If He chooses to live in darkness, you must pray to the night." . . . .

"Yes," said Marjorie, "I suppose one must."

She thought. "I suppose in the end one does," she said. . .

## § 18

Mixed up with this entirely characteristic theology of theirs and their elaborate planning-out of a new life in London were other strands of thought. Queer memories of London and old times together would flash with a peculiar brightness across their contemplation of the infinities and the needs of mankind. Out of nowhere, quite disconnectedly, would come the human, finite : "Do you remember—— ? "

Two things particularly pressed into their minds. One was the thought of their children, and I do not care to tell how often in the day now they calculated the time in England, and tried to guess to a half-mile or so where those young people might be and what they might be doing. "The shops are bright for Christmas now," said Marjorie. "This year Dick was to have had his first fireworks. I wonder if he did ? I wonder if he burned his dear little funny stumps of fingers ? I hope not."

"Oh, just a little," said Trafford. "I remember how a squib made my glove smoulder and singed me, and how my mother kissed me for taking it like a man. It was the best part of the adventure."

"Dick shall burn his fingers when his mother's home to kiss him. But spare his fingers now, Dadda."

The other topic was food.

It was only after they had been doing it for a week or so that they remarked how steadily they gravitated to reminiscences, suggestions, descriptions, and long discussions of eatables—sound, solid eatables. They told over the particulars of dinners they had imagined altogether forgotten ; neither hosts nor conversations seemed to matter now in the slightest degree, but every item in the menu had its place. They nearly quarrelled one day about *hors-d'œuvre*. Trafford wanted to dwell on them when Marjorie was eager for the soup.

" It's niggling with food," said Marjorie.

" Oh, but there's no reason," said Trafford, " why you shouldn't take a Lot of *hors-d'œuvre*. Three or four sardines, and potato salad and a big piece of smoked salmon, and some of that Norwegian herring, and so on, and keep the olives by you to pick at. It's a beginning."

" It's—it's immoral," said Marjorie, " that's what I feel. If one needs a whet to eat, one shouldn't eat. The proper beginning of a dinner is soup—good, hot, *rich* soup. Thick soup—with things in it, vegetables and meat and things. Bits of oxtail."

" Not peas."

" No, not peas. Pea-soup is tiresome. I never knew anything one tired of so soon. I wish we hadn't relied on it so much."

" Thick soup's all very well," said Trafford, " but how about that clear stuff they give you in the little pavement restaurants in Paris ? You know—*Croûte-au-pot*, with lovely great crusts and big leeks and lettuce leaves and so on ! Tremendous aroma of onions, and beautiful little beads of fat ! And being a clear soup, you see what there is. That's—interesting. Twenty-five centimes, Marjorie. Lord ! I'd give a guinea a plate for it. I'd give five pounds for one of those jolly white-metal tureens full—you know, *full*, with little drops all over the outside of it, and the ladle sticking out under the lid."

" Have you ever tasted turtle soup ? "

" Rather. They give it you in the City. The fat's—ripping. But they're rather precious with it, you know. For my own part, I don't think soup should be *doled* out. I always liked the soup we used to get at the Harts' ; but then they never give you enough, you know—not nearly enough."

" About a tablespoonful," said Marjorie. " It's mocking an appetite."

" Still, there's things to follow," said Trafford. . . .

They discussed the proper order of a dinner very carefully. They decided that sorbets and ices were not only unwholesome, but nasty. " In London," said Trafford, " one's taste gets—vitiated." . . .

They weighed the merits of French cookery, modern international cookery, and produced alternatives. Trafford became very eloquent about old English food. " Dinners," said Trafford, " should be feasting, not the mere satisfaction of a necessity. There should be—*amplitude*. I remember a recipe for a pie ; I think it was in one of those books that man Lucas used to compile. If I remember rightly, it began with : ' Take a swine and hew it into gobbets.' Gobbets ! That's something like a beginning. It was a big pie with tiers and tiers of things, and it kept it up all the way in that key. . . . And then what could be better than prime British-fed roast beef, reddish, just a shade on the side of underdone, and not too finely cut ? Mutton can't touch it."

" Beef is the best," she said.

" Then our English cold meat again. What can equal it ? Such stuff as they give in a good country inn, a huge joint of beef—you cut from it yourself, you know, as much as you like —with mustard, pickles, celery, a tankard of stout, let us say. Pressed beef, such as they'll give you at the Reform, too, that's good eating for a man. With chutney, and then old cheese to follow. And boiled beef, with little carrots and turnips and a dumpling or so. Eh ? "

" Of course," said Marjorie, " one must do justice to a well-chosen turkey, a *fat* turkey."

" Or a good goose, for the matter of that—with honest, well-thought-out stuffing. I like the little sausages round the dish of a turkey, too ; like cherubs they are, round the feet of a Madonna. . . . There's much to be said for sausage, Marjorie. It concentrates."

Sausage led to Germany. " I'm not one of those patriots," he was saying presently, " who run down other countries by way of glorifying their own. While I was in Germany I tasted many good things. There's their Leberwurst ; it's never bad, and, at its best, it's splendid. It's only a fool would reproach Germany with sausage. Devonshire black-pudding, of course, is the master of any Blutwurst, but there's all those others on the German side. Frankfurter, big reddish sausage stuff again with great crystalline lumps of white fat. And how well they cook their rich hashes, and the thick gravies they make ! Curious, how much better the cooking of Teutonic peoples is than the cooking of the South Europeans ! It's as if one needed a colder climate to brace a cook to his business. The Frenchman and the Italian trifle and stimulate. It's as if they'd never met a hungry man. No German would have thought of *soufflé*. Ugh ! it's vicious eating. There's much that's fine, though, in Austria and Hungary. I wish I had travelled in Hungary. Do you remember how once or twice we've lunched at that Viennese place in Regent Street, and how they've given us stuffed Paprika, eh ? "

" That was a good place. I remember there was stewed beef once with a lot of barley—such *good* barley ! "

" Every country has its glories. One talks of the cookery of northern countries and then suddenly one thinks of curry, with lots of rice."

" And lots of chicken ! "

" And lots of hot curry powder, *very* hot. And look at America ! Here's a people who haven't any of them been out of Europe for centuries, and yet they have as different a table as you could well imagine. There's a kind of fish, planked shad, that they cook on resinous wood—roast it, I suppose. It's substantial, like nothing else in the world. And how good, too, with turkey are sweet potatoes ! Then they have such a multitude of cereal things ; stuff like their buckwheat cakes, all swimming in golden syrup. And Indian corn, again ! "

" Of course, corn is being Anglicised. I've often given you corn—latterly, before we came away."

" That sort of separated grain—out of tins. Like chicken's food ! It's not the real thing. You should eat corn on the cob—American fashion ! It's fine. I had it when I was in the States. You know, you take it up in your hands by both ends —you've seen the cobs ?—and gnaw."

The craving air of Labrador at a temperature of $-20°$ Fahrenheit, and methodically stinted rations, make great changes in the outward qualities of the mind. " *I'd* like to do that," said Marjorie.

Her face flushed a little at a guilty thought, her eyes sparkled. She leaned forward and spoke in a confidential undertone.

" *I'd like to eat a mutton chop like that,*" said Marjorie.

## § 19

One morning Marjorie broached something she had had on her mind for several days.

" Old man," she said, " I can't stand it any longer. I'm going to thaw my scissors and cut your hair. . . . And then you'll have to trim that beard of yours."

" You'll have to dig out that looking-glass."

" I know," said Marjorie. She looked at him. " You'll never be a pretty man again," she said. " But there's a sort of wild splendour. . . . And I love every inch and scrap of you." . . .

Their eyes met. " We're a thousand deeps now below the look of things," said Trafford. " We'd love each other minced."

She broke into that smiling laugh of hers. " Oh ! it won't come to *that*," she said. " Trust my housekeeping ! "

# CHAPTER FIVE

## THE TRAIL TO THE SEA

### § 1

ONE astonishing afternoon in January a man came out of the wilderness to Lonely Hut. He was a French-Indian half-breed, a trapper up and down the Green River and across the Height of Land to Seal Lake. He arrived in a sort of shy silence, and squatted amiably on a log to thaw. " Much snow," he said, " and little fur."

After he had sat at their fire for an hour and eaten and drunk, his purpose in coming thawed out. He explained he had just come on to them to see how they were. He was, he said, a planter furring ; he had a line of traps, about a hundred and twenty miles in length. The nearest trap in his path before he turned northward over the divide was a good forty miles down the river. He had come on from there. Just to have a look. His name, he said, was Louis Napoleon Partington. He had carried a big pack, a rifle and a dead marten—they lay beside him—and out of his shapeless mass of caribou skins and woollen clothing and wrappings, peeped a genial, oily, brown face, very dirty, with a strand of blue-black hair across one eye, irregular teeth in its friendly smile, and little, squeezed-up eyes.

Conversation developed. There had been doubts of his linguistic range at first, but he had an understanding expression, and his English seemed guttural rather than really bad.

He was told the tremendous story of Trafford's leg ; was shown it, and felt it ; he interpolated thick and whistling noises to show how completely he followed their explanations, and then suddenly he began a speech that made all his earlier taciturnity seem but the dam of a great reservoir of mixed and partly incomprehensible English. He complimented Marjorie so effusively and relentlessly and shamelessly as to produce a pause when he had done. " Yes," he said, and nodded to button up the whole. He sucked his pipe, well satisfied with his eloquence. Trafford spoke in this silence. " We are coming down," he said.

(" I thought, perhaps——" whispered Louis Napoleon.)

" Yes," said Trafford, " we are coming down with you. Why not ? We can get a sledge over the snow now ? It's hard ? I mean a flat sledge—like *this*. See ? Like this." He got up and dragged Marjorie's old arrangement into view. " We shall bring all the stuff we can down with us, grub, blankets—not the tent, it's too bulky ; we'll leave a lot of the heavy gear."

" You'd have to leave the tent," said Louis Napoleon.

" I *said* leave the tent."

" And you'd have to leave . . . some of those tins."

" Nearly all of them."

" And the ammunition, there—except just a little."

" Just enough for the journey down."

" Perhaps a gun ? "

" No, not a gun. Though, after all—well, we'd return one of the guns. Give it you to bring back here."

" Bring back here ? "

" If you liked."

For some moments Louis Napoleon was intently silent. When he spoke his voice was guttural with emotion. " After," he said thoughtfully and paused, and then resolved to have it over forthwith, " all you leave will be mine ? Eh ? "

Trafford said that was the idea.

Louis Napoleon's eye brightened, but his face preserved its Indian calm.

" I will take you right to Hammond's," he said, " where they have dogs. And then I can come back here. . . ."

§ 2

They had talked out nearly every particular of their return before they slept that night ; they yarned away three hours over the first generous meal that any one of them had eaten for many weeks. Louis Napoleon stayed in the hut as a matter of course, and reposed with snores and choking upon Marjorie's sledge and within a yard of her. It struck her as she lay awake and listened that the housemaids in Sussex Square would have thought things a little congested for a lady's bedroom, and then she reflected that after all it wasn't much worse than a crowded carriage in an all-night train from Switzerland. She tried to count how many people there had been in that compartment, and failed. How stuffy that had been—the smell of cheese and all ! And with that, after a dream that she was whaling and had harpooned a particularly short-winded whale, she fell very peacefully into oblivion.

Next day was spent in the careful preparation of the two sledges. They intended to take a full provision for six weeks, although they reckoned that with good weather they ought to be down at Hammond's in four.

The day after was Sunday, and Louis Napoleon would not look at the sledges or packing. Instead he held a kind of re-ligious service which consisted partly in making Trafford read aloud out of a very oily old New Testament he produced, a selected passage from the Book of Corinthians, and partly in moaning rather than singing several hymns. He was rather disappointed that they did not join in with him. In the after-noon he heated some water, went into the tent with it and, it would appear, partially washed his face. In the evening, after they had supped, he discussed religion, being curious by this time about their beliefs and procedure.

He spread his mental and spiritual equipment before them very artlessly. Their isolation and their immense concentration on each other had made them sensitive to personal quality, and they listened to the broken English and the queer tangential starts into new topics of this dirty mongrel creature with the keenest appreciation of its quality. It was inconsistent, miscellaneous, simple, honest, and human. It was as touching as the medley in the pocket of a dead schoolboy. He was superstitious and sceptical and sensual and spiritual, and very, very earnest. The things he believed, even if they were just beliefs about the weather or drying venison or filling pipes, he believed with emotion. He flushed as he told them. For all his intellectual muddle, they felt he knew how to live honestly and die if need be very finely.

He was more than a little distressed at their apparent ignorance of the truths of revealed religion as it is taught in the Moravian schools upon the coast, and indeed it was manifest that he had had far more careful and infinitely more sincere religious teaching than either Trafford or Marjorie. For a time the missionary spirit inspired him, and then he quite forgot his solicitude for their conversion in a number of increasingly tall anecdotes about hunters and fishermen, illustrating at first the extreme dangers of any departure from a rigid Sabbatarianism, but presently becoming just stories illustrating the uncertainty of life. Thence he branched off to the general topic of life upon the coast and the relative advantages of " planter " and fisherman.

And then with a kindling eye he spoke of women, and how that some day he would marry. His voice softened, and he addressed himself more particularly to Marjorie. He didn't so much introduce the topic of the lady as allow the destined young woman suddenly to pervade his discourse. She was, it seemed, a servant, an Esquimaux girl at the Moravian Mission station at Manivikovik. He had been plighted to her for nine years. He described a gramophone he had purchased down at Port Dupré and brought back to her three hundred miles up the coast—it seemed to Marjorie an odd gift for an Esquimaux maiden—and he gave his views upon its mechanism. He said God was with the man who invented the gramophone " truly." They would have found one a very great relief to the tediums of their sojourn at Lonely Hut. The gramophone he had given his betrothed possessed records of the Rev. Capel Gumm's preaching and of Madame Melba's singing, a revival hymn called " Sowing the Seed," and a comic song—they could not make out his pronunciation of the title—that made you die of laughter. " It goes gobble, gobble, gobble," he said, with a solemn appreciative reflection of those distant joys.

" It's good to be jolly at times," he said, with his bright eyes scanning Marjorie's face a little doubtfully, as if such ideas were better left for week-day expression.

## § 3

Their return was a very different journey from the toilsome ascent of the summer. An immense abundance of snow masked the world, snow that made them regret acutely they had not equipped themselves with ski. With ski and a good circulation, a man may go about Labrador in winter six times more easily than. by the canoes and slow trudging of summer travel. As it was they were glad of their Canadian snow-shoes. One needs only shelters after the Alpine Club hut fashion, and all that vast solitary country would be open in the winter-time. Its shortest day is no shorter than the shortest day in Cumberland or Dublin.

This is no place to tell of the beauty and wonder of snow and ice, the soft contours of gentle slopes, the rippling of fine snow under a steady wind, the long shadow ridges of shining powder on the lee of trees and stones and rocks, the delicate wind streaks over broad surfaces like the marks of a chisel on marble, the crests and cornices, the vivid brightness of edges in the sun, the glowing yellowish light on sunlit surfaces, the long blue shadows, the flush of sunset and sunrise and the pallid unearthly desolation of snow beneath the moon. Nor need the broken snow in woods and amidst tumbled stony slopes be described, nor the vast soft overhanging crests on every outstanding rock beside the icebound river, nor the huge stalactites and stalagmites of green-blue ice below the cliffs, nor trees burthened and broken by frost and snow, nor snow upon ice, nor the blue pools at midday upon the surface of the ice-stream. Across the smooth wind-swept ice of the open tarns they would find a growth of ice flowers, six-rayed and complicated, more abundant and more beautiful than the Alpine summer flowers.

But the wind was very bitter, and the sun had scarcely passed its zenith before the thought of fuel and shelter came back into their minds.

As they approached Partington's tilt, at the point where his trapping ground turned out of the Green River gorge, he became greatly obsessed by the thought of his traps. He began to talk of all that he might find in them, all he hoped to find, and the " dallars " that might ensue. They slept the third night, Marjorie within and the two men under the lee of the little cabin, and Partington was up and away before dawn to a trap towards the ridge. He had infected Marjorie and Trafford with a sympathetic keenness, but when they saw his killing of a marten that was still alive in its trap, they suddenly conceived a distaste for trapping.

They insisted they must witness no more. They would wait while he went to a trap. . . .

" Think what he's doing ! " said Trafford, as they sat together under the lee of a rock waiting for him. " We imagined this was a free, simple-souled man leading an unsophisticated life on the very edge of humanity, and really he is as much a dependent of your woman's world, Marjorie, as any sweated seamstress in a Marylebone slum.   Lord ! how far those pretty wasteful hands of women reach !   All these poor broken and starving beasts he finds and slaughters are, from the point of view of our world, just furs.   Furs !   Poor little snarling unfortunates !   Their pelts will be dressed and prepared because women who have never dreamt of this bleak wilderness desire them.   They will get at last into Regent Street shops, and Bond Street shops, and shops in Fifth Avenue and Paris and Berlin, they will make delightful deep muffs, with scent and little bags and powder puffs and all sorts of things tucked away inside, and long wraps for tall women, and jolly little frames of soft fur for pretty faces, and dainty coats and rugs for expensive little babies in Kensington Gardens." . . .

" I wonder," reflected Marjorie, " if I could buy one perhaps ?   As a memento."

He looked at her with eyes of quiet amusement.

" Oh ! " she cried, " I didn't mean to !   The old Eve ! "

" The old Adam is with her," said Trafford.   " He's wanting to give it her. . . .   We don't cease to be human, Madge, you know, because we've got an idea now of just where we are.   I wonder which would you like ?   I dare say we could arrange it."

" No," said Marjorie, and thought.   " It would be jolly," she said.   " All the same, you know—and just to show you— I'm not going to let you buy me that fur."

" I'd like to," said Trafford.

" No," said Marjorie, with a decision that was almost fierce. " I mean it.   I've got more to do than you in the way of reforming.   It's just because always I've let my life be made up of such little things that I mustn't.   Indeed I mustn't.   Don't make things hard for me."

He looked at her for a moment.   " Very well," he said. " But I'd have liked to." . . .

" You're right," he added, five seconds later.

" Oh ! I'm right."

## § 4

One day Louis Napoleon sent them on along the trail while he went up the mountain to a trap among the trees.   He rejoined them—not as his custom was, shouting inaudible conversation for the last hundred yards or so, but in silence.   They wondered at that, and at the one clumsy gesture that flourished something darkly grey at them.   What had happened to the man ?   Whatever he had caught he was hugging it as one hugs a cat, and stroking it.   " Ugh ! " he said deeply, drawing near. " Oh ! "   A solemn joy irradiated his face, an almost religious ecstasy found expression.

He had got a silver fox, a beautifully marked silver fox, the best luck of Labrador ! One goes for years without one, in hope, and when it comes it pays the trapper's debts, it clears his life—for years !

They tried poor inadequate congratulations. . . .

As they sat about the fire that night a silence came upon Louis Napoleon. It was manifest that his mind was preoccupied. He got up, walked about, inspected the miracle of fur that had happened to him, returned, regarded them. "M'm," he said, and stroked his chin with his forefinger. A certain diffidence and yet a certain dignity of assurance mingled in his manner. It wasn't so much a doubt of his own correctness as of some possible ignorance of the finer shades on their part that might embarrass him. He coughed a curt preface, and intimated he had a request to make. Behind the Indian calm of his face glowed tremendous feeling, like the light of a foundry furnace shining through chinks in the door. He spoke in a small flat voice, exercising great self-control. His wish he said, in view of all that had happened, was a little thing. . . . This was nearly a perfect day for him, and one thing only remained. . . . " Well," he said, and hung. " Well ? " said Trafford. He plunged. Just simply this. Would they give him the brandy-bottle and let him get drunk ? Mr. Grenfell was a good man, a very good man. but he had made brandy dear—dear beyond the reach of common men altogether—along the coast. . . .

He explained, dear bundle of clothes and dirt ! that he was always perfectly respectable when he was drunk.

### § 5

It seemed strange to Trafford that now that Marjorie was going home, a wild impatience to see her children should possess her. So long as it had been probable that they would stay out their year in Labrador, that separation had seemed mainly a sentimental trouble ; now at times it was like an animal craving. She would talk of them for hours at a stretch, and when she was not talking he could see her eyes fixed ahead, and knew that she was anticipating a meeting. And for the first time it seemed the idea of possible misadventure troubled her. . . .

They reached Hammond's in one-and-twenty days from Lonely Hut, three days they had been forced to camp because of a blizzard, and three because Louis Napoleon was rigidly Sabbatarian. They parted from him reluctantly, and the next day Hammond's produced its dogs, twelve stout but extremely hungry dogs, and sent the Traffords on to the Green River pulp mills, where there were good beds and a copious supply of hot water. Thence they went to Manivikovok, and thence the new Marconi station sent their inquiries home, inquiries that were answered next day with matter-of-fact brevity : " Every one well, love from all."

When the operator hurried with that to Marjorie she re-

ceived it off-handedly, glanced at it carelessly, asked him to
smoke, remarked that wireless telegraphy was a wonderful
thing, and then, in the midst of some unfinished commonplace
about the temperature, broke down and wept wildly and uncontrollably. . . .

### § 6

Then came the long, wonderful ride southward day after day
along the coast to Port Dupré, a ride from headland to headland across the frozen bays behind long teams of straining,
furry dogs, that leaped and yelped as they ran.   Sometimes
over the land the brutes shirked and loitered and called for the
whip ;   they were a quarrelsome crew to keep waiting ;   but
across the sea-ice they went like the wind, and downhill the
komatic chased their waving tails.   The sledges swayed and
leaped depressions, and shot athwart icy stretches.   The
Traffords, spectacled and wrapped to their noses, had all the
sensations then of hunting an unknown quarry behind a pack
of wolves.   The snow blazed under the sun, out to sea beyond
the ice the water glittered, and it wasn't so much air they
breathed as a sort of joyous hunger.

One day their teams insisted upon racing.

Marjorie's team was the heavier, her driver more skilful, and
her sledge the lighter, and she led in that wild chase from start
to finish, but ever and again Trafford made wild spurts that
brought him almost level.   Once, as he came alongside, she
heard him laughing joyously.

" Marjorie," he shouted, " d'you remember ?   Old donkey-
cart ? "

Her team yawed away, and as he swept near again, behind
his pack of whimpering, straining, furious dogs, she heard him
shouting, " You know, that old cart !   Under the overhanging
trees !   So thick and green they met overhead !   You know !
When you and I had our first talk together !   In the lane.   It
wasn't so fast as this, eh ? " . . .

### § 7

At Port Dupré they stayed ten days—days that Marjorie
could only make tolerable by knitting absurd garments for the
children (her knitting was atrocious) ;   and then one afternoon
they heard the gun of the *Grenfell*, the new winter steamer from
St. John's, signalling as it came in through the fog, very slowly,
from that great wasteful world of men and women beyond the
seaward grey.

THE END